Mary Shelley

THE DOVER READER

Mary Shelley

DOVER PUBLICATIONS, INC.
Mineola, New York

DOVER THRIFT EDITIONS

General Editor: Mary Carolyn Waldrep

Editor of This Volume: Susan L. Rattiner

Copyright

Bibliographical Note

Mary Shelley: The Dover Reader, first published by Dover Publications, Inc., in 2015, is a new compilation of novels and short fiction by Mary Shelley, reprinted from authoritative sources. The Note has been specially prepared for the Dover edition.

Please note that some archaic spellings that appear throughout the text derive from the original editions of the works and have been retained here for the sake of authenticity.

Library of Congress Cataloging-in-Publication Data

Shelley, Mary Wollstonecraft, 1797–1851.
[Works. Selections.]
Mary Shelley : the Dover reader / Mary Shelley.
pages cm. — (Dover thrift editions)
ISBN-13: 978-0-486-80249-7 (paperback) — ISBN-10: 0-486-80249-3 (paperback)
I. Title.
PR5397.A1 2016
823'.7—dc23

2015025213

Manufactured in the United States by RR Donnelley
80249301 2015
www.doverpublications.com

Note

English Romantic novelist Mary Wollstonecraft Godwin Shelley, by her own account, was "the daughter of two persons of distinguished literary celebrity," Mary Wollstonecraft and William Godwin. Although her mother died eleven days after her birth, Mary was profoundly influenced by Wollstonecraft's reputation and writings. Godwin, who encouraged his daughter's intellectual development, was an emotionally distant parent, and Mary's own reminiscences of her childhood acknowledge an "excessive and romantic attachment" to her father, perhaps borne out of his neglect.

At the age of 16, Mary eloped with Percy Bysshe Shelley, who was married at the time to Harriet Westbrook. In December 1816—following the suicide of Shelley's first wife earlier that month—the two were married. Mary Shelley began writing *Frankenstein* (1818), her first and arguably best work of fiction, earlier that same year, when she was not yet nineteen years old.

After her husband drowned in a sailing accident, Shelley, now a young widow at 24 years old, lived in poverty for many years. No strangers to tragedy, Shelley and her husband suffered the loss of three of their children, and only one son survived to adulthood. Shelley produced several novels such as the science fiction tale *The Last Man* (1826), short stories, travelogues, and works of criticism. She was also instrumental in promoting her husband's poetry and upholding his place in literary history.

With her Gothic novel, *Frankenstein,* Shelley brilliantly achieved her self-defined—and most challenging—aspiration to create a story that "would speak to the mysterious fears of our nature and awaken thrilling horror—one to make the reader dread to look round, to curdle the blood, and quicken the beatings of the heart." Embraced by popular culture, Mary Shelley's famed novel endures as her foremost literary legacy.

Contents

Frankenstein

CONTENTS

AUTHOR'S INTRODUCTION

THE PUBLISHERS OF the Standard Novels, in selecting *Frankenstein* for one of their series, expressed a wish that I should furnish them with some account of the origin of the story. I am the more willing to comply, because I shall thus give a general answer to the question, so very frequently asked me—"How I, then a young girl, came to think of and to dilate upon so very hideous an idea?" It is true that I am very averse to bringing myself forward in print; but as my account will only appear as an appendage to a former production, and as it will be confined to such topics as have connexion with my authorship alone, I can scarcely accuse myself of a personal intrusion.

It is not singular that, as the daughter of two persons of distinguished literary celebrity,[1] I should very early in life have thought of writing. As a child I scribbled; and my favourite pastime during the hours given me for recreation was to "write stories." Still, I had a dearer pleasure than this, which was the formation of castles in the air—the indulging in waking dreams—the following up trains of thought, which had for their subject the formation of a succession of imaginary incidents. My dreams were at once more fantastic and agreeable than my writings. In the latter I was a close imitator—rather doing as others had done than putting down the suggestions of my own mind. What I wrote was intended at least for one other eye—my childhood's companion and friend; but my dreams were all my own; I accounted for them to nobody; they were my refuge when annoyed—my dearest pleasure when free.

---

[1] *two persons . . . celebrity*] Mary Wollstonecraft (1759–97), author of A *Vindication of the Rights of Woman,* and William Godwin (1756–1836), author of An *Enquiry Concerning Political Justice* and *Caleb Williams.*

I lived principally in the country as a girl, and passed a considerable time in Scotland. I made occasional visits to the more picturesque parts; but my habitual residence was on the blank and dreary northern shores of the Tay, near Dundee. Blank and dreary on retrospection I call them; they were not so to me then. They were the eyry[2] of freedom, and the pleasant region where unheeded I could commune with the creatures of my fancy. I wrote then—but in a most common-place style. It was beneath the trees of the grounds belonging to our house, or on the bleak sides of the woodless mountains near, that my true compositions, the airy flights of my imagination, were born and fostered. I did not make myself the heroine of my tales. Life appeared to me too common-place an affair as regarded myself. I could not figure to myself that romantic woes or wonderful events would ever be my lot; but I was not confined to my own identity, and I could people the hours with creations far more interesting to me at that age than my own sensations.

After this my life became busier, and reality stood in place of fiction. My husband, however, was from the first, very anxious that I should prove myself worthy of my parentage, and enrol myself on the page of fame. He was for ever inciting me to obtain literary reputation, which even on my own part I cared for then, though since I have become infinitely indifferent to it. At this time he desired that I should write, not so much with the idea that I could produce any thing worthy of notice, but that he might himself judge how far I possessed the promise of better things hereafter. Still I did nothing. Travelling, and the cares of a family, occupied my time; and study, in the way of reading or improving my ideas in communication with his far more cultivated mind, was all of literary employment that engaged my attention.

In the summer of 1816, we visited Switzerland and became the neighbours of Lord Byron. At first we spent our pleasant hours on the lake, or wandering on its shores; and Lord Byron, who was writing the third canto of *Childe Harold,* was the only one among us who put his thoughts upon paper. These, as he brought them successively to us, clothed in all the light and harmony of poetry,

[2] *eyry*] eyrie or aerie.

seemed to stamp as divine the glories of heaven and earth, whose influences we partook with him.

But it proved a wet, ungenial summer, and incessant rain often confined us for days to the house. Some volumes of ghost stories, translated from the German into French, fell into our hands. There was the *History of the Inconstant Lover,* who, when he thought to clasp the bride to whom he had pledged his vows, found himself in the arms of the pale ghost of her whom he had deserted. There was the tale of the sinful founder of his race whose miserable doom it was to bestow the kiss of death on all the younger sons of his fated house, just when they reached the age of promise. His gigantic, shadowy form, clothed like the ghost in *Hamlet,* in complete armour, but with the beaver up, was seen at midnight, by the moon's fitful beams, to advance slowly along the gloomy avenue. The shape was lost beneath the shadow of the castle walls; but soon a gate swung back, a step was heard, the door of the chamber opened, and he advanced to the couch of the blooming youths, cradled in healthy sleep. Eternal sorrow sat upon his face as he bent down and kissed the forehead of the boys, who from that hour withered like flowers snapt upon the stalk. I have not seen these stories since then; but their incidents are as fresh in my mind as if I had read them yesterday.

"We will each write a ghost story," said Lord Byron; and his proposition was acceded to. There were four of us. The noble author began a tale, a fragment of which he printed at the end of his poem of *Mazeppa.* Shelley, more apt to embody ideas and sentiments in the radiance of brilliant imagery, and in the music of the most melodious verse that adorns our language, than to invent the machinery of a story, commenced one founded on the experiences of his early life. Poor Polidori had some terrible idea about a skull-headed lady who was so punished for peeping through a key-hole—what to see I forget—something very shocking and wrong of course; but when she was reduced to a worse condition than the renowned Tom of Coventry, he did not know what to do with her and was obliged to dispatch her to the tomb of the Capulets, the only place for which she was fitted. The illustrious poets also, annoyed by the platitude of prose, speedily relinquished their uncongenial task.

I busied myself *to think of a story,*—a story to rival those which had excited us to this task. One which would speak to the mysterious fears of our nature and awaken thrilling horror—one to make the reader dread to look round, to curdle the blood, and quicken the beatings of the heart. If I did not accomplish these things, my ghost story would be unworthy of its name. I thought and pondered—vainly. I felt that blank incapability of invention which is the greatest misery of authorship, when dull Nothing replies to our anxious invocations. "Have you thought of a story?" I was asked each morning, and each morning I was forced to reply with a mortifying negative.

Every thing must have a beginning, to speak in Sanchean[3] phrase; and that beginning must be linked to something that went before. The Hindoos give the world an elephant to support it, but they make the elephant stand upon a tortoise. Invention, it must be humbly admitted, does not consist in creating out of void, but out of chaos; the materials must, in the first place, be afforded: it can give form to dark, shapeless substances, but cannot bring into being the substance itself. In all matters of discovery and invention, even of those that appertain to the imagination, we are continually reminded of the story of Columbus and his egg. Invention consists in the capacity of seizing on the capabilities of a subject: and in the power of moulding and fashioning ideas suggested to it.

Many and long were the conversations between Lord Byron and Shelley, to which I was a devout but nearly silent listener. During one of these, various philosophical doctrines were discussed, and among others the nature of the principle of life, and whether there was any probability of its ever being discovered and communicated. They talked of the experiments of Dr Darwin[4] (I speak not of what the Doctor really did, or said that he did, but, as more to my purpose, of what was then spoken of as having been done by him), who preserved a piece of vermicelli in a glass case, till by some extraordinary means it began to move with voluntary motion. Not thus, after all, would life be given. Perhaps a corpse would be reanimated; galvanism had given token of such things: perhaps the component parts of a creature might be manufactured, brought together, and endued with vital warmth.

---

[3] *Sanchean*] like Sancho Panza in *Don Quixote*.
[4] *Dr Darwin*] Erasmus Darwin (1731–1802), grandfather of Charles Darwin.

Night waned upon this talk, and even the witching hour had gone by, before we retired to rest. When I placed my head on my pillow, I did not sleep, nor could I be said to think. My imagination, unbidden, possessed and guided me, gifting the successive images that arose in my mind with a vividness far beyond the usual bounds of reverie. I saw—with shut eyes, but acute mental vision—I saw the pale student of unhallowed arts kneeling beside the thing he had put together. I saw the hideous phantasm of a man stretched out, and then, on the working of some powerful engine, show signs of life, and stir with an uneasy, half-vital motion. Frightful must it be; for supremely frightful would be the effect of any human endeavour to mock the stupendous mechanism of the Creator of the world. His success would terrify the artist; he would rush away from his odious handywork, horror-stricken. He would hope that, left to itself, the slight spark of life which he had communicated would fade; that this thing, which had received such imperfect animation would subside into dead matter; and he might sleep in the belief that the silence of the grave would quench forever the transient existence of the hideous corpse which he had looked upon as the cradle of life. He sleeps; but he is awakened; he opens his eyes; behold, the horrid thing stands at his bedside, opening his curtains and looking on him with yellow, watery, but speculative eyes.

I opened mine in terror. The idea so possessed my mind, that a thrill of fear ran through me, and I wished to exchange the ghastly image of my fancy for the realities around. I see them still; the very room, the dark *parquet,* the closed shutters, with the moonlight struggling through, and the sense I had that the glassy lake and white high Alps were beyond. I could not so easily get rid of my hideous phantom; still it haunted me. I must try to think of something else. I recurred to my ghost story—my tiresome, unlucky ghost story! O! if I could only contrive one which would frighten my reader as I myself had been frightened that night!

Swift as light and as cheering was the idea that broke in upon me. "I have found it! What terrified me will terrify others; and I need only describe the spectre which had haunted my midnight pillow." On the morrow I announced that I had *thought of a story.* I began that day with the words, "It was on a dreary night of November," making only a transcript of the grim terrors of my waking dream.

At first I thought but a few pages—of a short tale; but Shelley urged me to develope the idea at greater length. I certainly did not owe the suggestion of one incident, nor scarcely of one train of feeling, to my husband, and yet but for his incitement it would never have taken the form in which it was presented to the world. From this declaration I must except the preface.[5] As far as I can recollect, it was entirely written by him.

And now, once again, I bid my hideous progeny go forth and prosper. I have an affection for it, for it was the offspring of happy days, when death and grief were but words, which found no true echo in my heart. Its several pages speak of many a walk, many a drive, and many a conversation, when I was not alone; and my companion was one who, in this world, I shall never see more. But this is for myself; my readers have nothing to do with these associations.

I will add but one word as to the alterations I have made. They are principally those of style. I have changed no portion of the story nor introduced any new ideas or circumstances. I have mended the language where it was so bald as to interfere with the interest of the narrative; and these changes occur almost exclusively in the beginning of the first volume. Throughout they are entirely confined to such parts as are mere adjuncts to the story, leaving the core and substance of it untouched.

M.W.S.

London, October 15th, 1831.

---

[5] *preface*] Percy Shelley had written the preface (signed "Marlow") for the anonymous 1818 edition.

LETTER I

To Mrs Saville, England.

St Petersburgh, Dec. 11th, 17—.

You will rejoice to hear that no disaster has accompanied the commencement of an enterprise which you have regarded with such evil forebodings. I arrived here yesterday; and my first task is to assure my dear sister of my welfare, and increasing confidence in the success of my undertaking.

I am already far north of London; and as I walk in the streets of Petersburgh, I feel a cold northern breeze play upon my cheeks, which braces my nerves, and fills me with delight. Do you understand this feeling? This breeze, which has travelled from the regions towards which I am advancing, gives me a foretaste of those icy climes. Inspirited by this wind of promise, my day dreams become more fervent and vivid. I try in vain to be persuaded that the pole is the seat of frost and desolation; it ever presents itself to my imagination as the region of beauty and delight. There, Margaret, the sun is for ever visible, its broad disk just skirting the horizon, and diffusing a perpetual splendour. There—for with your leave, my sister, I will put some trust in preceding navigators—there snow and frost are banished; and, sailing over a calm sea, we may be wafted to a land surpassing in wonders and in beauty every region hitherto discovered on the habitable globe. Its productions and features may be without example, as the phenomena of the heavenly bodies undoubtedly are in those undiscovered solitudes. What may not be expected in a country of eternal light? I may there discover the wondrous power which attracts the needle; and may regulate a thousand celestial observations, that require only this voyage to render their seeming eccentricities consistent for ever. I shall satiate my ardent curiosity with the sight of a part of the world never before visited, and may tread a land never before imprinted by the foot of man. These are my enticements, and they are sufficient to conquer all fear of danger or death, and to induce me to commence this laborious voyage with the joy a child feels when he embarks in a little boat, with his holiday mates, on an expedition of discovery up his native river. But, supposing all these conjectures to be false, you cannot contest the inestimable benefit which I shall confer on all mankind to the last generation, by discovering a passage near the pole to those countries, to reach which at present so many months are requisite; or by ascertaining the secret of the magnet, which, if at all possible, can only be effected by an undertaking such as mine.

These reflections have dispelled the agitation with which I began my letter, and I feel my heart glow with an enthusiasm which elevates me to heaven; for nothing contributes so much to tranquillize the mind as a steady purpose—a point on which the soul may fix its intellectual eye. This expedition has been the favourite dream of my early years. I have read with ardour the accounts of the various voyages which have been made in the prospect of arriving at the North Pacific Ocean through the seas which surround the pole. You may remember that a history of all the voyages made for purposes of discovery composed the whole of our good uncle Thomas's library. My education was neglected, yet I was passionately fond of reading. These volumes were my study day and night, and my familiarity with them increased that regret which I had felt, as a child, on learning that my father's dying injunction had forbidden my uncle to allow me to embark in a seafaring life.

These visions faded when I perused, for the first time, those poets whose effusions entranced my soul, and lifted it to heaven. I also became a poet, and for one year lived in a Paradise of my own creation; I imagined that I also might obtain a niche in the temple where the names of Homer and Shakespeare are consecrated. You are well acquainted with my failure, and how heavily I bore the disappointment. But just at that time I inherited the fortune of my cousin, and my thoughts were turned into the channel of their earlier bent.

Six years have passed since I resolved on my present undertaking. I can, even now, remember the hour from which I dedicated myself to this great enterprise. I commenced by inuring my body to hardship. I accompanied the whale-fishers on several expeditions to the North Sea; I voluntarily endured cold, famine, thirst, and want of sleep; I often worked harder than the common sailors during the day, and devoted my nights to the study of mathematics, the theory of medicine, and those branches of physical science from which a naval adventure might derive the greatest practical advantage. Twice I actually hired myself as an under-mate in a Greenland whaler, and acquitted myself to admiration. I must own I felt a little proud, when my captain offered me the second dignity in the vessel and intreated me to remain with the greatest earnestness so valuable did he consider my services.

And now, dear Margaret, do I not deserve to accomplish some great purpose? My life might have been passed in ease and luxury; but I preferred glory to every enticement that wealth placed in my path. Oh, that some encouraging voice would answer in the affirmative! My courage and my resolution is firm; but my hopes fluctuate, and my spirits are often depressed. I am about to proceed on a long and difficult voyage, the emergencies of which will demand all my fortitude: I am required not only to raise the spirits of others, but sometimes to sustain my own, when theirs are failing.

This is the most favourable period for travelling in Russia. They fly quickly over the snow in their sledges; the motion is pleasant, and, in my opinion, far more agreeable than that of an English stage-coach. The cold is not excessive, if you are wrapped in furs—a dress which I have already adopted; for there is a great difference between walking the deck and remaining seated motionless for hours, when no exercise prevents the blood from actually freezing in your veins. I have no ambition to lose my life on the post-road between St Petersburgh and Archangel.

I shall depart for the latter town in a fortnight or three weeks; and my intention is to hire a ship there, which can easily be done by paying the insurance for the owner, and to engage as many sailors as I think necessary among those who are accustomed to the whale-fishing. I do not intend to sail until the month of June; and when shall I return? Ah, dear sister, how can I answer this question? If I succeed, many, many months, perhaps years, will pass before you and I may meet. If I fail, you will see me again soon, or never.

Farewell, my dear, excellent Margaret. Heaven shower down blessings on you, and save me, that I may again and again testify my gratitude for all your love and kindness.

Your affectionate brother,
R. Walton.

LETTER II

To Mrs Saville, England.

Archangel, March 28th, 17—.

How slowly the time passes here, encompassed as I am by frost and snow! yet a second step is taken towards my enterprise. I have hired a vessel, and am occupied in collecting my sailors; those whom I have already engaged, appear to be men on whom I can depend and are certainly possessed of dauntless courage.

But I have one want which I have never yet been able to satisfy; and the absence of the object of which I now feel as a most severe evil. I have no friend, Margaret: when I am glowing with the enthusiasm of success, there will be none to participate my joy; if I am assailed by disappointment, no one will endeavour to sustain me in dejection. I shall commit my thoughts to paper, it is true; but that is a poor medium for the communication of feeling. I desire the company of a man who could sympathise with me; whose eyes would reply to mine. You may deem me romantic, my dear sister, but I bitterly feel the want of a friend. I have no one near me, gentle yet courageous, possessed of a cultivated as well as of a capacious mind, whose tastes are like my own, to approve or amend my plans. How would such a friend repair the faults of your poor brother! I am too ardent in execution, and too impatient of difficulties. But it is a still greater evil to me that I am self-educated: for the first fourteen years of my life I ran wild on a common, and read nothing but our uncle Thomas's books of voyages. At that age I became acquainted with the celebrated poets of our own country; but it was only when it had ceased to be in my power to derive its most important benefits from such a conviction, that I perceived the necessity of becoming acquainted with more languages than that of my native country. Now I am twenty-eight and am in reality more illiterate than many schoolboys of fifteen. It is true that I have thought more, and that my day dreams are more extended and magnificent, but they want (as the painters call it) *keeping*; and I greatly need a friend who would have sense enough not to despise me as romantic, and affection enough for me to endeavour to regulate my mind.

Well, these are useless complaints; I shall certainly find no friend on the wide ocean, nor even here in Archangel, among merchants and seamen. Yet some feelings, unallied to the dross of human nature, beat even in these rugged bosoms. My lieutenant, for instance, is a man of wonderful courage and enterprise; he is madly desirous of glory: or rather, to word my phrase more characteristically, of advancement in his profession. He is an Englishman, and in the midst of national and professional prejudices, unsoftened by cultivation, retains some of the noblest endowments of humanity. I first became acquainted with him on board a whale vessel: finding that he was unemployed in this city, I easily engaged him to assist in my enterprise.

The master is a person of an excellent disposition, and is remarkable in the ship for his gentleness and the mildness of his discipline. This circumstance, added to his well-known integrity and dauntless courage, made me very desirous to engage him. A youth passed in solitude, my best years spent under your gentle and feminine fosterage, has so refined the groundwork of my character that I cannot overcome an intense distaste to the usual brutality exercised on board ship: I have never believed it to be necessary, and when I heard of a mariner equally noted for his kindliness of heart and the respect and obedience paid to him by his crew, I felt myself peculiarly fortunate in being able to secure his services. I heard of him first in rather a romantic manner, from a lady who owes to him the happiness of her life. This, briefly, is his story. Some years ago he loved a young Russian lady of moderate fortune; and having amassed a considerable sum in prize-money, the father of the girl consented to the match. He saw his mistress once before the destined ceremony; but she was bathed in tears, and, throwing herself at his feet, intreated him to spare her, confessing at the time that she loved another, but that he was poor, and that her father would never consent to the union. My generous friend reassured the suppliant, and on being informed of the name of her lover, instantly abandoned his pursuit. He had already bought a farm with his money, on which he had designed to pass the remainder of his life; but he bestowed the whole on his rival, together with the remains of his prize-money to purchase stock, and then himself solicited the young woman's father to consent to her marriage with her lover. But the old man decidedly refused, thinking himself bound in honour to my friend; who, when he found the father inexorable, quitted his country, nor returned until he heard that his former mistress was married according to her inclinations. "What a noble fellow!" you will exclaim. He is so; but then he is wholly uneducated: he is as silent as a Turk, and a kind of ignorant carelessness attends him, which, while it renders his conduct the more astonishing, detracts from the interest and sympathy which otherwise he would command.

Yet do not suppose, because I complain a little, or because I can conceive a consolation for my toils which I may never know, that I am wavering in my resolutions. Those are as fixed as fate, and my voyage is only now delayed until the weather shall permit my embarkation. The winter has been dreadfully severe, but the spring promises well, and it is considered as a remarkably early season; so that perhaps I may sail sooner than I expected. I shall do nothing rashly: you know me sufficiently to confide in my prudence and considerateness whenever the safety of others is committed to my care.

I cannot describe to you my sensations on the near prospect of my undertaking. It is impossible to communicate to you a conception of the trembling sensation, half pleasurable and half fearful, with which I am preparing to depart. I am going to unexplored regions to "the land of mist and snow"; but I shall kill no albatross, therefore do not be alarmed for my safety, or if I should come back to you as worn and woeful as the "Ancient Mariner." You will smile at my allusion; but I will disclose a secret. I have often attributed my attachment to, my passionate enthusiasm for, the dangerous mysteries of the ocean, to that production of the most imaginative of modern poets. There is something at work in my soul, which I do not understand. I am practically industrious—painstaking;—a workman to execute with perseverance and labour:—but besides this, there is a love for the marvellous, a belief in the marvellous, intertwined in all my projects, which hurries me out of the common pathways of men, even to the wild sea and unvisited regions I am about to explore.

But to return to dearer considerations. Shall I meet you again, after having traversed immense seas, and returned by the most southern cape of Africa or America? I dare not expect such success, yet I cannot bear to look on the reverse of the picture. Continue for the present to write to me by every opportunity: I may receive your letters on some occasions when I need them most to support my spirits. I love you very tenderly. Remember me with affection, should you never hear from me again.

Your affectionate brother,
Robert Walton.

LETTER III

To Mrs Saville, England.

July 7th, 17—.

My dear Sister,

I write a few lines in haste to say that I am safe—and well advanced on my voyage. This letter will reach England by a merchantman now on its homeward voyage from Archangel; more fortunate than I, who may not see my native land, perhaps, for many years. I am, however, in good spirits: my men are bold, and apparently firm of purpose, nor do the floating sheets of ice that continually pass us, indicating the dangers of the region towards which we are advancing, appear to dismay them. We have already reached a very high latitude; but it is the height of summer, and although not so warm as in England, the southern gales, which blow us speedily towards those shores which I so ardently desire to attain, breathe a degree of renovating warmth which I had not expected.

No incidents have hitherto befallen us that would make a figure in a letter. One or two stiff gales, and the springing of a leak, are accidents which experienced navigators scarcely remember to record; and I shall be well content if nothing worse happen to us during our voyage.

Adieu, my dear Margaret. Be assured, that for my own sake, as well as yours, I will not rashly encounter danger. I will be cool, persevering and prudent.

But success *shall* crown my endeavours. Wherefore not? Thus far I have gone, tracing a secure way over the pathless seas: the very stars themselves being witnesses and testimonies of my triumph. Why not still proceed over the untamed yet obedient element? What can stop the determined heart and resolved will of man?

My swelling heart involuntarily pours itself out thus. But I must finish. Heaven bless my beloved sister!

R.W.

LETTER IV

To Mrs Saville, England.

August 5th, 17—.

So strange an accident has happened to us that I cannot forbear recording it, although it is very probable that you will see me before these papers can come into your possession.

Last Monday (July 31st) we were nearly surrounded by ice, which closed in the ship on all sides, scarcely leaving her the sea-room in which she floated. Our situation was somewhat dangerous, especially as we were compassed round by a very thick fog. We accordingly lay to, hoping that some change would take place in the atmosphere and weather.

About two o'clock the mist cleared away, and we beheld, stretched out in every direction, vast and irregular plains of ice, which seemed to have no end. Some of my comrades groaned, and my own mind began to grow watchful with anxious thoughts, when a strange sight suddenly attracted our attention, and diverted our solicitude from our own situations. We perceived a low carriage, fixed on a sledge and drawn by dogs, pass on towards the north, at the distance of half a mile; a being which had the shape of a man, but apparently of gigantic stature, sat in the sledge, and guided the dogs. We watched the rapid progress of the traveller with our telescopes until he was lost among the distant inequalities of the ice.

This appearance excited our unqualified wonder. We were, as we believed, many hundred miles from any land; but this apparition seemed to denote that it was not, in reality, so distant as we had supposed. Shut in, however, by ice, it was impossible to follow his track, which we had observed with the greatest attention.

About two hours after this occurrence we heard the ground sea;[1] and before night the ice broke, and freed our ship. We, however, lay to until the morning, fearing to encounter in the dark those large loose masses which float about after the breaking up of the ice. I profited of this time to rest for a few hours.

In the morning, however, as soon as it was light, I went upon deck and found all the sailors busy on one side of the vessel, apparently talking to some one in the sea. It was, in fact, a sledge, like that we had seen before, which had drifted towards us in the night on a large fragment of ice. Only one dog remained alive; but there was a human being within it, whom the sailors were persuading to enter the vessel. He was not as the other traveller seemed to be, a savage inhabitant of some undiscovered island, but an European. When I appeared on deck, the master said, "Here is our captain, and he will not allow you to perish on the open sea."

On perceiving me, the stranger addressed me in English, although with a foreign accent. "Before I come on board your vessel," said he, "will you have the kindness to inform me whither you are bound?"

You may conceive my astonishment on hearing such a question addressed to me from a man on the brink of destruction and to whom I should have supposed that my vessel would have been a resource which he would not have exchanged for the most precious wealth the earth can afford. I replied, however, that we were on a voyage of discovery towards the northern pole.

Upon hearing this he appeared satisfied, and consented to come on board. Good God! Margaret, if you had seen the man who thus capitulated for his safety, your surprise would have been boundless. His limbs were nearly frozen, and his body dreadfully emaciated by fatigue and suffering. I never saw a man in so wretched a condition. We attempted to carry him into the cabin; but as soon as he had quitted the fresh air, he fainted. We accordingly brought him back to the deck, and restored him to animation by rubbing him with brandy and forcing him to swallow a small quantity. As soon as he showed signs of life, we wrapped him up in blankets and placed

[1] *ground sea*] a swell of the ocean, which occurs in calm weather and without obvious cause, breaking on the shore in heavy rollers.

him near the chimney of the kitchen stove. By slow degrees he recovered, and ate a little soup which restored him wonderfully.

Two days passed in this manner before he was able to speak; and I often feared that his sufferings had deprived him of understanding. When he had in some measure recovered, I removed him to my own cabin, and attended on him as much as my duty would permit. I never saw a more interesting creature; his eyes have generally an expression of wildness, and even madness, but there are moments when, if any one performs an act of kindness towards him or does him any the most trifling service, his whole countenance is lighted up, as it were, with a beam of benevolence and sweetness that I never saw equalled. But he is generally melancholy and despairing; and sometimes he gnashes his teeth; as if impatient of the weight of woes that oppresses him.

When my guest was a little recovered, I had great trouble to keep off the men, who wished to ask him a thousand questions; but I would not allow him to be tormented by their idle curiosity, in a state of body and mind whose restoration evidently depended upon entire repose. Once, however, the lieutenant asked why he had come so far upon the ice in so strange a vehicle?

His countenance instantly assumed an aspect of the deepest gloom; and he replied, "To seek one who fled from me."

"And did the man whom you pursued travel in the same fashion?"

"Yes."

"Then I fancy we have seen him, for the day before we picked you up, we saw some dogs drawing a sledge, with a man in it, across the ice."

This aroused the stranger's attention, and he asked a multitude of questions concerning the route which the daemon, as he called him, had pursued. Soon after, when he was alone with me, he said, "I have, doubtless, excited your curiosity, as well as that of these good people; but you are too considerate to make enquiries."

"Certainly; it would indeed be very impertinent and inhuman in me to trouble you with any inquisitiveness of mine."

"And yet you rescued me from a strange and perilous situation: you have benevolently restored me to life."

Soon after this he enquired if I thought that the breaking up of the ice had destroyed the other sledge? I replied, that I could not answer with any degree of certainty, for the ice had not broken until near midnight, and the traveller might have arrived at a place of safety before that time; but of this I could not judge.

From this time a new spirit of life animated the decaying frame of the stranger. He manifested the greatest eagerness to be upon deck, to watch for the sledge which had before appeared; but I have persuaded him to remain in the cabin, for he is far too weak to sustain the rawness of the atmosphere. I have promised that some one should watch for him and give him instant notice if any new object should appear in sight.

Such is my journal of what relates to this strange occurrence up to the present day. The stranger has gradually improved in health, but is very silent, and appears uneasy when anyone except myself enters the cabin. Yet his manners are so conciliating and gentle, that the sailors are all interested in him, although they have had very little communication with him. For my own part, I begin to love him as a brother; and his constant and deep grief fills me with sympathy and compassion. He must have been a noble creature in his better days, being even now in wreck so attractive and amiable.

I said in one of my letters, my dear Margaret, that I should find no friend on the wide ocean; yet I have found a man who, before his spirit had been broken by misery, I should have been happy to have possessed as the brother of my heart.

I shall continue my journal concerning the stranger at intervals, should I have any fresh incidents to record.

August 13th, 17—.

My affection for my guest increases every day. He excites at once my admiration and my pity to an astonishing degree. How can I see so noble a creature destroyed by misery, without feeling the most poignant grief? He is so gentle, yet so wise; his mind is so cultivated, and when he speaks, although his words are culled with the choicest art, yet they flow with rapidity and unparalleled eloquence.

He is now much recovered from his illness, and is continually on the deck, apparently watching for the sledge that preceded his own. Yet, although unhappy, he is not so utterly occupied by his own misery but that he interests himself deeply in the projects of others. He has frequently conversed with me on mine, which I have communicated to him without disguise. He entered attentively into all my arguments in favour of my eventual success, and into every minute detail of the measures I had taken to secure it. I was easily led by the sympathy which he evinced, to use the language of my heart, to give utterance to the burning ardour of my soul; and to say, with all the fervour that warmed me, how gladly I would sacrifice my fortune, my existence, my every hope, to the furtherance of my enterprise. One man's life or death were but a small price to pay for the acquirement of the knowledge which I sought for the dominion I should acquire and transmit over the elemental foes of our race. As I spoke, a dark gloom spread over my listener's countenance. At first I perceived that he tried to suppress his emotion; he placed his hands before his eyes, and my voice quivered and failed me as I beheld tears trickle fast from between his fingers,—a groan burst from his heaving breast. I paused;—at length he spoke, in broken accents:—"Unhappy man! Do you share my madness? Have you drunk also of the intoxicating draught? Hear me,—let me reveal my tale, and you will dash the cup from your lips!"

Such words, you may imagine, strongly excited my curiosity; but the paroxysm of grief that had seized the stranger overcame his weakened powers, and many hours of repose and tranquil conversation were necessary to restore his composure.

Having conquered the violence of his feelings, he appeared to despise himself for being the slave of passion; and quelling the dark tyranny of despair, he led me again to converse concerning myself personally. He asked me the history of my earlier years. The tale was quickly told: but it awakened various trains of reflection. I spoke of my desire of finding a friend—of my thirst for a more intimate sympathy with a fellow mind than had ever fallen to my lot; and expressed my conviction that a man could boast of little happiness, who did not enjoy this blessing.

"I agree with you," replied the stranger; "we are unfashioned creatures, but half made up, if one wiser, better, dearer than ourselves—such a friend ought to be—do not lend his aid to perfectionate our weak and faulty natures. I once had a friend, the most noble of human creatures, and am entitled, therefore, to judge respecting friendship. You have hope, and the world before you, and have no cause for despair. But I—I have lost every thing and cannot begin life anew."

As he said this his countenance became expressive of a calm, settled grief, that touched me to the heart. But he was silent, and presently retired to his cabin.

Even broken in spirit as he is, no one can feel more deeply than he does the beauties of nature. The starry sky, the sea, and every sight afforded by these wonderful regions, seems still to have the power of elevating his soul from earth. Such a man has a double existence: he may suffer misery and be overwhelmed by disappointments, yet, when he has retired into himself, he will be like a celestial spirit, that has a halo around him, within whose circle no grief or folly ventures.

Will you smile at the enthusiasm I express concerning this divine wanderer? You would not, if you saw him. You have been tutored and refined by books and retirement from the world, and you are therefore somewhat fastidious; but this only renders you the more fit to appreciate the extraordinary merits of this wonderful man. Sometimes I have endeavoured to discover what quality it is which he possesses, that elevates him so immeasurably above any other person I ever knew. I believe it to be an intuitive discernment; a quick but never-failing power of judgment; a penetration into the causes of things, unequalled for clearness and precision; add to this a facility of expression, and a voice whose varied intonations are soul-subduing music.

August 19th, 17—.

Yesterday the stranger said to me, "You may easily perceive, Captain Walton, that I have suffered great and unparalleled misfortunes. I had determined, at one time, that the memory of these evils should die with me, but you have won me to alter my determination. You seek for knowledge and wisdom, as I once did; and I ardently hope that the gratification of your wishes may not be a serpent to sting you, as mine has been. I do not know that the relation of my disasters will be useful to you; yet, when I reflect that you are pursuing the same course, exposing yourself to the same dangers which have rendered me what I am, I imagine that you may deduce an apt moral from my tale; one that may direct you if you succeed in your undertaking, and console you in case of failure. Prepare to hear of occurrences which are usually deemed marvellous. Were we among the tamer scenes of nature, I might fear to encounter your unbelief, perhaps your ridicule; but many things will appear possible in these wild and mysterious regions, which would provoke the laughter of those unacquainted with the ever-varied powers of nature:—nor can I doubt but that my tale conveys in its series internal evidence of the truth of the events of which it is composed."

You may easily imagine that I was much gratified by the offered communication, yet I could not endure that he should renew his grief by a recital of his misfortunes. I felt the greatest eagerness to hear the promised narrative, partly from curiosity, and partly from a strong desire to ameliorate his fate, if it were in my power. I expressed these feelings in my answer.

"I thank you," he replied, "for your sympathy, but it is useless; my fate is nearly fulfilled. I wait but for one event, and then I shall repose in peace. I understand your feeling," continued he, perceiving that I wished to interrupt him: "but you are mistaken, my friend, if thus you will allow me to name you; nothing can alter my destiny; listen to my history, and you will perceive how irrevocably it is determined."

He then told me, that he would commence his narrative the next day, when I should be at leisure. This promise drew from me the warmest thanks. I have resolved every night, when I am not imperatively occupied by my duties, to record, as nearly as possible in his own words, what he has related during the day. If I should be engaged, I will at least make notes. This manuscript will doubtless afford you the greatest pleasure: but to me, who know him and who hear it from his own lips—with what interest and sympathy shall I read it in some future day! Even now, as I commence my task, his full-toned voice swells in my ears; his lustrous eyes dwell on me with all their melancholy sweetness; I see his thin hand raised in animation, while the lineaments of his face are irradiated by the soul within. Strange and harrowing must be his story, frightful the storm which embraced the gallant vessel on its course and wrecked it—thus!

Chapter I

I AM BY birth a Genevese, and my family is one of the most distinguished of that republic. My ancestors had been for many years counsellors and syndics;[1] and my father had filled several public situations with honour and reputation. He was respected by all who knew him, for his integrity and indefatigable attention to public business. He passed his younger days perpetually occupied by the affairs of his country; a variety of circumstances had prevented his marrying early, nor was it until the decline of life that he became a husband and the father of a family.

As the circumstances of his marriage illustrate his character, I cannot refrain from relating them. One of his most intimate friends was a merchant who, from a flourishing state, fell, through numerous mischances, into poverty. This man, whose name was Beaufort, was of a proud and unbending disposition and could not bear to live in poverty and oblivion in the same country where he had formerly been distinguished for his rank and magnificence. Having paid his debts, therefore, in the most honourable manner, he retreated with his daughter to the town of Lucerne, where he lived unknown and in wretchedness. My father loved Beaufort with the truest friendship, and was deeply grieved by his retreat in these unfortunate circumstances. He bitterly deplored the false pride which led his friend to a conduct so little worthy of the affection that united them. He lost no time in endeavouring to seek him out, with the hope of persuading him to begin the world again through his credit and assistance.

Beaufort had taken effectual measures to conceal himself; and it was ten months before my father discovered his abode. Overjoyed

[1] *syndics*] municipal magistrates.

at this discovery, he hastened to the house, which was situated in a mean street near the Reuss. But when he entered, misery and despair alone welcomed him. Beaufort had saved but a very small sum of money from the wreck of his fortunes, but it was sufficient to provide him with sustenance for some months, and in the mean time he hoped to procure some respectable employment in a merchant's house. The interval was, consequently, spent in inaction; his grief only became more deep and rankling, when he had leisure for reflection; and at length it took so fast hold of his mind, that at the end of three months he lay on a bed of sickness, incapable of any exertion.

His daughter attended him with the greatest tenderness; but she saw with despair that their little fund was rapidly decreasing, and that there was no other prospect of support. But Caroline Beaufort possessed a mind of an uncommon mould, and her courage rose to support her in her adversity. She procured plain work; she plaited straw; and by various means contrived to earn a pittance scarcely sufficient to support life.

Several months passed in this manner. Her father grew worse; her time was more entirely occupied in attending him; her means of subsistence decreased; and in the tenth month her father died in her arms, leaving her an orphan and a beggar. This last blow overcame her, and she knelt by Beaufort's coffin, weeping bitterly, when my father entered the chamber. He came like a protecting spirit to the poor girl, who committed herself to his care; and after the interment of his friend he conducted her to Geneva, and placed her under the protection of a relation. Two years after this event Caroline became his wife.

There was a considerable difference between the ages of my parents, but this circumstance seemed to unite them only closer in bonds of devoted affection. There was a sense of justice in my father's upright mind, which rendered it necessary that he should approve highly to love strongly. Perhaps during former years he had suffered from the late-discovered unworthiness of one beloved, and so was disposed to set a greater value on tried worth. There was a show of gratitude and worship in his attachment to my mother, differing wholly from the doating fondness of age, for it was inspired by reverence for her virtues and a desire to be the means of, in some degree, recompensing her for the sorrows she had endured, but which gave inexpressible grace to his behaviour to her. Every thing was made to yield to her wishes and her convenience. He strove to shelter her, as a fair exotic is sheltered by the gardener, from every rougher wind, and to surround her with all that could tend to excite pleasurable emotion in her soft and benevolent mind. Her health, and even the tranquillity of her hitherto constant spirit, had been shaken by what she had gone through. During the two years that had elapsed previous to their marriage my father had gradually relinquished all his public functions; and immediately after their union they sought the pleasant climate of Italy, and the change of scene and interest attendant on a tour through that land of wonders, as a restorative for her weakened frame.

From Italy they visited Germany and France. I, their eldest child, was born at Naples, and as an infant accompanied them in their rambles. I remained for several years their only child. Much as they were attached to each other, they seemed to draw inexhaustible stores of affection from a very mine of love to bestow them upon me. My mother's tender caresses and my father's smile of benevolent pleasure while regarding me, are my first recollections. I was their plaything and their idol, and something better—their child, the innocent and helpless creature bestowed on them by Heaven, whom to bring up to good, and whose future lot it was in their hands to direct to happiness or misery, according as they fulfilled their duties towards me. With this deep consciousness of what they owed towards the being to which they had given life, added to the active spirit of tenderness that animated both, it may be imagined that while during every hour of my infant life I received a lesson of patience, of charity, and of self-control, I was so guided by a silken cord that all seemed but one train of enjoyment to me.

For a long time I was their only care. My mother had much desire to have a daughter, but I continued their single offspring. When I was about five years old, while making an excursion beyond the frontiers of Italy, they passed a week on the shores of the Lake of Como. Their benevolent disposition often made them enter the cottages of the poor. This, to my mother, was more than a duty; it was a necessity, a passion,—remembering what she had suffered, and how she had been relieved,—for her to act in her turn the guardian angel to the afflicted. During one of their walks a poor cot in the foldings of a vale attracted their notice as being singularly disconsolate, while the number of half-clothed children gathered about it spoke of penury in its worst shape. One day, when my father had gone by himself to Milan, my mother, accompanied by me, visited this abode. She found a peasant and his wife, hard working, bent down by care and labour, distributing a scanty meal to five hungry babes. Among these there was one which attracted my mother far above all the rest. She appeared of a different stock. The four others were dark-eyed, hardy little vagrants; this child was thin, and very fair. Her hair was the brightest living gold, and despite the poverty of her clothing, seemed to set a crown of distinction on her head. Her brow was clear and ample, her blue eyes cloudless, and her lips and the moulding of her face so expressive of sensibility and sweetness that none could behold her without looking on her as of a distinct species, a being heaven-sent, and bearing a celestial stamp in all her features.

The peasant woman, perceiving that my mother fixed eyes of wonder and admiration on this lovely girl, eagerly communicated her history. She was not her child, but the daughter of a Milanese nobleman. Her mother was a German, and had died on giving her birth. The infant had been placed with these good people to nurse: they were better off then. They had not been long married, and their eldest child was but just born. The father of their charge was one of those Italians nursed in the memory of the antique glory of Italy—one among the *schiavi ognor frementi,*[2] who exerted himself to obtain the liberty of his country. He became the victim of its weakness. Whether he had died, or still lingered in the dungeons of Austria, was not known. His property was confiscated; his child became an orphan and a beggar. She continued with her foster parents, and bloomed in their rude abode, fairer than a garden rose among dark-leaved brambles.

When my father returned from Milan, he found playing with me in the hall of our villa a child fairer than a pictured cherub—a creature who seemed to shed radiance from her looks and whose form and motions were lighter than the chamois of the hills. The apparition was soon explained. With his permission my mother prevailed on her rustic guardians to yield their charge to her. They were fond of the sweet orphan. Her presence had seemed a blessing to them, but it would be unfair to her to keep her in poverty and want, when Providence afforded her such powerful protection.

[2] *schiavi ognor frementi*] always restless slaves.

They consulted their village priest, and the result was that Elizabeth Lavenza became the inmate of my parents' house—my more than sister—the beautiful and adored companion of all my occupations and my pleasures.

Every one loved Elizabeth. The passionate and most reverential attachment with which all regarded her became, while I shared it, my pride and my delight. On the evening previous to her being brought to my home, my mother had said playfully,—"I have a pretty present for my Victor—tomorrow he shall have it." And when, on the morrow, she presented Elizabeth to me as her promised gift, I, with childish seriousness, interpreted her words literally and looked upon Elizabeth as mine—mine to protect, love, and cherish. All praises bestowed on her I received as made to a possession of my own. We called each other familiarly by the name of cousin. No word, no expression could body forth the kind of relation in which she stood to me—my more than sister, since till death she was to be mine only.

Chapter II

WE WERE BROUGHT up together; there was not quite a year difference in our ages. I need not say that we were strangers to any species of disunion or dispute. Harmony was the soul of our companionship, and the diversity and contrast that subsisted in our characters drew us nearer together. Elizabeth was of a calmer and more concentrated disposition; but, with all my ardour, I was capable of a more intense application, and was more deeply smitten with the thirst for knowledge. She busied herself with following the aerial creations of the poets; and in the majestic and wondrous scenes which surrounded our Swiss home—the sublime shapes of the mountains; the changes of the seasons; tempest and calm; the silence of winter, and the life and turbulence of our Alpine summers—she found ample scope for admiration and delight. While my companion contemplated with a serious and satisfied spirit the magnificent appearances of things, I delighted in investigating their causes. The world was to me a secret which I desired to divine. Curiosity, earnest research to learn the hidden laws of nature, gladness akin to rapture, as they were unfolded to me, are among the earliest sensations I can remember.

On the birth of a second son, my junior by seven years, my parents gave up entirely their wandering life, and fixed themselves in their native country. We possessed a house in Geneva, and a *campagne*[1] on Belrive, the eastern shore of the lake, at the distance of rather more than a league from the city. We resided principally in the latter, and the lives of my parents were passed in considerable seclusion. It was my temper to avoid a crowd, and to attach

[1] *campagne*] country place.

myself fervently to a few. I was indifferent, therefore, to my schoolfellows in general; but I united myself in the bonds of the closest friendship to one among them. Henry Clerval was the son of a merchant of Geneva. He was a boy of singular talent and fancy. He loved enterprise, hardship, and even danger for its own sake. He was deeply read in books of chivalry and romance. He composed heroic songs, and began to write many a tale of enchantment and knightly adventure. He tried to make us act plays and to enter into masquerades, in which the characters were drawn from the heroes of Roncesvalles, of the Round Table of King Arthur, and the chivalrous train who shed their blood to redeem the holy sepulchre from the hands of the infidels.

No human being could have passed a happier childhood than myself. My parents were possessed by the very spirit of kindness and indulgence. We felt that they were not the tyrants to rule our lot according to their caprice, but the agents and creators of all the many delights which we enjoyed. When I mingled with other families, I distinctly discerned how peculiarly fortunate my lot was, and gratitude assisted the development of filial love.

My temper was sometimes violent, and my passions vehement; but by some law in my temperature[2] they were turned not towards childish pursuits but to an eager desire to learn, and not to learn all things indiscriminately. I confess that neither the structure of languages, nor the code of governments, nor the politics of various states possessed attractions for me. It was the secrets of heaven and earth that I desired to learn; and whether it was the outward substance of things, or the inner spirit of nature and the mysterious soul of man that occupied me, still my enquiries were directed to the metaphysical, or in its highest sense, the physical secrets of the world.

Meanwhile Clerval occupied himself, so to speak, with the moral relations of things. The busy stage of life, the virtues of heroes, and the actions of men were his theme; and his hope and his dream was to become one among those whose names are recorded in story, as the gallant and adventurous benefactors of our species. The saintly soul of Elizabeth shone like a shrine-dedicated lamp in our peaceful home. Her sympathy was ours; her smile, her soft voice, the sweet

---

[2] *temperature*] temperament.

glance of her celestial eyes, were ever there to bless and animate us. She was the living spirit of love to soften and attract: I might have become sullen in my study, rough through the ardour of my nature, but that she was there to subdue me to a semblance of her own gentleness. And Clerval—could aught ill entrench on the noble spirit of Clerval?—yet he might not have been so perfectly humane, so thoughtful in his generosity—so full of kindness and tenderness amidst his passion for adventurous exploit, had she not unfolded to him the real loveliness of beneficence, and made the doing good the end and aim of his soaring ambition.

I feel exquisite pleasure in dwelling on the recollections of childhood, before misfortune had tainted my mind, and changed its bright visions of extensive usefulness into gloomy and narrow reflections upon self. Besides, in drawing the picture of my early days, I also record those events which led, by insensible steps, to my after tale of misery: for when I would account to myself for the birth of that passion, which afterwards ruled my destiny, I find it arise, like a mountain river, from ignoble and almost forgotten sources; but, swelling as it proceeded, it became the torrent which, in its course, has swept away all my hopes and joys.

Natural philosophy is the genius that has regulated my fate; I desire, therefore, in this narration, to state those facts which led to my predilection for that science. When I was thirteen years of age we all went on a party of pleasure to the baths near Thonon: the inclemency of the weather obliged us to remain a day confined to the inn. In this house I chanced to find a volume of the works of Cornelius Agrippa.[3] I opened it with apathy; the theory which he attempts to demonstrate, and the wonderful facts which he relates soon changed this feeling into enthusiasm. A new light seemed to dawn upon my mind, and, bounding with joy, I communicated my discovery to my father. My father looked carelessly at the title-page of my book and said, "Ah! Cornelius Agrippa! My dear Victor, do not waste your time upon this; it is sad trash."

If, instead of this remark, my father had taken the pains to explain to me that the principles of Agrippa had been entirely exploded,

[3] *Cornelius Agrippa*] Heinrich Cornelius Agrippa von Nettesheim (1486–1535), author of *De occulta philosophia,* in which he claimed that the study of magic was the best means to know God and nature.

and that a modern system of science had been introduced, which possessed much greater powers than the ancient, because the powers of the latter were chimerical, while those of the former were real and practical; under such circumstances I should certainly have thrown Agrippa aside and have contented my imagination, warmed as it was, by returning with greater ardour to my former studies. It is even possible that the train of my ideas would never have received the fatal impulse that led to my ruin. But the cursory glance my father had taken of my volume by no means assured me that he was acquainted with its contents; and I continued to read with the greatest avidity.

When I returned home my first care was to procure the whole works of this author, and afterwards of Paracelsus and Albertus Magnus.[4] I read and studied the wild fancies of these writers with delight; they appeared to me treasures known to few besides myself. I have described myself as always having been imbued with a fervent longing to penetrate the secrets of nature. In spite of the intense labour and wonderful discoveries of modern philosophers, I always came from my studies discontented and unsatisfied. Sir Isaac Newton is said to have avowed that he felt like a child picking up shells beside the great and unexplored ocean of truth. Those of his successors in each branch of natural philosophy with whom I was acquainted, appeared even to my boy's apprehensions, as tyros engaged in the same pursuit.

The untaught peasant beheld the elements around him, and was acquainted with their practical uses. The most learned philosopher knew little more. He had partially unveiled the face of Nature, but her immortal lineaments were still a wonder and a mystery. He might dissect, anatomise, and give names; but, not to speak of a final cause, causes in their secondary and tertiary grades were utterly unknown to him. I had gazed upon the fortifications and impediments that seemed to keep human beings from entering the citadel of nature, and rashly and ignorantly I had repined.

But here were books, and here were men who had penetrated deeper and knew more. I took their word for all that they averred,

[4] *Paracelsus and Albertus Magnus*] Paracelsus (1493–1541), or Theophrastus Bombastus Hohenheim, was a Swiss alchemist and physician; Albertus Magnus (1193?–1280) was a philosopher and natural scientist.

and I became their disciple. It may appear strange that such should arise in the eighteenth century; but while I followed the routine of education in the schools of Geneva, I was, to a great degree, self-taught with regard to my favourite studies. My father was not scientific, and I was left to struggle with a child's blindness, added to a student's thirst for knowledge. Under the guidance of my new preceptors, I entered with the greatest diligence into the search of the philosopher's stone and the elixir of life; but the latter soon obtained my undivided attention. Wealth was an inferior object; but what glory would attend the discovery, if I could banish disease from the human frame and render man invulnerable to any but a violent death!

Nor were these my only visions. The raising of ghosts or devils was a promise liberally accorded by my favourite authors, the fulfilment of which I most eagerly sought; and if my incantations were always unsuccessful, I attributed the failure rather to my own inexperience and mistake, than to a want of skill or fidelity in my instructors. And thus for a time I was occupied by exploded systems, mingling, like an unadept, a thousand contradictory theories, and floundering desperately in a very slough of multifarious knowledge, guided by an ardent imagination and childish reasoning, till an accident again changed the current of my ideas.

When I was about fifteen years old we had retired to our house near Belrive, when we witnessed a most violent and terrible thunder-storm. It advanced from behind the mountains of Jura; and the thunder burst at once with frightful loudness from various quarters of the heavens. I remained, while the storm lasted, watching its progress with curiosity and delight. As I stood at the door, on a sudden I beheld a stream of fire issue from an old and beautiful oak, which stood about twenty yards from our house; and so soon as the dazzling light vanished, the oak had disappeared, and nothing remained but a blasted stump. When we visited it the next morning, we found the tree shattered in a singular manner. It was not splintered by the shock, but entirely reduced to thin ribbons of wood. I never beheld anything so utterly destroyed.

Before this I was not unacquainted with the more obvious laws of electricity. On this occasion a man of great research in natural philosophy was with us, and, excited by this catastrophe, he entered on the explanation of a theory which he had formed on the subject of electricity and galvanism, which was at once new and astonishing to me. All that he said threw greatly into the shade Cornelius Agrippa, Albertus Magnus, and Paracelsus, the lords of my imagination; but by some fatality the overthrow of these men disinclined me to pursue my accustomed studies. It seemed to me as if nothing would or could ever be known. All that had so long engaged my attention suddenly grew despicable. By one of those caprices of the mind, which we are perhaps most subject to in early youth, I at once gave up my former occupations, set down natural history and all its progeny as a deformed and abortive creation, and entertained the greatest disdain for a would-be science which could never even step within the threshold of real knowledge. In this mood of mind I betook myself to the mathematics, and the branches of study appertaining to that science, as being built upon secure foundations, and so worthy of my consideration.

Thus strangely are our souls constructed, and by such slight ligaments are we bound to prosperity or ruin. When I look back, it seems to me as if this almost miraculous change of inclination and will was the immediate suggestion of the guardian angel of my life—the last effort made by the spirit of preservation to avert the storm that was even then hanging in the stars, and ready to envelope me. Her victory was announced by an unusual tranquillity and gladness of soul, which followed the relinquishing of my ancient and latterly tormenting studies. It was thus that I was to be taught to associate evil with their prosecution, happiness with their disregard.

It was a strong effort of the spirit of good; but it was ineffectual. Destiny was too potent, and her immutable laws had decreed my utter and terrible destruction.

Chapter III

When I had attained the age of seventeen, my parents resolved, that I should become a student at the university of Ingolstadt. I had hitherto attended the schools of Geneva; but my father thought it necessary, for the completion of my education, that I should be made acquainted with other customs than those of my native country. My departure was therefore fixed at an early date; but, before the day resolved upon could arrive, the first misfortune of my life occurred—an omen, as it were, of my future misery.

Elizabeth had caught the scarlet fever; her illness was severe, and she was in the greatest danger. During her illness, many arguments had been urged to persuade my mother to refrain from attending upon her. She had, at first, yielded to our intreaties, but when she heard that the life of her favourite was menaced, she could no longer control her anxiety. She attended her sickbed,—her watchful attentions triumphed over the malignity of the distemper,—Elizabeth was saved, but the consequences of this imprudence were fatal to her preserver. On the third day my mother sickened; her fever was accompanied by the most alarming symptoms, and the looks of her medical attendants prognosticated the worst event. On her death-bed the fortitude and benignity of this best of women did not desert her. She joined the hands of Elizabeth and myself:—"My children," she said, "my firmest hopes of future happiness were placed on the prospect of your union. This expectation will now be the consolation of your father. Elizabeth, my love, you must supply my place to my younger children. Alas! I regret that I am taken from you; and, happy and beloved as I have been, is it not hard to quit you all? But these are not thoughts befitting me; I will endeavour to resign myself cheerfully to death, and will indulge a hope of meeting you in another world."

She died calmly; and her countenance expressed affection even in death. I need not describe the feelings of those whose dearest ties are rent by that most irreparable evil; the void that presents itself to the soul; and the despair that is exhibited on the countenance. It is so long before the mind can persuade itself that she, whom we saw every day, and whose very existence appeared a part of our own, can have departed forever—that the brightness of a beloved eye can have been extinguished, and the sound of a voice so familiar and dear to the ear can be hushed, never more to be heard. These are the reflections of the first days; but when the lapse of time proves the reality of the evil, then the actual bitterness of grief commences. Yet from whom has not that rude hand rent away some dear connexion? and why should I describe a sorrow which all have felt, and must feel? The time at length arrives when grief is rather an indulgence than a necessity; and the smile that plays upon the lips, although it may be deemed a sacrilege, is not banished. My mother was dead, but we had still duties which we ought to perform; we must continue our course with the rest, and learn to think ourselves fortunate, whilst one remains whom the spoiler has not seized.

My departure for Ingolstadt, which had been deferred by these events, was now again determined upon. I obtained from my father a respite of some weeks. It appeared to me sacrilege so soon to leave the repose, akin to death, of the house of mourning and to rush into the thick of life. I was new to sorrow, but it did not the less alarm me. I was unwilling to quit the sight of those that remained to me; and above all, I desired to see my sweet Elizabeth in some degree consoled.

She indeed veiled her grief, and strove to act the comforter to us all. She looked steadily on life, and assumed its duties with courage and zeal. She devoted herself to those whom she had been taught to call her uncle and cousins. Never was she so enchanting as at this time, when she recalled the sunshine of her smiles and spent them upon us. She forgot even her own regret in her endeavours to make us forget.

The day of my departure at length arrived. Clerval spent the last evening with us. He had endeavoured to persuade his father to permit him to accompany me, and to become my fellow student; but in vain. His father was a narrow-minded trader, and saw idleness and ruin in the aspirations and ambition of his son. Henry deeply felt the misfortune of being debarred from a liberal education. He said little; but when he spoke, I read in his kindling eye and in his animated glance a restrained but firm resolve, not to be chained to the miserable details of commerce.

We sat late. We could not tear ourselves away from each other, nor persuade ourselves to say the word "Farewell!" It was said; and we retired under the pretence of seeking repose, each fancying that the other was deceived: but when at morning's dawn I descended to the carriage which was to convey me away, they were all there—my father again to bless me, Clerval to press my hand once more, my Elizabeth to renew her intreaties that I would write often, and to bestow the last feminine attentions on her playmate and friend.

I threw myself into the chaise that was to convey me away and indulged in the most melancholy reflections. I, who had ever been surrounded by amiable companions, continually engaged in endeavouring to bestow mutual pleasure, I was now alone. In the university, whither I was going, I must form my own friends and be my own protector. My life had hitherto been remarkably secluded and domestic; and this had given me invincible repugnance to new countenances. I loved my brothers, Elizabeth, and Clerval; these were "old familiar faces," but I believed myself totally unfitted for the company of strangers. Such were my reflections as I commenced my journey; but as I proceeded, my spirits and hopes rose. I ardently desired the acquisition of knowledge. I had often, when at home, thought it hard to remain during my youth cooped up in one place, and had longed to enter the world, and take my station among other human beings. Now my desires were complied with, and it would, indeed, have been folly to repent.

I had sufficient leisure for these and many other reflections during my journey to Ingolstadt, which was long and fatiguing. At length the high white steeple of the town met my eyes. I alighted, and was conducted to my solitary apartment, to spend the evening as I pleased.

The next morning I delivered my letters of introduction, and paid a visit to some of the principal professors. Chance—or rather the evil influence, the Angel of Destruction, which asserted omnipotent sway over me from the moment I turned my reluctant steps from my father's door—led me first to M. Krempe, professor of natural philosophy. He was an uncouth man, but deeply imbued in the secrets of his science. He asked me several questions concerning my progress in the different branches of science appertaining to natural philosophy. I replied carelessly; and, partly in contempt, mentioned the names of my alchymists as the principal authors I had studied. The professor stared. "Have you," he said, "really spent your time in studying such nonsense?"

I replied in the affirmative. "Every minute," continued M. Krempe with warmth, "every instant that you have wasted on those books is utterly and entirely lost. You have burdened your memory with exploded systems and useless names. Good God! In what desert land have you lived, where no one was kind enough to inform you that these fancies which you have so greedily imbibed are a thousand years old and as musty as they are ancient? I little expected, in this enlightened and scientific age, to find a disciple of Albertus Magnus and Paracelsus. My dear sir, you must begin your studies entirely anew."

So saying, he stept aside, and wrote down a list of several books treating of natural philosophy, which he desired me to procure; and dismissed me after mentioning that in the beginning of the following week he intended to commence a course of lectures upon natural philosophy in its general relations, and that M. Waldman, a fellow-professor, would lecture upon chemistry the alternate days that he omitted.

I returned home, not disappointed, for I have said that I had long considered those authors useless whom the professor reprobated; but I returned, not at all the more inclined to recur to these studies in any shape. M. Krempe was a little squat man, with a gruff voice and a repulsive countenance; the teacher, therefore, did not prepossess me in favour of his pursuits. In rather a too philosophical and connected a strain, perhaps, I have given an account of the conclusions I had come to concerning them in my early years. As a child, I had not been content with the results promised by the modern professors of natural science. With a confusion of ideas only to be accounted for by my extreme youth, and my want of a guide on such matters, I had retrod the steps of knowledge along the paths of time, and exchanged the discoveries of recent enquirers for the dreams of forgotten alchymists. Besides, I had a contempt for the uses of modern natural philosophy. It was very different, when the masters of the science sought immortality and power; such views, although futile, were grand; but now the scene was changed. The ambition of the enquirer seemed to limit itself to the annihilation of those visions on which my interest in science was chiefly founded. I was required to exchange chimeras of boundless grandeur for realities of little worth.

Such were my reflections during the first two or three days of my residence at Ingolstadt, which were chiefly spent in becoming acquainted with the localities, and the principal residents in my new abode. But as the ensuing week commenced, I thought of the information which M. Krempe had given me concerning the lectures. And although I could not consent to go and hear that little conceited fellow deliver sentences out of a pulpit, I recollected what he had said of M. Waldman, whom I had never seen, as he had hitherto been out of town.

Partly from curiosity, and partly from idleness, I went into the lecturing room, which M. Waldman entered shortly after. This professor was very unlike his colleague. He appeared about fifty years of age, but with an aspect expressive of the greatest benevolence; a few grey hairs covered his temples, but those at the back of his head were nearly black. His person was short, but remarkably erect; and his voice the sweetest I had ever heard. He began his lecture by a recapitulation of the history of chemistry and the various improvements made by different men of learning, pronouncing with fervour the names of the most distinguished discoverers. He then took a cursory view of the present state of the science, and explained many of its elementary terms. After having made a few preparatory experiments, he concluded with a panegyric upon modern chemistry, the terms of which I shall never forget:—

"The ancient teachers of this science," said he, "promised impossibilities, and performed nothing. The modern masters promise very little; they know that metals cannot be transmuted, and that the elixir of life is a chimera. But these philosophers, whose hands seem only made to dabble in dirt, and their eyes to pore over the microscope or crucible, have indeed performed miracles. They penetrate into the recesses of nature, and show how she works in her hiding-places. They ascend into the heavens; they have discovered how the blood circulates, and the nature of the air we breathe. They have acquired new and almost unlimited powers; they can command the thunders of heaven, mimic the earthquake, and even mock the invisible world with its own shadows."

Such were the professor's words—rather let me say such the words of the fate, enounced to destroy me. As he went on, I felt as if my soul were grappling with a palpable enemy; one by one the various keys were touched which formed the mechanism of my being: chord after chord was sounded, and soon my mind was filled with one thought, one conception, one purpose. So much has been done, exclaimed the soul of Frankenstein,—more, far more, will I achieve: treading in the steps already marked, I will pioneer a new way, explore unknown powers, and unfold to the world the deepest mysteries of creation.

I closed not my eyes that night. My internal being was in a state of insurrection and turmoil; I felt that order would thence arise, but I had no power to produce it. By degrees, after the morning's dawn, sleep came. I awoke, and my yesternight's thoughts were as a dream. There only remained a resolution to return to my ancient studies, and to devote myself to a science for which I believed myself to possess a natural talent. On the same day, I paid M. Waldman a visit. His manners in private were even more mild and attractive than in public; for there was a certain dignity in his mien during his lecture, which in his own house was replaced by the greatest affability and kindness. I gave him pretty nearly the same account of my former pursuits as I had given to his fellow-professor. He heard with attention the little narration concerning my studies, and smiled at the names of Cornelius Agrippa and Paracelsus, but without the contempt that M. Krempe had exhibited. He said that "these were men to whose indefatigable zeal modern philosophers were indebted for most of the foundations of their knowledge. They had left to us, as an easier task, to give new names, and arrange in connected classifications the facts which they in a great degree had been the instruments of bringing to light. The labours of men of genius, however erroneously directed, scarcely ever fail in ultimately turning to the solid advantage of mankind." I listened to his statement, which was delivered without any presumption or affectation; and then added that his lecture had removed any prejudices against modern chemists; I expressed myself in measured terms, with the modesty and deference due from a youth to his instructor, without letting escape (inexperience in life would have made me ashamed) any of the enthusiasm which stimulated my intended labours. I requested his advice concerning the books I ought to procure.

"I am happy," said M. Waldman, "to have gained a disciple; and if your application equals your ability, I have no doubt of your success. Chemistry is that branch of natural philosophy in which the greatest improvements have been and may be made; it is on that account that I have made it my peculiar study; but at the same time, I have not neglected the other branches of science. A man would make but a very sorry chemist if he attended to that department of human knowledge alone. If your wish is to become really a man of science, and not merely a petty experimentalist, I should advise you to apply to every branch of natural philosophy, including mathematics."

He then took me into his laboratory and explained to me the uses of his various machines; instructing me as to what I ought to procure, and promising me the use of his own when I should have advanced far enough in the science not to derange their mechanism. He also gave me the list of books which I had requested; and I took my leave.

Thus ended a day memorable to me: it decided my future destiny.

Chapter IV

From this day natural philosophy, and particularly chemistry, in the most comprehensive sense of the term, became nearly my sole occupation. I read with ardour those works, so full of genius and discrimination, which modern enquirers have written on these subjects. I attended the lectures, and cultivated the acquaintance, of the men of science of the university; and I found even in M. Krempe a great deal of sound sense and real information, combined, it is true, with a repulsive physiognomy and manners, but not on that account the less valuable. In M. Waldman I found a true friend. His gentleness was never tinged by dogmatism, and his instructions were given with an air of frankness and good nature, that banished every idea of pedantry. In a thousand ways he smoothed for me the path of knowledge, and made the most abstruse enquiries clear and facile to my apprehension. My application was at first fluctuating and uncertain; it gained strength as I proceeded, and soon became so ardent and eager, that the stars often disappeared in the light of morning whilst I was yet engaged in my laboratory.

As I applied so closely, it may be easily conceived that my progress was rapid. My ardour was indeed the astonishment of the students, and my proficiency that of the masters. Professor Krempe often asked me, with a sly smile, how Cornelius Agrippa went on? whilst M. Waldman expressed the most heartfelt exultation in my progress. Two years passed in this manner, during which I paid no visit to Geneva, but was engaged, heart and soul, in the pursuit of some discoveries which I hoped to make. None but those who have experienced them can conceive of the enticements of science. In other studies you go as far as others have gone before you, and there is nothing more to know; but in a scientific pursuit there is continual food for discovery and wonder. A mind of moderate capacity, which closely pursued one study must infallibly arrive at great proficiency in that study; and I, who continually sought the attainment of one object of pursuit and was solely wrapt up in this, improved so rapidly, that, at the end of two years, I made some discoveries in the improvement of some chemical instruments, which procured me great esteem and admiration at the university. When I had arrived at this point and had become as well acquainted with the theory and practice of natural philosophy as depended on the lessons of any of the professors at Ingolstadt, my residence there being no longer conducive to my improvements, I thought of returning to my friends and my native town, when an incident happened that protracted my stay.

One of the phenomena which had peculiarly attracted my attention was the structure of the human frame, and, indeed, any animal endued with life. Whence, I often asked myself, did the principle of life proceed? It was a bold question, and one which has ever been considered as a mystery; yet with how many things are we upon the brink of becoming acquainted, if cowardice or carelessness did not restrain our enquiries. I revolved these circumstances in my mind, and determined thenceforth to apply myself more particularly to those branches of natural philosophy which relate to physiology. Unless I had been animated by an almost supernatural enthusiasm, my application to this study would have been irksome, and almost intolerable. To examine the causes of life, we must first have recourse to death. I became acquainted with the science of anatomy: but this was not sufficient; I must also observe the natural decay and corruption of the human body. In my education my father had taken the greatest precautions that my mind should be impressed with no supernatural horrors. I do not ever remember to have trembled at a tale of superstition, or to have feared the apparition of a spirit. Darkness had no effect upon my fancy; and a churchyard was to me merely the receptacle of bodies deprived of life, which, from being the seat of beauty and strength, had become food for the worm. Now I was led to examine the cause and progress of this decay, and forced to spend days and nights in vaults and charnel-houses. My attention was fixed upon every object the most insupportable to the delicacy of the human feelings. I saw how the fine form of man was degraded and wasted; I beheld the corruption of death succeed to the blooming cheek of life; I saw how the worm inherited the wonders of the eye and brain. I paused, examining and analysing all the minutiae of causation, as exemplified in the change from life to death, and death to life, until from the midst of this darkness a sudden light broke in upon me—a light so brilliant and wondrous, yet so simple, that while I became dizzy with the immensity of the prospect which it illustrated, I was surprised, that among so many men of genius who had directed their enquiries towards the same science, that I alone should be reserved to discover so astonishing a secret.

Remember, I am not recording the vision of a madman. The sun does not more certainly shine in the heavens, than that which I now affirm is true. Some miracle might have produced it, yet the stages of the discovery were distinct and probable. After days and nights of incredible labour and fatigue, I succeeded in discovering the cause of generation and life; nay, more, I became myself capable of bestowing animation upon lifeless matter.

The astonishment which I had at first experienced on this discovery soon gave place to delight and rapture. After so much time spent in painful labour, to arrive at once at the summit of my desires, was the most gratifying consummation of my toils. But this discovery was so great and overwhelming, that all the steps by which I had been progressively led to it were obliterated, and I beheld only the result. What had been the study and desire of the wisest men since the creation of the world was now within my grasp. Not that, like a magic scene, it all opened upon me at once: the information I had obtained was of a nature rather to direct my endeavours so soon as I should point them towards the object of my search, than to exhibit that object already accomplished. I was like the Arabian who had been buried with the dead[1] and found a passage to life, aided only by one glimmering and seemingly ineffectual light.

I see by your eagerness and the wonder and hope which your eyes express, my friend, that you expect to be informed of the secret with which I am acquainted; that cannot be: listen patiently until the end of my story, and you will easily perceive why I am reserved upon that subject. I will not lead you on, unguarded and

[1] *the Arabian . . . dead*] a reference to Sinbad the Sailor's Fourth Voyage in *The Thousand and One Nights.*

ardent as I then was, to your destruction and infallible misery. Learn from me, if not by my precepts, at least by my example, how dangerous is the acquirement of knowledge and how much happier that man is who believes his native town to be the world, than he who aspires to become greater than his nature will allow.

When I found so astonishing a power placed within my hands, I hesitated a long time concerning the manner in which I should employ it. Although I possessed the capacity of bestowing animation, yet to prepare a frame for the reception of it, with all its intricacies of fibres, muscles, and veins, still remained a work of inconceivable difficulty and labour. I doubted at first whether I should attempt the creation of a being like myself, or one of simpler organisation; but my imagination was too much exalted by my first success to permit me to doubt of my ability to give life to an animal as complex and wonderful as man. The materials at present within my command hardly appeared adequate to so arduous an undertaking; but I doubted not that I should ultimately succeed. I prepared myself for a multitude of reverses; my operations might be incessantly baffled, and at last my work be imperfect: yet, when I considered the improvement which every day takes place in science and mechanics, I was encouraged to hope my present attempts would at least lay the foundations of future success. Nor could I consider the magnitude and complexity of my plan as any argument of its impracticability. It was with these feelings that I began the creation of a human being. As the minuteness of the parts formed a great hindrance to my speed, I resolved, contrary to my first intention, to make the being of a gigantic stature; that is to say, about eight feet in height, and proportionably large. After having formed this determination and having spent some months in successfully collecting and arranging my materials, I began.

No one can conceive the variety of feelings which bore me onwards, like a hurricane, in the first enthusiasm of success. Life and death appeared to me ideal bounds, which I should first break through, and pour a torrent of light into our dark world. A new species would bless me as its creator and source; many happy and excellent natures would owe their being to me. No father could claim the gratitude of his child so completely as I should deserve theirs. Pursuing these reflections, I thought, that if I could bestow animation upon lifeless matter, I might in process of time (although

I now found it impossible) renew life where death had apparently devoted the body to corruption.

These thoughts supported my spirits, while I pursued my undertaking with unremitting ardour. My cheek had grown pale with study, and my person had become emaciated with confinement. Sometimes, on the very brink of certainty, I failed; yet still I clung to the hope which the next day or the next hour might realise. One secret which I alone possessed was the hope to which I had dedicated myself; and the moon gazed on my midnight labours, while, with unrelaxed and breathless eagerness, I pursued nature to her hiding-places. Who shall conceive the horrors of my secret toil as I dabbled among the unhallowed damps of the grave or tortured the living animal to animate the lifeless clay? My limbs now tremble, and my eyes swim with the remembrance; but then a resistless, and almost frantic impulse, urged me forward; I seemed to have lost all soul or sensation but for this one pursuit. It was indeed but a passing trance, that only made me feel with renewed acuteness so soon as, the unnatural stimulus ceasing to operate, I had returned to my old habits. I collected bones from charnel-houses and disturbed, with profane fingers, the tremendous secrets of the human frame. In a solitary chamber, or rather cell, at the top of the house, and separated from all the other apartments by a gallery and staircase, I kept my workshop of filthy creation: my eyeballs were starting from their sockets in attending to the details of my employment. The dissecting room and the slaughter-house furnished many of my materials; and often did my human nature turn with loathing from my occupation, whilst, still urged on by an eagerness which perpetually increased, I brought my work near to a conclusion.

The summer months passed while I was thus engaged, heart and soul, in one pursuit. It was a most beautiful season; never did the fields bestow a more plentiful harvest, or the vines yield a more luxuriant vintage: but my eyes were insensible to the charms of nature. And the same feelings which made me neglect the scenes around me caused me also to forget those friends who were so many miles absent, and whom I had not seen for so long a time. I knew my silence disquieted them; and I well remembered the words of my father: "I know that while you are pleased with yourself, you will think of us with affection, and we shall hear regularly from you. You must pardon me if I regard any interruption in your correspondence as a proof that your other duties are equally neglected."

I knew well therefore what would be my father's feelings; but I could not tear my thoughts from my employment, loathsome in itself, but which had taken an irresistible hold of my imagination. I wished, as it were, to procrastinate all that related to my feelings of affection until the great object, which swallowed up every habit of my nature, should be completed.

I then thought that my father would be unjust if he ascribed my neglect to vice, or faultiness on my part, but I am now convinced that he was justified in conceiving that I should not be altogether free from blame. A human being in perfection ought always to preserve a calm and peaceful mind, and never to allow passion or a transitory desire to disturb his tranquillity. I do not think that the pursuit of knowledge is an exception to this rule. If the study to which you apply yourself has a tendency to weaken your affections, and to destroy your taste for those simple pleasures in which no alloy can possibly mix, then that study is certainly unlawful, that is to say, not befitting the human mind. If this rule were always observed; if no man allowed any pursuit whatsoever to interfere with the tranquillity of his domestic affections, Greece had not been enslaved; Caesar would have spared his country; America would have been discovered more gradually; and the empires of Mexico and Peru had not been destroyed.

But I forget that I am moralising in the most interesting part of my tale, and your looks remind me to proceed.

My father made no reproach in his letters, and only took notice of my silence by enquiring into my occupations more particularly than before. Winter, spring, and summer passed away during my labours; but I did not watch the blossom or the expanding leaves—sights which before always yielded me supreme delight—so deeply was I engrossed in my occupation. The leaves of that year had withered before my work drew to a close; and now every day showed me more plainly how well I had succeeded. But my enthusiasm was checked by my anxiety, and I appeared rather like one doomed by slavery to toil in the mines, or any other unwholesome trade than an artist occupied by his favourite employment. Every night I was oppressed by a slow fever, and I became nervous to a most painful degree; the fall of a leaf startled me, and I shunned my fellow-creatures as if I had been guilty of a crime. Sometimes I grew alarmed at the wreck I perceived that I had become; the energy of my purpose alone sustained me: my labours would soon end, and I believed that exercise and amusement would then drive away incipient disease; and I promised myself both of these when my creation should be complete.

Chapter V

It was on a dreary night of November, that I beheld the accomplishment of my toils. With an anxiety that almost amounted to agony, I collected the instruments of life around me, that I might infuse a spark of being into the lifeless thing that lay at my feet. It was already one in the morning; the rain pattered dismally against the panes, and my candle was nearly burnt out, when, by the glimmer of the half-extinguished light, I saw the dull yellow eye of the creature open; it breathed hard, and a convulsive motion agitated its limbs.

How can I describe my emotions at this catastrophe, or how delineate the wretch whom with such infinite pains and care I had endeavoured to form? His limbs were in proportion, and I had selected his features as beautiful. Beautiful!—Great God! His yellow skin scarcely covered the work of muscles and arteries beneath; his hair was of a lustrous black, and flowing; his teeth of pearly whiteness; but these luxuriances only formed a more horrid contrast with his watery eyes, that seemed almost of the same colour as the dun-white sockets in which they were set, his shrivelled complexion and straight black lips.

The different accidents of life are not so changeable as the feelings of human nature. I had worked hard for nearly two years, for the sole purpose of infusing life into an inanimate body. For this I had deprived myself of rest and health. I had desired it with an ardour that far exceeded moderation; but now that I had finished, the beauty of the dream vanished, and breathless horror and disgust filled my heart. Unable to endure the aspect of the being I had created, I rushed out of the room, and continued a long time traversing my bedchamber, unable to compose my mind to sleep. At length lassitude succeeded to the tumult I had before endured; and

I threw myself on the bed in my clothes, endeavouring to seek a few moments of forgetfulness. But it was in vain: I slept, indeed, but I was disturbed by the wildest dreams. I thought I saw Elizabeth, in the bloom of health, walking in the streets of Ingolstadt. Delighted and surprised, I embraced her, but as I imprinted the first kiss on her lips, they became livid with the hue of death; her features appeared to change, and I thought that I held the corpse of my dead mother in my arms; a shroud enveloped her form, and I saw the grave-worms crawling in the folds of flannel. I started from my sleep with horror; a cold dew covered my forehead, my teeth chattered, and every limb became convulsed: when, by the dim and yellow light of the moon, as it forced its way through the window shutters, I beheld the wretch—the miserable monster whom I had created. He held up the curtain of the bed; and his eyes, if eyes they may be called, were fixed on me. His jaws opened, and he muttered some inarticulate sounds, while a grin wrinkled his cheeks. He might have spoken, but I did not hear; one hand was stretched out, seemingly to detain me, but I escaped, and rushed downstairs. I took refuge in the courtyard belonging to the house which I inhabited; where I remained during the rest of the night, walking up and down in the greatest agitation, listening attentively, catching and fearing each sound as if it were to announce the approach of the demoniacal corpse to which I had so miserably given life.

Oh! no mortal could support the horror of that countenance. A mummy again endued with animation could not be so hideous as that wretch. I had gazed on him while unfinished; he was ugly then; but when those muscles and joints were rendered capable of motion, it became a thing such as even Dante could not have conceived.

I passed the night wretchedly. Sometimes my pulse beat so quickly and hardly that I felt the palpitation of every artery; at others, I nearly sank to the ground through languor and extreme weakness. Mingled with this horror, I felt the bitterness of disappointment; dreams that had been my food and pleasant rest for so long a space were now become a hell to me; and the change was so rapid, the overthrow so complete!

Morning, dismal and wet, at length dawned, and discovered to my sleepless and aching eyes the church of Ingolstadt, its white steeple and clock, which indicated the sixth hour. The porter opened the gates of the court, which had that night been my asylum, and I issued into the streets, pacing them with quick steps, as if I sought to avoid the wretch whom I feared every turning of the street would present to my view. I did not dare return to the apartment which I inhabited, but felt impelled to hurry on, although drenched by the rain which poured from a black and comfortless sky.

I continued walking in this manner for some time, endeavouring by bodily exercise to ease the load that weighed upon my mind. I traversed the streets without any clear conception of where I was or what I was doing. My heart palpitated in the sickness of fear, and I hurried on with irregular steps, not daring to look about me:

Like one, on a lonesome road who,
Doth walk in fear and dread,
And, having once turned round, walks on,
And turns no more his head;
Because he knows a frightful fiend
Doth close behind him tread.*

Continuing thus, I came at length opposite to the inn at which the various diligences and carriages usually stopped. Here I paused, I knew not why; but I remained some minutes with my eyes fixed on a coach that was coming towards me from the other end of the street. As it drew nearer I observed that it was the Swiss diligence: it stopped just where I was standing; and, on the door being opened, I perceived Henry Clerval, who, on seeing me, instantly sprung out. "My dear Frankenstein," exclaimed he, "how glad I am to see you! how fortunate that you should be here at the very moment of my alighting!"

Nothing could equal my delight on seeing Clerval; his presence brought back to my thoughts my father, Elizabeth, and all those scenes of home so dear to my recollection. I grasped his hand, and in a moment forgot my horror and misfortune; I felt suddenly, and for the first time during many months, calm and serene joy. I welcomed my friend, therefore, in the most cordial manner, and we walked towards my college. Clerval continued talking for some

* Coleridge's *Ancient Mariner* [author's footnote].

time about our mutual friends and his own good fortune in being permitted to come to Ingolstadt. "You may easily believe," said he, "how great was the difficulty to persuade my father that all necessary knowledge was not comprised in the noble art of book-keeping; and, indeed, I believe I left him incredulous to the last, for his constant answer to my unwearied intreaties was the same as that to the Dutch schoolmaster in *The Vicar of Wakefield:* 'I have ten thousand florins a year without Greek, I eat heartily without Greek.' But his affection for me at length overcame his dislike of learning, and he has permitted me to undertake a voyage of discovery to the land of knowledge."

"It gives me the greatest delight to see you; but tell me how you left my father, brothers, and Elizabeth."

"Very well, and very happy, only a little uneasy that they hear from you so seldom. By the by, I mean to lecture you a little upon their account myself.—But, my dear Frankenstein," continued he, stopping short, and gazing full in my face, "I did not before remark how very ill you appear; so thin and pale; you look as if you had been watching for several nights."

"You have guessed right; I have lately been so deeply engaged in one occupation, that I have not allowed myself sufficient rest, as you see; but I hope, I sincerely hope, that all these employments are now at an end, and that I am at length free."

I trembled excessively; I could not endure to think of, and far less to allude to, the occurrences of the preceding night. I walked with a quick pace, and we soon arrived at my college. I then reflected, and the thought made me shiver, that the creature whom I had left in my apartment might still be there, alive and walking about. I dreaded to behold this monster; but I feared still more that Henry should see him. Intreating him, therefore, to remain a few minutes at the bottom of the stairs, I darted up towards my own room. My hand was already on the lock of the door before I recollected myself. I then paused; and a cold shivering came over me. I threw the door forcibly open, as children are accustomed to do when they expect a spectre to stand in waiting for them on the other side; but nothing appeared. I stepped fearfully in: the apartment was empty; and my bedroom was also freed from its hideous guest. I could hardly believe that so great a good fortune could have befallen me; but when I became assured that my enemy had indeed fled, I clapped my hands for joy and ran down to Clerval.

We ascended into my room, and the servant presently brought breakfast; but I was unable to contain myself. It was not joy only that possessed me; I felt my flesh tingle with excess of sensitiveness, and my pulse beat rapidly. I was unable to remain for a single instant in the same place; I jumped over the chairs, clapped my hands, and laughed aloud. Clerval at first attributed my unusual spirits to joy on his arrival, but when he observed me more attentively, he saw a wildness in my eyes for which he could not account; and my loud, unrestrained, heartless laughter frightened and astonished him.

"My dear Victor," cried he, "what, for God's sake, is the matter? Do not laugh in that manner. How ill you are! What is the cause of all this?"

"Do not ask me," cried I, putting my hands before my eyes, for I thought I saw the dreaded spectre glide into the room; "*he* can tell.—Oh, save me! save me!" I imagined that the monster seized me; I struggled furiously and fell down in a fit.

Poor Clerval! what must have been his feelings? A meeting, which he anticipated with such joy, so strangely turned to bitterness. But I was not the witness of his grief; for I was lifeless, and did not recover my senses for a long, long time.

This was the commencement of a nervous fever, which confined me for several months. During all that time Henry was my only nurse. I afterwards learned that, knowing my father's advanced age, and unfitness for so long a journey, and how wretched my sickness would make Elizabeth, he spared them this grief by concealing the extent of my disorder. He knew that I could not have a more kind and attentive nurse than himself; and, firm in the hope he felt of my recovery, he did not doubt that, instead of doing harm, he performed the kindest action that he could towards them.

But I was in reality very ill; and surely nothing but the unbounded and unremitting attentions of my friend could have restored me to life. The form of the monster on whom I had bestowed existence was forever before my eyes, and I raved incessantly concerning him. Doubtless my words surprised Henry; he at first believed them to be the wanderings of my disturbed imagination; but the pertinacity with which I continually recurred to the same subject, persuaded him that my disorder indeed owed its origin to some uncommon and terrible event.

By very slow degrees, and with frequent relapses that alarmed and grieved my friend, I recovered. I remember the first time

I became capable of observing outward objects with any kind of pleasure, I perceived that the fallen leaves had disappeared and that the young buds were shooting forth from the trees that shaded my window. It was a divine spring; and the season contributed greatly to my convalescence. I felt also sentiments of joy and affection revive in my bosom; my gloom disappeared, and in a short time I became as cheerful as before I was attacked by the fatal passion.

"Dearest Clerval," exclaimed I, "how kind, how very good you are to me. This whole winter, instead of being spent in study, as you promised yourself, has been consumed in my sick room. How shall I ever repay you? I feel the greatest remorse for the disappointment of which I have been the occasion; but you will forgive me."

"You will repay me entirely, if you do not discompose yourself, but get well as fast as you can; and since you appear in such good spirits, I may speak to you on one subject, may I not?"

I trembled. One subject! What could it be? Could he allude to an object on whom I dared not even think?

"Compose yourself," said Clerval, who observed my change of colour, "I will not mention it if it agitates you; but your father and cousin would be very happy if they received a letter from you in your own handwriting. They hardly know how ill you have been, and are uneasy at your long silence."

"Is that all, my dear Henry? How could you suppose that my first thought would not fly towards those dear, dear friends whom I love, and who are so deserving of my love?"

"If this is your present temper, my friend, you will perhaps be glad to see a letter that has been lying here some days for you: it is from your cousin, I believe."

Chapter VI

Clerval then put the following letter into my hands. It was from my own Elizabeth:—

My dearest Cousin,

You have been ill, very ill, and even the constant letters of dear kind Henry are not sufficient to reassure me on your account. You are forbidden to write—to hold a pen; yet one word from you, dear Victor, is necessary to calm our apprehensions. For a long time I have thought that each post would bring this line, and my persuasions have restrained my uncle from undertaking a journey to Ingolstadt. I have prevented his encountering the inconveniences and perhaps dangers of so long a journey, yet how often have I regretted not being able to perform it myself! I figure to myself that the task of attending on your sickbed has devolved on some mercenary old nurse, who could never guess your wishes, nor minister to them with the care and affection of your poor cousin. Yet that is over now: Clerval writes that indeed you are getting better. I eagerly hope that you will confirm this intelligence soon in your own handwriting.

Get well—and return to us. You will find a happy, cheerful home, and friends who love you dearly. Your father's health is vigorous, and he asks but to see you, but to be assured that you are well; and not a care will ever cloud his benevolent countenance. How pleased you would be to remark the improvement of our Ernest! He is now sixteen, and full of activity and spirit. He is desirous to be a true Swiss, and to enter into foreign service, but we cannot part with him, at least until his elder brother return to us. My uncle is not pleased with the idea of a military career in a distant country, but Ernest never had your powers of application. He looks upon study as an odious fetter; his time is spent in the open air, climbing the hills or rowing on the lake. I fear that he will become an idler, unless we yield the point, and permit him to enter on the profession which he has selected.

Little alteration, except the growth of our dear children, has taken place since you left us. The blue lake, and snow-clad mountains—they never change; and I think our placid home and our contented hearts are regulated by the same immutable laws. My trifling occupations take up my time and amuse me, and I am rewarded for any exertions by seeing none but happy, kind faces around me. Since you left us, but one change has taken place in our little household. Do you remember on what occasions Justine Moritz entered our family? Probably you do not; I will relate her history, therefore, in a few words. Madame Moritz, her mother, was a widow with four children, of whom Justine was the third. This girl had always been the favourite of her father; but, through a strange perversity, her mother could not endure her, and after the death of M. Moritz, treated her very ill. My aunt observed this, and when Justine was twelve years of age, prevailed on her mother to allow her to live at our house. The republican institutions of our country have produced simpler and happier manners than those which prevail in the great monarchies that surround it. Hence there is less distinction between the several classes of its inhabitants; and the lower orders, being neither so poor nor so despised, their manners are more refined and moral. A servant in Geneva does not mean the same thing as a servant in France and England. Justine, thus received in our family, learned the duties of a servant; a condition which, in our fortunate country, does not include the idea of ignorance, and a sacrifice of the dignity of a human being.

Justine, you may remember, was a great favourite of yours; and I recollect you once remarked that if you were in an ill humour, one glance from Justine could dissipate it, for the same reason that Ariosto gives concerning the beauty of Angelica[1]—she looked so frank-hearted and happy. My aunt conceived a great attachment for her, by which she was induced to give her an education superior to

[1] *Ariosto . . . Angelica*] Angelica is one of the chief heroines of Ariosto's *Orlando Furioso*.

that which she had at first intended. This benefit was fully repaid; Justine was the most grateful little creature in the world: I do not mean that she made any professions; I never heard one pass her lips, but you could see by her eyes that she almost adored her protectress. Although her disposition was gay, and in many respects inconsiderate, yet she paid the greatest attention to every gesture of my aunt. She thought her the model of all excellence and endeavoured to imitate her phraseology and manners, so that even now she often reminds me of her.

When my dearest aunt died, every one was too much occupied in their own grief to notice poor Justine, who had attended her illness with the most anxious affection. Poor Justine was very ill, but other trials were reserved for her.

One by one, her brothers and sister died; and her mother, with the exception of her neglected daughter, was left childless. The conscience of the woman was troubled; she began to think that the deaths of her favourites were a judgment from heaven to chastise her partiality. She was a Roman Catholic; and I believe her confessor confirmed the idea which she had conceived. Accordingly, a few months after your departure for Ingolstadt, Justine was called home by her repentant mother. Poor girl! she wept when she quitted our house; she was much altered since the death of my aunt; grief had given softness and a winning mildness to her manners which had before been remarkable for vivacity. Nor was her residence at her mother's house of a nature to restore her gaiety. The poor woman was very vacillating in her repentance. She sometimes begged Justine to forgive her unkindness but much oftener accused her of having caused the deaths of her brothers and sister. Perpetual fretting at length threw Madame Moritz into a decline, which at first increased her irritability, but she is now at peace forever. She died on the first approach of cold weather, at the beginning of this last winter. Justine has returned to us, and I assure you I love her tenderly. She is very clever and gentle, and extremely pretty; as I mentioned before, her mien and her expressions continually remind me of my dear aunt.

I must say also a few words to you, my dear cousin, of little darling William. I wish you could see him; he is very tall of his age, with sweet laughing blue eyes, dark eyelashes, and curling hair. When he smiles, two little dimples appear on each cheek, which are rosy with health. He has already had one or two little *wives,* but Louisa Biron is his favourite, a pretty little girl of five years of age.

Now, dear Victor, I dare say you wish to be indulged in a little gossip concerning the good people of Geneva. The pretty Miss Mansfield has already received the congratulatory visits on her approaching marriage with a young Englishman, John Melbourne, Esq. Her ugly sister, Manon, married M. Duvillard, the rich banker, last autumn. Your favourite school-fellow, Louis Manoir, has suffered misfortunes since the departure of Clerval from Geneva. But he has already recovered his spirits and is reported to be on the point of marrying a very lively, pretty Frenchwoman, Madame Tavernier. She is a widow, and much older than Manoir; but she is very much admired and a favourite with every body.

I have written myself into better spirits, dear cousin; but my anxiety returns upon me as I conclude. Write, dearest Victor—one line—one word will be a blessing to us. Ten thousand thanks to Henry for his kindness, his affection, and his many letters: we are sincerely grateful. Adieu! my cousin; take care of yourself; and, I intreat you, write!

Elizabeth Lavenza
Geneva, March 18th, 17—.

"Dear, dear Elizabeth!" I exclaimed, when I had read her letter, "I will write instantly, and relieve them from the anxiety they must feel." I wrote, and this exertion greatly fatigued me; but my convalescence had commenced, and proceeded regularly. In another fortnight I was able to leave my chamber.

One of my first duties on my recovery was to introduce Clerval to the several professors of the university. In doing this, I underwent a kind of rough usage, ill befitting the wounds that my mind had sustained. Ever since the fatal night, the end of my labours, and the beginning of my misfortunes, I had conceived a violent antipathy even to the name of natural philosophy. When I was otherwise quite restored to health, the sight of a chemical instrument would renew all the agony of my nervous symptoms. Henry saw this and had removed all my apparatus from my view. He had also changed my apartment, for he perceived that I had acquired a dislike for the room which had previously been my laboratory. But these cares of

Clerval were made of no avail when I visited the professors. M. Waldman inflicted torture when he praised, with kindness and warmth, the astonishing progress I had made in the sciences. He soon perceived that I disliked the subject; but not guessing the real cause, he attributed my feelings to modesty and changed the subject from my improvement to the science itself, with a desire, as I evidently saw, of drawing me out. What could I do? He meant to please, and he tormented me. I felt as if he had placed carefully, one by one, in my view those instruments which were to be afterwards used in putting me to a slow and cruel death. I writhed under his words, yet dared not exhibit the pain I felt. Clerval, whose eyes and feelings were always quick in discerning the sensations of others, declined the subject, alleging, in excuse, his total ignorance; and the conversation took a more general turn. I thanked my friend from my heart, but I did not speak. I saw plainly that he was surprised, but he never attempted to draw my secret from me; and although I loved him with a mixture of affection and reverence that knew no bounds, yet I could never persuade myself to confide to him that event which was so often present to my recollection, but which I feared the detail to another would only impress more deeply.

M. Krempe was not equally docile; and in my condition at that time, of almost insupportable sensitiveness, his harsh, blunt encomiums gave me even more pain than the benevolent approbation of M. Waldman. "D—n the fellow!" cried he; "why, M. Clerval, I assure you he has outstript us all. Ay, stare if you please; but it is nevertheless true. A youngster who, but a few years ago, believed in Cornelius Agrippa as firmly as in the Gospel, has now set himself at the head of the university; and if he is not soon pulled down, we shall all be out of countenance.—Ay, ay," continued he, observing my face expressive of suffering, "M. Frankenstein is modest, an excellent quality in a young man. Young men should be diffident of themselves, you know, M. Clerval: I was myself when young, but that wears out in a very short time."

M. Krempe had now commenced a eulogy on himself, which happily turned the conversation from a subject that was so annoying to me.

Clerval had never sympathised in my tastes for natural science; and his literary pursuits differed wholly from those which had occupied me. He came to the university with the design of making himself complete master of the Oriental languages, as thus he should open a field for the plan of life he had marked out for himself. Resolved to pursue no inglorious career, he turned his eyes towards the East as affording scope for his spirit of enterprise. The Persian, Arabic, and Sanscrit languages engaged his attention, and I was easily induced to enter on the same studies. Idleness had ever been irksome to me, and now that I wished to fly from reflection and hated my former studies, I felt great relief in being the fellow pupil with my friend, and found not only instruction but consolation in the works of the Orientalists. I did not, like him, attempt a critical knowledge of their dialects, for I did not contemplate making any other use of them than temporary amusement. I read merely to understand their meaning, and they well repaid my labours. Their melancholy is soothing, and their joy elevating, to a degree I never experienced in studying the authors of any other country. When you read their writings, life appears to consist in a warm sun and a garden of roses, in the smiles and frowns of a fair enemy, and the fire that consumes your own heart. How different from the manly and heroical poetry of Greece and Rome!

Summer passed away in these occupations, and my return to Geneva was fixed for the latter end of autumn; but being delayed by several accidents, winter and snow arrived, the roads were deemed impassable, and my journey was retarded until the ensuing spring. I felt this delay very bitterly; for I longed to see my native town and my beloved friends. My return had only been delayed so long from an unwillingness to leave Clerval in a strange place before he had become acquainted with any of its inhabitants. The winter, however, was spent cheerfully, and although the spring was uncommonly late, when it came its beauty compensated for its dilatoriness.

The month of May had already commenced, and I expected the letter daily which was to fix the date of my departure, when Henry proposed a pedestrian tour in the environs of Ingolstadt, that I might bid a personal farewell to the country I had so long inhabited. I acceded with pleasure to this proposition: I was fond of exercise, and Clerval had always been my favourite companion in the rambles of this nature that I had taken among the scenes of my native country.

We passed a fortnight in these perambulations: my health and spirits had long been restored, and they gained additional strength from the salubrious air I breathed, the natural incidents of our progress, and the conversation of my friend. Study had before secluded me from the intercourse of my fellow-creatures, and rendered me unsocial, but Clerval called forth the better feelings of my heart; he again taught me to love the aspect of nature, and the cheerful faces of children. Excellent friend! how sincerely did you love me and endeavour to elevate my mind until it was on a level with your own! A selfish pursuit had cramped and narrowed me, until your gentleness and affection warmed and opened my senses; I became the same happy creature who, a few years ago, loved and beloved by all, had no sorrow or care. When happy, inanimate nature had the power of bestowing on me the most delightful sensations. A serene sky and verdant fields filled me with ecstasy. The present season was indeed divine; the flowers of spring bloomed in the hedges, while those of summer were already in bud. I was undisturbed by thoughts which during the preceding year had pressed upon me, notwithstanding my endeavours to throw them off, with an invincible burden.

Henry rejoiced in my gaiety, and sincerely sympathised in my feelings: he exerted himself to amuse me, while he expressed the sensations that filled his soul. The resources of his mind on this occasion were truly astonishing: his conversation was full of imagination; and very often, in imitation of the Persian and Arabic writers, he invented tales of wonderful fancy and passion. At other times, he repeated my favourite poems, or drew me out into arguments, which he supported with great ingenuity.

We returned to our college on a Sunday afternoon: the peasants were dancing, and everyone we met appeared gay and happy. My own spirits were high, and I bounded along with feelings of unbridled joy and hilarity.

Chapter VII

On my return, I found the following letter from my father:—

My dear Victor,

You have probably waited impatiently for a letter to fix the date of your return to us; and I was at first tempted to write only a few lines, merely mentioning the day on which I should expect you. But that would be a cruel kindness, and I dare not do it. What would be your surprise, my son, when you expect a happy and glad welcome, to behold, on the contrary, tears and wretchedness? And how, Victor, can I relate our misfortune? Absence cannot have rendered you callous to our joys and griefs; and how shall I inflict pain on my long-absent son? I wish to prepare you for the woeful news, but I know it is impossible; even now your eye skims over the page, to seek the words which are to convey to you the horrible tidings.

William is dead!—that sweet child, whose smiles delighted and warmed my heart, who was so gentle, yet so gay! Victor, he is murdered!

I will not attempt to console you; but will simply relate the circumstances of the transaction.

Last Thursday (May 7th) I, my niece, and your two brothers went to walk in Plainpalais. The evening was warm and serene, and we prolonged our walk farther than usual. It was already dusk before we thought of returning; and then we discovered that William and Ernest, who had gone on before, were not to be found. We accordingly rested on a seat until they should return. Presently Ernest came, and enquired if we had seen his brother: he said that he had been playing with him, that William had run away to hide himself, and that he vainly sought for him, and afterwards waited for him a long time, but he did not return.

This account rather alarmed us, and we continued to search for him until night fell, when Elizabeth conjectured that he might have returned to the house. He was not there. We returned again, with torches, for I could not rest when I thought that my sweet boy had lost himself and was exposed to all the damps and dews of night; Elizabeth also suffered extreme anguish. About five in the morning I discovered my lovely boy, whom the night before I had seen blooming and active in health, stretched on the grass livid and motionless: the print of the murderer's finger was on his neck.

He was conveyed home, and the anguish that was visible in my countenance betrayed the secret to Elizabeth. She was very earnest to see the corpse. At first I attempted to prevent her, but she persisted, and entering the room where it lay, hastily examined the neck of the victim, and clasping her hands, exclaimed, "Oh, God! I have murdered my darling child!"

She fainted, and was restored with extreme difficulty. When she again lived, it was only to weep and sigh. She told me that that same evening William had teased her to let him wear a very valuable miniature that she possessed of your mother. This picture is gone, and was doubtless the temptation which urged the murderer to the deed. We have no trace of him at present, although our exertions to discover him are unremitted; but they will not restore my beloved William!

Come, dearest Victor; you alone can console Elizabeth. She weeps continually and accuses herself unjustly as the cause of his death; her words pierce my heart. We are all unhappy, but will not that be an additional motive for you, my son, to return and be our comforter? Your dear mother! Alas, Victor! I now say, Thank God she did not live to witness the cruel, miserable death of her youngest darling!

Come, Victor; not brooding thoughts of vengeance against the assassin, but with feelings of peace and gentleness, that will heal, instead of festering, the wounds of our minds. Enter the house of mourning, my friend, but with kindness and affection for those who love you, and not with hatred for your enemies.

Your affectionate and afflicted father,
Alphonse Frankenstein
Geneva, May 12th, 17—.

Clerval, who had watched my countenance as I read this letter, was surprised to observe the despair that succeeded to the joy I at first expressed on receiving news from my friends. I threw the letter on the table, and covered my face with my hands.

"My dear Frankenstein," exclaimed Henry, when he perceived me weep with bitterness, "are we always to be unhappy? My dear friend, what has happened?"

I motioned to him to take up the letter, while I walked up and down the room in the extremest agitation. Tears also gushed from the eyes of Clerval, as he read the account of my misfortune.

"I can offer you no consolation, my friend," said he; "your disaster is irreparable. What do you intend to do?"

"To go instantly to Geneva: come with me, Henry, to order the horses."

During our walk Clerval endeavoured to say a few words of consolation; he could only express his heartfelt sympathy. "Poor William!" said he. "Dear lovely child, he now sleeps with his angel mother! Who that had seen him bright and joyous in his young beauty, but must weep over his untimely loss! To die so miserably; to feel the murderer's grasp! How much more a murderer, that could destroy such radiant innocence! Poor little fellow! one only consolation have we; his friends mourn and weep, but he is at rest. The pang is over, his sufferings are at an end forever. A sod covers his gentle form, and he knows no pain. He can no longer be a subject for pity; we must reserve that for his miserable survivors."

Clerval spoke thus as we hurried through the streets; the words impressed themselves on my mind, and I remembered them afterwards in solitude. But now, as soon as the horses arrived, I hurried into a cabriolet and bade farewell to my friend.

My journey was very melancholy. At first I wished to hurry on, for I longed to console and sympathise with my loved and sorrowing friends; but when I drew near my native town, I slackened my progress. I could hardly sustain the multitude of feelings that crowded into my mind. I passed through scenes familiar to my youth, but which I had not seen for nearly six years. How altered every thing might be during that time! One sudden and desolating change had taken place; but a thousand little circumstances might have by degrees worked other alterations, which, although they were done more tranquilly, might not be the less decisive. Fear overcame me;

I dared not advance, dreading a thousand nameless evils that made me tremble, although I was unable to define them.

I remained two days at Lausanne, in this painful state of mind. I contemplated the lake: the waters were placid; all around was calm, and the snowy mountains, "the palaces of nature,"[1] were not changed. By degrees the calm and heavenly scene restored me, and I continued my journey towards Geneva.

The road ran by the side of the lake, which became narrower as I approached my native town. I discovered more distinctly the black sides of Jura, and the bright summit of Mont Blanc. I wept like a child. "Dear mountains! My own beautiful lake! How do you welcome your wanderer? Your summits are dear; the sky and lake are blue and placid. Is this to prognosticate peace, or to mock at my unhappiness?"

I fear, my friend, that I shall render myself tedious by dwelling on these preliminary circumstances; but they were days of comparative happiness, and I think of them with pleasure. My country, my beloved country! who but a native can tell the delight I took in again beholding thy streams, thy mountains, and, more than all, thy lovely lake!

Yet, as I drew nearer home, grief and fear again overcame me. Night also closed around; and when I could hardly see the dark mountains, I felt still more gloomily. The picture appeared a vast and dim scene of evil, and I foresaw obscurely that I was destined to become the most wretched of human beings. Alas! I prophesied truly, and failed only in one single circumstance, that in all the misery I imagined and dreaded, I did not conceive the hundredth part of the anguish I was destined to endure.

It was completely dark when I arrived in the environs of Geneva; the gates of the town were already shut; and I was obliged to pass the night at Secheron, a village at the distance of half a league from the city. The sky was serene; and as I was unable to rest, I resolved to visit the spot where my poor William had been murdered. As I could not pass through the town, I was obliged to cross the lake in a boat to arrive at Plainpalais. During this short voyage I saw the lightnings playing on the summit of Mont Blanc

[1] "*the palaces of nature*"] from Canto III, line lxii, of Byron's *Childe Harold's Pilgrimage.*

in the most beautiful figures. The storm appeared to approach rapidly; and, on landing, I ascended a low hill, that I might observe its progress. It advanced; the heavens were clouded, and I soon felt the rain coming slowly in large drops, but its violence quickly increased.

I quitted my seat and walked on, although the darkness and storm increased every minute and the thunder burst with a terrific crash over my head. It was echoed from Salêve, the Juras, and the Alps of Savoy; vivid flashes of lightning dazzled my eyes, illuminating the lake, making it appear like a vast sheet of fire; then for an instant every thing seemed of a pitchy darkness, until the eye recovered itself from the preceding flash. The storm, as is often the case in Switzerland, appeared at once in various parts of the heavens. The most violent storm hung exactly north of the town, over that part of the lake which lies between the promontory of Belrive and the village of Copêt. Another storm enlightened Jura with faint flashes; and another darkened and sometimes disclosed the Môle, a peaked mountain to the east of the lake.

While I watched the tempest, so beautiful yet terrific, I wandered on with a hasty step. This noble war in the sky elevated my spirits; I clasped my hands and exclaimed aloud, "William, dear angel! this is thy funeral, this thy dirge!" As I said these words, I perceived in the gloom a figure which stole from behind a clump of trees near me; I stood fixed, gazing intently: I could not be mistaken. A flash of lightning illuminated the object, and discovered its shape plainly to me; its gigantic stature, and the deformity of its aspect, more hideous than belongs to humanity, instantly informed me that it was the wretch, the filthy daemon to whom I had given life. What did he there? Could he be (I shuddered at the conception) the murderer of my brother? No sooner did that idea cross my imagination, than I became convinced of its truth; my teeth chattered, and I was forced to lean against a tree for support. The figure passed me quickly, and I lost it in the gloom. Nothing in human shape could have destroyed that fair child. *He* was the murderer! I could not doubt it. The mere presence of the idea was an irresistible proof of the fact. I thought of pursuing the devil; but it would have been in vain, for another flash discovered him to me hanging among the rocks of the nearly perpendicular ascent of Mont Salêve, a hill that bound Plainpalais on the south. He soon reached the summit, and disappeared.

I remained motionless. The thunder ceased, but the rain still continued, and the scene was enveloped in an impenetrable darkness. I revolved in my mind the events which I had until now sought to forget: the whole train of my progress towards the creation; the appearance of the work of my own hands alive at my bedside; its departure. Two years had now nearly elapsed since the night on which he first received life; and was this his first crime? Alas! I had turned loose into the world a depraved wretch, whose delight was in carnage and misery; had he not murdered my brother?

No one can conceive the anguish I suffered during the remainder of the night, which I spent, cold and wet, in the open air. But I did not feel the inconvenience of the weather; my imagination was busy in scenes of evil and despair. I considered the being whom I had cast among mankind, and endowed with the will and power to effect purposes of horror, such as the deed which he had now done, nearly in the light of my own vampire, my own spirit let loose from the grave, and forced to destroy all that was dear to me.

Day dawned; and I directed my steps towards the town. The gates were open, and I hastened to my father's house. My first thought was to discover what I knew of the murderer, and cause instant pursuit to be made. But I paused when I reflected on the story that I had to tell. A being whom I myself had formed, and endued with life, had met me at midnight among the precipices of an inaccessible mountain. I remembered also the nervous fever with which I had been seized just at the time that I dated my creation, and which would give an air of delirium to a tale otherwise so utterly improbable. I well knew that if any other had communicated such a relation to me, I should have looked upon it as the ravings of insanity. Besides, the strange nature of the animal would elude all pursuit, even if I were so far credited as to persuade my relatives to commence it. And then of what use would be pursuit? Who could arrest a creature capable of scaling the overhanging sides of Mont Salêve? These reflections determined me, and I resolved to remain silent.

It was about five in the morning when I entered my father's house. I told the servants not to disturb the family, and went into the library to attend their usual hour of rising.

Six years had elapsed, passed as a dream but for one indelible trace, and I stood in the same place where I had last embraced my father before my departure for Ingolstadt. Beloved and venerable parent! He still remained to me. I gazed on the picture of my mother which stood over the mantle-piece. It was an historical subject, painted at my father's desire, and represented Caroline Beaufort in an agony of despair, kneeling by the coffin of her dead father. Her garb was rustic, and her cheek pale; but there was an air of dignity and beauty, that hardly permitted the sentiment of pity. Below this picture was a miniature of William; and my tears flowed when I looked upon it. While I was thus engaged, Ernest entered: he had heard me arrive, and hastened to welcome me. He expressed a sorrowful delight to see me. "Welcome, my dearest Victor," said he. "Ah! I wish you had come three months ago, and then you would have found us all joyous and delighted. You come to us now to share a misery which nothing can alleviate; yet your presence will, I hope, revive our father, who seems sinking under his misfortune; and your persuasions will induce poor Elizabeth to cease her vain and tormenting self-accusations.—Poor William! he was our darling and our pride!"

Tears, unrestrained, fell from my brother's eyes; a sense of mortal agony crept over my frame. Before, I had only imagined the wretchedness of my desolated home; the reality came on me as a new, and a not less terrible, disaster. I tried to calm Ernest; I enquired more minutely concerning my father, and her I named my cousin.

"She most of all," said Ernest, "requires consolation; she accused herself of having caused the death of my brother, and that made her very wretched. But since the murderer has been discovered—"

"The murderer discovered! Good God! how can that be? who could attempt to pursue him? It is impossible; one might as well try to overtake the winds or confine a mountain-stream with a straw. I saw him too; he was free last night!"

"I do not know what you mean," replied my brother, in accents of wonder, "but to us the discovery we have made completes our misery. No one would believe it at first; and even now Elizabeth will not be convinced, notwithstanding all the evidence. Indeed, who would credit that Justine Moritz, who was so amiable and fond of all the family, could suddenly become capable of so frightful, so appalling a crime?"

"Justine Moritz! Poor, poor girl, is she the accused? But it is wrongfully; every one knows that; no one believes it, surely, Ernest?"

"No one did at first; but several circumstances came out that have almost forced conviction upon us; and her own behaviour has been so confused as to add to the evidence of facts a weight that, I fear, leaves no hope for doubt. But she will be tried today, and you will then hear all."

He related that, the morning on which the murder of poor William had been discovered, Justine had been taken ill, and confined to her bed for several days. During this interval one of the servants, happening to examine the apparel she had worn on the night of the murder, had discovered in her pocket the picture of my mother, which had been judged to be the temptation of the murderer. The servant instantly showed it to one of the others, who, without saying a word to any of the family, went to a magistrate; and, upon their deposition, Justine was apprehended. On being charged with the fact, the poor girl confirmed the suspicion in a great measure by her extreme confusion of manner.

This was a strange tale, but it did not shake my faith, and I replied earnestly, "You are all mistaken; I know the murderer. Justine, poor, good Justine, is innocent."

At that instant my father entered. I saw unhappiness deeply impressed on his countenance, but he endeavoured to welcome me cheerfully; and after we had exchanged our mournful greeting, would have introduced some other topic than that of our disaster, had not Ernest exclaimed, "Good God, Papa! Victor says that he knows who was the murderer of poor William."

"We do also, unfortunately," replied my father; "for indeed I had rather have been forever ignorant than have discovered so much depravity and ingratitude in one I valued so highly."

"My dear father, you are mistaken; Justine is innocent."

"If she is, God forbid that she should suffer as guilty. She is to be tried today, and I hope, I sincerely hope, that she will be acquitted."

This speech calmed me. I was firmly convinced in my own mind that Justine, and indeed every human being, was guiltless of this murder. I had no fear, therefore, that any circumstantial evidence could be brought forward strong enough to convict her. My tale was not one to announce publicly; its astounding horror would be looked upon as madness by the vulgar. Did any one indeed exist, except I, the creator, who would believe, unless his senses convinced him, in the existence of the living monument of presumption and rash ignorance which I had let loose upon the world?

We were soon joined by Elizabeth. Time had altered her since I last beheld her; it had endowed her with loveliness surpassing the beauty of her childish years. There was the same candour, the same vivacity, but it was allied to an expression more full of sensibility and intellect. She welcomed me with the greatest affection. "Your arrival, my dear cousin," said she, "fills me with hope. You perhaps will find some means to justify my poor guiltless Justine. Alas! who is safe, if she be convicted of crime? I rely on her innocence as certainly as I do upon my own. Our misfortune is doubly hard to us; we have not only lost that lovely darling boy, but this poor girl, whom I sincerely love, is to be torn away by even a worse fate. If she is condemned, I never shall know joy more. But she will not, I am sure she will not; and then I shall be happy again, even after the sad death of my little William."

"She is innocent, my Elizabeth," said I, "and that shall be proved; fear nothing, but let your spirits be cheered by the assurance of her acquittal."

"How kind and generous you are! every one else believes in her guilt, and that made me wretched, for I knew that it was impossible: and to see every one else prejudiced in so deadly a manner rendered me hopeless and despairing." She wept.

"Dearest niece," said my father, "dry your tears. If she is, as you believe, innocent, rely on the justice of our laws, and the activity with which I shall prevent the slightest shadow of partiality."

Chapter VIII

We passed a few sad hours, until eleven o'clock, when the trial was to commence. My father and the rest of the family being obliged to attend as witnesses, I accompanied them to the court. During the whole of this wretched mockery of justice I suffered living torture. It was to be decided, whether the result of my curiosity and lawless devices would cause the death of my fellow-beings: one a smiling babe full of innocence and joy; the other far more dreadfully murdered, with every aggravation of infamy that could make the murder memorable in horror. Justine also was a girl of merit, and possessed qualities which promised to render her life happy; now all was to be obliterated in an ignominious grave, and I the cause! A thousand times rather would I have confessed myself guilty of the crime ascribed to Justine; but I was absent when it was committed, and such a declaration would have been considered as the ravings of a madman, and would not have exculpated her who suffered through me.

The appearance of Justine was calm. She was dressed in mourning; and her countenance, always engaging, was rendered, by the solemnity of her feelings, exquisitely beautiful. Yet she appeared confident in innocence and did not tremble, although gazed on and execrated by thousands; for all the kindness which her beauty might otherwise have excited was obliterated in the minds of the spectators by the imagination of the enormity she was supposed to have committed. She was tranquil, yet her tranquillity was evidently constrained; and as her confusion had before been adduced as a proof of her guilt, she worked up her mind to an appearance of courage. When she entered the court she threw her eyes round it, and quickly discovered where we were seated. A tear seemed to dim her eye when she saw us; but she quickly recovered herself, and a look of sorrowful affection seemed to attest her utter guiltlessness.

The trial began; and after the advocate against her had stated the charge, several witnesses were called. Several strange facts combined against her, which might have staggered any one who had not such proof of her innocence as I had. She had been out the whole of the night on which the murder had been committed, and towards morning had been perceived by a market-woman not far from the spot where the body of the murdered child had been afterwards found. The woman asked her what she did there; but she looked very strangely, and only returned a confused and unintelligible answer. She returned to the house about eight o'clock; and when one enquired where she had passed the night, she replied that she had been looking for the child and demanded earnestly if any thing had been heard concerning him. When shown the body, she fell into violent hysterics, and kept her bed for several days. The picture was then produced, which the servant had found in her pocket; and when Elizabeth, in a faltering voice, proved that it was the same which, an hour before the child had been missed, she had placed round his neck, a murmur of horror and indignation filled the court.

Justine was called on for her defence. As the trial proceeded, her countenance had altered. Surprise, horror, and misery were strongly expressed. Sometimes she struggled with her tears; but when she was desired to plead, she collected her powers, and spoke in an audible although variable voice:—

"God knows," she said, "how entirely I am innocent. But I do not pretend that my protestations should acquit me: I rest my innocence on a plain and simple explanation of the facts which have been adduced against me; and I hope the character I have always borne will incline my judges to a favourable interpretation, where any circumstance appears doubtful or suspicious."

She then related that, by the permission of Elizabeth, she had passed the evening of the night on which the murder had been committed at the house of an aunt at Chêne, a village situated at about a league from Geneva. On her return, at about nine o'clock, she met a man who asked her if she had seen any thing of the child who was lost. She was alarmed by this account, and passed several hours looking for him, when the gates of Geneva were shut, and she was forced to remain several hours of the night in a barn belonging to a cottage, being unwilling to call up the inhabitants, to whom she was well known. Most of the night she spent here watching; towards morning she believed that she slept for a few minutes; some steps disturbed her, and she awoke. It was dawn, and she quitted her asylum, that she might again endeavour to find my brother. If she had gone near the spot where his body lay, it was without her knowledge. That she had been bewildered when questioned by the market-woman was not surprising, since she had passed a sleepless night and the fate of poor William was yet uncertain. Concerning the picture she could give no account.

"I know," continued the unhappy victim, "how heavily and fatally this one circumstance weighs against me, but I have no power of explaining it; and when I have expressed my utter ignorance, I am only left to conjecture concerning the probabilities by which it might have been placed in my pocket. But here also I am checked. I believe that I have no enemy on earth, and none surely would have been so wicked as to destroy me wantonly. Did the murderer place it there? I know of no opportunity afforded him for so doing; or, if I had, why should he have stolen the jewel, to part with it again so soon?

"I commit my cause to the justice of my judges, yet I see no room for hope. I beg permission to have a few witnesses examined concerning my character; and if their testimony shall not overweigh my supposed guilt, I must be condemned, although I would pledge my salvation on my innocence."

Several witnesses were called, who had known her for many years, and they spoke well of her; but fear and hatred of the crime of which they supposed her guilty rendered them timorous, and unwilling to come forward. Elizabeth saw even this last resource, her excellent dispositions and irreproachable conduct, about to fail the accused, when, although violently agitated, she desired permission to address the court.

"I am," said she, "the cousin of the unhappy child who was murdered, or rather his sister, for I was educated by and have lived with his parents ever since and even long before, his birth. It may therefore be judged indecent in me to come forward on this occasion; but when I see a fellow creature about to perish through the cowardice of her pretended friends, I wish to be allowed to speak, that I may say what I know of her character. I am well acquainted with the accused. I have lived in the same house with her, at one time for five, and at another for nearly two years. During all that period she appeared to me the most amiable and benevolent of human creatures. She nursed Madame Frankenstein, my aunt, in her last illness, with the greatest affection and care, and afterwards attended her own mother during a tedious illness, in a manner that excited the admiration of all who knew her; after which she again lived in my uncle's house, where she was beloved by all the family. She was warmly attached to the child who is now dead, and acted towards him like a most affectionate mother. For my own part, I do not hesitate to say that, notwithstanding all the evidence produced against her, I believe and rely on her perfect innocence. She had no temptation for such an action: as to the bauble on which the chief proof rests, if she had earnestly desired it, I should have willingly given it to her; so much do I esteem and value her."

A murmur of approbation followed Elizabeth's simple and powerful appeal; but it was excited by her generous interference, and not in favour of poor Justine, on whom the public indignation was turned with renewed violence, charging her with the blackest ingratitude. She herself wept as Elizabeth spoke, but she did not answer. My own agitation and anguish was extreme during the whole trial. I believed in her innocence; I knew it. Could the daemon who had (I did not for a minute doubt) murdered my brother also in his hellish sport have betrayed the innocent to death and ignominy? I could not sustain the horror of my situation, and when I perceived that the popular voice and the countenances of the judges had already condemned my unhappy victim, I rushed out of the court in agony. The tortures of the accused did not equal mine; she was sustained by innocence, but the fangs of remorse tore my bosom and would not forego their hold.

I passed a night of unmingled wretchedness. In the morning I went to the court; my lips and throat were parched. I dared not ask the fatal question; but I was known, and the officer guessed the cause of my visit. The ballots had been thrown; they were all black, and Justine was condemned.

I cannot pretend to describe what I then felt. I had before experienced sensations of horror; and I have endeavoured to bestow upon them adequate expressions, but words cannot convey an idea of the heart-sickening despair that I then endured. The person to whom I addressed myself added, that Justine had already confessed her guilt. "That evidence," he observed, "was hardly required in so glaring a case, but I am glad of it; and, indeed, none of our judges like to condemn a criminal upon circumstantial evidence, be it ever so decisive."

This was strange and unexpected intelligence; what could it mean? Had my eyes deceived me? And was I really as mad as the whole world would believe me to be, if I disclosed the object of my suspicions? I hastened to return home, and Elizabeth eagerly demanded the result.

"My cousin," replied I, "it is decided as you may have expected; all judges had rather that ten innocent should suffer than that one guilty should escape. But she has confessed."

This was a dire blow to poor Elizabeth, who had relied with firmness upon Justine's innocence. "Alas!" said she, "how shall I ever again believe in human goodness? Justine, whom I loved and esteemed as my sister, how could she put on those smiles of innocence only to betray? her mild eyes seemed incapable of any severity or guile, and yet she has committed a murder."

Soon after we heard that the poor victim had expressed a desire to see my cousin. My father wished her not to go, but said that he left it to her own judgment and feelings to decide. "Yes," said Elizabeth, "I will go, although she is guilty; and you, Victor, shall accompany me: I cannot go alone." The idea of this visit was torture to me, yet I could not refuse.

We entered the gloomy prison chamber and beheld Justine sitting on some straw at the farther end; her hands were manacled, and her head rested on her knees. She rose on seeing us enter; and when we were left alone with her, she threw herself at the feet of Elizabeth, weeping bitterly. My cousin wept also.

"Oh, Justine!" said she, "why did you rob me of my last consolation? I relied on your innocence, and although I was then very wretched, I was not so miserable as I am now."

"And do you also believe that I am so very, very wicked? Do you also join with my enemies to crush me, to condemn me as a murderer?" Her voice was suffocated with sobs.

"Rise, my poor girl," said Elizabeth, "why do you kneel, if you are innocent? I am not one of your enemies; I believed you guiltless, notwithstanding every evidence, until I heard that you had yourself declared your guilt. That report, you say, is false; and be assured, dear Justine, that nothing can shake my confidence in you for a moment, but your own confession."

"I did confess; but I confessed a lie. I confessed, that I might obtain absolution; but now that falsehood lies heavier at my heart than all my other sins. The God of heaven forgive me! Ever since I was condemned, my confessor has besieged me; he threatened and menaced, until I almost began to think that I was the monster that he said I was. He threatened excommunication and hell fire in my last moments if I continued obdurate. Dear lady, I had none to support me; all looked on me as a wretch doomed to ignominy and perdition. What could I do? In an evil hour I subscribed to a lie; and now only am I truly miserable."

She paused, weeping, and then continued—"I thought with horror, my sweet lady, that you should believe your Justine, whom your blessed aunt had so highly honoured and whom you loved, was a creature capable of a crime which none but the devil himself could have perpetrated. Dear William! dearest blessed child! I soon shall see you again in heaven, where we shall all be happy; and that consoles me, going as I am to suffer ignominy and death."

"Oh, Justine! forgive me for having for one moment distrusted you. Why did you confess? But do not mourn, dear girl. Do not fear. I will proclaim, I will prove your innocence. I will melt the stony hearts of your enemies by my tears and prayers. You shall not die!—You, my play-fellow, my companion, my sister, perish on the scaffold! No! no! I never could survive so horrible a misfortune."

Justine shook her head mournfully. "I do not fear to die," she said; "that pang is past. God raises my weakness, and gives me courage to endure the worst. I leave a sad and bitter world; and if you remember me, and think of me as of one unjustly condemned, I am resigned to the fate awaiting me. Learn from me, dear lady, to submit in patience to the will of Heaven!"

During this conversation I had retired to the corner of the prison room, where I could conceal the horrid anguish that possessed me. Despair! Who dared talk of that? The poor victim, who on the morrow was to pass the awful boundary between life and death, felt not, as I did, such deep and bitter agony. I gnashed my teeth and ground them together, uttering a groan that came from my inmost soul. Justine started. When she saw who it was, she approached me, and said, "Dear Sir, you are very kind to visit me; you, I hope, do not believe that I am guilty."

I could not answer. "No, Justine," said Elizabeth; "he is more convinced of your innocence than I was; for even when he heard that you had confessed, he did not credit it."

"I truly thank him. In these last moments I feel the sincerest gratitude towards those who think of me with kindness. How sweet is the affection of others to such a wretch as I am! It removes more than half my misfortune; and I feel as if I could die in peace, now that my innocence is acknowledged by you, dear lady, and your cousin."

Thus the poor sufferer tried to comfort others and herself. She indeed gained the resignation she desired. But I, the true murderer, felt the never-dying worm alive in my bosom, which allowed of no hope or consolation. Elizabeth also wept and was unhappy; but hers also was the misery of innocence, which, like a cloud that passes over the fair moon, for a while hides but cannot tarnish its brightness. Anguish and despair had penetrated into the core of my heart; I bore a hell within me which nothing could extinguish. We stayed several hours with Justine; and it was with great difficulty that Elizabeth could tear herself away. "I wish," cried she, "that I were to die with you; I cannot live in this world of misery."

Justine assumed an air of cheerfulness, while she with difficulty repressed her bitter tears. She embraced Elizabeth and said, in a voice of half-suppressed emotion, "Farewell, sweet lady, dearest Elizabeth, my beloved and only friend; may Heaven, in its bounty, bless and preserve you; may this be the last misfortune that you will ever suffer! Live, and be happy, and make others so."

And on the morrow Justine died. Elizabeth's heart-rending eloquence failed to move the judges from their settled conviction in the criminality of the saintly sufferer. My passionate and indignant appeals were lost upon them. And when I received their cold answers and heard the harsh, unfeeling reasoning of these men, my purposed avowal died away on my lips. Thus I might proclaim myself a madman, but not revoke the sentence passed upon my wretched victim. She perished on the scaffold as a murderess!

From the tortures of my own heart, I turned to contemplate the deep and voiceless grief of my Elizabeth. This also was my doing! And my father's woe, and the desolation of that late so smiling home—all was the work of my thrice-accursed hands! Ye weep, unhappy ones; but these are not your last tears! Again shall you raise the funeral wail, and the sound of your lamentations shall again and again be heard! Frankenstein, your son, your kinsman, your early, much-loved friend; he who would spend each vital drop of blood for your sakes—who has no thought nor sense of joy, except as it is mirrored also in your dear countenances—who would fill the air with blessings and spend his life in serving you—he bids you weep—to shed countless tears; happy beyond his hopes, if thus inexorable fate be satisfied, and if the destruction pause before the peace of the grave have succeeded to your sad torments!

Thus spoke my prophetic soul, as, torn by remorse, horror, and despair, I beheld those I loved spend vain sorrow upon the graves of William and Justine, the first hapless victims to my unhallowed arts.[1]

[1] The end of Chapter VIII marked the end of Volume I of the first edition of 1818.

Chapter IX

Nothing is more painful to the human mind than, after the feelings have been worked up by a quick succession of events, the dead calmness of inaction and certainty which follows and deprives the soul both of hope and fear. Justine died; she rested; and I was alive. The blood flowed freely in my veins, but a weight of despair and remorse pressed on my heart, which nothing could remove. Sleep fled from my eyes; I wandered like an evil spirit, for I had committed deeds of mischief beyond description horrible, and more, much more (I persuaded myself) was yet behind. Yet my heart overflowed with kindness, and the love of virtue. I had begun life with benevolent intentions, and thirsted for the moment when I should put them in practice and make myself useful to my fellow beings. Now all was blasted: instead of that serenity of conscience which allowed me to look back upon the past with self-satisfaction, and from thence to gather promise of new hopes, I was seized by remorse and the sense of guilt, which hurried me away to a hell of intense tortures, such as no language can describe.

This state of mind preyed upon my health, which had perhaps never entirely recovered from the first shock it had sustained. I shunned the face of man; all sound of joy or complacency was torture to me; solitude was my only consolation—deep, dark, deathlike solitude.

My father observed with pain the alteration perceptible in my disposition and habits, and endeavoured by arguments, deduced from the feelings of his serene conscience and guiltless life, to inspire me with fortitude, and awaken in me the courage to dispel the dark cloud which brooded over me. "Do you think, Victor," said he, "that I do not suffer also? No one could love a child more than I loved your brother"—tears came into his eyes as he spoke—"but is it not a duty to the survivors that we should refrain from augmenting their unhappiness by an appearance of immoderate grief? It is also a duty owed to yourself; for excessive sorrow prevents improvement or enjoyment, or even the discharge of daily usefulness, without which no man is fit for society."

This advice, although good, was totally inapplicable to my case; I should have been the first to hide my grief and console my friends, if remorse had not mingled its bitterness, and terror its alarm, with my other sensations. Now I could only answer my father with a look of despair, and endeavour to hide myself from his view.

About this time we retired to our house at Belrive. This change was particularly agreeable to me. The shutting of the gates regularly at ten o'clock and the impossibility of remaining on the lake after that hour, had rendered our residence within the walls of Geneva very irksome to me. I was now free. Often, after the rest of the family had retired for the night, I took the boat and passed many hours upon the water. Sometimes, with my sails set, I was carried by the wind; and sometimes, after rowing into the middle of the lake, I left the boat to pursue its own course, and gave way to my own miserable reflections. I was often tempted, when all was at peace around me, and I the only unquiet thing that wandered restless in a scene so beautiful and heavenly—if I except some bat, or the frogs, whose harsh and interrupted croaking was heard only when I approached the shore—often, I say, I was tempted to plunge into the silent lake, that the waters might close over me and my calamities forever. But I was restrained, when I thought of the heroic and suffering Elizabeth, whom I tenderly loved, and whose existence was bound up in mine. I thought also of my father and surviving brother: should I by my base desertion leave them exposed and unprotected to the malice of the fiend whom I had let loose among them?

At these moments I wept bitterly, and wished that peace would revisit my mind only that I might afford them consolation and happiness. But that could not be. Remorse extinguished every hope. I had been the author of unalterable evils, and I lived in daily fear lest the monster whom I had created should perpetrate some new wickedness. I had an obscure feeling that all was not over, and that he would still commit some signal crime, which by its enormity should almost efface the recollection of the past. There was always scope for fear, so long as anything I loved remained behind.

My abhorrence of this fiend cannot be conceived. When I thought of him I gnashed my teeth, my eyes became inflamed, and I ardently wished to extinguish that life which I had so thoughtlessly bestowed. When I reflected on his crimes and malice, my hatred and revenge burst all bounds of moderation. I would have made a pilgrimage to the highest peak of the Andes, could I, when there, have precipitated him to their base. I wished to see him again, that I might wreak the utmost extent of abhorrence on his head, and avenge the deaths of William and Justine.

Our house was the house of mourning. My father's health was deeply shaken by the horror of the recent events. Elizabeth was sad and desponding; she no longer took delight in her ordinary occupations; all pleasure seemed to her sacrilege toward the dead; eternal woe and tears she then thought was the just tribute she should pay to innocence so blasted and destroyed. She was no longer that happy creature who, in earlier youth wandered with me on the banks of the lake, and talked with ecstasy of our future prospects. The first of these sorrows which are sent to wean us from the earth, had visited her, and its dimming influence quenched her dearest smiles.

"When I reflect, my dear cousin," said she, "on the miserable death of Justine Moritz, I no longer see the world and its works as they before appeared to me. Before, I looked upon the accounts of vice and injustice, that I read in books or heard from others as tales of ancient days or imaginary evils; at least they were remote, and more familiar to reason than to the imagination; but now misery has come home, and men appear to me as monsters thirsting for each other's blood. Yet I am certainly unjust. Every body believed that poor girl to be guilty; and if she could have committed the crime for which she suffered, assuredly she would have been the most depraved of human creatures. For the sake of a few jewels, to have murdered the son of her benefactor and friend, a child whom she had nursed from its birth, and appeared to love as if it had been her own! I could not consent to the death of any human being; but certainly I should have thought such a creature unfit to remain in the society of men. But she was innocent. I know, I feel, she was innocent; you are of the same opinion, and that confirms me. Alas! Victor, when falsehood can look so like the truth, who can assure themselves of certain happiness? I feel as if I were walking on the edge of a precipice, towards which thousands are crowding, and endeavouring to plunge me into the abyss. William and Justine were assassinated, and the murderer escapes; he walks about the world free, and perhaps respected. But even if I were condemned to suffer on the scaffold for the same crimes, I would not change places with such a wretch."

I listened to this discourse with the extremest agony. I, not in deed, but in effect, was the true murderer. Elizabeth read my anguish in my countenance, and kindly taking my hand, said, "My dearest friend, you must calm yourself. These events have affected me, God knows how deeply; but I am not so wretched as you are. There is an expression of despair, and sometimes of revenge, in your countenance that makes me tremble. Dear Victor, banish these dark passions. Remember the friends around you, who centre all their hopes in you. Have we lost the power of rendering you happy? Ah! while we love—while we are true to each other, here in this land of peace and beauty, your native country, we may reap every tranquil blessing,—what can disturb our peace?"

And could not such words from her whom I fondly prized before every other gift of fortune, suffice to chase away the fiend that lurked in my heart? Even as she spoke I drew near to her, as if in terror; lest at that very moment the destroyer had been near to rob me of her.

Thus not the tenderness of friendship, nor the beauty of earth, nor of heaven, could redeem my soul from woe: the very accents of love were ineffectual. I was encompassed by a cloud which no beneficial influence could penetrate. The wounded deer dragging its fainting limbs to some untrodden brake, there to gaze upon the arrow which had pierced it, and to die—was but a type of me.

Sometimes I could cope with the sullen despair that overwhelmed me: but sometimes the whirlwind passions of my soul drove me to seek, by bodily exercise and by change of place, some relief from my intolerable sensations. It was during an access of this kind that I suddenly left my home, and bending my steps towards the near Alpine valleys, sought in the magnificence, the eternity of such scenes, to forget myself and my ephemeral, because human, sorrows. My wanderings were directed towards the valley of Chamounix. I had visited it frequently during my boyhood. Six years had passed since then: *I* was a wreck—but nought had changed in those savage and enduring scenes.

I performed the first part of my journey on horseback. I afterwards hired a mule, as the more sure-footed and least liable to receive injury on these rugged roads. The weather was fine: it was about the middle of the month of August, nearly two months after the death of Justine; that miserable epoch from which I dated all my woe. The weight upon my spirit was sensibly lightened as I plunged yet deeper in the ravine of Arve. The immense mountains and precipices that overhung me on every side—the sound of the river raging among the rocks, and the dashing of the waterfalls around, spoke of a power mighty as Omnipotence—and I ceased to fear, or to bend before any being less almighty than that which had created and ruled the elements, here displayed in their most terrific guise. Still, as I ascended higher, the valley assumed a more magnificent and astonishing character. Ruined castles hanging on the precipices of piny mountains; the impetuous Arve, and cottages every here and there peeping forth from among the trees, formed a scene of singular beauty. But it was augmented and rendered sublime by the mighty Alps, whose white and shining pyramids and domes towered above all, as belonging to another earth, the habitations of another race of beings.

I passed the bridge of Pélissier, where the ravine, which the river forms, opened before me, and I began to ascend the mountain that overhangs it. Soon after I entered the valley of Chamounix. This valley is more wonderful and sublime, but not so beautiful and picturesque, as that of Servox, through which I had just passed. The high and snowy mountains were its immediate boundaries; but I saw no more ruined castles and fertile fields. Immense glaciers approached the road; I heard the rumbling thunder of the falling avalanche and marked the smoke of its passage. Mont Blanc, the supreme and magnificent Mont Blanc, raised itself from the surrounding *aiguilles,*[1] and its tremendous *dôme* overlooked the valley.

A tingling long-lost sense of pleasure often came across me during this journey. Some turn in the road, some new object suddenly perceived and recognised, reminded me of days gone by, and were associated with the light-hearted gaiety of boyhood. The very winds whispered in soothing accents, and maternal nature bade me weep no more. Then again the kindly influence ceased to act—I found myself fettered again to grief, and indulging in all the misery of reflection. Then I spurred on my animal, striving so to forget the

[1] *aiguilles*] sharp-pointed pinnacles of rock.

world, my fears, and, more than all, myself—or, in a more desperate fashion, I alighted, and threw myself on the grass, weighed down by horror and despair.

At length I arrived at the village of Chamounix. Exhaustion succeeded to the extreme fatigue both of body and of mind which I had endured. For a short space of time I remained at the window, watching the pallid lightnings that played above Mont Blanc, and listening to the rushing of the Arve, which pursued its noisy way beneath. The same lulling sounds acted as a lullaby to my too keen sensations: when I placed my head upon my pillow, sleep crept over me; I felt it as it came and blest the giver of oblivion.

Chapter X

I SPENT THE following day roaming through the valley. I stood beside the sources of the Arveiron, which take their rise in a glacier, that with slow pace is advancing down from the summit of the hills, to barricade the valley. The abrupt sides of vast mountains were before me; the icy wall of the glacier overhung me; a few shattered pines were scattered around; and the solemn silence of this glorious presence-chamber of imperial Nature was broken only by the brawling waves or the fall of some vast fragment, the thunder sound of the avalanche or the cracking, reverberated along the mountains of the accumulated ice, which, through the silent working of immutable laws, was ever and anon rent and torn, as if it had been but a plaything in their hands. These sublime and magnificent scenes afforded me the greatest consolation that I was capable of receiving. They elevated me from all littleness of feeling; and although they did not remove my grief, they subdued and tranquillised it. In some degree, also, they diverted my mind from the thoughts over which it had brooded for the last month. I retired to rest at night; my slumbers, as it were, waited on and ministered to by the assemblance of grand shapes which I had contemplated during the day. They congregated round me; the unstained snowy mountain-top, the glittering pinnacle, the pine woods, and ragged bare ravine, the eagle, soaring amidst the clouds—they all gathered round me and bade me be at peace.

Where had they fled when the next morning I awoke? All of soul-inspiriting fled with sleep, and dark melancholy clouded every thought. The rain was pouring in torrents, and thick mists hid the summits of the mountains, so that I even saw not the faces of those mighty friends. Still I would penetrate their misty veil and seek them in their cloudy retreats. What were rain and storm to me? My mule was brought to the door, and I resolved to ascend to the summit of Montanvert. I remembered the effect that the view of the tremendous and ever-moving glacier had produced upon my mind when I first saw it. It had then filled me with a sublime ecstasy, that gave wings to the soul, and allowed it to soar from the obscure world to light and joy. The sight of the awful and majestic in nature had indeed always the effect of solemnising my mind and causing me to forget the passing cares of life. I determined to go without a guide, for I was well acquainted with the path, and the presence of another would destroy the solitary grandeur of the scene.

The ascent is precipitous, but the path is cut into continual and short windings, which enable you to surmount the perpendicularity of the mountain. It is a scene terrifically desolate. In a thousand spots the traces of the winter avalanche may be perceived, where trees lie broken and strewed on the ground; some entirely destroyed, others bent, leaning upon the jutting rocks of the mountain or transversely upon other trees. The path, as you ascend higher, is intersected by ravines of snow, down which stones continually roll from above; one of them is particularly dangerous, as the slightest sound, such as even speaking in a loud voice, produces a concussion of air sufficient to draw destruction upon the head of the speaker. The pines are not tall or luxuriant, but they are sombre and add an air of severity to the scene. I looked on the valley beneath; vast mists were rising from the rivers which ran through it and curling in thick wreaths around the opposite mountains, whose summits were hid in the uniform clouds, while rain poured from the dark sky, and added to the melancholy impression I received from the objects around me. Alas! why does man boast of sensibilities superior to those apparent in the brute; it only renders them more necessary beings. If our impulses were confined to hunger, thirst, and desire, we might be nearly free; but now we are moved by every wind that blows and a chance word or scene that that word may convey to us.

We rest; a dream has power to poison sleep.
  We rise; one wand'ring thought pollutes the day.
We feel, conceive, or reason; laugh or weep,
  Embrace fond woe, or cast our cares away;
It is the same: for, be it joy or sorrow,
  The path of its departure still is free.

Man's yesterday may ne'er be like his morrow;
Nought may endure but mutability![1]

It was nearly noon when I arrived at the top of the ascent. For some time I sat upon the rock that overlooks the sea of ice. A mist covered both that and the surrounding mountains. Presently a breeze dissipated the cloud, and I descended upon the glacier. The surface is very uneven, rising like the waves of a troubled sea, descending low, and interspersed by rifts that sink deep. The field of ice is almost a league in width, but I spent nearly two hours in crossing it. The opposite mountain is a bare perpendicular rock. From the side where I now stood Montanvert was exactly opposite, at the distance of a league; and above it rose Mont Blanc, in awful majesty. I remained in a recess of the rock, gazing on this wonderful and stupendous scene. The sea, or rather the vast river of ice, wound among its dependent mountains, whose aerial summits hung over its recesses. Their icy and glittering peaks shone in the sunlight over the clouds. My heart, which was before sorrowful, now swelled with something like joy; I exclaimed—"Wandering spirits, if indeed ye wander, and do not rest in your narrow beds, allow me this faint happiness, or take me, as your companion, away from the joys of life."

As I said this, I suddenly beheld the figure of a man, at some distance, advancing towards me with superhuman speed. He bounded over the crevices in the ice, among which I had walked with caution; his stature, also, as he approached, seemed to exceed that of man. I was troubled: a mist came over my eyes, and I felt a faintness seize me; but I was quickly restored by the cold gale of the mountains. I perceived, as the shape came nearer (sight tremendous and abhorred!) that it was the wretch whom I had created. I trembled with rage and horror, resolving to wait his approach, and then close with him in mortal combat. He approached; his countenance bespoke bitter anguish, combined with disdain and malignity, while its unearthly ugliness rendered it almost too horrible for human eyes. But I scarcely observed this; rage and hatred had at first deprived me of utterance, and I recovered only to overwhelm him with words expressive of furious detestation and contempt.

---

[1] *We rest . . . mutability!*] last lines of Percy Bysshe Shelley's "Mutability."

"Devil," I exclaimed, "do you dare approach me? and do not you fear the fierce vengeance of my arm wreaked on your miserable head? Begone, vile insect! or rather, stay, that I may trample you to dust! and, oh! that I could, with the extinction of your miserable existence, restore those victims whom you have so diabolically murdered!"

"I expected this reception," said the daemon. "All men hate the wretched; how, then, must I be hated, who am miserable beyond all living things! Yet you, my creator, detest and spurn me, thy creature, to whom thou art bound by ties only dissoluble by the annihilation of one of us. You purpose to kill me. How dare you sport thus with life? Do your duty towards me, and I will do mine towards you and the rest of mankind. If you will comply with my conditions, I will leave them and you at peace; but if you refuse, I will glut the maw of death, until it be satiated with the blood of your remaining friends."

"Abhorred monster! fiend that thou art! the tortures of hell are too mild a vengeance for thy crimes. Wretched devil! you reproach me with your creation; come on, then, that I may extinguish the spark which I so negligently bestowed."

My rage was without bounds; I sprang on him, impelled by all the feelings which can arm one being against the existence of another.

He easily eluded me, and said,—

"Be calm! I intreat you to hear me, before you give vent to your hatred on my devoted head. Have I not suffered enough, that you seek to increase my misery? Life, although it may only be an accumulation of anguish, is dear to me, and I will defend it. Remember, thou hast made me more powerful than thyself; my height is superior to thine, my joints more supple. But I will not be tempted to set myself in opposition to thee. I am thy creature, and I will be even mild and docile to my natural lord and king, if thou wilt also perform thy part, the which thou owest me. Oh, Frankenstein, be not equitable to every other and trample upon me alone, to whom thy justice, and even thy clemency and affection, is most due. Remember, that I am thy creature; I ought to be thy Adam, but I am rather the fallen angel, whom thou drivest from joy for no misdeed. Everywhere I see bliss, from which I alone am irrevocably excluded. I was benevolent and good; misery made me a fiend. Make me happy, and I shall again be virtuous."

"Begone! I will not hear you. There can be no community between you and me; we are enemies. Begone, or let us try our strength in a fight in which one must fall."

"How can I move thee? Will no intreaties cause thee to turn a favourable eye upon thy creature, who implores thy goodness and compassion? Believe me, Frankenstein: I was benevolent; my soul glowed with love and humanity; but am I not alone, miserably alone? You, my creator, abhor me; what hope can I gather from your fellow-creatures, who owe me nothing? they spurn and hate me. The desert mountains and dreary glaciers are my refuge. I have wandered here many days; the caves of ice, which I only do not fear, are a dwelling to me, and the only one which man does not grudge. These bleak skies I hail, for they are kinder to me than your fellow beings. If the multitude of mankind knew of my existence, they would do as you do, and arm themselves for my destruction. Shall I not then hate them who abhor me? I will keep no terms with my enemies. I am miserable, and they shall share my wretchedness. Yet it is in your power to recompense me, and deliver them from an evil which it only remains for you to make so great, that not only you and your family, but thousands of others, shall be swallowed up in the whirlwinds of its rage. Let your compassion be moved, and do not disdain me. Listen to my tale: when you have heard that, abandon or commiserate me, as you shall judge that I deserve. But hear me. The guilty are allowed, by human laws, bloody as they are, to speak in their own defence before they are condemned. Listen to me, Frankenstein. You accuse me of murder, and yet you would, with a satisfied conscience, destroy your own creature. Oh, praise the eternal justice of man! Yet I ask you not to spare me: listen to me; and then, if you can, and if you will, destroy the work of your hands."

"Why do you call to my remembrance," I rejoined, "circumstances, of which I shudder to reflect, that I have been the miserable origin and author? Cursed be the day, abhorred devil, in which you first saw light! Cursed (although I curse myself) be the hands that formed you! You have made me wretched beyond expression. You have left me no power to consider whether I am just to you, or not. Begone! relieve me from the sight of your detested form."

'Thus I relieve thee, my creator," he said, and placed his hated hands before my eyes, which I flung from me with violence; "thus I take from thee a sight which you abhor. Still thou canst listen to me and grant me thy compassion. By the virtues that I once possessed, I demand this from you. Hear my tale; it is long and strange, and the temperature of this place is not fitting to your fine sensations; come to the hut upon the mountain. The sun is yet high in the heavens; before it descends to hide itself beyond yon snowy precipices, and illuminate another world, you will have heard my story and can decide. On you it rests, whether I quit forever the neighbourhood of man and lead a harmless life, or become the scourge of your fellow creatures, and the author of your own speedy ruin."

As he said this, he led the way across the ice: I followed. My heart was full, and I did not answer him; but as I proceeded, I weighed the various arguments that he had used, and determined at least to listen to his tale. I was partly urged by curiosity, and compassion confirmed my resolution. I had hitherto supposed him to be the murderer of my brother, and I eagerly sought a confirmation or denial of this opinion. For the first time, also, I felt what the duties of a creator towards his creature were, and that I ought to render him happy before I complained of his wickedness. These motives urged me to comply with his demand. We crossed the ice, therefore, and ascended the opposite rock. The air was cold, and the rain again began to descend: we entered the hut, the fiend with an air of exultation, I with a heavy heart and depressed spirits. But I consented to listen, and seating myself by the fire which my odious companion had lighted, he thus began his tale.

Chapter XI

"IT IS WITH considerable difficulty that I remember the original era of my being: all the events of that period appear confused and indistinct. A strange multiplicity of sensations seized me, and I saw, felt, heard, and smelt at the same time; and it was, indeed, a long time before I learned to distinguish between the operations of my various senses. By degrees, I remember, a stronger light pressed upon my nerves, so that I was obliged to shut my eyes. Darkness then came over me, and troubled me; but hardly had I felt this when, by opening my eyes, as I now suppose, the light poured in upon me again. I walked and, I believe, descended; but I presently found a great alteration in my sensations. Before, dark and opaque bodies had surrounded me, impervious to my touch or sight; but I now found that I could wander on at liberty, with no obstacles which I could not either surmount or avoid. The light became more and more oppressive to me; and the heat wearying me as I walked, I sought a place where I could receive shade. This was the forest near Ingolstadt; and here I lay by the side of a brook resting from my fatigue, until I felt tormented by hunger and thirst. This roused me from my nearly dormant state, and I ate some berries which I found hanging on the trees or lying on the ground. I slaked my thirst at the brook; and then lying down, was overcome by sleep.

"It was dark when I awoke; I felt cold also, and half frightened, as it were, instinctively, finding myself so desolate. Before I had quitted your apartment, on a sensation of cold, I had covered myself with some clothes; but these were insufficient to secure me from the dews of night. I was a poor, helpless, miserable wretch; I knew, and could distinguish, nothing; but feeling pain invade me on all sides, I sat down and wept.

"Soon a gentle light stole over the heavens, and gave me a sensation of pleasure. I started up and beheld a radiant form rise from among the trees.[1] I gazed with a kind of wonder. It moved slowly, but it enlightened my path, and I again went out in search of berries. I was still cold when under one of the trees I found a huge cloak, with which I covered myself, and sat down upon the ground. No distinct ideas occupied my mind; all was confused. I felt light, and hunger, and thirst, and darkness; innumerable sounds rang in my ears, and on all sides various scents saluted me: the only object that I could distinguish was the bright moon, and I fixed my eyes on that with pleasure.

"Several changes of day and night passed, and the orb of night had greatly lessened, when I began to distinguish my sensations from each other. I gradually saw plainly the clear stream that supplied me with drink, and the trees that shaded me with their foliage. I was delighted when I first discovered that a pleasant sound, which often saluted my ears, proceeded from the throats of the little winged animals who had often intercepted the light from my eyes. I began also to observe, with greater accuracy, the forms that surrounded me, and to perceive the boundaries of the radiant roof of light which canopied me. Sometimes I tried to imitate the pleasant songs of the birds, but was unable. Sometimes I wished to express my sensations in my own mode, but the uncouth and inarticulate sounds which broke from me frightened me into silence again.

"The moon had disappeared from the night, and again, with a lessened form, showed itself, while I still remained in the forest. My sensations had by this time become distinct, and my mind received every day additional ideas. My eyes became accustomed to the light and to perceive objects in their right forms; I distinguished the insect from the herb, and by degrees, one herb from another. I found that the sparrow uttered none but harsh notes, whilst those of the blackbird and thrush were sweet and enticing.

"One day, when I was oppressed by cold, I found a fire which had been left by some wandering beggars, and was overcome with delight at the warmth I experienced from it. In my joy I thrust my hand into the live embers, but quickly drew it out again with a cry of pain. How strange, I thought, that the same cause should produce

---

[1] The moon [author's footnote].

such opposite effects! I examined the materials of the fire, and to my joy found it to be composed of wood. I quickly collected some branches; but they were wet and would not burn. I was pained at this; and sat still watching the operation of the fire. The wet wood which I had placed near the heat dried, and itself became inflamed. I reflected on this; and by touching the various branches, I discovered the cause, and busied myself in collecting a great quantity of wood, that I might dry it and have a plentiful supply of fire. When night came on and brought sleep with it, I was in the greatest fear lest my fire should be extinguished. I covered it carefully with dry wood and leaves, and placed wet branches upon it; and then, spreading my cloak, I lay on the ground, and sunk into sleep.

"It was morning when I awoke, and my first care was to visit the fire. I uncovered it, and a gentle breeze quickly fanned it into a flame. I observed this also and contrived a fan of branches, which roused the embers when they were nearly extinguished. When night came again I found, with pleasure, that the fire gave light as well as heat; and that the discovery of this element was useful to me in my food, for I found some of the offals that the travellers had left had been roasted, and tasted much more savoury than the berries I gathered from the trees. I tried, therefore, to dress my food in the same manner, placing it on the live embers. I found that the berries were spoiled by this operation, and the nuts and roots much improved.

"Food, however, became scarce; and I often spent the whole day searching in vain for a few acorns to assuage the pangs of hunger. When I found this, I resolved to quit the place that I had hitherto inhabited, to seek for one where the few wants I experienced would be more easily satisfied. In this emigration, I exceedingly lamented the loss of the fire which I had obtained through accident, and knew not how to reproduce it. I gave several hours to the serious consideration of this difficulty; but I was obliged to relinquish all attempts to supply it; and, wrapping myself up in my cloak, I struck across the wood towards the setting sun. I passed three days in these rambles, and at length discovered the open country. A great fall of snow had taken place the night before, and the fields were of one uniform white; the appearance was disconsolate, and I found my feet chilled by the cold damp outside that covered the ground.

"It was about seven in the morning, and I longed to obtain food and shelter; at length I perceived a small hut, on a rising ground, which had doubtless been built for the convenience of some shepherd. This was a new sight to me; and I examined the structure with great curiosity. Finding the door open, I entered. An old man sat in it, near a fire, over which he was preparing his breakfast. He turned on hearing a noise; and perceiving me, shrieked loudly, and quitting the hut, ran across the fields with a speed of which his debilitated form hardly appeared capable. His appearance, different from any I had ever before seen, and his flight, somewhat surprised me. But I was enchanted by the appearance of the hut: here the snow and rain could not penetrate; the ground was dry; and it presented to me then as exquisite and divine a retreat as Pandaemonium appeared to the daemons of hell after their sufferings in the lake of fire. I greedily devoured the remnants of the shepherd's breakfast, which consisted of bread, cheese, milk, and wine; the latter, however, I did not like. Then, overcome by fatigue, I lay down among some straw, and fell asleep.

"It was noon when I awoke; and, allured by the warmth of the sun, which shone brightly on the white ground, I determined to recommence my travels; and, depositing the remains of the peasant's breakfast in a wallet I found, I proceeded across the fields for several hours, until at sunset I arrived at a village. How miraculous did this appear! the huts, the neater cottages, and stately houses engaged my admiration by turns. The vegetables in the gardens, the milk and cheese that I saw placed at the windows of some of the cottages, allured my appetite. One of the best of these I entered; but I had hardly placed my foot within the door before the children shrieked, and one of the women fainted. The whole village was roused; some fled, some attacked me, until, grievously bruised by stones and many other kinds of missile weapons, I escaped to the open country and fearfully took refuge in a low hovel, quite bare, and making a wretched appearance after the palaces I had beheld in the village. This hovel, however, joined a cottage of a neat and pleasant appearance; but, after my late dearly bought experience, I dared not enter it. My place of refuge was constructed of wood, but so low that I could with difficulty sit upright in it. No wood, however, was placed on the earth which formed the floor, but it was dry; and although the wind entered it by innumerable chinks, I found it an agreeable asylum from the snow and rain.

"Here then I retreated, and lay down happy to have found a shelter, however miserable, from the inclemency of the season, and still more from the barbarity of man.

"As soon as morning dawned, I crept from my kennel, that I might view the adjacent cottage and discover if I could remain in the habitation I had found. It was situated against the back of the cottage and surrounded on the sides which were exposed by a pig-stye and a clear pool of water. One part was open, and by that I had crept in; but now I covered every crevice by which I might be perceived with stones and wood, yet in such a manner that I might move them on occasion to pass out: all the light I enjoyed came through the sty, and that was sufficient for me.

"Having thus arranged my dwelling and carpeted it with clean straw, I retired; for I saw the figure of a man at a distance, and I remembered too well my treatment the night before, to trust myself in his power. I had first, however, provided for my sustenance for that day by a loaf of coarse bread, which I purloined, and a cup with which I could drink, more conveniently than from my hand, of the pure water which flowed by my retreat. The floor was a little raised, so that it was kept perfectly dry, and by its vicinity to the chimney of the cottage it was tolerably warm.

"Being thus provided, I resolved to reside in this hovel until something should occur which might alter my determination. It was indeed a paradise compared to the bleak forest, my former residence, the rain-dropping branches, and dank earth. I ate my breakfast with pleasure and was about to remove a plank to procure myself a little water when I heard a step, and looking through a small chink, I beheld a young creature, with a pail on her head, passing before my hovel. The girl was young and of gentle demeanour, unlike what I have since found cottagers and farm-house servants to be. Yet she was meanly dressed, a coarse blue petticoat and a linen jacket being her only garb; her fair hair was plaited, but not adorned: she looked patient, yet sad. I lost sight of her; and in about a quarter of an hour she returned bearing the pail, which was now partly filled with milk. As she walked along, seemingly incommoded by the burden, a young man met her, whose countenance expressed a deeper despondence. Uttering a few sounds with an air of melancholy, he took the pail from her head and bore it to the cottage himself. She followed, and they disappeared. Presently I saw the young man again, with some tools in his hand, cross the field behind the cottage; and the girl was also busied, sometimes in the house and sometimes in the yard.

"On examining my dwelling, I found that one of the windows of the cottage had formerly occupied a part of it, but the panes had been filled up with wood. In one of these was a small and almost imperceptible chink, through which the eye could just penetrate. Through this crevice a small room was visible, whitewashed and clean, but very bare of furniture. In one corner, near a small fire, sat an old man, leaning his head on his hands in a disconsolate attitude. The young girl was occupied in arranging the cottage; but presently she took something out of a drawer, which employed her hands, and she sat down beside the old man, who, taking up an instrument, began to play, and to produce sounds sweeter than the voice of the thrush or the nightingale. It was a lovely sight, even to me, poor wretch! who had never beheld aught beautiful before. The silver hair and benevolent countenance of the aged cottager won my reverence, while the gentle manners of the girl enticed my love. He played a sweet mournful air, which I perceived drew tears from the eyes of his amiable companion, of which the old man took no notice, until she sobbed audibly; he then pronounced a few sounds, and the fair creature, leaving her work, knelt at his feet. He raised her, and smiled with such kindness and affection that I felt sensations of a peculiar and overpowering nature: they were a mixture of pain and pleasure, such as I had never before experienced, either from hunger or cold, warmth or food; and I withdrew from the window, unable to bear these emotions.

"Soon after this the young man returned, bearing on his shoulders a load of wood. The girl met him at the door, helped to relieve him of his burden, and taking some of the fuel into the cottage, placed it on the fire; then she and the youth went apart into a nook of the cottage, and he showed her a large loaf and a piece of cheese. She seemed pleased, and went into the garden for some roots and plants, which she placed in water, and then upon the fire. She afterwards continued her work, whilst the young man went into the garden, and appeared busily employed in digging and pulling up roots. After he had been employed thus about an hour, the young woman joined him, and they entered the cottage together.

"The old man had, in the mean time, been pensive; but on the appearance of his companions he assumed a more cheerful air, and they sat down to eat. The meal was quickly despatched. The young woman was again occupied in arranging the cottage; the old man walked before the cottage in the sun for a few minutes, leaning on the arm of the youth. Nothing could exceed in beauty the contrast between these two excellent creatures. One was old, with silver hairs and a countenance beaming with benevolence and love: the younger was slight and graceful in his figure, and his features were moulded with the finest symmetry; yet his eyes and attitude expressed the utmost sadness and despondency. The old man returned to the cottage; and the youth, with tools different from those he had used in the morning, directed his steps across the fields.

"Night quickly shut in; but to my extreme wonder, I found that the cottagers had a means of prolonging light by the use of tapers, and was delighted to find that the setting of the sun did not put an end to the pleasure I experienced in watching my human neighbours. In the evening, the young girl and her companion were employed in various occupations which I did not understand; and the old man again took up the instrument which produced the divine sounds that had enchanted me in the morning. So soon as he had finished the youth began, not to play, but to utter sounds that were monotonous, and neither resembling the harmony of the old man's instrument nor the songs of the birds: I since found that he read aloud, but at that time I knew nothing of the science of words or letters.

"The family, after having been thus occupied for a short time, extinguished their lights and retired, as I conjectured, to rest."

Chapter XII

"I LAY ON my straw, but I could not sleep. I thought of the occurrences of the day. What chiefly struck me was the gentle manners of these people; and I longed to join them, but dared not. I remembered too well the treatment I had suffered the night before from the barbarous villagers, and resolved, whatever course of conduct I might hereafter think it right to pursue, that for the present I would remain quietly in my hovel, watching, and endeavouring to discover the motives which influenced their actions.

"The cottagers arose the next morning before the sun. The young woman arranged the cottage and prepared the food; and the youth departed after the first meal.

"This day was passed in the same routine as that which preceded it. The young man was constantly employed out of doors, and the girl in various laborious occupations within. The old man, whom I soon perceived to be blind, employed his leisure hours on his instrument or in contemplation. Nothing could exceed the love and respect which the younger cottagers exhibited towards their venerable companion. They performed towards him every little office of affection and duty with gentleness; and he rewarded them by his benevolent smiles.

"They were not entirely happy. The young man and his companion often went apart, and appeared to weep. I saw no cause for their unhappiness; but I was deeply affected by it. If such lovely creatures were miserable, it was less strange that I, an imperfect and solitary being, should be wretched. Yet why were these gentle beings unhappy? They possessed a delightful house (for such it was in my eyes) and every luxury; they had a fire to warm them when chill, and delicious viands when hungry; they were dressed in excellent clothes; and, still more, they enjoyed one another's company and speech, interchanging each day looks of affection and kindness. What did their tears imply? Did they really express pain? I was at first unable to solve these questions; but perpetual attention and time explained to me many appearances which were at first enigmatic.

"A considerable period elapsed before I discovered one of the causes of the uneasiness of this amiable family: it was poverty, and they suffered that evil in a very distressing degree. Their nourishment consisted entirely of the vegetables of their garden and the milk of one cow, which gave very little during the winter, when its masters could scarcely procure food to support it. They often, I believe, suffered the pangs of hunger very poignantly, especially the two younger cottagers; for several times they placed food before the old man when they reserved none for themselves.

"This trait of kindness moved me sensibly. I had been accustomed, during the night, to steal a part of their store for my own consumption; but when I found that in doing this I inflicted pain on the cottagers, I abstained, and satisfied myself with berries, nuts, and roots, which I gathered from a neighbouring wood.

"I discovered also another means through which I was enabled to assist their labours. I found that the youth spent a great part of each day in collecting wood for the family fire; and, during the night I often took his tools, the use of which I quickly discovered, and brought home firing sufficient for the consumption of several days.

"I remember, the first time that I did this, the young woman, when she opened the door in the morning, appeared greatly astonished on seeing a great pile of wood on the outside. She uttered some words in a loud voice, and the youth joined her, who also expressed surprise. I observed, with pleasure, that he did not go to the forest that day, but spent it in repairing the cottage and cultivating the garden.

"By degrees I made a discovery of still greater moment. I found that these people possessed a method of communicating their experience and feelings to one another by articulate sounds. I perceived that the words they spoke sometimes produced pleasure or pain, smiles or sadness, in the minds and countenances of the hearers. This was indeed a godlike science, and I ardently desired to become acquainted with it. But I was baffled in every attempt I made for this purpose. Their pronunciation was quick; and the words they uttered, not having any apparent connection with visible objects, I was unable to discover any clue by which I could unravel the mystery of their reference. By great application, however, and after having remained during the space of several revolutions of the moon in my hovel, I discovered the names that were given to some of the most familiar objects of discourse; I learned and applied the words, 'fire', 'milk,' 'bread,' and 'wood.' I learned also the names of the cottagers themselves. The youth and his companion had each of them several names, but the old man had only one, which was 'father.' The girl was called 'sister,' or 'Agatha,' and the youth 'Felix,' 'brother,' or 'son.' I cannot describe the delight I felt when I learned the ideas appropriated to each of these sounds, and was able to pronounce them. I distinguished several other words without being able as yet to understand or apply them; such as 'good,' 'dearest,' 'unhappy.'

"I spent the winter in this manner. The gentle manners and beauty of the cottagers greatly endeared them to me: when they were unhappy, I felt depressed; when they rejoiced, I sympathised in their joys. I saw few human beings besides them; and if any other happened to enter the cottage, their harsh manners and rude gait only enhanced to me the superior accomplishments of my friends. The old man, I could perceive, often endeavoured to encourage his children, as sometimes I found that he called them, to cast off their melancholy. He would talk in a cheerful accent, with an expression of goodness that bestowed pleasure even upon me. Agatha listened with respect, her eyes sometimes filled with tears, which she endeavoured to wipe away unperceived; but I generally found that her countenance and tone were more cheerful after having listened to the exhortations of her father. It was not thus with Felix. He was always the saddest of the group, and, even to my unpractised senses, he appeared to have suffered more deeply than his friends. But if his countenance was more sorrowful, his voice was more cheerful than that of his sister, especially when he addressed the old man.

"I could mention innumerable instances which, although slight, marked the dispositions of these amiable cottagers. In the midst of poverty and want, Felix carried with pleasure to his sister the first little white flower that peeped out from beneath the snowy ground. Early in the morning, before she had risen, he cleared away the snow that obstructed her path to the milk-house, drew water from the well, and brought the wood from the out-house, where, to his perpetual astonishment, he found his store always replenished by an invisible hand. In the day, I believe, he worked sometimes for a neighbouring farmer, because he often went forth and did not return until dinner, yet brought no wood with him. At other times he worked in the garden; but as there was little to do in the frosty season, he read to the old man and Agatha.

"This reading had puzzled me extremely at first; but, by degrees, I discovered that he uttered many of the same sounds when he read, as when he talked. I conjectured, therefore, that he found on the paper signs for speech which he understood, and I ardently longed to comprehend these also; but how was that possible when I did not even understand the sounds for which they stood as signs? I improved, however, sensibly in this science, but not sufficiently to follow up any kind of conversation, although I applied my whole mind to the endeavour: for I easily perceived that, although I eagerly longed to discover[1] myself to the cottagers, I ought not to make the attempt until I had first become master of their language; which knowledge might enable me to make them overlook the deformity of my figure; for with this also the contrast perpetually presented to my eyes had made me acquainted.

"I had admired the perfect forms of my cottagers—their grace, beauty, and delicate complexions: but how was I terrified, when I viewed myself in a transparent pool! At first I started back, unable to believe that it was indeed I who was reflected in the mirror; and when I became fully convinced that I was in reality the monster that I am, I was filled with the bitterest sensations of despondence and mortification. Alas! I did not yet entirely know the fatal effects of this miserable deformity.

"As the sun became warmer, and the light of day longer, the snow vanished, and I beheld the bare trees and the black earth. From this time Felix was more employed; and the heart-moving indications of impending famine disappeared. Their food, as I afterwards found, was coarse, but it was wholesome; and they procured a sufficiency of it. Several new kinds of plants sprang up in the garden, which they dressed; and these signs of comfort increased daily as the season advanced.

---

[1] *discover*] reveal.

"The old man, leaning on his son, walked each day at noon, when it did not rain, as I found it was called when the heavens poured forth its water. This frequently took place; but a high wind quickly dried the earth, and the season became far more pleasant than it had been.

"My mode of life in my hovel was uniform. During the morning I attended the motions of the cottagers; and when they were dispersed in various occupations, I slept: the remainder of the day was spent in observing my friends. When they had retired to rest, if there was any moon or the night was star-light, I went into the woods and collected my own food and fuel for the cottage. When I returned, as often as it was necessary, I cleared their path from the snow and performed those offices that I had seen done by Felix. I afterwards found that these labours, performed by an invisible hand, greatly astonished them; and once or twice I heard them, on these occasions, utter the words 'good spirit,' 'wonderful'; but I did not then understand the signification of these terms.

"My thoughts now became more active, and I longed to discover the motives and feelings of these lovely creatures; I was inquisitive to know why Felix appeared so miserable and Agatha so sad. I thought (foolish wretch!) that it might be in my power to restore happiness to these deserving people. When I slept or was absent, the forms of the venerable blind father, the gentle Agatha, and the excellent Felix, flitted before me. I looked upon them as superior beings, who would be the arbiters of my future destiny. I formed in my imagination a thousand pictures of presenting myself to them, and their reception of me. I imagined that they would be disgusted, until, by my gentle demeanour and conciliating words, I should first win their favour, and afterwards their love.

"These thoughts exhilarated me and led me to apply with fresh ardour to the acquiring the art of language. My organs were indeed harsh, but supple; and although my voice was very unlike the soft music of their tones, yet I pronounced such words as I understood with tolerable ease. It was as the ass and the lap-dog;[2] yet surely the gentle ass whose intentions were affectionate, although his manners were rude, deserved better treatment than blows and execration.

---

[2] *the ass and the lap-dog*] in the fable, the ass tries to gain his master's affection by imitating the lap-dog, but is beaten for his behavior.

"The pleasant showers and genial warmth of spring greatly altered the aspect of the earth. Men, who before this change seemed to have been hid in caves, dispersed themselves, and were employed in various arts of cultivation. The birds sang in more cheerful notes, and the leaves began to bud forth on the trees. Happy, happy earth! fit habitation for gods, which, so short a time before, was bleak, damp, and unwholesome. My spirits were elevated by the enchanting appearance of nature; the past was blotted from my memory, the present was tranquil, and the future gilded by bright rays of hope, and anticipations of joy."

Chapter XIII

"I NOW HASTEN to the more moving part of my story. I shall relate events, that impressed me with feelings which, from what I had been, have made me what I am.

"Spring advanced rapidly; the weather became fine and the skies cloudless. It surprised me, that what before was desert and gloomy should now bloom with the most beautiful flowers and verdure. My senses were gratified and refreshed by a thousand scents of delight, and a thousand sights of beauty.

"It was on one of these days, when my cottagers periodically rested from labour—the old man played on his guitar, and the children listened to him—that I observed the countenance of Felix was melancholy beyond expression; he sighed frequently; and once his father paused in his music, and I conjectured by his manner that he enquired the cause of his son's sorrow. Felix replied in a cheerful accent, and the old man was recommencing his music when some one tapped at the door.

"It was a lady on horseback, accompanied by a countryman as a guide. The lady was dressed in a dark suit, and covered with a thick black veil. Agatha asked a question, to which the stranger only replied by pronouncing, in a sweet accent, the name of Felix. Her voice was musical but unlike that of either of my friends. On hearing this word, Felix came up hastily to the lady, who, when she saw him, threw up her veil, and I beheld a countenance of angelic beauty and expression. Her hair of a shining raven black, and curiously braided; her eyes were dark, but gentle, although animated; her features of a regular proportion, and her complexion wondrously fair, each cheek tinged with a lovely pink.

"Felix seemed ravished with delight when he saw her, every trait of sorrow vanished from his face, and it instantly expressed a degree of ecstatic joy, of which I could hardly have believed it capable; his eyes sparkled, as his cheek flushed with pleasure; and at that moment I thought him as beautiful as the stranger. She appeared affected by different feelings; wiping a few tears from her lovely eyes, she held out her hand to Felix, who kissed it rapturously and called her, as well as I could distinguish, his sweet Arabian. She did not appear to understand him, but smiled. He assisted her to dismount, and dismissing her guide, conducted her into the cottage. Some conversation took place between him and his father; and the young stranger knelt at the old man's feet and would have kissed his hand, but he raised her, and embraced her affectionately.

"I soon perceived, that although the stranger uttered articulate sounds, and appeared to have a language of her own, she was neither understood by, nor herself understood, the cottagers. They made many signs which I did not comprehend; but I saw that her presence diffused gladness through the cottage, dispelling their sorrow as the sun dissipates the morning mists. Felix seemed peculiarly happy, and with smiles of delight welcomed his Arabian. Agatha, the ever-gentle Agatha, kissed the hands of the lovely stranger; and pointing to her brother, made signs which appeared to me to mean that he had been sorrowful until she came. Some hours passed thus, while they, by their countenances, expressed joy, the cause of which I did not comprehend. Presently I found, by the frequent recurrence of some sound which the stranger repeated after them, that she was endeavouring to learn their language; and the idea instantly occurred to me that I should make use of the same instructions to the same end. The stranger learned about twenty words at the first lesson, most of them, indeed, were those which I had before understood, but I profited by the others.

"As night came on, Agatha and the Arabian retired early. When they separated, Felix kissed the hand of the stranger and said, 'Good night, sweet Safie.' He sat up much longer, conversing with his father; and by the frequent repetition of her name, I conjectured that their lovely guest was the subject of their conversation. I ardently desired to understand them, and bent every faculty towards that purpose, but found it utterly impossible.

"The next morning Felix went out to his work; and, after the usual occupations of Agatha were finished, the Arabian sat at the feet of the old man, and taking his guitar, played some airs so entrancingly beautiful that they at once drew tears of sorrow and delight from my eyes. She sang, and her voice flowed in a rich cadence, swelling or dying away, like a nightingale of the woods.

"When she had finished, she gave the guitar to Agatha, who at first declined it. She played a simple air, and her voice accompanied it in sweet accents, but unlike the wondrous strain of the stranger. The old man appeared enraptured and said some words, which Agatha endeavoured to explain to Safie, and by which he appeared to wish to express that she bestowed on him the greatest delight by her music.

"The days now passed as peaceably as before, with the sole alteration that joy had taken place of sadness in the countenances of my friends. Safie was always gay and happy; she and I improved rapidly in the knowledge of language, so that in two months I began to comprehend most of the words uttered by my protectors.

"In the meanwhile also the black ground was covered with herbage, and the green banks interspersed with innumerable flowers, sweet to the scent and the eyes, stars of pale radiance among the moonlight woods; the sun became warmer, the nights clear and balmy; and my nocturnal rambles were an extreme pleasure to me, although they were considerably shortened by the late setting and early rising of the sun, for I never ventured abroad during daylight, fearful of meeting with the same treatment I had formerly endured in the first village which I entered.

"My days were spent in close attention, that I might more speedily master the language; and I may boast that I improved more rapidly than the Arabian, who understood very little and conversed in broken accents, whilst I comprehended and could imitate almost every word that was spoken.

"While I improved in speech, I also learned the science of letters as it was taught to the stranger; and this opened before me a wide field for wonder and delight.

"The book from which Felix instructed Safie was Volney's *Ruins of Empires*.[1] I should not have understood the purport of this book had not Felix, in reading it, given very minute explanations. He had chosen this work, he said, because the declamatory style was framed in imitation of the eastern authors. Through this work I obtained a cursory knowledge of history and a view of the several

[1] *Volney's* Ruins of Empires] an essay on the philosophy of history written by the Comte de Volney in 1791.

empires at present existing in the world; it gave me an insight into the manners, governments, and religions of the different nations of the earth. I heard of the slothful Asiatics; of the stupendous genius and mental activity of the Grecians; of the wars and wonderful virtue of the early Romans—of their subsequent degenerating—of the decline of that mighty empire, of chivalry, Christianity, and kings. I heard of the discovery of the American hemisphere and wept with Safie over the hapless fate of its original inhabitants.

"These wonderful narrations inspired me with strange feelings. Was man, indeed, at once so powerful, so virtuous, and magnificent, yet so vicious and base? He appeared at one time a mere scion of the evil principle, and at another as all that can be conceived as noble and godlike. To be a great and virtuous man appeared the highest honour that can befall a sensitive being; to be base and vicious, as many on record have been, appeared the lowest degradation, a condition more abject than that of the blind mole or harmless worm. For a long time I could not conceive how one man could go forth to murder his fellow, or even why there were laws and governments; but when I heard details of vice and bloodshed, my wonder ceased, and I turned away with disgust and loathing.

"Every conversation of the cottagers now opened new wonders to me. While I listened to the instructions which Felix bestowed upon the Arabian, the strange system of human society was explained to me. I heard of the division of property, of immense wealth and squalid poverty; of rank, descent, and noble blood.

"The words induced me to turn towards myself. I learned that the possessions most esteemed by your fellow creatures were high and unsullied descent united with riches. A man might be respected with only one of these advantages; but without either he was considered, except in very rare instances, as a vagabond and a slave, doomed to waste his powers for the profits of the chosen few! And what was I? Of my creation and creator I was absolutely ignorant, but I knew that I possessed no money, no friends, no kind of property. I was, besides, endued with a figure hideously deformed and loathsome; I was not even of the same nature as man. I was more agile than they and could subsist upon coarser diet; I bore the extremes of heat and cold with less injury to my frame; my stature far exceeded theirs. When I looked around I saw and heard of none like me. Was I, then, a monster, a blot upon the earth, from which all men fled and whom all men disowned?

"I cannot describe to you the agony that these reflections inflicted upon me: I tried to dispel them, but sorrow only increased with knowledge. Oh, that I had forever remained in my native wood, nor known nor felt beyond the sensations of hunger, thirst and heat!

"Of what a strange nature is knowledge! It clings to the mind, when it has once seized on it, like a lichen on the rock. I wished sometimes to shake off all thought and feeling; but I learned that there was but one means to overcome the sensation of pain, and that was death—a state which I feared yet did not understand. I admired virtue and good feelings and loved the gentle manners and amiable qualities of my cottagers, but I was shut out from intercourse with them, except through means which I obtained by stealth, when I was unseen and unknown, and which rather increased than satisfied the desire I had of becoming one among my fellows. The gentle words of Agatha and the animated smiles of the charming Arabian, were not for me. The mild exhortations of the old man, and the lively conversation of the loved Felix were not for me. Miserable, unhappy wretch!

"Other lessons were impressed upon me even more deeply. I heard of the difference of sexes; and the birth and growth of children; how the father doated on the smiles of the infant, and the lively sallies of the older child; how all the life and cares of the mother were wrapped up in the precious charge; how the mind of youth expanded and gained knowledge; of brother, sister, and all the various relationships which bind one human being to another in mutual bonds.

"But where were my friends and relations? No father had watched my infant days, no mother had blessed me with smiles and caresses; or if they had, all my past life was now a blot, a blind vacancy in which I distinguished nothing. From my earliest remembrance I had been as I then was in height and proportion. I had never yet seen a being resembling me, or who claimed any intercourse with me. What was I? The question again recurred, to be answered only with groans.

"I will soon explain to what these feelings tended; but allow me now to return to the cottagers, whose story excited in me such various feelings of indignation, delight, and wonder, but which all terminated in additional love and reverence for my protectors (for so I loved, in an innocent, half-painful self-deceit, to call them)."

Chapter XIV

"Some time elapsed before I learned the history of my friends. It was one which could not fail to impress itself deeply on my mind, unfolding as it did a number of circumstances, each interesting and wonderful to one so utterly inexperienced as I was.

"The name of the old man was De Lacey. He was descended from a good family in France, where he had lived for many years in affluence, respected by his superiors and beloved by his equals. His son was bred in the service of his country; and Agatha had ranked with ladies of the highest distinction. A few months before my arrival they had lived in a large and luxurious city called Paris, surrounded by friends and possessed of every enjoyment which virtue, refinement of intellect, or taste, accompanied by a moderate fortune, could afford.

"The father of Safie had been the cause of their ruin. He was a Turkish merchant, and had inhabited Paris for many years, when, for some reason which I could not learn, he became obnoxious to the government. He was seized and cast into prison the very day that Safie arrived from Constantinople to join him. He was tried and condemned to death. The injustice of his sentence was very flagrant; all Paris was indignant; and it was judged that his religion and wealth rather than the crime alleged against him had been the cause of his condemnation.

"Felix had accidentally been present at the trial; his horror and indignation were uncontrollable when he heard the decision of the court. He made, at that moment, a solemn vow to deliver him and then looked around for the means. After many fruitless attempts to gain admittance to the prison, he found a strongly grated window in an unguarded part of the building, which lighted the dungeon of the unfortunate Mahometan; who, loaded with chains, waited in despair the execution of the barbarous sentence. Felix visited the grate at night and made known to the prisoner his intentions in his favour. The Turk, amazed and delighted, endeavoured to kindle the zeal of his deliverer by promises of reward and wealth. Felix rejected his offers with contempt; yet when he saw the lovely Safie, who was allowed to visit her father and who, by her gestures, expressed her lively gratitude, the youth could not help owning to his own mind that the captive possessed a treasure which would fully reward his toil and hazard.

"The Turk quickly perceived the impression that his daughter had made on the heart of Felix and endeavoured to secure him more entirely in his interests by the promise of her hand in marriage, so soon as he should be conveyed to a place of safety. Felix was too delicate to accept his offer; yet he looked forward to the probability of the event as to the consummation of his happiness.

"During the ensuing days, while the preparations were going forward for the escape of the merchant, the zeal of Felix was warmed by several letters that he received from this lovely girl, who found means to express her thoughts in the language of her lover by the aid of an old man, a servant of her father who understood French. She thanked him in the most ardent terms for his intended services towards her parent; and at the same time she gently deplored her own fate.

"I have copies of these letters; for I found means, during my residence in the hovel, to procure the implements of writing; and the letters were often in the hands of Felix or Agatha. Before I depart, I will give them to you, they will prove the truth of my tale; but at present, as the sun is already far declined, I shall only have time to repeat the substance of them to you.

"Safie related that her mother was a Christian Arab, seized and made a slave by the Turks; recommended by her beauty, she had won the heart of the father of Safie, who married her. The young girl spoke in high and enthusiastic terms of her mother, who, born in freedom, spurned the bondage to which she was now reduced. She instructed her daughter in the tenets of her religion and taught her to aspire to higher powers of intellect and an independence of spirit forbidden to the female followers of Mahomet. This lady died; but her lessons were indelibly impressed on the mind of Safie, who sickened at the prospect of again returning to Asia and being immured within the walls of a harem, allowed only to occupy herself with infantile amusements, ill-suited to the temper of her soul, now accustomed to grand ideas and a noble emulation of virtue. The prospect of marrying a Christian and remaining in a country where women were allowed to take a rank in society was enchanting to her.

"The day for the execution of the Turk was fixed; but on the night previous to it he quitted his prison, and before morning was distant many leagues from Paris. Felix had procured passports in the name of his father, sister, and himself. He had previously communicated his plan to the former, who aided the deceit by quitting his house, under the pretence of a journey and concealing himself, with his daughter, in an obscure part of Paris.

"Felix conducted the fugitives through France to Lyons and across Mont Cenis to Leghorn, where the merchant had decided to wait a favourable opportunity of passing into some part of the Turkish dominions.

"Safie resolved to remain with her father until the moment of his departure, before which time the Turk renewed his promise that she should be united to his deliverer; and Felix remained with them in expectation of that event; and in the mean time he enjoyed the society of the Arabian, who exhibited towards him the simplest and tenderest affection. They conversed with one another through the means of an interpreter, and sometimes with the interpretation of looks; and Safie sang to him the divine airs of her native country.

"The Turk allowed this intimacy to take place, and encouraged the hopes of the youthful lovers, while in his heart he had formed far other plans. He loathed the idea that his daughter should be united to a Christian; but he feared the resentment of Felix if he should appear lukewarm; for he knew that he was still in the power of his deliverer if he should choose to betray him to the Italian state which they inhabited. He revolved a thousand plans by which he should be enabled to prolong the deceit until it might be no longer necessary, and secretly to take his daughter with him when he departed. His plans were facilitated by the news which arrived from Paris.

"The government of France were greatly enraged at the escape of their victim and spared no pains to detect and punish his deliverer. The plot of Felix was quickly discovered, and De Lacey and Agatha were thrown into prison. The news reached Felix and roused him from his dream of pleasure. His blind and aged father and his gentle sister lay in a noisome dungeon while he enjoyed the free air and the society of her whom he loved. This idea was torture to him. He quickly arranged with the Turk that if the latter should find a favourable opportunity for escape before Felix could return to Italy, Safie should remain as a boarder at a convent at Leghorn; and then, quitting the lovely Arabian, he hastened to Paris, and delivered himself up to the vengeance of the law, hoping to free De Lacey and Agatha by this proceeding.

"He did not succeed. They remained confined for five months before the trial took place; the result of which deprived them of their fortune and condemned them to a perpetual exile from their native country.

"They found a miserable asylum in the cottage in Germany, where I discovered them. Felix soon learned that the treacherous Turk, for whom he and his family endured such unheard-of oppression, on discovering that his deliverer was thus reduced to poverty and ruin, became a traitor to good feeling and honour and had quitted Italy with his daughter, insultingly sending Felix a pittance of money to aid him, as he said, in some plan of future maintenance.

"Such were the events that preyed on the heart of Felix and rendered him, when I first saw him, the most miserable of his family. He could have endured poverty; and while this distress had been the meed of his virtue, he gloried in it; but the ingratitude of the Turk and the loss of his beloved Safie, were misfortunes more bitter and irreparable. The arrival of the Arabian now infused new life into his soul.

"When the news reached Leghorn that Felix was deprived of his wealth and rank, the merchant commanded his daughter to think no more of her lover, but to prepare to return to her native country. The generous nature of Safie was outraged by this command; she attempted to expostulate with her father, but he left her angrily, reiterating his tyrannical mandate.

"A few days after, the Turk entered his daughter's apartment and told her hastily that he had reason to believe that his residence at Leghorn had been divulged and that he should speedily be delivered up to the French government; he had, consequently, hired a vessel to convey him to Constantinople, for which city he should sail in a few hours. He intended to leave his daughter under the care of a confidential servant, to follow at her leisure with the greater part of his property, which had not yet arrived at Leghorn.

"When alone, Safie resolved in her own mind the plan of conduct that it would become her to pursue in this emergency. A residence in Turkey was abhorrent to her; her religion and her feelings were alike averse to it. By some papers of her father which fell into her hands she heard of the exile of her lover and learnt the name of the spot where he then resided. She hesitated some time, but at length she formed her determination. Taking with her some jewels that belonged to her and a sum of money, she quitted Italy with an attendant, a native of Leghorn, but who understood the common language of Turkey, and departed for Germany.

"She arrived in safety at a town about twenty leagues from the cottage of De Lacey, when her attendant fell dangerously ill. Safie nursed her with the most devoted affection; but the poor girl died, and the Arabian was left alone, unacquainted with the language of the country and utterly ignorant of the customs of the world. She fell, however, into good hands. The Italian had mentioned the name of the spot for which they were bound; and after her death, the woman of the house in which they had lived took care that Safie should arrive in safety at the cottage of her lover."

Chapter XV

"SUCH WAS THE history of my beloved cottagers. It impressed me deeply. I learned, from the views of social life which it developed, to admire their virtues and to deprecate the vices of mankind.

"As yet I looked upon crime as a distant evil; benevolence and generosity were ever present before me, inciting within me a desire to become an actor in the busy scene where so many admirable qualities were called forth and displayed. But in giving an account of the progress of my intellect, I must not omit a circumstance which occurred in the beginning of the month of August of the same year.

"One night, during my accustomed visit to the neighbouring wood, where I collected my own food and brought home firing for my protectors, I found on the ground a leathern portmanteau, containing several articles of dress and some books. I eagerly seized the prize, and returned with it to my hovel. Fortunately the books were written in the language, the elements of which I had acquired at the cottage; they consisted of *Paradise Lost,* a volume of Plutarch's *Lives,* and the *Sorrows of Werter.* The possession of these treasures gave me extreme delight; I now continually studied and exercised my mind upon these histories, whilst my friends were employed in their ordinary occupations.

"I can hardly describe to you the effect of these books. They produced in me an infinity of new images and feelings, that sometimes raised me to ecstasy, but more frequently sunk me into the lowest dejection. In the *Sorrows of Werter,* besides the interest of its simple and affecting story, so many opinions are canvassed, and so many lights thrown upon what had hitherto been to me obscure subjects, that I found in it a never-ending source of speculation and astonishment. The gentle and domestic manners it described, combined with lofty sentiments and feelings, which had for their object something out of self, accorded well with my experience among my protectors, and with the wants which were forever alive in my own bosom. But I thought Werter himself a more divine being than I had ever beheld or imagined; his character contained no pretension, but it sunk deep. The disquisitions upon death and suicide were calculated to fill me with wonder. I did not pretend to enter into the merits of the case, yet I inclined towards the opinions of the hero, whose extinction I wept, without precisely understanding it.

"As I read, however, I applied much personally to my own feelings and condition. I found myself similar, yet at the same time strangely unlike to the beings concerning whom I read, and to whose conversation I was a listener. I sympathised with and partly understood them, but I was unformed in mind; I was dependent on none, and related to none. 'The path of my departure was free,'[1] and there was none to lament my annihilation. My person was hideous and my stature gigantic. What did this mean? Who was I? What was I? Whence did I come? What was my destination? These questions continually recurred, but I was unable to solve them.

"The volume of Plutarch's *Lives* which I possessed, contained the histories of the first founders of the ancient republics. This book had a far different effect upon me from the *Sorrows of Werter*. I learned from Werter's imaginations despondency and gloom: but Plutarch taught me high thoughts; he elevated me above the wretched sphere of my own reflections, to admire and love the heroes of past ages. Many things I read surpassed my understanding and experience. I had a very confused knowledge of kingdoms, wide extents of country, mighty rivers, and boundless seas. But I was perfectly unacquainted with towns, and large assemblages of men. The cottage of my protectors had been the only school in which I had studied human nature; but this book developed new and mightier scenes of action. I read of men concerned in public affairs, governing or massacring their species. I felt the greatest ardour for virtue rise within me, and abhorrence for vice, as far as I understood the signification of those terms, relative as they were, as

[1] "*The path . . . free*"] perhaps based on line 14 of Shelley's "Mutability" ("The path of its departure still is free").

I applied them, to pleasure and pain alone. Induced by these feelings, I was of course led to admire peaceable lawgivers, Numa, Solon, and Lycurgus, in preference to Romulus and Theseus. The patriarchal lives of my protectors caused these impressions to take a firm hold on my mind; perhaps, if my first introduction to humanity had been made by a young soldier, burning for glory and slaughter, I should have been imbued with different sensations.

"But *Paradise Lost* excited different and far deeper emotions. I read it, as I had read the other volumes which had fallen into my hands, as a true history. It moved every feeling of wonder and awe, that the picture of an omnipotent God warring with his creatures was capable of exciting. I often referred the several situations, as their similarity struck me, to my own. Like Adam, I was apparently united by no link to any other being in existence; but his state was far different from mine in every other respect. He had come forth from the hands of God a perfect creature, happy and prosperous, guarded by the especial care of his Creator; he was allowed to converse with and acquire knowledge from beings of a superior nature: but I was wretched, helpless, and alone. Many times I considered Satan as the fitter emblem of my condition; for often, like him, when I viewed the bliss of my protectors, the bitter gall of envy rose within me.

"Another circumstance strengthened and confirmed these feelings. Soon after my arrival in the hovel, I discovered some papers in the pocket of the dress which I had taken from your laboratory. At first I had neglected them; but now that I was able to decipher the characters in which they were written, I began to study them with diligence. It was your journal of the four months that preceded my creation. You minutely described in these papers every step you took in the progress of your work; this history was mingled with accounts of domestic occurrences. You, doubtless, recollect these papers. Here they are. Every thing is related in them which bears reference to my accursed origin; the whole detail of that series of disgusting circumstances which produced it is set in view; the minutest description of my odious and loathsome person is given, in language which painted your own horrors, and rendered mine indelible. I sickened as I read. 'Hateful day when I received life!' I exclaimed in agony. 'Accursed creator! Why did you form a monster so hideous that even *you* turned from me in disgust? God, in pity, made man beautiful and alluring, after his own image;

but my form is a filthy type of yours, more horrid even from the very resemblance. Satan had his companions, fellow-devils, to admire and encourage him; but I am solitary and abhorred.'

"These were the reflections of my hours of despondency and solitude; but when I contemplated the virtues of the cottagers, their amiable and benevolent dispositions, I persuaded myself that when they should become acquainted with my admiration of their virtues, they would compassionate me and overlook my personal deformity. Could they turn from their door one, however monstrous, who solicited their compassion and friendship? I resolved, at least, not to despair, but in every way to fit myself for an interview with them, which would decide my fate. I postponed this attempt for some months longer; for the importance attached to its success inspired me with a dread lest I should fail. Besides, I found that my understanding improved so much with every day's experience that I was unwilling to commence this undertaking until a few more months should have added to my sagacity.

"Several changes, in the mean time, took place in the cottage. The presence of Safie diffused happiness among its inhabitants; and I also found that a greater degree of plenty reigned there. Felix and Agatha spent more time in amusement and conversation, and were assisted in their labours by servants. They did not appear rich, but they were contented and happy; their feelings were serene and peaceful, while mine became every day more tumultuous. Increase of knowledge only discovered to me more clearly what a wretched outcast I was. I cherished hope, it is true; but it vanished when I beheld my person reflected in water, or my shadow in the moonshine, even as that frail image and that inconstant shade.

"I endeavoured to crush these fears, and to fortify myself for the trial which in a few months I resolved to undergo; and sometimes I allowed my thoughts, unchecked by reason, to ramble in the fields of Paradise, and dared to fancy amiable and lovely creatures sympathising with my feelings and cheering my gloom; their angelic countenances breathed smiles of consolation. But it was all a dream; no Eve soothed my sorrows nor shared my thoughts; I was alone. I remembered Adam's supplication to his Creator. But where was mine? He had abandoned me, and in the bitterness of my heart I cursed him.

"Autumn passed thus. I saw, with surprise and grief, the leaves decay and fall, and nature again assume the barren and bleak appearance it had worn when I first beheld the woods and the lovely moon. Yet I did not heed the bleakness of the weather; I was better fitted by my conformation for the endurance of cold than heat. But my chief delights were the sight of the flowers, the birds, and all the gay apparel of summer; when those deserted me, I turned with more attention towards the cottagers. Their happiness was not decreased by the absence of summer. They loved and sympathised with one another; and their joys, depending on each other, were not interrupted by the casualties that took place around them. The more I saw of them, the greater became my desire to claim their protection and kindness; my heart yearned to be known and loved by these amiable creatures; to see their sweet looks directed towards me with affection was the utmost limit of my ambition. I dared not think that they would turn them from me with disdain and horror. The poor that stopped at their door were never driven away. I asked, it is true, for greater treasures than a little food or rest; I required kindness and sympathy; but I did not believe myself unworthy of it.

"The winter advanced, and an entire revolution of the seasons had taken place since I awoke into life. My attention, at this time, was solely directed towards my plan of introducing myself into the cottage of my protectors. I revolved many projects; but that on which I finally fixed was, to enter the dwelling when the blind old man should be alone. I had sagacity enough to discover, that the unnatural hideousness of my person was the chief object of horror with those who had formerly beheld me. My voice, although harsh, had nothing terrible in it; I thought, therefore, that if in the absence of his children, I could gain the good-will and mediation of the old De Lacey, I might by his means be tolerated by my younger protectors.

"One day, when the sun shone on the red leaves that strewed the ground, and diffused cheerfulness, although it denied warmth, Safie, Agatha, and Felix departed on a long country walk, and the old man, at his own desire, was left alone in the cottage. When his children had departed, he took up his guitar, and played several mournful but sweet airs, more sweet and mournful than I had ever heard him play before. At first his countenance was illuminated with pleasure, but, as he continued, thoughtfulness and sadness succeeded; at length, laying aside the instrument, he sat absorbed in reflection.

"My heart beat quick; this was the hour and moment of trial, which would decide my hopes, or realise my fears. The servants were gone to a neighbouring fair. All was silent in and around the cottage: it was an excellent opportunity; yet, when I proceeded to execute my plan, my limbs failed me, and I sank to the ground. Again I rose; and, exerting all the firmness of which I was master, removed the planks which I had placed before my hovel to conceal my retreat. The fresh air revived me, and, with renewed determination, I approached the door of their cottage.

"I knocked. 'Who is there?' said the old man—'Come in.'

"I entered; 'Pardon this intrusion,' said I; 'I am a traveller in want of a little rest; you would greatly oblige me if you would allow me to remain a few minutes before the fire.'

" 'Enter,' said De Lacey, 'and I will try in what manner I can to relieve your wants; but, unfortunately, my children are from home, and as I am blind, I am afraid I shall find it difficult to procure food for you.'

" 'Do not trouble yourself, my kind host; I have food; it is warmth and rest only that I need.'

"I sat down, and a silence ensued. I knew that every minute was precious to me, yet I remained irresolute in what manner to commence the interview; when the old man addressed me—

" 'By your language, stranger, I suppose you are my countryman;—are you French?'

" 'No; but I was educated by a French family, and understand that language only. I am now going to claim the protection of some friends, whom I sincerely love, and of whose favour I have some hopes.'

" 'Are they Germans?'

" 'No, they are French. But let us change the subject. I am an unfortunate and deserted creature; I look around, and I have no relation or friend upon earth. These amiable people to whom I go have never seen me, and know little of me. I am full of fears, for if I fail there, I am an outcast in the world forever.'

" 'Do not despair. To be friendless is indeed to be unfortunate; but the hearts of men, when unprejudiced by any obvious self-interest, are full of brotherly love and charity. Rely, therefore, on your hopes; and if these friends are good and amiable, do not despair.'

" 'They are kind—they are the most excellent creatures in the world; but unfortunately, they are prejudiced against me. I have good dispositions; my life has been hitherto harmless and in some degree beneficial; but a fatal prejudice clouds their eyes, and where they ought to see a feeling and kind friend, they behold only a detestable monster.'

"'That is indeed unfortunate; but if you are really blameless, cannot you undeceive them?'

"'I am about to undertake that task; and it is on that account that I feel so many overwhelming terrors. I tenderly love these friends; I have, unknown to them, been for many months in the habits of daily kindness towards them; but they believe that I wish to injure them, and it is that prejudice which I wish to overcome.'

"'Where do these friends reside?'

"'Near this spot.'

"The old man paused and then continued, 'If you will unreservedly confide to me the particulars of your tale, I perhaps may be of use in undeceiving them. I am blind and cannot judge of your countenance, but there is something in your words which persuades me that you are sincere. I am poor and an exile, but it will afford me true pleasure to be in any way serviceable to a human creature.'

"'Excellent man! I thank you and accept your generous offer. You raise me from the dust by this kindness; and I trust that, by your aid, I shall not be driven from the society and sympathy of your fellow-creatures.'

"'Heaven forbid! Even if you were really criminal, for that can only drive you to desperation, and not instigate you to virtue. I also am unfortunate; I and my family have been condemned, although innocent; judge, therefore, if I do not feel for your misfortunes.'

"'How can I thank you, my best and only benefactor? From your lips first have I heard the voice of kindness directed towards me; I shall be forever grateful; and your present humanity assures me of success with those friends whom I am on the point of meeting.'

"'May I know the names and residence of those friends?'

"I paused. This, I thought, was the moment of decision, which was to rob me of, or bestow happiness on me forever. I struggled vainly for firmness sufficient to answer him, but the effort destroyed all my remaining strength; I sank on the chair and sobbed aloud. At that moment I heard the steps of my younger protectors. I had not a moment to lose, but, seizing the hand of the old man, I cried, 'Now is the time!—save and protect me! You and your family are the friends whom I seek. Do not you desert me in the hour of trial!'

"'Great God!' exclaimed the old man, 'who are you?'

"At that instant the cottage door was opened, and Felix, Safie, and Agatha entered. Who can describe their horror and consternation on beholding me? Agatha fainted; and Safie, unable to attend to her friend, rushed out of the cottage. Felix darted forward, and with supernatural force tore me from his father, to whose knees I clung: in a transport of fury, he dashed me to the ground and struck me violently with a stick. I could have torn him limb from limb, as the lion rends the antelope. But my heart sunk within me as with bitter sickness, and I refrained. I saw him on the point of repeating his blow, when, overcome by pain and anguish, I quitted the cottage, and in the general tumult escaped unperceived to my hovel."

Chapter XVI

"CURSED, CURSED CREATOR! Why did I live? Why, in that instant, did I not extinguish the spark of existence which you had so wantonly bestowed? I know not; despair had not yet taken possession of me; my feelings were those of rage and revenge. I could with pleasure have destroyed the cottage and its inhabitants, and have glutted myself with their shrieks and misery.

"When night came I quitted my retreat and wandered in the wood; and now, no longer restrained by the fear of discovery, I gave vent to my anguish in fearful howlings. I was like a wild beast that had broken the toils, destroying the objects that obstructed me, and ranging through the wood with a stag-like swiftness. Oh! what a miserable night I passed! the cold stars shone in mockery, and the bare trees waved their branches above me: now and then the sweet voice of a bird burst forth amidst the universal stillness. All, save I, were at rest or in enjoyment: I, like the arch-fiend, bore a hell within me; and, finding myself unsympathised with, wished to tear up the trees, spread havoc and destruction around me, and then to have sat down and enjoyed the ruin.

"But this was a luxury of sensation that could not endure; I became fatigued with excess of bodily exertion, and sank on the damp grass in the sick impotence of despair. There was none among the myriads of men that existed who would pity or assist me; and should I feel kindness towards my enemies? No: from that moment I declared ever-lasting war against the species, and, more than all, against him who had formed me, and sent me forth to this insupportable misery.

"The sun rose; I heard the voices of men, and knew that it was impossible to return to my retreat during that day. Accordingly I hid myself in some thick underwood, determining to devote the ensuing hours to reflection on my situation.

"The pleasant sunshine, and the pure air of day, restored me to some degree of tranquillity; and when I considered what had passed at the cottage, I could not help believing that I had been too hasty in my conclusions. I had certainly acted imprudently. It was apparent that my conversation had interested the father in my behalf, and I was a fool in having exposed my person to the horror of his children. I ought to have familiarised the old De Lacey to me, and by degrees to have discovered myself to the rest of his family, when they should have been prepared for my approach. But I did not believe my errors to be irretrievable; and, after much consideration, I resolved to return to the cottage, seek the old man, and by my representations win him to my party.

"These thoughts calmed me, and in the afternoon I sank into a profound sleep; but the fever of my blood did not allow me to be visited by peaceful dreams. The horrible scene of the preceding day was forever acting before my eyes; the females were flying, and the enraged Felix tearing me from his father's feet. I awoke exhausted; and, finding that it was already night, I crept forth from my hiding-place, and went in search of food.

"When my hunger was appeased, I directed my steps towards the well-known path that conducted to the cottage. All there was at peace. I crept into my hovel, and remained in silent expectation of the accustomed hour when the family arose. That hour passed, the sun mounted high in the heavens, but the cottagers did not appear. I trembled violently, apprehending some dreadful misfortune. The inside of the cottage was dark, and I heard no motion; I cannot describe the agony of this suspense.

"Presently two countrymen passed by; but pausing near the cottage, they entered into conversation, using violent gesticulations; but I did not understand what they said, as they spoke the language of the country, which differed from that of my protectors. Soon after, however, Felix approached with another man; I was surprised, as I knew that he had not quitted the cottage that morning, and waited anxiously to discover, from his discourse, the meaning of these unusual appearances.

"'Do you consider,' said his companion to him, 'that you will be obliged to pay three months' rent and to lose the produce of your garden? I do not wish to take any unfair advantage, and I beg therefore that you will take some days to consider of your determination.'

"'It is utterly useless,' replied Felix; 'we can never again inhabit your cottage. The life of my father is in the greatest danger, owing to the dreadful circumstance that I have related. My wife and my sister will never recover from their horror. I intreat you not to reason with me any more. Take possession of your tenement, and let me fly from this place.'

"Felix trembled violently as he said this. He and his companion entered the cottage, in which they remained for a few minutes, and then departed. I never saw any of the family of De Lacey more.

"I continued for the remainder of the day in my hovel in a state of utter and stupid despair. My protectors had departed, and had broken the only link that held me to the world. For the first time the feelings of revenge and hatred filled my bosom, and I did not strive to control them; but, allowing myself to be borne away by the stream, I bent my mind towards injury and death. When I thought of my friends, of the mild voice of De Lacey, the gentle eyes of Agatha, and the exquisite beauty of the Arabian, these thoughts vanished, and a gush of tears somewhat soothed me. But again, when I reflected that they had spurned and deserted me, anger returned, a rage of anger; and, unable to injure anything human, I turned my fury towards inanimate objects. As night advanced I placed a variety of combustibles around the cottage; and, after having destroyed every vestige of cultivation in the garden, I waited with forced impatience until the moon had sunk to commence my operations.

"As the night advanced, a fierce wind arose from the woods, and quickly dispersed the clouds that had loitered in the heavens: the blast tore along like a mighty avalanche and produced a kind of insanity in my spirits, that burst all bounds of reason and reflection. I lighted the dry branch of a tree and danced with fury around the devoted cottage, my eyes still fixed on the western horizon, the edge of which the moon nearly touched. A part of its orb was at length hid, and I waved my brand; it sank, and with a loud scream I fired the straw, and heath, and bushes, which I had collected. The wind fanned the fire, and the cottage was quickly enveloped by the flames, which clung to it and licked it with their forked and destroying tongues.

"As soon as I was convinced that no assistance could save any part of the habitation, I quitted the scene, and sought for refuge in the woods.

"And now, with the world before me, whither should I bend my steps? I resolved to fly far from the scene of my misfortunes; but to me, hated and despised, every country must be equally horrible. At length the thought of you crossed my mind. I learned from your papers that you were my father, my creator; and to whom could I apply with more fitness than to him who had given me life? Among the lessons that Felix had bestowed upon Safie, geography had not been omitted: I had learned from these the relative situations of the different countries of the earth. You had mentioned Geneva as the name of your native town; and towards this place I resolved to proceed.

"But how was I to direct myself? I knew that I must travel in a southwesterly direction to reach my destination; but the sun was my only guide. I did not know the names of the towns that I was to pass through, nor could I ask information from a single human being; but I did not despair. From you only could I hope for succour, although towards you I felt no sentiment but that of hatred. Unfeeling, heartless creator! you had endowed me with perceptions and passions and then cast me abroad an object for the scorn and horror of mankind. But on you only had I any claim for pity and redress, and from you I determined to seek that justice which I vainly attempted to gain from any other being that wore the human form.

"My travels were long, and the sufferings I endured intense. It was late in autumn when I quitted the district where I had so long resided. I travelled only at night, fearful of encountering the visage of a human being. Nature decayed around me, and the sun became heatless; rain and snow poured around me; mighty rivers were frozen; the surface of the earth was hard, and chill, and bare, and I found no shelter. Oh, earth! how often did I imprecate curses on the cause of my being! The mildness of my nature had fled, and all within me was turned to gall and bitterness. The nearer I approached to your habitation, the more deeply did I feel the spirit of revenge enkindled in my heart. Snow fell, and the waters were hardened, but I rested not. A few incidents now and then directed me, and I possessed a map of the country; but I often wandered wide from my path. The agony of my feelings allowed me no respite: no incident occurred from which my rage and misery could not extract its food; but a circumstance that happened when I arrived on the confines of Switzerland, when the sun had recovered its warmth, and the earth again began to look green, confirmed in an especial manner the bitterness and horror of my feelings.

"I generally rested during the day, and travelled only when I was secured by night from the view of man. One morning, however, finding that my path lay through a deep wood, I ventured to continue my journey after the sun had risen; the day, which was one of the first of spring, cheered even me by the loveliness of its sunshine and the balminess of the air. I felt emotions of gentleness and pleasure, that had long appeared dead, revive within me. Half surprised by the novelty of these sensations, I allowed myself to be borne away by them; and, forgetting my solitude and deformity, dared to be happy. Soft tears again bedewed my cheeks, and I even raised my humid eyes with thankfulness towards the blessed sun, which bestowed such joy upon me.

"I continued to wind among the paths of the wood, until I came to its boundary, which was skirted by a deep and rapid river, into which many of the trees bent their branches, now budding with the fresh spring. Here I paused, not exactly knowing what path to pursue, when I heard the sound of voices, that induced me to conceal myself under the shade of a cypress. I was scarcely hid, when a young girl came running towards the spot where I was concealed, laughing, as if she ran from some one in sport. She continued her course along the precipitous sides of the river, when suddenly her foot slipt, and she fell into the rapid stream. I rushed from my hiding-place, and, with extreme labour from the force of the current, saved her, and dragged her to shore. She was senseless; and I endeavoured, by every means in my power, to restore animation, when I was suddenly interrupted by the approach of a rustic, who was probably the person from whom she had playfully fled. On seeing me, he darted towards me, and tearing the girl from my arms, hastened towards the deeper parts of the wood. I followed speedily, I hardly knew why; but when the man saw me draw near, he aimed a gun, which he carried, at my body, and fired. I sank to the ground, and my injurer, with increased swiftness, escaped into the wood.

"This was then the reward of my benevolence! I had saved a human being from destruction, and as a recompense I now writhed under the miserable pain of a wound which shattered the flesh and bone. The feelings of kindness and gentleness, which I had entertained but a few moments before, gave place to hellish rage and gnashing of teeth. Inflamed by pain, I vowed eternal hatred and vengeance to all mankind. But the agony of my wound overcame me; my pulses paused, and I fainted.

"For some weeks I led a miserable life in the woods, endeavouring to cure the wound which I had received. The ball had entered my shoulder, and I knew not whether it had remained there or passed through; at any rate I had no means of extracting it. My sufferings were augmented also by the oppressive sense of the injustice and ingratitude of their infliction. My daily vows rose for revenge—a deep and deadly revenge, such as would alone compensate for the outrages and anguish I had endured.

"After some weeks my wound healed, and I continued my journey. The labours I endured were no longer to be alleviated by the bright sun or gentle breezes of spring; all joy was but a mockery which insulted my desolate state, and made me feel more painfully that I was not made for the enjoyment of pleasure.

"But my toils now drew near a close, and in two months from this time, I reached the environs of Geneva.

"It was evening when I arrived, and I retired to a hiding-place among the fields that surround it, to meditate in what manner I should apply to you. I was oppressed by fatigue and hunger, and far too unhappy to enjoy the gentle breezes of evening, or the prospect of the sun setting behind the stupendous mountains of Jura.

"At this time a slight sleep relieved me from the pain of reflection, which was disturbed by the approach of a beautiful child, who came running into the recess I had chosen, with all the sportiveness of infancy. Suddenly, as I gazed on him, an idea seized me that this little creature was unprejudiced, and had lived too short a time to have imbibed a horror of deformity. If, therefore, I could seize him and educate him as my companion and friend, I should not be so desolate in this peopled earth.

"Urged by this impulse, I seized on the boy as he passed and drew him towards me. As soon as he beheld my form, he placed his hands before his eyes, and uttered a shrill scream; I drew his hand forcibly from his face and said, 'Child, what is the meaning of this? I do not intend to hurt you; listen to me.'

"He struggled violently. 'Let me go,' he cried; 'monster! ugly wretch! you wish to eat me and tear me to pieces—You are an ogre—Let me go, or I will tell my papa.'

"'Boy, you will never see your father again; you must come with me.'

"'Hideous monster! let me go. My papa is a Syndic—he is M. Frankenstein—he will punish you. You dare not keep me.'

"'Frankenstein! you belong then to my enemy—to him towards whom I have sworn eternal revenge; you shall be my first victim.'

"The child still struggled, and loaded me with epithets which carried despair to my heart: I grasped his throat to silence him, and in a moment he lay dead at my feet.

"I gazed on my victim, and my heart swelled with exultation and hellish triumph; clapping my hands, I exclaimed, 'I too can create desolation; my enemy is not invulnerable; this death will carry despair to him, and a thousand other miseries shall torment and destroy him.'

"As I fixed my eyes on the child, I saw something glittering on his breast. I took it; it was a portrait of a most lovely woman. In spite of my malignity, it softened and attracted me. For a few moments I gazed with delight on her dark eyes, fringed by deep lashes, and her lovely lips; but presently my rage returned: I remembered that I was forever deprived of the delights that such beautiful creatures could bestow; and that she whose resemblance I contemplated would, in regarding me, have changed that air of divine benignity to one expressive of disgust and affright.

"Can you wonder that such thoughts transported me with rage? I only wonder that at that moment, instead of venting my sensations in exclamations and agony, I did not rush among mankind, and perish in the attempt to destroy them.

"While I was overcome by these feelings, I left the spot where I had committed the murder, and seeking a more secluded hiding-place, I entered a barn which had appeared to me to be empty. A woman was sleeping on some straw; she was young: not indeed so beautiful as her whose portrait I held; but of an agreeable aspect and blooming in the loveliness of youth and health. Here, I thought, is one of those whose joy-imparting smiles are bestowed on all but me. And then I bent over her, and whispered, 'Awake, fairest, thy lover is near—he who would give his life but to obtain one look of affection from thine eyes: my beloved, awake!'

"The sleeper stirred; a thrill of terror ran through me. Should she indeed awake, and see me, and curse me, and denounce the murderer? Thus would she assuredly act, if her darkened eyes opened, and she beheld me. The thought was madness; it stirred the fiend within me—not I, but she, shall suffer; the murder I have committed because I am forever robbed of all that she could give me, she shall atone. The crime had its source in her: be hers the punishment! Thanks to the lessons of Felix and the sanguinary laws of man, I had learned how to work mischief. I bent over her and placed the portrait securely in one of the folds of her dress. She moved again, and I fled.

"For some days I haunted the spot where these scenes had taken place; sometimes wishing to see you, sometimes resolved to quit the world and its miseries forever. At length I wandered towards these mountains, and have ranged through their immense recesses, consumed by a burning passion which you alone can gratify. We may not part until you have promised to comply with my requisition. I am alone, and miserable; man will not associate with me; but one as deformed and horrible as myself would not deny herself to me. My companion must be of the same species, and have the same defects. This being you must create."

Chapter XVII

THE BEING FINISHED speaking, and fixed his looks upon me in the expectation of a reply. But I was bewildered, perplexed, and unable to arrange my ideas sufficiently to understand the full extent of his proposition. He continued.

"You must create a female for me, with whom I can live in the interchange of those sympathies necessary for my being. This you alone can do; and I demand it of you as a right which you must not refuse to concede."

The latter part of his tale had kindled anew in me the anger that had died away while he narrated his peaceful life among the cottagers, and, as he said this, I could no longer suppress the rage that burned within me.

"I do refuse it," I replied; "and no torture shall ever extort a consent from me. You may render me the most miserable of men, but you shall never make me base in my own eyes. Shall I create another like yourself, whose joint wickedness might desolate the world? Begone! I have answered you; you may torture me, but I will never consent."

"You are in the wrong," replied the fiend; "and, instead of threatening, I am content to reason with you. I am malicious because I am miserable. Am I not shunned and hated by all mankind? You, my creator, would tear me to pieces, and triumph; remember that, and tell me why I should pity man more than he pities me? You would not call it murder, if you could precipitate me into one of those ice-rifts, and destroy my frame, the work of your own hands. Shall I respect man when he contemns me? Let him live with me in the interchange of kindness; and, instead of injury I would bestow every benefit upon him with tears of gratitude at his acceptance. But that cannot be; the human senses are insurmountable barriers to our union. Yet mine shall not be the submission of abject slavery. I will revenge my injuries: if I cannot inspire love, I will cause fear, and chiefly towards you my arch-enemy, because my creator, do I swear inextinguishable hatred. Have a care: I will work at your destruction, nor finish until I desolate your heart, so that you shall curse the hour of your birth."

A fiendish rage animated him as he said this; his face was wrinkled into contortions too horrible for human eyes to behold; but presently he calmed himself and proceeded—

"I intended to reason. This passion is detrimental to me; for you do not reflect that you are the cause of its excess. If any being felt emotions of benevolence towards me, I should return them an hundred and an hundredfold; for that one creature's sake, I would make peace with the whole kind! But I now indulge in dreams of bliss that cannot be realised. What I ask of you is reasonable and moderate; I demand a creature of another sex, but as hideous as myself; the gratification is small, but it is all that I can receive, and it shall content me. It is true, we shall be monsters, cut off from all the world; but on that account we shall be more attached to one another. Our lives will not be happy, but they will be harmless, and free from the misery I now feel. Oh! my creator, make me happy; let me feel gratitude towards you for one benefit! Let me see that I excite the sympathy of some existing thing; do not deny me my request!"

I was moved. I shuddered when I thought of the possible consequences of my consent, but I felt that there was some justice in his argument. His tale, and the feelings he now expressed, proved him to be a creature of fine sensations; and did I not as his maker, owe him all the portion of happiness that it was in my power to bestow? He saw my change of feeling and continued.

"If you consent, neither you nor any other human being shall ever see us again: I will go to the vast wilds of South America. My food is not that of man; I do not destroy the lamb and the kid to glut my appetite; acorns and berries afford me sufficient nourishment. My companion will be of the same nature as myself, and will be content with the same fare. We shall make our bed of dried leaves; the sun will shine on us as on man, and will ripen our food. The picture I present to you is peaceful and human, and you must feel that you could deny it only in the wantonness of power and cruelty. Pitiless as you have been towards me, I now see compassion in your eyes; let me seize the favourable moment and persuade you to promise what I so ardently desire."

"You propose," replied I, "to fly from the habitations of man, to dwell in those wilds where the beasts of the field will be your only companions. How can you, who long for the love and sympathy of man, persevere in this exile? You will return, and again seek their kindness, and you will meet with their detestation; your evil passions will be renewed, and you will then have a companion to aid you in the task of destruction. This may not be: cease to argue the point, for I cannot consent."

"How inconstant are your feelings! but a moment ago you were moved by my representations, and why do you again harden yourself to my complaints? I swear to you, by the earth which I inhabit, and by you that made me, that with the companion you bestow I will quit the neighbourhood of man, and dwell, as it may chance, in the most savage of places. My evil passions will have fled, for I shall meet with sympathy! my life will flow quietly away, and in my dying moments I shall not curse my maker."

His words had a strange effect upon me. I compassionated him and sometimes felt a wish to console him; but when I looked upon him, when I saw the filthy mass that moved and talked, my heart sickened and my feelings were altered to those of horror and hatred. I tried to stifle these sensations; I thought, that as I could not sympathise with him, I had no right to withhold from him the small portion of happiness which was yet in my power to bestow.

"You swear," I said, "to be harmless; but have you not already shown a degree of malice that should reasonably make me distrust you? May not even this be a feint that will increase your triumph by affording a wider scope for your revenge?"

"How is this? I must not be trifled with: and I demand an answer. If I have no ties and no affections, hatred and vice must be my portion; the love of another will destroy the cause of my crimes, and I shall become a thing of whose existence every one will be ignorant. My vices are the children of a forced solitude that I abhor; and my virtues will necessarily arise when I live in communion with an equal. I shall feel the affections of a sensitive being, and become linked to the chain of existence and events, from which I am now excluded."

I paused some time to reflect on all he had related, and the various arguments which he had employed. I thought of the promise of virtues which he had displayed on the opening of his existence, and the subsequent blight of all kindly feeling by the loathing and scorn which his protectors had manifested towards him. His power and threats were not omitted to my calculations: a creature who could exist in the ice-caves of the glaciers, and hide himself from pursuit among the ridges of inaccessible precipices, was a being possessing faculties it would be vain to cope with. After a long pause of reflection, I concluded that the justice due both to him and my fellow creatures demanded of me that I should comply with his request. Turning to him, therefore, I said—

"I consent to your demand, on your solemn oath to quit Europe forever, and every other place in the neighbourhood of man, as soon as I shall deliver into your hands a female who will accompany you in your exile."

"I swear," he cried, "by the sun, and by the blue sky of Heaven, and by the fire of love that burns my heart, that if you grant my prayer, while they exist you shall never behold me again. Depart to your home, and commence your labours: I shall watch their progress with unutterable anxiety; and fear not but that when you are ready I shall appear."

Saying this, he suddenly quitted me, fearful, perhaps, of any change in my sentiments. I saw him descend the mountain with greater speed than the flight of an eagle, and quickly lost among the undulations of the sea of ice.

His tale had occupied the whole day, and the sun was upon the verge of the horizon when he departed. I knew that I ought to hasten my descent towards the valley, as I should soon be encompassed in darkness; but my heart was heavy, and my steps slow. The labour of winding among the little paths of the mountain and fixing my feet firmly as I advanced, perplexed me, occupied as I was by the emotions which the occurrences of the day had produced. Night was far advanced when I came to the half-way resting-place and seated myself beside the fountain. The stars shone at intervals, as the clouds passed from over them; the dark pines rose before me, and every here and there a broken tree lay on the ground: it was a scene of wonderful solemnity and stirred strange thoughts within me. I wept bitterly; and clasping my hands in agony, I exclaimed, "Oh! stars and clouds and winds, ye are all about to mock me: if ye really pity me, crush sensation and memory; let me become as nought; but if not, depart, depart, and leave me in darkness."

These were wild and miserable thoughts; but I cannot describe to you how the eternal twinkling of the stars weighed upon me, and how I listened to every blast of wind, as if it were a dull ugly siroc[1] on its way to consume me.

Morning dawned before I arrived at the village of Chamounix; I took no rest, but returned immediately to Geneva. Even in my own heart I could give no expression to my sensations—they weighed on me with a mountain's weight, and their excess destroyed my agony beneath them.

Thus I returned home, and entering the house, presented myself to the family. My haggard and wild appearance awoke intense alarm; but I answered no questions, scarcely did I speak. I felt as if I were placed under a ban—as if I had no right to claim their sympathies—as if never more might I enjoy companionship with them. Yet even thus I loved them to adoration; and to save them, I resolved to dedicate myself to my most abhorred task. The prospect of such an occupation made every other circumstance of existence pass before me like a dream, and that thought only had to me the reality of life.[2]

---

[1] *siroc*] sirocco; a hot, oppressive wind.

[2] The end of Chapter XVII marks the end of Volume II of the 1818 edition.

Chapter XVIII

Day after day, week after week, passed away on my return to Geneva; and I could not collect the courage to recommence my work. I feared the vengeance of the disappointed fiend, yet I was unable to overcome my repugnance to the task which was enjoined me. I found that I could not compose a female without again devoting several months to profound study and laborious disquisition. I had heard of some discoveries having been made by an English philosopher, the knowledge of which was material to my success, and I sometimes thought of obtaining my father's consent to visit England for this purpose; but I clung to every pretence of delay, and shrank from taking the first step in an undertaking whose immediate necessity began to appear less absolute to me. A change indeed had taken place in me: my health, which had hitherto declined, was now much restored; and my spirits, when unchecked by the memory of my unhappy promise, rose proportionably. My father saw this change with pleasure, and he turned his thoughts towards the best method of eradicating the remains of my melancholy, which every now and then would return by fits, and with a devouring blackness overcast the approaching sunshine. At these moments I took refuge in the most perfect solitude. I passed whole days on the lake alone in a little boat, watching the clouds, and listening to the rippling of the waves, silent and listless. But the fresh air and bright sun seldom failed to restore me to some degree of composure; and, on my return, I met the salutations of my friends with a readier smile and a more cheerful heart.

It was after my return from one of these rambles that my father, calling me aside, thus addressed me—

"I am happy to remark, my dear son, that you have resumed your former pleasures, and seem to be returning to yourself. And yet you are still unhappy, and still avoid our society. For some time I was lost in conjecture as to the cause of this; but yesterday an idea struck me, and if it is well founded, I conjure you to avow it. Reserve on such a point would be not only useless, but draw down treble misery on us all."

I trembled violently at his exordium, and my father continued—

"I confess, my son, that I have always looked forward to your marriage with our dear Elizabeth as the tie of our domestic comfort, and the stay of my declining years. You were attached to each other from your earliest infancy; you studied together, and appeared, in dispositions and tastes, entirely suited to one another. But so blind is the experience of man, that what I conceived to be the best assistants to my plan may have entirely destroyed it. You, perhaps, regard her as your sister, without any wish that she might become your wife. Nay, you may have met with another whom you may love; and, considering yourself as bound in honour to Elizabeth, this struggle may occasion the poignant misery which you appear to feel."

"My dear father, re-assure yourself. I love my cousin tenderly and sincerely. I never saw any woman who excited, as Elizabeth does, my warmest admiration and affection. My future hopes and prospects are entirely bound up in the expectation of our union."

"The expression of your sentiments of this subject, my dear Victor, gives me more pleasure than I have for some time experienced. If you feel thus, we shall assuredly be happy, however present events may cast a gloom over us. But it is this gloom, which appears to have taken so strong a hold of your mind, that I wish to dissipate. Tell me, therefore, whether you object to an immediate solemnisation of the marriage. We have been unfortunate, and recent events have drawn us from that every-day tranquillity befitting my years and infirmities. You are younger; yet I do not suppose, possessed as you are of a competent fortune, that an early marriage would at all interfere with any future plans of honour and utility that you may have formed. Do not suppose, however, that I wish to dictate happiness to you, or that a delay on your part would cause me any serious uneasiness. Interpret my words with candour, and answer me, I conjure you, with confidence and sincerity."

I listened to my father in silence, and remained for some time incapable of offering any reply. I revolved rapidly in my mind a multitude of thoughts, and endeavoured to arrive at some conclusion.

Alas! to me the idea of an immediate union with my Elizabeth was one of horror and dismay. I was bound by a solemn promise, which I had not yet fulfilled, and dared not break; or, if I did, what manifold miseries might not impend over me and my devoted family! Could I enter into a festival with this deadly weight yet hanging round my neck, and bowing me to the ground? I must perform my engagement, and let the monster depart with his mate, before I allowed myself to enjoy the delight of a union from which I expected peace.

I remembered also the necessity imposed upon me of either journeying to England, or entering into a long correspondence with those philosophers of that country, whose knowledge and discoveries were of indispensable use to me in my present undertaking. The latter method of obtaining the desired intelligence was dilatory and unsatisfactory: besides, I had an insurmountable aversion to the idea of engaging myself in my loathsome task in my father's house, while in habits of familiar intercourse with those I loved. I knew that a thousand fearful accidents might occur, the slightest of which would disclose a tale to thrill all connected with me with horror. I was aware also that I should often lose all self-command, all capacity of hiding the harrowing sensations that would possess me during the progress of my unearthly occupation. I must absent myself from all I loved while thus employed. Once commenced, it would quickly be achieved, and I might be restored to my family in peace and happiness. My promise fulfilled, the monster would depart forever. Or (so my fond fancy imaged) some accident might meanwhile occur to destroy him, and put an end to my slavery forever.

These feelings dictated my answer to my father. I expressed a wish to visit England; but concealing the true reasons of this request, I clothed my desires under a guise which excited no suspicion, while I urged my desire with an earnestness that easily induced my father to comply. After so long a period of an absorbing melancholy, that resembled madness in its intensity and effects, he was glad to find that I was capable of taking pleasure in the idea of such a journey, and he hoped that change of scene and varied amusement would, before my return, have restored me entirely to myself.

The duration of my absence was left to my own choice; a few months, or at most a year, was the period contemplated. One paternal kind precaution he had taken to ensure my having a companion. Without previously communicating with me, he had, in concert with Elizabeth, arranged that Clerval should join me in Strasburgh. This interfered with the solitude I coveted for the prosecution of my task; yet at the commencement of my journey the presence of my friend could in no way be an impediment, and truly I rejoiced that thus I should be saved many hours of lonely, maddening reflection. Nay, Henry might stand between me and the intrusion of my foe. If I were alone, would he not at times force his abhorred presence on me, to remind me of my task or to contemplate its progress?

To England, therefore, I was bound, and it was understood that my union with Elizabeth should take place immediately on my return. My father's age rendered him extremely averse to delay. For myself, there was one reward I promised myself from my detested toils—one consolation for my unparalleled sufferings; it was the prospect of that day when, enfranchised from my miserable slavery, I might claim Elizabeth, and forget the past in union with her.

I now made arrangements for my journey; but one feeling haunted me, which filled me with fear and agitation. During my absence I should leave my friends unconscious of the existence of their enemy, and unprotected from his attacks, exasperated as he might be by my departure. But he had promised to follow me wherever I might go; and would he not accompany me to England? This imagination was dreadful in itself, but soothing, inasmuch as it supposed the safety of my friends. I was agonised with the idea of the possibility that the reverse of this might happen. But through the whole period during which I was the slave of my creature I allowed myself to be governed by the impulses of the moment; and my present sensations strongly intimated that the fiend would follow me, and exempt my family from the danger of his machinations.

It was in the latter end of September that I again quitted my native country. My journey had been my own suggestion, and Elizabeth, therefore, acquiesced; but she was filled with disquiet at the idea of my suffering, away from her, the inroads of misery and grief. It had been her care which provided me a companion in Clerval—and yet a man is blind to a thousand minute circumstances, which call forth a woman's sedulous attention. She longed to bid me hasten my return—a thousand conflicting emotions rendered her mute, as she bade me a tearful, silent farewell.

I threw myself into the carriage that was to convey me away, hardly knowing whither I was going, and careless of what was passing around. I remembered only, and it was with a bitter anguish that I reflected on it, to order that my chemical instruments should be packed to go with me. Filled with dreary imaginations, I passed through many beautiful and majestic scenes, but my eyes were fixed and unobserving. I could only think of the bourne of my travels, and the work which was to occupy me whilst they endured.

After some days spent in listless indolence, during which I traversed many leagues, I arrived at Strasburgh, where I waited two days for Clerval. He came. Alas, how great was the contrast between us! He was alive to every new scene; joyful when he saw the beauties of the setting sun, and more happy when he beheld it rise, and recommence a new day. He pointed out to me the shifting colours of the landscape, and the appearances of the sky. "This is what it is to live," he cried; "now I enjoy existence! But you, my dear Frankenstein, wherefore are you desponding and sorrowful?" In truth, I was occupied by gloomy thoughts, and neither saw the descent of the evening star, nor the golden sun-rise reflected in the Rhine.—And you, my friend, would be far more amused with the journal of Clerval, who observed the scenery with an eye of feeling and delight, than in listening to my reflections. I, a miserable wretch, haunted by a curse that shut up every avenue to enjoyment.

We had agreed to descend the Rhine in a boat from Strasburgh to Rotterdam, whence we might take shipping for London. During this voyage we passed many willowy islands, and saw several beautiful towns. We stayed a day at Mannheim, and, on the fifth from our departure from Strasburgh, arrived at Mayence.[1] The course of the Rhine below Mayence becomes much more picturesque. The river descends rapidly, and winds between hills, not high, but steep, and of beautiful forms. We saw many ruined castles standing on the edges of precipices, surrounded by black woods, high and inaccessible. This part of the Rhine, indeed, presents a singularly variegated landscape. In one spot you view rugged hills, ruined castles

[1] *Mayence*] Mainz.

overlooking tremendous precipices, with the dark Rhine rushing beneath; and, on the sudden turn of a promontory, flourishing vineyards with green sloping banks and a meandering river and populous towns occupy the scene.

We travelled at the time of the vintage, and heard the song of the labourers, as we glided down the stream. Even I, depressed in mind, and my spirits continually agitated by gloomy feelings, even I was pleased. I lay at the bottom of the boat, and, as I gazed on the cloudless blue sky, I seemed to drink in a tranquillity to which I had long been a stranger. And if these were my sensations, who can describe those of Henry? He felt as if he had been transported to Fairy-land and enjoyed a happiness seldom tasted by man. "I have seen," he said, "the most beautiful scenes of my own country; I have visited the lakes of Lucerne and Uri, where the snowy mountains descend almost perpendicularly to the water, casting black and impenetrable shades, which would cause a gloomy and mournful appearance were it not for the most verdant islands that relieve the eye by their gay appearance; I have seen this lake agitated by a tempest, when the wind tore up whirlwinds of water and gave you an idea of what the water-spout must be on the great ocean; and the waves dash with fury the base of the mountain, where the priest and his mistress were overwhelmed by an avalanche and where their dying voices are still said to be heard amid the pauses of the nightly wind; I have seen the mountains of La Valais, and the Pays de Vaud: but this country, Victor, pleases me more than all those wonders. The mountains of Switzerland are more majestic and strange; but there is a charm in the banks of this divine river, that I never before saw equalled. Look at that castle which overhangs yon precipice; and that also on the island, almost concealed amongst the foliage of those lovely trees; and now that group of labourers coming from among their vines; and that village half hid in the recess of the mountain. Oh, surely the spirit that inhabits and guards this place has a soul more in harmony with man than those who pile the glacier, or retire to the inaccessible peaks of the mountains of our own country."

Clerval! beloved friend! Even now it delights me to record your words, and to dwell on the praise of which you are so eminently deserving. He was a being formed in the "very poetry of nature."[2]

---

[2] "*very poetry of nature*"] from *The Story of Rimini* by Leigh Hunt (1784–1859).

His wild and enthusiastic imagination was chastened by the sensibility of his heart. His soul overflowed with ardent affections, and his friendship was of that devoted and wondrous nature that the worldly-minded teach us to look for only in the imagination. But even human sympathies were not sufficient to satisfy his eager mind. The scenery of external nature, which others regard only with admiration, he loved with ardour:—

> The sounding cataract
> Haunted him like a passion: the tall rock,
> The mountain, and the deep and gloomy wood,
> Their colours and their forms, were then to him
> An appetite; a feeling, and a love,
> That had no need of a remoter charm,
> By thought supplied, or any interest
> Unborrow'd from the eye.*

And where does he now exist? Is this gentle and lovely being lost forever? Has this mind, so replete with ideas, imaginations fanciful and magnificent, which formed a world, whose existence depended on the life of its creator; has this mind perished? Does it now only exist in my memory? No, it is not thus; your form so divinely wrought, and beaming with beauty, has decayed, but your spirit still visits and consoles your unhappy friend.

Pardon this gush of sorrow; these ineffectual words are but a slight tribute to the unexampled worth of Henry, but they soothe my heart, overflowing with the anguish which his remembrance creates. I will proceed with my tale.

Beyond Cologne we descended to the plains of Holland; and we resolved to post the remainder of our way; for the wind was contrary, and the stream of the river was too gentle to aid us.

Our journey here lost the interest arising from beautiful scenery, but we arrived in a few days at Rotterdam; whence we proceeded by sea to England. It was on a clear morning, in the latter days of December, that I first saw the white cliffs of Britain. The banks of the Thames presented a new scene; they were flat, but fertile, and almost every town was marked by the remembrance of

* Wordsworth's Tintern Abbey [author's footnote].

some story. We saw Tilbury Fort, and remembered the Spanish Armada; Gravesend, Woolwich, and Greenwich—places which I had heard of even in my country.

At length we saw the numerous steeples of London, St Paul's towering above all, and the Tower, famed in English history.

Chapter XIX

London was our present point of rest; we determined to remain several months in this wonderful and celebrated city. Clerval desired the intercourse of the men of genius and talent who flourished at this time; but this was with me a secondary object; I was principally occupied with the means of obtaining the information necessary for the completion of my promise, and quickly availed myself of the letters of introduction that I had brought with me, addressed to the most distinguished natural philosophers.

If this journey had taken place during my days of study and happiness, it would have afforded me inexpressible pleasure. But a blight had come over my existence, and I only visited these people for the sake of the information they might give me on the subject in which my interest was so terribly profound. Company was irksome to me; when alone, I could fill my mind with the sights of heaven and earth; the voice of Henry soothed me, and I could thus cheat myself into a transitory peace. But busy, uninteresting, joyous faces brought back despair to my heart. I saw an insurmountable barrier placed between me and my fellow-men; this barrier was sealed with the blood of William and Justine, and to reflect on the events connected with those names filled my soul with anguish.

But in Clerval I saw the image of my former self; he was inquisitive, and anxious to gain experience and instruction. The difference of manners which he observed was to him an inexhaustible source of instruction and amusement. He was also pursuing an object he had long had in view. His design was to visit India, in the belief that he had in his knowledge of its various languages, and in the views he had taken of its society, the means of materially assisting the progress of European colonisation and trade. In Britain only could he further the execution of his plan. He was forever busy; and the only check to his enjoyments was my sorrowful and dejected mind. I tried to conceal this as much as possible, that I might not debar him from the pleasures natural to one who was entering on a new scene of life, undisturbed by any care or bitter recollection. I often refused to accompany him, alleging another engagement, that I might remain alone. I now also began to collect the materials necessary for my new creation, and this was to me like the torture of single drops of water continually falling on the head. Every thought that was devoted to it was an extreme anguish, and every word that I spoke in allusion to it caused my lips to quiver, and my heart to palpitate.

After passing some months in London, we received a letter from a person in Scotland, who had formerly been our visitor at Geneva. He mentioned the beauties of his native country, and asked us if those were not sufficient allurements to induce us to prolong our journey as far north as Perth, where he resided. Clerval eagerly desired to accept this invitation; and I, although I abhorred society, wished to view again mountains and streams, and all the wondrous works with which Nature adorns her chosen dwelling-places.

We had arrived in England at the beginning of October, and it was now February. We accordingly determined to commence our journey towards the north at the expiration of another month. In this expedition we did not intend to follow the great road to Edinburgh, but to visit Windsor, Oxford, Matlock, and the Cumberland lakes, resolving to arrive at the completion of this tour about the end of July. I packed up my chemical instruments and the materials I had collected, resolving to finish my labours in some obscure nook in the northern highlands of Scotland.

We quitted London on the 27th of March and remained a few days at Windsor, rambling in its beautiful forest. This was a new scene to us mountaineers; the majestic oaks, the quantity of game, and the herds of stately deer, were all novelties to us.

From thence we proceeded to Oxford. As we entered this city, our minds were filled with the remembrance of the events that had been transacted there more than a century and a half before. It was here that Charles I had collected his forces. This city had remained faithful to him, after the whole nation had forsaken his cause to join the standard of parliament and liberty. The memory of that unfortunate king, and his companions, the amiable Falkland, the insolent

Goring,[1] his queen and son, gave a peculiar interest to every part of the city, which they might be supposed to have inhabited. The spirit of elder days found a dwelling here, and we delighted to trace its footsteps. If these feelings had not found an imaginary gratification, the appearance of the city had yet in itself sufficient beauty to obtain our admiration. The colleges are ancient and picturesque; the streets are almost magnificent; and the lovely Isis, which flows beside it through meadows of exquisite verdure, is spread forth into a placid expanse of waters, which reflects its majestic assemblage of towers, and spires, and domes, embosomed among aged trees.

I enjoyed this scene; and yet my enjoyment was embittered both by the memory of the past, and the anticipation of the future. I was formed for peaceful happiness. During my youthful days discontent never visited my mind; and if I was ever overcome by *ennui,* the sight of what is beautiful in nature, or the study of what is excellent and sublime in the productions of man, could always interest my heart, and communicate elasticity to my spirits. But I am a blasted tree; the bolt has entered my soul; and I felt then that I should survive to exhibit what I shall soon cease to be—a miserable spectacle of wrecked humanity, pitiable to others, and intolerable to myself.

We passed a considerable period at Oxford, rambling among its environs, and endeavouring to identify every spot which might relate to the most animating epoch of English history. Our little voyages of discovery were often prolonged by the successive objects that presented themselves. We visited the tomb of the illustrious Hampden, and the field on which that patriot fell.[2] For a moment my soul was elevated from its debasing and miserable fears, to contemplate the divine ideas of liberty and self-sacrifice, of which these sights were the monuments and the remembrancers. For an instant I dared to shake off my chains, and look around me with a free and lofty spirit; but the iron had eaten into my flesh, and I sank again, trembling and hopeless, into my miserable self.

---

[1] *Falkland . . . Goring*] Lucius Cary, second Viscount Falkland (1610?–1643) and Lord George Goring (1608–1657), both of whom were Royalists during the Civil War (1642–1651).

[2] *illustrious Hampden . . . patriot fell*] John Hampden (1594–1643) was a cousin and ally of Oliver Cromwell; he was killed in a skirmish near Oxford.

We left Oxford with regret, and proceeded to Matlock, which was our next place of rest. The country in the neighbourhood of this village resembled, to a greater degree, the scenery of Switzerland; but every thing is on a lower scale, and the green hills want the crown of distant white Alps, which always attend on the piny mountains of my native country. We visited the wondrous cave, and the little cabinets of natural history, where the curiosities are disposed in the same manner as in the collections at Servox and Chamounix. The latter name made me tremble when pronounced by Henry; and I hastened to quit Matlock, with which that terrible scene was thus associated.

From Derby, still journeying northwards, we passed two months in Cumberland and Westmorland. I could now almost fancy myself among the Swiss mountains. The little patches of snow which yet lingered on the northern sides of the mountains, the lakes, and the dashing of the rocky streams, were all familiar and dear sights to me. Here also we made some acquaintances, who almost contrived to cheat me into happiness. The delight of Clerval was proportionably greater than mine; his mind expanded in the company of men of talent, and he found in his own nature greater capacities and resources than he could have imagined himself to have possessed while he associated with his inferiors. "I could pass my life here," said he to me; "and among these mountains I should scarcely regret Switzerland and the Rhine."

But he found that a traveller's life is one that includes much pain amidst its enjoyments. His feelings are forever on the stretch; and when he begins to sink into repose, he finds himself obliged to quit that on which he rests in pleasure for something new, which again engages his attention, and which also he forsakes for other novelties.

We had scarcely visited various lakes of Cumberland and Westmorland, and conceived an affection for some of the inhabitants, when the period of our appointment with our Scotch friend approached, and we left them to travel on. For my own part I was not sorry. I had now neglected my promise for some time, and I feared the effects of the daemon's disappointment. He might remain in Switzerland, and wreak his vengeance on my relatives. This idea pursued me, and tormented me at every moment from which I might otherwise have snatched repose and peace. I waited for my letters with feverish impatience: if they were delayed, I was miserable, and overcome by a thousand fears; and when they arrived and I saw the superscription of Elizabeth or my father, I hardly dared to read and ascertain my fate. Sometimes I thought that the fiend followed me, and might expedite my remissness by murdering my companion. When these thoughts possessed me, I would not quit Henry for a moment, but followed him as his shadow, to protect him from the fancied rage of his destroyer. I felt as if I had committed some great crime, the consciousness of which haunted me. I was guiltless, but I had indeed drawn down a horrible curse upon my head, as mortal as that of crime.

I visited Edinburgh with languid eyes and mind; and yet that city might have interested the most unfortunate being. Clerval did not like it so well as Oxford: for the antiquity of the latter city was more pleasing to him. But the beauty and regularity of the new town of Edinburgh, its romantic castle and its environs, the most delightful in the world, Arthur's Seat, St Bernard's Well, and the Pentland Hills, compensated him for the change, and filled him with cheerfulness and admiration. But I was impatient to arrive at the termination of my journey.

We left Edinburgh in a week, passing through Coupar, St Andrew's, and along the banks of the Tay, to Perth, where our friend expected us. But I was in no mood to laugh and talk with strangers, or enter into their feelings or plans with the good humour expected from a guest; and accordingly I told Clerval that I wished to make the tour of Scotland alone. "Do you," said I, "enjoy yourself, and let this be our rendezvous. I may be absent a month or two; but do not interfere with my motions, I intreat you: leave me to peace and solitude for a short time; and when I return, I hope it will be with a lighter heart, more congenial to your own temper."

Henry wished to dissuade me; but seeing me bent on this plan, ceased to remonstrate. He intreated me to write often. "I had rather be with you," he said, "in your solitary rambles, than with these Scotch people, whom I do not know: hasten, then, my dear friend, to return, that I may again feel myself somewhat at home, which I cannot do in your absence."

Having parted from my friend, I determined to visit some remote spot of Scotland, and finish my work in solitude. I did not doubt but that the monster followed me, and would discover himself to me when I should have finished, that he might receive his companion.

With this resolution I traversed the northern highlands, and fixed on one of the remotest of the Orkneys as the scene of my labours. It was a place fitted for such a work, being hardly more than a rock, whose high sides were continually beaten upon by the waves. The soil was barren, scarcely affording pasture for a few miserable cows, and oatmeal for its inhabitants, which consisted of five persons, whose gaunt and scraggy limbs gave tokens of their miserable fare. Vegetables and bread, when they indulged in such luxuries, and even fresh water, was to be procured from the mainland, which was about five miles distant..

On the whole island there were but three miserable huts, and one of these was vacant when I arrived. This I hired. It contained but two rooms, and these exhibited all the squalidness of the most miserable penury. The thatch had fallen in, the walls were unplastered, and the door was off its hinges. I ordered it to be repaired, bought some furniture, and took possession; an incident which would, doubtless, have occasioned some surprise had not all the senses of the cottagers been benumbed by want and squalid poverty. As it was, I lived ungazed at and unmolested, hardly thanked for the pittance of food and clothes which I gave; so much does suffering blunt even the coarsest sensations of men.

In this retreat I devoted the morning to labour; but in the evening, when the weather permitted, I walked on the stony beach of the sea to listen to the waves as they roared and dashed at my feet. It was a monotonous yet ever-changing scene. I thought of Switzerland; it was far different from this desolate and appalling landscape. Its hills are covered with veins, and its cottages are scattered thickly in the plains. Its fair lakes reflect a blue and gentle sky; and, when troubled by the winds, their tumult is but as the play of a lively infant, when compared to the roarings of the giant ocean.

In this manner I distributed my occupations when I first arrived; but as I proceeded in my labour, it became every day more horrible and irksome to me. Sometimes I could not prevail on myself to enter my laboratory for several days; and at other times I toiled day and night in order to complete my work. It was, indeed, a filthy process in which I was engaged. During my first experiment, a kind of enthusiastic frenzy had blinded me to the horror of my employment; my mind was intently fixed on the consummation of my labour, and my eyes shut to the horror of my proceedings. But now

I went to it in cold blood, and my heart often sickened at the work of my hands.

Thus situated, employed in the most detestable occupation, immersed in a solitude where nothing could for an instant call my attention from the actual scene in which I was engaged, my spirits became unequal; I grew restless and nervous. Every moment I feared to meet my persecutor. Sometimes I sat with my eyes fixed on the ground, fearing to raise them, lest they should encounter the object which I so much dreaded to behold. I feared to wander from the sight of my fellow-creatures, lest when alone he should come to claim his companion.

In the mean time I worked on, and my labour was already considerably advanced. I looked towards its completion with a tremulous and eager hope, which I dared not trust myself to question, but which was intermixed with obscure forebodings of evil, that made my heart sicken in my bosom.

Chapter XX

I SAT ONE evening in my laboratory; the sun had set, and the moon was just rising from the sea; I had not sufficient light for my employment, and I remained idle, in a pause of consideration of whether I should leave my labour for the night, or hasten its conclusion by an unremitting attention to it. As I sat, a train of reflection occurred to me, which led me to consider the effects of what I was now doing. Three years before I was engaged in the same manner, and had created a fiend whose unparalleled barbarity had desolated my heart, and filled it forever with the bitterest remorse. I was now about to form another being, of whose dispositions I was alike ignorant; she might become ten thousand times more malignant than her mate, and delight, for its own sake, in murder and wretchedness. He had sworn to quit the neighbourhood of man, and hide himself in deserts; but she had not; and she, who in all probability was to become a thinking and reasoning animal, might refuse to comply with a compact made before her creation. They might even hate each other; the creature who already lived loathed his own deformity, and might he not conceive a greater abhorrence for it when it came before his eyes in the female form? She also might turn with disgust from him to the superior beauty of man; she might quit him, and he be again alone, exasperated by the fresh provocation of being deserted by one of his own species.

Even if they were to leave Europe, and inhabit the deserts of the new world, yet one of the first results of those sympathies for which the daemon thirsted would be children, and a race of devils would be propagated upon the earth, who might make the very existence of the species of man a condition precarious and full of terror. Had I a right, for my own benefit, to inflict this curse upon everlasting generations? I had before been moved by the sophisms of the being

I had created; I had been struck senseless by his fiendish threats: but now, for the first time, the wickedness of my promise burst upon me; I shuddered to think that future ages might curse me as their pest, whose selfishness had not hesitated to buy its own peace at the price, perhaps, of the existence of the whole human race.

I trembled, and my heart failed within me, when, on looking up, I saw, by the light of the moon, the daemon at the casement. A ghastly grin wrinkled his lips as he gazed on me, where I sat fulfilling the task which he had allotted to me. Yes, he had followed me in my travels; he had loitered in forests, hid himself in caves, or taken refuge in wide and desert heaths; and he now came to mark my progress, and claim the fulfilment of my promise.

As I looked on him, his countenance expressed the utmost extent of malice and treachery. I thought with a sensation of madness on my promise of creating another like to him, and trembling with passion, tore to pieces the thing on which I was engaged. The wretch saw me destroy the creature on whose future existence he depended for happiness, and, with a howl of devilish despair and revenge, withdrew.

I left the room, and, locking the door, made a solemn vow in my own heart never to resume my labours; and then, with trembling steps, I sought my own apartment. I was alone; none were near me to dissipate the gloom, and relieve me from the sickening oppression of the most terrible reveries.

Several hours passed, and I remained near my window gazing on the sea; it was almost motionless, for the winds were hushed, and all nature reposed under the eye of the quiet moon. A few fishing vessels alone specked the water, and now and then the gentle breeze wafted the sound of voices as the fishermen called to one another. I felt the silence, although I was hardly conscious of its extreme profundity, until my ear was suddenly arrested by the paddling of oars near the shore, and a person landed close to my house.

In a few minutes after, I heard the creaking of my door, as if some one endeavoured to open it softly. I trembled from head to foot; I felt a presentiment of who it was, and wished to rouse one of the peasants who dwelt in a cottage not far from mine; but I was overcome by the sensation of helplessness, so often felt in frightful dreams, when you in vain endeavour to fly from an impending danger, and was rooted to the spot.

Presently I heard the sound of footsteps along the passage; the door opened, and the wretch whom I dreaded appeared. Shutting the door, he approached me, and said, in a smothered voice—

"You have destroyed the work which you began; what is it that you intend? Do you dare to break your promise? I have endured toil and misery: I left Switzerland with you; I crept along the shores of the Rhine, among its willow islands, and over the summits of its hills. I have dwelt many months in the heaths of England, and among the deserts of Scotland. I have endured incalculable fatigue, and cold, and hunger; do you dare destroy my hopes?"

"Begone! I do break my promise; never will I create another like yourself, equal in deformity and wickedness."

"Slave, I before reasoned with you, but you have proved yourself unworthy of my condescension. Remember that I have power; you believe yourself miserable, but I can make you so wretched that the light of day will be hateful to you. You are my creator, but I am your master;—obey!"

"The hour of my irresolution is past, and the period of your power is arrived. Your threats cannot move me to do an act of wickedness; but they confirm me in a determination of not creating you a companion in vice. Shall I, in cool blood, set loose upon the earth a daemon, whose delight is in death and wretchedness? Begone! I am firm, and your words will only exasperate my rage."

The monster saw my determination in my face, and gnashed his teeth in the impotence of anger. "Shall each man," cried he, "find a wife for his bosom, and each beast have his mate, and I be alone? I had feelings of affection, and they were requited by detestation and scorn. Man! you may hate; but beware! Your hours will pass in dread and misery, and soon the bolt will fall which must ravish from you your happiness forever. Are you to be happy, while I grovel in the intensity of my wretchedness? You can blast my other passions; but revenge remains—revenge, henceforth dearer than light or food! I may die; but first you, my tyrant and tormentor, shall curse the sun that gazes on your misery. Beware; for I am fearless, and therefore powerful. I will watch with the wiliness of a snake, that I may sting with its venom. Man, you shall repent of the injuries you inflict."

"Devil, cease; and do not poison the air with these sounds of malice. I have declared my resolution to you, and I am no coward to bend beneath words. Leave me; I am inexorable."

"It is well. I go; but remember, I shall be with you on your wedding-night."

I started forward, and exclaimed, "Villain! before you sign my death-warrant, be sure that you are yourself safe."

I would have seized him; but he eluded me, and quitted the house with precipitation: in a few moments I saw him in his boat, which shot across the waters with an arrowy swiftness, and was soon lost amidst the waves.

All was again silent; but his words rung in my ears. I burned with rage to pursue the murderer of my peace, and precipitate him into the ocean. I walked up and down my room hastily and perturbed, while my imagination conjured up a thousand images to torment and sting me. Why had I not followed him, and closed with him in mortal strife? But I had suffered him to depart, and he had directed his course towards the main land. I shuddered to think who might be the next victim sacrificed to his insatiate revenge. And then I thought again of his words—"*I will be with you on your wedding-night.*" That then was the period fixed for the fulfilment of my destiny. In that hour I should die, and at once satisfy and extinguish his malice. The prospect did not move me to fear; yet when I thought of my beloved Elizabeth,—of her tears and endless sorrow, when she should find her lover so barbarously snatched from her,—tears, the first I had shed for many months, streamed from my eyes, and I resolved not to fall before my enemy without a bitter struggle.

The night passed away, and the sun rose from the ocean; my feelings became calmer, if it may be called calmness, when the violence of rage sinks into the depths of despair. I left the house, the horrid scene of the last night's contention, and walked on the beach of the sea, which I almost regarded as an insuperable barrier between me and my fellow-creatures; nay, a wish that such should prove the fact stole across me. I desired that I might pass my life on that barren rock, wearily, it is true, but uninterrupted by any sudden shock of misery. If I returned, it was to be sacrificed, or to see those whom I most loved die under the grasp of a daemon whom I had myself created.

I walked about the isle like a restless spectre, separated from all it loved, and miserable in the separation. When it became noon, and the sun rose higher, I lay down on the grass, and was overpowered by a deep sleep. I had been awake the whole of the preceding night, my nerves were agitated, and my eyes inflamed by watching and misery. The sleep into which I now sunk refreshed me; and when I awoke, I again felt as if I belonged to a race of human beings like myself, and I began to reflect upon what had passed with greater composure; yet still the words of the fiend rung in my ears like a death-knell; they appeared like a dream, yet distinct and oppressive as a reality.

The sun had far descended, and I still sat on the shore, satisfying my appetite, which had become ravenous, with an oaten cake, when I saw a fishing-boat land close to me, and one of the men brought me a packet; it contained letters from Geneva, and one from Clerval, entreating me to join him. He said that he was wearing away his time fruitlessly where he was; that letters from the friends he had formed in London desired his return to complete the negotiation they had entered into for his Indian enterprise. He could not any longer delay his departure; but as his journey to London might be followed, even sooner than he now conjectured, by his longer voyage, he entreated me to bestow as much of my society on him as I could spare. He besought me, therefore, to leave my solitary isle, and to meet him at Perth, that we might proceed southwards together. This letter in a degree recalled me to life, and I determined to quit my island at the expiration of two days.

Yet, before I departed, there was a task to perform, on which I shuddered to reflect: I must pack up my chemical instruments; and for that purpose I must enter the room which had been the scene of my odious work, and I must handle those utensils, the sight of which was sickening to me. The next morning, at daybreak, I summoned sufficient courage, and unlocked the door of my laboratory. The remains of the half-finished creature, whom I had destroyed, lay scattered on the floor, and I almost felt as if I had mangled the living flesh of a human being. I paused to collect myself, and then entered the chamber. With trembling hand I conveyed the instruments out of the room; but I reflected that I ought not to leave the relics of my work to excite the horror and suspicion of the peasants; and I accordingly put them into a basket, with a great quantity of stones, and, laying them up, determined to throw them into the sea that very night; and in the mean time I sat upon the beach, employed in cleaning and arranging my chemical apparatus.

Nothing could be more complete than the alteration that had taken place in my feelings since the night of the appearance of the daemon. I had before regarded my promise with a gloomy despair, as a thing that, with whatever consequences, must be fulfilled; but I now felt as if a film had been taken from before my eyes, and that I, for the first time, saw clearly. The idea of renewing my labours did not for one instant occur to me; the threat I had heard weighed on my thoughts, but I did not reflect that a voluntary act of mine could avert it. I had resolved in my own mind, that to create another like the fiend I had first made would be an act of the basest and most atrocious selfishness; and I banished from my mind every thought that could lead to a different conclusion.

Between two and three in the morning the moon rose; and I then, putting my basket aboard a little skiff, sailed out about four miles from the shore. The scene was perfectly solitary: a few boats were returning towards land, but I sailed away from them. I felt as if I was about the commission of a dreadful crime, and avoided with shuddering anxiety any encounter with my fellow-creatures. At one time the moon, which had before been clear, was suddenly overspread by a thick cloud, and I took advantage of the moment of darkness and cast my basket into the sea; I listened to the gurgling sound as it sunk, and then sailed away from the spot. The sky became clouded; but the air was pure, although chilled by the north-east breeze that was then rising. But it refreshed me, and filled me with such agreeable sensations, that I resolved to prolong my stay on the water; and, fixing the rudder in a direct position, stretched myself at the bottom of the boat. Clouds hid the moon, everything was obscure, and I heard only the sound of the boat, as its keel cut through the waves; the murmur lulled me, and in a short time I slept soundly.

I do not know how long I remained in this situation, but when I awoke I found that the sun had already mounted considerably. The wind was high, and the waves continually threatened the safety of my little skiff. I found that the wind was north-east, and must have driven me far from the coast from which I had embarked. I endeavoured to change my course, but quickly found that if I again made the attempt, the boat would be instantly filled with water.

Thus situated, my only resource was to drive before the wind. I confess that I felt a few sensations of terror. I had no compass with me, and was so slenderly acquainted with the geography of this part of the world, that the sun was of little benefit to me. I might be driven into the wide Atlantic, and feel all the tortures of starvation, or be swallowed up in the immeasurable waters that roared and buffeted around me. I had already been out many hours, and felt the torment of a burning thirst, a prelude to my other sufferings. I looked on the heavens, which were covered by clouds that flew before the wind, only to be replaced by others: I looked upon the sea, it was to be my grave. "Fiend," I exclaimed, "your task is already fulfilled!" I thought of Elizabeth, of my father, and of Clerval; all left behind, on whom the monster might satisfy his sanguinary and merciless passions. This idea plunged me into a reverie, so despairing and frightful, that even now, when the scene is on the point of closing before me forever, I shudder to reflect on it.

Some hours passed thus; but by degrees, as the sun declined towards the horizon, the wind died away into a gentle breeze, and the sea became free from breakers. But these gave place to a heavy swell; I felt sick, and hardly able to hold the rudder, when suddenly I saw a line of high land towards the south.

Almost spent, as I was, by fatigue, and the dreadful suspense I endured for several hours, this sudden certainty of life rushed like a flood of warm joy to my heart, and tears gushed from my eyes.

How mutable are our feelings, and how strange is that clinging love we have of life even in the excess of misery! I constructed another sail with a part of my dress, and eagerly steered my course towards the land. It had a wild and rocky appearance, but, as I approached nearer, I easily perceived the traces of cultivation. I saw vessels near the shore, and found myself suddenly transported back to the neighbourhood of civilised man. I carefully traced the windings of the land, and hailed a steeple which I at length saw issuing from behind a small promontory. As I was in a state of extreme debility, I resolved to sail directly towards the town, as a place where I could most easily procure nourishment. Fortunately I had money with me. As I turned the promontory, I perceived a small neat town and a good harbour, which I entered, my heart bounding with joy at my unexpected escape.

As I was occupied in fixing the boat and arranging the sails, several people crowded towards the spot. They seemed much surprised at my appearance, but instead of offering me any assistance, whispered together with gestures that at any other time might have produced in me a slight sensation of alarm. As it was, I merely remarked that they spoke English; and I therefore addressed them in that language. "My good friends," said I, "will you be so kind as to tell me the name of this town, and inform me where I am?"

"You will know that soon enough," replied a man with a hoarse voice. "May be you are come to a place that will not prove much to your taste; but you will not be consulted as to your quarters, I promise you."

I was exceedingly surprised on receiving so rude an answer from a stranger; and I was also disconcerted on perceiving the frowning and angry countenances of his companions. "Why do you answer me so roughly?" I replied; "surely it is not the custom of Englishmen to receive strangers so inhospitably."

"I do not know," said the man, "what the custom of the English may be; but it is the custom of the Irish to hate villains."

While this strange dialogue continued, I perceived the crowd rapidly increase. Their faces expressed a mixture of curiosity and anger, which annoyed, and in some degree alarmed me. I enquired the way to the inn; but no one replied. I then moved forward, and a murmuring sound arose from the crowd as they followed and surrounded me; when an ill-looking man approaching, tapped me on the shoulder, and said, "Come, sir, you must follow me to Mr Kirwin's, to give an account of yourself."

"Who is Mr Kirwin? Why am I to give an account of myself? Is not this a free country?"

"Ay, sir, free enough for honest folks. Mr Kirwin is a magistrate; and you are to give an account of the death of a gentleman who was found murdered here last night."

This answer startled me; but I presently recovered myself. I was innocent; that could easily be proved: accordingly I followed my conductor in silence and was led to one of the best houses in the town. I was ready to sink from fatigue and hunger; but, being surrounded by a crowd, I thought it politic to rouse all my strength, that no physical debility might be construed into apprehension or conscious guilt. Little did I then expect the calamity that was in a few moments to overwhelm me, and extinguish in horror and despair all fear of ignominy or death.

I must pause here; for it requires all my fortitude to recall the memory of the frightful events which I am about to relate, in proper detail, to my recollection.

Chapter XXI

I WAS SOON introduced into the presence of the magistrate, an old benevolent man, with calm and mild manners. He looked upon me, however, with some degree of severity; and then, turning towards my conductors, he asked who appeared as witnesses on this occasion.

About half a dozen men came forward; and, one being selected by the magistrate, he deposed, that he had been out fishing the night before with his son and brother-in-law, Daniel Nugent, when, about ten o'clock, they observed a strong northerly blast rising, and they accordingly put in for port. It was a very dark night, as the moon had not yet risen; they did not land at the harbour, but, as they had been accustomed, at a creek about two miles below. He walked on first, carrying a part of the fishing tackle, and his companions followed him at some distance. As he was proceeding along the sands, he struck his foot against something, and fell at his length on the ground. His companions came up to assist him; and, by the light of their lantern, they found that he had fallen on the body of a man, who was to all appearance dead. Their first supposition was, that it was the corpse of some person who had been drowned, and was thrown on shore by the waves, but, on examination, they found that the clothes were not wet, and even that the body was not then cold. They instantly carried it to the cottage of an old woman near the spot, and endeavoured, but in vain, to restore it to life. It appeared to be a handsome young man, about five and twenty years of age. He had apparently been strangled; for there was no sign of any violence, except the black mark of fingers on his neck.

The first part of his deposition did not in the least interest me; but when the mark of the fingers was mentioned, I remembered the murder of my brother, and felt myself extremely agitated; my limbs trembled, and a mist came over my eyes, which obliged me to lean on a chair for support. The magistrate observed me with a keen eye, and of course drew an unfavourable augury from my manner.

The son confirmed his father's account: but when Daniel Nugent was called, he swore positively that, just before the fall of his companion, he saw a boat, with a single man in it, at a short distance from the shore; and, as far as he could judge by the light of a few stars, it was the same boat in which I had just landed.

A woman deposed, that she lived near the beach, and was standing at the door of her cottage, waiting for the return of the fishermen, about an hour before she heard of the discovery of the body, when she saw a boat with only one man in it, push off from that part of the shore where the corpse was afterwards found.

Another woman confirmed the account of the fishermen having brought the body into her house; it was not cold. They put it into a bed, and rubbed it; and Daniel went to the town for an apothecary, but life was quite gone.

Several other men were examined concerning my landing; and they agreed that, with the strong north wind that had arisen during the night, it was very probable that I had beaten about for many hours, and had been obliged to return nearly to the same spot from which I had departed. Besides, they observed that it appeared that I had brought the body from another place, and it was likely, that as I did not appear to know the shore, I might have put into the harbour ignorant of the distance of the town of * * * from the place where I had deposited the corpse.

Mr Kirwin, on hearing this evidence, desired that I should be taken into the room where the body lay for interment, that it might be observed what effect the sight of it would produce upon me. This idea was probably suggested by the extreme agitation I had exhibited when the mode of the murder had been described. I was accordingly conducted, by the magistrate and several other persons, to the inn. I could not help being struck by the strange coincidences that had taken place during this eventful night; but, knowing that I had been conversing with several persons in the island I had inhabited about the time that the body had been found, I was perfectly tranquil as to the consequences of the affair.

I entered the room where the corpse lay, and was led up to the coffin. How can I describe my sensations of beholding it? I feel yet parched with horror, nor can I reflect on that terrible moment without shuddering and agony. The examination, the presence of the magistrate and witnesses, passed like a dream from my memory, when I saw the lifeless form of Henry Clerval stretched before me. I gasped for breath; and, throwing myself on the body, I exclaimed, "Have my murderous machinations deprived you also, my dearest Henry, of life? Two I have already destroyed; other victims await their destiny: but you, Clerval, my friend, my benefactor—"

The human frame could no longer support the agonies that I endured, and I was carried out of the room in strong convulsions.

A fever succeeded to this. I lay for two months on the point of death: my ravings, as I afterwards heard, were frightful; I called myself the murderer of William, of Justine, and of Clerval. Sometimes I intreated my attendants to assist me in the destruction of the fiend by whom I was tormented; and, at others, I felt the fingers of the monster already grasping my neck, and screamed aloud with agony and terror. Fortunately, as I spoke my native language, Mr Kirwin alone understood me; but my gestures and bitter cries were sufficient to affright the other witnesses.

Why did I not die? More miserable than man ever was before, why did I not sink into forgetfulness and rest? Death snatches away many blooming children, the only hopes of their doating parents: how many brides and youthful lovers have been one day in the bloom of health and hope, and the next a prey for worms and the decay of the tomb! Of what materials was I made, that I could thus resist so many shocks, which, like the turning of the wheel, continually renewed the torture?

But I was doomed to live; and, in two months, found myself as awaking from a dream, in a prison, stretched on a wretched bed, surrounded by gaolers, turnkeys, bolts, and all the miserable apparatus of a dungeon. It was morning, I remember, when I thus awoke to understanding: I had forgotten the particulars of what had happened, and only felt as if some great misfortune had suddenly overwhelmed me; but when I looked around, and saw the barred windows, and the squalidness of the room in which I was, all flashed across my memory, and I groaned bitterly.

This sound disturbed an old woman who was sleeping in a chair beside me. She was a hired nurse, the wife of one of the turnkeys, and her countenance expressed all those bad qualities which often characterise that class. The lines of her face were hard and rude, like that of persons accustomed to see without sympathising in sights of misery. Her tone expressed her entire indifference; she addressed me in English, and the voice struck me as one that I had heard during my sufferings:—

"Are you better now, sir?" said she.

I replied in the same language, with a feeble voice, "I believe I am; but if it all be true, if indeed I did not dream, I am sorry that I am still alive to feel this misery and horror."

"For that matter," replied the old woman, "if you mean about the gentleman you murdered, I believe that it were better for you if you were dead, for I fancy it will go hard with you! However, that's none of my business; I am sent to nurse you and get you well; I do my duty with a safe conscience; it were well if everybody did the same."

I turned with loathing from the woman who could utter so unfeeling a speech to a person just saved, on the very edge of death; but I felt languid, and unable to reflect on all that had passed. The whole series of my life appeared to me as a dream; I sometimes doubted if indeed it were all true, for it never presented itself to my mind with the force of reality.

As the images that floated before me became more distinct, I grew feverish; a darkness pressed around me; no one was near me who soothed me with the gentle voice of love; no dear hand supported me. The physician came and prescribed medicines, and the old woman prepared them for me; but utter carelessness was visible in the first, and the expression of brutality was strongly marked in the visage of the second. Who could be interested in the fate of a murderer, but the hangman who would gain his fee?

These were my first reflections; but I soon learned that Mr Kirwin had shown me extreme kindness. He had caused the best room in the prison to be prepared for me (wretched indeed was the best); and it was he who had provided a physician and a nurse. It is true, he seldom came to see me, for although he ardently desired to relieve the sufferings of every human creature, he did not wish to be present at the agonies and miserable ravings of a murderer. He came, therefore, sometimes to see that I was not neglected; but his visits were short, and with long intervals.

One day, while I was gradually recovering, I was seated in a chair, my eyes half open, and my cheeks livid like those in death. I was overcome by gloom and misery, and often reflected I had better seek death than desire to remain in a world which to me was replete with wretchedness. At one time I considered whether I should not declare myself guilty, and suffer the penalty of the law, less innocent than poor Justine had been. Such were my thoughts, when the door of my apartment was opened, and Mr Kirwin entered. His countenance expressed sympathy and compassion; he drew a chair close to mine and addressed me in French—

"I fear that this place is very shocking to you; can I do anything to make you more comfortable?"

"I thank you; but all that you mention is nothing to me: on the whole earth there is no comfort which I am capable of receiving."

"I know that the sympathy of a stranger can be but of little relief to one borne down as you are by so strange a misfortune. But you will, I hope, soon quit this melancholy abode; for, doubtless, evidence can easily be brought to free you from the criminal charge."

"That is my least concern: I am, by a course of strange events, become the most miserable of mortals. Persecuted and tortured as I am and have been, can death be any evil to me?"

"Nothing indeed could be more unfortunate and agonising than the strange chances that have lately occurred. You were thrown, by some surprising accident, on this shore, renowned for its hospitality; seized immediately, and charged with murder. The first sight that was presented to your eyes was the body of your friend, murdered in so unaccountable a manner, and placed, as it were, by some fiend across your path."

As Mr Kirwin said this, notwithstanding the agitation I endured on this retrospect of my sufferings, I also felt considerable surprise at the knowledge he seemed to possess concerning me. I suppose some astonishment was exhibited in my countenance; for Mr Kirwin hastened to say—

"Immediately upon your being taken ill, all the papers that were on your person were brought me, and I examined them that I might discover some trace by which I could send to your relations an account of your misfortune and illness. I found several letters, and, among others, one which I discovered from its commencement to be from your father. I instantly wrote to Geneva: nearly two months have elapsed since the departure of my letter.—But you are ill; even now you tremble: you are unfit for agitation of any kind."

"This suspense is a thousand times worse than the most horrible event: tell me what new scene of death has been acted, and whose I am now to lament?"

"Your family is perfectly well," said Mr Kirwin, with gentleness; "and some one, a friend, is come to visit you."

I know not by what chain of thought the idea presented itself, but it instantly darted into my mind that the murderer had come to mock at my misery, and taunt me with the death of Clerval, as a new incitement for me to comply with his hellish desires. I put my hand before my eyes, and cried out in agony—

"Oh! take him away! I cannot see him; for God's sake, do not let him enter!"

Mr Kirwin regarded me with a troubled countenance. He could not help regarding my exclamation as a presumption of my guilt, and said, in rather a severe tone—

"I should have thought, young man, that the presence of your father would have been welcome instead of inspiring such violent repugnance."

"My father!" cried I, while every feature and every muscle was relaxed from anguish to pleasure: "is my father indeed come? How kind, how very kind! But where is he, why does he not hasten to me?"

My change of manner surprised and pleased the magistrate; perhaps he thought that my former exclamation was a momentary return of delirium, and now he instantly resumed his former benevolence. He rose, and quitted the room with my nurse, and in a moment my father entered it.

Nothing, at this moment, could have given me greater pleasure than the arrival of my father. I stretched out my hand to him and cried—

"Are you, then, safe—and Elizabeth—and Ernest?"

My father calmed me with assurances of their welfare, and endeavoured, by dwelling on these subjects so interesting to my heart, to raise my desponding spirits; but he soon felt that a prison cannot be the abode of cheerfulness. "What a place is this that you inhabit, my son!" said he, looking mournfully at the barred windows, and wretched appearance of the room. "You travelled to seek happiness, but a fatality seems to pursue you. And poor Clerval—"

The name of my unfortunate and murdered friend was an agitation too great to be endured in my weak state; I shed tears.

"Alas! yes, my father," replied I; "some destiny of the most horrible kind hangs over me, and I must live to fulfil it, or surely I should have died on the coffin of Henry."

We were not allowed to converse for any length of time, for the precarious state of my health rendered every precaution necessary that could ensure tranquillity. Mr Kirwin came in, and insisted that my strength should not be exhausted by too much exertion. But the appearance of my father was to me like that of my good angel, and I gradually recovered my health.

As my sickness quitted me, I was absorbed by a gloomy and black melancholy, that nothing could dissipate. The image of Clerval was forever before me, ghastly and murdered. More than once the agitation into which these reflections threw me made my friends dread a dangerous relapse. Alas! why did they preserve so miserable and detested a life? It was surely that I might fill my destiny, which is now drawing to a close. Soon, oh! very soon, will death extinguish these throbbings, and relieve me from the mighty weight of anguish that bears me to the dust; and, in executing the award of justice, I shall also sink to rest. Then the appearance of death was distant, although the wish was ever present to my thoughts; and I often sat for hours motionless and speechless, wishing for some mighty revolution that might bury me and my destroyer in its ruins.

The season of the assizes approached. I had already been three months in prison; and although I was still weak and in continual danger of a relapse, I was obliged to travel nearly a hundred miles to the county-town, where the court was held. Mr Kirwin charged himself with every care of collecting witnesses, and arranging my defence. I was spared the disgrace of appearing publicly as a criminal, as the case was not brought before the court that decides on life and death. The grand jury rejected the bill, on its being proved that I was on the Orkney Islands at the hour the body of my friend was found, and a fortnight after my removal I was liberated from prison.

My father was enraptured on finding me freed from the vexations of a criminal charge, that I was again allowed to breathe the fresh atmosphere, and permitted to return to my native country. I did not participate in these feelings; for to me the walls of a dungeon or a palace were alike hateful. The cup of life was poisoned for ever; and although the sun shone upon me, as upon the happy and gay of heart, I saw around me nothing but a dense and frightful darkness, penetrated by no light but the glimmer of two eyes that glared upon me. Sometimes they were the expressive eyes of Henry, languishing in death, the dark orbs nearly covered by the lids, and the long black lashes that fringed them; sometimes it was the watery, clouded eyes of the monster, as I first saw them in my chamber at Ingolstadt.

My father tried to awaken in me the feelings of affection. He talked of Geneva, which I should soon visit—of Elizabeth and Ernest; but these words only drew deep groans from me. Sometimes, indeed, I felt a wish for happiness; and thought, with melancholy delight of my beloved cousin; or longed, with a devouring *maladie du pays,*[1] to see once more the blue lake and rapid Rhône, that had been so dear to me in early childhood: but my general state of feeling was a torpor, in which a prison was as welcome a residence as the divinest scene in nature; and these fits were seldom interrupted but by paroxysms of anguish and despair. At these moments I often endeavoured to put an end to the existence I loathed; and it required unceasing attendance and vigilance to restrain me from committing some dreadful act of violence.

Yet one duty remained to me, the recollection of which finally triumphed over my selfish despair. It was necessary that I should return without delay to Geneva, there to watch over the lives of those I so fondly loved; and to lie in wait for the murderer, that if any chance led me to the place of his concealment, or if he dared again to blast me by his presence, I might, with unfailing aim, put an end to the existence of the monstrous Image which I had endued with the mockery of a soul still more monstrous. My father still desired to delay our departure, fearful that I could not sustain the fatigues of a journey: for I was a shattered wreck,—the shadow of a human being. My strength was gone. I was a mere skeleton; and fever night and day preyed upon my wasted frame.

Still, as I urged our leaving Ireland with such inquietude and impatience, my father thought it best to yield. We took our passage

[1] *maladie du pays*] homesickness, particularly for one's homeland.

on board a vessel bound for Havre-de-Grâce, and sailed with a fair wind from the Irish shores. It was midnight. I lay on the deck, looking at the stars, and listening to the dashing of the waves. I hailed the darkness that shut Ireland from my sight, and my pulse beat with a feverish joy when I reflected that I should soon see Geneva. The past appeared to me in the light of a frightful dream; yet the vessel in which I was, the wind that blew me from the detested shore of Ireland, and the sea which surrounded me, told me too forcibly that I was deceived by no vision, and that Clerval, my friend and dearest companion, had fallen a victim to me and the monster of my creation. I repassed, in my memory, my whole life—my quiet happiness while residing with my family in Geneva, the death of my mother, and my departure for Ingolstadt. I remembered, shuddering, the mad enthusiasm that hurried me on to the creation of my hideous enemy, and I called to mind the night in which he first lived. I was unable to pursue the train of thought; a thousand feelings pressed upon me, and I wept bitterly.

Ever since my recovery from the fever, I had been in the custom of taking every night a small quantity of laudanum; for it was by means of this drug only that I was enabled to gain the rest necessary for the preservation of life. Oppressed by the recollection of my various misfortunes, I now swallowed double my usual quantity, and soon slept profoundly. But sleep did not afford me respite from thought and misery; my dreams presented a thousand objects that scared me. Towards morning I was possessed by a kind of nightmare; I felt the fiend's grasp in my neck, and could not free myself from it; groans and cries rang in my ears. My father, who was watching over me, perceiving my restlessness, awoke me; the dashing waves were around: the cloudy sky above; the fiend was not here: a sense of security, a feeling that a truce was established between the present hour and the irresistible, disastrous future, imparted to me a kind of calm forgetfulness, of which the human mind is by its structure peculiarly susceptible.

Chapter XXII

The voyage came to an end. We landed, and proceeded to Paris. I soon found that I had overtaxed my strength, and that I must repose before I could continue my journey. My father's care and attentions were indefatigable; but he did not know the origin of my sufferings, and sought erroneous methods to remedy the incurable ill. He wished me to seek amusement in society. I abhorred the face of man. Oh, not abhorred! they were my brethren, my fellow beings, and I felt attracted even to the most repulsive among them, as to creatures of an angelic nature and celestial mechanism. But I felt that I had no right to share their intercourse. I had unchained an enemy among them, whose joy it was to shed their blood, and to revel in their groans. How they would, each and all, abhor me, and hunt me from the world, did they know my unhallowed acts, and the crimes which had their source in me!

My father yielded at length to my desire to avoid society, and strove by various arguments to banish my despair. Sometimes he thought that I felt deeply the degradation of being obliged to answer a charge of murder, and he endeavoured to prove to me the futility of pride.

"Alas! my father," said I, "how little do you know me. Human beings, their feelings and passions, would indeed be degraded, if such a wretch as I felt pride. Justine, poor unhappy Justine, was as innocent as I, and she suffered the same charge; she died for it; and I am the cause of this—I murdered her. William, Justine, and Henry—they all died by my hands."

My father had often, during my imprisonment, heard me make the same assertion; when I thus accused myself, he sometimes seemed to desire an explanation, and at others he appeared to consider it as the offspring of delirium, and that, during my illness, some idea of this kind had presented itself to my imagination, the remembrance of which I preserved in my convalescence. I avoided explanation, and maintained a continual silence concerning the wretch I had created. I had a persuasion that I should be supposed mad, and this in itself would forever have chained my tongue. But, besides, I could not bring myself to disclose a secret which would fill my hearer with consternation, and make fear and unnatural horror the inmates of his breast. I checked, therefore, my impatient thirst for sympathy, and was silent when I would have given the world to have confided that fatal secret. Yet still words like those I have recorded would burst uncontrollably from me. I could offer no explanation of them; but their truth in part relieved the burden of my mysterious woe.

Upon this occasion, my father said, with an expression of unbounded wonder, "My dearest Victor, what infatuation is this? My dear son, I entreat you never to make such an assertion again."

"I am not mad," I cried energetically; "the sun and the heavens, who have viewed my operations, can bear witness of my truth. I am the assassin of those most innocent victims; they died by my machinations. A thousand times would I have shed my own blood, drop by drop, to have saved their lives; but I could not, my father, indeed I could not sacrifice the whole human race."

The conclusion of this speech convinced my father that my ideas were deranged, and he instantly changed the subject of our conversation, and endeavoured to alter the course of my thoughts. He wished as much as possible to obliterate the memory of the scenes that had taken place in Ireland, and never alluded to them, or suffered me to speak of my misfortunes.

As time passed away I became more calm; misery had her dwelling in my heart, but I no longer talked in the same incoherent manner of my own crimes; sufficient for me was the consciousness of them. By the utmost self-violence I curbed the imperious voice of wretchedness, which sometimes desired to declare itself to the whole world; and my manners were calmer and more composed than they had ever been since my journey to the sea of ice.

A few days before we left Paris on our way to Switzerland, I received the following letter from Elizabeth:—

My dear Friend,

It gave me the greatest pleasure to receive a letter from my uncle dated at Paris; you are no longer at a formidable distance, and I may hope to see you in less than a fortnight. My poor cousin, how much you must have suffered! I expect to see you looking even more ill than when you quitted Geneva. This winter has been passed most miserably, tortured as I have been by anxious suspense; yet I hope to see peace in your countenance, and to find that your heart is not totally void of comfort and tranquillity.

Yet I fear that the same feelings now exist that made you so miserable a year ago, even perhaps augmented by time. I would not disturb you at this period, when so many misfortunes weigh upon you; but a conversation that I had with my uncle previous to his departure renders some explanation necessary before we meet.

Explanation! you may possibly say; what can Elizabeth have to explain? If you really say this, my questions are answered, and all my doubts satisfied. But you are distant from me, and it is possible that you may dread, and yet be pleased with this explanation; and, in a probability of this being the case, I dare not any longer postpone writing what, during your absence, I have often wished to express to you, but have never had the courage to begin.

You well know, Victor, that our union had been the favourite plan of your parents ever since our infancy. We were told this when young, and taught to look forward to it as an event that would certainly take place. We were affectionate playfellows during childhood, and, I believe, dear and valued friends to one another as we grew older. But as brother and sister often entertain a lively affection towards each other, without desiring a more intimate union, may not such also be our case? Tell me, dearest Victor. Answer me, I conjure you, by our mutual happiness, with simple truth—do you not love another?

You have travelled: you have spent several years of your life at Ingolstadt; and I confess to you, my friend, that when I saw you last autumn so unhappy, flying to solitude, from the society of every creature, I could not help supposing that you might regret our connection, and believe yourself bound in honour to fulfil the wishes of your parents, although they opposed themselves to your inclinations. But this is false reasoning. I confess to you, my friend, that I love you, and that in my airy dreams of futurity you have been my constant friend and companion. But it is your happiness I desire as well as my own, when I declare to you that our marriage would render me eternally miserable, unless it were the dictate of your own free choice. Even now I weep to think that, borne down as you are by the cruellest misfortunes, you may stifle, by the word "honour," all hope of that love and happiness which would alone restore you to yourself. I, who have so disinterested an affection for you, may increase your miseries tenfold by being an obstacle to your wishes. Ah! Victor, be assured that your cousin and playmate has too sincere a love for you not to be made miserable by this supposition. Be happy, my friend; and if you obey me in this one request, remain satisfied that nothing on earth will have the power to interrupt my tranquillity.

Do not let this letter disturb you; do not answer tomorrow, or the next day, or even until you come, if it will give you pain. My uncle will send me news of your health; and if I see but one smile on your lips when we meet, occasioned by this or any other exertion of mine, I shall need no other happiness.

Elizabeth Lavenza
Geneva, May 18th, 17—

This letter revived in my memory what I had before forgotten, the threat of the fiend—"*I will be with you on your wedding-night.*" Such was my sentence, and on that night would the daemon employ every art to destroy me, and tear me from the glimpse of happiness which promised partly to console my sufferings. On that night he had determined to consummate his crimes by my death. Well, be it so; a deadly struggle would then assuredly take place, in which if he were victorious I should be at peace, and his power over me be at an end. If he were vanquished, I should be a free man. Alas! what freedom? Such as the peasant enjoys when his family have been massacred before his eyes, his cottage burnt, his lands laid waste, and he is turned adrift, homeless, penniless, and alone, but free. Such would be my liberty, except that in my Elizabeth I possessed a treasure; alas! balanced by those horrors of remorse and guilt, which would pursue me until death.

Sweet and beloved Elizabeth! I read and re-read her letter, and some softened feelings stole into my heart, and dared to whisper paradisiacal dreams of love and joy; but the apple was already eaten, and the angel's arm bared to drive me from all hope. Yet I would die to make her happy. If the monster executed his threat, death was inevitable; yet, again, I considered whether my marriage would hasten my fate. My destruction might indeed arrive a few months sooner; but if my torturer should suspect that I postponed it, influenced by his menaces, he would surely find other and perhaps more dreadful means of revenge. He had vowed *to be with me on my wedding-night,* yet he did not consider that threat as binding him to peace in the mean time; for as if to show me that he was not yet satiated with blood, he had murdered Clerval immediately after the enunciation of his threats. I resolved, therefore, that if my immediate union with my cousin would conduce either to hers or my father's happiness, my adversary's designs against my life should not retard it a single hour.

In this state of mind I wrote to Elizabeth. My letter was calm and affectionate. "I fear, my beloved girl," I said, "little happiness remains for us on earth; yet all that I may one day enjoy is centred in you. Chase away your idle fears; to you alone do I consecrate my life, and my endeavours for contentment. I have one secret, Elizabeth, a dreadful one; when revealed to you, it will chill your frame with horror, and then, far from being surprised at my misery, you will only wonder that I survive what I have endured. I will confide this tale of misery and terror to you the day after our marriage shall take place; for, my sweet cousin, there must be perfect confidence between us. But until then, I conjure you, do not mention or allude to it. This I most earnestly intreat, and I know you will comply."

In about a week after the arrival of Elizabeth's letter, we returned to Geneva. The sweet girl welcomed me with warm affection; yet tears were in her eyes, as she beheld my emaciated frame and feverish cheeks. I saw a change in her also. She was thinner, and had lost much of that heavenly vivacity that had before charmed me; but her gentleness, and soft looks of compassion, made her a more fit companion for one blasted and miserable as I was.

The tranquillity which I now enjoyed did not endure. Memory brought madness with it; and when I thought of what had passed, a real insanity possessed me; sometimes I was furious, and burnt with rage, sometimes low and despondent. I neither spoke, nor looked at any one, but sat motionless, bewildered by the multitude of miseries that overcame me.

Elizabeth alone had the power to draw me from these fits; her gentle voice would soothe me when transported by passion, and inspire me with human feelings when sunk in torpor. She wept with me, and for me. When reason returned, she would remonstrate, and endeavour to inspire me with resignation. Ah! it is well for the unfortunate to be resigned, but for the guilty there is no peace. The agonies of remorse poison the luxury there is otherwise sometimes found in indulging the excess of grief.

Soon after my arrival, my father spoke of my immediate marriage with Elizabeth. I remained silent.

"Have you, then, some other attachment?"

"None on earth. I love Elizabeth and look forward to our union with delight. Let the day therefore be fixed; and on it I will consecrate myself, in life or death, to the happiness of my cousin."

"My dear Victor, do not speak thus. Heavy misfortunes have befallen us, but let us only cling closer to what remains, and transfer our love for those whom we have lost to those who yet live. Our circle will be small, but bound close by the ties of affection and mutual misfortune. And when time shall have softened your despair, new and dear objects of care will be born to replace those of whom we have been so cruelly deprived."

Such were the lessons of my father. But to me the remembrance of the threat returned: nor can you wonder that, omnipotent as the fiend had yet been in his deeds of blood, I should almost regard him as invincible; and that when he had pronounced the words, "*I shall be with you on your wedding-night,*" I should regard the threatened fate as unavoidable. But death was no evil to me, if the loss of Elizabeth were balanced with it; and I therefore, with a contented and even cheerful countenance, agreed with my father, that if my cousin would consent, the ceremony should take place in ten days, and thus put, as I imagined, the seal to my fate.

Great God! if for one instant I had thought what might be the hellish intention of my fiendish adversary, I would rather have banished myself for ever from my native country, and wandered a friendless outcast over the earth, than have consented to this miserable marriage. But, as if possessed of magic powers, the monster had blinded me to his real intentions; and when I thought that I had prepared only my own death, I hastened that of a far dearer victim.

As the period fixed for our marriage drew nearer, whether from cowardice or a prophetic feeling, I felt my heart sink within me. But I concealed my feelings by an appearance of hilarity, that brought smiles and joy to the countenance of my father, but hardly deceived the ever-watchful and nicer eye of Elizabeth. She looked forward to our union with placid contentment, not unmingled with a little fear, which past misfortunes had impressed, that what now appeared certain and tangible happiness, might soon dissipate into an airy dream, and leave no trace but deep and everlasting regret.

Preparations were made for the event, congratulatory visits were received, and all wore a smiling appearance. I shut up, as well as I could, in my own heart the anxiety that preyed there, and entered with seeming earnestness into the plans of my father, although they might only serve as the decorations of my tragedy. Through my father's exertions, a part of the inheritance of Elizabeth had been restored to her by the Austrian government. A small possession on the shores of Como belonged to her. It was agreed that, immediately after our union, we should proceed to Villa Lavenza, and spend our first days of happiness beside the beautiful lake near which it stood.

In the mean time I took every precaution to defend my person, in case the fiend should openly attack me. I carried pistols and a dagger constantly about me, and was ever on the watch to prevent artifice; and by these means gained a greater degree of tranquillity. Indeed, as the period approached, the threat appeared more as a delusion, not to be regarded as worthy to disturb my peace, while the happiness I hoped for in my marriage wore a greater appearance of certainty, as the day fixed for its solemnisation drew nearer, and I heard it continually spoken of as an occurrence which no accident could possibly prevent.

Elizabeth seemed happy; my tranquil demeanour contributed greatly to calm her mind. But on the day that was to fulfil my wishes and my destiny, she was melancholy, and a presentiment of evil pervaded her; and perhaps also she thought of the dreadful secret, which I had promised to reveal to her on the following day. My father was in the mean time overjoyed, and in the bustle of preparation only recognised in the melancholy of his niece the diffidence of a bride.

After the ceremony was performed, a large party assembled at my father's; but it was agreed that Elizabeth and I should commence our journey by water, sleeping that night at Evian, and continuing our voyage on the following day. The day was fair, the wind favourable, all smiled on our nuptial embarkation.

Those were the last moments of my life during which I enjoyed the feeling of happiness. We passed rapidly along: the sun was hot, but we were sheltered from its rays by a kind of canopy, while we enjoyed the beauty of the scene, sometimes on one side of the lake, where we saw Mont Salêve, the pleasant banks of Montalègre, and at a distance, surmounting all, the beautiful Mont Blanc, and the assemblage of snowy mountains that in vain endeavour to emulate her; sometimes coasting the opposite banks, we saw the mighty Jura opposing its dark side to the ambition that would quit its native country, and an almost insurmountable barrier to the invader who should wish to enslave it.

I took the hand of Elizabeth. "You are sorrowful, my love. Ah! if you knew what I have suffered, and what I may yet endure, you would endeavour to let me taste the quiet and freedom from despair that this one day at least permits me to enjoy."

"Be happy, my dear Victor," replied Elizabeth; "there is, I hope, nothing to distress you; and be assured that if a lively joy is not painted in my face, my heart is contented. Something whispers to me not to depend too much on the prospect that is opened before us, but I will not listen to such a sinister voice. Observe how fast we move along, and how the clouds, which sometimes obscure and sometimes rise above the dome of Mont Blanc, render this scene of beauty still more interesting. Look also at the innumerable fish that are swimming in the clear waters, where we can distinguish every pebble that lies at the bottom. What a divine day! how happy and serene all nature appears!"

Thus Elizabeth endeavoured to divert her thoughts and mine from all reflection upon melancholy subjects. But her temper was fluctuating; joy for a few instants shone in her eyes, but it continually gave place to distraction and reverie.

The sun sank lower in the heavens; we passed the river Drance, and observed its path through the chasms of the higher, and the glens of the lower hills. The Alps here come closer to the lake, and we approached the amphitheatre of mountains which forms its eastern boundary. The spire of Evian shone under the woods that surrounded it, and the range of mountain above mountain by which it was overhung.

The wind, which had hitherto carried us along with amazing rapidity, sunk at sunset to a light breeze; the soft air just ruffled the water, and caused a pleasant motion among the trees as we approached the shore, from which it wafted the most delightful scent of flowers and hay. The sun sunk beneath the horizon as we landed; and as I touched the shore, I felt those cares and fears revive, which soon were to clasp me, and cling to me forever.

Chapter XXIII

IT WAS EIGHT o'clock when we landed; we walked for a short time on the shore, enjoying the transitory light, and then retired to the inn, and contemplated the lovely scene of waters, woods, and mountains, obscured in darkness, yet still displaying their black outlines.

The wind, which had fallen in the south, now rose with great violence in the west. The moon had reached her summit in the heavens and was beginning to descend; the clouds swept across it swifter than the flight of the vulture, and dimmed her rays, while the lake reflected the scene of the busy heavens, rendered still busier by the restless waves that were beginning to rise. Suddenly a heavy storm of rain descended.

I had been calm during the day; but so soon as night obscured the shapes of objects, a thousand fears arose in my mind. I was anxious and watchful, while my right hand grasped a pistol which was hidden in my bosom; every sound terrified me; but I resolved that I would sell my life dearly, and not shrink from the conflict until my own life, or that of my adversary, was extinguished.

Elizabeth observed my agitation for some time in timid and fearful silence, but there was something in my glance which communicated terror to her, and trembling, she asked, "What is it that agitates you, my dear Victor? What is it you fear?"

"Oh! peace, peace, my love," replied I; "this night, and all will be safe: but this night is dreadful, very dreadful."

I passed an hour in this state of mind, when suddenly I reflected how fearful the combat which I momentarily expected would be to my wife, and I earnestly intreated her to retire, resolving not to join her until I had obtained some knowledge as to the situation of my enemy.

She left me, and I continued some time walking up and down the passages of the house, and inspecting every corner that might afford a retreat to my adversary. But I discovered no trace of him, and was beginning to conjecture that some fortunate chance had intervened to prevent the execution of his menaces; when suddenly I heard a shrill and dreadful scream. It came from the room into which Elizabeth had retired. As I heard it, the whole truth rushed into my mind, my arms dropped, the motion of every muscle and fibre was suspended; I could feel the blood trickling in my veins, and tingling in the extremities of my limbs. This state lasted but for an instant; the scream was repeated, and I rushed into the room.

Great God! why did I not then expire! Why am I here to relate the destruction of the best hope, and the purest creature of earth? She was there, lifeless and inanimate, thrown across the bed, her head hanging down, and her pale and distorted features half covered by her hair. Every where I turn I see the same figure—her bloodless arms and relaxed form flung by the murderer on its bridal bier. Could I behold this, and live? Alas! life is obstinate, and clings closest where it is most hated. For a moment only did I lose recollection; I fell senseless on the ground.

When I recovered, I found myself surrounded by the people of the inn; their countenances expressed a breathless terror: but the horror of others appeared only as a mockery, a shadow of the feelings that oppressed me. I escaped from them to the room where lay the body of Elizabeth, my love, my wife, so lately living, so dear, so worthy. She had been moved from the posture in which I had first beheld her; and now, as she lay, her head upon her arm, and a handkerchief thrown across her face and neck, I might have supposed her asleep. I rushed towards her, and embraced her with ardour; but the deadly langour and coldness of the limbs told me, that what I now held in my arms had ceased to be the Elizabeth whom I had loved and cherished. The murderous mark of the fiend's grasp was on her neck, and the breath had ceased to issue from her lips.

While I still hung over her in the agony of despair, I happened to look up. The windows of the room had before been darkened, and I felt a kind of panic on seeing the pale yellow light of the moon illuminate the chamber. The shutters had been thrown back; and, with a sensation of horror not to be described, I saw at the open window a figure the most hideous and abhorred. A grin was on the face of the monster; he seemed to jeer, as with his fiendish finger he pointed towards the corpse of my wife. I rushed towards the window, and drawing a pistol from my bosom, fired: but he eluded me, leaped from his station, and, running with the swiftness of lightning, plunged into the lake.

The report of the pistol brought a crowd into the room. I pointed to the spot where he had disappeared, and we followed the track with boats; nets were cast, but in vain. After passing several hours, we returned hopeless, most of my companions believing it to have been a form conjured up by my fancy. After having landed, they proceeded to search the country, parties going in different directions among the woods and vines.

I attempted to accompany them, and proceeded a short distance from the house; but my head whirled round, my steps were like those of a drunken man, I fell at last in a state of utter exhaustion; a film covered my eyes, and my skin was parched with the heat of fever. In this state I was carried back, and placed on a bed, hardly conscious of what had happened; my eyes wandered round the room, as if to seek something that I had lost.

After an interval I arose, and, as if by instinct, crawled into the room where the corpse of my beloved lay. There were women weeping around—I hung over it, and joined my sad tears to theirs—all this time no distinct idea presented itself to my mind; but my thoughts rambled to various subjects, reflecting confusedly on my misfortunes and their cause. I was bewildered, in a cloud of wonder and horror. The death of William, the execution of Justine, the murder of Clerval, and lastly of my wife; even at that moment I knew not that my only remaining friends were safe from the malignity of the fiend; my father even now might be writhing under his grasp, and Ernest might be dead at his feet. This idea made me shudder, and recalled me to action. I started up, and resolved to return to Geneva with all possible speed.

There were no horses to be procured, and I must return by the lake; but the wind was unfavourable, and the rain fell in torrents. However, it was hardly morning, and I might reasonably hope to arrive by night. I hired men to row and took an oar myself, for I had always experienced relief from mental torment in bodily exercise. But the overflowing misery I now felt, and the excess of agitation that I endured, rendered me incapable of any exertion. I threw down the oar; and leaning my head upon my hands, gave way to every gloomy idea that arose. If I looked up, I saw scenes which were familiar to me in my happier time, and which I had contemplated but the day before in the company of her who was now but a shadow and a recollection. Tears streamed from my eyes. The rain had ceased for a moment, and I saw the fish play in the waters as they had done a few hours before; they had then been observed by Elizabeth. Nothing is so painful to the human mind as a great and sudden change. The sun might shine, or the clouds might lour: but nothing could appear to me as it had done the day before. A fiend had snatched from me every hope of future happiness: no creature had ever been so miserable as I was; so frightful an event is single in the history of man.

But why should I dwell upon the incidents that followed this last overwhelming event? Mine has been a tale of horrors; I have reached their *acme,* and what I must now relate can but be tedious to you. Know that, one by one, my friends were snatched away; I was left desolate. My own strength is exhausted; and I must tell, in a few words, what remains of my hideous narration.

I arrived at Geneva. My father and Ernest yet lived; but the former sunk under the tidings that I bore. I see him now, excellent and venerable old man! his eyes wandered in vacancy, for they had lost their charm and their delight—his Elizabeth, his more than daughter, whom he doated on with all that affection which a man feels, who, in the decline of life, having few affections, clings more earnestly to those that remain. Cursed, cursed be the fiend that brought misery on his grey hairs, and doomed him to waste in wretchedness! He could not live under the horrors that were accumulated around him; the springs of existence suddenly gave way: he was unable to rise from his bed, and in a few days he died in my arms.

What then became of me? I know not; I lost sensation and chains and darkness were the only objects that pressed upon me. Sometimes, indeed, I dreamt that I wandered in flowery meadows and pleasant vales with the friends of my youth; but I awoke, and found myself in a dungeon. Melancholy followed, but by degrees I gained a clear conception of my miseries and situation, and was then released from my prison. For they had called me mad; and during many months, as I understood, a solitary cell had been my habitation.

Liberty, however, had been an useless gift to me had I not, as I awakened to reason, at the same time awakened to revenge. As the memory of past misfortunes pressed upon me, I began to reflect on their cause—the monster whom I had created, the miserable daemon whom I had sent abroad into the world for my destruction. I was possessed by a maddening rage when I thought of him, and desired and ardently prayed that I might have him within my grasp to wreak a great and signal revenge on his cursed head.

Nor did my hate long confine itself to useless wishes; I began to reflect on the best means of securing him; and for this purpose, about a month after my release, I repaired to a criminal judge in the town, and told him that I had an accusation to make; that I knew the destroyer of my family; and that I required him to exert his whole authority for the apprehension of the murderer.

The magistrate listened to me with attention and kindness:—"Be assured sir," said he, "no pains or exertions on my part shall be spared to discover the villain."

"I thank you," replied I; "listen, therefore, to the deposition that I have to make. It is indeed a tale so strange, that I should fear you would not credit it were there not something in truth which, however wonderful, forces conviction. The story is too connected to be mistaken for a dream, and I have no motive for falsehood." My manner, as I thus addressed him, was impressive, but calm; I had formed in my own heart a resolution to pursue my destroyer to death; and this purpose quieted my agony, and for an interval reconciled me to life. I now related my history briefly, but with firmness and precision, marking the dates with accuracy, and never deviating into invective or exclamation.

The magistrate appeared at first perfectly incredulous, but as I continued he became more attentive and interested; I saw him sometimes shudder with horror; at others a lively surprise, unmingled with disbelief, was painted on his countenance.

When I had concluded my narration, I said, "This is the being whom I accuse, and for whose seizure and punishment I call upon you to exert your whole power. It is your duty as a magistrate, and I believe and hope that your feelings as a man will not revolt from the execution of those functions on this occasion."

This address caused a considerable change in the physiognomy of my own auditor. He had heard my story with that half kind of belief that is given to a tale of spirits and supernatural events; but when he was called upon to act officially in consequence, the whole tide of his incredulity returned. He, however, answered mildly, "I would willingly afford you every aid in your pursuit; but the creature of whom you speak appears to have powers which would put all my exertions to defiance. Who can follow an animal which can traverse the sea of ice, and inhabit caves and dens where no man would venture to intrude? Besides, some months have elapsed since the commission of his crimes, and no one can conjecture to what place he has wandered, or what region he may now inhabit."

"I do not doubt that he hovers near the spot which I inhabit; and if he has indeed taken refuge in the Alps, he may be hunted like the chamois, and destroyed as a beast of prey. But I perceive your thoughts: you do not credit my narrative, and do not intend to pursue my enemy with the punishment which is his desert."

As I spoke, rage sparkled in my eyes; the magistrate was intimidated:—"You are mistaken," said he. "I will exert myself; and if it is in my power to seize the monster, be assured that he shall suffer punishment proportionate to his crimes. But I fear, from what you have yourself described to be his properties, that this will prove impracticable; and thus, while every proper measure is pursued, you should make up your mind to disappointment."

"That cannot be; but all that I can say will be of little avail. My revenge is of no moment to you; yet, while I allow it to be a vice, I confess that it is the devouring and only passion of my soul. My rage is unspeakable, when I reflect that the murderer, whom I have turned loose upon society, still exists. You refuse my just demand: I have but one resource; and I devote myself, either in my life or death, to his destruction."

I trembled with excess of agitation as I said this; there was a frenzy in my manner, and something, I doubt not, of that haughty fierceness which the martyrs of old are said to have possessed. But to a Genevan magistrate, whose mind was occupied by far other ideas than those of devotion and heroism, this elevation of mind had much the appearance of madness. He endeavoured to soothe me as a nurse does a child, and reverted to my tale as the effects of delirium.

"Man," I cried, "how ignorant art thou in thy pride of wisdom! Cease; you know not what it is you say."

I broke from the house angry and disturbed, and retired to meditate on some other mode of action.

Chapter XXIV

My present situation was one in which all voluntary thought was swallowed up and lost. I was hurried away by fury; revenge alone endowed me with strength and composure; it moulded my feelings, and allowed me to be calculating and calm, at periods when otherwise delirium or death would have been my portion.

My first resolution was to quit Geneva forever; my country, which, when I was happy and beloved, was dear to me, now, in my adversity, became hateful, I provided myself with a sum of money, together with a few jewels which had belonged to my mother, and departed.

And now my wanderings began, which are to cease but with life. I have traversed a vast portion of the earth, and have endured all the hardships which travellers, in deserts and barbarous countries, are wont to meet. How I have lived I hardly know; many times have I stretched my failing limbs upon the sandy plain, and prayed for death. But revenge kept me alive; I dared not die, and leave my adversary in being.

When I quitted Geneva, my first labour was to gain some clue by which I might trace the steps of my fiendish enemy. But my plan was unsettled; and I wandered many hours round the confines of the town, uncertain what path I should pursue. As night approached, I found myself at the entrance of the cemetery where William, Elizabeth, and my father reposed. I entered it, and approached the tomb which marked their graves. Every thing was silent, except the leaves of the trees, which were gently agitated by the wind; the night was nearly dark; and the scene would have been solemn and affecting even to an uninterested observer. The spirits of the departed seemed to flit around, and to cast a shadow, which was felt but not seen, around the head of the mourner.

The deep grief which this scene had at first excited quickly gave way to rage and despair. They were dead, and I lived; their murderer also lived, and to destroy him I must drag out my weary existence. I knelt on the grass, and kissed the earth, and with quivering lips exclaimed, "By the sacred earth on which I kneel, by the shades that wander near me, by the deep and eternal grief that I feel, I swear; and by thee, O Night, and the spirits that preside over thee, to pursue the daemon, who caused this misery, until he or I shall perish in mortal conflict. For this purpose I will preserve my life: to execute this dear revenge will I again behold the sun, and tread the green herbage of earth, which otherwise should vanish from my eyes forever. And I call on you, spirits of the dead; and on you, wandering ministers of vengeance, to aid and conduct me in my work. Let the cursed and hellish monster drink deep of agony; let him feel the despair that now torments me."

I had begun my adjuration with solemnity, and an awe which almost assured me that the shades of my murdered friends heard and approved my devotion; but the furies possessed me as I concluded, and rage choked my utterance.

I was answered through the stillness of night by a loud and fiendish laugh. It rang on my ears long and heavily; the mountains re-echoed it, and I felt as if all hell surrounded me with mockery and laughter. Surely in that moment I should have been possessed by frenzy, and have destroyed my miserable existence, but that my vow was heard, and that I was reserved for vengeance. The laughter died away; when a well-known and abhorred voice, apparently close to my ear, addressed me in an audible whisper—"I am satisfied: miserable wretch! you have determined to live, and I am satisfied."

I darted towards the spot from which the sound proceeded; but the devil eluded my grasp. Suddenly the broad disk of the moon arose, and shone full upon his ghastly and distorted shape, as he fled with more than mortal speed.

I pursued him; and for many months this has been my task. Guided by a slight clue, I followed the windings of the Rhône, but vainly. The blue Mediterranean appeared; and, by a strange chance, I saw the fiend enter by night, and hide himself in a vessel bound for the Black Sea. I took my passage in the same ship; but he escaped, I know not how.

Amidst the wilds of Tartary and Russia, although he still evaded me, I have ever followed in his track. Sometimes the peasants, scared by this horrid apparition, informed me of his path; sometimes he himself, who feared that if I lost all trace of him, I should despair and die, left some mark to guide me. The snows descended on my head, and I saw the print of his huge step on the white plain. To you first entering on life, to whom care is new, and agony unknown, how can you understand what I have felt, and still feel? Cold, want, and fatigue, were the least pains which I was destined to endure; I was cursed by some devil, and carried about with me my eternal hell; yet still a spirit of good followed and directed my steps and, when I most murmured, would suddenly extricate me from seemingly insurmountable difficulties. Sometimes, when nature, overcome by hunger, sunk under the exhaustion, a repast was prepared for me in the desert, that restored and inspirited me. The fare was indeed coarse, such as the peasants of the country ate; but I will not doubt that it was set there by the spirits that I had invoked to aid me. Often, when all was dry, the heavens cloudless, and I was parched by thirst, a slight cloud would bedim the sky, shed the few drops that revived me, and vanish.

I followed, when I could, the courses of the rivers; but the daemon generally avoided these, as it was here that the population of the country chiefly collected. In other places human beings were seldom seen; and I generally subsisted on the wild animals that crossed my path. I had money with me, and gained the friendship of the villagers by distributing it, or I brought with me some food that I had killed, which, after taking a small part, I always presented to those who had provided me with fire and utensils for cooking.

My life, as it passed thus, was indeed hateful to me, and it was during sleep alone that I could taste joy. O blessed sleep! often, when most miserable, I sank to repose, and my dreams lulled me even to rapture. The spirits that guarded me had provided these moments, or rather hours, of happiness that I might retain strength to fulfil my pilgrimage. Deprived of this respite, I should have sunk under my hardships. During the day I was sustained and inspirited by the hope of night: for in sleep I saw my friends, my wife, and my beloved country; again I saw the benevolent countenance of my father, heard the silver tones of my Elizabeth's voice, and beheld Clerval enjoying health and youth. Often, when wearied by a toilsome march, I persuaded myself that I was dreaming until night should come, and that I should then enjoy reality in the arms of my dearest friends. What agonising fondness did I feel for them! how did I cling to their dear forms, as sometimes they haunted even my waking hours, and persuade myself that they still lived! At such moments vengeance, that burned within me, died in my heart, and I pursued my path towards the destruction of the daemon, more as a task enjoined by heaven, as the mechanical impulse of some power of which I was unconscious, than as the ardent desire of my soul.

What his feelings were whom I pursued I cannot know. Sometimes, indeed, he left marks in writing on the barks of the trees, or cut in stone, that guided me, and instigated my fury. "My reign is not yet over"—these words were legible in one of these inscriptions—"you live, and my power is complete. Follow me; I seek the everlasting ices of the north, where you will feel the misery of cold and frost, to which I am impassive. You will find near this place, if you follow not too tardily, a dead hare; eat, and be refreshed. Come on, my enemy; we have yet to wrestle for our lives; but many hard and miserable hours must you endure until that period shall arrive."

Scoffing devil! Again do I vow vengeance; again do I devote thee, miserable fiend, to torture and death. Never will I give up my search, until he or I perish; and then with what ecstasy shall I join my Elizabeth and my departed friends, who even now prepare for me the reward of my tedious toil and horrible pilgrimage!

As I still pursued my journey to the northward, the snows thickened, and the cold increased in a degree almost too severe to support. The peasants were shut up in their hovels, and only a few of the most hardy ventured forth to seize the animals whom starvation had forced from their hiding-places to seek for prey. The rivers were covered with ice, and no fish could be procured; and thus I was cut off from my chief article of maintenance.

The triumph of my enemy increased with the difficulty of my labours. One inscription that he left was in these words:—"Prepare! your toils only begin; wrap yourself in furs, and provide food, for we shall soon enter upon a journey where your sufferings will satisfy my everlasting hatred."

My courage and perseverance were invigorated by these scoffing words; I resolved not to fail in my purpose; and, calling on heaven to support me, I continued with unabated fervour to traverse immense deserts, until the ocean appeared at a distance, and formed the utmost boundary of the horizon. Oh! how unlike it was to the blue seasons of the south! Covered with ice, it was only to be distinguished from land by its superior wildness and ruggedness. The Greeks wept for joy when they beheld the Mediterranean from the hills of Asia, and hailed with rapture the boundary of their toils. I did not weep; but I knelt down, and, with a full heart, thanked my guiding spirit for conducting me in safety to the place where I hoped, notwithstanding my adversary's gibe, to meet and grapple with him.

Some weeks before this period I had procured a sledge and dogs, and thus traversed the snows with inconceivable speed. I know not whether the fiend possessed the same advantages; but I found that, as before I had daily lost ground in the pursuit, I now gained on him, so much so that when I first saw the ocean he was but one day's journey in advance, and I hoped to intercept him before he should reach the beach. With new courage, therefore, I pressed on, and in two days arrived at a wretched hamlet on the sea-shore. I enquired of the inhabitants concerning the fiend, and gained accurate information. A gigantic monster, they said, had arrived the night before, armed with a gun and many pistols; putting to flight the inhabitants of a solitary cottage, through fear of his terrific appearance. He had carried off their store of winter food, and, placing it in a sledge, to draw which he had seized on a numerous drove of trained dogs, he had harnessed them, and the same night, to the joy of the horror-struck villagers, had pursued his journey across the sea in a direction that led to no land; and they conjectured that he must speedily be destroyed by the breaking of the ice, or frozen by the eternal frosts.

On hearing this information, I suffered a temporary access of despair. He had escaped me; and I must commence a destructive and almost endless journey across the mountainous ices of the ocean,—amidst cold that few of the inhabitants could long endure and which I, the native of a genial and sunny climate, could not hope to survive. Yet at the idea that the fiend should live and be triumphant, my rage and vengeance returned, and, like a mighty tide, overwhelmed every other feeling. After a slight repose, during which the spirits of the dead hovered round, and instigated me to toil and revenge, I prepared for my journey.

I exchanged my land-sledge for one fashioned for the inequalities of the Frozen Ocean; and purchasing a plentiful stock of provisions, I departed from land.

I cannot guess how many days have passed since then; but I have endured misery, which nothing but the eternal sentiment of a just retribution burning within my heart could have enabled me to support. Immense and rugged mountains of ice often barred up my passage, and I often heard the thunder of the ground sea, which threatened my destruction. But again the frost came, and made the paths of the sea secure.

By the quantity of provision which I had consumed, I should guess that I had passed three weeks in this journey; and the continual protraction of hope, returning back upon the heart, often wrung bitter drops of despondency and grief from my eyes. Despair had indeed almost secured her prey, and I should soon have sunk beneath this misery. Once, after the poor animals that conveyed me had with incredible toil gained the summit of a sloping ice-mountain, and one, sinking under his fatigue, died, I viewed the expanse before me with anguish, when suddenly my eye caught a dark speck upon the dusky plain. I strained my sight to discover what it could be, and uttered a wild cry of ecstasy when I distinguished a sledge, and the distorted proportions of a well-known form within. Oh! with what a burning gush did hope revisit my heart! warm tears filled my eyes, which I hastily wiped away, that they might not intercept the view I had of the daemon; but still my sight was dimmed by the burning drops, until, giving way to the emotions that oppressed me, I wept aloud.

But this was not the time for delay: I disencumbered the dogs of their dead companion, gave them a plentiful portion of food; and, after an hour's rest, which was absolutely necessary, and yet which was bitterly irksome to me, I continued my route. The sledge was still visible; nor did I again lose sight of it, except at the moments when for a short time some ice-rock concealed it with its intervening crags. I indeed perceptibly gained on it; and when, after nearly two days' journey, I beheld my enemy at no more than a mile distant, my heart bounded within me.

But now, when I appeared almost within grasp of my foe, my hopes were suddenly extinguished, and I lost all trace of him more utterly than I had ever done before. A ground sea was heard; the thunder of its progress, as the waters rolled and swelled beneath me, became every moment more ominous and terrific. I pressed on, but in vain. The wind arose; the sea roared; and, as with the mighty shock of an earthquake, it split, and cracked with a tremendous and overwhelming sound. The work was soon finished: in a few minutes a tumultuous sea rolled between me and my enemy, and I was left drifting on a scattered piece of ice, that was continually lessening, and thus preparing for me a hideous death.

In this manner many appalling hours passed; several of my dogs died; and I myself was about to sink under the accumulation of distress, when I saw your vessel riding at anchor, and holding forth to me hopes of succour and life. I had no conception that vessels ever came so far north, and was astounded at the sight. I quickly destroyed part of my sledge to construct oars; and by these means was enabled, with infinite fatigue, to move my ice-raft in the direction of your ship. I had determined, if you were going southward, still to trust myself to the mercy of the seas rather than abandon my purpose. I hoped to induce you to grant me a boat with which I could pursue my enemy. But your direction was northward. You took me on board when my vigour was exhausted, and I should soon have sunk under my multiplied hardships into a death which I still dread,—for my task is unfulfilled.

Oh! when will my guiding spirit, in conducting me to the daemon, allow me the rest I so much desire; or must I die, and he yet live? If I do, swear to me, Walton, that he shall not escape; that you will seek him, and satisfy my vengeance in his death. And do I dare to ask of you to undertake my pilgrimage, to endure the hardships that I have undergone? No; I am not so selfish. Yet, when I am dead, if he should appear; if the ministers of vengeance should conduct him to you, swear that he shall not live—swear that he shall not triumph over my accumulated woes and survive to add to the list of his dark crimes. He is eloquent and persuasive; and once his words had even power over my heart: but trust him not. His soul is as hellish as his form, full of treachery and fiend-like malice. Hear him not; call on the manes[1] of William, Justine, Clerval, Elizabeth, my father, and of the wretched Victor, and thrust your sword into his heart. I will hover near, and direct the steel aright.

[1] *manes*] spirits of the dead.

Walton, *in continuation.*

August 26th, 17—.

You have read this strange and terrific story, Margaret; and do you not feel your blood congeal with horror, like that which even now curdles mine? Sometimes, seized with sudden agony, he could not continue his tale; at others, his voice broken, yet piercing, uttered with difficulty the words so replete with anguish. His fine and lovely eyes were now lighted up with indignation, now subdued to downcast sorrow, and quenched in infinite wretchedness. Sometimes he commanded his countenance and tones, and related the most horrible incidents with a tranquil voice, suppressing every mark of agitation; then, like a volcano bursting forth, his face would suddenly change to an expression of the wildest rage, as he shrieked out imprecations on his persecutor.

His tale is connected, and told with an appearance of the simplest truth; yet I own to you that the letters of Felix and Safie, which he showed me, and the apparition of the monster seen from our ship, brought to me a greater conviction of the truth of his narrative than his asseverations, however earnest and connected. Such a monster has, then, real existence! I cannot doubt it; yet I am lost in surprise and admiration. Sometimes I endeavoured to gain from Frankenstein the particulars of his creature's formation: but on this point he was impenetrable.

"Are you mad, my friend?" said he; "or whither does your senseless curiosity lead you? Would you also create for yourself and the world a demoniacal enemy? Peace, peace! learn my miseries, and do not seek to increase your own."

Frankenstein discovered that I made notes concerning his history: he asked to see them, and then himself corrected and augmented them in many places; but principally in giving the life and spirit to the conversations he held with his enemy. "Since you have preserved my narration," said he, "I would not that a mutilated one should go down to posterity."

Thus has a week passed away, while I have listened to the strangest tale that ever imagination formed. My thoughts, and every feeling of my soul, have been drunk up by the interest for my guest, which this tale, and his own elevated and gentle manners, have created. I wish to soothe him; yet can I counsel one so infinitely miserable, so destitute of every hope of consolation, to live? Oh, no! the only joy that he can now know will be when he composes his shattered spirit to peace and death. Yet he enjoys one comfort, the offspring of solitude and delirium: he believes, that when in dreams he holds converse with his friends, and derives from that communion consolation for his miseries, or excitements to his vengeance, that they are not the creations of his fancy, but the beings themselves who visit him from the regions of a remote world. This faith gives a solemnity to his reveries that render them to me almost as imposing and interesting as truth.

Our conversations are not always confined to his own history and misfortunes. On every point of general literature he displays unbounded knowledge, and a quick and piercing apprehension. His eloquence is forcible and touching; nor can I hear him, when he relates a pathetic incident, or endeavours to move the passions of pity or love, without tears. What a glorious creature must he have been in the days of his prosperity, when he is thus noble and godlike in ruin! He seems to feel his own worth, and the greatness of his fall.

"When younger," said he, "I believed myself destined for some great enterprise. My feelings are profound; but I possessed a coolness of judgment that fitted me for illustrious achievements. This sentiment of the worth of my nature supported me, when others would have been oppressed; for I deemed it criminal to throw away in useless grief those talents that might be useful to my fellow-creatures. When I reflected on the work I had completed, no less a one than the creation of a sensitive and rational animal, I could not rank myself with the herd of common projectors. But this thought, which supported me in the commencement of my career, now serves only to plunge me lower in the dust. All my speculations and hopes are as nothing; and, like the archangel who aspired to omnipotence, I am chained in an eternal hell. My imagination was vivid, yet my powers of analysis and application were intense; by the union of these qualities I conceived the idea, and executed the creation of a man. Even now I cannot recollect, without passion, my reveries while the work was incomplete. I trod heaven in my thoughts, now exulting in my powers, now burning with the idea of their effects. From my infancy I was imbued with high hopes and a lofty ambition; but how am I sunk! Oh! my friend, if you had known me as I once was, you would not recognise me in this state of degradation. Despondency rarely visited my heart; a high destiny seemed to bear me on, until I fell, never, never again to rise."

Must I then lose this admirable being? I have longed for a friend; I have sought one who would sympathise with and love me. Behold, on these desert seas I have found such a one; but, I fear, I have gained him only to know his value, and lose him. I would reconcile him to life, but he repulses the idea.

"I thank you, Walton," he said, "for your kind intentions towards so miserable a wretch; but when you speak of new ties, and fresh affections, think you that any can replace those who are gone? Can any man be to me as Clerval was; or any woman another Elizabeth? Even where the affections are not strongly moved by any superior excellence, the companions of our childhood always possess a certain power over our minds, which hardly any later friend can obtain. They know our infantine dispositions, which, however they may be afterwards modified, are never eradicated; and they can judge of our actions with more certain conclusions as to the integrity of our motives. A sister or a brother can never, unless indeed such symptoms have been shown early, suspect the other of fraud or false dealing, when another friend, however strongly he may be attached, may, in spite of himself, be contemplated with suspicion. But I enjoyed friends, dear not only through habit and association, but from their own merits; and, wherever I am, the soothing voice of my Elizabeth, and the conversation of Clerval, will be ever whispered in my ear. They are dead; and but one feeling in such a solitude can persuade me to preserve my life. If I were engaged in any high undertaking or design, fraught with extensive utility to my fellow-creatures, then could I live to fulfil it. But such is not my destiny; I must pursue and destroy the being to whom I gave existence; then my lot on earth will be fulfilled, and I may die."

September 2nd.

My beloved Sister,

I write to you, encompassed by peril, and ignorant whether I am ever doomed to see again dear England, and the dearer friends that inhabit it. I am surrounded by mountains of ice, which admit of no escape, and threaten every moment to crush my vessel. The brave fellows, whom I have persuaded to be my companions, look towards me for aid; but I have none to bestow. There is something terribly appalling in our situation, yet my courage and hopes do not desert me. Yet it is terrible to reflect that the lives of all these men are endangered through me. If we are lost, my mad schemes are the cause.

And what, Margaret, will be the state of your mind? You will not hear of my destruction, and you will anxiously await my return. Years will pass, and you will have visitings of despair, and yet be tortured by hope. Oh! my beloved sister, the sickening failing of your heart-felt expectations is, in prospect, more terrible to me than my own death. But you have a husband, and lovely children; you may be happy: Heaven bless you, and make you so!

My unfortunate guest regards me with the tenderest compassion. He endeavours to fill me with hope; and talks as if life were a possession which he valued. He reminds me how often the same accidents have happened to other navigators, who have attempted this sea, and in spite of myself, he fills me with cheerful auguries. Even the sailors feel the power of his eloquence; when he speaks, they no longer despair; he rouses their energies, and, while they hear his voice, they believe these vast mountains of ice are mole-hills, which will vanish before the resolutions of man. These feelings are transitory; each day of expectation delayed fills them with fear, and I almost dread a mutiny caused by this despair.

September 5th.

A scene has just passed of such uncommon interest, that although it is highly probable that these papers may never reach you, yet I cannot forbear recording it.

We are still surrounded by mountains of ice, still in imminent danger of being crushed in their conflict. The cold is excessive, and many of my unfortunate comrades have already found a grave amidst this scene of desolation. Frankenstein has daily declined in health: a feverish fire still glimmers in his eyes; but he is exhausted, and, when suddenly roused to any exertion, he speedily sinks again into apparent lifelessness.

I mentioned in my last letter the fears I entertained of a mutiny. This morning, as I sat watching the wan countenance of my friend—his eyes half closed, and his limbs hanging listlessly,—I was roused by half a dozen of the sailors, who demanded admission into the cabin. They entered, and their leader addressed me. He told me that he and his companions had been chosen by the other sailors to come in deputation to me, to make me a requisition, which, in justice, I could not refuse. We were immured in ice, and should probably never escape; but they feared that if, as was possible, the ice should dissipate and a free passage be opened, I should be rash enough to continue my voyage, and lead them into fresh dangers, after they might happily have surmounted this. They insisted, therefore, that I should engage with a solemn promise, that if the vessel should be freed I would instantly direct my course southward.

This speech troubled me. I had not despaired; nor had I yet conceived the idea of returning, if set free. Yet could I, in justice, or even in possibility, refuse this demand? I hesitated before I answered; when Frankenstein, who had at first been silent, and, indeed, appeared hardly to have force enough to attend, now roused himself; his eyes sparkled, and his cheeks flushed with momentary vigour. Turning towards the men, he said—

"What do you mean? What do you demand of your captain? Are you then so easily turned from your design? Did you not call this a glorious expedition? And wherefore was it glorious? Not because the way was smooth and placid as a southern sea, but because it was full of dangers and terror; because, at every new incident, your fortitude was to be called forth, and your courage exhibited; because danger and death surrounded it, and these you were to brave and overcome. For this was it a glorious, for this was it an honourable undertaking. You were hereafter to be hailed as the benefactors of your species; your names adored, as belonging to brave men who encountered death for honour, and the benefit of mankind. And now, behold, with the first imagination of danger, or, if you will, the first mighty and terrific trial of your courage, you shrink away, and are content to be handed down as men who had not strength enough to endure cold and peril; and so, poor souls, they were chilly and returned to their warm firesides. Why, that requires not this preparation; ye need not have come thus far, and dragged your captain to the shame of a defeat, merely to prove yourselves cowards. Oh! be men, or be more than men. Be steady to your purposes, and firm as a rock. This ice is not made of such stuff as your hearts may be; it is mutable, and cannot withstand you, if you say that it shall not. Do not return to your families with the stigma of disgrace marked on your brows. Return as heroes who have fought and conquered, and who know not what it is to turn their backs on the foe."

He spoke this with a voice so modulated to the different feelings expressed in his speech, with an eye so full of lofty design and heroism, that can you wonder that these men were moved? They looked at one another, and were unable to reply. I spoke; I told them to retire, and consider of what had been said: that I would not lead them farther north if they strenuously desired the contrary; but that I hoped that, with reflection, their courage would return.

They retired, and I turned towards my friend, but he was sunk in languor, and almost deprived of life.

How all this will terminate, I know not; but I had rather die than return shamefully,—my purpose unfulfilled. Yet I fear such will be my fate; the men, unsupported by ideas of glory and honour, can never willingly continue to endure their present hardships.

September 7th.

The die is cast; I have consented to return, if we are not destroyed. Thus are my hopes blasted by cowardice and indecision: I come back ignorant and disappointed. It requires more philosophy than I possess, to bear this injustice with patience.

September 12th.

It is past; I am returning to England. I have lost my hopes of utility and glory;—I have lost my friend. But I will endeavour to detail these bitter circumstances to you, my dear sister; and, while I am wafted towards England, and towards you, I will not despond.

September 9th, the ice began to move, and roarings like thunder were heard at a distance, as the islands split and cracked in every direction. We were in the most imminent peril; but, as we could only remain passive, my chief attention was occupied by my unfortunate guest, whose illness increased in such a degree, that he was entirely confined to his bed. The ice cracked behind us, and was driven with force towards the north; a breeze sprung from the west, and on the 11th the passage towards the south became perfectly free. When the sailors saw this, and that their return to their native country was apparently assured, a shout of tumultuous joy broke from them, loud and long-continued. Frankenstein, who was dozing, awoke and asked the cause of the tumult. "They shout," I said, "because they will soon return to England."

"Do you then really return?"

"Alas! yes; I cannot withstand their demands. I cannot lead them unwillingly to danger, and I must return."

"Do so, if you will; but I will not. You may give up your purpose, but mine is assigned to me by heaven, and I dare not. I am weak; but surely the spirits who assist my vengeance will endow me with sufficient strength." Saying this, he endeavoured to spring from the bed, but the exertion was too great for him; he fell back and fainted.

It was long before he was restored; and I often thought that life was entirely extinct. At length he opened his eyes; he breathed with difficulty, and was unable to speak. The surgeon gave him a composing draught, and ordered us to leave him undisturbed. In the mean time he told me, that my friend had certainly not many hours to live.

His sentence was pronounced; and I could only grieve, and be patient. I sat by his bed, watching him; his eyes were closed, and I thought he slept; but presently he called to me in a feeble voice, and bidding me come near, said—"Alas! the strength I relied on is gone; I feel that I shall soon die, and he, my enemy and persecutor, may still be in being. Think not, Walton, that in the last moments of my existence I feel that burning hatred, and ardent desire of revenge, I once expressed, but I feel myself justified in desiring the death of my adversary. During these last days I have been occupied in examining my past conduct; nor do I find it blameable. In a fit of enthusiastic madness I created a rational creature, and was bound towards him, to assure, as far as was in my power, his happiness and well-being. This was my duty; but there was another still paramount to that. My duties towards the beings of my own species had greater claims to my attention, because they included a greater proportion of happiness or misery. Urged by this view, I refused, and I did right in refusing, to create a companion for the first creature. He showed unparalleled malignity and selfishness, in evil; he destroyed my friends; he devoted to destruction beings who possessed exquisite sensations, happiness, and wisdom; nor do I know where this thirst for vengeance may end. Miserable himself, that he may render no other wretched, he ought to die. The task of his destruction was mine, but I have failed. When actuated by selfish and vicious motives, I asked you to undertake my unfinished work; and I renew this request now, when I am only induced by reason and virtue.

"Yet I cannot ask you to renounce your country and friends, to fulfil this task; and now that you are returning to England, you will have little chance of meeting with him. But the consideration of these points, and the well balancing of what you may esteem your duties, I leave to you; my judgment and ideas are already disturbed by the near approach of death. I dare not ask you to do what I think right, for I may still be misled by passion.

"That he should live to be an instrument of mischief disturbs me; in other respects, this hour, when I momentarily expect my release, is the only happy one which I have enjoyed for several years. The forms of the beloved dead flit before me, and I hasten to their arms. Farewell, Walton! Seek happiness in tranquillity, and avoid ambition, even if it be only the apparently innocent one of distinguishing yourself in science and discoveries. Yet why do I say this? I have myself been blasted in these hopes, yet another may succeed."

His voice became faint as he spoke; and at length, exhausted by his effort, he sunk into silence. About half an hour afterwards he attempted again to speak, but was unable; he pressed my hand feebly, and his eyes closed for ever, while the irradiation of a gentle smile passed away from his lips.

Margaret, what comment can I make on the untimely extinction of this glorious spirit? What can I say, that will enable you to understand the depth of my sorrow? All that I should express would be inadequate and feeble. My tears flow; my mind is overshadowed by a cloud of disappointment. But I journey towards England, and I may there find consolation.

I am interrupted. What do these sounds portend? It is midnight; the breeze blows fairly, and the watch on deck scarcely stir. Again; there is a sound as of a human voice, but hoarser; it comes from the cabin where the remains of Frankenstein still lie. I must arise, and examine. Good night, my sister.

Great God! what a scene has just taken place! I am yet dizzy with the remembrance of it. I hardly know whether I shall have the power to detail it; yet the tale which I have recorded would be incomplete without this final and wonderful catastrophe.

I entered the cabin where lay the remains of my ill-fated and admirable friend. Over him hung a form which I cannot find words to describe:—gigantic in stature, yet uncouth and distorted in its proportions. As he hung over the coffin, his face was concealed by long locks of ragged hair; but one vast hand was extended, in colour and apparent texture like that of a mummy. When he heard the sound of my approach, he ceased to utter exclamations of grief and horror, and sprung towards the window. Never did I behold a vision so horrible as his face, of such loathsome, yet appalling hideousness. I shut my eyes involuntarily, and endeavoured to recollect what were my duties with regard to this destroyer. I called on him to stay.

He paused, looking on me with wonder; and, again turning towards the lifeless form of his creator, he seemed to forget my presence, and every feature and gesture seemed instigated by the wildest rage of some uncontrollable passion.

"That is also my victim!" he exclaimed; "in his murder my crimes are consummated; the miserable series of my being is wound to its close! Oh, Frankenstein! generous and self-devoted being! what does it avail that I now ask thee to pardon me? I, who irretrievably destroyed thee by destroying all thou lovedst. Alas! he is cold, he cannot answer me."

His voice seemed suffocated; and my first impulses, which had suggested to me the duty of obeying the dying request of my friend, in destroying his enemy, were now suspended by a mixture of curiosity and compassion. I approached this tremendous being; I dared not again raise my eyes to his face, there was something so scaring and unearthly in his ugliness. I attempted to speak, but the words died away on my lips. The monster continued to utter wild and incoherent self-reproaches. At length I gathered resolution to address him in a pause of the tempest of his passion: "Your repentance," I said, "is now superfluous. If you had listened to the voice of conscience, and heeded the stings of remorse, before you had urged your diabolical vengeance to this extremity, Frankenstein would yet have lived."

"And do you dream?" said the daemon; "do you think that I was then dead to agony and remorse?—He," he continued, pointing to the corpse, "he suffered not in the consummation of the deed;—oh! not the ten-thousandth portion of the anguish that was mine during the lingering detail of its execution. A frightful selfishness hurried me on, while my heart was poisoned with remorse. Think you that the groans of Clerval were music to my ears? My heart was fashioned to be susceptible of love and sympathy; and when wrenched by misery to vice and hatred, it did not endure the violence of the change, without torture such as you cannot even imagine.

"After the murder of Clerval, I returned to Switzerland, heart-broken and overcome. I pitied Frankenstein; my pity amounted to horror: I abhorred myself. But when I discovered that he, the author at once of my existence and of its unspeakable torments, dared to hope for happiness; that while he accumulated wretchedness and despair upon me, he sought his own enjoyment in feelings and passions from the indulgence of which I was for ever barred, then impotent envy and bitter indignation filled me with an insatiable thirst for vengeance. I recollected my threat, and resolved that it should be accomplished. I knew that I was preparing for myself a deadly torture; but I was the slave, not the master, of an impulse, which I detested, yet could not disobey. Yet when she died!—nay, then I was not miserable. I had cast off all feeling, subdued all anguish, to riot in the excess of my despair. Evil thenceforth became my good. Urged thus far, I had no choice but to adapt my nature to an element which I had willingly chosen. The completion of my demoniacal design became an insatiable passion. And now it is ended; there is my last victim!"

I was at first touched by the expressions of his misery; yet, when I called to mind what Frankenstein had said of his powers of eloquence and persuasion, and when I again cast my eyes on the lifeless form of my friend, indignation was rekindled within me. "Wretch!" I said, "it is well that you come here to whine over the desolation that you have made. You throw a torch into a pile of buildings; and when they are consumed, you sit among the ruins, and lament the fall. Hypocritical fiend! if he whom you mourn still lived, still would he be the object, again would he become the prey, of your accursed vengeance. It is not pity that you feel; you lament only because the victim of your malignity is withdrawn from your power."

"Oh, it is not thus—not thus," interrupted the being; "yet such must be the impression conveyed to you by what appears to be the purport of my actions. Yet I seek not a fellow-feeling in my misery. No sympathy may I ever find. When I first sought it, it was the love of virtue, the feelings of happiness and affection with which my whole being overflowed, that I wished to be participated. But now, that virtue has become to me a shadow, and that happiness and affection are turned into bitter and loathing despair, in what should I seek for sympathy? I am content to suffer alone, while my sufferings shall endure; when I die, I am well satisfied that abhorrence and opprobrium should load my memory. Once my fancy was soothed with dreams of virtue, of fame, and of enjoyment. Once I falsely hoped to meet with beings who, pardoning my outward form, would love me for the excellent qualities which I was capable of unfolding. I was nourished with high thoughts of honour and devotion. But now crime has degraded me beneath the meanest animal. No guilt, no mischief, no malignity, no misery, can be found comparable to mine. When I run over the frightful catalogue of my sins, I cannot believe that I am the same creature whose thoughts were once filled with sublime and transcendent visions of the beauty and the majesty of goodness. But it is even so; the fallen angel becomes a malignant devil. Yet even that enemy of God and man had friends and associates in his desolation; I am alone.

"You, who call Frankenstein your friend, seem to have a knowledge of my crimes and his misfortunes. But, in the detail which he gave you of them, he could not sum up the hours and months of misery which I endured, wasting in impotent passions. For while I destroyed his hopes, I did not satisfy my own desires. They were for ever ardent and craving; still I desired love and fellowship, and I was still spurned. Was there no injustice in this? Am I to be thought the only criminal, when all human kind sinned against me? Why do you not hate Felix, who drove his friend from the door with contumely? Why do you not execrate the rustic who sought to destroy the saviour of his child? Nay, these are virtuous and immaculate beings! I, the miserable and the abandoned, am an abortion, to be spurned at, and kicked, and trampled on. Even now my blood boils at the recollection of this injustice.

"But it is true that I am a wretch. I have murdered the lovely and the helpless; I have strangled the innocent as they slept, and grasped to death his throat who never injured me or any other living thing. I have devoted my creator, the select specimen of all that is worthy of love and admiration among men, to misery; I have pursued him even to that irremediable ruin. There he lies, white and cold in death. You hate me; but your abhorrence cannot equal that with which I regard myself. I look on the hands which executed the deed; I think on the heart in which the imagination of it was conceived, and long for the moment when these hands will meet my eyes, when that imagination will haunt my thoughts no more.

"Fear not that I shall be the instrument of future mischief. My work is nearly complete. Neither yours nor any man's death is needed to consummate the series of my being, and accomplish that which must be done; but it requires my own. Do not think that I shall be slow to perform this sacrifice. I shall quit your vessel on the ice-raft which brought me thither, and shall seek the most northern extremity of the globe; I shall collect my funeral pile, and consume to ashes this miserable frame, that its remains may afford no light to any curious and unhallowed wretch, who would create such another as I have been. I shall die. I shall no longer feel the agonies which now consume me, or be the prey of feelings unsatisfied, yet unquenched. He is dead who called me into being; and when I shall be no more, the very remembrance of us both will speedily vanish. I shall no longer see the sun or stars, or feel the winds play on my cheeks. Light, feeling, and sense will pass away; and in this condition must I find my happiness. Some years ago, when the images which this world affords first opened upon me, when I felt the cheering warmth of summer, and heard the rustling of the leaves and the warbling of the birds, and these were all to me, I should have wept to die; now it is my only consolation. Polluted by crimes, and torn by the bitterest remorse, where can I find rest but in death?

"Farewell! I leave you, and in you the last of human-kind whom these eyes will ever behold. Farewell, Frankenstein! If thou wert yet alive and yet cherished a desire of revenge against me, it would be better satiated in my life than in my destruction. But it was not so; thou didst seek my extinction, that I might not cause greater wretchedness; and if yet, in some mode unknown to me, thou hadst not ceased to think and feel, thou wouldst not desire against me a vengeance greater than that which I feel. Blasted as thou wert, my agony was still superior to thine; for the bitter sting of remorse will not cease to rankle in my wounds until death shall close them for ever.

"But soon," he cried, with sad and solemn enthusiasm, "I shall die, and what I now feel be no longer felt. Soon these burning miseries will be extinct. I shall ascend my funeral pile triumphantly, and exult in the agony of the torturing flames. The light of that conflagration will fade away; my ashes will be swept into the sea by the winds. My spirit will sleep in peace; or if it thinks, it will not surely think thus. Farewell."

He sprung from the cabin window, as he said this, upon the ice-raft which lay close to the vessel. He was soon borne away by the waves, and lost in darkness and distance.

THE END.

Mathilda

CONTENTS

Chapter I

It is only four o'clock; but it is winter and the sun has already set: there are no clouds in the clear, frosty sky to reflect its slant beams, but the air itself is tinged with a slight roseate colour which is again reflected on the snow that covers the ground. I live in a lone cottage on a solitary, wide heath: no voice of life reaches me. I see the desolate plain covered with white, save a few black patches that the noonday sun has made at the top of those sharp pointed hillocks from which the snow, sliding as it fell, lay thinner than on the plain ground: a few birds are pecking at the hard ice that covers the pools—for the frost has been of long continuance.

I am in a strange state of mind. I am alone—quite alone—in the world—the blight of misfortune has passed over me and withered me; I know that I am about to die and I feel happy—joyous.—I feel my pulse; it beats fast: I place my thin hand on my cheek; it burns: there is a slight, quick spirit within me which is now emitting its last sparks. I shall never see the snows of another winter—I do believe that I shall never again feel the vivifying warmth of another summer sun; and it is in this persuasion that I begin to write my tragic history. Perhaps a history such as mine had better die with me, but a feeling that I cannot define leads me on and I am too weak both in body and mind to resist the slightest impulse. While life was strong within me I thought indeed that there was a sacred horror in my tale that rendered it unfit for utterance, and now about to die I pollute its mystic terrors. It is as the wood of the Eumenides none but the dying may enter; and Oedipus is about to die.

What am I writing?—I must collect my thoughts. I do not know that any will peruse these pages except you, my friend, who will receive them at my death. I do not address them to you alone because it will give me pleasure to dwell upon our friendship in a way that would be needless if you alone read what I shall write. I shall relate my tale therefore as if I wrote for strangers. You have often asked me the cause of my solitary life; my tears; and above all of my impenetrable and unkind silence. In life I dared not; in death I unveil the mystery. Others will toss these pages lightly over: to you, Woodville, kind, affectionate friend, they will be dear—the precious memorials of a heart-broken girl who, dying, is still warmed by gratitude towards you: your tears will fall on the words that record my misfortunes; I know they will—and while I have life I thank you for your sympathy.

But enough of this. I will begin my tale: it is my last task, and I hope I have strength sufficient to fulfill it. I record no crimes; my faults may easily be pardoned; for they proceeded not from evil motive but from want of judgement; and I believe few would say that they could, by a different conduct and superior wisdom, have avoided the misfortunes to which I am the victim. My fate has been governed by necessity, a hideous necessity. It required hands stronger than mine; stronger I do believe than any human force to break the thick, adamantine chain that has bound me, once breathing nothing but joy, ever possessed by a warm love and delight in goodness,—to misery only to be ended, and now about to be ended, in death. But I forget myself, my tale is yet untold. I will pause a few moments, wipe my dim eyes, and endeavour to lose the present obscure but heavy feeling of unhappiness in the more acute emotions of the past.

I was born in England. My father was a man of rank: he had lost his father early, and was educated by a weak mother with all the indulgence she thought due to a nobleman of wealth. He was sent to Eton and afterwards to college; and allowed from childhood the free use of large sums of money; thus enjoying from his earliest youth the independance which a boy with these advantages, always acquires at a public school.

Under the influence of these circumstances his passions found a deep soil wherein they might strike their roots and flourish either as flowers or weeds as was their nature. By being always allowed to act for himself his character became strongly and early marked and exhibited a various surface on which a quick sighted observer might see the seeds of virtues and of misfortunes. His careless extravagance, which made him squander immense sums of money to satisfy passing whims, which from their apparent energy he dignified with the name of passions, often displayed itself in unbounded generosity. Yet while he earnestly occupied himself about the wants of others his own desires were gratified to their fullest extent. He gave his money, but none of his own wishes were sacrifised to his gifts; he gave his time, which he did not value, and his affections which he was happy in any manner to have called into action.

I do not say that if his own desires had been put in competition with those of others that he would have displayed undue selfishness, but this trial was never made. He was nurtured in prosperity and attended by all its advantages; every one loved him and wished to gratify him. He was ever employed in promoting the pleasures of his companions—but their pleasures were his; and if he bestowed more attention upon the feelings of others than is usual with schoolboys it was because his social temper could never enjoy itself if every brow was not as free from care as his own.

While at school, emulation and his own natural abilities made him hold a conspicuous rank in the forms among his equals; at college he discarded books; he believed that he had other lessons to learn than those which they could teach him. He was now to enter into life and he was still young enough to consider study as a school-boy shackle, employed merely to keep the unruly out of mischief but as having no real connexion with life—whose wisdom of riding—gaming &c. he considered with far deeper interest—So he quickly entered into all college follies although his heart was too well moulded to be contaminated by them—it might be light but it was never cold. He was a sincere and sympathizing friend—but he had met with none who superior or equal to himself could aid him in unfolding his mind, or make him seek for fresh stores of thought by exhausting the old ones. He felt himself superior in quickness of judgement to those around him: his talents, his rank and wealth made him the chief of his party, and in that station he rested not only contented but glorying, conceiving it to be the only ambition worthy for him to aim at in the world.

By a strange narrowness of ideas he viewed all the world in connexion only as it was or was not related to his little society. He considered queer and out of fashion all opinions that were exploded by his circle of intimates, and he became at the same time dogmatic and yet fearful of not coinciding with the only sentiments he could consider orthodox. To the generality of spectators he appeared careless of censure, and with high disdain to throw aside all dependance on public prejudices; but at the same time that he strode with a triumphant stride over the rest of the world, he cowered, with self-disguised lowliness, to his own party, and although its chief never dared express an opinion or a feeling until he was assured that it would meet with the approbation of his companions.

Yet he had one secret hidden from these dear friends; a secret he had nurtured from his earliest years, and although he loved his fellow collegiates he would not trust it to the delicacy or sympathy of any one among them. He loved. He feared that the intensity of his passion might become the subject of their ridicule; and he could not bear that they should blaspheme it by considering that trivial and transitory which he felt was the life of his life.

There was a gentleman of small fortune who lived near his family mansion who had three lovely daughters. The eldest was far the most beautiful, but her beauty was only an addition to her other qualities—her understanding was clear and strong and her disposition angelically gentle. She and my father had been playmates from infancy: Diana, even in her childhood had been a favourite with his mother; this partiality encreased with the years of this beautiful and lively girl and thus during his school and college vacations they were perpetually together. Novels and all the various methods by which youth in civilized life are led to a knowledge of the existence of passions before they really feel them, had produced a strong effect on him who was so peculiarly susceptible of every impression. At eleven years of age Diana was his favourite playmate but he already talked the language of love. Although she was elder than he by nearly two years the nature of her education made her more childish at least in the knowledge and expression of feeling; she received his warm protestations with innocence, and returned them unknowing of what they meant. She had read no novels and associated only with her younger sisters, what could she know of the difference between love and friendship? And when the development of her understanding disclosed the true nature of this intercourse to her, her affections were already engaged to her friend, and all she feared was lest other attractions and fickleness might make him break his infant vows.

But they became every day more ardent and tender. It was a passion that had grown with his growth; it had become entwined with every faculty and every sentiment and only to be lost with life. None knew of their love except their own two hearts; yet although in all things else and even in this he dreaded the censure of his companions, for thus truly loving one inferior to him in fortune, nothing was ever able for a moment to shake his purpose of uniting himself to her as soon as he could muster courage sufficient to meet those difficulties he was determined to surmount.

Diana was fully worthy of his deepest affection. There were few who could boast of so pure a heart, and so much real humbleness of soul joined to a firm reliance on her own integrity and a belief in that of others. She had from her birth lived a retired life. She had lost her mother when very young, but her father had devoted himself to the care of her education—He had many peculiar ideas which influenced the system he had adopted with regard to her—She was well acquainted with the heroes of Greece and Rome or with those of England who had lived some hundred years ago, while she was nearly ignorant of the passing events of the day: she had read few authors who had written during at least the last fifty years but her reading with this exception was very extensive. Thus although she appeared to be less initiated in the mysteries of life and society than he, her knowledge was of a deeper kind and laid on firmer foundations; and if even her beauty and sweetness had not fascinated him, her understanding would ever have held his in thrall. He looked up to her as his guide, and such was his adoration that he delighted to augment to his own mind the sense of inferiority with which she sometimes impressed him.

When he was nineteen his mother died. He left college on this event and shaking off for a while his old friends he retired to the neighbourhood of his Diana and received all his consolation from her sweet voice and dearer caresses. This short separation from his companions gave him courage to assert his independance. He had a feeling that however they might express ridicule of his intended marriage they would not dare display it when it had taken place; therefore seeking the consent of his guardian which with some difficulty he obtained, and of the father of his mistress which was more easily given, without acquainting any one else of his intention, by the time he had attained his twentieth birthday he had become the husband of Diana.

He loved her with passion and her tenderness had a charm for him that would not permit him to think of aught but her. He invited some of his college friends to see him but their frivolity disgusted him. Diana had torn the veil which had before kept him in his boyhood: he was become a man and he was surprised how he could ever have joined in the cant words and ideas of his fellow collegiates or how for a moment he had feared the censure of such as these. He discarded his old friendships not from fickleness but because they were indeed unworthy of him. Diana filled up all his heart: he felt as if by his union with her he had received a new and better soul. She was his monitress as he learned what were the true ends of life. It was through her beloved lessons that he cast off his old pursuits and gradually formed himself to become one among his fellow men; a distinguished member of society, a Patriot; and an enlightened lover of truth and virtue.—He loved her for her beauty and for her amiable disposition but he seemed to love her more for what he considered her superior wisdom. They studied, they rode together; they were never seperate and seldom admitted a third to their society.

Thus my father, born in affluence, and always prosperous, clombe without the difficulty and various disappointments that all human beings seem destined to encounter, to the very topmost pinacle of happiness. Around him was sunshine, and clouds whose shapes of beauty made the prospect divine concealed from him the barren reality which lay hidden below them. From this dizzy point he was dashed at once as he unawares congratulated himself on his felicity. Fifteen months after their marriage I was born, and my mother died a few days after my birth.

A sister of my father was with him at this period. She was nearly fifteen years older than he, and was the offspring of a former marriage of his father. When the latter died this sister was taken by her maternal relations: they had seldom seen one another, and were quite unlike in disposition. This aunt, to whose care I was afterwards consigned, has often related to me the effect that this catastrophe had on my father's strong and susceptible character. From the moment of my mother's death until his departure she never heard him utter a single word: buried in the deepest melancholy he took no notice of any one; often for hours his eyes streamed tears or a more fearful gloom overpowered him. All outward things seemed to have lost their existence relatively to him and only one circumstance could in any degree recall him from his motionless and mute despair: he would never see me. He seemed insensible to the presence of any one else, but if, as a trial to awaken his sensibility, my aunt brought me into the room he would instantly rush out with every symptom of fury and distraction. At the end of a month he suddenly quitted his house and, unattended by any servant, departed from that part of the country without by word or writing informing any one of his intentions. My aunt was only relieved of her anxiety concerning his fate by a letter from him dated Hamburgh.

How often have I wept over that letter which until I was sixteen was the only relick I had to remind me of my parents. "Pardon me," it said, "for the uneasiness I have unavoidably given you: but while in that unhappy island, where every thing breathes *her* spirit whom I have lost for ever, a spell held me. It is broken: I have quitted England for many years, perhaps for ever. But to convince you that selfish feeling does not entirely engross me I shall remain in this town until you have made by letter every arrangement that you judge necessary. When I leave this place do not expect to hear from me: I must break all ties that at present exist. I shall become a wanderer, a miserable outcast—alone! alone!"—In another part of the letter he mentioned me—"As for that unhappy little being whom I could not see, and hardly dare mention, I leave her under your protection. Take care of her and cherish her: one day I may claim her at your hands; but futurity is dark, make the present happy to her."

My father remained three months at Hamburgh; when he quitted it he changed his name, my aunt could never discover that which he adopted and only by faint hints, could conjecture that he had taken the road of Germany and Hungary to Turkey.

Thus this towering spirit who had excited interest and high expectation in all who knew and could value him became at once, as it were, extinct. He existed from this moment for himself only. His friends remembered him as a brilliant vision which would never again return to them. The memory of what he had been faded away as years passed; and he who before had been as a part of themselves and of their hopes was now no longer counted among the living.

Chapter II

I NOW COME to my own story. During the early part of my life there is little to relate, and I will be brief; but I must be allowed to dwell a little on the years of my childhood that it may be apparent how when one hope failed all life was to be a blank; and how when the only affection I was permitted to cherish was blasted my existence was extinguished with it.

I have said that my aunt was very unlike my father. I believe that without the slightest tinge of a bad heart she had the coldest that ever filled a human breast: it was totally incapable of any affection. She took me under her protection because she considered it her duty; but she had too long lived alone and undisturbed by the noise and prattle of children to allow that I should disturb her quiet. She had never been married; and for the last five years had lived perfectly alone on an estate, that had descended to her through her mother, on the shores of Loch Lomond in Scotland. My father had expressed a wish in his letters that she should reside with me at his family mansion which was situated in a beautiful country near Richmond in Yorkshire. She would not consent to this proposition, but as soon as she had arranged the affairs which her brother's departure had caused to fall to her care, she quitted England and took me with her to her Scotch estate.

The care of me while a baby, and afterwards until I had reached my eighth year devolved on a servant of my mother's, who had accompanied us in our retirement for that purpose. I was placed in a remote part of the house, and only saw my aunt at stated hours. These occurred twice a day; once about noon she came to my nursery, and once after her dinner I was taken to her. She never caressed me, and seemed all the time I stayed in the room to fear that I should annoy her by some childish freak. My good nurse always schooled me with the greatest care before she ventured into the parlour—and the awe my aunt's cold looks and few constrained words inspired was so great that I seldom disgraced her lessons or was betrayed from the exemplary stillness which I was taught to observe during these short visits.

Under my good nurse's care I ran wild about our park and the neighbouring fields. The offspring of the deepest love, I displayed from my earliest years the greatest sensibility of disposition. I cannot say with what passion I loved every thing, even the inanimate objects that surrounded me. I believe that I bore an individual attachment to every tree in our park; every animal that inhabited it knew me and I loved them. Their occasional deaths filled my infant heart with anguish. I cannot number the birds that I have saved during the long and severe winters of that climate; or the hares and rabbits that I have defended from the attacks of our dogs, or have nursed when accidentally wounded.

When I was seven years of age my nurse left me. I now forget the cause of her departure if indeed I ever knew it. She returned to England, and the bitter tears she shed at parting were the last I saw flow for love of me for many years. My grief was terrible: I had no friend but her in the whole world. By degrees I became reconciled to solitude but no one supplied her place in my affections. I lived in a desolate country where

——— there were none to praise
And very few to love.

It is true that I now saw a little more of my aunt, but she was in every way an unsocial being; and to a timid child she was as a plant beneath a thick covering of ice; I should cut my hands in endeavouring to get at it. So I was entirely thrown upon my own resources. The neighbouring minister was engaged to give me lessons in reading, writing, and French, but he was without family and his manners even to me were always perfectly characteristic of the profession in the exercise of whose functions he chiefly shone, that of a schoolmaster. I sometimes strove to form friendships with the most attractive of the girls who inhabited the neighbouring village; but I believe I should never have succeeded [even] had not my aunt interposed her authority to prevent all intercourse between me and the peasantry; for she was fearful lest I should acquire the Scotch accent and dialect; a little of it I had, although great pains was taken that my tongue should not disgrace my English origin.

As I grew older my liberty encreased with my desires, and my wanderings extended from our park to the neighbouring country. Our house was situated on the shores of the lake and the lawn came down to the water's edge. I rambled amidst the wild scenery of this lovely country and became a complete mountaineer: I passed hours on the steep brow of a mountain that overhung a waterfall or rowed myself in a little skiff to some one of the islands. I wandered for ever about these lovely solitudes, gathering flower after flower

Ond' era pinta tutta la mia via

singing as I might the wild melodies of the country, or occupied by pleasant day dreams. My greatest pleasure was the enjoyment of a serene sky amidst these verdant woods: yet I loved all the changes of Nature; and rain, and storm, and the beautiful clouds of heaven brought their delights with them. When rocked by the waves of the lake my spirits rose in triumph as a horseman feels with pride the motions of his high fed steed.

But my pleasures arose from the contemplation of nature alone, I had no companion: my warm affections finding no return from any other human heart were forced to run waste on inanimate objects. Sometimes indeed I wept when my aunt received my caresses with repulsive coldness, and when I looked round and found none to love; but I quickly dried my tears. As I grew older books in some degree supplied the place of human intercourse: the library of my aunt was very small; Shakespear, Milton, Pope and Cowper were the strangely assorted poets of her collection; and among the prose authors a translation of Livy and Rollin's ancient history were my chief favourites although as I emerged from childhood I found others highly interesting which I had before neglected as dull.

When I was twelve years old it occurred to my aunt that I ought to learn music; she herself played upon the harp. It was with great hesitation that she persuaded herself to undertake my instruction; yet believing this accomplishment a necessary part of my education, and balancing the evils of this measure or of having some one in the house to instruct me she submitted to the inconvenience. A harp was sent for that my playing might not interfere with hers, and I began: she found me a docile and, when I had conquered the first rudiments, a very apt scholar. I had acquired in my harp a companion in rainy days; a sweet soother of my feelings when any untoward accident ruffled them: I often addressed it as my only friend; I could pour forth to it my hopes and loves, and I fancied that its sweet accents answered me. I have now mentioned all my studies.

I was a solitary being, and from my infant years, ever since my dear nurse left me, I had been a dreamer. I brought Rosalind and Miranda and the lady of Comus to life to be my companions, or on my isle acted over their parts imagining myself to be in their situations. Then I wandered from the fancies of others and formed affections and intimacies with the aerial creations of my own brain—but still clinging to reality I gave a name to these conceptions and nursed them in the hope of realization. I clung to the memory of my parents; my mother I should never see, she was dead: but the idea of [my] unhappy, wandering father was the idol of my imagination. I bestowed on him all my affections; there was a miniature of him that I gazed on continually; I copied his last letter and read it again and again. Sometimes it made me weep; and at others I repeated with transport those words,—"One day I may claim her at your hands." I was to be his consoler, his companion in after years. My favourite vision was that when I grew up I would leave my aunt, whose coldness lulled my conscience, and disguised like a boy I would seek my father through the world. My imagination hung upon the scene of recognition; his miniature, which I should continually wear exposed on my breast, would be the means and I imaged the moment to my mind a thousand and a thousand times, perpetually varying the circumstances. Sometimes it would be in a desart; in a populous city; at a ball; we should perhaps meet in a vessel; and his first words constantly were, "My daughter, I love thee!" What extatic moments have I passed in these dreams! How many tears I have shed; how often have I laughed aloud.

This was my life for sixteen years. At fourteen and fifteen I often thought that the time was come when I should commence my pilgrimage, which I had cheated my own mind into believing was my imperious duty: but a reluctance to quit my aunt; a remorse for the grief which, I could not conceal from myself, I should occasion her for ever withheld me. Sometimes when I had planned the next morning for my escape a word of more than usual affection from her lips made me postpone my resolution. I reproached myself bitterly for what I called a culpable weakness; but this weakness returned upon me whenever the critical moment approached, and I never found courage to depart.

Chapter III

It was on my sixteenth birthday that my aunt received a letter from my father. I cannot describe the tumult of emotions that arose within me as I read it. It was dated from London; he had returned! I could only relieve my transports by tears, tears of unmingled joy. He had returned, and he wrote to know whether my aunt would come to London or whether he should visit her in Scotland. How delicious to me were the words of his letter that concerned me: "I cannot tell you," it said, "how ardently I desire to see my Mathilda. I look on her as the creature who will form the happiness of my future life: she is all that exists on earth that interests me. I can hardly prevent myself from hastening immediately to you but I am necessarily detained a week and I write because if you come here I may see you somewhat sooner." I read these words with devouring eyes; I kissed them, wept over them and exclaimed, "He will love me!"—

My aunt would not undertake so long a journey, and in a fortnight we had another letter from my father, it was dated Edinburgh: he wrote that he should be with us in three days. As he approached, his desire of seeing me, he said, became more and more ardent, and he felt that the moment when he should first clasp me in his arms would be the happiest of his life.

How irksome were these three days to me! All sleep and appetite fled from me; I could only read and re-read his letter, and in the solitude of the woods imagine the moment of our meeting. On the eve of the third day I retired early to my room; I could not sleep but paced all night about my chamber and, as you may in Scotland at midsummer, watched the crimson track of the sun as it almost skirted the northern horizon. At day break I hastened to the woods; the hours past on while I indulged in wild dreams that gave wings to the slothful steps of time, and beguiled my eager impatience. My father was expected at noon but when I wished to return to meet him I found that I had lost my way: it seemed that in every attempt to find it I only became more involved in the intricacies of the woods, and the trees hid all trace by which I might be guided. I grew impatient, I wept, and wrung my hands but still I could not discover my path.

It was past two o'clock when by a sudden turn I found myself close to the lake near a cove where a little skiff was moored—It was not far from our house and I saw my father and aunt walking on the lawn. I jumped into the boat, and well accustomed to such feats, I pushed it from shore, and exerted all my strength to row swiftly across. As I came, dressed in white, covered only by my tartan *rachan,* my hair streaming on my shoulders, and shooting across with greater speed than it could be supposed I could give to my boat, my father has often told me that I looked more like a spirit than a human maid. I approached the shore, my father held the boat, I leapt lightly out, and in a moment was in his arms.

And now I began to live. All around me was changed from a dull uniformity to the brightest scene of joy and delight. The happiness I enjoyed in the company of my father far exceeded my sanguine expectations. We were for ever together; and the subjects of our conversations were inexhaustible. He had passed the sixteen years of absence among nations nearly unknown to Europe; he had wandered through Persia, Arabia and the north of India and had penetrated among the habitations of the natives with a freedom permitted to few Europeans. His relations of their manners, his anecdotes and descriptions of scenery whiled away delicious hours, when we were tired of talking of our own plans of future life.

The voice of affection was so new to me that I hung with delight upon his words when he told me what he had felt concerning me during these long years of apparent forgetfulness. "At first"—said he, "I could not bear to think of my poor little girl; but afterwards as grief wore off and hope again revisited me I could only turn to her, and amidst cities and desarts her little fairy form, such as I imagined it, for ever flitted before me. The northern breeze as it refreshed me was sweeter and more balmy for it seemed to carry some of your spirit along with it. I often thought that I would instantly return and take you along with me to some fertile island where we should live at peace for ever. As I returned my fervent hopes were dashed by so many fears; my impatience became in the highest degree painful. I dared not think that the sun should shine and the moon rise not on your living form but on your grave. But, no, it is not so; I have my Mathilda, my consolation, and my hope."—

My father was very little changed from what he described himself to be before his misfortunes. It is intercourse with civilized society; it is the disappointment of cherished hopes, the falsehood of friends, or the perpetual clash of mean passions that changes the heart and damps the ardour of youthful feelings; lonely wanderings in a wild country among people of simple or savage manners may inure the body but will not tame the soul, or extinguish the ardour and freshness of feeling incident to youth. The burning sun of India, and the freedom from all restraint had rather encreased the energy of his character: before he bowed under, now he was impatient of any censure except that of his own mind. He had seen so many customs and witnessed so great a variety of moral creeds that he had been obliged to form an independant one for himself which had no relation to the peculiar notions of any one country: his early prejudices of course influenced his judgement in the formation of his principles, and some raw college ideas were strangely mingled with the deepest deductions of his penetrating mind.

The vacuity his heart endured of any deep interest in life during his long absence from his native country had had a singular effect upon his ideas. There was a curious feeling of unreality attached by him to his foreign life in comparison with the years of his youth. All the time he had passed out of England was as a dream, and all the interest of his soul, all his affections belonged to events which had happened and persons who had existed sixteen years before. It was strange when you heard him talk to see how he passed over this lapse of time as a night of visions; while the remembrances of his youth standing seperate as they did from his after life had lost none of their vigour. He talked of my mother as if she had lived but a few weeks before; not that he expressed poignant grief, but his description of her person, and his relation of all anecdotes connected with her was thus fervent and vivid.

In all this there was a strangeness that attracted and enchanted me. He was, as it were, now awakened from his long, visionary sleep, and he felt somewhat like one of the seven sleepers, or like Nourjahad, in that sweet imitation of an eastern tale: Diana was gone; his friends were changed or dead, and now on his awakening I was all that he had to love on earth.

How dear to me were the waters, and mountains, and woods of Loch Lomond now that I had so beloved a companion for my rambles. I visited with my father every delightful spot, either on the islands, or by the side of the tree-sheltered waterfalls; every shady path, or dingle entangled with underwood and fern. My ideas were enlarged by his conversation. I felt as if I were recreated and had about me all the freshness and life of a new being: I was, as it were, transported since his arrival from a narrow spot of earth into a universe boundless to the imagination and the understanding. My life had been before as a pleasing country rill, never destined to leave its native fields, but when its task was fulfilled quietly to be absorbed, and leave no trace. Now it seemed to me to be as a various river flowing through a fertile and lovely landscape, ever changing and ever beautiful. Alas! I knew not the desart it was about to reach; the rocks that would tear its waters, and the hideous scene that would be reflected in a more distorted manner in its waves. Life was then brilliant; I began to learn to hope and what brings a more bitter despair to the heart than hope destroyed?

Is it not strange that grief should quickly follow so divine a happiness? I drank of an enchanted cup but gall was at the bottom of its long drawn sweetness. My heart was full of deep affection, but it was calm from its very depth and fulness. I had no idea that misery could arise from love, and this lesson that all at last must learn was taught me in a manner few are obliged to receive it. I lament now, I must ever lament, those few short months of Paradisaical bliss; I disobeyed no command, I ate no apple, and yet I was ruthlessly driven from it. Alas! my companion did, and I was precipitated in his fall. But I wander from my relation—let woe come at its appointed time; I may at this stage of my story still talk of happiness.

Three months passed away in this delightful intercourse, when my aunt fell ill. I passed a whole month in her chamber nursing her, but her disease was mortal and she died, leaving me for some time inconsolable. Death is so dreadful to the living; the chains of habit are so strong even when affection does not link them that the heart must be agonized when they break. But my father was beside me to console me and to drive away bitter memories by bright hopes: methought that it was sweet to grieve that he might dry my tears.

Then again he distracted my thoughts from my sorrow by comparing it with his despair when he lost my mother. Even at that time I shuddered at the picture he drew of his passions: he had the imagination of a poet, and when he described the whirlwind that then tore his feelings he gave his words the impress of life so vividly that I believed while I trembled. I wondered how he could ever again have entered into the offices of life after his wild thoughts seemed to have given him affinity with the unearthly; while he spoke, so tremendous were the ideas which he conveyed that it appeared as if the human heart were far too bounded for their conception. His feelings seemed better fitted for a spirit whose habitation is the earthquake and the volcano than for one confined to a mortal body and human lineaments. But these were merely memories; he was changed since then. He was now all love, all softness: and when I raised my eyes in wonder at him as he spoke the smile on his lips told me that his heart was possessed by the gentlest passions.

Two months after my aunt's death we removed to London where I was led by my father to attend to deeper studies than had before occupied me. My improvement was his delight; he was with me during all my studies and assisted or joined with me in every lesson. We saw a great deal of society, and no day passed that my father did not endeavour to embellish by some new enjoyment. The tender attachment that he bore me, and the love and veneration with which I returned it cast a charm over every moment. The hours were slow for each minute was employed; we lived more in one week than many do in the course of several months, and the variety and novelty of our pleasures gave zest to each.

We perpetually made excursions together. And whether it were to visit beautiful scenery, or to see fine pictures, or sometimes for no object but to seek amusement as it might chance to arise, I was always happy when near my father. It was a subject of regret to me whenever we were joined by a third person, yet if I turned with a disturbed look towards my father, his eyes fixed on me and beaming with tenderness instantly restored joy to my heart. O, hours of intense delight! Short as ye were ye are made as long to me as a whole life when looked back upon through the mist of grief that rose immediately after as if to shut ye from my view. Alas! ye were the last of happiness that I ever enjoyed; a few, a very few weeks and all was destroyed. Like Psyche I lived for awhile in an enchanted palace, amidst odours, and music, and every luxurious delight; when suddenly I was left on a barren rock; a wide ocean of despair rolled around me: above all was black, and my eyes closed while I still inhabited a universal death. Still I would not hurry on; I would pause for ever on the recollections of these happy weeks; I would repeat every word, and how many do I remember, record every enchantment of the faery habitation. But, no, my tale must not pause; it must be as rapid as was my fate,—I can only describe in short although strong expressions my precipitate and irremediable change from happiness to despair.

Chapter IV

Among our most assiduous visitors was a young man of rank, well informed, and agreeable in his person. After we had spent a few weeks in London his attentions towards me became marked and his visits more frequent. I was too much taken up by my own occupations and feelings to attend much to this, and then indeed I hardly noticed more than the bare surface of events as they passed around me; but I now remember that my father was restless and uneasy whenever this person visited us, and when we talked together watched us with the greatest apparent anxiety although he himself maintained a profound silence. At length these obnoxious visits suddenly ceased altogether, but from that moment I must date the change of my father: a change that to remember makes me shudder and then filled me with the deepest grief. There were no degrees which could break my fall from happiness to misery; it was as the stroke of lightning—sudden and entire. Alas! I now met frowns where before I had been welcomed only with smiles: he, my beloved father, shunned me, and either treated me with harshness or a more heart-breaking coldness. We took no more sweet counsel together; and when I tried to win him again to me, his anger, and the terrible emotions that he exhibited drove me to silence and tears.

And this was sudden. The day before we had passed alone together in the country; I remember we had talked of future travels that we should undertake together—there was an eager delight in our tones and gestures that could only spring from deep and mutual love joined to the most unrestrained confidence; and now the next day, the next hour, I saw his brows contracted, his eyes fixed in sullen fierceness on the ground, and his voice so gentle and so dear made me shiver when he addressed me. Often, when my wandering fancy brought by its various images now consolation and now aggravation of grief to my heart, I have compared my self to Proserpine who was gaily and heedlessly gathering flowers on the sweet plain of Enna, when the King of Hell snatched her away to the abodes of death and misery. Alas! I who so lately knew of nought but the joy of life; who had slept only to dream sweet dreams and awoke to incomparable happiness, I now passed my days and nights in tears. I who sought and had found joy in the love-breathing countenance of my father now when I dared fix on him a supplicating look it was ever answered by an angry frown. I dared not speak to him; and when sometimes I had worked up courage to meet him and to ask an explanation, one glance at his face where a chaos of mighty passion seemed for ever struggling made me tremble and shrink to silence. I was dashed down from heaven to earth as a silly sparrow when pounced on by a hawk; my eyes swam and my head was bewildered by the sudden apparition of grief. Day after day passed marked only by my complaints and my tears; often I lifted my soul in vain prayer for a softer descent from joy to woe, or if that were denied me that I might be allowed to die, and fade for ever under the cruel blast that swept over me,

——for what should I do here,
Like a decaying flower, still withering
Under his bitter words, whose kindly heat
Should give my poor heart life?

Sometimes I said to myself, this is an enchantment, and I must strive against it. My father is blinded by some malignant vision which I must remove. And then, like David, I would try music to win the evil spirit from him; and once while singing I lifted my eyes towards him and saw his fixed on me and filled with tears; all his muscles seemed relaxed to softness. I sprung towards him with a cry of joy and would have thrown myself into his arms, but he pushed me roughly from him and left me. And even from this slight incident he contracted fresh gloom and an additional severity of manner.

There are many incidents that I might relate which shewed the diseased yet incomprehensible state of his mind; but I will mention one that occurred while we were in company with several other persons. On this occasion I chanced to say that I thought Myrrha the best of Alfieri's tragedies; as I said this I chanced to cast my eyes on my father and met his: for the first time the expression of those beloved eyes displeased me, and I saw with affright that his whole frame shook with some concealed emotion that in spite of his efforts half conquered him: as this tempest faded from his soul he became melancholy and silent. Every day some new scene occurred and displayed in him a mind working as [it] were with an unknown horror that now he could master but which at times threatened to overturn his reason, and to throw the bright seat of his intelligence into a perpetual chaos.

I will not dwell longer than I need on these disastrous circumstances. I might waste days in describing how anxiously I watched every change of fleeting circumstance that promised better days, and with what despair I found that each effort of mine aggravated his seeming madness. To tell all my grief I might as well attempt to count the tears that have fallen from these eyes, or every sign that has torn my heart. I will be brief for there is in all this a horror that will not bear many words, and I sink almost a second time to death while I recall these sad scenes to my memory. Oh, my beloved father! Indeed you made me miserable beyond all words, but how truly did I even then forgive you, and how entirely did you possess my whole heart while I endeavoured, as a rainbow gleams upon a cataract, to soften thy tremendous sorrows.

Thus did this change come about. I seem perhaps to have dashed too suddenly into the description, but thus suddenly did it happen. In one sentence I have passed from the idea of unspeakable happiness to that of unspeakable grief but they were thus closely linked together. We had remained five months in London, three of joy and two of sorrow. My father and I were now seldom alone or if we were he generally kept silence with his eyes fixed on the ground—the dark full orbs in which before I delighted to read all sweet and gentle feeling shadowed from my sight by their lids and the long lashes that fringed them. When we were in company he affected gaiety but I wept to hear his hollow laugh—begun by an empty smile and often ending in a bitter sneer such as never before this fatal period had wrinkled his lips. When others were there he often spoke to me and his eyes perpetually followed my slightest motion. His accents whenever he addressed me were cold and constrained although his voice would tremble when he perceived that my full heart choked the answer to words proffered with a mien yet new to me.

But days of peaceful melancholy were of rare occurrence: they were often broken in upon by gusts of passion that drove me as a weak boat on a stormy sea to seek a cove for shelter; but the winds blew from my native harbour and I was cast far, far out until shattered I perished when the tempest had passed and the sea was apparently calm. I do not know that I can describe his emotions: sometimes he only betrayed them by a word or gesture, and then retired to his chamber and I crept as near it as I dared and listened with fear to every sound, yet still more dreading a sudden silence—dreading I knew not what, but ever full of fear.

It was after one tremendous day when his eyes had glared on me like lightning—and his voice sharp and broken seemed unable to express the extent of his emotion—that in the evening when I was alone he joined me with a calm countenance, and not noticing my tears which I quickly dried when he approached, told me that in three days that he intended to remove with me to his estate in Yorkshire, and bidding me prepare left me hastily as if afraid of being questioned.

This determination on his part indeed surprised me. This estate was that which he had inhabited in childhood and near which my mother resided while a girl; this was the scene of their youthful loves and where they had lived after their marriage; in happier days my father had often told me that however he might appear weaned from his widow sorrow, and free from bitter recollections elsewhere, yet he would never dare visit the spot where he had enjoyed her society or trust himself to see the rooms that so many years ago they had inhabited together; her favourite walks and the gardens the flowers of which she had delighted to cultivate. And now while he suffered intense misery he determined to plunge into still more intense, and strove for greater emotion than that which already tore him. I was perplexed, and most anxious to know what this portended; ah, what could it portend but ruin!

I saw little of my father during this interval, but he appeared calmer although not less unhappy than before. On the morning of the third day he informed me that he had determined to go to Yorkshire first alone, and that I should follow him in a fortnight unless I heard any thing from him in the mean time that should contradict this command. He departed the same day, and four days afterwards I received a letter from his steward telling me in his name to join him with as little delay as possible. After travelling day and night I arrived with an anxious, yet a hoping heart, for why should he send for me if it were only to avoid me and to treat me with the apparent aversion that he had in London. I met him at the distance of thirty miles from our mansion. His demeanour was sad; for a moment he appeared glad to see me and then he checked himself as if unwilling to betray his feelings. He was silent during our ride, yet his manner was kinder than before and I thought I beheld a softness in his eyes that gave me hope.

When we arrived, after a little rest, he led me over the house and pointed out to me the rooms which my mother had inhabited. Although more than sixteen years had passed since her death nothing had been changed; her work box, her writing desk were still there and in her room a book lay open on the table as she had left it. My father pointed out these circumstances with a serious and unaltered mien, only now and then fixing his deep and liquid eyes upon me; there was something strange and awful in his look that overcame me, and in spite of myself I wept, nor did he attempt to console me, but I saw his lips quiver and the muscles of his countenance seemed convulsed.

We walked together in the gardens and in the evening when I would have retired he asked me to stay and read to him; and first said, "When I was last here your mother read Dante to me; you shall go on where she left off." And then in a moment he said, "No, that must not be; you must not read Dante. Do you choose a book." I took up Spenser and read the descent of Sir Guyon to the halls of Avarice; while he listened his eyes fixed on me in sad profound silence.

I heard the next morning from the steward that upon his arrival he had been in a most terrible state of mind: he had passed the first night in the garden lying on the damp grass; he did not sleep but groaned perpetually. "Alas!" said the old man who gave me this account with tears in his eyes, "it wrings my heart to see my lord in this state: when I heard that he was coming down here with you, my young lady, I thought we should have the happy days over again that we enjoyed during the short life of my lady your mother—But that would be too much happiness for us poor creatures born to tears—and that was why she was taken from us so soon. She was too beautiful and good for us. It was a happy day as we all thought it when my lord married her: I knew her when she was a child and many a good turn has she done for me in my old lady's time—You are like her although there is more of my lord in you—But has he been thus ever since his return? All my joy turned to sorrow when I first beheld him with that melancholy countenance enter these doors as it were the day after my lady's funeral—He seemed to recover himself a little after he had bidden me write to you—but still it is a woful thing to see him so unhappy." These were the feelings of an old, faithful servant: what must be those of an affectionate daughter. Alas! Even then my heart was almost broken.

We spent two months together in this house. My father spent the greater part of his time with me; he accompanied me in my walks, listened to my music, and leant over me as I read or painted. When he conversed with me his manner was cold and constrained; his eyes only seemed to speak, and as he turned their black, full lustre towards me they expressed a living sadness. There was something in those dark deep orbs so liquid, and intense that even in happiness I could never meet their full gaze that mine did not overflow. Yet it was with sweet tears; now there was a depth of affliction in their gentle appeal that rent my heart with sympathy; they seemed to desire peace for me; for himself, a heart patient to suffer; a craving for sympathy, yet a perpetual self denial. It was only when he was absent from me that his passion subdued him,—that he clinched his hands—knit his brows—and with haggard looks called for death to his despair, raving wildly, until exhausted he sank down nor was revived until I joined him.

While we were in London there was a harshness and sulleness in his sorrow which had now entirely disappeared. There I shrunk and fled from him, now I only wished to be with him that I might soothe him to peace. When he was silent I tried to divert him, and when sometimes I stole to him during the energy of his passion I wept but did not desire to leave him. Yet he suffered fearful agony; during the day he was more calm, but at night when I could not be with him he seemed to give the reins to his grief: he often passed his nights either on the floor in my mother's room, or in the garden; and when in the morning he saw me view with poignant grief his exhausted frame, and his person languid almost to death with watching, he wept; but during all this time he spoke no word by which I might guess the cause of his unhappiness. If I ventured to enquire he would either leave me or press his finger on his lips, and with a deprecating look that I could not resist, turn away. If I wept he would gaze on me in silence but he was no longer harsh and although he repulsed every caress yet it was with gentleness.

He seemed to cherish a mild grief and softer emotions although sad as a relief from despair—He contrived in many ways to nurse his melancholy as an antidote to wilder passion. He perpetually frequented the walks that had been favourites with him when he and my mother wandered together talking of love and happiness; he collected every relick that remained of her and always sat opposite her picture which hung in the room fixing on it a look of sad despair—and all this was done in a mystic and awful silence. If his passion subdued him he locked himself in his room; and at night when he wandered restlessly about the house, it was when every other creature slept.

It may easily be imagined that I wearied myself with conjecture to guess the cause of his sorrow. The solution that seemed to me the most probable was that during his residence in London he had fallen in love with some unworthy person, and that his passion mastered him although he would not gratify it: he loved me too well to sacrifise me to this inclination, and that he had now visited this house that by reviving the memory of my mother whom he so passionately adored he might weaken the present impression. This was possible; but it was a mere conjecture unfounded on any fact. Could there be guilt in it? He was too upright and noble to *do* aught that his conscience would not approve; I did not yet know of the crime there may be in involuntary feeling and therefore ascribed his tumultuous starts and gloomy looks wholly to the struggles of his mind and not any as they were partly due to the worst fiend of all—Remorse.

But still do I flatter myself that this would have passed away. His paroxisms of passion were terrific but his soul bore him through them triumphant, though almost destroyed by victory; but the day would finally have been won had not I, foolish and presumptuous wretch! hurried him on until there was no recall, no hope. My rashness gave the victory in this dreadful fight to the enemy who triumphed over him as he lay fallen and vanquished. I! I alone was the cause of his defeat and justly did I pay the fearful penalty. I said to myself, let him receive sympathy and these struggles will cease. Let him confide his misery to another heart and half the weight of it will be lightened. I will win him to me; he shall not deny his grief to me and when I know his secret then will I pour a balm into his soul and again I shall enjoy the ravishing delight of beholding his smile, and of again seeing his eyes beam if not with pleasure at least with gentle love and thankfulness. This will I do, I said. Half I accomplished; I gained his secret and we were both lost for ever.

Chapter V

NEARLY A YEAR had passed since my father's return, and the seasons had almost finished their round—It was now the end of May; the woods were clothed in their freshest verdure, and the sweet smell of the new mown grass was in the fields. I thought that the balmy air and the lovely face of Nature might aid me in inspiring him with mild sensations, and give him gentle feelings of peace and love preparatory to the confidence I determined to win from him.

I chose therefore the evening of one of these days for my attempt. I invited him to walk with me, and led him to a neighbouring wood of beech trees whose light shade shielded us from the slant and dazzling beams of the descending sun—after walking for some time in silence I seated myself with him on a mossy hillock—It is strange but even now I seem to see the spot—the slim and smooth trunks were many of them wound round by ivy whose shining leaves of the darkest green contrasted with the white bark and the light leaves of the young sprouts of beech that grew from their parent trunks—the short grass was mingled with moss and was partly covered by the dead leaves of the last autumn that driven by the winds had here and there collected in little hillocks—there were a few moss grown stumps about—The leaves were gently moved by the breeze and through their green canopy you could see the bright blue sky—As evening came on the distant trunks were reddened by the sun and the wind died entirely away while a few birds flew past us to their evening rest.

Well it was here we sat together, and when you hear all that passed—all that of terrible tore our souls even in this placid spot, which but for strange passions might have been a paradise to us, you will not wonder that I remember it as I looked on it that its calm might give me calm, and inspire me not only with courage but with persuasive words. I saw all these things and in a vacant manner noted them in my mind while I endeavoured to arrange my thoughts in fitting order for my attempt. My heart beat fast as I worked myself up to speak to him, for I was determined not to be repulsed but I trembled to imagine what effect my words might have on him; at length, with much hesitation I began:

"Your kindness to me, my dearest father, and the affection—the excessive affection—that you had for me when you first returned will I hope excuse me in your eyes that I dare speak to you, although with the tender affection of a daughter, yet also with the freedom of a friend and equal. But pardon me, I entreat you and listen to me: do not turn away from me; do not be impatient; you may easily intimidate me into silence, but my heart is bursting, nor can I willingly consent to endure for one moment longer the agony of uncertitude which for the last four months has been my portion.

"Listen to me, dearest friend, and permit me to gain your confidence. Are the happy days of mutual love which have passed to be to me as a dream never to return? Alas! You have a secret grief that destroys us both: but you must permit me to win this secret from you. Tell me, can I do nothing? You well know that on the whole earth there is no sacrifise that I would not make, no labour that I would not undergo with the mere hope that I might bring you ease. But if no endeavour on my part can contribute to your happiness, let me at least know your sorrow, and surely my earnest love and deep sympathy must soothe your despair.

"I fear that I speak in a constrained manner: my heart is overflowing with the ardent desire I have of bringing calm once more to your thoughts and looks; but I fear to aggravate your grief, or to raise that in you which is death to me, anger and distaste. Do not then continue to fix your eyes on the earth; raise them on me for I can read your soul in them: speak to me, and pardon my presumption. Alas! I am a most unhappy creature!"

I was breathless with emotion, and I paused fixing my earnest eyes on my father, after I had dashed away the intrusive tears that dimmed them. He did not raise his, but after a short silence he replied to me in a low voice: "You are indeed presumptuous, Mathilda, presumptuous and very rash. In the heart of one like me there are secret thoughts working, and secret tortures which you ought not to seek to discover. I cannot tell you how it adds to my grief to know that I am the cause of uneasiness to you; but this will pass away, and I hope that soon we shall be as we were a few months ago. Restrain your impatience or you may mar what you attempt to alleviate. Do not again speak to me in this strain; but wait in submissive patience the event of what is passing around you."

"Oh, yes!" I passionately replied, "I will be very patient; I will not be rash or presumptuous: I will see the agonies, and tears, and despair of my father, my only friend, my hope, my shelter, I will see it all with folded arms and downcast eyes. You do not treat me with candour; it is not true what you say; this will not soon pass away, it will last for ever if you deign not to speak to me; to admit my consolations.

"Dearest, dearest father, pity me and pardon me: I entreat you do not drive me to despair; indeed I must not be repulsed; there is one thing that although it may torture me to know, yet that you must tell me. I demand, and most solemnly I demand if in any way I am the cause of your unhappiness. Do you not see my tears which I in vain strive against—You hear unmoved my voice broken by sobs—Feel how my hand trembles: my whole heart is in the words I speak and you must not endeavour to silence me by mere words barren of meaning: the agony of my doubt hurries me on, and you must reply. I beseech you; by your former love for me now lost, I adjure you to answer that one question. Am I the cause of your grief?"

He raised his eyes from the ground, but still turning them away from me, said: "Besought by that plea I will answer your rash question. Yes, you are the sole, the agonizing cause of all I suffer, of all I must suffer until I die. Now, beware! Be silent! Do not urge me to your destruction. I am struck by the storm, rooted up, laid waste: but you can stand against it; you are young and your passions are at peace. One word I might speak and then you would be implicated in my destruction; yet that word is hovering on my lips. Oh! There is a fearful chasm; but I adjure you to beware!"

"Ah, dearest friend!" I cried, "do not fear! Speak that word; it will bring peace, not death. If there is a chasm our mutual love will give us wings to pass it, and we shall find flowers, and verdure, and delight on the other side." I threw myself at his feet, and took his hand, "Yes, speak, and we shall be happy; there will no longer be doubt, no dreadful uncertainty; trust me, my affection will soothe your sorrow; speak that word and all danger will be past, and we shall love each other as before, and for ever."

He snatched his hand from me, and rose in violent disorder: "What do you mean? You know not what you mean. Why do you bring me out, and torture me, and tempt me, and kill me—Much happier would [it] be for you and for me if in your frantic curiosity you tore my heart from my breast and tried to read its secrets in it as its life's blood was dropping from it. Thus you may console me by reducing me to nothing—but your words I cannot bear; soon they will make me mad, quite mad, and then I shall utter strange words, and you will believe them, and we shall be both lost for ever. I tell you I am on the very verge of insanity; why, cruel girl, do you drive me on: you will repent and I shall die."

When I repeat his words I wonder at my pertinacious folly; I hardly know what feelings resistlessly impelled me. I believe it was that coming out with a determination not to be repulsed I went right forward to my object without well weighing his replies: I was led by passion and drew him with frantic heedlessness into the abyss that he so fearfully avoided—I replied to his terrific words: "You fill me with affright it is true, dearest father, but you only confirm my resolution to put an end to this state of doubt. I will not be put off thus: do you think that I can live thus fearfully from day to day—the sword in my bosom yet kept from its mortal wound by a hair—a word!—I demand that dreadful word; though it be as a flash of lightning to destroy me, speak it.

"Alas! Alas! What am I become? But a few months have elapsed since I believed that I was all the world to you; and that there was no happiness or grief for you on earth unshared by your Mathilda—your child: that happy time is no longer, and what I most dreaded in this world is come upon me. In the despair of my heart I see what you cannot conceal: you no longer love me. I adjure you, my father, has not an unnatural passion seized upon your heart? Am I not the most miserable worm that crawls? Do I not embrace your knees, and you most cruelly repulse me? I know it—I see it—you hate me!"

I was transported by violent emotion, and rising from his feet, at which I had thrown myself, I leant against a tree, wildly raising my eyes to heaven. He began to answer with violence: "Yes, yes, I hate you! You are my bane, my poison, my disgust! Oh! No!" And then his manner changed, and fixing his eyes on me with an expression that convulsed every nerve and member of my frame—"you are none of all these; you are my light, my only one, my life.—My daughter, I love you!" The last words died away in a hoarse whisper, but I heard them and sunk on the ground, covering my face and almost dead with excess of sickness and fear: a cold perspiration covered my forehead and I shivered in every limb—But he continued, clasping his hands with a frantic gesture:

"Now I have dashed from the top of the rock to the bottom! Now I have precipitated myself down the fearful chasm! The danger is over; she is alive! Oh, Mathilda, lift up those dear eyes in the light of which I live. Let me hear the sweet tones of your beloved voice in peace and calm. Monster as I am, you are still, as you ever were, lovely, beautiful beyond expression. What I have become since this last moment I know not; perhaps I am changed in mien as the fallen archangel. I do believe I am for I have surely a new soul within me, and my blood riots through my veins: I am burnt up with fever. But these are precious moments; devil as I am become, yet that is my Mathilda before me whom I love as one was never before loved: and she knows it now; she listens to these words which I thought, fool as I was, would blast her to death. Come, come, the worst is past: no more grief, tears or despair; were not those the words you uttered?—We have leapt the chasm I told you of, and now, mark me, Mathilda, we are to find flowers, and verdure and delight, or is it hell, and fire, and tortures? Oh! Beloved One, I am borne away; I can no longer sustain myself; surely this is death that is coming. Let me lay my head near your heart; let me die in your arms!"—He sunk to the earth fainting, while I, nearly as lifeless, gazed on him in despair.

Yes it was despair I felt; for the first time that phantom seized me; the first and only time for it has never since left me—After the first moments of speechless agony I felt her fangs on my heart: I tore my hair; I raved aloud; at one moment in pity for his sufferings I would have clasped my father in my arms; and then starting back with horror I spurned him with my foot; I felt as if stung by a serpent, as if scourged by a whip of scorpions which drove me—Ah! Whither—Whither?

Well, this could not last. One idea rushed on my mind; never, never may I speak to him again. As this terrible conviction came upon *him* [*me*?] it melted my soul to tenderness and love—I gazed on him as to take my last farewell—he lay insensible—his eyes closed as [and?] his cheeks deathly pale—Above, the leaves of the beech wood cast a flickering shadow on his face, and waved in mournful melody over him—I saw all these things and said, "Aye, this is his grave!" And then I wept aloud, and raised my eyes to heaven to entreat for a respite to my despair and an alleviation for his unnatural suffering—the tears that gushed in a warm and healing stream from my eyes relieved the burthen that oppressed my heart almost to madness. I wept for a long time until I saw him about to revive, when horror and misery again recurred, and the tide of my sensations rolled back to their former channel: with a terror I could not restrain—I sprung up and fled, with winged speed, along the paths of the wood and across the fields until nearly dead I reached our house and just ordering the servants to seek my father at the spot I indicated, I shut myself up in my own room.

Chapter VI

My chamber was in a retired part of the house, and looked upon the garden so that no sound of the other inhabitants could reach it; and here in perfect solitude I wept for several hours. When a servant came to ask me if I would take food I learnt from him that my father had returned, and was apparently well and this relieved me from a load of anxiety, yet I did not cease to weep bitterly. At first, as the memory of former happiness contrasted to my present despair came across me, I gave relief to the oppression of heart that I felt by words, and groans, and heart rending sighs: but nature became wearied, and this more violent grief gave place to a passionate but mute flood of tears: my whole soul seemed to dissolve them. I did not wring my hands, or tear my hair, or utter wild exclamations, but as Boccaccio describes the intense and quiet grief [of] Ghismunda over the heart of Guiscardo, I sat with my hands folded, silently letting fall a perpetual stream from my eyes. Such was the depth of my emotion that I had no feeling of what caused my distress, my thoughts even wandered to many indifferent objects; but still neither moving limb or feature my tears fell until, as if the fountains were exhausted, they gradually subsided, and I awoke to life as from a dream.

When I had ceased to weep, reason and memory returned upon me, and I began to reflect with greater calmness on what had happened, and how it became me to act—A few hours only had passed but a mighty revolution had taken place with regard to me—the natural work of years had been transacted since the morning: my father was as dead to me, and I felt for a moment as if he with white hairs were laid in his coffin and I—youth vanished in approaching age, were weeping at his timely dissolution. But it was not so, I was yet young, Oh! far too young, nor was he dead to others; but I, most miserable, must never see or speak to him again. I must fly from him with more earnestness than from my greatest enemy: in solitude or in cities I must never more behold him. That consideration made me breathless with anguish, and impressing itself on my imagination I was unable for a time to follow up any train of ideas. Ever after this, I thought, I would live in the most dreary seclusion. I would retire to the Continent and become a nun; not for religion's sake, for I was not a Catholic, but that I might be for ever shut out from the world. I should there find solitude where I might weep, and the voices of life might never reach me.

But my father; my beloved and most wretched father? Would he die? Would he never overcome the fierce passion that now held pityless dominion over him? Might he not many, many years hence, when age had quenched the burning sensations that he now experienced, might he not then be again a father to me? This reflection unwrinkled my brow, and I could feel (and I wept to feel it) a half melancholy smile draw from my lips their expression of suffering: I dared indulge better hopes for my future life; years must pass but they would speed lightly away winged by hope, or if they passed heavily, still they would pass and I had not lost my father for ever. Let him spend another sixteen years of desolate wandering: let him once more utter his wild complaints to the vast woods and the tremendous cataracts of another clime: let him again undergo fearful danger and soul-quelling hardships: let the hot sun of the south again burn his passion worn cheeks and the cold night rains fall on him and chill his blood.

To this life, miserable father, I devote thee!—Go!—Be thy days passed with savages, and thy nights under the cope of heaven! Be thy limbs worn and thy heart chilled, and all youth be dead within thee! Let thy hairs be as snow; thy walk trembling and thy voice have lost its mellow tones! Let the liquid lustre of thine eyes be quenched; and then return to me, return to thy Mathilda, thy child, who may then be clasped in thy loved arms, while thy heart beats with sinless emotion. Go, Devoted One, and return thus!—This is my curse, a daughter's curse: go, and return pure to thy child, who will never love aught but thee.

These were my thoughts; and with trembling hands I prepared to begin a letter to my unhappy parent. I had now spent many hours in tears and mournful meditation; it was past twelve o'clock; all was at peace in the house, and the gentle air that stole in at my window did not rustle the leaves of the twining plants that shadowed it. I felt the entire tranquillity of the hour when my own breath and involuntary sobs were all the sounds that struck upon the air. On a sudden I heard a gentle step ascending the stairs; I paused breathless, and as it approached glided into an obscure corner of the room; the steps paused at my door, but after a few moments they again receded, descended the stairs and I heard no more.

This slight incident gave rise in me to the most painful reflections; nor do I now dare express the emotions I felt. That he should be restless I understood; that he should wander as an unlaid ghost and find no quiet from the burning hell that consumed his heart. But why approach my chamber? Was not that sacred? I felt almost ready to faint while he had stood there, but I had not betrayed my wakefulness by the slightest motion, although I had heard my own heart beat with violent fear. He had withdrawn. Oh, never, never, may I see him again! Tomorrow night the same roof may not cover us; he or I must depart. The mutual link of our destinies is broken; we must be divided by seas—by land. The stars and the sun must not rise at the same period to us: he must not say, looking at the setting crescent of the moon, "Mathilda now watches its fall."—No, all must be changed. Be it light with him when it is darkness with me! Let him feel the sun of summer while I am chilled by the snows of winter! Let there be the distance of the antipodes between us!

At length the east began to brighten, and the comfortable light of morning streamed into my room. I was weary with watching and for some time I had combated with the heavy sleep that weighed down my eyelids: but now, no longer fearful, I threw myself on my bed. I sought for repose although I did not hope for forgetfulness; I knew I should be pursued by dreams, but did not dread the frightful one that I really had. I thought that I had risen and went to seek my father to inform him of my determination to seperate myself from him. I sought him in the house, in the park, and then in the fields and the woods, but I could not find him. At length I saw him at some distance, seated under a tree, and when he perceived me he waved his hand several times, beckoning me to approach; there was something unearthly in his mien that awed and chilled me, but I drew near. When at a short distance from him I saw that he was dead-lily pale, and clothed in flowing garments of white. Suddenly he started up and fled from me; I pursued him: we sped over the fields, and by the skirts of woods, and on the banks of rivers; he flew fast and I followed. We came at last, methought, to the brow of a huge cliff that over hung the sea which, troubled by the winds, dashed against its base, at a distance. I heard the roar of the waters: he held his course right on towards the brink and I became breathless with fear lest he should plunge down the dreadful precipice; I tried to augment my speed, but my knees failed beneath me, yet I had just reached him; just caught a part of his flowing robe, when he leapt down and I awoke with a violent scream. I was trembling and my pillow was wet with my tears; for a few moments my heart beat hard, but the bright beams of the sun and the chirping of the birds quickly restored me to myself, and I rose with a languid spirit, yet wondering what events the day would bring forth. Some time passed before I summoned courage to ring the bell for my servant, and when she came I still dared not utter my father's name. I ordered her to bring my breakfast to my room, and was again left alone—yet still I could make no resolve, but only thought that I might write a note to my father to beg his permission to pay a visit to a relation who lived about thirty miles off, and who had before invited me to her house, but I had refused for then I could not quit my suffering father. When the servant came back she gave me a letter.

"From whom is this letter," I asked trembling.

"Your father left it, madam, with his servant, to be given to you when you should rise."

"My father left it! Where is he? Is he not here?"

"No; he quitted the house before four this morning."

"Good God! He is gone! But tell how this was; speak quick!" Her relation was short. He had gone in the carriage to the nearest town where he took a post chaise and horses with orders for the London road. He dismissed his servants there, only telling them that he had a sudden call of business and that they were to obey me as their mistress until his return.

Chapter VII

WITH A BEATING heart and fearful, I knew not why, I dismissed the servant and locking my door, sat down to read my father's letter. These are the words that it contained.

"My dear Child

"I have betrayed your confidence; I have endeavoured to pollute your mind, and have made your innocent heart acquainted with the looks and language of unlawful and monstrous passion. I must expiate these crimes, and must endeavour in some degree to proportionate my punishment to my guilt. You are I doubt not prepared for what I am about to announce; we must seperate and be divided for ever.

"I deprive you of your parent and only friend. You are cast out shelterless on the world: your hopes are blasted; the peace and security of your pure mind destroyed; memory will bring to you frightful images of guilt, and the anguish of innocent love betrayed. Yet I who draw down all this misery upon you; I who cast you forth and remorselessly have set the seal of distrust and agony on the heart and brow of my own child, who with devilish levity have endeavoured to steal away her loveliness to place in its stead the foul deformity of sin; I, in the overflowing anguish of my heart, supplicate you to forgive me.

"I do not ask your pity; you must and do abhor me: but pardon me, Mathilda, and let not your thoughts follow me in my banishment with unrelenting anger. I must never more behold you; never more hear your voice; but the soft whisperings of your forgiveness will reach me and cool the burning of my disordered brain and heart; I am sure I should feel it even in my grave. And I dare enforce this request by relating how miserably I was betrayed into this net of fiery anguish and all my struggles to release myself: indeed if your soul were less pure and bright I would not attempt to exculpate myself to you; I should fear that if I led you to regard me with less abhorrence you might hate vice less: but in addressing you I feel as if I appealed to an angelic judge. I cannot depart without your forgiveness and I must endeavour to gain it, or I must despair. I conjure you therefore to listen to my words, and if with the good guilt may be in any degree extenuated by sharp agony and remorse that rends the brain as madness, perhaps you may think, though I dare not, that I have some claim to your compassion.

"I entreat you to call to your remembrance our first happy life on the shores of Loch Lomond. I had arrived from a weary wandering of sixteen years, during which, although I had gone through many dangers and misfortunes, my affections had been an entire blank. If I grieved it was for your mother, if I loved it was your image; these sole emotions filled my heart in quietness. The human creatures around me excited in me no sympathy and I thought that the mighty change that the death of your mother had wrought within me had rendered me callous to any future impression. I saw the lovely and I did not love, I imagined therefore that all warmth was extinguished in my heart except that which led me ever to dwell on your then infantine image.

"It is a strange link in my fate that without having seen you I should passionately love you. During my wanderings I never slept without first calling down gentle dreams on your head. If I saw a lovely woman, I thought, does my Mathilda resemble her? All delightful things, sublime scenery, soft breezes, exquisite music seemed to me associated with you and only through you to be pleasant to me. At length I saw you. You appeared as the deity of a lovely region, the ministering Angel of a Paradise to which of all human kind you admitted only me. I dared hardly consider you as my daughter; your beauty, artlessness, and untaught wisdom seemed to belong to a higher order of beings; your voice breathed forth only words of love: if there was aught of earthly in you it was only what you derived from the beauty of the world; you seemed to have gained a grace from the mountain breezes—the waterfalls and the lake; and this was all of earthly except your affections that you had; there was no dross, no bad feeling in the composition. You yet even have not seen enough of the world to know the stupendous difference that exists between the women we meet in daily life and a nymph of the woods such as you were, in whose eyes alone mankind may study for centuries and grow wiser and purer. Those divine lights which shone on me as did those of Beatrice upon Dante, and well might I say with him yet with what different feelings

E quasi mi perdei con gli occhi chini.

Can you wonder, Mathilda, that I dwelt on your looks, your words, your motions, and drank in unmixed delight?

"But I am afraid that I wander from my purpose. I must be more brief for night draws on apace and all my hours in this house are counted. Well, we removed to London, and still I felt only the peace of sinless passion. You were ever with me, and I desired no more than to gaze on your countenance, and to know that I was all the world to you; I was lapped in a fool's paradise of enjoyment and security. Was my love blamable? If it was I was ignorant of it; I desired only that which I possessed, and if I enjoyed from your looks, and words, and most innocent caresses a rapture usually excluded from the feelings of a parent towards his child, yet no uneasiness, no wish, no casual idea awoke me to a sense of guilt. I loved you as a human father might be supposed to love a daughter borne to him by a heavenly mother; as Anchises might have regarded the child of Venus if the sex had been changed; love mingled with respect and adoration. Perhaps also my passion was lulled to content by the deep and exclusive affection you felt for me.

"But when I saw you become the object of another's love; when I imagined that you might be loved otherwise than as a sacred type and image of loveliness and excellence; or that you might love another with a more ardent affection than that which you bore to me, then the fiend awoke within me; I dismissed your lover; and from that moment I have known no peace. I have sought in vain for sleep and rest; my lids refused to close, and my blood was for ever in a tumult. I awoke to a new life as one who dies in hope might wake in Hell. I will not sully your imagination by recounting my combats, my self-anger, and my despair. Let a veil be drawn over the unimaginable sensations of a guilty father; the secrets of so agonized a heart may not be made vulgar. All was uproar, crime, remorse, and hate, yet still the tenderest love; and what first awoke me to the firm resolve of conquering my passion and of restoring her father to my child was the sight of your bitter and sympathizing sorrows. It was this that led me here: I thought that if I could again awaken in my heart the grief I had felt at the loss of your mother, and the many associations with her memory which had been laid to sleep for seventeen years, that all love for her child would become extinct. In a fit of heroism I determined to go alone; to quit you, the life of my life, and not to see you again until I might guiltlessly. But it would not do: I rated my fortitude too high, or my love too low. I should certainly have died if you had not hastened to me. Would that I had been indeed extinguished!

"And now, Mathilda I must make you my last confession. I have been miserably mistaken in imagining that I could conquer my love for you; I never can. The sight of this house, these fields and woods which my first love inhabited seems to have encreased it: in my madness I dared say to myself—Diana died to give her birth; her mother's spirit was transferred into her frame, and she ought to be as Diana to me. With every effort to cast it off, this love clings closer, this guilty love more unnatural than hate, that withers your hopes and destroys me for ever.

Better have loved despair, and safer kissed her.

No time or space can tear from my soul that which makes a part of it. Since my arrival here I have not for a moment ceased to feel the hell of passion which has been implanted in me to burn until all be cold, and stiff, and dead. Yet I will not die; alas! how dare I go where I may meet Diana, when I have disobeyed her last request; her last words said in a faint voice when all feeling but love, which survives all things else, was already dead, she then bade me make her child happy: that thought alone gives a double sting to death. I will wander away from you, away from all life—in the solitude I shall seek I alone shall breathe of human kind. I must endure life; and as it is my duty so I shall until the grave, dreaded yet desired, receive me free from pain: for while I feel it will be pain that must make up the whole sum of my sensations. Is not this a fearful curse that I labour under? Do I not look forward to a miserable future? My child, if after this life I am permitted to see you again, if pain can purify the heart, mine will be pure: if remorse may expiate guilt, I shall be guiltless.

"I have been at the door of your chamber: every thing is silent. You sleep. Do you indeed sleep, Mathilda? Spirits of Good, behold the tears of my earnest prayer! Bless my child! Protect her from the selfish among her fellow creatures: protect her from the agonies of passion, and the despair of disappointment! Peace, Hope, and Love be thy guardians, oh, thou soul of my soul: thou in whom I breathe!

"I dare not read my letter over for I have no time to write another, and yet I fear that some expressions in it might displease me. Since I last saw you I have been constantly employed in writing letters, and have several more to write; for I do not intend that any one shall hear of me after I depart. I need not conjure you to look upon me as one of whom all links that once existed between us are broken. Your own delicacy will not allow you, I am convinced, to attempt to trace me. It is far better for your peace that you should be ignorant of my destination. You will not follow me, for when I banish myself would you nourish guilt by obtruding yourself upon me? You will not do this, I know you will not. You must forget me and all the evil that I have taught you. Cast off the only gift that I have bestowed upon you, your grief, and rise from under my blighting influence as no flower so sweet ever did rise from beneath so much evil.

"You will never hear from me again: receive these then as the last words of mine that will ever reach you; and although I have forfeited your filial love, yet regard them I conjure you as a father's command. Resolutely shake off the wretchedness that this first misfortune in early life must occasion you. Bear boldly up against the storm: continue wise and mild, but believe it, and indeed it is, your duty to be happy. You are very young; let not this check for more than a moment retard your glorious course; hold on, beloved one. The sun of youth is not set for you; it will restore vigour and life to you; do not resist with obstinate grief its beneficent influence, oh, my child! bless me with the hope that I have not utterly destroyed you.

"Farewell, Mathilda. I go with the belief that I have your pardon. Your gentle nature would not permit you to hate your greatest enemy and though I be he, although I have rent happiness from your grasp; though I have passed over your young love and hopes as the angel of destruction, finding beauty and joy, and leaving blight and despair, yet you will forgive me, and with eyes overflowing with tears I thank you; my beloved one, I accept your pardon with a gratitude that will never die, and that will, indeed it will, outlive guilt and remorse.

"Farewell for ever!"

The moment I finished this letter I ordered the carriage and prepared to follow my father. The words of his letter by which he had dissuaded me from this step were those that determined me. Why did he write them? He must know that if I believed that his intention was merely to absent himself from me that instead of opposing him it would be that which I should myself require—or if he thought that any lurking feeling, yet he could not think that, should lead me to him would he endeavour to overthrow the only hope he could have of ever seeing me again; a lover, there was madness in the thought, yet he was my lover, would not act thus. No, he had determined to die, and he wished to spare me the misery of knowing it. The few ineffectual words he had said concerning his duty were to me a further proof—and the more I studied the letter the more did I perceive a thousand slight expressions that could only indicate a knowledge that life was now over for him. He was about to die! My blood froze at the thought: a sickening feeling of horror came over me that allowed not of tears. As I waited for the carriage I walked up and down with a quick pace; then kneeling and passionately clasping my hands I tried to pray but my voice was choked by convulsive sobs—Oh the sun shone, the air was balmy—he must yet live for if he were dead all would surely be black as night to me!

The motion of the carriage knowing that it carried me towards him and that I might perhaps find him alive somewhat revived my courage: yet I had a dreadful ride. Hope only supported me, the hope that I should not be too late. I did not weep, but I wiped the perspiration from my brow, and tried to still my brain and heart beating almost to madness. Oh! I must not be mad when I see him; or perhaps it were as well that I should be, my distraction might calm his, and recall him to the endurance of life. Yet until I find him I must force reason to keep her seat, and I pressed my forehead hard with my hands—Oh do not leave me; or I shall forget what I am about—instead of driving on as we ought with the speed of lightning they will attend to me, and we shall be too late. Oh! God help me! Let him be alive! It is all dark; in my abject misery I demand no more: no hope, no good: only passion, and guilt, and horror; but alive! Alive! My sensations choked me—No tears fell yet I sobbed, and breathed short and hard; one only thought possessed me, and I could only utter one word, that half screaming was perpetually on my lips: Alive! Alive!—

I had taken the steward with me for he, much better than I, could make the requisite enquiries—the poor old man could not restrain his tears as he saw my deep distress and knew the cause—he sometimes uttered a few broken words of consolation: in moments like these the mistress and servant become in a manner equals and when I saw his old dim eyes wet with sympathizing tears; his gray hair thinly scattered on an age-wrinkled brow I thought oh if my father were as he is—decrepid and hoary—then I should be spared this pain—

When I had arrived at the nearest town I took post horses and followed the road my father had taken. At every inn where we changed horses we heard of him, and I was possessed by alternate hope and fear. At length I found that he had altered his route; at first he had followed the London road; but now he changed it, and upon enquiry I found that the one which he now pursued led *towards the sea*. My dream recurred to my thoughts; I was not usually superstitious but in wretchedness every one is so. The sea was fifty miles off, yet it was towards it that he fled. The idea was terrible to my half-crazed imagination, and almost overturned the little self possession that still remained to me. I journeyed all day; every moment my misery encreased and the fever of my blood became intolerable. The summer sun shone in an unclouded sky; the air was close but all was cool to me except my own scorching skin. Towards evening dark thunder clouds arose above the horizon and I heard its distant roll—after sunset they darkened the whole sky and it began to rain, the lightning lighted up the whole country, and the thunder drowned the noise of our carriage. At the next inn my father had not taken horses; he had left a box there saying he would return, and had walked over the fields to the town of ——— a seacoast town eight miles off.

For a moment I was almost paralized by fear; but my energy returned and I demanded a guide to accompany me in following his steps. The night was tempestuous but my bribe was high and I easily procured a countryman. We passed through many lanes and over fields and wild downs; the rain poured down in torrents, and the loud thunder broke in terrible crashes over our heads. Oh! What a night it was! And I passed on with quick steps among the high, dank grass amid the rain and tempest. My dream was for ever in my thoughts, and with a kind of half insanity that often possesses the mind in despair, I said aloud: "Courage! We are not near the sea; we are yet several miles from the ocean"—Yet it was towards the sea that our direction lay and that heightened the confusion of my ideas. Once, overcome by fatigue, I sunk on the wet earth; about two hundred yards distant, alone in a large meadow stood a magnificent oak; the lightnings shewed its myriad boughs torn by the storm. A strange idea seized me; a person must have felt all the agonies of doubt concerning the life and death of one who is the whole world to them before they can enter into my feelings—for in that state, the mind working unrestrained by the will makes strange and fanciful combinations with outward circumstances and weaves the chances and changes of nature into an immediate connexion with the event they dread. It was with this feeling that I turned to the old steward who stood pale and trembling beside me; "Mark, Gaspar, if the next flash of lightning rend not that oak my father will be alive."

I had scarcely uttered these words than a flash instantly followed by a tremendous peal of thunder descended on it; and when my eyes recovered their sight after the dazzling light, the oak no longer stood in the meadow—The old man uttered a wild exclamation of horror when he saw so sudden an interpretation given to my prophecy. I started up, my strength returned with my terror; I cried, "Oh, God! Is this thy decree? Yet perhaps I shall not be too late."

Although still several miles distant we continued to approach the sea. We came at last to the road that led to the town of——— and at an inn there we heard that my father had passed by somewhat before sunset; he had observed the approaching storm and had hired a horse for the next town which was situated a mile from the sea that he might arrive there before it should commence: this town was five miles off. We hired a chaise here, and with four horses drove with speed through the storm. My garments were wet and clung around me, and my hair hung in straight locks on my neck when not blown aside by the wind. I shivered, yet my pulse was high with fever. Great God! What agony I endured. I shed no tears but my eyes wild and inflamed were starting from my head; I could hardly support the weight that pressed upon my brain. We arrived at the town of——— in a little more than half an hour. When my father had arrived the storm had already begun, but he had refused to stop and leaving his horse there he walked on—*towards the sea.* Alas! it was double cruelty in him to have chosen the sea for his fatal resolve; it was adding madness to my despair.

The poor old servant who was with me endeavoured to persuade me to remain here and to let him go alone—I shook my head silently and sadly; sick almost to death I leant upon his arm, and as there was no road for a chaise dragged my weary steps across the desolate downs to meet my fate, now too certain for the agony of doubt. Almost fainting I slowly approached the fatal waters; when we had quitted the town we heard their roaring. I whispered to myself in a muttering voice—"The sound is the same as that which I heard in my dream. It is the knell of my father which I hear."

The rain had ceased; there was no more thunder and lightning; the wind had paused. My heart no longer beat wildly; I did not feel any fever: but I was chilled; my knees sunk under me—I almost slept as I walked with excess of weariness; every limb trembled. I was silent: all was silent except the roaring of the sea which became louder and more dreadful. Yet we advanced slowly: sometimes I thought that we should never arrive; that the sound of waves would still allure us, and that we should walk on for ever and ever: field succeeding field, never would our weary journey cease, nor night nor day; but still we should hear the dashing of the sea, and to all this there would be no end. Wild beyond the imagination of the happy are the thoughts bred by misery and despair.

At length we reached the overhanging beach; a cottage stood beside the path; we knocked at the door and it was opened: the bed within instantly caught my eye; something stiff and straight lay on it, covered by a sheet; the cottagers looked aghast. The first words that they uttered confirmed what I before knew. I did not feel shocked or overcome: I believe that I asked one or two questions and listened to the answers. I hardly know, but in a few moments I sank lifeless to the ground; and so would that then all had been at an end!

Chapter VIII

I WAS CARRIED to the next town: fever succeeded to convulsions and faintings, and for some weeks my unhappy spirit hovered on the very verge of death. But life was yet strong within me; I recovered: nor did it a little aid my returning health that my recollections were at first vague, and that I was too weak to feel any violent emotion. I often said to myself, my father is dead. He loved me with a guilty passion, and stung by remorse and despair he killed himself. Why is it that I feel no horror? Are these circumstances not dreadful? Is it not enough that I shall never more meet the eyes of my beloved father; never more hear his voice; no caress, no look? All cold, and stiff, and dead! Alas! I am quite callous: the night I was out in was fearful and the cold rain that fell about my heart has acted like the waters of the cavern of Antiparos and has changed it to stone. I do not weep or sigh; but I must reason with myself, and force myself to feel sorrow and despair. This is not resignation that I feel, for I am dead to all regret.

I communed in this manner with myself, but I was silent to all around me. I hardly replied to the slightest question, and was uneasy when I saw a human creature near me. I was surrounded by my female relations, but they were all of them nearly strangers to me: I did not listen to their consolations; and so little did they work their designed effect that they seemed to me to be spoken in an unknown tongue. I found if sorrow was dead within me, so was love and desire of sympathy. Yet sorrow only slept to revive more fierce, but love never woke again—its ghost, ever hovering over my father's grave, alone survived—since his death all the world was to me a blank except where woe had stampt its burning words telling me to smile no more—the living were not fit companions for me, and I was ever meditating by what means I might shake them all off, and never be heard of again.

My convalescence rapidly advanced, yet this was the thought that haunted me, and I was for ever forming plans how I might hereafter contrive to escape the tortures that were prepared for me when I should mix in society, and to find that solitude which alone could suit one whom an untold grief seperated from her fellow creatures. Who can be more solitary even in a crowd than one whose history and the never ending feelings and remembrances arising from it is known to no living soul. There was too deep a horror in my tale for confidence; I was on earth the sole depository of my own secret. I might tell it to the winds and to the desart heaths but I must never among my fellow creatures, either by word or look give allowance to the smallest conjecture of the dread reality: I must shrink before the eye of man lest he should read my father's guilt in my glazed eyes: I must be silent lest my faltering voice should betray unimagined horrors. Over the deep grave of my secret I must heap an impenetrable heap of false smiles and words: cunning frauds, treacherous laughter, and a mixture of all light deceits would form a mist to blind others and be as the poisonous simoon to me. I, the offspring of love, the child of the woods, the nursling of Nature's bright self was to submit to this? I dared not.

How must I escape? I was rich and young, and had a guardian appointed for me; and all about me would act as if I were one of their great society, while I must keep the secret that I really was cut off from them for ever. If I fled I should be pursued; in life there was no escape for me: why then I must die. I shuddered; I dared not die even though the cold grave held all I loved; although I might say with Job

> Where is now my hope? For my hope who shall see it?
> They shall go down together to the bars of the pit,
> when our rest together is in the dust—

Yes my hope was corruption and dust and all to which death brings us.—Or after life—No, no, I will not persuade myself to die, I may not, dare not. And then I wept; yes, warm tears once more struggled into my eyes soothing yet bitter; and after I had wept much and called with unavailing anguish, with outstretched arms, for my cruel father; after my weak frame was exhausted by all variety of plaint I sank once more into reverie, and once more reflected on how I might find that which I most desired; dear to me if aught were dear, a death-like solitude.

I dared not die, but I might feign death, and thus escape from my comforters: they will believe me united to my father, and so indeed I shall be. For alone, when no voice can disturb my dream, and no cold eye meet mine to check its fire, then I may commune with his spirit; on a lone heath, at noon or at midnight, still I should be near him. His last injunction to me was that I should be happy; perhaps he did not mean the shadowy happiness that I promised myself, yet it was that alone which I could taste. He did not conceive that never again I could make one of the smiling hunters that go coursing after bubbles that break to nothing when caught, and then after a new one with brighter colours; my hope also had proved a bubble, but it had been so lovely, so adorned that I saw none that could attract me after it; besides I was wearied with the pursuit, nearly dead with weariness.

I would feign to die; my contented heirs would seize upon my wealth, and I should purchase freedom. But then my plan must be laid with art; I would not be left destitute, I must secure some money. Alas! to what loathsome shifts must I be driven? Yet a whole life of falsehood was otherwise my portion: and when remorse at being the contriver of any cheat made me shrink from my design I was irresistibly led back and confirmed in it by the visit of some aunt or cousin, who would tell me that death was the end of all men. And then say that my father had surely lost his wits ever since my mother's death; that he was mad and that I was fortunate, for in one of his fits he might have killed me instead of destroying his own crazed being. And all this, to be sure, was delicately put; not in broad words for my feelings might be hurt but

Whispered so and so
In dark hint soft and low

with downcast eyes, and sympathizing smiles or whimpers; and I listened with quiet countenance while every nerve trembled; I that dared not utter aye or no to all this blasphemy. Oh, this was a delicious life quite void of guile! I with my dove's look and fox's heart: for indeed I felt only the degradation of falsehood, and not any sacred sentiment of conscious innocence that might redeem it. I who had before clothed myself in the bright garb of sincerity must now borrow one of divers colours: it might sit awkwardly at first, but use would enable me to place it in elegant folds, to lie with grace. Aye,

I might die my soul with falsehood until I had quite hid its native colour. Oh, beloved father! Accept the pure heart of your unhappy daughter; permit me to join you unspotted as I was or you will not recognize my altered semblance. As grief might change Constance so would deceit change me until in heaven you would say, "This is not my child"—My father, to be happy both now and when again we meet I must fly from all this life which is mockery to one like me. In solitude only shall I be myself; in solitude I shall be thine.

Alas! I even now look back with disgust at my artifices and contrivances by which, after many painful struggles, I effected my retreat. I might enter into a long detail of the means I used, first to secure myself a slight maintenance for the remainder of my life, and afterwards to ensure the conviction of my death: I might, but I will not. I even now blush at the falsehoods I uttered; my heart sickens: I will leave this complication of what I hope I may in a manner call innocent deceit to be imagined by the reader. The remembrance haunts me like a crime—I know that if I were to endeavour to relate it my tale would at length remain unfinished. I was led to London, and had to endure for some weeks cold looks, cold words and colder consolations: but I escaped; they tried to bind me with fetters that they thought silken, yet which weighed on me like iron, although I broke them more easily than a girth formed of a single straw and fled to freedom.

The few weeks that I spent in London were the most miserable of my life: a great city is a frightful habitation to one sorrowing. The sunset and the gentle moon, the blessed motion of the leaves and the murmuring of waters are all sweet physicians to a distempered mind. The soul is expanded and drinks in quiet, a lulling medecine—to me it was as the sight of the lovely water snakes to the bewitched mariner—in loving and blessing Nature I unawares, called down a blessing on my own soul. But in a city all is closed shut like a prison, a wiry prison from which you can peep at the sky only. I cannot describe to you what were the frantic nature of my sensations while I resided there; I was often on the verge of madness. Nay, when I look back on many of my wild thoughts, thoughts with which actions sometimes endeavoured to keep pace; when I tossed my hands high calling down the cope of heaven to fall on me and bury me; when I tore my hair and throwing it to the winds cried, "Ye are free, go seek my father!" And then, like the unfortunate Constance, catching at them again and tying them up, that nought might find him if I might not. How, on my knees I have fancied myself close to my father's grave and struck the ground in anger that it should cover him from me. Oft when I have listened with gasping attention for the sound of the ocean mingled with my father's groans; and then wept until my strength was gone and I was calm and faint, when I have recollected all this I have asked myself if this were not madness. While in London these and many other dreadful thoughts too harrowing for words were my portion: I lost all this suffering when I was free; when I saw the wild heath around me, and the evening star in the west, then I could weep, gently weep, and be at peace.

Do not mistake me; I never was really mad. I was always conscious of my state when my wild thoughts seemed to drive me to insanity, and never betrayed them to aught but silence and solitude. The people around me saw nothing of all this. They only saw a poor girl broken in spirit, who spoke in a low and gentle voice, and from underneath whose downcast lids tears would sometimes steal which she strove to hide. One who loved to be alone, and shrunk from observation; who never smiled; oh, no! I never smiled—and that was all.

Well, I escaped. I left my guardian's house and I was never heard of again; it was believed from the letters that I left and other circumstances that I planned that I had destroyed myself. I was sought after therefore with less care than would otherwise have been the case; and soon all trace and memory of me was lost. I left London in a small vessel bound for a port in the north of England. And now having succeeded in my attempt, and being quite alone peace returned to me. The sea was calm and the vessel moved gently onwards, I sat upon deck under the open canopy of heaven and methought I was an altered creature. Not the wild, raving and most miserable Mathilda but a youthful Hermitess dedicated to seclusion and whose bosom she must strive to keep free from all tumult and unholy despair—The fanciful nun-like dress that I had adopted; the knowledge that my very existence was a secret known only to myself; the solitude to which I was for ever hereafter destined nursed gentle thoughts in my wounded heart. The breeze that played in my hair revived me, and I watched with quiet eyes the sunbeams that glittered on the waves, and the birds that coursed each other over the waters just brushing them with their plumes. I slept too undisturbed by dreams; and awoke refreshed to again enjoy my tranquil freedom.

In four days we arrived at the harbour to which we were bound. I would not remain on the sea coast, but proceeded immediately inland. I had already planned the situation where I would live. It should be a solitary house on a wide plain near no other habitation: where I could behold the whole horizon, and wander far without molestation from the sight of my fellow creatures. I was not misanthropic, but I felt that the gentle current of my feelings depended upon my being alone. I fixed myself on a wide solitude. On a dreary heath bestrewn with stones, among which short grass grew; and here and there a few rushes beside a little pool. Not far from my cottage was a small cluster of pines the only trees to be seen for many miles: I had a path cut through the furze from my door to this little wood, from whose topmost branches the birds saluted the rising sun and awoke me to my daily meditation. My view was bounded only by the horizon except on one side where a distant wood made a black spot on the heath, that every where else stretched out its faint hues as far as the eye could reach, wide and very desolate. Here I could mark the net work of the clouds as they wove themselves into thick masses: I could watch the slow rise of the heavy thunder clouds and could see the rack as it was driven across the heavens, or under the pine trees I could enjoy the stillness of the azure sky.

My life was very peaceful. I had one female servant who spent the greater part of the day at a village two miles off. My amusements were simple and very innocent; I fed the birds who built on the pines or among the ivy that covered the wall of my little garden, and they soon knew me: the bolder ones pecked the crumbs from my hands and perched on my fingers to sing their thankfulness. When I had lived here some time other animals visited me and a fox came every day for a portion of food appropriated for him and would suffer me to pat his head. I had besides many books and a harp with which when despairing I could soothe my spirits, and raise myself to sympathy and love.

Love! What had I to love? Oh many things: there was the moonshine, and the bright stars; the breezes and the refreshing rains; there was the whole earth and the sky that covers it: all lovely forms that visited my imagination, all memories of heroism and virtue. Yet this was very unlike my early life although as then I was confined to Nature and books. Then I bounded across the fields; my spirit often seemed to ride upon the winds, and to mingle in joyful sympathy with the ambient air. Then if I wandered slowly I cheered myself with a sweet song or sweeter day dreams. I felt a holy rapture spring from all I saw. I drank in joy with life; my steps were light; my eyes, clear from the love that animated them, sought the heavens, and with my long hair loosened to the winds I gave my body and my mind to sympathy and delight. But now my walk was slow—My eyes were seldom raised and often filled with tears; no song; no smiles; no careless motion that might bespeak a mind intent on what surrounded it—I was gathered up into myself—a selfish solitary creature ever pondering on my regrets and faded hopes.

Mine was an idle, useless life; it was so; but say not to the lily laid prostrate by the storm, "Arise, and bloom as before." My heart was bleeding from its death's wound; I could live no otherwise—Often amid apparent calm I was visited by despair and melancholy; gloom that nought could dissipate or overcome; a hatred of life; a carelessness of beauty; all these would by fits hold me nearly annihilated by their powers. Never for one moment when most placid did I cease to pray for death. I could be found in no state of mind which I would not willingly have exchanged for nothingness. And morning and evening my tearful eyes raised to heaven, my hands clasped tight in the energy of prayer, I have repeated with the poet—

Before I see another day
Oh, let this body die away!

Let me not be reproached then with inutility; I believed that by suicide I should violate a divine law of nature, and I thought that I sufficiently fulfilled my part in submitting to the hard task of enduring the crawling hours and minutes—in bearing the load of time that weighed miserably upon me and that in abstaining from what I in my calm moments considered a crime, I deserved the reward of virtue. There were periods, dreadful ones, during which I despaired—and doubted the existence of all duty and the reality of crime—but I shudder, and turn from the rememberance.

Chapter IX

THUS I PASSED two years. Day after day so many hundreds wore on; they brought no outward changes with them, but some few slowly operated on my mind as I glided on towards death. I began to study more; to sympathize more in the thoughts of others as expressed in books; to read history, and to lose my individuality among the crowd that had existed before me. Thus perhaps as the sensation of immediate suffering wore off, I became more human. Solitude also lost to me some of its charms: I began again to wish for sympathy; not that I was ever tempted to seek the crowd, but I wished for one friend to love me. You will say perhaps that I gradually became fitted to return to society. I do not think so. For the sympathy that I desired must be so pure, so divested of influence from outward circumstances that in the world I could not fail of being balked by the gross materials that perpetually mingle even with its best feelings. Believe me, I was then less fitted for any communion with my fellow creatures than before. When I left them they had tormented me but it was in the same way as pain and sickness may torment; something extraneous to the mind that galled it, and that I wished to cast aside. But now I should have desired sympathy; I should wish to knit my soul to some one of theirs, and should have prepared for myself plentiful draughts of disappointment and suffering; for I was tender as the sensitive plant, all nerve. I did not desire sympathy and aid in ambition or wisdom, but sweet and mutual affection; smiles to cheer me and gentle words of comfort. I wished for one heart in which I could pour unrestrained my plaints, and by the heavenly nature of the soil blessed fruit might spring from such bad seed. Yet how could I find this? The love that is the soul of friendship is a soft spirit seldom found except when two amiable creatures are knit from early youth, or when bound by mutual suffering and pursuits; it comes to some of the elect unsought and unaware; it descends as gentle dew on chosen spots which however barren they were before become under its benign influence fertile in all sweet plants; but when desired it flies; it scoffs at the prayers of its votaries; it will bestow, but not be sought.

I knew all this and did not go to seek sympathy; but there on my solitary heath, under my lowly roof where all around was desart, it came to me as a sunbeam in winter to adorn while it helps to dissolve the drifted snow.—Alas the sun shone on blighted fruit; I did not revive under its radiance for I was too utterly undone to feel its kindly power. My father had been and his memory was the life of my life. I might feel gratitude to another but I never more could love or hope as I had done; it was all suffering; even my pleasures were endured, not enjoyed. I was as a solitary spot among mountains shut in on all sides by steep black precipices; where no ray of heat could penetrate; and from which there was no outlet to sunnier fields. And thus it was that although the spirit of friendship soothed me for a while it could not restore me. It came as some gentle visitation; it went and I hardly felt the loss. The spirit of existence was dead within me; be not surprised therefore that when it came I welcomed not more gladly, or when it departed I lamented not more bitterly the best gift of heaven—a friend.

The name of my friend was Woodville. I will briefly relate his history that you may judge how cold my heart must have been not to be warmed by his eloquent words and tender sympathy; and how he also being most unhappy we were well fitted to be a mutual consolation to each other, if I had not been hardened to stone by the Medusa head of Misery. The misfortunes of Woodville were not of the heart's core like mine; his was a natural grief, not to destroy but to purify the heart and from which he might, when its shadow had passed from over him, shine forth brighter and happier than before.

Woodville was the son of a poor clergyman and had received a classical education. He was one of those very few whom fortune favours from their birth; on whom she bestows all gifts of intellect and person with a profusion that knew no bounds, and whom under her peculiar protection, no imperfection however slight, or disappointment however transitory has leave to touch. She seemed to have formed his mind of that excellence which no dross can tarnish, and his understanding was such that no error could pervert.

His genius was transcendant, and when it rose as a bright star in the east all eyes were turned towards it in admiration. He was a Poet. That name has so often been degraded that it will not convey the idea of all that he was. He was like a poet of old whom the muses had crowned in his cradle, and on whose lips bees had fed. As he walked among other men he seemed encompassed with a heavenly halo that divided him from and lifted him above them. It was his surpassing beauty, the dazzling fire of his eyes, and his words whose rich accents wrapt the listener in mute and extatic wonder, that made him transcend all others so that before him they appeared only formed to minister to his superior excellence.

He was glorious from his youth. Every one loved him; no shadow of envy or hate cast even from the meanest mind ever fell upon him. He was, as one the peculiar delight of the gods, railed and fenced in by his own divinity, so that nought but love and admiration could approach him. His heart was simple like a child, unstained by arrogance or vanity. He mingled in society unknowing of his superiority over his companions, not because he undervalued himself but because he did not perceive the inferiority of others. He seemed incapable of conceiving of the full extent of the power that selfishness and vice possesses in the world: when I knew him, although he had suffered disappointment in his dearest hopes, he had not experienced any that arose from the meanness and self-love of men: his station was too high to allow of his suffering through their hard-heartedness; and too low for him to have experienced ingratitude and encroaching selfishness: it is one of the blessings of a moderate fortune, that by preventing the possessor from conferring pecuniary favours it prevents him also from diving into the arcana of human weakness or malice—To bestow on your fellow men is a godlike attribute—So indeed it is and as such not one fit for mortality;—the giver like Adam and Prometheus, must pay the penalty of rising above his nature by being the martyr to his own excellence. Woodville was free from all these evils; and if slight examples did come across him he did not notice them but passed on in his course as an angel with winged feet might glide along the earth unimpeded by all those little obstacles over which we of earthly origin stumble. He was a believer in the divinity of genius and always opposed a stern disbelief to the objections of those petty cavillers and minor critics who wish to reduce all men to their own miserable level—"I will make a scientific simile" he would say, "in the manner, if you will, of Dr. Darwin—I consider the alledged errors of a man of genius as the aberrations of the fixed stars. It is our distance from them and our imperfect means of communication that makes them appear to move; in truth they always remain stationary, a glorious centre, giving us a fine lesson of modesty if we would thus receive it."—

I have said that he was a poet: when he was three and twenty years of age he first published a poem, and it was hailed by the whole nation with enthusiasm and delight. His good star perpetually shone upon him; a reputation had never before been made so rapidly: it was universal. The multitude extolled the same poems that formed the wonder of the sage in his closet: there was not one dissentient voice.

It was at this time, in the height of his glory, that he became acquainted with Elinor. She was a young heiress of exquisite beauty who lived under the care of her guardian: from the moment they were seen together they appeared formed for each other. Elinor had not the genius of Woodville but she was generous and noble, and exalted by her youth and the love that she every where excited above the knowledge of aught but virtue and excellence. She was lovely; her manners were frank and simple; her deep blue eyes swam in a lustre which could only be given by sensibility joined to wisdom.

They were formed for one another and they soon loved. Woodville for the first time felt the delight of love; and Elinor was enraptured in possessing the heart of one so beautiful and glorious among his fellow men. Could any thing but unmixed joy flow from such a union?

Woodville was a Poet—he was sought for by every society and all eyes were turned on him alone when he appeared; but he was the son of a poor clergyman and Elinor was a rich heiress. Her guardian was not displeased with their mutual affection: the merit of Woodville was too eminent to admit of cavil on account of his inferior wealth; but the dying will of her father did not allow her to marry before she was of age and her fortune depended upon her obeying this injunction. She had just entered her twentieth year, and she and her lover were obliged to submit to this delay. But they were ever together and their happiness seemed that of Paradise: they studied together: formed plans of future occupations, and drinking in love and joy from each other's eyes and words they hardly repined at the delay to their entire union. Woodville for ever rose in glory; and Elinor become more lovely and wise under the lessons of her accomplished lover.

In two months Elinor would be twenty one: every thing was prepared for their union. How shall I relate the catastrophe to so much joy; but the earth would not be the earth it is, covered with blight and sorrow, if one such pair as these angelic creatures had been suffered to exist for one another: search through the world and you will not find the perfect happiness which their marriage would have caused them to enjoy; there must have been a revolution in the order of things as established among us miserable earth-dwellers to have admitted of such consummate joy. The chain of necessity ever bringing misery must have been broken and the malignant fate that presides over it would not permit this breach of her eternal laws. But why should I repine at this? Misery was my element, and nothing but what was miserable could approach me; if Woodville had been happy I should never have known him. And can I who for many years was fed by tears, and nourished under the dew of grief, can I pause to relate a tale of woe and death?

Woodville was obliged to make a journey into the country and was detained from day to day in irksome absence from his lovely bride. He received a letter from her to say that she was slightly ill, but telling him to hasten to her, that from his eyes she would receive health and that his company would be her surest medecine. He was detained three days longer and then he hastened to her. His heart, he knew not why, prognosticated misfortune; he had not heard from her again; he feared she might be worse and this fear made him impatient and restless for the moment of beholding her once more stand before him arrayed in health and beauty; for a sinister voice seemed always to whisper to him, "You will never more behold her as she was."

When he arrived at her habitation all was silent in it: he made his way through several rooms; in one he saw a servant weeping bitterly: he was faint with fear and could hardly ask, "Is she dead?" and just listened to the dreadful answer, "Not yet." These astounding words came on him as of less fearful import than those which he had expected; and to learn that she was still in being, and that he might still hope was an alleviation to him. He remembered the words of her letter and he indulged the wild idea that his kisses breathing warm love and life would infuse new spirit into her, and that with him near her she could not die; that his presence was the talisman of her life.

He hastened to her sick room; she lay, her cheeks burning with fever, yet her eyes were closed and she was seemingly senseless. He wrapt her in his arms; he imprinted breathless kisses on her burning lips; he called to her in a voice of subdued anguish by the tenderest names; "Return Elinor; I am with you; your life, your love. Return; dearest one, you promised me this boon, that I should bring you health. Let your sweet spirit revive; you cannot die near me: What is death? To see you no more? To part with what is a part of myself; without whom I have no memory and no futurity? Elinor die! This is frenzy and the most miserable despair: you cannot die while I am near."

And again he kissed her eyes and lips, and hung over her inanimate form in agony, gazing on her countenance still lovely although changed, watching every slight convulsion, and varying colour which denoted life still lingering although about to depart. Once for a moment she revived and recognized his voice; a smile, a last lovely smile, played upon her lips. He watched beside her for twelve hours and then she died.

Chapter X

It was six months after this miserable conclusion to his long nursed hopes that I first saw him. He had retired to a part of the country where he was not known that he might peacefully indulge his grief. All the world, by the death of his beloved Elinor, was changed to him, and he could no longer remain in any spot where he had seen her or where her image mingled with the most rapturous hopes had brightened all around with a light of joy which would now be transformed to a darkness blacker than midnight since she, the sun of his life, was set for ever.

He lived for some time never looking on the light of heaven but shrouding his eyes in a perpetual darkness far from all that could remind him of what he had been; but as time softened his grief, like a true child of Nature he sought in the enjoyment of her beauties for a consolation in his unhappiness. He came to a part of the country where he was entirely unknown and where in the deepest solitude he could converse only with his own heart. He found a relief to his impatient grief in the breezes of heaven and in the sound of waters and woods. He became fond of riding; this exercise distracted his mind and elevated his spirits; on a swift horse he could for a moment gain respite from the image that else for ever followed him; Elinor on her death bed, her sweet features changed, and the soft spirit that animated her gradually waning into extinction. For many months Woodville had in vain endeavoured to cast off this terrible remembrance; it still hung on him until memory was too great a burthen for his loaded soul, but when on horseback the spell that seemingly held him to this idea was snapt; then if he thought of his lost bride he pictured her radiant in beauty; he could hear her voice, and fancy her "a sylvan Huntress by his side," while his eyes brightened as he thought he gazed on her cherished form. I had several times seen him ride across the heath and felt angry that my solitude should be disturbed. It was so long [since] I had spoken to any but peasants that I felt a disagreeable sensation at being gazed on by one of superior rank. I feared also that it might be some one who had seen me before: I might be recognized, my impostures discovered and I dragged back to a life of worse torture than that I had before endured. These were dreadful fears and they even haunted my dreams.

I was one day seated on the verge of the clump of pines when Woodville rode past. As soon as I perceived him I suddenly rose to escape from his observation by entering among the trees. My rising startled his horse; he reared and plunged and the rider was at length thrown. The horse then galloped swiftly across the heath and the stranger remained on the ground stunned by his fall. He was not materially hurt, a little fresh water soon recovered him. I was struck by his exceeding beauty, and as he spoke to thank me the sweet but melancholy cadence of his voice brought tears into my eyes.

A short conversation passed between us, but the next day he again stopped at my cottage and by degrees an intimacy grew between us. It was strange to him to see a female in extreme youth. I was not yet twenty, evidently belonging to the first classes of society and possessing every accomplishment an excellent education could bestow, living alone on a desolate heath—One on whose forehead the impress of grief was strongly marked, and whose words and motions betrayed that her thoughts did not follow them but were intent on far other ideas; bitter and overwhelming miseries. I was dressed also in a whimsical nun-like habit which denoted that I did not retire to solitude from necessity, but that I might indulge in a luxury of grief, and fanciful seclusion.

He soon took great interest in me, and sometimes forgot his own grief to sit beside me and endeavour to cheer me. He could not fail to interest even one who had shut herself from the whole world, whose hope was death, and who lived only with the departed. His personal beauty; his conversation which glowed with imagination and sensibility; the poetry that seemed to hang upon his lips and to make the very air mute to listen to him were charms that no one could resist. He was younger, less worn, more passionless than my father and in no degree reminded me of him: he suffered under immediate grief yet its gentle influence instead of calling feelings otherwise dormant into action, seemed only to veil that which otherwise would have been too dazzling for me. When we were together I spoke little, yet my selfish mind was sometimes borne away by the rapid course of his ideas; I would lift my eyes with momentary brilliancy until memories that never died and seldom slept would recur, and a tear would dim them.

Woodville for ever tried to lead me to the contemplation of what is beautiful and happy in the world. His own mind was constitutionally bent to a firmer belief in good than in evil and this feeling which must even exhilarate the hopeless ever shone forth in his words. He would talk of the wonderful powers of man, of their present state and of their hopes: of what they had been and what they were, and when reason could no longer guide him, his imagination as if inspired shed light on the obscurity that veils the past and the future. He loved to dwell on what might have been the state of the earth before man lived on it, and how he first arose and gradually became the strange, complicated, but as he said, the glorious creature he now is. Covering the earth with their creations and forming by the power of their minds another world more lovely than the visible frame of things, even all the world that we find in their writings. A beautiful creation, he would say, which may claim this superiority to its model, that good and evil is more easily seperated: the good rewarded in the way they themselves desire; the evil punished as all things evil ought to be punished, not by pain which is revolting to all philanthropy to consider but by quiet obscurity, which simply deprives them of their harmful qualities; why kill the serpent when you have extracted his fangs?

The poetry of his language and ideas which my words ill convey held me enchained to his discourses. It was a melancholy pleasure to me to listen to his inspired words; to catch for a moment the light of his eyes; to feel a transient sympathy and then to awaken from the delusion, again to know that all this was nothing,—a dream—a shadow for which there was no reality for me; my father had for ever deserted me, leaving me only memories which set an eternal barrier between me and my fellow creatures. I was indeed fellow to none. He—Woodville, mourned the loss of his bride: others wept the various forms of misery as they visited them: but infamy and guilt was mingled with my portion; unlawful and detestable passion had poured its poison into my ears and changed all my blood, so that it was no longer the kindly stream that supports life but a cold fountain of bitterness corrupted in its very source. It must be the excess of madness that could make me imagine that I could ever be aught but one alone; struck off from humanity; bearing no affinity to man or woman; a wretch on whom Nature had set her ban.

Sometimes Woodville talked to me of himself. He related his history brief in happiness and woe and dwelt with passion on his and Elinor's mutual love. "She was," he said, "the brightest vision that ever came upon the earth: there was something in her frank countenance, in her voice, and in every motion of her graceful form that overpowered me, as if it were a celestial creature that deigned to mingle with me in intercourse more sweet than man had ever before enjoyed. Sorrow fled before her; and her smile seemed to possess an influence like light to irradiate all mental darkness. It was not like a human loveliness that these gentle smiles went and came; but as a sunbeam on a lake, now light and now obscure, flitting before as you strove to catch them, and fold them for ever to your heart. I saw this smile fade for ever. Alas! I could never have believed that it was indeed Elinor that died if once when I spoke she had not lifted her almost benighted eyes, and for one moment like nought beside on earth, more lovely than a sunbeam, slighter, quicker than the waving plumage of a bird, dazzling as lightning and like it giving day to night, yet mild and faint, that smile came; it went, and then there was an end of all joy to me."

Thus his own sorrows, or the shapes copied from nature that dwelt in his mind with beauty greater than their own, occupied our talk while I railed in my own griefs with cautious secresy. If for a moment he shewed curiosity, my eyes fell, my voice died away and my evident suffering made him quickly endeavour to banish the ideas he had awakened; yet he for ever mingled consolation in his talk, and tried to soften my despair by demonstrations of deep sympathy and compassion. "We are both unhappy—" he would say to me; "I have told you my melancholy tale and we have wept together the loss of that lovely spirit that has so cruelly deserted me; but you hide your griefs: I do not ask you to disclose them, but tell me if I may not console you. It seems to me a wild adventure to find in this desart one like you quite solitary: you are young and lovely; your manners are refined and attractive; yet there is in your settled melancholy, and something, I know not what, in your expressive eyes that seems to seperate you from your kind: you shudder; pardon me, I entreat you but I cannot help expressing this once at least the lively interest I feel in your destiny.

"You never smile: your voice is low, and you utter your words as if you were afraid of the slight sound they would produce: the expression of awful and intense sorrow never for a moment fades from your countenance. I have lost for ever the loveliest companion that any man could ever have possessed, one who rather appears to have been a superior spirit who by some strange accident wandered among us earthly creatures, than as belonging to our kind. Yet I smile, and sometimes I speak almost forgetful of the change I have endured. But your sad mien never alters; your pulses beat and you breathe, yet you seem already to belong to another world; and sometimes, pray pardon my wild thoughts, when you touch my hand I am surprised to find your hand warm when all the fire of life seems extinct within you.

"When I look upon you, the tears you shed, the soft deprecating look with which you withstand enquiry; the deep sympathy your voice expresses when I speak of my lesser sorrows add to my interest for you. You stand here shelterless. You have cast yourself from among us and you wither on this wild plain forlorn and helpless: some dreadful calamity must have befallen you. Do not turn from me; I do not ask you to reveal it: I only entreat you to listen to me and to become familiar with the voice of consolation and kindness. If pity, and admiration, and gentle affection can wean you from despair let me attempt the task. I cannot see your look of deep grief without endeavouring to restore you to happier feelings. Unbend your brow; relax the stern melancholy of your regard; permit a friend, a sincere, affectionate friend, I will be one, to convey some relief, some momentary pause to your sufferings.

"Do not think that I would intrude upon your confidence: I only ask your patience. Do not for ever look sorrow and never speak it; utter one word of bitter complaint and I will reprove it with gentle exhortation and pour on you the balm of compassion. You must not shut me from all communion with you: do not tell me why you grieve but only say the words, 'I am unhappy,' and you will feel relieved as if for some time excluded from all intercourse by some magic spell you should suddenly enter again the pale of human sympathy. I entreat you to believe in my most sincere professions and to treat me as an old and tried friend: promise me never to forget me, never causelessly to banish me; but try to love me as one who would devote all his energies to make you happy. Give me the name of friend; I will fulfill its duties; and if for a moment complaint and sorrow would shape themselves into words, let me be near to speak peace to your vext soul."

I repeat his persuasions in faint terms and cannot give you at the same time the tone and gesture that animated them. Like a refreshing shower on an arid soil they revived me, and although I still kept their cause secret he led me to pour forth my bitter complaints and to clothe my woe in words of gall and fire. With all the energy of desperate grief I told him how I had fallen at once from bliss to misery; how that for me there was no joy, no hope; that death however bitter would be the welcome seal to all my pangs; death the skeleton was to be beautiful as love. I know not why but I found it sweet to utter these words to human ears; and though I derided all consolation yet I was pleased to see it offered me with gentleness and kindness. I listened quietly, and when he paused would again pour out my misery in expressions that shewed how far too deep my wounds were for any cure.

But now also I began to reap the fruits of my perfect solitude. I had become unfit for any intercourse, even with Woodville the most gentle and sympathizing creature that existed. I had become captious and unreasonable: my temper was utterly spoilt. I called him my friend but I viewed all he did with jealous eyes. If he did not visit me at the appointed hour I was angry, very angry, and told him that if indeed he did feel interest in me it was cold, and could not be fitted for me, a poor worn creature, whose deep unhappiness demanded much more than his worldly heart could give. When for a moment I imagined that his manner was cold I would fretfully say to him—"I was at peace before you came; why have you disturbed me? You have given me new wants and now you trifle with me as if my heart were as whole as yours, as if I were not in truth a shorn lamb thrust out on the bleak hill side, tortured by every blast. I wished for no friend, no sympathy. I avoided you, you know I did, but you forced yourself upon me and gave me those wants which you see with triumph give you power over me. Oh the brave power of the bitter north wind which freezes the tears it has caused to shed! But I will not bear this; go: the sun will rise and set as before you came, and I shall sit among the pines or wander on the heath weeping and complaining without wishing for you to listen. You are cruel, very cruel, to treat me who bleed at every pore in this rough manner."

And then, when in answer to my peevish words, I saw his countenance bent with living pity on me. When I saw him

> Gli occhi drizzo ver me con quel sembiante
> Che madre fa sopra figlioul deliro

I wept and said, "Oh, pardon me! You are good and kind but I am not fit for life. Why am I obliged to live? To drag hour after hour, to see the trees wave their branches restlessly, to feel the air, and to suffer in all I feel keenest agony. My frame is strong, but my soul sinks beneath this endurance of living anguish. Death is the goal that I would attain, but, alas! I do not even see the end of the course. Do you, my compassionate friend, tell me how to die peacefully and innocently and I will bless you: all that I, poor wretch, can desire is a painless death."

But Woodville's words had magic in them, when beginning with the sweetest pity, he would raise me by degrees out of myself and my sorrows until I wondered at my own selfishness: but he left me and despair returned; the work of consolation was ever to begin anew. I often desired his entire absence; for I found that I was grown out of the ways of life and that by long seclusion, although I could support my accustomed grief, and drink the bitter daily draught with some degree of patience, yet I had become unfit for the slightest novelty of feeling. Expectation, and hopes, and affection were all too much for me. I knew this, but at other times I was unreasonable and laid the blame upon him, who was most blameless, and peevishly thought that if his gentle soul were more gentle, if his intense sympathy were more intense, he could drive the fiend from my soul and make me more human. I am, I thought, a tragedy; a character that he comes to see act: now and then he gives me my cue that I may make a speech more to his purpose: perhaps he is already planning a poem in which I am to figure. I am a farce and play to him, but to me this is all dreary reality: he takes all the profit and I bear all the burthen.

Chapter XI

It is a strange circumstance but it often occurs that blessings by their use turn to curses; and that I who in solitude had desired sympathy as the only relief I could enjoy should now find it an additional torture to me. During my father's life time I had always been of an affectionate and forbearing disposition, but since those days of joy alas! I was much changed. I had become arrogant, peevish, and above all suspicious. Although the real interest of my narration is now ended and I ought quickly to wind up its melancholy catastrophe, yet I will relate one instance of my sad suspicion and despair and how Woodville with the goodness and almost the power of an angel, softened my rugged feelings and led me back to gentleness.

He had promised to spend some hours with me one afternoon but a violent and continual rain prevented him. I was alone the whole evening. I had passed two whole years alone unrepining, but now I was miserable. He could not really care for me, I thought, for if he did the storm would rather have made him come even if I had not expected him, than, as it did, prevent a promised visit. He would well know that this drear sky and gloomy rain would load my spirit almost to madness: if the weather had been fine I should not have regretted his absence as heavily as I necessarily must, shut up in this miserable cottage with no companions but my own wretched thoughts. If he were truly my friend he would have calculated all this; and let me now calculate this boasted friendship, and discover its real worth. He got over his grief for Elinor, and the country became dull to him, so he was glad to find even me for amusement; and when he does not know what else to do he passes his lazy hours here, and calls this friendship—It is true that his presence is a consolation to me, and that his words are sweet, and, when he will, he can pour forth thoughts that win me from despair.

His words are sweet,—and so, truly, is the honey of the bee, but the bee has a sting, and unkindness is a worse smart than that received from an insect's venom. I will put him to the proof. He says all hope is dead to him, and I know that it is dead to me, so we are both equally fitted for death. Let me try if he will die with me; and as I fear to die alone, if he will accompany to cheer me, and thus he can shew himself my friend in the only manner my misery will permit.

It was madness I believe, but I so worked myself up to this idea that I could think of nothing else. If he dies with me it is well, and there will be an end of two miserable beings; and if he will not, then will I scoff at his friendship and drink the poison before him to shame his cowardice. I planned the whole scene with an earnest heart and franticly set my soul on this project. I procured Laudanum and placing it in two glasses on the table, filled my room with flowers and decorated the last scene of my tragedy with the nicest care. As the hour for his coming approached, my heart softened and I wept; not that I gave up my plan, but even when resolved the mind must undergo several revolutions of feeling before it can drink its death.

Now all was ready and Woodville came. I received him at the door of my cottage and leading him solemnly into the room, I said: "My friend, I wish to die. I am quite weary of enduring the misery which hourly I do endure, and I will throw it off. What slave will not, if he may, escape from his chains? Look, I weep; for more than two years I have never enjoyed one moment free from anguish. I have often desired to die; but I am a very coward. It is hard for one so young who was once so happy as I was voluntarily to divest themselves of all sensation and to go alone to the dreary grave; I dare not. I must die, yet my fear chills me; I pause and shudder and then for months I endure my excess of wretchedness. But now the time is come when I may quit life. I have a friend who will not refuse to accompany me in this dark journey; such is my request: earnestly do I entreat and implore you to die with me. Then we shall find Elinor and what I have lost. Look, I am prepared; there is the death draught, let us drink it together and willingly and joyfully quit this hated round of daily life.

"You turn from me; yet before you deny me reflect, Woodville, how sweet it were to cast off the load of tears and misery under which we now labour: and surely we shall find light after we have passed the dark valley. That drink will plunge us in a sweet slumber, and when we awaken what joy will be ours to find all our sorrows and fears past. *A little patience, and all will be over,* aye, a very little patience; for, look, there is the key of our prison; we hold it in our own hands, and are we more debased than slaves to cast it away and give ourselves up to voluntary bondage? Even now if we had courage we might be free. Behold, my cheek is flushed with pleasure at the imagination of death; all that we love are dead. Come, give me your hand, one look of joyous sympathy and we will go together and seek them; a lulling journey; where our arrival will bring bliss and our waking be that of angels. Do you delay? Are you a coward, Woodville? Oh fie! Cast off this blank look of human melancholy. Oh! that I had words to express the luxury of death that I might win you. I tell you we are no longer miserable mortals; we are about to become gods; spirits free and happy as gods. What fool on a bleak shore, seeing a flowery isle on the other side with his lost love beckoning to him from it would pause because the wave is dark and turbid?

> What if some little payne the passage have
> That makes frayle flesh to fear the bitter wave?
> Is not short payne well borne that brings long ease,
> And lays the soul to sleep in quiet grave?

"Do you mark my words; I have learned the language of despair: I have it all by heart, for I am Despair; and a strange being am I, joyous, triumphant Despair. But those words are false, for the wave may be dark but it is not bitter. We lie down, and close our eyes with a gentle good night, and when we wake, we are free. Come then, no more delay, thou tardy one! Behold the pleasant potion! Look, I am a spirit of good, and not a human maid that invites thee, and with winning accents (oh, that they would win thee!) says, Come and drink."

As I spoke I fixed my eyes upon his countenance, and his exquisite beauty, the heavenly compassion that beamed from his eyes, his gentle yet earnest look of deprecation and wonder even before he spoke wrought a change in my high-strained feelings taking from me all the sternness of despair and filling me only with the softest grief. I saw his eyes humid also as he took both my hands in his; and sitting down near me, he said:

"This is a sad deed to which you would lead me, dearest friend, and your woe must indeed be deep that could fill you with these unhappy thoughts. You long for death and yet you fear it and wish me to be your companion. But I have less courage than you and even thus accompanied I dare not die. Listen to me, and then reflect if you ought to win me to your project, even if with the overbearing eloquence of despair you could make black death so inviting that the fair heaven should appear darkness. Listen I entreat you to the words of one who has himself nurtured desperate thoughts, and longed with impatient desire for death, but who has at length trampled the phantom under foot, and crushed his sting. Come, as you have played Despair with me I will play the part of Una with you and bring you hurtless from his dark cavern. Listen to me, and let yourself be softened by words in which no selfish passion lingers.

"We know not what all this wide world means; its strange mixture of good and evil. But we have been placed here and bid live and hope. I know not what we are to hope; but there is some good beyond us that we must seek; and that is our earthly task. If misfortune come against us we must fight with her; we must cast her aside, and still go on to find out that which it is our nature to desire. Whether this prospect of future good be the preparation for another existence I know not; or whether that it is merely that we, as workmen in God's vineyard, must lend a hand to smooth the way for our posterity. If it indeed be that; if the efforts of the virtuous now, are to make the future inhabitants of this fair world more happy; if the labours of those who cast aside selfishness, and try to know the truth of things, are to free the men of ages, now far distant but which will one day come, from the burthen under which those who now live groan, and like you weep bitterly; if they free them but from one of what are now the necessary evils of life, truly I will not fail but will with my whole soul aid the work. From my youth I have said, I will be virtuous; I will dedicate my life for the good of others; I will do my best to extirpate evil and if the spirit who protects ill should so influence circumstances that I should suffer through my endeavour, yet while there is hope, and hope there ever must be, of success, cheerfully do I gird myself to my task.

"I have powers; my countrymen think well of them. Do you think I sow my seed in the barren air, and have no end in what I do? Believe me, I will never desert life until this last hope is torn from my bosom, that in some way my labours may form a link in the chain of gold with which we ought all to strive to drag Happiness from where she sits enthroned above the clouds, now far beyond our reach, to inhabit the earth with us. Let us suppose that Socrates, or Shakespear, or Rousseau had been seized with despair and died in youth when they were as young as I am; do you think that we and all the world should not have lost incalculable improvement in our good feelings and our happiness through their destruction? I am not like one of these; they influenced millions: but if I can influence but a hundred, but ten, but one solitary individual, so as in any way to lead him from ill to good, that will be a joy to repay me for all my sufferings, though they were a million times multiplied; and that hope will support me to bear them.

"And those who do not work for posterity; or working, as may be my case, will not be known by it; yet they, believe me, have also their duties. You grieve because you are unhappy; it is happiness you seek but you despair of obtaining it. But if you can bestow happiness on another; if you can give one other person only one hour of joy ought you not to live to do it? And every one has it in their power to do that. The inhabitants of this world suffer so much pain. In crowded cities, among cultivated plains, or on the desart mountains, pain is thickly sown, and if we can tear up but one of these noxious weeds, or more, if in its stead we can sow one seed of corn, or plant one fair flower, let that be motive sufficient against suicide. Let us not desert our task while there is the slightest hope that we may in a future day do this.

"Indeed I dare not die. I have a mother whose support and hope I am. I have a friend who loves me as his life, and in whose breast I should infix a mortal sting if I ungratefully left him. So I will not die. Nor shall you, my friend; cheer up; cease to weep, I entreat you. Are you not young, and fair, and good? Why should you despair? Or if you must for yourself, why for others? If you can never be happy, can you never bestow happiness? Oh! believe me, if you beheld on lips pale with grief one smile of joy and gratitude, and knew that you were parent of that smile, and that without you it had never been, you would feel so pure and warm a happiness that you would wish to live for ever again and again to enjoy the same pleasure.

"Come, I see that you have already cast aside the sad thoughts you before franticly indulged. Look in that mirror; when I came your brow was contracted, your eyes deep sunk in your head, your lips quivering; your hands trembled violently when I took them; but now all is tranquil and soft. You are grieved and there is grief in the expression of your countenance but it is gentle and sweet. You allow me to throw away this cursed drink; you smile. Oh! Congratulate me, hope is triumphant, and I have done some good."

These words are shadowy as I repeat them but they were indeed words of fire and produced a warm hope in me (I, miserable wretch, to hope!) that tingled like pleasure in my veins. He did not leave me for many hours; not until he had improved the spark that he had kindled, and with an angelic hand fostered the return of something that seemed like joy. He left me but I still was calm, and after I had saluted the starry sky and dewy earth with eyes of love and a contented good night, I slept sweetly, visited by dreams, the first of pleasure I had had for many long months.

But this was only a momentary relief and my old habits of feeling returned; for I was doomed while in life to grieve, and to the natural sorrow of my father's death and its most terrific cause, imagination added a ten-fold weight of woe. I believed myself to be polluted by the unnatural love I had inspired, and that I was a creature cursed and set apart by nature. I thought that like another Cain, I had a mark set on my forehead to shew mankind that there was a barrier between me and them. Woodville had told me that there was in my countenance an expression as if I belonged to another world; so he had seen that sign: and there it lay a gloomy mark to tell the world that there was that within my soul that no silence could render sufficiently obscure. Why when fate drove me to become this outcast from human feeling; this monster with whom none might mingle in converse and love; why had she not from that fatal and most accursed moment, shrouded me in thick mists and placed real darkness between me and my fellows so that I might never more be seen; and as I passed, like a murky cloud loaded with blight, they might only perceive me by the cold chill I should cast upon them; telling them, how truly, that something unholy was near? Then I should have lived upon this dreary heath unvisited, and blasting none by my unhallowed gaze. Alas! I verily believe that if the near prospect of death did not dull and soften my bitter feelings, if for a few months longer I had continued to live as I then lived, strong in body, but my soul corrupted to its core by a deadly cancer, if day after day I had dwelt on these dreadful sentiments I should have become mad, and should have fancied myself a living pestilence: so horrible to my own solitary thoughts did this form, this voice, and all this wretched self appear; for had it not been the source of guilt that wants a name?

This was superstition. I did not feel thus franticly when first I knew that the holy name of father was become a curse to me: but my lonely life inspired me with wild thoughts; and then when I saw Woodville and day after day he tried to win my confidence and I never dared give words to my dark tale, I was impressed more strongly with the withering fear that I was in truth a marked creature, a pariah, only fit for death.

Chapter XII

As I WAS perpetually haunted by these ideas, you may imagine that the influence of Woodville's words was very temporary; and that although I did not again accuse him of unkindness, yet I soon became as unhappy as before. Soon after this incident we parted. He heard that his mother was ill, and he hastened to her. He came to take leave of me, and we walked together on the heath for the last time. He promised that he would come and see me again; and bade me take cheer, and to encourage what happy thoughts I could, until time and fortitude should overcome my misery, and I could again mingle in society.

"Above all other admonition on my part," he said, "cherish and follow this one: do not despair. That is the most dangerous gulph on which you perpetually totter; but you must reassure your steps, and take hope to guide you. Hope, and your wounds will be already half healed: but if you obstinately despair, there never more will be comfort for you. Believe me, my dearest friend, that there is a joy that the sun and earth and all its beauties can bestow that you will one day feel. The refreshing bliss of Love will again visit your heart, and undo the spell that binds you to woe, until you wonder how your eyes could be closed in the long night that burthens you. I dare not hope that I have inspired you with sufficient interest that the thought of me, and the affection that I shall ever bear you, will soften your melancholy and decrease the bitterness of your tears. But if my friendship can make you look on life with less disgust, beware how you injure it with suspicion. Love is a delicate sprite and easily hurt by rough jealousy. Guard, I entreat you, a firm persuasion of my sincerity in the inmost recesses of your heart out of the reach of the casual winds that may disturb its surface. Your temper is made unequal by suffering, and the tenor of your mind is, I fear, sometimes shaken by unworthy causes; but let your confidence in my sympathy and love be deeper far, and incapable of being reached by these agitations that come and go, and if they touch not your affections leave you uninjured."

These were some of Woodville's last lessons. I wept as I listened to him; and after we had taken an affectionate farewell, I followed him far with my eyes until they saw the last of my earthly comforter. I had insisted on accompanying him across the heath towards the town where he dwelt: the sun was yet high when he left me, and I turned my steps towards my cottage. It was at the latter end of the month of September when the nights have become chill. But the weather was serene, and as I walked on I fell into no unpleasing reveries. I thought of Woodville with gratitude and kindness and did not, I know not why, regret his departure with any bitterness. It seemed that after one great shock all other change was trivial to me; and I walked on wondering when the time would come when we should all four, my dearest father restored to me, meet in some sweet Paradise. I pictured to myself a lovely river such as that on whose banks Dante describes Mathilda gathering flowers, which ever flows

——— bruna, bruna,
Sotto l'ombra perpetua, che mai
Raggiar non lascia sole ivi, nè Luna.

And then I repeated to myself all that lovely passage that relates the entrance of Dante into the terrestrial Paradise; and thought it would be sweet when I wandered on those lovely banks to see the car of light descend with my long lost parent to be restored to me. As I waited there in expectation of that moment, I thought how, of the lovely flowers that grew there, I would wind myself a chaplet and crown myself for joy: I would sing *sul margine d'un rio,* my father's favourite song, and my voice gliding through the windless air would announce to him, in whatever bower he sat expecting the moment of our union, that his daughter was come. Then the mark of misery would have faded from my brow, and I should raise my eyes fearlessly to meet his, which ever beamed with the soft lustre of innocent love. When I reflected on the magic look of those deep eyes I wept, but gently, lest my sobs should disturb the fairy scene.

I was so entirely wrapt in this reverie that I wandered on, taking no heed of my steps until I actually stooped down to gather a flower for my wreath on that bleak plain where no flower grew, when I awoke from my day dream and found myself I knew not where.

The sun had set and the roseate hue which the clouds had caught from him in his descent had nearly died away. A wind swept across the plain, I looked around me and saw no object that told me where I was; I had lost myself, and in vain attempted to find my path. I wandered on, and the coming darkness made every trace indistinct by which I might be guided. At length all was veiled in the deep obscurity of blackest night; I became weary and knowing that my servant was to sleep that night at the neighbouring village, so that my absence would alarm no one; and that I was safe in this wild spot from every intruder, I resolved to spend the night where I was. Indeed I was too weary to walk further: the air was chill but I was careless of bodily inconvenience, and I thought that I was well inured to the weather during my two years of solitude, when no change of seasons prevented my perpetual wanderings.

I lay upon the grass surrounded by a darkness which not the slightest beam of light penetrated—There was no sound for the deep night had laid to sleep the insects, the only creatures that lived on the lone spot where no tree or shrub could afford shelter to aught else—There was a wondrous silence in the air that calmed my senses yet which enlivened my soul; my mind hurried from image to image and seemed to grasp an eternity. All in my heart was shadowy yet calm, until my ideas became confused and at length died away in sleep.

When I awoke it rained: I was already quite wet, and my limbs were stiff and my head giddy with the chill of night. It was a drizzling, penetrating shower; as my dank hair clung to my neck and partly covered my face, I had hardly strength to part with my fingers, the long straight locks that fell before my eyes. The darkness was much dissipated and in the east where the clouds were least dense the moon was visible behind the thin grey cloud—

> The moon is behind, and at the full
> And yet she looks both small and dull.

Its presence gave me a hope that by its means I might find my home. But I was languid and many hours passed before I could reach the cottage, dragging as I did my slow steps, and often resting on the wet earth unable to proceed.

I particularly mark this night, for it was that which has hurried on the last scene of my tragedy, which else might have dwindled on through long years of listless sorrow. I was very ill when I arrived and quite incapable of taking off my wet clothes that clung about me. In the morning, on her return, my servant found me almost lifeless, while possessed by a high fever I was lying on the floor of my room.

I was very ill for a long time, and when I recovered from the immediate danger of fever, every symptom of a rapid consumption declared itself. I was for some time ignorant of this and thought that my excessive weakness was the consequence of the fever. But my strength became less and less; as winter came on I had a cough; and my sunken cheek, before pale, burned with a hectic fever. One by one these symptoms struck me; and I became convinced that the moment I had so much desired was about to arrive and that I was dying. I was sitting by my fire, the physician who had attended me ever since my fever had just left me, and I looked over his prescription in which digitalis was the prominent medecine. "Yes," I said, "I see how this is, and it is strange that I should have deceived myself so long; I am about to die an innocent death, and it will be sweeter even than that which the opium promised."

I rose and walked slowly to the window; the wide heath was covered by snow which sparkled under the beams of the sun that shone brightly through the pure, frosty air: a few birds were pecking some crumbs under my window. I smiled with quiet joy; and in my thoughts, which through long habit would for ever connect themselves into one train, as if I shaped them into words, I thus addressed the scene before me:

"I salute thee, beautiful Sun, and thou, white Earth, fair and cold! Perhaps I shall never see thee again covered with green, and the sweet flowers of the coming spring will blossom on my grave. I am about to leave thee; soon this living spirit which is ever busy among strange shapes and ideas, which belong not to thee, soon it will have flown to other regions and this emaciated body will rest insensate on thy bosom

Rolled round in earth's diurnal course
With rocks, and stones, and trees.

"For it will be the same with thee, who art called our Universal Mother, when I am gone. I have loved thee; and in my days both of happiness and sorrow I have peopled your solitudes with wild fancies of my own creation. The woods, and lakes, and mountains which I have loved, have for me a thousand associations; and thou, oh, Sun! hast smiled upon, and borne your part in many imaginations that sprung to life in my soul alone, and which will die with me. Your solitudes, sweet land, your trees and waters will still exist, moved by your winds, or still beneath the eye of noon, though what I have felt about ye, and all my dreams which have often strangely deformed thee, will die with me. You will exist to reflect other images in other minds, and ever will remain the same, although your reflected semblance vary in a thousand ways, changeable as the hearts of those who view thee. One of these fragile mirrors, that ever doted on thine image, is about to be broken, crumbled to dust. But ever teeming Nature will create another and another, and thou wilt lose nought by my destruction.

"Thou wilt ever be the same. Receive then the grateful farewell of a fleeting shadow who is about to disappear, who joyfully leaves thee, yet with a last look of affectionate thankfulness. Farewell! Sky, and fields and woods; the lovely flowers that grow on thee; thy mountains and thy rivers; to the balmy air and the strong wind of the north, to all, a last farewell. I shall shed no more tears for my task is almost fulfilled, and I am about to be rewarded for long and most burthensome suffering. Bless thy child even in death, as I bless thee; and let me sleep at peace in my quiet grave."

I feel death to be near at hand and I am calm. I no longer despair, but look on all around me with placid affection. I find it sweet to watch the progressive decay of my strength, and to repeat to myself, another day and yet another, but again I shall not see the red leaves of autumn; before that time I shall be with my father. I am glad Woodville is not with me for perhaps he would grieve, and I desire to see smiles alone during the last scene of my life; when I last wrote to him I told him of my ill health but not of its mortal tendency, lest he should conceive it to be his duty to come to me for I fear lest the tears of friendship should destroy the blessed calm of my mind. I take pleasure in arranging all the little details which will occur when I shall no longer be. In truth I am in love with death; no maiden ever took more pleasure in the contemplation of her bridal attire than I in fancying my limbs already enwrapt in their shroud: is it not my marriage dress? Alone it will unite me to my father when in an eternal mental union we shall never part.

I will not dwell on the last changes that I feel in the final decay of nature. It is rapid but without pain: I feel a strange pleasure in it. For long years these are the first days of peace that have visited me. I no longer exhaust my miserable heart by bitter tears and frantic complaints; I no longer reproach the sun, the earth, the air, for pain and wretchedness. I wait in quiet expectation for the closing hours of a life which has been to me most sweet and bitter. I do not die not having enjoyed life; for sixteen years I was happy: during the first months of my father's return I had enjoyed ages of pleasure: now indeed I am grown old in grief; my steps are feeble like those of age; I have become peevish and unfit for life; so having passed little more than twenty years upon the earth I am more fit for my narrow grave than many are when they reach the natural term of their lives.

Again and again I have passed over in my remembrance the different scenes of my short life: if the world is a stage and I merely an actor on it my part has been strange, and, alas! tragical. Almost from infancy I was deprived of all the testimonies of affection which children generally receive; I was thrown entirely upon my own resources, and I enjoyed what I may almost call unnatural pleasures, for they were dreams and not realities. The earth was to me a magic lantern and I [a] gazer, and a listener but no actor; but then came the transporting and soul-reviving era of my existence: my father returned and I could pour my warm affections on a human heart; there was a new sun and a new earth created to me; the waters of existence sparkled: joy! joy! but, alas! what grief! My bliss was more rapid than the progress of a sunbeam on a mountain, which discloses its glades and woods, and then leaves it dark and blank; to my happiness followed madness and agony, closed by despair.

This was the drama of my life which I have now depicted upon paper. During three months I have been employed in this task. The memory of sorrow has brought tears; the memory of happiness a warm glow the lively shadow of that joy. Now my tears are dried; the glow has faded from my cheeks, and with a few words of farewell to you, Woodville, I close my work; the last that I shall perform.

Farewell, my only living friend; you are the sole tie that binds me to existence, and now I break it. It gives me no pain to leave you; nor can our seperation give you much. You never regarded me as one of this world, but rather as a being, who for some penance was sent from the Kingdom of Shadows; and she passed a few days weeping on the earth and longing to return to her native soil. You will weep but they will be tears of gentleness. I would, if I thought that it would lessen your regret, tell you to smile and congratulate me on my departure from the misery you beheld me endure. I would say: Woodville, rejoice with your friend, I triumph now and am most happy. But I check these expressions; these may not be the consolations of the living; they weep for their own misery, and not for that of the being they have lost. No; shed a few natural tears due to my memory: and if you ever visit my grave, pluck from thence a flower, and lay it to your heart; for your heart is the only tomb in which my memory will be interred.

My death is rapidly approaching and you are not near to watch the flitting and vanishing of my spirit. Do not regret this; for death is too terrible an object for the living. It is one of those adversities which hurt instead of purifying the heart; for it is so intense a misery that it hardens and dulls the feelings. Dreadful as the time was when I pursued my father towards the ocean, and found there only his lifeless corpse; yet for my own sake I should prefer that to the watching one by one his senses fade; his pulse weaken—and sleeplessly as it were devour his life in gazing. To see life in his limbs and to know that soon life would no longer be there; to see the warm breath issue from his lips and to know they would soon be chill—I will not continue to trace this frightful picture; you suffered this torture once; I never did. And the remembrance fills your heart sometimes with bitter despair when otherwise your feelings would have melted into soft sorrow.

So day by day I become weaker, and life flickers in my wasting form, as a lamp about to lose its vivifying oil. I now behold the glad sun of May. It was May, four years ago, that I first saw my beloved father; it was in May, three years ago that my folly destroyed the only being I was doomed to love. May is returned, and I die. Three days ago, the anniversary of our meeting; and, alas! of our eternal seperation, after a day of killing emotion, I caused myself to be led once more to behold the face of nature. I caused myself to be carried to some meadows some miles distant from my cottage; the grass being mowed, and there was the scent of hay in the fields; all the earth looked fresh and its inhabitants happy. Evening approached and I beheld the sun set. Three years ago and on that day and hour it shone through the branches and leaves of the beech wood and its beams flickered upon the countenance of him whom I then beheld for the last time. I now saw that divine orb, gilding all the clouds with unwonted splendour, sink behind the horizon; it disappeared from a world where he whom I would seek exists not; it approached a world where he exists not. Why do I weep so bitterly? Why does my heart heave with vain endeavour to cast aside the bitter anguish that covers it "as the waters cover the sea." I go from this world where he is no longer and soon I shall meet him in another.

Farewell, Woodville, the turf will soon be green on my grave; and the violets will bloom on it. *There* is my hope and my expectation; yours are in this world; may they be fulfilled.

Excerpt from
The Last Man

CONTENTS

Chapter I

I AM THE native of a sea-surrounded nook, a cloud-enshadowed land, which, when the surface of the globe, with its shoreless ocean and trackless continents, presents itself to my mind, appears only as an inconsiderable speck in the immense whole; and yet, when balanced in the scale of mental power, far outweighed countries of larger extent and more numerous population. So true it is, that man's mind alone was the creator of all that was good or great to man, and that Nature herself was only his first minister. England, seated far north in the turbid sea, now visits my dreams in the semblance of a vast and well-manned ship, which mastered the winds and rode proudly over the waves. In my boyish days she was the universe to me. When I stood on my native hills, and saw plain and mountain stretch out to the utmost limits of my vision, speckled by the dwellings of my countrymen, and subdued to fertility by their labours, the earth's very centre was fixed for me in that spot, and the rest of her orb was as a fable, to have forgotten which would have cost neither my imagination nor understanding an effort.

My fortunes have been, from the beginning, an exemplification of the power that mutability may possess over the varied tenor of man's life. With regard to myself, this came almost by inheritance. My father was one of those men on whom nature had bestowed to prodigality the envied gifts of wit and imagination, and then left his bark of life to be impelled by these winds, without adding reason as the rudder, or judgment as the pilot for the voyage. His extraction was obscure; but circumstances brought him early into public notice, and his small paternal property was soon dissipated in the splendid scene of fashion and luxury in which he was an actor. During the short years of thoughtless youth, he was adored by the high-bred triflers of the day, nor least by the youthful sovereign, who escaped from the intrigues of party, and the arduous duties of kingly business, to find never-failing amusement and exhilaration of spirit in his society. My father's impulses, never under his own controul, perpetually led him into difficulties from which his ingenuity alone could extricate him; and the accumulating pile of debts of honour and of trade, which would have bent to earth any other, was supported by him with a light spirit and tameless hilarity; while his company was so necessary at the tables and assemblies of the rich, that his derelictions were considered venial, and he himself received with intoxicating flattery.

This kind of popularity, like every other, is evanescent: and the difficulties of every kind with which he had to contend, increased in a frightful ratio compared with his small means of extricating himself. At such times the king, in his enthusiasm for him, would come to his relief, and then kindly take his friend to task; my father gave the best promises for amendment, but his social disposition, his craving for the usual diet of admiration, and more than all, the fiend of gambling, which fully possessed him, made his good resolutions transient, his promises vain. With the quick sensibility peculiar to his temperament, he perceived his power in the brilliant circle to be on the wane. The king married; and the haughty princess of Austria, who became, as queen of England, the head of fashion, looked with harsh eyes on his defects, and with contempt on the affection her royal husband entertained for him. My father felt that his fall was near; but so far from profiting by this last calm before the storm to save himself, he sought to forget anticipated evil by making still greater sacrifices to the deity of pleasure, deceitful and cruel arbiter of his destiny.

The king, who was a man of excellent dispositions, but easily led, had now become a willing disciple of his imperious consort. He was induced to look with extreme disapprobation, and at last with distaste, on my father's imprudence and follies. It is true that his presence dissipated these clouds; his warm-hearted frankness, brilliant sallies, and confiding demeanour were irresistible: it was only when at a distance, while still renewed tales of his errors were poured into his royal friend's ear, that he lost his influence. The queen's dextrous management was employed to prolong these absences, and gather together accusations. At length the king was brought to see in him a source of perpetual disquiet, knowing that he should pay for the short-lived pleasure of his society by tedious homilies, and more painful narrations of excesses, the truth of which he could not disprove. The result was, that he would make one more attempt to reclaim him, and in case of ill success, cast him off for ever.

Such a scene must have been one of deepest interest and high-wrought passion. A powerful king, conspicuous for a goodness which had heretofore made him meek, and now lofty in his admonitions, with alternate entreaty and reproof, besought his friend to attend to his real interests, resolutely to avoid those fascinations which in fact were fast deserting him, and to spend his great powers on a worthy field, in which he, his sovereign, would be his prop, his stay, and his pioneer. My father felt this kindness; for a moment ambitious dreams floated before him; and he thought that it would be well to exchange his present pursuits for nobler duties. With sincerity and fervour he gave the required promise: as a pledge of continued favour, he received from his royal master a sum of money to defray pressing debts, and enable him to enter under good auspices his new career. That very night, while yet full of gratitude and good resolves, this whole sum, and its amount doubled, was lost at the gaming-table. In his desire to repair his first losses, my father risked double stakes, and thus incurred a debt of honour he was wholly unable to pay. Ashamed to apply again to the king, he turned his back upon London, its false delights and clinging miseries; and, with poverty for his sole companion, buried himself in solitude among the hills and lakes of Cumberland. His wit, his bon mots, the record of his personal attractions, fascinating manners, and social talents, were long remembered and repeated from mouth to mouth. Ask where now was this favourite of fashion, this companion of the noble, this excelling beam, which gilt with alien splendour the assemblies of the courtly and the gay—you heard that he was under a cloud, a lost man; not one thought it belonged to him to repay pleasure by real services, or that his long reign of brilliant wit deserved a pension on retiring. The king lamented his absence; he loved to repeat his sayings, relate the adventures they had had together, and exalt his talents—but here ended his reminiscence.

Meanwhile my father, forgotten, could not forget. He repined for the loss of what was more necessary to him than air or food—the excitements of pleasure, the admiration of the noble, the luxurious and polished living of the great. A nervous fever was the consequence; during which he was nursed by the daughter of a poor cottager, under whose roof he lodged. She was lovely, gentle, and, above all, kind to him; nor can it afford astonishment, that the late idol of high-bred beauty should, even in a fallen state, appear a being of an elevated and wondrous nature to the lowly cottage-girl. The attachment between them led to the ill-fated marriage, of which I was the offspring.

Notwithstanding the tenderness and sweetness of my mother, her husband still deplored his degraded state. Unaccustomed to industry, he knew not in what way to contribute to the support of his increasing family. Sometimes he thought of applying to the king; pride and shame for a while withheld him; and, before his necessities became so imperious as to compel him to some kind of exertion, he died. For one brief interval before this catastrophe, he looked forward to the future, and contemplated with anguish the desolate situation in which his wife and children would be left. His last effort was a letter to the king, full of touching eloquence, and of occasional flashes of that brilliant spirit which was an integral part of him. He bequeathed his widow and orphans to the friendship of his royal master, and felt satisfied that, by this means, their prosperity was better assured in his death than in his life. This letter was enclosed to the care of a nobleman, who, he did not doubt, would perform the last and inexpensive office of placing it in the king's own hand.

He died in debt, and his little property was seized immediately by his creditors. My mother, pennyless and burthened with two children, waited week after week, and month after month, in sickening expectation of a reply, which never came. She had no experience beyond her father's cottage; and the mansion of the lord of the manor was the chiefest type of grandeur she could conceive. During my father's life, she had been made familiar with the name of royalty and the courtly circle; but such things, ill according with her personal experience, appeared, after the loss of him who gave substance and reality to them, vague and fantastical. If, under any circumstances, she could have acquired sufficient courage to address the noble persons mentioned by her husband, the ill success of his own application caused her to banish the idea. She saw therefore no escape from dire penury: perpetual care, joined to sorrow for the loss of the wondrous being, whom she continued to contemplate with ardent admiration, hard labour, and naturally delicate health, at length released her from the sad continuity of want and misery.

The condition of her orphan children was peculiarly desolate. Her own father had been an emigrant from another part of the country, and had died long since: they had no one relation to take them by the hand; they were outcasts, paupers, unfriended beings, to whom the most scanty pittance was a matter of favour, and who were treated merely as children of peasants, yet poorer than the poorest, who, dying, had left them, a thankless bequest, to the close-handed charity of the land.

I, the elder of the two, was five years old when my mother died. A remembrance of the discourses of my parents, and the communications which my mother endeavoured to impress upon me concerning my father's friends, in slight hope that I might one day derive benefit from the knowledge, floated like an indistinct dream through my brain. I conceived that I was different and superior to my protectors and companions, but I knew not how or wherefore. The sense of injury, associated with the name of king and noble, clung to me; but I could draw no conclusions from such feelings, to serve as a guide to action. My first real knowledge of myself was as an unprotected orphan among the valleys and fells of Cumberland. I was in the service of a farmer; and with crook in hand, my dog at my side, I shepherded a numerous flock on the near uplands. I cannot say much in praise of such a life; and its pains far exceeded its pleasures. There was freedom in it, a companionship with nature, and a reckless loneliness; but these, romantic as they were, did not accord with the love of action and desire of human sympathy, characteristic of youth. Neither the care of my flock, nor the change of seasons, were sufficient to tame my eager spirit; my out-door life and unemployed time were the temptations that led me early into lawless habits. I associated with others friendless like myself; I formed them into a band, I was their chief and captain. All shepherd-boys alike, while our flocks were spread over the pastures, we schemed and executed many a mischievous prank, which drew on us the anger and revenge of the rustics. I was the leader and protector of my comrades, and as I became distinguished among them, their misdeeds were usually visited upon me. But while I endured punishment and pain in their defence with the spirit of an hero, I claimed as my reward their praise and obedience.

In such a school my disposition became rugged, but firm. The appetite for admiration and small capacity for self-controul which I inherited from my father, nursed by adversity, made me daring and reckless. I was rough as the elements, and unlearned as the animals I tended. I often compared myself to them, and finding that my chief superiority consisted in power, I soon persuaded myself that it was in power only that I was inferior to the chiefest potentates of the earth. Thus untaught in refined philosophy, and pursued by a restless feeling of degradation from my true station in society, I wandered among the hills of civilized England as uncouth a savage as the wolf-bred founder of old Rome. I owned but one law, it was that of the strongest, and my greatest deed of virtue was never to submit.

Yet let me a little retract from this sentence I have passed on myself. My mother, when dying, had, in addition to her other half-forgotten and misapplied lessons, committed, with solemn exhortation, her other child to my fraternal guardianship; and this one duty I performed to the best of my ability, with all the zeal and affection of which my nature was capable. My sister was three years younger than myself; I had nursed her as an infant, and when the difference of our sexes, by giving us various occupations, in a great measure divided us, yet she continued to be the object of my careful love. Orphans, in the fullest sense of the term, we were poorest among the poor, and despised among the unhonoured. If my daring and courage obtained for me a kind of respectful aversion, her youth and sex, since they did not excite tenderness, by proving her to be weak, were the causes of numberless mortifications to her; and her own disposition was not so constituted as to diminish the evil effects of her lowly station.

She was a singular being, and, like me, inherited much of the peculiar disposition of our father. Her countenance was all expression; her eyes were not dark, but impenetrably deep; you seemed to discover space after space in their intellectual glance, and to feel that the soul which was their soul, comprehended an universe of thought in its ken. She was pale and fair, and her golden hair clustered on her temples, contrasting its rich hue with the living marble beneath. Her coarse peasant-dress, little consonant apparently with the refinement of feeling which her face expressed, yet in a strange manner accorded with it. She was like one of Guido's saints, with heaven in her heart and in her look, so that when you saw her you only thought of that within, and costume and even feature were secondary to the mind that beamed in her countenance.

Yet though lovely and full of noble feeling, my poor Perdita (for this was the fanciful name my sister had received from her dying parent), was not altogether saintly in her disposition. Her manners were cold and repulsive. If she had been nurtured by those who had regarded her with affection, she might have been different; but unloved and neglected, she repaid want of kindness with distrust and silence. She was submissive to those who held authority over her, but a perpetual cloud dwelt on her brow; she looked as if she expected enmity from every one who approached her, and her actions were instigated by the same feeling. All the time she could command she spent in solitude. She would ramble to the most unfrequented places, and scale dangerous heights, that in those unvisited spots she might wrap herself in loneliness. Often she passed whole hours walking up and down the paths of the woods; she wove garlands of flowers and ivy, or watched the flickering of the shadows and glancing of the leaves; sometimes she sat beside a stream, and as her thoughts paused, threw flowers or pebbles into the waters, watching how those swam and these sank; or she would set afloat boats formed of bark of trees or leaves, with a feather for a sail, and intensely watch the navigation of her craft among the rapids and shallows of the brook. Meanwhile her active fancy wove a thousand combinations; she dreamt "of moving accidents by flood and field"—she lost herself delightedly in these self-created wanderings, and returned with unwilling spirit to the dull detail of common life.

Poverty was the cloud that veiled her excellencies, and all that was good in her seemed about to perish from want of the genial dew of affection. She had not even the same advantage as I in the recollection of her parents; she clung to me, her brother, as her only friend, but her alliance with me completed the distaste that her protectors felt for her; and every error was magnified by them into crimes. If she had been bred in that sphere of life to which by inheritance the delicate framework of her mind and person was adapted, she would have been the object almost of adoration, for her virtues were as eminent as her defects. All the genius that ennobled the blood of her father illustrated hers; a generous tide flowed in her veins; artifice, envy, or meanness, were at the antipodes of her nature; her countenance, when enlightened by amiable feeling, might have belonged to a queen of nations; her eyes were bright; her look fearless.

Although by our situation and dispositions we were almost equally cut off from the usual forms of social intercourse, we formed a strong contrast to each other. I always required the stimulants of companionship and applause. Perdita was all-sufficient to herself. Notwithstanding my lawless habits, my disposition was sociable, hers recluse. My life was spent among tangible realities, hers was a dream. I might be said even to love my enemies, since by exciting me they in a sort bestowed happiness upon me; Perdita almost disliked her friends, for they interfered with her visionary moods. All my feelings, even of exultation and triumph, were changed to bitterness, if unparticipated; Perdita, even in joy, fled to loneliness, and could go on from day to day, neither expressing her emotions, nor seeking a fellow-feeling in another mind. Nay, she could love and dwell with tenderness on the look and voice of her friend, while her demeanour expressed the coldest reserve. A sensation with her became a sentiment, and she never spoke until she had mingled her perceptions of outward objects with others which were the native growth of her own mind. She was like a fruitful soil that imbibed the airs and dews of heaven, and gave them forth again to light in loveliest forms of fruits and flowers; but then she was often dark and rugged as that soil, raked up, and new sown with unseen seed.

She dwelt in a cottage whose trim grass-plat sloped down to the waters of the lake of Ulswater; a beech wood stretched up the hill behind, and a purling brook gently falling from the acclivity ran through poplar-shaded banks into the lake. I lived with a farmer whose house was built higher up among the hills: a dark crag rose behind it, and, exposed to the north, the snow lay in its crevices the summer through. Before dawn I led my flock to the sheep-walks, and guarded them through the day. It was a life of toil; for rain and cold were more frequent than sunshine; but it was my pride to contemn the elements. My trusty dog watched the sheep as I slipped away to the rendezvous of my comrades, and thence to the accomplishment of our schemes. At noon we met again, and we threw away in contempt our peasant fare, as we built our fire-place and kindled the cheering blaze destined to cook the game stolen from the neighbouring preserves. Then came the tale of hair-breadth escapes, combats with dogs, ambush and flight, as gipsey-like we encompassed our pot. The search after a stray lamb, or the devices by which we elude or endeavoured to elude punishment, filled up the hours of afternoon; in the evening my flock went to its fold, and I to my sister.

It was seldom indeed that we escaped, to use an old-fashioned phrase, scot free. Our dainty fare was often exchanged for blows and imprisonment. Once, when thirteen years of age, I was sent for a month to the county jail. I came out, my morals unimproved, my hatred to my oppressors encreased tenfold. Bread and water did not tame my blood, nor solitary confinement inspire me with gentle thoughts. I was angry, impatient, miserable; my only happy hours were those during which I devised schemes of revenge; these were perfected in my forced solitude, so that during the whole of the following season, and I was freed early in September, I never failed to provide excellent and plenteous fare for myself and my comrades. This was a glorious winter. The sharp frost and heavy snows tamed the animals, and kept the country gentlemen by their firesides; we got more game than we could eat, and my faithful dog grew sleek upon our refuse.

Thus years passed on; and years only added fresh love of freedom, and contempt for all that was not as wild and rude as myself. At the age of sixteen I had shot up in appearance to man's estate; I was tall and athletic; I was practised to feats of strength, and inured to the inclemency of the elements. My skin was embrowned by the sun; my step was firm with conscious power. I feared no man, and loved none. In after life I looked back with wonder to what I then was; how utterly worthless I should have become if I had pursued my lawless career. My life was like that of an animal, and my mind was in danger of degenerating into that which informs brute nature. Until now, my savage habits had done me no radical mischief; my physical powers had grown up and flourished under their influence, and my mind, undergoing the same discipline, was imbued with all the hardy virtues. But now my boasted independence was daily instigating me to acts of tyranny, and freedom was becoming licentiousness. I stood on the brink of manhood; passions, strong as the trees of a forest, had already taken root within me, and were about to shadow with their noxious overgrowth, my path of life.

I panted for enterprises beyond my childish exploits, and formed distempered dreams of future action. I avoided my ancient comrades, and I soon lost them. They arrived at the age when they were sent to fulfil their destined situations in life; while I, an outcast, with none to lead or drive me forward, paused. The old began to point at me as an example, the young to wonder at me as a being distinct from themselves; I hated them, and began, last and worst degradation, to hate myself. I clung to my ferocious habits, yet half despised them; I continued my war against civilization, and yet entertained a wish to belong to it.

I revolved again and again all that I remembered my mother to have told me of my father's former life; I contemplated the few relics I possessed belonging to him, which spoke of greater refinement than could be found among the mountain cottages; but nothing in all this served as a guide to lead me to another and pleasanter way of life. My father had been connected with nobles, but all I knew of such connection was subsequent neglect. The name of the king,—he to whom my dying father had addressed his latest prayers, and who had barbarously slighted them, was associated only with the ideas of unkindness, injustice, and consequent resentment. I was born for something greater than I was—and greater I would become; but greatness, at least to my distorted perceptions, was no necessary associate of goodness, and my wild thoughts were unchecked by moral considerations when they rioted in dreams of distinction. Thus I stood upon a pinnacle, a sea of evil rolled at my feet; I was about to precipitate myself into it, and rush like a torrent over all obstructions to the object of my wishes—when a stranger influence came over the current of my fortunes, and changed their boisterous course to what was in comparison like the gentle meanderings of a meadow-encircling streamlet.

Chapter II

I LIVED FAR from the busy haunts of men, and the rumour of wars or political changes came worn to a mere sound, to our mountain abodes. England had been the scene of momentous struggles, during my early boyhood. In the year 2073, the last of its kings, the ancient friend of my father, had abdicated in compliance with the gentle force of the remonstrances of his subjects, and a republic was instituted. Large estates were secured to the dethroned monarch and his family; he received the title of Earl of Windsor, and Windsor Castle, an ancient royalty, with its wide demesnes were a part of his allotted wealth. He died soon after, leaving two children, a son and a daughter.

The ex-queen, a princess of the house of Austria, had long impelled her husband to withstand the necessity of the times. She was haughty and fearless; she cherished a love of power, and a bitter contempt for him who had despoiled himself of a kingdom. For her children's sake alone she consented to remain, shorn of regality, a member of the English republic. When she became a widow, she turned all her thoughts to the educating her son Adrian, second Earl of Windsor, so as to accomplish her ambitious ends; and with his mother's milk he imbibed, and was intended to grow up in the steady purpose of re-acquiring his lost crown. Adrian was now fifteen years of age. He was addicted to study, and imbued beyond his years with learning and talent: report said that he had already begun to thwart his mother's views, and to entertain republican principles. However this might be, the haughty Countess entrusted none with the secrets of her family-tuition. Adrian was bred up in solitude, and kept apart from the natural companions of his age and rank. Some unknown circumstance now induced his mother to send him from under her immediate tutelage; and we heard that he was about to visit Cumberland. A thousand tales were rife, explanatory of the Countess of Windsor's conduct; none true probably; but each day it became more certain that we should have the noble scion of the late regal house of England among us.

There was a large estate with a mansion attached to it, belonging to this family, at Ulswater. A large park was one of its appendages, laid out with great taste, and plentifully stocked with game. I had often made depredations on these preserves; and the neglected state of the property facilitated my incursions. When it was decided that the young Earl of Windsor should visit Cumberland, workmen arrived to put the house and grounds in order for his reception. The apartments were restored to their pristine splendour, and the park, all disrepairs restored, was guarded with unusual care.

I was beyond measure disturbed by this intelligence. It roused all my dormant recollections, my suspended sentiments of injury, and gave rise to the new one of revenge. I could no longer attend to my occupations; all my plans and devices were forgotten; I seemed about to begin life anew, and that under no good auspices. The tug of war, I thought, was now to begin. He would come triumphantly to the district to which my parent had fled broken-hearted; he would find the ill-fated offspring, bequeathed with such vain confidence to his royal father, miserable paupers. That he should know of our existence, and treat us, near at hand, with the same contumely which his father had practised in distance and absence, appeared to me the certain consequence of all that had gone before. Thus then I should meet this titled stripling—the son of my father's friend. He would be hedged in by servants; nobles, and the sons of nobles, were his companions; all England rang with his name; and his coming, like a thunderstorm, was heard from far: while I, unlettered and unfashioned, should, if I came in contact with him, in the judgment of his courtly followers, bear evidence in my very person to the propriety of that ingratitude which had made me the degraded being I appeared.

With my mind fully occupied by these ideas, I might be said as if fascinated, to haunt the destined abode of the young Earl. I watched the progress of the improvements, and stood by the unlading waggons, as various articles of luxury, brought from London, were taken forth and conveyed into the mansion. It was part of the Ex-Queen's plan, to surround her son with princely magnificence. I beheld rich carpets and silken hangings, ornaments of gold, richly embossed metals, emblazoned furniture, and all the appendages of high rank arranged, so that nothing but what was regal in splendour should reach the eye of one of royal descent. I looked on these; I turned my gaze to my own mean dress.—Whence sprung this difference? Whence but from ingratitude, from falsehood, from a dereliction on the part of the prince's father, of all noble sympathy and generous feeling. Doubtless, he also, whose blood received a mingling tide from his proud mother—he, the acknowledged focus of the kingdom's wealth and nobility, had been taught to repeat my father's name with disdain, and to scoff at my just claims to protection. I strove to think that all this grandeur was but more glaring infamy, and that, by planting his gold-enwoven flag beside my tarnished and tattered banner, he proclaimed not his superiority, but his debasement. Yet I envied him. His stud of beautiful horses, his arms of costly workmanship, the praise that attended him, the adoration, ready servitor, high place and high esteem,—I considered them as forcibly wrenched from me, and envied them all with novel and tormenting bitterness.

To crown my vexation of spirit, Perdita, the visionary Perdita, seemed to awake to real life with transport, when she told me that the Earl of Windsor was about to arrive.

"And this pleases you?" I observed, moodily.

"Indeed it does, Lionel," she replied; "I quite long to see him; he is the descendant of our kings, the first noble of the land: every one admires and loves him, and they say that his rank is his least merit; he is generous, brave, and affable."

"You have learnt a pretty lesson, Perdita," said I, "and repeat it so literally, that you forget the while the proofs we have of the Earl's virtues; his generosity to us is manifest in our plenty, his bravery in the protection he affords us, his affability in the notice he takes of us. His rank his least merit, do you say? Why, all his virtues are derived from his station only; because he is rich, he is called generous; because he is powerful, brave; because he is well served, he is affable. Let them call him so, let all England believe him to be thus—we know him—he is our enemy—our penurious, dastardly, arrogant enemy; if he were gifted with one particle of the virtues you call his, he would do justly by us, if it were only to shew, that if he must strike, it should not be a fallen foe. His father injured my father—his father, unassailable on his throne, dared despise him who only stooped beneath himself, when he deigned to associate with the royal ingrate. We, descendants from the one and the other, must be enemies also. He shall find that I can feel my injuries; he shall learn to dread my revenge!"

A few days after he arrived. Every inhabitant of the most miserable cottage, went to swell the stream of population that poured forth to meet him: even Perdita, in spite of my late philippic, crept near the highway, to behold this idol of all hearts. I, driven half mad, as I met party after party of the country people, in their holiday best, descending the hills, escaped to their cloud-veiled summits, and looking on the sterile rocks about me, exclaimed—"*They* do not cry, long live the Earl!" Nor, when night came, accompanied by drizzling rain and cold, would I return home; for I knew that each cottage rang with the praises of Adrian; as I felt my limbs grow numb and chill, my pain served as food for my insane aversion; nay, I almost triumphed in it, since it seemed to afford me reason and excuse for my hatred of my unheeding adversary. All was attributed to him, for I confounded so entirely the idea of father and son, that I forgot that the latter might be wholly unconscious of his parent's neglect of us; and as I struck my aching head with my hand, I cried: "He shall hear of this! I will be revenged! I will not suffer like a spaniel! He shall know, beggar and friendless as I am, that I will not tamely submit to injury!"

Each day, each hour added to these exaggerated wrongs. His praises were so many adder's stings infixed in my vulnerable breast. If I saw him at a distance, riding a beautiful horse, my blood boiled with rage; the air seemed poisoned by his presence, and my very native English was changed to a vile jargon, since every phrase I heard was coupled with his name and honour. I panted to relieve this painful heart-burning by some misdeed that should rouse him to a sense of my antipathy. It was the height of his offending, that he should occasion in me such intolerable sensations, and not deign himself to afford any demonstration that he was aware that I even lived to feel them.

It soon became known that Adrian took great delight in his park and preserves. He never sported, but spent hours in watching the tribes of lovely and almost tame animals with which it was stocked, and ordered that greater care should be taken of them than ever. Here was an opening for my plans of offence, and I made use of it with all the brute impetuosity I derived from my active mode of life. I proposed the enterprize of poaching on his demesne to my few remaining comrades, who were the most determined and lawless of the crew; but they all shrunk from the peril; so I was left to achieve my revenge myself. At first my exploits were unperceived; I increased in daring; footsteps on the dewy grass, torn boughs, and marks of slaughter, at length betrayed me to the gamekeepers. They kept better watch; I was taken, and sent to prison. I entered its gloomy walls in a fit of triumphant extasy: "He feels me now," I cried, "and shall, again and again!"—I passed but one day in confinement; in the evening I was liberated, as I was told, by the order of the Earl himself. This news precipitated me from my self-raised pinnacle of honour. He despises me, I thought; but he shall learn that I despise him, and hold in equal contempt his punishments and his clemency. On the second night after my release, I was again taken by the gamekeepers—again imprisoned, and again released; and again, such was my pertinacity, did the fourth night find me in the forbidden park. The gamekeepers were more enraged than their lord by my obstinacy. They had received orders that if I were again taken, I should be brought to the Earl; and his lenity made them expect a conclusion which they considered ill befitting my crime. One of them, who had been from the first the leader among those who had seized me, resolved to satisfy his own resentment, before he made me over to the higher powers.

The late setting of the moon, and the extreme caution I was obliged to use in this my third expedition, consumed so much time, that something like a qualm of fear came over me when I perceived dark night yield to twilight. I crept along by the fern, on my hands and knees, seeking the shadowy coverts of the underwood, while the birds awoke with unwelcome song above, and the fresh morning wind, playing among the boughs, made me suspect a footfall at each turn. My heart beat quick as I approached the palings; my hand was on one of them, a leap would take me to the other side, when two keepers sprang from an ambush upon me: one knocked me down, and proceeded to inflict a severe horse-whipping. I started up—a knife was in my grasp; I made a plunge at his raised right arm, and inflicted a deep, wide wound in his hand. The rage and yells of the wounded man, the howling execrations of his comrade, which I answered with equal bitterness and fury, echoed through the dell; morning broke more and more, ill accordant in its celestial beauty with our brute and noisy contest. I and my enemy were still struggling, when the wounded man exclaimed,

"The Earl!" I sprang out of the herculean hold of the keeper, panting from my exertions; I cast furious glances on my persecutors, and placing myself with my back to a tree, resolved to defend myself to the last. My garments were torn, and they, as well as my hands, were stained with the blood of the man I had wounded; one hand grasped the dead birds—my hard-earned prey, the other held the knife; my hair was matted; my face besmeared with the same guilty signs that bore witness against me on the dripping instrument I clenched; my whole appearance was haggard and squalid. Tall and muscular as I was in form, I must have looked like, what indeed I was, the merest ruffian that ever trod the earth.

The name of the Earl startled me, and caused all the indignant blood that warmed my heart to rush into my cheeks; I had never seen him before; I figured to myself a haughty, assuming youth, who would take me to task, if he deigned to speak to me, with all the arrogance of superiority. My reply was ready; a reproach I deemed calculated to sting his very heart. He came up the while; and his appearance blew aside, with gentle western breath, my cloudy wrath: a tall, slim, fair boy, with a physiognomy expressive of the excess of sensibility and refinement stood before me; the morning sunbeams tinged with gold his silken hair, and spread light and glory over his beaming countenance. "How is this?" he cried. The men eagerly began their defence; he put them aside, saying, "Two of you at once on a mere lad—for shame!" He came up to me: "Verney," he cried, "Lionel Verney, do we meet thus for the first time? We were born to be friends to each other; and though ill fortune has divided us, will you not acknowledge the hereditary bond of friendship which I trust will hereafter unite us?"

As he spoke, his earnest eyes, fixed on me, seemed to read my very soul: my heart, my savage revengeful heart, felt the influence of sweet benignity sink upon it; while his thrilling voice, like sweetest melody, awoke a mute echo within me, stirring to its depths the life-blood in my frame. I desired to reply, to acknowledge his goodness, accept his proffered friendship; but words, fitting words, were not afforded to the rough mountaineer; I would have held out my hand, but its guilty stain restrained me. Adrian took pity on my faltering mien: "Come with me," he said, "I have much to say to you; come home with me—you know who I am?"

"Yes," I exclaimed, "I do believe that I now know you, and that you will pardon my mistakes—my crime."

Adrian smiled gently; and after giving his orders to the gamekeepers, he came up to me; putting his arm in mine, we walked together to the mansion.

It was not his rank—after all that I have said, surely it will not be suspected that it was Adrian's rank, that, from the first, subdued my heart of hearts, and laid my entire spirit prostrate before him. Nor was it I alone who felt thus intimately his perfections, his sensibility and courtesy fascinated every one. His vivacity, intelligence, and active spirit of benevolence, completed the conquest. Even at this early age, he was deep read and imbued with the spirit of high philosophy. This spirit gave a tone of irresistible persuasion to his intercourse with others, so that he seemed like an inspired musician, who struck, with unerring skill, the "lyre of mind," and produced thence divine harmony. In person, he hardly appeared of this world; his slight frame was overinformed by the soul that dwelt within; he was all mind; "Man but a rush against" his breast, and it would have conquered his strength; but the might of his smile would have tamed an hungry lion, or caused a legion of armed men to lay their weapons at his feet.

I spent the day with him. At first he did not recur to the past, or indeed to any personal occurrences. He wished probably to inspire me with confidence, and give me time to gather together my scattered thoughts. He talked of general subjects, and gave me ideas I had never before conceived. We sat in his library, and he spoke of the old Greek sages, and of the power which they had acquired over the minds of men, through the force of love and wisdom only. The room was decorated with the busts of many of them, and he described their characters to me. As he spoke, I felt subject to him; and all my boasted pride and strength were subdued by the honeyed accents of this blue-eyed boy. The trim and paled demesne of civilization, which I had before regarded from my wild jungle as inaccessible, had its wicket opened by him; I stepped within, and felt, as I entered, that I trod my native soil.

As evening came on, he reverted to the past. "I have a tale to relate," he said, "and much explanation to give concerning the past; perhaps you can assist me to curtail it. Do you remember your father? I had never the happiness of seeing him, but his name is one of my earliest recollections: he stands written in my mind's tablets as the type of all that was gallant, amiable, and fascinating in man. His wit was not more conspicuous than the overflowing goodness of his heart, which he poured in such full measure on his friends, as to leave, alas! small remnant for himself."

Encouraged by this encomium, I proceeded, in answer to his inquiries, to relate what I remembered of my parent; and he gave an account of those circumstances which had brought about a neglect of my father's testamentary letter. When, in after times, Adrian's father, then king of England, felt his situation become more perilous, his line of conduct more embarrassed, again and again he wished for his early friend, who might stand a mound against the impetuous anger of his queen, a mediator between him and the parliament. From the time that he had quitted London, on the fatal night of his defeat at the gaming-table, the king had received no tidings concerning him; and when, after the lapse of years, he exerted himself to discover him, every trace was lost. With fonder regret than ever, he clung to his memory; and gave it in charge to his son, if ever he should meet this valued friend, in his name to bestow every succour, and to assure him that, to the last, his attachment survived separation and silence.

A short time before Adrian's visit to Cumberland, the heir of the nobleman to whom my father had confided his last appeal to his royal master, put this letter, its seal unbroken, into the young Earl's hands. It had been found cast aside with a mass of papers of old date, and accident alone brought it to light. Adrian read it with deep interest; and found there that living spirit of genius and wit he had so often heard commemorated. He discovered the name of the spot whither my father had retreated, and where he died; he learnt the existence of his orphan children; and during the short interval between his arrival at Ulswater and our meeting in the park, he had been occupied in making inquiries concerning us, and arranging a variety of plans for our benefit, preliminary to his introducing himself to our notice.

The mode in which he spoke of my father was gratifying to my vanity; the veil which he delicately cast over his benevolence, in alledging a duteous fulfilment of the king's latest will, was soothing to my pride. Other feelings, less ambiguous, were called into play by his conciliating manner and the generous warmth of his expressions, respect rarely before experienced, admiration, and love—he had touched my rocky heart with his magic power, and the stream of affection gushed forth, imperishable and pure. In the evening we parted; he pressed my hand: "We shall meet again; come to me to-morrow." I clasped that kind hand; I tried to answer; a fervent "God bless you!" was all my ignorance could frame of speech, and I darted away, oppressed by my new emotions.

I could not rest. I sought the hills; a west wind swept them, and the stars glittered above. I ran on, careless of outward objects, but trying to master the struggling spirit within me by means of bodily fatigue. "This," I thought, "is power! Not to be strong of limb, hard of heart, ferocious, and daring; but kind, compassionate and soft."—Stopping short, I clasped my hands, and with the fervour of a new proselyte, cried, "Doubt me not, Adrian, I also will become wise and good!" and then quite overcome, I wept aloud.

As this gust of passion passed from me, I felt more composed. I lay on the ground, and giving the reins to my thoughts, repassed in my mind my former life; and began, fold by fold, to unwind the many errors of my heart, and to discover how brutish, savage, and worthless I had hitherto been. I could not however at that time feel remorse, for methought I was born anew; my soul threw off the burthen of past sin, to commence a new career in innocence and love. Nothing harsh or rough remained to jar with the soft feelings which the transactions of the day had inspired; I was as a child lisping its devotions after its mother, and my plastic soul was remoulded by a master hand, which I neither desired nor was able to resist.

This was the first commencement of my friendship with Adrian, and I must commemorate this day as the most fortunate of my life. I now began to be human. I was admitted within that sacred boundary which divides the intellectual and moral nature of man from that which characterizes animals. My best feelings were called into play to give fitting responses to the generosity, wisdom, and amenity of my new friend. He, with a noble goodness all his own, took infinite delight in bestowing to prodigality the treasures of his mind and fortune on the long-neglected son of his father's friend, the offspring of that gifted being whose excellencies and talents he had heard commemorated from infancy.

After his abdication the late king had retreated from the sphere of politics, yet his domestic circle afforded him small content. The ex-queen had none of the virtues of domestic life, and those of courage and daring which she possessed were rendered null by the secession of her husband: she despised him, and did not care to conceal her sentiments. The king had, in compliance with her exactions, cast off his old friends, but he had acquired no new ones under her guidance. In this dearth of sympathy, he had recourse to his almost infant son; and the early development of talent and sensibility rendered Adrian no unfitting depository of his father's confidence. He was never weary of listening to the latter's often repeated accounts of old times, in which my father had played a distinguished part; his keen remarks were repeated to the boy, and remembered by him; his wit, his fascinations, his very faults were hallowed by the regret of affection; his loss was sincerely deplored. Even the queen's dislike of the favourite was ineffectual to deprive him of his son's admiration: it was bitter, sarcastic, contemptuous—but as she bestowed her heavy censure alike on his virtues as his errors, on his devoted friendship and his ill-bestowed loves, on his disinterestedness and his prodigality, on his pre-possessing grace of manner, and the facility with which he yielded to temptation, her double shot proved too heavy, and fell short of the mark. Nor did her angry dislike prevent Adrian from imaging my father, as he had said, the type of all that was gallant, amiable, and fascinating in man. It was not strange therefore, that when he heard of the existence of the offspring of this celebrated person, he should have formed the plan of bestowing on them all the advantages his rank made him rich to afford. When he found me a vagabond shepherd of the hills, a poacher, an unlettered savage, still his kindness did not fail. In addition to the opinion he entertained that his father was to a degree culpable of neglect towards us, and that he was bound to every possible reparation, he was pleased to say that under all my ruggedness there glimmered forth an elevation of spirit, which could be distinguished from mere animal courage, and that I inherited a similarity of countenance to my father, which gave proof that all his virtues and talents had not died with him. Whatever those might be which descended to me, my noble young friend resolved should not be lost for want of culture.

Acting upon this plan in our subsequent intercourse, he led me to wish to participate in that cultivation which graced his own intellect. My active mind, when once it seized upon this new idea, fastened on it with extreme avidity. At first it was the great object of my ambition to rival the merits of my father, and render myself worthy of the friendship of Adrian. But curiosity soon awoke, and an earnest love of knowledge, which caused me to pass days and nights in reading and study. I was already well acquainted with what I may term the panorama of nature, the change of seasons, and the various appearances of heaven and earth. But I was at once startled and enchanted by my sudden extension of vision, when the curtain, which had been drawn before the intellectual world, was withdrawn, and I saw the universe, not only as it presented itself to my outward senses, but as it had appeared to the wisest among men. Poetry and its creations, philosophy and its researches and classifications, alike awoke the sleeping ideas in my mind, and gave me new ones.

I felt as the sailor, who from the topmast first discovered the shore of America; and like him I hastened to tell my companions of my discoveries in unknown regions. But I was unable to excite in any breast the same craving appetite for knowledge that existed in mine. Even Perdita was unable to understand me. I had lived in what is generally called the world of reality, and it was awakening to a new country to find that there was a deeper meaning in all I saw, besides that which my eyes conveyed to me. The visionary Perdita beheld in all this only a new gloss upon an old reading, and her own was sufficiently inexhaustible to content her. She listened to me as she had done to the narration of my adventures, and sometimes took an interest in this species of information; but she did not, as I did, look on it as an integral part of her being, which having obtained, I could no more put off than the universal sense of touch.

We both agreed in loving Adrian: although she not having yet escaped from childhood could not appreciate as I did the extent of his merits, or feel the same sympathy in his pursuits and opinions. I was for ever with him. There was a sensibility and sweetness in his disposition, that gave a tender and unearthly tone to our converse. Then he was gay as a lark carolling from its skiey tower, soaring in thought as an eagle, innocent as the mild-eyed dove. He could dispel the seriousness of Perdita, and take the sting from the torturing activity of my nature. I looked back to my restless desires and painful struggles with my fellow beings as to a troubled dream, and felt myself as much changed as if I had transmigrated into another form, whose fresh sensorium and mechanism of nerves had altered the reflection of the apparent universe in the mirror of mind. But it was not so; I was the same in strength, in earnest craving for sympathy, in my yearning for active exertion. My manly virtues did not desert me, for the witch Urania spared the locks of Sampson, while he reposed at her feet; but all was softened and humanized. Nor did Adrian instruct me only in the cold truths of history and philosophy. At the same time that he taught me by their means to subdue my own reckless and uncultured spirit, he opened to my view the living page of his own heart, and gave me to feel and understand its wondrous character.

The ex-queen of England had, even during infancy, endeavoured to implant daring and ambitious designs in the mind of her son. She saw that he was endowed with genius and surpassing talent; these she cultivated for the sake of afterwards using them for the furtherance of her own views. She encouraged his craving for knowledge and his impetuous courage; she even tolerated his tameless love of freedom, under the hope that this would, as is too often the case, lead to a passion for command. She endeavoured to bring him up in a sense of resentment towards, and a desire to revenge himself upon, those who had been instrumental in bringing about his father's abdication. In this she did not succeed. The accounts furnished him, however distorted, of a great and wise nation asserting its right to govern itself, excited his admiration: in early days he became a republican from principle. Still his mother did not despair. To the love of rule and haughty pride of birth she added determined ambition, patience, and self-control. She devoted herself to the study of her son's disposition. By the application of praise, censure, and exhortation, she tried to seek and strike the fitting chords; and though the melody that followed her touch seemed discord to her, she built her hopes on his talents, and felt sure that she would at last win him. The kind of banishment he now experienced arose from other causes.

The ex-queen had also a daughter, now twelve years of age; his fairy sister, Adrian was wont to call her; a lovely, animated, little thing, all sensibility and truth. With these, her children, the noble widow constantly resided at Windsor; and admitted no visitors, except her own partizans, travellers from her native Germany, and a few of the foreign ministers. Among these, and highly distinguished by her, was Prince Zaimi, ambassador to England from the free States of Greece; and his daughter, the young Princess Evadne, passed much of her time at Windsor Castle. In company with this sprightly and clever Greek girl, the Countess would relax from her usual state. Her views with regard to her own children, placed all her words and actions relative to *them* under restraint: but Evadne was a plaything she could in no way fear; nor were her talents and vivacity slight alleviations to the monotony of the Countess's life.

Evadne was eighteen years of age. Although they spent much time together at Windsor, the extreme youth of Adrian prevented any suspicion as to the nature of their intercourse. But he was ardent and tender of heart beyond the common nature of man, and had already learnt to love, while the beauteous Greek smiled benignantly on the boy. It was strange to me, who, though older than Adrian, had never loved, to witness the whole heart's sacrifice of my friend. There was neither jealousy, inquietude, or mistrust in his sentiment; it was devotion and faith. His life was swallowed up in the existence of his beloved; and his heart beat only in unison with the pulsations that vivified hers. This was the secret law of his life—he loved and was beloved. The universe was to him a dwelling, to inhabit with his chosen one; and not either a scheme of society or an enchainment of events, that could impact to him either happiness or misery. What, though life and the system of social intercourse were a wilderness, a tiger-haunted jungle! Through the midst of its errors, in the depths of its savage recesses, there was a disentangled and flowery pathway, through which they might journey in safety and delight. Their track would be like the passage of the Red Sea, which they might traverse with unwet feet, though a wall of destruction were impending on either side.

Alas! why must I record the hapless delusion of this matchless specimen of humanity? What is there in our nature that is for ever urging us on towards pain and misery? We are not formed for enjoyment; and, however we may be attuned to the reception of pleasureable emotion, disappointment is the never-failing pilot of our life's bark, and ruthlessly carries us on to the shoals. Who was better framed than this highly-gifted youth to love and be beloved, and to reap unalienable joy from an unblamed passion? If his heart had slept but a few years longer, he might have been saved; but it awoke in its infancy; it had power, but no knowledge; and it was ruined, even as a too early-blowing bud is nipt by the killing frost.

I did not accuse Evadne of hypocrisy or a wish to deceive her lover; but the first letter that I saw of hers convinced me that she did not love him; it was written with elegance, and, foreigner as she was, with great command of language. The hand-writing itself was exquisitely beautiful; there was something in her very paper and its folds, which even I, who did not love, and was withal unskilled in such matters, could discern as being tasteful. There was much kindness, gratitude, and sweetness in her expression, but no love. Evadne was two years older than Adrian; and who, at eighteen, ever loved one so much their junior? I compared her placid epistles with the burning ones of Adrian. His soul seemed to distil itself into the words he wrote; and they breathed on the paper, bearing with them a portion of the life of love, which was his life. The very writing used to exhaust him; and he would weep over them, merely from the excess of emotion they awakened in his heart.

Adrian's soul was painted in his countenance, and concealment or deceit were at the antipodes to the dreadless frankness of his nature. Evadne made it her earnest request that the tale of their loves should not be revealed to his mother; and after for a while contesting the point, he yielded it to her. A vain concession; his demeanour quickly betrayed his secret to the quick eyes of the ex-queen. With the same wary prudence that characterized her whole conduct, she concealed her discovery, but hastened to remove her son from the sphere of the attractive Greek. He was sent to Cumberland; but the plan of correspondence between the lovers, arranged by Evadne, was effectually hidden from her. Thus the absence of Adrian, concerted for the purpose of separating, united them in firmer bonds than ever. To me he discoursed ceaselessly of his beloved Ionian. Her country, its ancient annals, its late memorable struggles, were all made to partake in her glory and excellence. He submitted to be away from her, because she commanded this submission; but for her influence, he would have declared his attachment before all England, and resisted, with unshaken constancy, his mother's opposition. Evadne's feminine prudence perceived how useless any assertion of his resolves would be, till added years gave weight to his power. Perhaps there was besides a lurking dislike to bind herself in the face of the world to one whom she did not love—not love, at least, with that passionate enthusiasm which her heart told her she might one day feel towards another. He obeyed her injunctions, and passed a year in exile in Cumberland.

Chapter III

HAPPY, THRICE HAPPY, were the months, and weeks, and hours of that year. Friendship, hand in hand with admiration, tenderness and respect, built a bower of delight in my heart, late rough as an untrod wild in America, as the homeless wind or herbless sea. Insatiate thirst for knowledge, and boundless affection for Adrian, combined to keep both my heart and understanding occupied, and I was consequently happy. What happiness is so true and unclouded, as the overflowing and talkative delight of young people. In our boat, upon my native lake, beside the streams and the pale bordering poplars—in valley and over hill, my crook thrown aside, a nobler flock to tend than silly sheep, even a flock of new-born ideas, I read or listened to Adrian; and his discourse, whether it concerned his love or his theories for the improvement of man, alike entranced me. Sometimes my lawless mood would return, my love of peril, my resistance to authority; but this was in his absence; under the mild sway of his dear eyes, I was obedient and good as a boy of five years old, who does his mother's bidding. After a residence of about a year at Ulswater, Adrian visited London, and came back full of plans for our benefit. You must begin life, he said: you are seventeen, and longer delay would render the necessary apprenticeship more and more irksome. He foresaw that his own life would be one of struggle, and I must partake his labours with him. The better to fit me for this task, we must now separate. He found my name a good passport to preferment, and he had procured for me the situation of private secretary to the Ambassador at Vienna, where I should enter on my career under the best auspices. In two years, I should return to my country, with a name well known and a reputation already founded.

And Perdita?—Perdita was to become the pupil, friend and younger sister of Evadne. With his usual thoughtfulness, he had provided for her independence in this situation. How refuse the offers of this generous friend?—I did not wish to refuse them; but in my heart of hearts, I made a vow to devote life, knowledge, and power, all of which, in as much as they were of any value, he had bestowed on me—all, all my capacities and hopes, to him alone I would devote.

Thus I promised myself, as I journied towards my destination with roused and ardent expectation: expectation of the fulfilment of all that in boyhood we promise ourselves of power and enjoyment in maturity. Methought the time was now arrived, when, childish occupations laid aside, I should enter into life. Even in the Elysian fields, Virgil describes the souls of the happy as eager to drink of the wave which was to restore them to this mortal coil. The young are seldom in Elysium, for their desires, outstripping possibility, leave them as poor as a moneyless debtor. We are told by the wisest philosophers of the dangers of the world, the deceits of men, and the treason of our own hearts: but not the less fearlessly does each put off his frail bark from the port, spread the sail, and strain his oar, to attain the multitudinous streams of the sea of life. How few in youth's prime, moor their vessels on the "golden sands," and collect the painted shells that strew them. But all at close of day, with riven planks and rent canvas make for shore, and are either wrecked ere they reach it, or find some wave-beaten haven, some desart strand, whereon to cast themselves and die unmourned.

A truce to philosophy!—Life is before me, and I rush into possession. Hope, glory, love, and blameless ambition are my guides, and my soul knows no dread. What has been, though sweet, is gone; the present is good only because it is about to change, and the to come is all my own. Do I fear, that my heart palpitates? high aspirations cause the flow of my blood; my eyes seem to penetrate the cloudy midnight of time, and to discern within the depths of its darkness, the fruition of all my soul desires.

Now pause!—During my journey I might dream, and with buoyant wings reach the summit of life's high edifice. Now that I am arrived at its base, my pinions are furled, the mighty stairs are before me, and step by step I must ascend the wondrous fane—

Speak!—What door is opened?

Behold me in a new capacity. A diplomatist: one among the pleasure-seeking society of a gay city; a youth of promise; favourite of the Ambassador. All was strange and admirable to the shepherd of Cumberland. With breathless amaze I entered on the gay scene, whose actors were

—— the lilies glorious as Solomon,
Who toil not, neither do they spin.

Soon, too soon, I entered the giddy whirl; forgetting my studious hours, and the companionship of Adrian. Passionate desire of sympathy, and ardent pursuit for a wished-for object still characterized me. The sight of beauty entranced me, and attractive manners in man or woman won my entire confidence. I called it rapture, when a smile made my heart beat; and I felt the life's blood tingle in my frame, when I approached the idol which for awhile I worshipped. The mere flow of animal spirits was Paradise, and at night's close I only desired a renewal of the intoxicating delusion. The dazzling light of ornamented rooms; lovely forms arrayed in splendid dresses; the motions of a dance, the voluptuous tones of exquisite music, cradled my senses in one delightful dream.

And is not this in its kind happiness? I appeal to moralists and sages. I ask if in the calm of their measured reveries, if in the deep meditations which fill their hours, they feel the extasy of a youthful tyro in the school of pleasure? Can the calm beams of their heaven-seeking eyes equal the flashes of mingling passion which blind his, or does the influence of cold philosophy steep their soul in a joy equal to his, engaged

In this dear work of youthful revelry.

But in truth, neither the lonely meditations of the hermit, nor the tumultuous raptures of the reveller, are capable of satisfying man's heart. From the one we gather unquiet speculation, from the other satiety. The mind flags beneath the weight of thought, and droops in the heartless intercourse of those whose sole aim is amusement. There is no fruition in their vacant kindness, and sharp rocks lurk beneath the smiling ripples of these shallow waters.

Thus I felt, when disappointment, weariness, and solitude drove me back upon my heart, to gather thence the joy of which it had become barren. My flagging spirits asked for something to speak to the affections; and not finding it, I drooped. Thus, notwithstanding the thoughtless delight that waited on its commencement, the impression I have of my life at Vienna is melancholy. Goethe has said, that in youth we cannot be happy unless we love. I did not love; but I was devoured by a restless wish to be something to others. I became the victim of ingratitude and cold coquetry—then I desponded, and imagined that my discontent gave me a right to hate the world. I receded to solitude; I had recourse to my books, and my desire again to enjoy the society of Adrian became a burning thirst.

Emulation, that in its excess almost assumed the venomous properties of envy, gave a sting to these feelings. At this period the name and exploits of one of my countrymen filled the world with admiration. Relations of what he had done, conjectures concerning his future actions, were the never-failing topics of the hour. I was not angry on my own account, but I felt as if the praises which this idol received were leaves torn from laurels destined for Adrian. But I must enter into some account of this darling of fame—this favourite of the wonder-loving world.

Lord Raymond was the sole remnant of a noble but impoverished family. From early youth he had considered his pedigree with complacency, and bitterly lamented his want of wealth. His first wish was aggrandisement; and the means that led towards this end were secondary considerations. Haughty, yet trembling to every demonstration of respect; ambitious, but too proud to shew his ambition; willing to achieve honour, yet a votary of pleasure,—he entered upon life. He was met on the threshold by some insult, real or imaginary; some repulse, where he least expected it; some disappointment, hard for his pride to bear. He writhed beneath an injury he was unable to revenge; and he quitted England with a vow not to return, till the good time should arrive, when she might feel the power of him she now despised.

He became an adventurer in the Greek wars. His reckless courage and comprehensive genius brought him into notice. He became the darling hero of this rising people. His foreign birth, and he refused to throw off his allegiance to his native country, alone prevented him from filling the first offices in the state. But, though others might rank higher in title and ceremony, Lord Raymond held a station above and beyond all this. He led the Greek armies to victory; their triumphs were all his own. When he appeared, whole towns poured forth their population to meet him; new songs were adapted to their national airs, whose themes were his glory, valour, and munificence.

A truce was concluded between the Greeks and Turks. At the same time, Lord Raymond, by some unlooked-for chance, became the possessor of an immense fortune in England, whither he returned, crowned with glory, to receive the meed of honour and distinction before denied to his pretensions. His proud heart rebelled against this change. In what was the despised Raymond not the same? If the acquisition of power in the shape of wealth caused this alteration, that power should they feel as an iron yoke. Power therefore was the aim of all his endeavours; aggrandizement the mark at which he for ever shot. In open ambition or close intrigue, his end was the same—to attain the first station in his own country.

This account filled me with curiosity. The events that in succession followed his return to England, gave me keener feelings. Among his other advantages, Lord Raymond was supremely handsome; every one admired him; of women he was the idol. He was courteous, honey-tongued—an adept in fascinating arts. What could not this man achieve in the busy English world? Change succeeded to change; the entire history did not reach me; for Adrian had ceased to write, and Perdita was a laconic correspondent. The rumour went that Adrian had become—how write the fatal word—mad: that Lord Raymond was the favourite of the ex-queen, her daughter's destined husband. Nay, more, that this aspiring noble revived the claim of the house of Windsor to the crown, and that, on the event of Adrian's incurable disorder and his marriage with the sister, the brow of the ambitious Raymond might be encircled with the magic ring of regality.

Such a tale filled the trumpet of many voiced fame; such a tale rendered my longer stay at Vienna, away from the friend of my youth, intolerable. Now I must fulfil my vow; now range myself at his side, and be his ally and support till death. Farewell to courtly pleasure; to politic intrigue; to the maze of passion and folly! All hail, England! Native England, receive thy child! thou art the scene of all my hopes, the mighty theatre on which is acted the only drama that can, heart and soul, bear me along with it in its development. A voice most irresistible, a power omnipotent, drew me thither. After an absence of two years I landed on its shores, not daring to make any inquiries, fearful of every remark. My first visit would be to my sister, who inhabited a little cottage, a part of Adrian's gift, on the borders of Windsor Forest. From her I should learn the truth concerning our protector; I should hear why she had withdrawn from the protection of the Princess Evadne, and be instructed as to the influence which this overtopping and towering Raymond exercised over the fortunes of my friend.

I had never before been in the neighbourhood of Windsor; the fertility and beauty of the country around now struck me with admiration, which encreased as I approached the antique wood. The ruins of majestic oaks which had grown, flourished, and decayed during the progress of centuries, marked where the limits of the forest once reached, while the shattered palings and neglected underwood shewed that this part was deserted for the younger plantations, which owed their birth to the beginning of the nineteenth century, and now stood in the pride of maturity. Perdita's humble dwelling was situated on the skirts of the most ancient portion; before it was stretched Bishopgate Heath, which towards the east appeared interminable, and was bounded to the west by Chapel Wood and the grove of Virginia Water. Behind, the cottage was shadowed by the venerable fathers of the forest, under which the deer came to graze, and which for the most part hollow and decayed, formed fantastic groups that contrasted with the regular beauty of the younger trees. These, the offspring of a later period, stood erect and seemed ready to advance fearlessly into coming time; while those out worn stragglers, blasted and broke, clung to each other, their weak boughs sighing as the wind buffetted them—a weather-beaten crew.

A light railing surrounded the garden of the cottage, which, low-roofed, seemed to submit to the majesty of nature, and cower amidst the venerable remains of forgotten time. Flowers, the children of the spring, adorned her garden and casements; in the midst of lowliness there was an air of elegance which spoke the graceful taste of the inmate. With a beating heart I entered the enclosure; as I stood at the entrance, I heard her voice, melodious as it had ever been, which before I saw her assured me of her welfare.

A moment more and Perdita appeared; she stood before me in the fresh bloom of youthful womanhood, different from and yet the same as the mountain girl I had left. Her eyes could not be deeper than they were in childhood, nor her countenance more expressive; but the expression was changed and improved; intelligence sat on her brow; when she smiled her face was embellished by the softest sensibility, and her low, modulated voice seemed tuned by love. Her person was formed in the most feminine proportions; she was not tall, but her mountain life had given freedom to her motions, so that her light step scarce made her foot-fall heard as she tript across the hall to meet me. When we had parted, I had clasped her to my bosom with unrestrained warmth; we met again, and new feelings were awakened; when each beheld the other, childhood passed, as full grown actors on this changeful scene. The pause was but for a moment; the flood of association and natural feeling which had been checked, again rushed in full tide upon our hearts, and with tenderest emotion we were swiftly locked in each other's embrace.

This burst of passionate feeling over, with calmed thoughts we sat together, talking of the past and present. I alluded to the coldness of her letters; but the few minutes we had spent together sufficiently explained the origin of this. New feelings had arisen within her, which she was unable to express in writing to one whom she had only known in childhood; but we saw each other again, and our intimacy was renewed as if nothing had intervened to check it. I detailed the incidents of my sojourn abroad, and then questioned her as to the changes that had taken place at home, the causes of Adrian's absence, and her secluded life.

The tears that suffused my sister's eyes when I mentioned our friend, and her heightened colour seemed to vouch for the truth of the reports that had reached me. But their import was too terrible for me to give instant credit to my suspicion. Was there indeed anarchy in the sublime universe of Adrian's thoughts, did madness scatter the well-appointed legions, and was he no longer the lord of his own soul? Beloved friend, this ill world was no clime for your gentle spirit; you delivered up its governance to false humanity, which stript it of its leaves ere winter-time, and laid bare its quivering life to the evil ministration of roughest winds. Have those gentle eyes, those "channels of the soul" lost their meaning, or do they only in their glare disclose the horrible tale of its aberrations?

Does that voice no longer "discourse excellent music?" Horrible, most horrible! I veil my eyes in terror of the change, and gushing tears bear witness to my sympathy for this unimaginable ruin.

In obedience to my request Perdita detailed the melancholy circumstances that led to this event.

The frank and unsuspicious mind of Adrian, gifted as it was by every natural grace, endowed with transcendant powers of intellect, unblemished by the shadow of defect (unless his dreadless independence of thought was to be construed into one), was devoted, even as a victim to sacrifice, to his love for Evadne. He entrusted to her keeping the treasures of his soul, his aspirations after excellence, and his plans for the improvement of mankind. As manhood dawned upon him, his schemes and theories, far from being changed by personal and prudential motives, acquired new strength from the powers he felt arise within him; and his love for Evadne became deep-rooted, as he each day became more certain that the path he pursued was full of difficulty, and that he must seek his reward, not in the applause or gratitude of his fellow creatures, hardly in the success of his plans, but in the approbation of his own heart, and in her love and sympathy, which was to lighten every toil and recompence every sacrifice.

In solitude, and through many wanderings afar from the haunts of men, he matured his views for the reform of the English government, and the improvement of the people. It would have been well if he had concealed his sentiments, until he had come into possession of the power which would secure their practical development. But he was impatient of the years that must intervene, he was frank of heart and fearless. He gave not only a brief denial to his mother's schemes, but published his intention of using his influence to diminish the power of the aristocracy, to effect a greater equalization of wealth and privilege, and to introduce a perfect system of republican government into England. At first his mother treated his theories as the wild ravings of inexperience. But they were so systematically arranged, and his arguments so well supported, that though still in appearance incredulous, she began to fear him. She tried to reason with him, and finding him inflexible, learned to hate him.

Strange to say, this feeling was infectious. His enthusiasm for good which did not exist; his contempt for the sacredness of authority; his ardour and imprudence were all at the antipodes of the usual routine of life; the worldly feared him; the young and inexperienced did not understand the lofty severity of his moral views, and disliked him as a being different from themselves. Evadne entered but coldly into his systems. She thought he did well to assert his own will, but she wished that will to have been more intelligible to the multitude. She had none of the spirit of a martyr, and did not incline to share the shame and defeat of a fallen patriot. She was aware of the purity of his motives, the generosity of his disposition, his true and ardent attachment to her; and she entertained a great affection for him. He repaid this spirit of kindness with the fondest gratitude, and made her the treasure-house of all his hopes.

At this time Lord Raymond returned from Greece. No two persons could be more opposite than Adrian and he. With all the incongruities of his character, Raymond was emphatically a man of the world. His passions were violent; as these often obtained the mastery over him, he could not always square his conduct to the obvious line of self-interest, but self-gratification at least was the paramount object with him. He looked on the structure of society as but a part of the machinery which supported the web on which his life was traced. The earth was spread out as an highway for him; the heavens built up as a canopy for him.

Adrian felt that he made a part of a great whole. He owned affinity not only with mankind, but all nature was akin to him; the mountains and sky were his friends; the winds of heaven and the offspring of earth his playmates; while he the focus only of this mighty mirror, felt his life mingle with the universe of existence. His soul was sympathy, and dedicated to the worship of beauty and excellence. Adrian and Raymond now came into contact, and a spirit of aversion rose between them. Adrian despised the narrow views of the politician, and Raymond held in supreme contempt the benevolent visions of the philanthropist.

With the coming of Raymond was formed the storm that laid waste at one fell blow the gardens of delight and sheltered paths which Adrian fancied that he had secured to himself, as a refuge from defeat and contumely. Raymond, the deliverer of Greece, the graceful soldier, who bore in his mien a tinge of all that, peculiar to her native clime, Evadne cherished as most dear—Raymond was loved by Evadne. Overpowered by her new sensations, she did not pause to examine them, or to regulate her conduct by any sentiments except the tyrannical one which suddenly usurped the empire of her heart. She yielded to its influence, and the too natural consequence in a mind unattuned to soft emotions was, that the attentions of Adrian became distasteful to her. She grew capricious; her gentle conduct towards him was exchanged for asperity and repulsive coldness. When she perceived the wild or pathetic appeal of his expressive countenance, she would relent, and for a while resume her ancient kindness. But these fluctuations shook to its depths the soul of the sensitive youth; he no longer deemed the world subject to him, because he possessed Evadne's love; he felt in every nerve that the dire storms of the mental universe were about to attack his fragile being, which quivered at the expectation of its advent.

Perdita, who then resided with Evadne, saw the torture that Adrian endured. She loved him as a kind elder brother; a relation to guide, protect, and instruct her, without the too frequent tyranny of parental authority. She adored his virtues, and with mixed contempt and indignation she saw Evadne pile drear sorrow on his head, for the sake of one who hardly marked her. In his solitary despair Adrian would often seek my sister, and in covered terms express his misery, while fortitude and agony divided the throne of his mind. Soon, alas! was one to conquer. Anger made no part of his emotion. With whom should he be angry? Not with Raymond, who was unconscious of the misery he occasioned; not with Evadne, for her his soul wept tears of blood—poor, mistaken girl, slave not tyrant was she, and amidst his own anguish he grieved for her future destiny. Once a writing of his fell into Perdita's hands; it was blotted with tears—well might any blot it with the like—

"Life"—it began thus—"is not the thing romance writers describe it; going through the measures of a dance, and after various evolutions arriving at a conclusion, when the dancers may sit down and repose. While there is life there is action and change. We go on, each thought linked to the one which was its parent, each act to a previous act. No joy or sorrow dies barren of progeny, which for ever generated and generating, weaves the chain that make our life:

> Un dia llama à otro dia
> y ass i llama, y encadena
> llanto à llanto, y pena à pena.[★]

[★] One day calls to another, / and in that manner is linked / a cry to a cry and a sorrow to a sorrow.

Truly disappointment is the guardian deity of human life; she sits at the threshold of unborn time, and marshals the events as they come forth. Once my heart sat lightly in my bosom; all the beauty of the world was doubly beautiful, irradiated by the sun-light shed from my own soul. O wherefore are love and ruin for ever joined in this our mortal dream? So that when we make our hearts a lair for that gently seeming beast, its companion enters with it, and pitilessly lays waste what might have been an home and a shelter."

By degrees his health was shaken by his misery, and then his intellect yielded to the same tyranny. His manners grew wild; he was sometimes ferocious, sometimes absorbed in speechless melancholy. Suddenly Evadne quitted London for Paris; he followed, and overtook her when the vessel was about to sail; none knew what passed between them, but Perdita had never seen him since; he lived in seclusion, no one knew where, attended by such persons as his mother selected for that purpose.

Chapter IV

The next day Lord Raymond called at Perdita's cottage, on his way to Windsor Castle. My sister's heightened colour and sparkling eyes half revealed her secret to me. He was perfectly self-possessed; he accosted us both with courtesy, seemed immediately to enter into our feelings, and to make one with us. I scanned his physiognomy, which varied as he spoke, yet was beautiful in every change. The usual expression of his eyes was soft, though at times he could make them even glare with ferocity; his complexion was colourless; and every trait spoke predominate self-will; his smile was pleasing, though disdain too often curled his lips—lips which to female eyes were the very throne of beauty and love. His voice, usually gentle, often startled you by a sharp discordant note, which shewed that his usual low tone was rather the work of study than nature. Thus full of contradictions, unbending yet haughty, gentle yet fierce, tender and again neglectful, he by some strange art found easy entrance to the admiration and affection of women; now caressing and now tyrannizing over them according to his mood, but in every change a despot.

At the present time Raymond evidently wished to appear amiable. Wit, hilarity, and deep observation were mingled in his talk, rendering every sentence that he uttered as a flash of light. He soon conquered my latent distaste; I endeavoured to watch him and Perdita, and to keep in mind every thing I had heard to his disadvantage. But all appeared so ingenuous, and all was so fascinating, that I forgot everything except the pleasure his society afforded me. Under the idea of initiating me in the scene of English politics and society, of which I was soon to become a part, he narrated a number of anecdotes, and sketched many characters; his discourse, rich and varied, flowed on, pervading all my senses with pleasure. But for one thing he would have been completely triumphant. He alluded to Adrian, and spoke of him with that disparagement that the worldly wise always attach to enthusiasm. He perceived the cloud gathering, and tried to dissipate it; but the strength of my feelings would not permit me to pass thus lightly over this sacred subject; so I said emphatically, "Permit me to remark, that I am devotedly attached to the Earl of Windsor; he is my best friend and benefactor. I reverence his goodness, I accord with his opinions, and bitterly lament his present, and I trust temporary, illness. That illness, from its peculiarity, makes it painful to me beyond words to hear him mentioned, unless in terms of respect and affection."

Raymond replied; but there was nothing conciliatory in his reply. I saw that in his heart he despised those dedicated to any but worldly idols. "Every man," he said, "dreams about something, love, honour, and pleasure; you dream of friendship, and devote yourself to a maniac; well, if that be your vocation, doubtless you are in the right to follow it."—

Some reflection seemed to sting him, and the spasm of pain that for a moment convulsed his countenance, checked my indignation. "Happy are dreamers," he continued, "so that they be not awakened! Would I could dream! but 'broad and garish day' is the element in which I live; the dazzling glare of reality inverts the scene for me. Even the ghost of friendship has departed, and love"—He broke off; nor could I guess whether the disdain that curled his lip was directed against the passion, or against himself for being its slave.

This account may be taken as a sample of my intercourse with Lord Raymond. I became intimate with him, and each day afforded me occasion to admire more and more his powerful and versatile talents, that together with his eloquence, which was graceful and witty, and his wealth now immense, caused him to be feared, loved, and hated beyond any other man in England.

My descent, which claimed interest, if not respect, my former connection with Adrian, the favour of the ambassador, whose secretary I had been, and now my intimacy with Lord Raymond, gave me easy access to the fashionable and political circles of England. To my inexperience we at first appeared on the eve of a civil war; each party was violent, acrimonious, and unyielding. Parliament was divided by three factions, aristocrats, democrats, and royalists. After Adrian's declared predeliction to the republican form of government, the latter party had nearly died away, chiefless, guideless; but, when Lord Raymond came forward as its leader, it revived with redoubled force. Some were royalists from prejudice and ancient affection, and there were many moderately inclined who feared alike the capricious tyranny of the popular party, and the unbending despotism of the aristocrats. More than a third of the members ranged themselves under Raymond, and their number was perpetually encreasing. The aristocrats built their hopes on their preponderant wealth and influence; the reformers on the force of the nation itself; the debates were violent, more violent the discourses held by each knot of politicians as they assembled to arrange their measures. Opprobrious epithets were bandied about, resistance even to the death threatened; meetings of the populace disturbed the quiet order of the country; except in war, how could all this end? Even as the destructive flames were ready to break forth, I saw them shrink back; allayed by the absence of the military, by the aversion entertained by every one to any violence, save that of speech, and by the cordial politeness and even friendship of the hostile leaders when they met in private society. I was from a thousand motives induced to attend minutely to the course of events, and watch each turn with intense anxiety.

I could not but perceive that Perdita loved Raymond; methought also that he regarded the fair daughter of Verney with admiration and tenderness. Yet I knew that he was urging forward his marriage with the presumptive heiress of the Earldom of Windsor, with keen expectation of the advantages that would thence accrue to him. All the ex-queen's friends were his friends; no week passed that he did not hold consultations with her at Windsor.

I had never seen the sister of Adrian. I had heard that she was lovely, amiable, and fascinating. Wherefore should I see her? There are times when we have an indefinable sentiment of impending change for better or for worse, to arise from an event; and, be it for better or for worse, we fear the change, and shun the event. For this reason I avoided this high-born damsel. To me she was everything and nothing; her very name mentioned by another made me start and tremble; the endless discussion concerning her union with Lord Raymond was real agony to me. Methought that, Adrian withdrawn from active life, and this beauteous Idris, a victim probably to her mother's ambitious schemes, I ought to come forward to protect her from undue influence, guard her from unhappiness, and secure to her freedom of choice, the right of every human being. Yet how was I to do this? She herself would disdain my interference. Since then I must be an object of indifference or contempt to her, better, far better avoid her, nor expose myself before her and the scornful world to the chance of playing the mad game of a fond, foolish Icarus.

One day, several months after my return to England, I quitted London to visit my sister. Her society was my chief solace and delight; and my spirits always rose at the expectation of seeing her. Her conversation was full of pointed remark and discernment; in her pleasant alcove, redolent with sweetest flowers, adorned by magnificent casts, antique vases, and copies of the finest pictures of Raphael, Correggio, and Claude, painted by herself, I fancied myself in a fairy retreat untainted by and inaccessible to the noisy contentions of politicians and the frivolous pursuits of fashion. On this occasion, my sister was not alone; nor could I fail to recognise her companion: it was Idris, the till now unseen object of my mad idolatry.

In what fitting terms of wonder and delight, in what choice expression and soft flow of language, can I usher in the loveliest, wisest, best? How in poor assemblage of words convey the halo of glory that surrounded her, the thousand graces that waited unwearied on her. The first thing that struck you on beholding that charming countenance was its perfect goodness and frankness; candour sat upon her brow, simplicity in her eyes, heavenly benignity in her smile. Her tall slim figure bent gracefully as a poplar to the breezy west, and her gait, goddess-like, was as that of a winged angel new alit from heaven's high floor; the pearly fairness of her complexion was stained by a pure suffusion; her voice resembled the low, subdued tenor of a flute. It is easiest perhaps to describe by contrast. I have detailed the perfections of my sister; and yet she was utterly unlike Idris. Perdita, even where she loved, was reserved and timid; Idris was frank and confiding. The one recoiled to solitude, that she might there entrench herself from disappointment and injury; the other walked forth in open day, believing that none would harm her. Wordsworth has compared a beloved female to two fair objects in nature; but his lines always appeared to me rather a contrast than a similitude:

A violet by a mossy stone
Half hidden from the eye,
Fair as a star when only one
Is shining in the sky.

Such a violet was sweet Perdita, trembling to entrust herself to the very air, cowering from observation, yet betrayed by her excellences; and repaying with a thousand graces the labour of those who sought her in her lonely bye-path. Idris was as the star, set in single splendour in the dim anadem of balmy evening; ready to enlighten and delight the subject world, shielded herself from every taint by her unimagined distance from all that was not like herself akin to heaven.

I found this vision of beauty in Perdita's alcove, in earnest conversation with its inmate. When my sister saw me, she rose, and taking my hand, said, "He is here, even at our wish; this is Lionel, my brother."

Idris arose also, and bent on me her eyes of celestial blue, and with grace peculiar said—"You hardly need an introduction; we have a picture, highly valued by my father, which declares at once your name. Verney, you will acknowledge this tie, and as my brother's friend, I feel that I may trust you."

Then, with lids humid with a tear and trembling voice, she continued—"Dear friends, do not think it strange that now, visiting you for the first time, I ask your assistance, and confide my wishes and fears to you. To you alone do I dare speak; I have heard you commended by impartial spectators; you are my brother's friends, therefore you must be mine. What can I say? if you refuse to aid me, I am lost indeed!" She cast up her eyes, while wonder held her auditors mute; then, as if carried away by her feelings, she cried—"My brother! beloved, ill-fated Adrian! how speak of your misfortunes? Doubtless you have both heard the current tale; perhaps believe the slander; but he is not mad! Were an angel from the foot of God's throne to assert it, never, never would I believe it. He is wronged, betrayed, imprisoned—save him! Verney, you must do this; seek him out in whatever part of the island he is immured; find him, rescue him from his persecutors, restore him to himself, to me—on the wide earth I have none to love but only him!"

Her earnest appeal, so sweetly and passionately expressed, filled me with wonder and sympathy; and, when she added, with thrilling voice and look, "Do you consent to undertake this enterprize?"

I vowed, with energy and truth, to devote myself in life and death to the restoration and welfare of Adrian. We then conversed on the plan I should pursue, and discussed the probable means of discovering his residence. While we were in earnest discourse, Lord Raymond entered unannounced: I saw Perdita tremble and grow deadly pale, and the cheeks of Idris glow with purest blushes. He must have been astonished at our conclave, disturbed by it I should have thought; but nothing of this appeared; he saluted my companions, and addressed me with a cordial greeting. Idris appeared suspended for a moment, and then with extreme sweetness, she said, "Lord Raymond, I confide in your goodness and honour."

Smiling haughtily, he bent his head, and replied, with emphasis, "Do you indeed confide, Lady Idris?"

She endeavoured to read his thought, and then answered with dignity, "As you please. It is certainly best not to compromise oneself by any concealment."

"Pardon me," he replied, "if I have offended. Whether you trust me or not, rely on my doing my utmost to further your wishes, whatever they may be."

Idris smiled her thanks, and rose to take leave. Lord Raymond requested permission to accompany her to Windsor Castle, to which she consented, and they quitted the cottage together. My sister and I were left—truly like two fools, who fancied that they had obtained a golden treasure, till daylight shewed it to be lead—two silly, luckless flies, who had played in sunbeams and were caught in a spider's web. I leaned against the casement, and watched those two glorious creatures, till they disappeared in the forest-glades; and then I turned. Perdita had not moved; her eyes fixed on the ground, her cheeks pale, her very lips white, motionless and rigid, every feature stamped by woe, she sat. Half frightened, I would have taken her hand; but she shudderingly withdrew it, and strove to collect herself. I entreated her to speak to me: "Not now," she replied, "nor do you speak to me, my dear Lionel; you *can* say nothing, for you know nothing. I will see you to-morrow; in the meantime, adieu!" She rose, and walked from the room; but pausing at the door, and leaning against it, as if her over-busy thoughts had taken from her the power of supporting herself, she said, "Lord Raymond will probably return. Will you tell him that he must excuse me to-day, for I am not well. I will see him to-morrow if he wishes it, and you also. You had better return to London with him; you can there make the enquiries agreed upon, concerning the Earl of Windsor and visit me again to-morrow, before you proceed on your journey—till then, farewell!"

She spoke falteringly, and concluded with a heavy sigh. I gave my assent to her request; and she left me. I felt as if, from the order of the systematic world, I had plunged into chaos, obscure, contrary, unintelligible. That Raymond should marry Idris was more than ever intolerable; yet my passion, though a giant from its birth, was too strange, wild, and impracticable, for me to feel at once the misery I perceived in Perdita. How should I act? She had not confided in me; I could not demand an explanation from Raymond without the hazard of betraying what was perhaps her most treasured secret. I would obtain the truth from her the following day—in the mean time—But, while I was occupied by multiplying reflections, Lord Raymond returned. He asked for my sister; and I delivered her message. After musing on it for a moment, he asked me if I were about to return to London, and if I would accompany him: I consented. He was full of thought, and remained silent during a considerable part of our ride; at length he said, "I must apologize to you for my abstraction; the truth is, Ryland's motion comes on to-night, and I am considering my reply."

Ryland was the leader of the popular party, a hard-headed man, and in his way eloquent; he had obtained leave to bring in a bill making it treason to endeavour to change the present state of the English government and the standing laws of the republic. This attack was directed against Raymond and his machinations for the restoration of the monarchy.

Raymond asked me if I would accompany him to the House that evening. I remembered my pursuit for intelligence concerning Adrian; and, knowing that my time would be fully occupied, I excused myself. "Nay," said my companion, "I can free you from your present impediment. You are going to make enquiries concerning the Earl of Windsor. I can answer them at once, he is at the Duke of Athol's seat at Dunkeld. On the first approach of his disorder, he travelled about from one place to another; until, arriving at that romantic seclusion he refused to quit it, and we made arrangements with the Duke for his continuing there."

I was hurt by the careless tone with which he conveyed this information, and replied coldly: "I am obliged to you for your intelligence, and will avail myself of it."

"You shall, Verney," said he, "and if you continue of the same mind, I will facilitate your views. But first witness, I beseech you, the result of this night's contest, and the triumph I am about to achieve, if I may so call it, while I fear that victory is to me defeat. What can I do? My dearest hopes appear to be near their fulfilment. The ex-queen gives me Idris; Adrian is totally unfitted to succeed to the earldom, and that earldom in my hands becomes a kingdom. By the reigning God it is true; the paltry earldom of Windsor shall no longer content him, who will inherit the rights which must for ever appertain to the person who possesses it. The Countess can never forget that she has been a queen, and she disdains to leave a diminished inheritance to her children; her power and my wit will rebuild the throne, and this brow will be clasped by a kingly diadem.—I can do this—I can marry Idris."——

He stopped abruptly, his countenance darkened, and its expression changed again and again under the influence of internal passion. I asked, "Does Lady Idris love you?"

"What a question," replied he laughing. "She will of course, as I shall her, when we are married."

"You begin late," said I, ironically, "marriage is usually considered the grave, and not the cradle of love. So you are about to love her, but do not already?"

"Do not catechise me, Lionel; I will do my duty by her, be assured. Love! I must steel my heart against *that*; expel it from its tower of strength, barricade it out: the fountain of love must cease to play, its waters be dried up, and all passionate thoughts attendant on it die—that is to say, the love which would rule me, not that which I rule. Idris is a gentle, pretty, sweet little girl; it is impossible not to have an affection for her, and I have a very sincere one; only do not speak of love—love, the tyrant and the tyrant-queller; love, until now my conqueror, now my slave; the hungry fire, the untameable beast, the fanged snake no—-no—I will have nothing to do with that love. Tell me, Lionel, do you consent that I should marry this young lady?"

He bent his keen eyes upon me, and my uncontrollable heart swelled in my bosom. I replied in a calm voice—but how far from calm was the thought imaged by my still words—"Never! I can never consent that Lady Idris should be united to one who does not love her."

"Because you love her yourself."

"Your Lordship might have spared that taunt; I do not, dare not love her."

"At least," he continued haughtily, "she does not love you. I would not marry a reigning sovereign, were I not sure that her heart was free. But, O, Lionel! a kingdom is a word of might, and gently sounding are the terms that compose the style of royalty. Were not the mightiest men of the olden times kings? Alexander was a king; Solomon, the wisest of men, was a king; Napoleon was a king; Caesar died in his attempt to become one, and Cromwell, the puritan and king-killer, aspired to regality. The father of Adrian yielded up the already broken sceptre of England; but I will rear the fallen plant, join its dismembered frame, and exalt it above all the flowers of the field.

"You need not wonder that I freely discover Adrian's abode. Do not suppose that I am wicked or foolish enough to found my purposed sovereignty on a fraud, and one so easily discovered as the truth or falsehood of the Earl's insanity. I am just come from him. Before I decided on my marriage with Idris, I resolved to see him myself again, and to judge of the probability of his recovery.—He is irrecoverably mad."

I gasped for breath—

"I will not detail to you," continued Raymond, "the melancholy particulars. You shall see him, and judge for yourself; although I fear this visit, useless to him, will be insufferably painful to you. It has weighed on my spirits ever since. Excellent and gentle as he is even in the downfall of his reason, I do not worship him as you do, but I would give all my hopes of a crown and my right hand to boot, to see him restored to himself."

His voice expressed the deepest compassion: "Thou most unaccountable being," I cried, "whither will thy actions tend, in all this maze of purpose in which thou seemest lost?"

"Whither indeed? To a crown, a golden begemmed crown, I hope; and yet I dare not trust and though I dream of a crown and wake for one, ever and anon a busy devil whispers to me, that it is but a fool's cap that I seek, and that were I wise, I should trample on it, and take in its stead, that which is worth all the crowns of the east and presidentships of the west."

"And what is that?"

"If I do make it my choice, then you shall know; at present I dare not speak, even think of it."

Again he was silent, and after a pause turned to me laughingly. When scorn did not inspire his mirth, when it was genuine gaiety that painted his features with a joyous expression, his beauty became super-eminent, divine. "Verney," said he, "my first act when I become King of England, will be to unite with the Greeks, take Constantinople, and subdue all Asia. I intend to be a warrior, a conqueror; Napoleon's name shall vail to mine; and enthusiasts, instead of visiting his rocky grave, and exalting the merits of the fallen, shall adore my majesty, and magnify my illustrious achievements."

I listened to Raymond with intense interest. Could I be other than all ear, to one who seemed to govern the whole earth in his grasping imagination, and who only quailed when he attempted to rule himself. Then on his word and will depended my own happiness—the fate of all dear to me. I endeavoured to divine the concealed meaning of his words. Perdita's name was not mentioned; yet I could not doubt that love for her caused the vacillation of purpose that he exhibited. And who was so worthy of love as my noble-minded sister? Who deserved the hand of this self-exalted king more than she whose glance belonged to a queen of nations? who loved him, as he did her; notwithstanding that disappointment quelled her passion, and ambition held strong combat with his.

We went together to the House in the evening. Raymond, while he knew that his plans and prospects were to be discussed and decided during the expected debate, was gay and careless. An hum, like that of ten thousand hives of swarming bees, stunned us as we entered the coffee-room. Knots of politicians were assembled with anxious brows and loud or deep voices. The aristocratical party, the richest and most influential men in England, appeared less agitated than the others, for the question was to be discussed without their interference. Near the fire was Ryland and his supporters. Ryland was a man of obscure birth and of immense wealth, inherited from his father, who had been a manufacturer. He had witnessed, when a young man, the abdication of the king, and the amalgamation of the two houses of Lords and Commons; he had sympathized with these popular encroachments, and it had been the business of his life to consolidate and encrease them. Since then, the influence of the landed proprietors had augmented; and at first Ryland was not sorry to observe the machinations of Lord Raymond, which drew off many of his opponent's partizans. But the thing was now going too far. The poorer nobility hailed the return of sovereignty, as an event which would restore them to their power and rights, now lost. The half extinct spirit of royalty roused itself in the minds of men; and they, willing slaves, self-constituted subjects, were ready to bend their necks to the yoke. Some erect and manly spirits still remained, pillars of state; but the word republic had grown stale to the vulgar ear; and many—the event would prove whether it was a majority—pined for the tinsel and show of royalty. Ryland was roused to resistance; he asserted that his sufferance alone had permitted the encrease of this party; but the time for indulgence was passed, and with one motion of his arm he would sweep away the cobwebs that blinded his countrymen.

When Raymond entered the coffee-room, his presence was hailed by his friends almost with a shout. They gathered round him, counted their numbers, and detailed the reasons why they were now to receive an addition of such and such members, who had not yet declared themselves. Some trifling business of the House having been gone through, the leaders took their seats in the chamber; the clamour of voices continued, till Ryland arose to speak, and then the slightest whispered observation was audible. All eyes were fixed upon him as he stood—ponderous of frame, sonorous of voice, and with a manner which, though not graceful, was impressive. I turned from his marked, iron countenance to Raymond, whose face, veiled by a smile, would not betray his care; yet his lips quivered somewhat, and his hand clasped the bench on which he sat, with a convulsive strength that made the muscles start again.

Ryland began by praising the present state of the British empire. He recalled past years to their memory; the miserable contentions which in the time of our fathers arose almost to civil war, the abdication of the late king, and the foundation of the republic. He described this republic; shewed how it gave privilege to each individual in the state, to rise to consequence, and even to temporary sovereignty. He compared the royal and republican spirit; shewed how the one tended to enslave the minds of men; while all the institutions of the other served to raise even the meanest among us to something great and good. He shewed how England had become powerful, and its inhabitants valiant and wise, by means of the freedom they enjoyed. As he spoke, every heart swelled with pride, and every cheek glowed with delight to remember, that each one there was English, and that each supported and contributed to the happy state of things now commemorated. Ryland's fervour increased—his eyes lighted up—his voice assumed the tone of passion. There was one man, he continued, who wished to alter all this, and bring us back to our days of impotence and contention:—one man, who would dare arrogate the honour which was due to all who claimed England as their birthplace, and set his name and style above the name and style of his country. I saw at this juncture that Raymond changed colour; his eyes were withdrawn from the orator, and cast on the ground; the listeners turned from one to the other; but in the meantime the speaker's voice filled their ears—the thunder of his denunciations influenced their senses. The very boldness of his language gave him weight; each knew that he spoke truth—a truth known, but not acknowledged. He tore from reality the mask with which she had been clothed; and the purposes of Raymond, which before had crept around, ensnaring by stealth, now stood a hunted stag—even at bay—as all perceived who watched the irrepressible changes of his countenance. Ryland ended by moving, that any attempt to re-erect the kingly power should be declared treason, and he a traitor who should endeavour to change the present form of government. Cheers and loud acclamations followed the close of his speech.

After his motion had been seconded, Lord Raymond rose,—his countenance bland, his voice softly melodious, his manner soothing, his grace and sweetness came like the mild breathing of a flute, after the loud, organ-like voice of his adversary. He rose, he said, to speak in favour of the honourable member's motion, with one slight amendment subjoined. He was ready to go back to old times, and commemorate the contests of our fathers, and the monarch's abdication. Nobly and greatly, he said, had the illustrious and last sovereign of England sacrificed himself to the apparent good of his country, and divested himself of a power which could only be maintained by the blood of his subjects—these subjects named so no more, these, his friends and equals, had in gratitude conferred certain favours and distinctions on him and his family for ever. An ample estate was allotted to them, and they took the first rank among the peers of Great Britain. Yet it might be conjectured that they had not forgotten their ancient heritage; and it was hard that his heir should suffer alike with any other pretender, if he attempted to regain what by ancient right and inheritance belonged to him. He did not say that he should favour such an attempt; but he did say that such an attempt would be venial; and, if the aspirant did not go so far as to declare war, and erect a standard in the kingdom, his fault ought to be regarded with an indulgent eye. In his amendment he proposed, that an exception should be made in the bill in favour of any person who claimed the sovereign power in right of the earls of Windsor.

Nor did Raymond make an end without drawing in vivid and glowing colours, the splendour of a kingdom, in opposition to the commercial spirit of republicanism. He asserted, that each individual under the English monarchy, was then as now, capable of attaining high rank and power—with one only exception, that of the function of chief magistrate; higher and nobler rank, than a bartering, timorous commonwealth could afford. And for this one exception, to what did it amount? The nature of riches and influence forcibly confined the list of candidates to a few of the wealthiest; and it was much to be feared, that the ill-humour and contention generated by this triennial struggle, would counterbalance its advantages in impartial eyes. I can ill record the flow of language and graceful turns of expression, the wit and easy raillery that gave vigour and influence to his speech. His manner, timid at first, became firm—his changeful face was lit up to superhuman brilliancy; his voice, various as music, was like that enchanting.

It were useless to record the debate that followed this harangue. Party speeches were delivered, which clothed the question in cant, and veiled its simple meaning in a woven wind of words. The motion was lost; Ryland withdrew in rage and despair; and Raymond, gay and exulting, retired to dream of his future kingdom.

Chapter IV(A)

IS THERE SUCH a feeling as love at first sight? And if there be, in what does its nature differ from love founded in long observation and slow growth? Perhaps its effects are not so permanent; but they are, while they last, as violent and intense. We walk the pathless mazes of society, vacant of joy, till we hold this clue, leading us through that labyrinth to paradise. Our nature dim, like to an unlighted torch, sleeps in formless blank till the fire attain it; this life of life, this light to moon, and glory to the sun. What does it matter, whether the fire be struck from flint and steel, nourished with care into a flame, slowly communicated to the dark wick, or whether swiftly the radiant power of light and warmth passes from a kindred power, and shines at once the beacon and the hope. In the deepest fountain of my heart the pulses were stirred; around, above, beneath, the clinging Memory as a cloak enwrapt me. In no one moment of coming time did I feel as I had done in time gone by. The spirit of Idris hovered in the air I breathed; her eyes were ever and for ever bent on mine; her remembered smile blinded my faint gaze, and caused me to walk as one, not in eclipse, not in darkness and vacancy—but in a new and brilliant light, too novel, too dazzling for my human senses. On every leaf, on every small division of the universe, (as on the hyacinth ας[★] is engraved) was imprinted the talisman of my existence—SHE LIVES! SHE IS!—I had not time yet to analyze my feeling, to take myself to task, and leash in the tameless passion; all was one idea, one feeling, one knowledge—it was my life!

[★] Undoubtedly a misprint for αι (cf. Ovid, *Metamorphoses,* X, 215), or "ai," the conventional cry of despair.

But the die was cast—Raymond would marry Idris. The merry marriage bells rung in my ears; I heard the nation's gratulation which followed the union; the ambitious noble uprose with swift eagle-flight, from the lowly ground to regal supremacy—and to the love of Idris. Yet, not so! She did not love him; she had called me her friend; she had smiled on me; to me she had entrusted her heart's dearest hope, the welfare of Adrian. This reflection thawed my congealing blood, and again the tide of life and love flowed impetuously onward, again to ebb as my busy thoughts changed.

The debate had ended at three in the morning. My soul was in tumults; I traversed the streets with eager rapidity. Truly, I was mad that night—love—which I have named a giant from its birth, wrestled with despair! My heart, the field of combat, was wounded by the iron heel of the one, watered by the gushing tears of the other. Day, hateful to me, dawned; I retreated to my lodgings—I threw myself on a couch—I slept—was it sleep?—for thought was still alive—love and despair struggled still, and I writhed with unendurable pain.

I awoke half stupefied; I felt a heavy oppression on me, but knew not wherefore; I entered, as it were, the council-chamber of my brain, and questioned the various ministers of thought therein assembled; too soon I remembered all; too soon my limbs quivered beneath the tormenting power; soon, too soon, I knew myself a slave!

Suddenly, unannounced, Lord Raymond entered my apartment. He came in gaily, singing the Tyrolese song of liberty; noticed me with a gracious nod, and threw himself on a sopha opposite the copy of a bust of the Apollo Belvidere. After one or two trivial remarks, to which I sullenly replied, he suddenly cried, looking at the bust, "I am called like that victor! Not a bad idea; the head will serve for my new coinage, and be an omen to all dutiful subjects of my future success."

He said this in his most gay, yet benevolent manner, and smiled, not disdainfully, but in playful mockery of himself. Then his countenance suddenly darkened, and in that shrill tone peculiar to himself, he cried, "I fought a good battle last night; higher conquest the plains of Greece never saw me achieve. Now I am the first man in the state, burthen of every ballad, and object of old women's mumbled devotions. What are your meditations? You, who fancy that you can read the human soul, as your native lake reads each crevice and folding of its surrounding hills—say what you think of me; king-expectant, angel or devil, which?"

This ironical tone was discord to my bursting, over-boiling-heart; I was nettled by his insolence, and replied with bitterness; "There is a spirit, neither angel or devil, damned to limbo merely." I saw his cheeks become pale, and his lips whiten and quiver; his anger served but to enkindle mine, and I answered with a determined look his eyes which glared on me; suddenly they were withdrawn, cast down, a tear, I thought, wetted the dark lashes; I was softened, and with involuntary emotion added, "Not that you are such, my dear lord."

I paused, even awed by the agitation he evinced; "Yes," he said at length, rising and biting his lip, as he strove to curb his passion; "Such am I! You do not know me, Verney; neither you, nor our audience of last night, nor does universal England know aught of me. I stand here, it would seem, an elected king; this hand is about to grasp a sceptre; these brows feel in each nerve the coming diadem. I appear to have strength, power, victory; standing as a dome-supporting column stands; and I am—a reed! I have ambition, and that attains its aim; my nightly dreams are realized, my waking hopes fulfilled; a kingdom awaits my acceptance, my enemies are overthrown. But here," and he struck his heart with violence, "here is the rebel, here the stumbling-block; this over-ruling heart, which I may drain of its living blood; but, while one fluttering pulsation remains, I am its slave."

He spoke with a broken voice, then bowed his head, and, hiding his face in his hands, wept. I was still smarting from my own disappointment; yet this scene oppressed me even to terror, nor could I interrupt his access of passion. It subsided at length; and, throwing himself on the couch, he remained silent and motionless, except that his changeful features shewed a strong internal conflict. At last he rose, and said in his usual tone of voice, "The time grows on us, Verney, I must away. Let me not forget my chiefest errand here. Will you accompany me to Windsor to-morrow? You will not be dishonoured by my society, and as this is probably the last service, or disservice you can do me, will you grant my request?"

He held out his hand with almost a bashful air. Swiftly I thought—Yes, I will witness the last scene of the drama. Beside which, his mien conquered me, and an affectionate sentiment towards him, again filled my heart—I bade him command me. "Aye, that I will," said he gaily, "that's my cue now; be with me to-morrow morning by seven; be secret and faithful; and you shall be groom of the stole ere long."

So saying, he hastened away, vaulted on his horse, and with a gesture as if he gave me his hand to kiss, bade me another laughing adieu. Left to myself, I strove with painful intensity to divine the motive of his request, and foresee the events of the coming day. The hours passed on unperceived; my head ached with thought, the nerves seemed teeming with the over full fraught—I clasped my burning brow, as if my fevered hand could medicine its pain.

I was punctual to the appointed hour on the following day, and found Lord Raymond waiting for me. We got into his carriage, and proceeded towards Windsor. I had tutored myself, and was resolved by no outward sign to disclose my internal agitation.

"What a mistake Ryland made," said Raymond, "when he thought to overpower me the other night. He spoke well, very well; such an harangue would have succeeded better addressed to me singly, than to the fools and knaves assembled yonder. Had I been alone, I should have listened to him with a wish to hear reason, but when he endeavoured to vanquish me in my own territory, with my own weapons, he put me on my mettle, and the event was such as all might have expected."

I smiled incredulously, and replied: "I am of Ryland's way of thinking, and will, if you please, repeat all his arguments; we shall see how far you will be induced by them, to change the royal for the patriotic style."

"The repetition would be useless," said Raymond, "since I well remember them, and have many others, self-suggested, which speak with unanswerable persuasion."

He did not explain himself, nor did I make any remark on his reply. Our silence endured for some miles, till the country with open fields, or shady woods and parks, presented pleasant objects to our view. After some observations on the scenery and seats, Raymond said: "Philosophers have called man a microcosm of nature, and find a reflection in the internal mind for all this machinery visibly at work around us. This theory has often been a source of amusement to me; and many an idle hour have I spent, exercising my ingenuity in finding resemblances. Does not Lord Bacon say that, 'the falling from a discord to a concord, which maketh great sweetness in music, hath an agreement with the affections, which are re-integrated to the better after some dislikes?' What a sea is the tide of passion, whose fountains are in our own nature! Our virtues are the quick-sands, which shew themselves at calm and low water; but let the waves arise and the winds buffet them, and the poor devil whose hope was in their durability, finds them sink from under him. The fashions of the world, its exigencies, educations and pursuits, are winds to drive our wills, like clouds all one way; but let a thunderstorm arise in the shape of love, hate, or ambition, and the rack goes backward, stemming the opposing air in triumph."

"Yet," replied I, "nature always presents to our eyes the appearance of a patient: while there is an active principle in man which is capable of ruling fortune, and at least of tacking against the gale, till it in some mode conquers it."

"There is more of what is specious than true in your distinction," said my companion. "Did we form ourselves, choosing our dispositions, and our powers? I find myself, for one, as a stringed instrument with chords and stops—but I have no power to turn the pegs, or pitch my thoughts to a higher or lower key."

"Other men," I observed, "may be better musicians."

"I talk not of others, but myself," replied Raymond, "and I am as fair an example to go by as another. I cannot set my heart to a particular tune, or run voluntary changes on my will. We are born; we choose neither our parents, nor our station; we are educated by others, or by the world's circumstance, and this cultivation, mingling with our innate disposition, is the soil in which our desires, passions, and motives grow."

"There is much truth in what you say," said I, "and yet no man ever acts upon this theory. Who, when he makes a choice, says, Thus I choose, because I am necessitated? Does he not on the contrary feel a freedom of will within him, which, though you may call it fallacious, still actuates him as he decides?"

"Exactly so," replied Raymond, "another link of the breakless chain. Were I now to commit an act which would annihilate my hopes, and pluck the regal garment from my mortal limbs, to clothe them in ordinary weeds, would this, think you, be an act of free-will on my part?"

As we talked thus, I perceived that we were not going the ordinary road to Windsor, but through Englefield Green, towards

Bishopgate Heath. I began to divine that Idris was not the object of our journey, but that I was brought to witness the scene that was to decide the fate of Raymond—and of Perdita. Raymond had evidently vacillated during his journey, and irresolution was marked in every gesture as we entered Perdita's cottage. I watched him curiously, determined that, if this hesitation should continue, I would assist Perdita to overcome herself, and teach her to disdain the wavering love of him, who balanced between the possession of a crown, and of her, whose excellence and affection transcended the worth of a kingdom.

We found her in her flower-adorned alcove; she was reading the newspaper report of the debate in parliament, that apparently doomed her to hopelessness. That heart-sinking feeling was painted in her sunk eyes and spiritless attitude; a cloud was on her beauty, and frequent sighs were tokens of her distress. This sight had an instantaneous effect on Raymond; his eyes beamed with tenderness, and remorse clothed his manners with earnestness and truth. He sat beside her; and, taking the paper from her hand, said, "Not a word more shall my sweet Perdita read of this contention of madmen and fools. I must not permit you to be acquainted with the extent of my delusion, lest you despise me; although, believe me, a wish to appear before you, not vanquished, but as a conqueror, inspired me during my wordy war."

Perdita looked at him like one amazed; her expressive countenance shone for a moment with tenderness; to see him only was happiness. But a bitter thought swiftly shadowed her joy; she bent her eyes on the ground, endeavouring to master the passion of tears that threatened to overwhelm her. Raymond continued, "I will not act a part with you, dear girl, or appear other than what I am, weak and unworthy, more fit to excite your disdain than your love. Yet you do love me; I feel and know that you do, and thence I draw my most cherished hopes. If pride guided you, or even reason, you might well reject me. Do so; if your high heart, incapable of my infirmity of purpose, refuses to bend to the lowness of mine. Turn from me, if you will,—if you can. If your whole soul does not urge you to forgive me—if your entire heart does not open wide its door to admit me to its very centre, forsake me, never speak to me again. I, though sinning against you almost beyond remission, I also am proud; there must be no reserve in your pardon—no drawback to the gift of your affection."

Perdita looked down, confused, yet pleased. My presence embarrassed her; so that she dared not turn to meet her lover's eye, or trust her voice to assure him of her affection; while a blush mantled her cheek, and her disconsolate air was exchanged for one expressive of deep-felt joy. Raymond encircled her waist with his arm, and continued, "I do not deny that I have balanced between you and the highest hope that mortal men can entertain; but I do so no longer. Take me—mould me to your will, possess my heart and soul to all eternity. If you refuse to contribute to my happiness, I quit England to-night, and will never set foot in it again.

"Lionel, you hear: witness for me: persuade your sister to forgive the injury I have done her; persuade her to be mine."

"There needs no persuasion," said the blushing Perdita, "except your own dear promises, and my ready heart, which whispers to me that they are true."

That same evening we all three walked together in the forest, and, with the garrulity which happiness inspires, they detailed to me the history of their loves. It was pleasant to see the haughty Raymond and reserved Perdita changed through happy love into prattling, playful children, both losing their characteristic dignity in the fulness of mutual contentment. A night or two ago Lord Raymond, with a brow of care, and a heart oppressed with thought, bent all his energies to silence or persuade the legislators of England that a sceptre was not too weighty for his hand, while visions of dominion, war, and triumph floated before him; now, frolicsome as a lively boy sporting under his mother's approving eye, the hopes of his ambition were complete, when he pressed the small fair hand of Perdita to his lips; while she, radiant with delight, looked on the still pool, not truly admiring herself, but drinking in with rapture the reflection there made of the form of herself and her lover, shewn for the first time in dear conjunction.

I rambled away from them. If the rapture of assured sympathy was theirs, I enjoyed that of restored hope. I looked on the regal towers of Windsor. High is the wall and strong the barrier that separate me from my Star of Beauty. But not impassible. She will not be his. A few more years dwell in thy native garden, sweet flower, till I by toil and time acquire a right to gather thee. Despair not, nor bid me despair! What must I do now? First I must seek Adrian, and restore him to her. Patience, gentleness, and untired affection, shall recall him, if it be true, as Raymond says, that he is mad; energy and courage shall rescue him, if he be unjustly imprisoned.

After the lovers again joined me, we supped together in the alcove. Truly it was a fairy's supper; for though the air was perfumed by the scent of fruits and wine, we none of us either ate or drank—even the beauty of the night was unobserved; their extasy could not be increased by outward objects, and I was wrapt in reverie. At about midnight Raymond and I took leave of my sister, to return to town. He was all gaiety; scraps of songs fell from his lips; every thought of his mind—every object about us, gleamed under the sunshine of his mirth. He accused me of melancholy, of ill-humour and envy.

"Not so," said I, "though I confess that my thoughts are not occupied as pleasantly as yours are. You promised to facilitate my visit to Adrian; I conjure you to perform your promise. I cannot linger here; I long to soothe—perhaps to cure the malady of my first and best friend. I shall immediately depart for Dunkeld."

"Thou bird of night," replied Raymond, "what an eclipse do you throw across my bright thoughts, forcing me to call to mind that melancholy ruin, which stands in mental desolation, more irreparable than a fragment of a carved column in a weed-grown field. You dream that you can restore him? Dædalus never wound so inextricable an error round Minotaur, as madness has woven about his imprisoned reason. Nor you, nor any other Theseus, can thread the labyrinth, to which perhaps some unkind Ariadne has the clue."

"You allude to Evadne Zaimi: but she is not in England."

"And were she," said Raymond, "I would not advise her seeing him. Better to decay in absolute delirium, than to be the victim of the methodical unreason of ill-bestowed love. The long duration of his malady has probably erased from his mind all vestige of her; and it were well that it should never again be imprinted. You will find him at Dunkeld; gentle and tractable he wanders up the hills, and through the wood, or sits listening beside the waterfall. You may see him—his hair stuck with wild flowers—his eyes full of untraceable meaning—his voice broken—his person wasted to a shadow. He plucks flowers and weeds, and weaves chaplets of them, or sails yellow leaves and bits of bark on the stream, rejoicing in their safety, or weeping at their wreck. The very memory half unmans me. By Heaven! the first tears I have shed since boyhood rushed scalding into my eyes when I saw him."

It needed not this last account to spur me on to visit him. I only doubted whether or not I should endeavour to see Idris again, before I departed. This doubt was decided on the following day. Early in the morning Raymond came to me; intelligence had arrived that Adrian was dangerously ill, and it appeared impossible that his failing strength should surmount the disorder. "To-morrow," said Raymond, "his mother and sister set out for Scotland to see him once again."

"And I go to-day," I cried; "this very hour I will engage a sailing balloon; I shall be there in forty-eight hours at furthest, perhaps in less, if the wind is fair. Farewell, Raymond; be happy in having chosen the better part in life. This turn of fortune revives me. I feared madness, not sickness—I have a presentiment that Adrian will not die; perhaps this illness is a crisis, and he may recover."

Everything favoured my journey. The balloon rose about half a mile from the earth, and with a favourable wind it hurried through the air, its feathered vans cleaving the unopposing atmosphere. Notwithstanding the melancholy object of my journey, my spirits were exhilarated by reviving hope, by the swift motion of the airy pinnace, and the balmy visitation of the sunny air. The pilot hardly moved the plumed steerage, and the slender mechanism of the wings, wide unfurled, gave forth a murmuring noise, soothing to the sense. Plain and hill, stream and corn-field, were discernible below, while we unimpeded sped on swift and secure, as a wild swan in his spring-tide flight. The machine obeyed the slightest motion of the helm; and, the wind blowing steadily, there was no let or obstacle to our course. Such was the power of man over the elements; a power long sought, and lately won; yet foretold in bygone time by the prince of poets, whose verses I quoted much to the astonishment of my pilot, when I told him how many hundred years ago they had been written:—

> Oh! human wit, thou can'st invent much ill,
> Thou searchest strange arts: who would think by skill,
> An heavy man like a light bird should stray,
> And through the empty heavens find a way?

I alighted at Perth; and, though much fatigued by a constant exposure to the air for many hours, I would not rest, but merely altering my mode of conveyance, I went by land instead of air, to Dunkeld. The sun was rising as I entered the opening of the hills. After the revolution of ages Birnam hill was again covered with a young forest, while more aged pines, planted at the very commencement of the nineteenth century by the then Duke of Athol, gave solemnity and beauty to the scene. The rising sun first tinged the pine tops; and my mind, rendered through my mountain education deeply susceptible of the graces of nature, and now on the eve of again beholding my beloved and perhaps dying friend, was strangely influenced by the sight of those distant beams: surely they were ominous, and as such I regarded them, good omens for Adrian, on whose life my happiness depended.

Poor fellow! he lay stretched on a bed of sickness, his cheeks glowing with the hues of fever, his eyes half closed, his breath irregular and difficult. Yet it was less painful to see him thus, than to find him fulfilling the animal functions uninterruptedly, his mind sick the while. I established myself at his bedside; I never quitted it day or night. Bitter task was it, to behold his spirit waver between death and life: to see his warm cheek, and know that the very fire which burned too fiercely there, was consuming the vital fuel; to hear his moaning voice, which might never again articulate words of love and wisdom; to witness the ineffectual motions of his limbs, soon to be wrapt in their mortal shroud. Such for three days and nights appeared the consummation which fate had decreed for my labours, and I became haggard and spectre-like, through anxiety and watching. At length his eyes unclosed faintly, yet with a look of returning life; he became pale and weak; but the rigidity of his features was softened by approaching convalescence. He knew me. What a brimful cup of joyful agony it was, when his face first gleamed with the glance of recognition—when he pressed my hand, now more fevered than his own, and when he pronounced my name! No trace of his past insanity remained, to dash my joy with sorrow.

This same evening his mother and sister arrived. The Countess of Windsor was by nature full of energetic feeling; but she had very seldom in her life permitted the concentrated emotions of her heart to shew themselves on her features. The studied immovability of her countenance; her slow, equable manner, and soft but unmelodious voice, were a mask, hiding her fiery passions, and the impatience of her disposition. She did not in the least resemble either of her children; her black and sparkling eye, lit up by pride, was totally unlike the blue lustre, and frank, benignant expression of either Adrian or Idris. There was something grand and majestic in her motions, but nothing persuasive, nothing amiable. Tall, thin, and strait, her face still handsome, her raven hair hardly tinged with grey, her forehead arched and beautiful, had not the eye-brows been somewhat scattered—it was impossible not to be struck by her, almost to fear her. Idris appeared to be the only being who could resist her mother, notwithstanding the extreme mildness of her character. But there was a fearlessness and frankness about her, which said that she would not encroach on another's liberty, but held her own sacred and unassailable.

The Countess cast no look of kindness on my worn-out frame, though afterwards she thanked me coldly for my attentions. Not so Idris; her first glance was for her brother; she took his hand, she kissed his eye-lids, and hung over him with looks of compassion and love. Her eyes glistened with tears when she thanked me, and the grace of her expressions was enhanced, not diminished, by the fervour, which caused her almost to falter as she spoke. Her mother, all eyes and ears, soon interrupted us; and I saw, that she wished to dismiss me quietly, as one whose services, now that his relatives had arrived, were of no use to her son. I was harassed and ill, resolved not to give up my post, yet doubting in what way I should assert it; when Adrian called me, and clasping my hand, bade me not leave him. His mother, apparently inattentive, at once understood what was meant, and seeing the hold we had upon her, yielded the point to us.

The days that followed were full of pain to me; so that I sometimes regretted that I had not yielded at once to the haughty lady, who watched all my motions, and turned my beloved task of nursing my friend to a work of pain and irritation. Never did any woman appear so entirely made of mind, as the Countess of Windsor. Her passions had subdued her appetites, even her natural wants; she slept little, and hardly ate at all; her body was evidently considered by her as a mere machine, whose health was necessary for the accomplishment of her schemes, but whose senses formed no part of her enjoyment. There is something fearful in one who can thus conquer the animal part of our nature, if the victory be not the effect of consummate virtue; nor was it without a mixture of this feeling, that I beheld the figure of the Countess awake when others slept, fasting when I, abstemious naturally, and rendered so by the fever that preyed on me, was forced to recruit myself with food. She resolved to prevent or diminish my opportunities of acquiring influence over her children, and circumvented my plans by a hard, quiet, stubborn resolution, that seemed not to belong to flesh and blood. War was at last tacitly acknowledged between us. We had many pitched battles, during which no word was spoken, hardly a look was interchanged, but in which each resolved not to submit to the other. The Countess had the advantage of position; so I was vanquished, though I would not yield.

I became sick at heart. My countenance was painted with the hues of ill health and vexation. Adrian and Idris saw this; they attributed it to my long watching and anxiety; they urged me to rest, and take care of myself, while I most truly assured them, that my best medicine was their good wishes; those, and the assured convalescence of my friend, now daily more apparent. The faint rose again blushed on his cheek; his brow and lips lost the ashy paleness of threatened dissolution; such was the dear reward of my unremitting attention—and bounteous heaven added overflowing recompence, when it gave me also the thanks and smiles of Idris.

After the lapse of a few weeks, we left Dunkeld. Idris and her mother returned immediately to Windsor, while Adrian and I followed by slow journies and frequent stoppages, occasioned by his continued weakness. As we traversed the various counties of fertile England, all wore an exhilirating appearance to my companion, who had been so long secluded by disease from the enjoyments of weather and scenery. We passed through busy towns and cultivated plains. The husbandmen were getting in their plenteous harvests, and the women and children, occupied by light rustic toils, formed groupes of happy, healthful persons, the very sight of whom carried cheerfulness to the heart. One evening, quitting our inn, we strolled down a shady lane, then up a grassy slope, till we came to an eminence, that commanded an extensive view of hill and dale, meandering rivers, dark woods, and shining villages. The sun was setting; and the clouds, straying, like new-shorn sheep, through the vast fields of sky, received the golden colour of his parting beams; the distant uplands shone out, and the busy hum of evening came, harmonized by distance, on our ear. Adrian, who felt all the fresh spirit infused by returning health, clasped his hands in delight, and exclaimed with transport:

"O happy earth, and happy inhabitants of earth! A stately palace has God built for you, O man! and worthy are you of your dwelling! Behold the verdant carpet spread at our feet, and the azure canopy above; the fields of earth which generate and nurture all things, and the track of heaven, which contains and clasps all things. Now, at this evening hour, at the period of repose and refection, methinks all hearts breathe one hymn of love and thanksgiving, and we, like priests of old on the mountain-tops, give a voice to their sentiment.

"Assuredly a most benignant power built up the majestic fabric we inhabit, and framed the laws by which it endures. If mere existence, and not happiness, had been the final end of our being, what need of the profuse luxuries which we enjoy? Why should our dwelling place be so lovely, and why should the instincts of nature minister pleasurable sensations? The very sustaining of our animal machine is made delightful; and our sustenance, the fruits of the field, is painted with transcendant hues, endued with grateful odours, and palatable to our taste. Why should this be, if HE were not good? We need houses to protect us from the seasons, and behold the materials with which we are provided; the growth of trees with their adornment of leaves; while rocks of stone piled above the plains variegate the prospect with their pleasant irregularity.

"Nor are outward objects alone the receptacles of the Spirit of Good. Look into the mind of man, where wisdom reigns enthroned; where imagination, the painter, sits, with his pencil dipt in hues lovelier than those of sunset, adorning familiar life with glowing tints. What a noble boon, worthy the giver, is the imagination! it takes from reality its leaden hue: it envelopes all thought and sensation in a radiant veil, and with an hand of beauty beckons us from the sterile seas of life, to her gardens, and bowers, and glades of bliss. And is not love a gift of the divinity? Love, and her child, Hope, which can bestow wealth on poverty, strength on the weak, and happiness on the sorrowing.

"My lot has not been fortunate. I have consorted long with grief, entered the gloomy labyrinth of madness, and emerged, but half alive. Yet I thank God that I have lived! I thank God, that I have beheld his throne, the heavens, and earth, his footstool. I am glad that I have seen the changes of his day; to behold the sun, fountain of light, and the gentle pilgrim moon; to have seen the fire bearing flowers of the sky, and the flowery stars of earth; to have witnessed the sowing and the harvest. I am glad that I have loved, and have experienced sympathetic joy and sorrow with my fellow-creatures. I am glad now to feel the current of thought flow through my mind, as the blood through the articulations of my frame; mere existence is pleasure; and I thank God that I live!

"And all ye happy nurslings of mother-earth, do ye not echo my words? Ye who are linked by the affectionate ties of nature; companions, friends, lovers! fathers, who toil with joy for their offspring; women, who while gazing on the living forms of their children, forget the pains of maternity; children, who neither toil nor spin, but love and are loved!

"Oh, that death and sickness were banished from our earthly home! that hatred, tyranny, and fear could no longer make their lair in the human heart! that each man might find a brother in his fellow, and a nest of repose amid the wide plains of his inheritance! that the source of tears were dry, and that lips might no longer form expressions of sorrow. Sleeping thus under the beneficent eye of heaven, can evil visit thee, O Earth, or grief cradle to their graves thy luckless children? Whisper it not, let the dæmons hear and rejoice! The choice is with us; let us will it, and our habitation becomes a paradise. For the will of man is omnipotent, blunting the arrows of death, soothing the bed of disease, and wiping away the tears of agony. And what is each human being worth, if he do not put forth his strength to aid his fellow-creatures? My soul is a fading spark, my nature frail as a spent wave; but I dedicate all of intellect and strength that remains to me, to that one work, and take upon me the task, as far as I am able, of bestowing blessings on my fellow-men!"

His voice trembled, his eyes were cast up, his hands clasped, and his fragile person was bent, as it were, with excess of emotion. The spirit of life seemed to linger in his form, as a dying flame on an altar flickers on the embers of an accepted sacrifice.

Chapter V

When we arrived at Windsor, I found that Raymond and Perdita had departed for the continent. I took possession of my sister's cottage, and blessed myself that I lived within view of Windsor Castle. It was a curious fact, that at this period, when by the marriage of Perdita I was allied to one of the richest individuals in England, and was bound by the most intimate friendship to its chiefest noble, I experienced the greatest excess of poverty that I had ever known. My knowledge of the worldly principles of Lord Raymond, would have ever prevented me from applying to him, however deep my distress might have been. It was in vain that I repeated to myself with regard to Adrian, that his purse was open to me; that one in soul, as we were, our fortunes ought also to be common. I could never, while with him, think of his bounty as a remedy to my poverty; and I even put aside hastily his offers of supplies, assuring him of a falsehood, that I needed them not. How could I say to this generous being, "Maintain me in idleness. You who have dedicated your powers of mind and fortune to the benefit of your species, shall you so misdirect your exertions, as to support in uselessness the strong, healthy, and capable?"

And yet I dared not request him to use his influence that I might obtain an honourable provision for myself—for then I should have been obliged to leave Windsor. I hovered for ever around the walls of its Castle, beneath its enshadowing thickets; my sole companions were my books and my loving thoughts. I studied the wisdom of the ancients, and gazed on the happy walls that sheltered the beloved of my soul. My mind was nevertheless idle. I pored over the poetry of old times; I studied the metaphysics of Plato and Berkley. I read the histories of Greece and Rome, and of England's former periods, and I watched the movements of the lady of my heart. At night I could see her shadow on the walls of her apartment; by day I viewed her in her flower-garden, or riding in the park with her usual companions. Methought the charm would be broken if I were seen, but I heard the music of her voice and was happy. I gave to each heroine of whom I read, her beauty and matchless excellences—such was Antigone, when she guided the blind Œdipus to the grove of the Eumenides, and discharged the funeral rites of Polynices; such was Miranda in the unvisited cave of Prospero; such Haidee, on the sands of the Ionian island. I was mad with excess of passionate devotion; but pride, tameless as fire, invested my nature, and prevented me from betraying myself by word or look.

In the mean time, while I thus pampered myself with rich mental repasts, a peasant would have disdained my scanty fare, which I sometimes robbed from the squirrels of the forest. I was, I own, often tempted to recur to the lawless feats of my boy-hood, and knock down the almost tame pheasants that perched upon the trees, and bent their bright eyes on me. But they were the property of Adrian, the nurslings of Idris; and so, although my imagination rendered sensual by privation, made me think that they would better become the spit in my kitchen, than the green leaves of the forest,

Nathelesse,
I checked my haughty will, and did not eat;

but supped upon sentiment, and dreamt vainly of "such morsels sweet," as I might not waking attain.

But, at this period, the whole scheme of my existence was about to change. The orphan and neglected son of Verney, was on the eve of being linked to the mechanism of society by a golden chain, and to enter into all the duties and affections of life. Miracles were to be wrought in my favour, the machine of social life pushed with vast effort backward. Attend, O reader! while I narrate this tale of wonders!

One day as Adrian and Idris were riding through the forest, with their mother and accustomed companions, Idris, drawing her brother aside from the rest of the cavalcade, suddenly asked him, "What had become of his friend, Lionel Verney?"

"Even from this spot," replied Adrian, pointing to my sister's cottage, "you can see his dwelling."

"Indeed!" said Idris, "and why, if he be so near, does he not come to see us, and make one of our society?"

"I often visit him," replied Adrian; "but you may easily guess the motives, which prevent him from coming where his presence may annoy any one among us."

"I do guess them," said Idris, "and such as they are, I would not venture to combat them. Tell me, however, in what way he passes his time; what he is doing and thinking in his cottage retreat?"

"Nay, my sweet sister," replied Adrian, "you ask me more than I can well answer; but if you feel interest in him, why not visit him? He will feel highly honoured, and thus you may repay a part of the obligation I owe him, and compensate for the injuries fortune has done him."

"I will most readily accompany you to his abode," said the lady, "not that I wish that either of us should unburthen ourselves of our debt, which, being no less than your life, must remain unpayable ever. But let us go; tomorrow we will arrange to ride out together, and proceeding towards that part of the forest, call upon him."

The next evening therefore, though the autumnal change had brought on cold and rain, Adrian and Idris entered my cottage. They found me Curius-like, feasting on sorry fruits for supper; but they brought gifts richer than the golden bribes of the Sabines, nor could I refuse the invaluable store of friendship and delight which they bestowed. Surely the glorious twins of Latona were not more welcome, when, in the infancy of the world, they were brought forth to beautify and enlighten this "sterile promontory," than were this angelic pair to my lowly dwelling and grateful heart. We sat like one family round my hearth. Our talk was on subjects, unconnected with the emotions that evidently occupied each; but we each divined the other's thought, and as our voices spoke of indifferent matters, our eyes, in mute language, told a thousand things no tongue could have uttered.

They left me in an hour's time. They left me happy—how unspeakably happy. It did not require the measured sounds of human language to syllable the story of my extasy. Idris had visited me; Idris I should again and again see—my imagination did not wander beyond the completeness of this knowledge. I trod air; no doubt, no fear, no hope even, disturbed me; I clasped with my soul the fulness of contentment, satisfied, undesiring, beatified.

For many days Adrian and Idris continued to visit me thus. In this dear intercourse, love, in the guise of enthusiastic friendship, infused more and more of his omnipotent spirit. Idris felt it. Yes, divinity of the world, I read your characters in her looks and gesture; I heard your melodious voice echoed by her—you prepared for us a soft and flowery path, all gentle thoughts adorned it—your name, O Love, was not spoken, but you stood the Genius of the Hour, veiled, and time, but no mortal hand, might raise the curtain. Organs of articulate sound did not proclaim the union of our hearts; for untoward circumstance allowed no opportunity for the expression that hovered on our lips.

Oh my pen! haste thou to write what was, before the thought of what is, arrests the hand that guides thee. If I lift up my eyes and see the desart earth, and feel that those dear eyes have spent their mortal lustre, and that those beauteous lips are silent, their "crimson leaves" faded, for ever I am mute!

But you live, my Idris, even now you move before me! There was a glade, O reader! a grassy opening in the wood; the retiring trees left its velvet expanse as a temple for love; the silver Thames bounded it on one side, and a willow bending down dipt in the water its Naiad hair, dishevelled by the wind's viewless hand. The oaks around were the home of a tribe of nightingales—there am I now; Idris, in youth's dear prime, is by my side—remember, I am just twenty-two, and seventeen summers have scarcely passed over the beloved of my heart. The river swollen by autumnal rains, deluged the low lands, and Adrian in his favourite boat is employed in the dangerous pastime of plucking the topmost bough from a submerged oak. Are you weary of life, O Adrian, that you thus play with danger?—

He has obtained his prize, and he pilots his boat through the flood; our eyes were fixed on him fearfully, but the stream carried him away from us; he was forced to land far lower down, and to make a considerable circuit before he could join us. "He is safe!" said Idris, as he leapt on shore, and waved the bough over his head in token of success; "we will wait for him here."

We were alone together; the sun had set; the song of the nightingales began; the evening star shone distinct in the flood of light, which was yet unfaded in the west. The blue eyes of my angelic girl were fixed on this sweet emblem of herself: "How the light palpitates," she said, "which is that star's life. Its vacillating effulgence seems to say that its state, even like ours upon earth, is wavering and inconstant; it fears, methinks, and it loves."

"Gaze not on the star, dear, generous friend," I cried, "read not love in *its* trembling rays; look not upon distant worlds; speak not of the mere imagination of a sentiment. I have long been silent; long even to sickness have I desired to speak to you, and submit my soul, my life, my entire being to you. Look not on the star, dear love, or do, and let that eternal spark plead for me; let it be my witness and my advocate, silent as it shines—love is to me as light to the star; even so long as that is uneclipsed by annihilation, so long shall I love you."

Veiled for ever to the world's callous eye must be the transport of that moment. Still do I feel her graceful form press against my full-fraught heart—still does sight, and pulse, and breath sicken and fail, at the remembrance of that first kiss. Slowly and silently we went to meet Adrian, whom we heard approaching.

I entreated Adrian to return to me after he had conducted his sister home. And that same evening, walking among the moon-lit forest paths, I poured forth my whole heart, its transport and its hope, to my friend. For a moment he looked disturbed—"I might have foreseen this," he said, "what strife will now ensue! Pardon me, Lionel, nor wonder that the expectation of contest with my mother should jar me, when else I should delightedly confess that my best hopes are fulfilled, in confiding my sister to your protection. If you do not already know it, you will soon learn the deep hate my mother bears to the name Verney. I will converse with Idris; then all that a friend can do, I will do; to her it must belong to play the lover's part, if she be capable of it."

While the brother and sister were still hesitating in what manner they could best attempt to bring their mother over to their party, she, suspecting our meetings, taxed her children with them; taxed her fair daughter with deceit, and an unbecoming attachment for one whose only merit was being the son of the profligate favourite of her imprudent father; and who was doubtless as worthless as he from whom he boasted his descent. The eyes of Idris flashed at this accusation; she replied, "I do not deny that I love Verney; prove to me that he is worthless; and I will never see him more."

"Dear Madam," said Adrian, "let me entreat you to see him, to cultivate his friendship. You will wonder then, as I do, at the extent of his accomplishments, and the brilliancy of his talents." (Pardon me, gentle reader, this is not futile vanity;—not futile, since to know that Adrian felt thus, brings joy even now to my lone heart).

"Mad and foolish boy!" exclaimed the angry lady, "you have chosen with dreams and theories to overthrow my schemes for your own aggrandizement; but you shall not do the same by those I have formed for your sister. I but too well understand the fascination you both labour under; since I had the same struggle with your father, to make him cast off the parent of this youth, who hid his evil propensities with the smoothness and subtlety of a viper. In those days how often did I hear of his attractions, his wide spread conquests, his wit, his refined manners. It is well when flies only are caught by such spiders' webs; but is it for the high-born and powerful to bow their necks to the flimsy yoke of these unmeaning pretensions? Were your sister indeed the insignificant person she deserves to be, I would willingly leave her to the fate, the wretched fate, of the wife of a man, whose very person, resembling as it does his wretched father, ought to remind you of the folly and vice it typifies—but remember, Lady Idris, it is not alone the once royal blood of England that colours your veins, you are a Princess of Austria, and every life-drop is akin to emperors and kings. Are you then a fit mate for an uneducated shepherd-boy, whose only inheritance is his father's tarnished name?"

"I can make but one defence," replied Idris, "the same offered by my brother; see Lionel, converse with my shepherd-boy"——.

The Countess interrupted her indignantly—"Yours!"—she cried: and then, smoothing her impassioned features to a disdainful smile, she continued—"We will talk of this another time. All I now ask, all your mother, Idris, requests is, that you will not see this upstart during the interval of one month."

"I dare not comply," said Idris, "it would pain him too much. I have no right to play with his feelings, to accept his proffered love, and then sting him with neglect."

"This is going too far," her mother answered, with quivering lips, and eyes again instinct by anger.

"Nay, Madam," said Adrian, "unless my sister consent never to see him again, it is surely an useless torment to separate them for a month."

"Certainly," replied the ex-queen, with bitter scorn, "his love, and her love, and both their childish flutterings, are to be put in fit comparison with my years of hope and anxiety, with the duties of the offspring of kings, with the high and dignified conduct which one of her descent ought to pursue. But it is unworthy of me to argue and complain. Perhaps you will have the goodness to promise me not to marry during that interval?"

This was asked only half ironically; and Idris wondered why her mother should extort from her a solemn vow not to do, what she had never dreamed of doing—but the promise was required and given.

All went on cheerfully now; we met as usual, and talked without dread of our future plans. The Countess was so gentle, and even beyond her wont, amiable with her children, that they began to entertain hopes of her ultimate consent. She was too unlike them, too utterly alien to their tastes, for them to find delight in her society, or in the prospect of its continuance, but it gave them pleasure to see her conciliating and kind. Once even, Adrian ventured to propose her receiving me. She refused with a smile, reminding him that for the present his sister had promised to be patient.

One day, after the lapse of nearly a month, Adrian received a letter from a friend in London, requesting his immediate presence for the furtherance of some important object. Guileless himself, Adrian feared no deceit. I rode with him as far as Staines: he was in high spirits; and, since I could not see Idris during his absence, he promised a speedy return. His gaiety, which was extreme, had the strange effect of awakening in me contrary feelings; a presentiment of evil hung over me; I loitered on my return; I counted the hours that must elapse before I saw Idris again. Wherefore should this be? What evil might not happen in the mean time? Might not her mother take advantage of Adrian's absence to urge her beyond her sufferance, perhaps to entrap her? I resolved, let what would befall, to see and converse with her the following day. This determination soothed me. To-morrow, loveliest and best, hope and joy of my life, to-morrow I will see thee—Fool, to dream of a moment's delay!

I went to rest. At past midnight I was awaked by a violent knocking. It was now deep winter; it had snowed, and was still snowing; the wind whistled in the leafless trees, despoiling them of the white flakes as they fell; its drear moaning, and the continued knocking, mingled wildly with my dreams—at length I was wide awake; hastily dressing myself, I hurried to discover the cause of this disturbance, and to open my door to the unexpected visitor. Pale as the snow that showered about her, with clasped hands, Idris stood before me. "Save me!" she exclaimed, and would have sunk to the ground had I not supported her. In a moment however she revived, and, with energy, almost with violence, entreated me to saddle horses, to take her away, away to London—to her brother—at least to save her. I had no horses—she wrung her hands. "What can I do?" she cried, "I am lost—we are both for ever lost! But come—come with me, Lionel; here I must not stay,—we can get a chaise at the nearest post-house; yet perhaps we have time!—come, O come with me to save and protect me!"

When I heard her piteous demands, while with disordered dress, dishevelled hair, and aghast looks, she wrung her hands—the idea shot across me—is she also mad?—"Sweet one," and I folded her to my heart, "better repose than wander further;—rest—my beloved, I will make a fire—you are chill."

"Rest!" she cried, "repose! you rave, Lionel! If you delay we are lost; come, I pray you, unless you would cast me off for ever."

That Idris, the princely born, nursling of wealth and luxury, should have come through the tempestuous winter-night from her regal abode, and standing at my lowly door, conjure me to fly with her through darkness and storm—was surely a dream—again her plaintive tones, the sight of her loveliness assured me that it was no vision. Looking timidly around, as if she feared to be overheard, she whispered: "I have discovered—to-morrow—that is, to-day—already the to-morrow is come—before dawn, foreigners, Austrians, my mother's hirelings, are to carry me off to Germany, to prison, to marriage—to anything, except you and my brother—take me away, or soon they will be here!"

I was frightened by her vehemence, and imagined some mistake in her incoherent tale; but I no longer hesitated to obey her. She had come by herself from the Castle, three long miles, at midnight, through the heavy snow; we must reach Englefield Green, a mile and a half further, before we could obtain a chaise. She told me, that she had kept up her strength and courage till her arrival at my cottage, and then both failed. Now she could hardly walk. Supporting her as I did, still she lagged: and at the distance of half a mile, after many stoppages, shivering fits, and half faintings, she slipt from my supporting arm on the snow, and with a torrent of tears averred that she must be taken, for that she could not proceed. I lifted her up in my arms; her light form rested on my breast.—I felt no burthen, except the internal one of contrary and contending emotions. Brimming delight now invested me. Again her chill limbs touched me as a torpedo; and I shuddered in sympathy with her pain and fright. Her head lay on my shoulder, her breath waved my hair, her heart beat near mine, transport made me tremble, blinded me, annihilated me—till a suppressed groan, bursting from her lips, the chattering of her teeth, which she strove vainly to subdue, and all the signs of suffering she evinced, recalled me to the necessity of speed and succour. At last I said to her, "There is Englefield Green; there the inn. But, if you are seen thus strangely circumstanced, dear Idris, even now your enemies may learn your flight too soon: were it not better that I hired the chaise alone? I will put you in safety meanwhile, and return to you immediately."

She answered that I was right, and might do with her as I pleased. I observed the door of a small out-house a-jar. I pushed it open; and, with some hay strewed about, I formed a couch for her, placing her exhausted frame on it, and covering her with my cloak. I feared to leave her, she looked so wan and faint—but in a moment she re-acquired animation, and, with that, fear; and again she implored me not to delay. To call up the people of the inn, and obtain a conveyance and horses, even though I harnessed them myself, was the work of many minutes; minutes, each freighted with the weight of ages. I caused the chaise to advance a little, waited till the people of the inn had retired, and then made the post-boy draw up the carriage to the spot where Idris, impatient, and now somewhat recovered, stood waiting for me. I lifted her into the chaise; I assured her that with our four horses we should arrive in London before five o'clock, the hour when she would be sought and missed. I besought her to calm herself; a kindly shower of tears relieved her, and by degrees she related her tale of fear and peril.

That same night after Adrian's departure, her mother had warmly expostulated with her on the subject of her attachment to me. Every motive, every threat, every angry taunt was urged in vain. She seemed to consider that through me she had lost Raymond; I was the evil influence of her life; I was even accused of encreasing and confirming the mad and base apostacy of Adrian from all views of advancement and grandeur; and now this miserable mountaineer was to steal her daughter. Never, Idris related, did the angry lady deign to recur to gentleness and persuasion; if she had, the task of resistance would have been exquisitely painful. As it was, the sweet girl's generous nature was roused to defend, and ally herself with, my despised cause. Her mother ended with a look of contempt and covert triumph, which for a moment awakened the suspicions of Idris. When they parted for the night, the Countess said, "To-morrow I trust your tone will be changed: be composed; I have agitated you; go to rest; and I will send you a medicine I always take when unduly restless—it will give you a quiet night."

By the time that she had with uneasy thoughts laid her fair cheek upon her pillow, her mother's servant brought a draught; a suspicion again crossed her at this novel proceeding, sufficiently alarming to determine her not to take the potion; but dislike of contention, and a wish to discover whether there was any just foundation for her conjectures, made her, she said, almost instinctively, and in contradiction to her usual frankness, pretend to swallow the medicine. Then, agitated as she had been by her mother's violence, and now by unaccustomed fears, she lay unable to sleep, starting at every sound. Soon her door opened softly, and on her springing up, she heard a whisper, "Not asleep yet," and the door again closed. With a beating heart she expected another visit, and when after an interval her chamber was again invaded, having first assured herself that the intruders were her mother and an attendant, she composed herself to feigned sleep. A step approached her bed, she dared not move, she strove to calm her palpitations, which became more violent, when she heard her mother say mutteringly, "Pretty simpleton, little do you think that your game is already at an end for ever."

For a moment the poor girl fancied that her mother believed that she had drank poison: she was on the point of springing up; when the Countess, already at a distance from the bed, spoke in a low voice to her companion, and again Idris listened: "Hasten," said she, "there is no time to lose—it is long past eleven; they will be here at five; take merely the clothes necessary for her journey, and her jewel-casket." The servant obeyed; few words were spoken on either side; but those were caught at with avidity by the intended victim. She heard the name of her own maid mentioned;—"No, no," replied her mother, "she does not go with us; Lady Idris must forget England, and all belonging to it." And again she heard, "She will not wake till late to-morrow, and we shall then be at sea."——"All is ready," at length the woman announced. The Countess again came to her daughter's bedside: "In Austria at least," she said, "you will obey. In Austria, where obedience can be enforced, and no choice left but between an honourable prison and a fitting marriage."

Both then withdrew; though, as she went, the Countess said, "Softly; all sleep; though all have not been prepared for sleep, like her. I would not have any one suspect, or she might be roused to resistance, and perhaps escape. Come with me to my room; we will remain there till the hour agreed upon." They went. Idris, panic-struck, but animated and strengthened even by her excessive fear, dressed herself hurriedly, and going down a flight of back-stairs, avoiding the vicinity of her mother's apartment, she contrived to escape from the castle by a low window, and came through snow, wind, and obscurity to my cottage; nor lost her courage, until she arrived, and, depositing her fate in my hands, gave herself up to the desperation and weariness that overwhelmed her.

I comforted her as well as I might. Joy and exultation, were mine, to possess, and to save her. Yet not to excite fresh agitation in her, "*per non turbar quel bel viso sereno,*" [★] I curbed my delight. I strove to quiet the eager dancing of my heart; I turned from her my eyes, beaming with too much tenderness, and proudly, to dark night, and the inclement atmosphere, murmured the expressions of my transport. We reached London, methought, all too soon; and yet I could not regret our speedy arrival, when I witnessed the extasy with which my beloved girl found herself in her brother's arms, safe from every evil, under his unblamed protection.

Adrian wrote a brief note to his mother, informing her that Idris was under his care and guardianship. Several days elapsed, and at last an answer came, dated from Cologne. "It was useless," the haughty and disappointed lady wrote, "for the Earl of Windsor and his sister to address again the injured parent, whose only expectation of tranquillity must be derived from oblivion of their existence. Her desires had been blasted, her schemes overthrown. She did not complain; in her brother's court she would find, not

[★] "in order not to disturb that serene and beautiful face."

compensation for their disobedience (filial unkindness admitted of none), but such a state of things and mode of life, as might best reconcile her to her fate. Under such circumstances, she positively declined any communication with them."

Such were the strange and incredible events, that finally brought about my union with the sister of my best friend, with my adored Idris. With simplicity and courage she set aside the prejudices and opposition which were obstacles to my happiness, nor scrupled to give her hand, where she had given her heart. To be worthy of her, to raise myself to her height through the exertion of talents and virtue, to repay her love with devoted, unwearied tenderness, were the only thanks I could offer for the matchless gift.

Chapter VI

And now let the reader, passing over some short period of time, be introduced to our happy circle. Adrian, Idris and I, were established in Windsor Castle; Lord Raymond and my sister, inhabited a house which the former had built on the borders of the Great Park, near Perdita's cottage, as was still named the low-roofed abode, where we two, poor even in hope, had each received the assurance of our felicity. We had our separate occupations and our common amusements. Sometimes we passed whole days under the leafy covert of the forest with our books and music. This occurred during those rare days in this country, when the sun mounts his etherial throne in unclouded majesty, and the windless atmosphere is as a bath of pellucid and grateful water, wrapping the senses in tranquillity. When the clouds veiled the sky, and the wind scattered them there and here, rending their woof, and strewing its fragments through the aerial plains—then we rode out, and sought new spots of beauty and repose. When the frequent rains shut us within doors, evening recreation followed morning study, ushered in by music and song. Idris had a natural musical talent; and her voice, which had been carefully cultivated, was full and sweet. Raymond and I made a part of the concert, and Adrian and Perdita were devout listeners. Then we were as gay as summer insects, playful as children; we ever met one another with smiles, and read content and joy in each other's countenances. Our prime festivals were held in Perdita's cottage; nor were we ever weary of talking of the past or dreaming of the future. Jealousy and disquiet were unknown among us; nor did a fear or hope of change ever disturb our tranquillity. Others said, We might be happy—we said—We are.

When any separation took place between us, it generally so happened, that Idris and Perdita would ramble away together, and we remained to discuss the affairs of nations, and the philosophy of life. The very difference of our dispositions gave zest to these conversations. Adrian had the superiority in learning and eloquence; but Raymond possessed a quick penetration, and a practical knowledge of life, which usually displayed itself in opposition to Adrian, and thus kept up the ball of discussion. At other times we made excursions of many days' duration, and crossed the country to visit any spot noted for beauty or historical association. Sometimes we went up to London, and entered into the amusements of the busy throng; sometimes our retreat was invaded by visitors from among them. This change made us only the more sensible to the delights of the intimate intercourse of our own circle, the tranquillity of our divine forest, and our happy evenings in the halls of our beloved Castle.

The disposition of Idris was peculiarly frank, soft, and affectionate. Her temper was unalterably sweet; and although firm and resolute on any point that touched her heart, she was yielding to those she loved. The nature of Perdita was less perfect; but tenderness and happiness improved her temper, and softened her natural reserve. Her understanding was clear and comprehensive, her imagination vivid; she was sincere, generous, and reasonable. Adrian, the matchless brother of my soul, the sensitive and excellent Adrian, loving all, and beloved by all, yet seemed destined not to find the half of himself, which was to complete his happiness. He often left us, and wandered by himself in the woods, or sailed in his little skiff, his books his only companions. He was often the gayest of our party, at the same time that he was the only one visited by fits of despondency; his slender frame seemed overcharged with the weight of life, and his soul appeared rather to inhabit his body than unite with it. I was hardly more devoted to my Idris than to her brother, and she loved him as her teacher, her friend, the benefactor who had secured to her the fulfilment of her dearest wishes. Raymond, the ambitious, restless Raymond, reposed midway on the great high-road of life, and was content to give up all his schemes of sovereignty and fame, to make one of us, the flowers of the field. His kingdom was the heart of Perdita, his subjects her thoughts; by her he was loved, respected as a superior being, obeyed, waited on. No office, no devotion, no watching was irksome to her, as it regarded him. She would sit apart from us and watch him; she would weep for joy to think that he was hers. She erected a temple for him in the depth of her being, and each faculty was a priestess vowed to his service. Sometimes she might be wayward and capricious; but her repentance was bitter, her return entire, and even this inequality of temper suited him who was not formed by nature to float idly down the stream of life.

During the first year of their marriage, Perdita presented Raymond with a lovely girl. It was curious to trace in this miniature model the very traits of its father. The same half-disdainful lips and smile of triumph, the same intelligent eyes, the same brow and chestnut hair; her very hands and taper fingers resembled his. How very dear she was to Perdita! In progress of time, I also became a father, and our little darlings, our playthings and delights, called forth a thousand new and delicious feelings.

Years passed thus,—even years. Each month brought forth its successor, each year one like to that gone by; truly, our lives were a living comment on that beautiful sentiment of Plutarch, that "our souls have a natural inclination to love, being born as much to love, as to feel, to reason, to understand and remember." We talked of change and active pursuits, but still remained at Windsor, incapable of violating the charm that attached us to our secluded life.

> Pareamo aver qui tutto il ben raccolto
> Che fra mortali in più parte si rimembra.[★]

Now also that our children gave us occupation, we found excuses for our idleness, in the idea of bringing them up to a more splendid career. At length our tranquillity was disturbed, and the course of events, which for five years had flowed on in hushing tranquillity, was broken by breakers and obstacles, that woke us from our pleasant dream.

A new Lord Protector of England was to be chosen; and, at Raymond's request, we removed to London, to witness, and even take a part in the election. If Raymond had been united to Idris, this post had been his stepping-stone to higher dignity; and his desire for power and fame had been crowned with fullest measure. He had exchanged a sceptre for a lute, a kingdom for Perdita.

[★] We appear to have gathered here all the good / That men will remember in greatest measure.

Did he think of this as we journeyed up to town? I watched him, but could make but little of him. He was particularly gay, playing with his child, and turning to sport every word that was uttered. Perhaps he did this because he saw a cloud upon Perdita's brow. She tried to rouse herself, but her eyes every now and then filled with tears, and she looked wistfully on Raymond and her girl, as if fearful that some evil would betide them. And so she felt. A presentiment of ill hung over her. She leaned from the window looking on the forest, and the turrets of the Castle, and as these became hid by intervening objects, she passionately exclaimed—"Scenes of happiness! scenes sacred to devoted love, when shall I see you again! and when I see ye, shall I be still the beloved and joyous Perdita, or shall I, heart-broken and lost, wander among your groves, the ghost of what I am!"

"Why, silly one," cried Raymond, "what is your little head pondering upon, that of a sudden you have become so sublimely dismal? Cheer up, or I shall make you over to Idris, and call Adrian into the carriage, who, I see by his gesture, sympathizes with my good spirits."

Adrian was on horseback; he rode up to the carriage, and his gaiety, in addition to that of Raymond, dispelled my sister's melancholy. We entered London in the evening, and went to our several abodes near Hyde Park.

The following morning Lord Raymond visited me early. "I come to you," he said, "only half assured that you will assist me in my project, but resolved to go through with it, whether you concur with me or not. Promise me secrecy however; for if you will not contribute to my success, at least you must not baffle me."

"Well, I promise. And now——"

"And now, my dear fellow, for what are we come to London? To be present at the election of a Protector, and to give our yea or nay for his shuffling Grace of ———? or for that noisy Ryland? Do you believe, Verney, that I brought you to town for that? No, we will have a Protector of our own. We will set up a candidate, and ensure his success. We will nominate Adrian, and do our best to bestow on him the power to which he is entitled by his birth, and which he merits through his virtues.

"Do not answer; I know all your objections, and will reply to them in order. First, Whether he will or will not consent to become a great man? Leave the task of persuasion on that point to me; I do not ask you to assist me there. Secondly, Whether he ought to exchange his employment of plucking blackberries, and nursing wounded partridges in the forest, for the command of a nation? My dear Lionel, *we* are married men, and find employment sufficient in amusing our wives, and dancing our children. But Adrian is alone, wifeless, childless, unoccupied. I have long observed him. He pines for want of some interest in life. His heart, exhausted by his early sufferings, reposes like a new-healed limb, and shrinks from all excitement. But his understanding, his charity, his virtues, want a field for exercise and display; and we will procure it for him. Besides, is it not a shame, that the genius of Adrian should fade from the earth like a flower in an untrod mountain-path, fruitless? Do you think Nature composed his surpassing machine for no purpose? Believe me, he was destined to be the author of infinite good to his native England. Has she not bestowed on him every gift in prodigality?—birth, wealth, talent, goodness? Does not every one love and admire him? and does he not delight singly in such efforts as manifest his love to all? Come, I see that you are already persuaded, and will second me when I propose him to-night in parliament."

"You have got up all your arguments in excellent order," I replied; "and, if Adrian consent, they are unanswerable. One only condition I would make,—that you do nothing without his concurrence."

"I believe you are in the right," said Raymond; "although I had thought at first to arrange the affair differently. Be it so. I will go instantly to Adrian; and, if he inclines to consent, you will not destroy my labour by persuading him to return, and turn squirrel again in Windsor Forest. Idris, you will not act the traitor towards me?"

"Trust me," replied she, "I will preserve a strict neutrality."

"For my part," said I, "I am too well convinced of the worth of our friend, and the rich harvest of benefits that all England would reap from his Protectorship, to deprive my countrymen of such a blessing, if he consent to bestow it on them."

In the evening Adrian visited us.—"Do you cabal also against me," said he, laughing; "and will you make common cause with Raymond, in dragging a poor visionary from the clouds to surround him with the fireworks and blasts of earthly grandeur, instead of heavenly rays and airs? I thought you knew me better."

"I do know you better," I replied "than to think that you would be happy in such a situation; but the good you would do to others may be an inducement, since the time is probably arrived when you can put your theories into practice, and you may bring about such reformation and change, as will conduce to that perfect system of government which you delight to portray."

"You speak of an almost-forgotten dream," said Adrian, his countenance slightly clouding as he spoke; "the visions of my boyhood have long since faded in the light of reality; I know now that I am not a man fitted to govern nations; sufficient for me, if I keep in wholesome rule the little kingdom of my own mortality.

"But do not you see, Lionel, the drift of our noble friend; a drift, perhaps, unknown to himself, but apparent to me. Lord Raymond was never born to be a drone in the hive, and to find content in our pastoral life. He thinks, that he ought to be satisfied; he imagines, that his present situation precludes the possibility of aggrandisement; he does not therefore, even in his own heart, plan change for himself. But do you not see, that, under the idea of exalting me, he is chalking out a new path for himself; a path of action from which he has long wandered?

"Let us assist him. He, the noble, the warlike, the great in every quality that can adorn the mind and person of man; he is fitted to be the Protector of England. If *I*—that is, if *we* propose him, he will assuredly be elected, and will find, in the functions of that high office, scope for the towering powers of his mind. Even Perdita will rejoice. Perdita, in whom ambition was a covered fire until she married Raymond, which event was for a time the fulfilment of her hopes; Perdita will rejoice in the glory and advancement of her lord—and, coyly and prettily, not be discontented with her share. In the mean time, we, the wise of the land, will return to our Castle, and, Cincinnatus-like, take to our usual labours, until our friend shall require our presence and assistance here."

The more Adrian reasoned upon this scheme, the more feasible it appeared. His own determination never to enter into public life was insurmountable, and the delicacy of his health was a sufficient argument against it. The next step was to induce Raymond to confess his secret wishes for dignity and fame. He entered while we were speaking. The way in which Adrian had received his project for setting him up as a candidate for the Protectorship, and his replies, had already awakened in his mind, the view of the subject which we were now discussing. His countenance and manner betrayed irresolution and anxiety; but the anxiety arose from a fear that we should not prosecute, or not succeed in our idea; and his irresolution, from a doubt whether we should risk a defeat. A few words from us decided him, and hope and joy sparkled in his eyes; the idea of embarking in a career, so congenial to his early habits and cherished wishes, made him as before energetic and bold. We discussed his chances, the merits of the other candidates, and the dispositions of the voters.

After all we miscalculated. Raymond had lost much of his popularity, and was deserted by his peculiar partizans. Absence from the busy stage had caused him to be forgotten by the people; his former parliamentary supporters were principally composed of royalists, who had been willing to make an idol of him when he appeared as the heir of the Earldom of Windsor; but who were indifferent to him, when he came forward with no other attributes and distinctions than they conceived to be common to many among themselves. Still he had many friends, admirers of his transcendent talents; his presence in the house, his eloquence, address and imposing beauty, were calculated to produce an electric effect. Adrian also, notwithstanding his recluse habits and theories, so adverse to the spirit of party, had many friends, and they were easily induced to vote for a candidate of his selection.

The Duke of ———, and Mr. Ryland, Lord Raymond's old antagonist, were the other candidates. The Duke was supported by all the aristocrats of the republic, who considered him their proper representative. Ryland was the popular candidate; when Lord Raymond was first added to the list, his chance of success appeared small. We retired from the debate which had followed on his nomination: we, his nominators, mortified; he dispirited to excess. Perdita reproached us bitterly. Her expectations had been strongly excited; she had urged nothing against our project, on the contrary, she was evidently pleased by it; but its evident ill success changed the current of her ideas. She felt, that, once awakened, Raymond would never return unrepining to Windsor. His habits were unhinged; his restless mind roused from its sleep, ambition must now be his companion through life; and if he did not succeed in his present attempt, she foresaw that unhappiness and cureless discontent would follow. Perhaps her own disappointment added a sting to her thoughts and words; she did not spare us, and our own reflections added to our disquietude.

It was necessary to follow up our nomination, and to persuade Raymond to present himself to the electors on the following evening. For a long time he was obstinate. He would embark in a balloon; he would sail for a distant quarter of the world, where his name and humiliation were unknown. But this was useless; his attempt was registered; his purpose published to the world; his shame could never be erased from the memories of men. It was as well to fail at last after a struggle, as to fly now at the beginning of his enterprise.

From the moment that he adopted this idea, he was changed. His depression and anxiety fled; he became all life and activity. The smile of triumph shone on his countenance; determined to pursue his object to the uttermost, his manner and expression seem ominous of the accomplishment of his wishes. Not so Perdita. She was frightened by his gaiety, for she dreaded a greater revulsion at the end. If his appearance even inspired us with hope, it only rendered the state of her mind more painful. She feared to lose sight of him; yet she dreaded to remark any change in the temper of his mind. She listened eagerly to him, yet tantalized herself by giving to his words a meaning foreign to their true interpretation, and adverse to her hopes. She dared not be present at the contest; yet she remained at home a prey to double solicitude. She wept over her little girl; she looked, she spoke, as if she dreaded the occurrence of some frightful calamity. She was half mad from the effects of uncontrollable agitation.

Lord Raymond presented himself to the house with fearless confidence and insinuating address. After the Duke of ——— and Mr. Ryland had finished their speeches, he commenced. Assuredly he had not conned his lesson; and at first he hesitated, pausing in his ideas, and in the choice of his expressions. By degrees he warmed; his words flowed with ease, his language was full of vigour, and his voice of persuasion. He reverted to his past life, his successes in Greece, his favour at home. Why should he lose this, now that added years, prudence, and the pledge which his marriage gave to his country, ought to encrease, rather than diminish his claims to confidence? He spoke of the state of England; the necessary measures to be taken to ensure its security, and confirm its prosperity. He drew a glowing picture of its present situation. As he spoke, every sound was hushed, every thought suspended by intense attention. His graceful elocution enchained the senses of his hearers. In some degree also he was fitted to reconcile all parties. His birth pleased the aristocracy; his being the candidate recommended by Adrian, a man intimately allied to the popular party, caused a number, who had no great reliance either on the Duke or Mr. Ryland, to range on his side.

The contest was keen and doubtful. Neither Adrian nor myself would have been so anxious, if our own success had depended on our exertions; but we had egged our friend on to the enterprise, and it became us to ensure his triumph. Idris, who entertained the highest opinion of his abilities, was warmly interested in the event: and my poor sister, who dared not hope, and to whom fear was misery, was plunged into a fever of disquietude.

Day after day passed while we discussed our projects for the evening, and each night was occupied by debates which offered no conclusion. At last the crisis came: the night when parliament, which had so long delayed its choice, must decide: as the hour of twelve passed, and the new day began, it was by virtue of the constitution dissolved, its power extinct.

We assembled at Raymond's house, we and our partizans. At half past five o'clock we proceeded to the House. Idris endeavoured to calm Perdita; but the poor girl's agitation deprived her of all power of self-command. She walked up and down the room,—gazed wildly when any one entered, fancying that they might be the announcers of her doom. I must do justice to my sweet sister: it was not for herself that she was thus agonized. She alone knew the weight which Raymond attached to his success. Even to us he assumed gaiety and hope, and assumed them so well, that we did not divine the secret workings of his mind. Sometimes a nervous trembling, a sharp dissonance of voice, and momentary fits of absence revealed to Perdita the violence he did himself; but we, intent on our plans, observed only his ready laugh, his joke intruded on all occasions, the flow of his spirits which seemed incapable of ebb. Besides, Perdita was with him in his retirement; she saw the moodiness that succeeded to this forced hilarity; she marked his disturbed sleep, his painful irritability—once she had seen his tears—hers had scarce ceased to flow, since she had beheld the big drops which disappointed pride had caused to gather in his eye, but which pride was unable to dispel. What wonder then, that her feelings were wrought to this pitch! I thus accounted to myself for her agitation; but this was not all, and the sequel revealed another excuse.

One moment we seized before our departure, to take leave of our beloved girls. I had small hope of success, and entreated Idris to watch over my sister. As I approached the latter, she seized my hand, and drew me into another apartment; she threw herself into my arms, and wept and sobbed bitterly and long. I tried to soothe her; I bade her hope; I asked what tremendous consequences would ensue even on our failure. "My brother," she cried, "protector of my childhood, dear, most dear Lionel, my fate hangs by a thread. I have you all about me now—you, the companion of my infancy; Adrian, as dear to me as if bound by the ties of blood; Idris, the sister of my heart, and her lovely offspring. This, O this may be the last time that you will surround me thus!"

Abruptly she stopped, and then cried: "What have I said?—foolish false girl that I am!" She looked wildly on me, and then suddenly calming herself, apologized for what she called her unmeaning words, saying that she must indeed be insane, for, while Raymond lived, she must be happy; and then, though she still wept, she suffered me tranquilly to depart. Raymond only took her hand when he went, and looked on her expressively; she answered by a look of intelligence and assent.

Poor girl! what she then suffered! I could never entirely forgive Raymond for the trials he imposed on her, occasioned as they were by a selfish feeling on his part. He had schemed, if he failed in his present attempt, without taking leave of any of us, to embark for Greece, and never again to revisit England. Perdita acceded to his wishes; for his contentment was the chief object of her life, the crown of her enjoyment; but to leave us all, her companions, the beloved partners of her happiest years, and in the interim to conceal this frightful determination, was a task that almost conquered her stength of mind. She had been employed in arranging for their departure; she had promised Raymond during this decisive evening, to take advantage of our absence, to go one stage of the journey, and he, after his defeat was ascertained, would slip away from us, and join her.

Although, when I was informed of this scheme, I was bitterly offended by the small attention which Raymond paid to my sister's feelings, I was led by reflection to consider, that he acted under the force of such strong excitement, as to take from him the consciousness, and, consequently, the guilt of a fault. If he had permitted us to witness his agitation, he would have been more under the guidance of reason; but his struggles for the shew of composure, acted with such violence on his nerves, as to destroy his power of self-command. I am convinced that, at the worst, he would have returned from the sea-shore to take leave of us, and to make us the partners of his council. But the task imposed on Perdita was not the less painful. He had extorted from her a vow of secrecy; and her part of the drama, since it was to be performed alone, was the most agonizing that could be devised. But to return to my narrative.

The debates had hitherto been long and loud; they had often been protracted merely for the sake of delay. But now each seemed fearful lest the fatal moment should pass, while the choice was yet undecided. Unwonted silence reigned in the house, the members spoke in whispers, and the ordinary business was transacted with celerity and quietness. During the first stage of the election, the Duke of——— had been thrown out; the question therefore lay between Lord Raymond and Mr. Ryland. The latter had felt secure of victory, until the appearance of Raymond; and, since his name had been inserted as a candidate, he had canvassed with eagerness. He had appeared each evening, impatience and anger marked in his looks, scowling on us from the opposite side of St. Stephen's, as if his mere frown would cast eclipse on our hopes.

Every thing in the English constitution had been regulated for the better preservation of peace. On the last day, two candidates only were allowed to remain; and to obviate, if possible, the last struggle between these, a bribe was offered to him who should voluntarily resign his pretensions; a place of great emolument and honour was given him, and his success facilitated at a future election. Strange to say however, no instance had yet occurred, where either candidate had had recourse to this expedient; in consequence the law had become obsolete, nor had been referred to by any of us in our discussions. To our extreme surprise, when it was moved that we should resolve ourselves into a committee for the election of the Lord Protector, the member who had nominated Ryland, rose and informed us that this candidate had resigned his pretensions. His information was at first received with silence; a confused murmur succeeded; and, when the chairman declared Lord Raymond duly chosen, it amounted to a shout of applause and victory. It seemed as if, far from any dread of defeat even if Mr. Ryland had not resigned, every voice would have been united in favour of our candidate. In fact, now that the idea of contest was dismissed, all hearts returned to their former respect and admiration of our accomplished friend. Each felt, that England had never seen a Protector so capable of fulfilling the arduous duties of that high office. One voice made of many voices, resounded through the chamber; it syllabled the name of Raymond.

He entered. I was on one of the highest seats, and saw him walk up the passage to the table of the speaker. The native modesty of his disposition conquered the joy of his triumph. He looked round timidly; a mist seemed before his eyes. Adrian, who was beside me, hastened to him, and jumping down the benches, was at his side in a moment. His appearance re-animated our friend; and, when he came to speak and act, his hesitation vanished, and he shone out supreme in majesty and victory. The former Protector tendered him the oaths, and presented him with the insignia of office, performing the ceremonies of installation. The house then dissolved. The chief members of the state crowded round the new magistrate, and conducted him to the palace of government. Adrian suddenly vanished; and, by the time that Raymond's supporters were reduced to our intimate friends merely, returned leading Idris to congratulate her friend on his success.

But where was Perdita? In securing solicitously an unobserved retreat in case of failure, Raymond had forgotten to arrange the mode by which she was to hear of his success; and she had been too much agitated to revert to this circumstance. When Idris entered, so far had Raymond forgotten himself, that he asked for my sister; one word, which told of her mysterious disappearance, recalled him. Adrian it is true had already gone to seek the fugitive, imagining that her tameless anxiety had led her to the purlieus of the House, and that some sinister event detained her. But Raymond, without explaining himself, suddenly quitted us, and in another moment we heard him gallop down the street, in spite of the wind and rain that scattered tempest over the earth. We did not know how far he had to go, and soon separated, supposing that in a short time he would return to the palace with Perdita, and that they would not be sorry to find themselves alone.

Perdita had arrived with her child at Darford, weeping and inconsolable. She directed everything to be prepared for the continuance of their journey, and placing her lovely sleeping charge on a bed, passed several hours in acute suffering. Sometimes she observed the war of elements, thinking that they also declared against her, and listened to the pattering of the rain in gloomy despair. Sometimes she hung over her child, tracing her resemblance to the father, and fearful lest in after life she should display the same passions and uncontrollable impulses, that rendered him unhappy. Again, with a gush of pride and delight, she marked in the features of her little girl, the same smile of beauty that often irradiated Raymond's countenance. The sight of it soothed her. She thought of the treasure she possessed in the affections of her lord; of his accomplishments, surpassing those of his contemporaries, his genius, his devotion to her.—Soon she thought, that all she possessed in the world, except him, might well be spared, nay, given with delight, a propitiatory offering, to secure the supreme good she retained in him. Soon she imagined, that fate demanded this sacrifice from her, as a mark she was devoted to Raymond, and that it must be made with cheerfulness. She figured to herself their life in the Greek isle he had selected for their retreat; her task of soothing him; her cares for the beauteous Clara, her rides in his company, her dedication of herself to his consolation. The picture then presented itself to her in such glowing colours, that she feared the reverse, and a life of magnificence and power in London; where Raymond would no longer be hers only, nor she the sole source of happiness to him. So far as she merely was concerned, she began to hope for defeat; and it was only on his account that her feelings vacillated, as she heard him gallop into the court-yard of the inn. That he should come to her alone, wetted by the storm, careless of every thing except speed, what else could it mean, than that, vanquished and solitary, they were to take their way from native England, the scene of shame, and hide themselves in the myrtle groves of the Grecian isles?

In a moment she was in his arms. The knowledge of his success had become so much a part of himself, that he forgot that it was necessary to impart it to his companion. She only felt in his embrace a dear assurance that while he possessed her, he would not despair. "This is kind," she cried; "this is noble, my own beloved! O fear not disgrace or lowly fortune, while you have your Perdita; fear not sorrow, while our child lives and smiles. Let us go even where you will; the love that accompanies us will prevent our regrets."

Locked in his embrace, she spoke thus, and cast back her head, seeking an assent to her words in his eyes—they were sparkling with ineffable delight. "Why, my little Lady Protectress," said he, playfully, "what is this you say? And what pretty scheme have you woven of exile and obscurity, while a brighter web, a gold-enwoven tissue, is that which, in truth, you ought to contemplate?"

He kissed her brow—but the wayward girl, half sorry at his triumph, agitated by swift change of thought, hid her face in his bosom and wept. He comforted her; he instilled into her his own hopes and desires; and soon her countenance beamed with sympathy. How very happy were they that night! How full even to bursting was their sense of joy!

Chapter VII

Having seen our friend properly installed in his new office, we turned our eyes towards Windsor. The nearness of this place to London was such, as to take away the idea of painful separation, when we quitted Raymond and Perdita. We took leave of them in the Protectoral Palace. It was pretty enough to see my sister enter as it were into the spirit of the drama, and endeavour to fill her station with becoming dignity. Her internal pride and humility of manner were now more than ever at war. Her timidity was not artificial, but arose from that fear of not being properly appreciated, that slight estimation of the neglect of the world, which also characterized Raymond. But then Perdita thought more constantly of others than he; and part of her bashfulness arose from a wish to take from those around her a sense of inferiority; a feeling which never crossed her mind. From the circumstances of her birth and education, Idris would have been better fitted for the formulæ of ceremony; but the very ease which accompanied such actions with her, arising from habit, rendered them tedious; while, with every drawback, Perdita evidently enjoyed her situation. She was too full of new ideas to feel much pain when we departed; she took an affectionate leave of us, and promised to visit us soon; but she did not regret the circumstances that caused our separation. The spirits of Raymond were unbounded; he did not know what to do with his new got power; his head was full of plans; he had as yet decided on none—but he promised himself, his friends, and the world, that the æra of his Protectorship should be signalized by some act of surpassing glory.

Thus, we talked of them, and moralized, as with diminished numbers we returned to Windsor Castle. We felt extreme delight at our escape from political turmoil, and sought our solitude with redoubled zest. We did not want for occupation; but my eager disposition was now turned to the field of intellectual exertion only; and hard study I found to be an excellent medicine to allay a fever of spirit with which in indolence, I should doubtless have been assailed. Perdita had permitted us to take Clara back with us to Windsor; and she and my two lovely infants were perpetual sources of interest and amusement.

The only circumstance that disturbed our peace, was the health of Adrian. It evidently declined, without any symptom which could lead us to suspect his disease, unless indeed his brightened eyes, animated look, and flustering cheeks, made us dread consumption; but he was without pain or fear. He betook himself to books with ardour, and reposed from study in the society he best loved, that of his sister and myself. Sometimes he went up to London to visit Raymond, and watch the progress of events. Clara often accompanied him in these excursions; partly that she might see her parents, partly because Adrian delighted in the prattle, and intelligent looks of this lovely child.

Meanwhile all went on well in London. The new elections were finished; parliament met, and Raymond was occupied in a thousand beneficial schemes. Canals, aqueducts, bridges, stately buildings, and various edifices for public utility, were entered upon; he was continually surrounded by projectors and projects, which were to render England one scene of fertility and magnificence; the state of poverty was to be abolished; men were to be transported from place to place almost with the same facility as the Princes Houssain, Ali, and Ahmed, in the Arabian Nights. The physical state of man would soon not yield to the beatitude of angels; disease was to be banished; labour lightened of its heaviest burden. Nor did this seem extravagant. The arts of life, and the discoveries of science had augmented in a ratio which left all calculation behind; food sprung up, so to say, spontaneously—machines existed to supply with facility every want of the population. An evil direction still survived; and men were not happy, not because they could not, but because they would not rouse themselves to vanquish self-raised obstacles. Raymond was to inspire them with his beneficial will, and the mechanism of society, once systematised according to faultless rules, would never again swerve into disorder. For these hopes he abandoned his long-cherished ambition of being enregistered in the annals of nations as a successful warrior; laying aside his sword, peace and its enduring glories became his aim—the title he coveted was that of the benefactor of his country.

Among other works of art in which he was engaged, he had projected the erection of a national gallery for statues and pictures. He possessed many himself, which he designed to present to the Republic; and, as the edifice was to be the great ornament of his Protectorship, he was very fastidious in his choice of the plan on which it would be built. Hundreds were brought to him and rejected. He sent even to Italy and Greece for drawings; but, as the design was to be characterized by originality as well as by perfect beauty, his endeavours were for a time without avail. At length a drawing came, with an address where communications might be sent, and no artist's name affixed. The design was new and elegant, but faulty; so faulty, that although drawn with the hand and eye of taste, it was evidently the work of one who was not an architect. Raymond contemplated it with delight; the more he gazed, the more pleased he was; and yet the errors multiplied under inspection. He wrote to the address given, desiring to see the draughtsman, that such alterations might be made, as should be suggested in a consultation between him and the original conceiver.

A Greek came. A middle-aged man, with some intelligence of manner, but with so common-place a physiognomy, that Raymond could scarcely believe that he was the designer. He acknowledged that he was not an architect; but the idea of the building had struck him, though he had sent it without the smallest hope of its being accepted. He was a man of few words. Raymond questioned him; but his reserved answers soon made him turn from the man to the drawing. He pointed out the errors, and the alterations that he wished to be made; he offered the Greek a pencil that he might correct the sketch on the spot; this was refused by his visitor, who said that he perfectly understood, and would work at it at home. At length Raymond suffered him to depart.

The next day he returned. The design had been re-drawn; but many defects still remained, and several of the instructions given had been misunderstood. "Come," said Raymond, "I yielded to you yesterday, now comply with my request—take the pencil."

The Greek took it, but he handled it in no artist-like way; at length he said: "I must confess to you, my Lord, that I did not make this drawing. It is impossible for you to see the real designer; your instructions must pass through me. Condescend therefore to have patience with my ignorance, and to explain your wishes to me; in time I am certain that you will be satisfied."

Raymond questioned vainly; the mysterious Greek would say no more. Would an architect be permitted to see the artist? This also was refused. Raymond repeated his instructions, and the visitor retired. Our friend resolved however not to be foiled in his wish. He suspected, that unaccustomed poverty was the cause of the mystery, and that the artist was unwilling to be seen in the garb and abode of want. Raymond was only the more excited by this consideration to discover him; impelled by the interest he took in obscure talent, he therefore ordered a person skilled in such matters, to follow the Greek the next time he came, and observe the house in which he should enter. His emissary obeyed, and brought the desired intelligence. He had traced the man to one of the most penurious streets in the metropolis. Raymond did not wonder, that, thus situated, the artist had shrunk from notice, but he did not for this alter his resolve.

On the same evening, he went alone to the house named to him. Poverty, dirt, and squalid misery characterized its appearance. Alas! thought Raymond, I have much to do before England becomes a Paradise. He knocked; the door was opened by a string from above—the broken, wretched staircase was immediately before him, but no person appeared; he knocked again, vainly—and then, impatient of further delay, he ascended the dark, creaking stairs. His main wish, more particularly now that he witnessed the abject dwelling of the artist, was to relieve one, possessed of talent, but depressed by want. He pictured to himself a youth, whose eyes sparkled with genius, whose person was attenuated by famine. He half feared to displease him; but he trusted that his generous kindness would be administered so delicately, as not to excite repulse. What human heart is shut to kindness? and though poverty, in its excess, might render the sufferer unapt to submit to the supposed degradation of a benefit, the zeal of the benefactor must at last relax him into thankfulness. These thoughts encouraged Raymond, as he stood at the door of the highest room of the house. After trying vainly to enter the other apartments, he perceived just within the threshold of this one, a pair of small Turkish slippers; the door was ajar, but all was silent within. It was probable that the inmate was absent, but secure that he had found the right person, our adventurous Protector was tempted to enter, to leave a purse on the table, and silently depart. In pursuance of this idea, he pushed open the door gently—but the room was inhabited.

Raymond had never visited the dwellings of want, and the scene that now presented itself struck him to the heart. The floor was sunk in many places; the walls ragged and bare—the ceiling weather-stained—a tattered bed stood in the corner; there were but two chairs in the room, and a rough broken table, on which was a light in a tin candlestick;—yet in the midst of such drear and heart sickening poverty, there was an air of order and cleanliness that surprised him. The thought was fleeting; for his attention was instantly drawn towards the inhabitant of this wretched abode. It was a female. She sat at the table; one small hand shaded her eyes from the candle; the other held a pencil; her looks were fixed on a drawing before her, which Raymond recognized as the design presented to him. Her whole appearance awakened his deepest interest. Her dark hair was braided and twined in thick knots like the head-dress of a Grecian statue; her garb was mean, but her attitude might have been selected as a model of grace. Raymond had a confused remembrance that he had seen such a form before; he walked across the room; she did not raise her eyes, merely asking in Romaic, who is there? "A friend," replied Raymond in the same dialect. She looked up wondering, and he saw that it was Evadne Zaimi. Evadne, once the idol of Adrian's affections; and who, for the sake of her present visitor, had disdained the noble youth, and then, neglected by him she loved, with crushed hopes and a stinging sense of misery, had returned to her native Greece. What revolution of fortune could have brought her to England, and housed her thus?

Raymond recognized her; and his manner changed from polite beneficence to the warmest protestations of kindness and sympathy. The sight of her, in her present situation, passed like an arrow into his soul. He sat by her, he took her hand, and said a thousand things which breathed the deepest spirit of compassion and affection. Evadne did not answer; her large dark eyes were cast down, at length a tear glimmered on the lashes. "Thus," she cried, "kindness can do, what no want, no misery ever effected; I weep." She shed indeed many tears; her head sunk unconsciously on the shoulder of Raymond; he held her hand: he kissed her sunken tear-stained cheek. He told her, that her sufferings were now over: no one possessed the art of consoling like Raymond; he did not reason or declaim, but his look shone with sympathy; he brought pleasant images before the sufferer; his caresses excited no distrust, for they arose purely from the feeling which leads a mother to kiss her wounded child; a desire to demonstrate in every possible way the truth of his feelings, and the keenness of his wish to pour balm into the lacerated mind of the unfortunate.

As Evadne regained her composure, his manner became even gay; he sported with the idea of her poverty. Something told him that it was not its real evils that lay heavily at her heart, but the debasement and disgrace attendant on it; as he talked, he divested it of these; sometimes speaking of her fortitude with energetic praise; then, alluding to her past state, he called her his Princess in disguise. He made her warm offers of service; she was too much occupied by more engrossing thoughts, either to accept or reject them; at length he left her, making a promise to repeat his visit the next day. He returned home, full of mingled feelings, of pain excited by Evadne's wretchedness, and pleasure at the prospect of relieving it. Some motive for which he did not account, even to himself, prevented him from relating his adventure to Perdita.

The next day he threw such disguise over his person as a cloak afforded, and revisited Evadne. As he went, he bought a basket of costly fruits, such as were natives of her own country, and throwing over these various beautiful flowers, bore it himself to the miserable garret of his friend. "Behold," cried he, as he entered, "what bird's food I have brought for my sparrow on the house-top."

Evadne now related the tale of her misfortunes. Her father, though of high rank, had in the end dissipated his fortune, and even destroyed his reputation and influence through a course of dissolute indulgence. His health was impaired beyond hope of cure; and it became his earnest wish, before he died, to preserve his daughter from the poverty which would be the portion of her orphan state. He therefore accepted for her, and persuaded her to accede to, a proposal of marriage, from a wealthy Greek merchant settled at Constantinople. She quitted her native Greece; her father died; by degrees she was cut off from all the companions and ties of her youth.

The war, which about a year before the present time had broken out between Greece and Turkey, brought about many reverses of fortune. Her husband became bankrupt, and then in a tumult and threatened massacre on the part of the Turks, they were obliged to fly at midnight, and reached in an open boat an English vessel under sail, which brought them immediately to this island. The few jewels they had saved, supported them awhile. The whole strength of Evadne's mind was exerted to support the failing spirits of her husband. Loss of property, hopelessness as to his future prospects, the inoccupation to which poverty condemned him, combined to reduce him to a state bordering on insanity. Five months after their arrival in England, he committed suicide.

"You will ask me," continued Evadne, "what I have done since; why I have not applied for succour to the rich Greeks resident here; why I have not returned to my native country? My answer to these questions must needs appear to you unsatisfactory, yet they have sufficed to lead me on, day after day, enduring every wretchedness, rather than by such means to seek relief. Shall the daughter of the noble, though prodigal Zaimi, appear a beggar before her compeers or inferiors—superiors she had none. Shall I bow my head before them, and with servile gesture sell my nobility for life? Had I a child, or any tie to bind me to existence, I might descend to this—but, as it is—the world has been to me a harsh step-mother; fain would I leave the abode she seems to grudge, and in the grave forget my pride, my struggles, my despair. The time will soon come; grief and famine have already sapped the foundations of my being; a very short time, and I shall have passed away; unstained by the crime of self-destruction, unstung by the memory of degradation, my spirit will throw aside the miserable coil, and find such recompense as fortitude and resignation may deserve. This may seem madness to you, yet you also have pride and resolution; do not then wonder that my pride is tameless, my resolution unalterable."

Having thus finished her tale, and given such an account as she deemed fit, of the motives of her abstaining from all endeavour to obtain aid from her countrymen, Evadne paused; yet she seemed to have more to say, to which she was unable to give words. In the mean time Raymond was eloquent. His desire of restoring his lovely friend to her rank in society, and to her lost prosperity, animated him, and he poured forth with energy, all his wishes and intentions on that subject. But he was checked; Evadne exacted a promise, that he should conceal from all her friends her existence in England. "The relatives of the Earl of Windsor," said she haughtily, "doubtless think that I injured him; perhaps the Earl himself would be the first to acquit me, but probably I do not deserve acquittal. I acted then, as I ever must, from impulse. This abode of penury may at least prove the disinterestedness of my conduct. No matter: I do not wish to plead my cause before any of them, not even before your Lordship, had you not first discovered me. The tenor of my actions will prove that I had rather die, than be a mark for scorn—behold the proud Evadne in her tatters! look on the beggar-princess! There is aspic venom in the thought—promise me that my secret shall not be violated by you."

Raymond promised; but then a new discussion ensued. Evadne required another engagement on his part, that he would not without her concurrence enter into any project for her benefit, nor himself offer relief. "Do not degrade me in my own eyes," she said; "poverty has long been my nurse; hard-visaged she is, but honest. If dishonour, or what I conceive to be dishonour, come near me, I am lost." Raymond adduced many arguments and fervent persuasions to overcome her feeling, but she remained unconvinced; and, agitated by the discussion, she wildly and passionately made a solemn vow, to fly and hide herself where he never could discover her, where famine would soon bring death to conclude her woes, if he persisted in his to her disgracing offers. She could support herself, she said. And then she shewed him how, by executing various designs and paintings, she earned a pittance for her support. Raymond yielded for the present. He felt assured, after he had for awhile humoured her self-will, that in the end friendship and reason would gain the day.

But the feelings that actuated Evadne were rooted in the depths of her being, and were such in their growth as he had no means of understanding. Evadne loved Raymond. He was the hero of her imagination, the image carved by love in the unchanged texture of her heart. Seven years ago, in her youthful prime, she had become attached to him; he had served her country against the Turks; he had in her own land acquired that military glory peculiarly dear to the Greeks, since they were still obliged inch by inch to fight for their security. Yet when he returned thence, and first appeared in public life in England, her love did not purchase his, which then vacillated between Perdita and a crown. While he was yet undecided, she had quitted England; the news of his marriage reached her, and her hopes, poorly nurtured blossoms, withered and fell. The glory of life was gone for her; the roseate halo of love, which had imbued every object with its own colour, faded;—she was content to take life as it was, and to make the best of leaden-coloured reality. She married; and, carrying her restless energy of character with her into new scenes, she turned her thoughts to ambition, and aimed at the title and power of Princess of Wallachia; while her patriotic feelings were soothed by the idea of the good she might do her country, when her husband should be chief of this principality. She lived to find ambition, as unreal a delusion as love. Her intrigues with Russia for the furtherance of her object, excited the jealousy of the Porte, and the animosity of the Greek government. She was considered a traitor by both, the ruin of her husband followed; they avoided death by a timely flight, and she fell from the height of her desires to penury in England. Much of this tale she concealed from Raymond; nor did she confess, that repulse and denial, as to a criminal convicted of the worst of crimes, that of bringing the scythe of foreign despotism to cut away the new springing liberties of her country, would have followed her application to any among the Greeks.

She knew that she was the cause of her husband's utter ruin; and she strung herself to bear the consequences. The reproaches which agony extorted; or worse, cureless, uncomplaining depression, when his mind was sunk in a torpor, not the less painful because it was silent and moveless. She reproached herself with the crime of his death; guilt and its punishments appeared to surround her; in vain she endeavoured to allay remorse by the memory of her real integrity; the rest of the world, and she among them, judged of her actions, by their consequences. She prayed for her husband's soul; she conjured the Supreme to place on her head the crime of his self-destruction—she vowed to live to expiate his fault.

In the midst of such wretchedness as must soon have destroyed her, one thought only was matter of consolation. She lived in the same country, breathed the same air as Raymond. His name as Protector was the burthen of every tongue; his achievements, projects, and magnificence, the argument of every story. Nothing is so precious to a woman's heart as the glory and excellence of him she loves; thus in every horror Evadne revelled in his fame and prosperity. While her husband lived, this feeling was regarded by her as a crime, repressed, repented of. When he died, the tide of love resumed its ancient flow, it deluged her soul with its tumultuous waves, and she gave herself up a prey to its uncontrollable power.

But never, O, never, should he see her in her degraded state. Never should he behold her fallen, as she deemed, from her pride of beauty, the poverty-stricken inhabitant of a garret, with a name which had become a reproach, and a weight of guilt on her soul. But though impenetrably veiled from him, his public office permitted her to become acquainted with all his actions, his daily course of life, even his conversation. She allowed herself one luxury, she saw the newspapers every day, and feasted on the praise and actions of the Protector. Not that this indulgence was devoid of accompanying grief. Perdita's name was for ever joined with his; their conjugal felicity was celebrated even by the authentic testimony of facts. They were continually together, nor could the unfortunate Evadne read the monosyllable that designated his name, without, at the same time, being presented with the image of her who was the faithful companion of all his labours and pleasures. *They, their Excellencies,* met her eyes in each line, mingling an evil potion that poisoned her very blood.

It was in the newspaper that she saw the advertisement for the design for a national gallery. Combining with taste her remembrance of the edifices which she had seen in the east, and by an effort of genius enduing them with unity of design, she executed the plan which had been sent to the Protector. She triumphed in the idea of bestowing, unknown and forgotten as she was, a benefit upon him she loved; and with enthusiastic pride looked forward to the accomplishment of a work of hers, which, immortalized in stone, would go down to posterity stamped with the name of Raymond. She awaited with eagerness the return of her messenger from the palace; she listened insatiate to his account of each word, each look of the Protector; she felt bliss in this communication with her beloved, although he knew not to whom he addressed his instructions. The drawing itself became ineffably dear to her. He had seen it, and praised it; it was again retouched by her, each stroke of her pencil was as a chord of thrilling music, and bore to her the idea of a temple raised to celebrate the deepest and most unutterable emotions of her soul. These contemplations engaged her, when the voice of Raymond first struck her ear, a voice, once heard, never to be forgotten; she mastered her gush of feelings, and welcomed him with quiet gentleness.

Pride and tenderness now struggled, and at length made a compromise together. She would see Raymond, since destiny had led him to her, and her constancy and devotion must merit his friendship. But her rights with regard to him, and her cherished independence, should not be injured by the idea of interest, or the intervention of the complicated feelings attendant on pecuniary obligation, and the relative situations of the benefactor, and benefited. Her mind was uncommon strength; she could subdue her sensible wants to her mental wishes, and suffer cold, hunger and misery, rather than concede to fortune a contested point. Alas! that in human nature such a pitch of mental discipline, and disdainful negligence of nature itself, should not have been allied to the extreme of moral excellence! But the resolution that permitted her to resist the pains of privation, sprung from the too great energy of her passions; and the concentrated self-will of which this was a sign, was destined to destroy even the very idol, to preserve whose respect she submitted to this detail of wretchedness.

Their intercourse continued. By degrees Evadne related to her friend the whole of her story, the stain her name had received in Greece, the weight of sin which had accrued to her from the death of her husband. When Raymond offered to clear her reputation, and demonstrate to the world her real patriotism, she declared that it was only through her present sufferings that she hoped for any relief to the stings of conscience; that, in her state of mind, diseased as he might think it, the necessity of occupation was salutary medicine; she ended by extorting a promise that for the space of one month he would refrain from the discussion of her interests, engaging after that time to yield in part to his wishes. She could not disguise to herself that any change would separate her from him; now she saw him each day. His connection with Adrian and Perdita was never mentioned; he was to her a meteor, a companionless star, which at its appointed hour rose in her hemisphere, whose appearance brought felicity, and which, although it set, was never eclipsed. He came each day to her abode of penury, and his presence transformed it to a temple redolent with sweets, radiant with heaven's own light; he partook of her delirium. "They built a wall between them and the world"——Without, a thousand harpies raved, remorse and misery, expecting the destined moment for their invasion. Within, was the peace as of innocence, reckless blindless, deluding joy, hope, whose still anchor rested on placid but unconstant water.

Thus, while Raymond had been wrapt in visions of power and fame, while he looked forward to entire dominion over the elements and the mind of man, the territory of his own heart escaped his notice; and from that unthought of source arose the mighty torrent that overwhelmed his will, and carried to the oblivious sea, fame, hope, and happiness.

CHAPTER VIII

In the mean time what did Perdita?

During the first months of his Protectorate, Raymond and she had been inseparable; each project was discussed with her, each plan approved by her. I never beheld any one so perfectly happy as my sweet sister. Her expressive eyes were two stars whose beams were love; hope and light-heartedness sat on her cloudless brow. She fed even to tears of joy on the praise and glory of her Lord; her whole existence was one sacrifice to him, and if in the humility of her heart she felt self-complacency, it arose from the reflection that she had won the distinguished hero of the age, and had for years preserved him, even after time had taken from love its usual nourishment. Her own feeling was as entire as at its birth. Five years had failed to destroy the dazzling unreality of passion. Most men ruthlessly destroy the sacred veil, with which the female heart is wont to adorn the idol of its affections. Not so Raymond; he was an enchanter, whose reign was for ever undiminished; a king whose power never was suspended: follow him through the details of common life, still the same charm of grace and majesty adorned him; nor could he be despoiled of the innate deification with which nature had invested him. Perdita grew in beauty and excellence under his eye; I no longer recognised my reserved abstracted sister in the fascinating and open-hearted wife of Raymond. The genius that enlightened her countenance, was now united to an expression of benevolence, which gave divine perfection to her beauty.

Happiness is in its highest degree the sister of goodness. Suffering and amiability may exist together, and writers have loved to depict their conjunction; there is a human and touching harmony in the picture. But perfect happiness is an attribute of angels; and those who possess it, appear angelic. Fear has been said to be the parent of religion: even of that religion is it the generator, which leads its votaries to sacrifice human victims at its altars; but the religion which springs from happiness is a lovelier growth; the religion which makes the heart breathe forth fervent thanksgiving, and causes us to pour out the overflowings of the soul before the author of our being; that which is the parent of the imagination and the nurse of poetry; that which bestows benevolent intelligence on the visible mechanism of the world, and makes earth a temple with heaven for its cope. Such happiness, goodness, and religion inhabited the mind of Perdita.

During the five years we had spent together, a knot of happy human beings at Windsor Castle, her blissful lot had been the frequent theme of my sister's conversation. From early habit, and natural affection, she selected me in preference to Adrian or Idris, to be the partner in her overflowings of delight; perhaps, though apparently much unlike, some secret point of resemblance, the offspring of consanguinity, induced this preference. Often at sunset, I have walked with her, in the sober, enshadowed forest paths, and listened with joyful sympathy. Security gave dignity to her passion; the certainty of a full return, left her with no wish unfulfilled. The birth of her daughter, embryo copy of her Raymond, filled up the measure of her content, and produced a sacred and indissoluble tie between them. Sometimes she felt proud that he had preferred her to the hopes of a crown. Sometimes she remembered that she had suffered keen anguish, when he hesitated in his choice. But this memory of past discontent only served to enhance her present joy. What had been hardly won, was now, entirely possessed, doubly dear. She would look at him at a distance with the same rapture, (O, far more exuberant rapture!) that one might feel, who after the perils of a tempest, should find himself in the desired port; she would hasten towards him, to feel more certain in his arms, the reality of her bliss. This warmth of affection, added to the depth of her understanding, and the brilliancy of her imagination, made her beyond words dear to Raymond.

If a feeling of dissatisfaction ever crossed her, it arose from the idea that he was not perfectly happy. Desire of renown, and presumptuous ambition, had characterized his youth. The one he had acquired in Greece; the other he had sacrificed to love. His intellect found sufficient field for exercise in his domestic circle, whose members, all adorned by refinement and literature, were many of them, like himself, distinguished by genius. Yet active life was the genuine soil for his virtues; and he sometimes suffered tedium from the monotonous succession of events in our retirement. Pride made him recoil from complaint; and gratitude and affection to Perdita, generally acted as an opiate to all desire, save that of meriting her love. We all observed the visitation of these feelings, and none regretted them so much as Perdita. Her life consecrated to him, was a slight sacrifice to reward his choice, but was not that sufficient—Did he need any gratification that she was unable to bestow? This was the only cloud in the azure of her happiness.

His passage to power had been full of pain to both. He however attained his wish; he filled the situation for which nature seemed to have moulded him. His activity was fed in wholesome measure, without either exhaustion or satiety; his taste and genius found worthy expression in each of the modes human beings have invented to encage and manifest the spirit of beauty; the goodness of his heart made him never weary of conducing to the well-being of his fellow-creatures; his magnificent spirit, and aspirations for the respect and love of mankind, now received fruition; true, his exaltation was temporary; perhaps it were better that it should be so. Habit would not dull his sense of the enjoyment of power; nor struggles, disappointment and defeat await the end of that which would expire at its maturity. He determined to extract and condense all of glory, power, and achievement, which might have resulted from a long reign, into the three years of his Protectorate.

Raymond was eminently social. All that he now enjoyed would have been devoid of pleasure to him, had it been unparticipated. But in Perdita he possessed all that his heart could desire. Her love gave birth to sympathy; her intelligence made her understand him at a word; her powers of intellect enabled her to assist and guide him. He felt her worth. During the early years of their union, the inequality of her temper, and yet unsubdued self-will which tarnished her character, had been a slight drawback to the fulness of his sentiment. Now that unchanged serenity, and gentle compliance were added to her other qualifications, his respect equalled his love. Years added to the strictness of their union. They did not now guess at, and totter on the pathway, divining the mode to please, hoping, yet fearing the continuance of bliss. Five years gave a sober certainty to their emotions, though it did not rob them of their etherial nature. It had given them a child; but it had not detracted from the personal attractions of my sister. Timidity, which in her had almost amounted to awkwardness, was exchanged for a graceful decision of manner; frankness, instead of reserve, characterized her physiognomy; and her voice was attuned to thrilling softness. She was now three and twenty, in the pride of womanhood, fulfilling the precious duties of wife and mother, possessed of all her heart had ever coveted. Raymond was ten years older; to his previous beauty, noble mien, and commanding aspect, he now added gentlest benevolence, winning tenderness, graceful and unwearied attention to the wishes of another.

The first secret that had existed between them was the visits of Raymond to Evadne. He had been struck by the fortitude and beauty of the ill-fated Greek; and, when her constant tenderness towards him unfolded itself, he asked with astonishment, by what act of his he had merited this passionate and unrequited love. She was for a while the sole object of his reveries; and Perdita became aware that his thoughts and time were bestowed on a subject unparticipated by her. My sister was by nature destitute of the common feelings of anxious, petulant jealousy. The treasure which she possessed in the affections of Raymond, was more necessary to her being, than the life-blood that animated her veins—more truly than Othello she might say,

To be once in doubt,
Is—once to be resolved.

On the present occasion she did not suspect any alienation of affection; but she conjectured that some circumstance connected with his high place, had occasioned this mystery. She was startled and pained. She began to count the long days, and months, and years which must elapse, before he would be restored to a private station, and unreservedly to her. She was not content that, even for a time, he should practice concealment with her. She often repined; but her trust in the singleness of his affection was undisturbed; and, when they were together, unchecked by fear, she opened her heart to the fullest delight.

Time went on. Raymond, stopping mid-way in his wild career, paused suddenly to think of consequences. Two results presented themselves in the view he took of the future. That his intercourse with Evadne should continue a secret to, or that finally it should be discovered by Perdita. The destitute condition, and highly wrought feelings of his friend prevented him from adverting to the possibility of exiling himself from her. In the first event he had bidden an eternal farewell to open-hearted converse, and entire sympathy with the companion of his life. The veil must be thicker than that invented by Turkish jealousy; the wall higher than the unscaleable tower of Vathek, which should conceal from her the workings of his heart, and hide from her view the secret of his actions. This idea was intolerably painful to him. Frankness and social feelings were the essence of Raymond's nature; without them his qualities became common-place; without these to spread glory over his intercourse with Perdita, his vaunted exchange of a throne for her love, was as weak and empty as the rainbow hues which vanish when the sun is down. But there was no remedy. Genius, devotion, and courage; the adornments of his mind, and the energies of his soul, all exerted to their uttermost stretch, could not roll back one hair's breadth the wheel of time's chariot; that which had been was written with the adamantine pen of reality, on the everlasting volume of the past; nor could agony and tears suffice to wash out one iota from the act fulfilled.

But this was the best side of the question. What, if circumstance should lead Perdita to suspect, and suspecting to be resolved? The fibres of his frame became relaxed, and cold dew stood on his forehead, at this idea. Many men may scoff at his dread; but he read the future; and the peace of Perdita was too dear to him, but speechless agony too certain, and too fearful, not to unman him. His course was speedily decided upon. If the worst befell; if she learnt the truth, he would neither stand her reproaches, or the anguish of her altered looks. He would forsake her, England, his friends, the scenes of his youth, the hopes of coming time, he would seek another country, and in other scenes begin life again. Having resolved on this, he became calmer. He endeavoured to guide with prudence the steeds of destiny through the devious road which he had chosen, and bent all his efforts the better to conceal what he could not alter.

The perfect confidence that subsisted between Perdita and him, rendered every communication common between them. They opened each other's letters, even as, until now, the inmost fold of the heart of each was disclosed to the other. A letter came unawares, Perdita read it. Had it contained confirmation, she must have been annihilated. As it was, trembling, cold, and pale, she sought Raymond. He was alone, examining some petitions lately presented. She entered silently, sat on a sofa opposite to him, and gazed on him with a look of such despair, that wildest shrieks and dire moans would have been tame exhibitions of misery, compared to the living incarnation of the thing itself exhibited by her.

At first he did not take his eyes from the papers; when he raised them, he was struck by the wretchedness manifest on her altered cheek; for a moment he forgot his own acts and fears, and asked with consternation—"Dearest girl, what is the matter; what has happened?"

"Nothing," she replied at first; "and yet not so," she continued, hurrying on in her speech; "you have secrets, Raymond; where have you been lately, whom have you seen, what do you conceal from me?—why am I banished from your confidence? Yet this is not it—I do not intend to entrap you with questions—one will suffice—am I completely a wretch?"

With tembling hand she gave him the paper, and sat white and motionless looking at him while he read it. He recognised the hand-writing of Evadne, and the colour mounted in his cheeks. With lightning-speed he conceived the contents of the letter; all was now cast on one die; falsehood and artifice were trifles in comparison with the impending ruin. He would either entirely dispel Perdita's suspicions, or quit her for ever. "My dear girl," he said, "I have been to blame; but you must pardon me. I was in the wrong to commence a system of concealment; but I did it for the sake of sparing you pain; and each day has rendered it more difficult for me to alter my plan. Besides, I was instigated by delicacy towards the unhappy writer of these few lines."

Perdita gasped: "Well," she cried, "well, go on!"

"That is all—this paper tells all. I am placed in the most difficult circumstances. I have done my best, though perhaps I have done wrong. My love for you is inviolate."

Perdita shook her head doubtingly: "It cannot be," she cried, "I know that it is not. You would deceive me, but I will not be deceived. I have lost you, myself, my life!"

"Do you not believe me?" said Raymond haughtily.

"To believe you," she exclaimed, "I would give up all, and expire with joy, so that in death I could feel that you were true—but that cannot be!"

"Perdita," continued Raymond, "you do not see the precipice on which you stand. You may believe that I did not enter on my present line of conduct without reluctance and pain. I knew that it was possible that your suspicions might be excited; but I trusted that my simple word would cause them to disappear. I built my hope on your confidence. Do you think that I will be questioned, and my replies disdainfully set aside? Do you think that I will be suspected, perhaps watched, cross-questioned, and disbelieved? I am not yet fallen so low; my honour is not yet so tarnished. You have loved me; I adored you. But all human sentiments come to an end. Let our affection expire—but let it not be exchanged for distrust and recrimination. Heretofore we have been friends—lovers—let us not become enemies, mutual spies. I cannot live the object of suspicion—you cannot believe me—let us part!"

"Exactly so," cried Perdita, "I knew that it would come to this! Are we not already parted? Does not a stream, boundless as ocean, deep as vacuum, yawn between us?"

Raymond rose, his voice was broken, his features convulsed, his manner calm as the earthquake-cradling atmosphere, he replied: "I am rejoiced that you take my decision so philosophically. Doubtless you will play the part of the injured wife to admiration. Sometimes you may be stung with the feeling that you have wronged me, but the condolence of your relatives, the pity of the world, the complacency which the consciousness of your own immaculate innocence will bestow, will be excellent balm;—me you will never see more!"

Raymond moved towards the door. He forgot that each word he spoke was false. He personated his assumption of innocence even to self-deception. Have not actors wept, as they pourtrayed imagined passion? A more intense feeling of the reality of fiction possessed Raymond. He spoke with pride; he felt injured. Perdita looked up; she saw his angry glance; his hand was on the lock of the door. She started up, she threw herself on his neck, she gasped and sobbed; he took her hand, and leading her to the sofa, sat down near her. Her head fell on his shoulder, she trembled, alternate changes of fire and ice ran through her limbs: observing her emotion he spoke with softened accents:

"The blow is given. I will not part from you in anger;—I owe you too much. I owe you six years of unalloyed happiness. But they are passed. I will not live the mark of suspicion, the object of jealousy. I love you too well. In an eternal separation only can either of us hope for dignity and propriety of action. We shall not then be degraded from our true characters. Faith and devotion have hitherto been the essence of our intercourse;—these lost, let us not cling to the seedless husk of life, the unkernelled shell. You have your child, your brother, Idris, Adrian"——

"And you," cried Perdita, "the writer of that letter."

Uncontrollable indignation flashed from the eyes of Raymond. He knew that this accusation at least was false. "Entertain this belief," he cried, "hug it to your heart—make it a pillow to your head, an opiate for your eyes—I am content. But, by the God that made me, hell is not more false than the word you have spoken!"

Perdita was struck by the impassioned seriousness of his asserverations. She replied with earnestness, "I do not refuse to believe you, Raymond; on the contrary I promise to put implicit faith in your simple word. Only assure me that your love and faith towards me have never been violated; and suspicion, and doubt, and jealousy will at once be dispersed. We shall continue as we have ever done, one heart, one hope, one life."

"I have already assured you of my fidelity," said Raymond with disdainful coldness, "triple assertions will avail nothing where one is despised. I will say no more; for I can add nothing to what I have already said, to what you before contemptuously set aside. This contention is unworthy of both of us; and I confess that I am weary of replying to charges at once unfounded and unkind."

Perdita tried to read his countenance, which he angrily averted. There was so much of truth and nature in his resentment, that her doubts were dispelled. Her countenance, which for years had not expressed a feeling unallied to affection, became again radiant and satisfied. She found it however no easy task to soften and reconcile Raymond. At first he refused to stay to hear her. But she would not be put off; secure of his unaltered love, she was willing to undertake any labour, use any entreaty, to dispel his anger. She obtained an hearing, he sat in haughty silence, but he listened. She first assured him of her boundless confidence; of this he must be conscious, since but for that she would not seek to detain him. She enumerated their years of happiness; she brought before him past scenes of intimacy and happiness; she pictured their future life, she mentioned their child—tears unbidden now filled her eyes. She tried to disperse them, but they refused to be checked—her utterance was choaked. She had not wept before. Raymond could not resist these signs of distress: he felt perhaps somewhat ashamed of the part he acted of the injured man, he who was in truth the injurer. And then he devoutly loved Perdita; the bend of her head, her glossy ringlets, the turn of her form were to him subjects of deep tenderness and admiration; as she spoke, her melodious tones entered his soul; he soon softened towards her, comforting and caressing her, and endeavouring to cheat himself into the belief that he had never wronged her.

Raymond staggered forth from this scene, as a man might do, who had been just put to the torture, and looked forward to when it would be again inflicted. He had sinned against his own honour, by affirming, swearing to, a direct falsehood; true this he had palmed on a woman, and it might therefore be deemed less base—by others—not by him;—for whom had he deceived?—his own trusting, devoted, affectionate Perdita, whose generous belief galled him doubly, when he remembered the parade of innocence with which it had been exacted. The mind of Raymond was not so rough cast, nor had been so rudely handled, in the circumstance of life, as to make him proof to these considerations—on the contrary, he was all nerve; his spirit was as a pure fire, which fades and shrinks from every contagion of foul atmosphere: but now the contagion had become incorporated with its essence, and the change was the more painful. Truth and falsehood, love and hate lost their eternal boundaries, heaven rushed in to mingle with hell; while his sensitive mind, turned to a field for such battle, was stung to madness. He heartily despised himself, he was angry with Perdita, and the idea of Evadne was attended by all that was hideous and cruel. His passions, always his masters, acquired fresh strength, from the long sleep in which love had cradled them, the clinging weight of destiny bent him down; he was goaded, tortured, fiercely impatient of that worst of miseries, the sense of remorse. This troubled state yielded by degrees, to sullen animosity, and depression of spirits. His dependants, even his equals, if in his present post he had any, were startled to find anger, derision, and bitterness in one, before distinguished for suavity and benevolence of manner. He transacted public business with distaste, and hastened from it to the solitude which was at once his bane and relief. He mounted a fiery horse, that which had borne him forward to victory in Greece; he fatigued himself with deadening exercise, losing the pangs of a troubled mind in animal sensation.

He slowly recovered himself; yet, at last, as one might from the effects of poison, he lifted his head from above the vapours of fever and passion into the still atmosphere of calm reflection. He meditated on what was best to be done. He was first struck by the space of time that had elapsed, since madness, rather than any reasonable impulse, had regulated his actions. A month had gone by, and during that time he had not seen Evadne. Her power, which was linked to few of the enduring emotions of his heart, had greatly decayed. He was no longer her slave—no longer her lover: he would never see her more, and by the completeness of his return, deserve the confidence of Perdita.

Yet, as he thus determined, fancy conjured up the miserable abode of the Greek girl. An abode, which from noble and lofty principle, she had refused to exchange for one of greater luxury. He thought of the splendour of her situation and appearance when he first knew her; he thought of her life at Constantinople, attended by every circumstance of oriental magnificence; of her present penury, her daily task of industry, her lorn state, her faded, famine-struck cheek. Compassion swelled his breast; he would see her once again; he would devise some plan for restoring her to society, and the enjoyment of her rank; their separation would then follow, as a matter of course.

Again he thought, how during this long month, he had avoided Perdita, flying from her as from the stings of his own conscience. But he was awake now; all this should be remedied; and future devotion erase the memory of this only blot on the serenity of their life. He became cheerful, as he thought of this, and soberly and resolutely marked out the line of conduct he would adopt. He remembered that he had promised Perdita to be present this very evening (the 19th of October, anniversary of his election as Protector) at a festival given in his honour. Good augury should this festival be of the happiness of future years. First, he would look in on Evadne; he would not stay; but he owed her some account, some compensation for his long and unannounced absence; and then to Perdita, to the forgotten world, to the duties of society, the splendour of rank, the enjoyment of power.

After the scene sketched in the preceding pages, Perdita had contemplated an entire change in the manners and conduct of

Raymond. She expected freedom of communication, and a return to those habits of affectionate intercourse which had formed the delight of her life. But Raymond did not join her in any of her avocations. He transacted the business of the day apart from her; he went out, she knew not whither. The pain inflicted by this disappointment was tormenting and keen. She looked on it as a deceitful dream, and tried to throw off the consciousness of it; but like the shirt of Nessus, it clung to her very flesh, and ate with sharp agony into her vital principle. She possessed that (though such an assertion may appear a paradox) which belongs to few, a capacity of happiness. Her delicate organization and creative imagination rendered her peculiarly susceptible of pleasurable emotion. The overflowing warmth of her heart, by making love a plant of deep root and stately growth, had attuned her whole soul to the reception of happiness, when she found in Raymond all that could adorn love and satisfy her imagination. But if the sentiment on which the fabric of her existence was founded, became common place through participation, the endless succession of attentions and graceful action snapt by transfer, his universe of love wrested from her, happiness must depart, and then be exchanged for its opposite. The same peculiarities of character rendered her sorrows agonies; her fancy magnified them, her sensibility made her for ever open to their renewed impression; love envenomed the heart-piercing sting. There was neither submission, patience, nor self-abandonment in her grief; she fought with it, struggled beneath it, and rendered every pang more sharp by resistance. Again and again the idea recurred, that he loved another. She did him justice; she believed that he felt a tender affection for her; but give a paltry prize to him who in some life-pending lottery has calculated on the possession of tens of thousands, and it will disappoint him more than a blank. The affection and amity of a Raymond might be inestimable; but, beyond that affection, embosomed deeper than friendship, was the indivisible treasure of love. Take the sum in its completeness, and no arithmetic can calculate its price; take from it the smallest portion, give it but the name of parts, separate it into degrees and sections, and like the magician's coin, the valuless gold of the mine, is turned to vilest substance. There is a meaning in the eye of love; a cadence in its voice, an irradiation in its smile, the talisman of whose enchantments one only can possess; its spirit is elemental, its essence single, its divinity an unit. The very heart and soul of Raymond and

Perdita had mingled, even as two mountain brooks that join in their descent, and murmuring and sparkling flow over shining pebbles, beside starry flowers; but let one desert its primal course, or be dammed up by choaking obstruction, and the other shrinks in its altered banks. Perdita was sensible of the failing of the tide that fed her life. Unable to support the slow withering of her hopes, she suddenly formed a plan, resolving to terminate at once the period of misery, and to bring to an happy conclusion the late disastrous events.

The anniversary was at hand of the exaltation of Raymond to the office of Protector; and it was customary to celebrate this day by a splendid festival. A variety of feelings urged Perdita to shed double magnificence over the scene; yet, as she arrayed herself for the evening gala, she wondered herself at the pains she took, to render sumptuous the celebration of an event which appeared to her the beginning of her sufferings. Woe befall the day, she thought, woe, tears, and mourning betide the hour, that gave Raymond another hope than love, another wish than my devotion; and thrice joyful the moment when he shall be restored to me! God knows, I put my trust in his vows, and believe his asserted faith—but for that, I would not seek what I am now resolved to attain. Shall two years more be thus passed, each day adding to our alienation, each act being another stone piled on the barrier which separates us? No, my Raymond, my only beloved, sole possession of Perdita! This night, this splendid assembly, these sumptuous apartments, and this adornment of your tearful girl, are all united to celebrate your abdication. Once for me, you relinquished the prospect of a crown. That was in days of early love, when I could only hold out the hope, not the assurance of happiness. Now you have the experience of all that I can give, the heart's devotion, taintless love, and unhesitating subjection to you. You must choose between these and your protectorate. This, proud noble, is your last night! Perdita has bestowed on it all of magnificent and dazzling that your heart best loves—but, from these gorgeous rooms, from this princely attendance, from power and elevation, you must return with to-morrow's sun to our rural abode; for I would not buy an immortality of joy, by the endurance of one more week sister to the last.

Brooding over this plan, resolved when the hour should come, to propose, and insist upon its accomplishment, secure of his consent, the heart of Perdita was lightened, or rather exalted. Her cheek was flushed by the expectation of struggle; her eyes sparkled with the hope of triumph. Having cast her fate upon a die, and feeling secure of winning, she, whom I have named as bearing the stamp of queen of nations on her noble brow, now rose superior to humanity, and seemed in calm power, to arrest with her finger, the wheel of destiny. She had never before looked so supremely lovely.

We, the Arcadian shepherds of the tale, had intended to be present at this festivity, but Perdita wrote to entreat us not to come, or to absent ourselves from Windsor; for she (though she did not reveal her scheme to us) resolved the next morning to return with Raymond to our dear circle, there to renew a course of life in which she had found entire felicity. Late in the evening she entered the apartments appropriated to the festival. Raymond had quitted the palace the night before; he had promised to grace the assembly, but he had not yet returned. Still she felt sure that he would come at last; and the wider the breach might appear at this crisis, the more secure she was of closing it for ever.

It was as I said, the nineteenth of October; the autumn was far advanced and dreary. The wind howled; the half bare trees were despoiled of the remainder of their summer ornament; the state of the air which induced the decay of vegetation, was hostile to cheerfulness or hope. Raymond had been exalted by the determination he had made; but with the declining day his spirits declined. First he was to visit Evadne, and then to hasten to the palace of the Protectorate. As he walked through the wretched streets in the neighbourhood of the luckless Greek's abode, his heart smote him for the whole course of his conduct towards her. First, his having entered into any engagement that should permit her to remain in such a state of degradation; and then, after a short wild dream, having left her to drear solitude, anxious conjecture, and bitter, still—disappointed expectation. What had she done the while, how supported his absence and neglect? Light grew dim in these close streets, and when the well known door was opened, the staircase was shrouded in perfect night. He groped his way up, he entered the garret, he found Evadne stretched speechless, almost lifeless on her wretched bed. He called for the people of the house, but could learn nothing from them, except that they knew nothing. Her story was plain to him, plain and distinct as the remorse and horror that darted their fangs into him. When she found herself forsaken by him, she lost the heart to pursue her usual avocations; pride forbade every application to him; famine was welcomed as the kind porter to the gates of death, within whose opening folds she should now, without sin, quickly repose. No creature came near her, as her strength failed.

If she died, where could there be found on record a murderer, whose cruel act might compare with his? What fiend more wanton in his mischief, what damned soul more worthy of perdition! But he was not reserved for this agony of self-reproach. He sent for medical assistance; the hours passed, spun by suspense into ages; the darkness of the long autumnal night yielded to day, before her life was secure. He had her then removed to a more commodious dwelling, and hovered about her, again and again to assure himself that she was safe.

In the midst of his greatest suspense and fear as to the event, he remembered the festival given in his honour, by Perdita; in his honour then, when misery and death were affixing indelible disgrace to his name, honour to him whose crimes deserved a scaffold; this was the worst mockery. Still Perdita would expect him; he wrote a few incoherent words on a scrap of paper, testifying that he was well, and bade the woman of the house take it to the palace, and deliver it into the hands of the wife of the Lord Protector. The woman, who did not know him, contemptuously asked, how he thought she should gain admittance, particularly on a festal night, to that lady's presence? Raymond gave her his ring to ensure the respect of the menials. Thus, while Perdita was entertaining her guests, and anxiously awaiting the arrival of her lord, his ring was brought her; and she was told that a poor woman had a note to deliver to her from its wearer.

The vanity of the old gossip was raised by her commission, which, after all, she did not understand, since she had no suspicion, even now that Evadne's visitor was Lord Raymond. Perdita dreaded a fall from his horse, or some similar accident—till the woman's answers woke other fears. From a feeling of cunning blindly exercised, the officious, if not malignant messenger, did not speak of Evadne's illness; but she garrulously gave an account of Raymond's frequent visits, adding to her narration such circumstances, as, while they convinced Perdita of its truth, exaggerated the unkindness and perfidy of Raymond. Worst of all, his absence now from the festival, his message wholly unaccounted for, except by the disgraceful hints of the woman, appeared the deadliest insult.

Again she looked at the ring, it was a small ruby, almost heart-shaped, which she had herself given him. She looked at the hand-writing, which she could not mistake, and repeated to herself the words—"Do not, I charge you, I entreat you, permit your guests to wonder at my absence:" the while the old crone going on with her talk, filled her ear with a strange medley of truth and falsehood. At length Perdita dismissed her.

The poor girl returned to the assembly, where her presence had not been missed. She glided into a recess somewhat obscured, and leaning against an ornamental column there placed, tried to recover herself. Her faculties were palsied. She gazed on some flowers that stood near in a carved vase: that morning she had arranged them, they were rare and lovely plants; even now all aghast as she was, she observed their brilliant colours and starry shapes.—"Divine infoliations of the spirit of beauty," she exclaimed, "Ye droop not, neither do ye mourn; the despair that clasps my heart, has not spread contagion over you!—Why am I not a partner of your insensibility, a sharer in your calm!"

She paused. "To my task," she continued mentally, "my guests must not perceive the reality, either as it regards him or me. I obey; they shall not, though I die the moment they are gone. They shall behold the antipodes of what is real—for I will appear to live—while I am—dead." It required all her self-command, to suppress the gush of tears self-pity caused at this idea. After many struggles, she succeeded, and turned to join the company.

All her efforts were now directed to the dissembling her internal conflict. She had to play the part of a courteous hostess; to attend to all; to shine the focus of enjoyment and grace. She had to do this, while in deep woe she sighed for loneliness, and would gladly have exchanged her crowded rooms for dark forest depths, or a drear, night-enshadowed heath. But she became gay. She could not keep in the medium, nor be, as was usual with her, placidly content. Every one remarked her exhilaration of spirits; as all actions appear graceful in the eye of rank, her guests surrounded her applaudingly, although there was a sharpness in her laugh, and an abruptness in her sallies, which might have betrayed her secret to an attentive observer. She went on, feeling that, if she had paused for a moment, the checked waters of misery would have deluged her soul, that her wrecked hopes would raise their wailing voices, and that those who now echoed her mirth, and provoked her repartees, would have shrunk in fear from her convulsive despair. Her only consolation during the violence which she did herself, was to watch the motions of an illuminated clock, and internally count the moments which must elapse before she could be alone.

At length the rooms began to thin. Mocking her own desires, she rallied her guests on their early departure. One by one they left her—at length she pressed the hand of her last visitor. "How cold and damp your hand is," said her friend; "you are over fatigued, pray hasten to rest." Perdita smiled faintly—her guest left her; the carriage rolling down the street assured the final departure. Then, as if pursued by an enemy, as if wings had been at her feet, she flew to her own apartment, she dismissed her attendants, she locked the doors, she threw herself wildly on the floor, she bit her lips even to blood to suppress her shrieks, and lay long a prey to the vulture of despair, striving not to think, while multitudinous ideas made a home of her heart; and ideas, horrid as furies, cruel as vipers, and poured in with such swift succession, that they seemed to jostle and wound each other, while they worked her up to madness.

At length she rose, more composed, not less miserable. She stood before a large mirror—she gazed on her reflected image; her light and graceful dress, the jewels that studded her hair, and encircled her beauteous arms and neck, her small feet shod in satin, her profuse and glossy tresses, all were to her clouded brow and woe-begone countenance like a gorgeous frame to a dark tempest-pourtraying picture. "Vase am I," she thought, "vase brimful of despair's direst essence. Farewell, Perdita! farewell, poor girl! never again will you see yourself thus; luxury and wealth are no longer yours; in the excess of your poverty you may envy the homeless beggar; most truly am I without a home! I live on a barren desart, which, wide and interminable, brings forth neither fruit or flower; in the midst is a solitary rock, to which thou, Perdita, art chained, and thou seest the dreary level stretch far away."

She threw open her window, which looked on the palace-garden. Light and darkness were struggling together, and the orient was streaked by roseate and golden rays. One star only trembled in the depth of the kindling atmosphere. The morning air blowing freshly over the dewy plants, rushed into the heated room. "All things go on," thought Perdita, "all things proceed, decay, and perish! When noontide has passed, and the weary day has driven her team to their western stalls, the fires of heaven rise from the East, moving in their accustomed path, they ascend and descend the skiey hill. When their course is fulfilled, the dial begins to cast westward an uncertain shadow; the eye-lids of day are opened, and birds and flowers, the startled vegetation, and fresh breeze awaken; the sun at length appears, and in majestic procession climbs the capitol of heaven. All proceeds, changes and dies, except the sense of misery in my bursting heart.

"Ay, all proceeds and changes: what wonder then, that love has journied on to its setting, and that the lord of my life has changed? We call the supernal lights fixed, yet they wander about yonder plain, and if I look again where I looked an hour ago, the face of the eternal heavens is altered. The silly moon and inconstant planets vary nightly their erratic dance; the sun itself, sovereign of the sky, ever and anon deserts his throne, and leaves his dominion to night and winter. Nature grows old, and shakes in her decaying limbs,—creation has become bankrupt! What wonder then, that eclipse and death have led to destruction the light of thy life, O Perdita!"

CHAPTER IX

THUS SAD AND disarranged were the thoughts of my poor sister, when she became assured of the infidelity of Raymond. All her virtues and all her defects tended to make the blow incurable. Her affection for me, her brother, for Adrian and Idris, was subject as it were to the reigning passion of her heart; even her maternal tenderness borrowed half its force from the delight she had in tracing Raymond's features and expression in the infant's countenance. She had been reserved and even stern in childhood; but love had softened the asperities of her character, and her union with Raymond had caused her talents and affections to unfold themselves; the one betrayed, and the other lost, she in some degree returned to her ancient disposition. The concentrated pride of her nature, forgotten during her blissful dream, awoke, and with its adder's sting pierced her heart; her humility of spirit augmented the power of the venom; she had been exalted in her own estimation, while distinguished by his love: of what worth was she, now that he thrust her from this preferment? She had been proud of having won and preserved him—but another had won him from her, and her exultation was as cold as a water quenched ember.

We, in our retirement, remained long in ignorance of her misfortune. Soon after the festival she had sent for her child, and then she seemed to have forgotten us. Adrian observed a change during a visit that he afterward paid them; but he could not tell its extent, or divine the cause. They still appeared in public together, and lived under the same roof. Raymond was as usual courteous, though there was, on occasions, an unbidden haughtiness, or painful abruptness in his manners, which startled his gentle friend; his brow was not clouded but disdain sat on his lips, and his voice was harsh. Perdita was all kindness and attention to her lord; but she was silent, and beyond words sad. She had grown thin and pale; and her eyes often filled with tears. Sometimes she looked at Raymond, as if to say—That it should be so! At others her countenance expressed—I will still do all I can to make you happy. But Adrian read with uncertain aim the charactery of her face, and might mistake.—Clara was always with her, and she seemed most at ease, when, in an obscure corner, she could sit holding her child's hand, silent and lonely. Still Adrian was unable to guess the truth; he entreated them to visit us at Windsor, and they promised to come during the following month.

It was May before they arrived: the season had decked the forest trees with leaves, and its paths with a thousand flowers. We had notice of their intention the day before; and, early in the morning, Perdita arrived with her daughter. Raymond would follow soon, she said; he had been detained by business. According to Adrian's account, I had expected to find her sad; but, on the contrary, she appeared in the highest spirits: true, she had grown thin, her eyes were somewhat hollow, and her cheeks sunk, though tinged by a bright glow. She was delighted to see us; caressed our children, praised their growth and improvement; Clara also was pleased to meet again her young friend Alfred; all kinds of childish games were entered into, in which Perdita joined. She communicated her gaiety to us, and as we amused ourselves on the Castle Terrace, it appeared that a happier, less care-worn party could not have been assembled. "This is better, Mamma," said Clara, "than being in that dismal London, where you often cry, and never laugh as you do now."—"Silence, little foolish thing," replied her mother, "and remember any one that mentions London is sent to Coventry for an hour."

Soon after, Raymond arrived. He did not join as usual in the playful spirit of the rest; but, entering into conversation with Adrian and myself, by degrees we seceded from our companions, and Idris and Perdita only remained with the children. Raymond talked of his new buildings; of his plan for an establishment for the better education of the poor; as usual Adrian and he entered into argument, and the time slipped away unperceived.

We assembled again towards evening, and Perdita insisted on our having recourse to music. She wanted, she said, to give us a specimen of her new accomplishment; for since she had been in London, she had applied herself to music, and sang, without much power, but with a great deal of sweetness. We were not permitted by her to select any but light-hearted melodies; and all the Operas of Mozart were called into service, that we might choose the most exhilarating of his airs. Among the other transcendant attributes of Mozart's music, it possesses more than any other that of appearing to come from the heart; you enter into the passions expressed by him, and are transported with grief, joy, anger, or confusion, as he, our soul's master, chooses to inspire. For some time, the spirit of hilarity was kept up; but, at length, Perdita receded from the piano, for Raymond had joined in the trio of "*Taci ingiusto core,*"[*] in Don Giovanni, whose arch entreaty was softened by him into tenderness, and thrilled her heart with memories of the changed past; it was the same voice, the same tone, the selfsame sounds and words, which often before she had received, as the homage of love to her—no longer was it that; and this concord of sound with its dissonance of expression penetrated her with regret and despair. Soon after Idris, who was at the harp, turned to that passionate and sorrowful air in Figaro, "*Porgi, amor, qualche ristoro,*"[†] in which the deserted Countess laments the change of the faithless Almaviva. The soul of tender sorrow is breathed forth in this strain; and the sweet voice of Idris, sustained by the mournful chords of her instrument, added to the expression of the words. During the pathetic appeal with which it concludes, a stifled sob attracted our attention to Perdita, the cessation of the music recalled her to herself, she hastened out of the hall—I followed her. At first, she seemed to wish to shun me; and then, yielding to my earnest questioning, she threw herself on my neck, and wept aloud:—"Once more," she cried, "once more on your friendly breast, my beloved brother, can the lost Perdita pour forth her sorrows. I had imposed a law of silence on myself; and for months I have kept it. I do wrong in weeping now, and greater wrong in giving words to my grief. I will not speak! Be [it] enough for you to know that I am miserable [—] be it enough for you to know, that the painted veil of life is rent, that I sit for ever shrouded in darkness and gloom, that grief is my sister, everlasting lamentation my mate!"

I endeavoured to console her; I did not question her! but I caressed her, assured her of my deepest affection and my intense

[*] "Be silent, unjust heart!"

[†] "Give me, love, some relief."

interest in the changes of her fortune:—"Dear words," she cried, "expressions of love come upon my ear, like the remembered sounds of forgotten music, that had been dear to me. They are vain, I know; how very vain in their attempt to soothe or comfort me. Dearest Lionel, you cannot guess what I have suffered during these long months. I have read of mourners in ancient days, who clothed themselves in sackcloth, scattered dust upon their heads, ate their bread mingled with ashes, and took up their abode on the bleak mountain tops, reproaching heaven and earth aloud with their misfortunes. Why this is the very luxury of sorrow! thus one might go on from day to day contriving new extravagances, revelling in the paraphernalia of woe, wedded to all the appurtenances of despair. Alas! I must for ever conceal the wretchedness that consumes me. I must weave a veil of dazzling falsehood to hide my grief from vulgar eyes, smoothe my brow, and paint my lips in deceitful smiles—even in solitude I dare not think how lost I am, lest I become insane and rave."

The tears and agitation of my poor sister had rendered her unfit to return to the circle we had left—so I persuaded her to let me drive her through the park; and, during the ride, I induced her to confide the tale of her unhappiness to me, fancying that talking of it would lighten the burthen, and certain that, if there were a remedy, it should be found and secured to her.

Several weeks had elapsed since the festival of the anniversary, and she had been unable to calm her mind, or to subdue her thoughts to any regular train. Sometimes she reproached herself for taking too bitterly to heart, that which many would esteem an imaginary evil; but this was no subject for reason; and, ignorant as she was of the motives and true conduct of Raymond, things assumed for her even a worse appearance, than the reality warranted. He was seldom at the palace; never, but when he was assured that his public duties would prevent his remaining alone with Perdita. They seldom addressed each other, shunning explanation, each fearing any communication the other might make. Suddenly, however, the manners of Raymond changed; he appeared to desire to find opportunities of bringing about a return to kindness and intimacy with my sister. The tide of love towards her appeared to flow again; he could never forget, how once he had been devoted to her, making her the shrine and storehouse wherein to place every thought and every sentiment. Shame seemed to hold him back; yet he evidently wished to establish a renewal of confidence and affection. From the moment Perdita had sufficiently recovered herself to form any plan of action, she had laid one down, which now she prepared to follow. She received these tokens of returning love with gentleness; she did not shun his company; but she endeavoured to place a barrier in the way of familiar intercourse or painful discussion, which mingled pride and shame prevented Raymond from surmounting. He began at last to shew signs of angry impatience, and Perdita became aware that the system she had adopted could not continue; she must explain herself to him; she could not summon courage to speak—she wrote thus:—

"Read this letter with patience, I entreat you. It will contain no reproaches. Reproach is indeed an idle word: for what should I reproach you?

"Allow me in some degree to explain my feeling; without that, we shall both grope in the dark, mistaking one another; erring from the path which may conduct, one of us at least, to a more eligible mode of life than that led by either during the last few weeks.

"I loved you—I love you—neither anger nor pride dictates these lines; but a feeling beyond, deeper, and more unalterable than either. My affections are wounded; it is impossible to heal them:—cease then the vain endeavour, if indeed that way your endeavours tend. Forgiveness! Return! Idle words are these! I forgive the pain I endure; but the trodden path cannot be retraced.

"Common affection might have been satisfied with common usages. I believed that you read my heart, and knew its devotion, its unalienable fidelity towards you. I never loved any but you. You came the embodied image of my fondest dreams. The praise of men, power and high aspirations attended your career. Love for you invested the world for me in enchanted light; it was no longer the earth I trod—the earth common mother, yielding only trite and stale repetition of objects and circumstances old and worn out. I lived in a temple glorified by intensest sense of devotion and rapture; I walked, a consecrated being, contemplating only your power, your excellence;

> For O, you stood beside me, like my youth,
> Transformed for me the real to a dream,
> Cloathing the palpable and familiar
> With golden exhalations of the dawn.

'The bloom has vanished from my life'—there is no morning to this all investing night; no rising to the set-sun of love. In those days the rest of the world was nothing to me: all other men—I never considered nor felt what they were; nor did I look on you as one of them. Separated from them; exalted in my heart; sole possessor of my affections; single object of my hopes, the best half of myself.

"Ah, Raymond, were we not happy? Did the sun shine on any, who could enjoy its light with purer and more intense bliss? It was not—it is not a common infidelity at which I repine. It is the disunion of an whole which may not have parts; it is the carelessness with which you have shaken off the mantle of election with which to me you were invested, and have become one among the many. Dream not to alter this. Is not love a divinity, because it is immortal? Did not I appear sanctified, even to myself, because this love had for its temple my heart? I have gazed on you as you slept, melted even to tears, as the idea filled my mind, that all I possessed lay cradled in those idolized, but mortal lineaments before me. Yet, even then, I have checked thick-coming fears with one thought; I would not fear death, for the emotions that linked us must be immortal.

"And now I do not fear death. I should be well pleased to close my eyes, never more to open them again. And yet I fear it; even as I fear all things; for in any state of being linked by the chain of memory with this, happiness would not return—even in Paradise, I must feel that your love was less enduring than the mortal beatings of my fragile heart, every pulse of which knells audibly,

The funeral note
Of love, deep buried, without resurrection.

No—no—me miserable; for love extinct there is no resurrection!

"Yet I love you. Yet, and for ever, would I contribute all I possess to your welfare. On account of a tattling world; for the sake of my—of our child, I would remain by you, Raymond, share your fortunes, partake your counsel. Shall it be thus? We are no longer lovers; nor can I call myself a friend to any; since, lost as I am, I have no thought to spare from my own wretched, engrossing self.

But it will please me to see you each day! to listen to the public voice praising you; to keep up your paternal love for our girl; to hear your voice; to know that I am near you, though you are no longer mine.

"If you wish to break the chains that bind us, say the word, and it shall be done—I will take all the blame on myself, of harshness or unkindness, in the world's eye.

"Yet, as I have said, I should be best pleased, at least for the present, to live under the same roof with you. When the fever of my young life is spent; when placid age shall tame the vulture that devours me, friendship may come, love and hope being dead. May this be true? Can my soul, inextricably linked to this perishable frame, become lethargic and cold, even as this sensitive mechanism shall lose its youthful elasticity? Then, with lack-lustre eyes, grey hairs, and wrinkled brow, though now the words sound hollow and meaningless, then, tottering on the grave's extreme edge, I may be—your affectionate and true friend,

"PERDITA."

Raymond's answer was brief. What indeed could he reply to her complaints, to her griefs which she jealously paled round, keeping out all thought of remedy. "Notwithstanding your bitter letter," he wrote, "for bitter I must call it, you are the chief person in my estimation, and it is your happiness that I would principally consult. Do that which seems best to you: and if you can receive gratification from one mode of life in preference to another, do not let me be any obstacle. I foresee that the plan which you mark out in your letter will not endure long; but you are mistress of yourself, and it is my sincere wish to contribute as far as you will permit me to your happiness."

"Raymond has prophesied well," said Perdita, "alas, that it should be so! our present mode of life cannot continue long, yet I will not be the first to propose alteration. He beholds in me one whom he has injured even unto death; and I derive no hope from his kindness; no change can possibly be brought about even by his best intentions. As well might Cleopatra have worn as an ornament the vinegar which contained her dissolved pearl, as I be content with the love that Raymond can now offer me."

I own that I did not see her misfortune with the same eyes as Perdita. At all events methought that the wound could be healed;

and, if they remained together, it would be so. I endeavoured therefore to sooth and soften her mind; and it was not until after many endeavours that I gave up the task as impracticable. Perdita listened to me impatiently, and answered with some asperity:—"Do you think that any of your arguments are new to me? or that my own burning wishes and intense anguish have not suggested them all a thousand times, with far more eagerness and subtlety than you can put into them? Lionel, you cannot understand what woman's love is. In days of happiness I have often repeated to myself, with a grateful heart and exalting spirit, all that Raymond sacrificed for me. I was a poor, uneducated, unbefriended, mountain girl, raised from nothingness by him. All that I possessed of the luxuries of life came from him. He gave me an illustrious name and noble station; the world's respect reflected from his own glory: all his joined to his own undying love, inspired me with sensations towards him, akin to those with which we regard the Giver of life. I gave him love only. I devoted myself to him: imperfect creature that I was, I took myself to task, that I might become worthy of him. I watched over my hasty temper, subdued my burning impatience of character, schooled my self-engrossing thoughts, educating myself to the best perfection I might attain, that the fruit of my exertions might be his happiness. I took no merit to myself for this. He deserved it all—all labour, all devotion, all sacrifice; I would have toiled up a scaleless Alp, to pluck a flower that would please him. I was ready to quit you all, my beloved and gifted companions, and to live only with him for him. I could not do otherwise, even if I had wished; for if we are said to have two souls, he was my better soul, to which the other was a perpetual slave. One only return did he owe me, even fidelity. I earned that; I deserved it. Because I was mountain bred, unallied to the noble and wealthy, shall he think to repay me by an empty name and station? Let him take them back; without his love they are nothing to me. Their only merit in my eyes was that they were his."

Thus passionately Perdita ran on. When I adverted to the question of their entire separation, she replied: "Be it so! One day the period will arrive; I know it, and feel it. But in this I am a coward. This imperfect companionship, and our masquerade of union, are strangely dear to me. It is painful, I allow, destructive, impracticable. It keeps up a perpetual fever in my veins; it frets my immedicable wound; it is instinct with poison. Yet I must cling to it; perhaps it will kill me soon, and thus perform a thankful office."

In the mean time, Raymond had remained with Adrian and Idris. He was naturally frank; the continued absence of Perdita and myself became remarkable; and Raymond soon found relief from the constraint of months, by an unreserved confidence with his two friends. He related to them the situation in which he had found Evadne. At first, from delicacy to Adrian he concealed her name; but it was divulged in the course of his narrative, and her former lover heard with the most acute agitation the history of her sufferings. Idris had shared Perdita's ill opinion of the Greek; but Raymond's account softened and interested her. Evadne's constancy, fortitude, even her ill-fated and ill-regulated love, were matter of admiration and pity; especially when, from the detail of the events of the nineteenth of October, it was apparent that she preferred suffering and death to any in her eyes degrading application for the pity and assistance of her lover. Her subsequent conduct did not diminish this interest. At first, relieved from famine and the grave, watched over by Raymond with the tenderest assiduity, with that feeling of repose peculiar to convalescence, Evadne gave herself up to rapturous gratitude and love. But reflection returned with health. She questioned him with regard to the motives which had occasioned his critical absence. She framed her enquiries with Greek subtlety; she formed her conclusions with the decision and firmness peculiar to her disposition. She could not divine, that the breach which she had occasioned between Raymond and Perdita was already irreparable: but she knew, that under the present system it would be widened each day, and that its result must be to destroy her lover's happiness, and to implant the fangs of remorse in his heart. From the moment that she perceived the right line of conduct, she resolved to adopt it, and to part from Raymond for ever. Conflicting passions, long-cherished love, and self-inflicted disappointment, made her regard death alone as sufficient refuge for her woe. But the same feelings and opinions which had before restrained her, acted with redoubled force; for she knew that the reflection that he had occasioned her death, would pursue Raymond through life, poisoning every enjoyment, clouding every prospect. Besides, though the violence of her anguish made life hateful, it had not yet produced that monotonous, lethargic sense of changeless misery which for the most part produces suicide. Her energy of character induced her still to combat with the ills of life; even those attendant on hopeless love presented themselves, rather in the shape of an adversary to be overcome, than of a victor to whom she must submit. Besides, she had memories of past tenderness to cherish, smiles, words, and even tears, to con over, which, though remembered in desertion and sorrow, were to be preferred to the forgetfulness of the grave. It was impossible to guess at the whole of her plan. Her letter to Raymond gave no clue for discovery; it assured him, that she was in no danger of wanting the means of life; she promised in it to preserve herself, and some future day perhaps to present herself to him in a station not unworthy of her. She then bade him, with the eloquence of despair and of unalterable love, a last farewell.

All these circumstances were now related to Adrian and Idris. Raymond then lamented the careless evil of his situation with Perdita. He declared, notwithstanding her harshness, he even called it coldness, that he loved her. He had been ready once with the humility of a penitent, and the duty of a vassal, to surrender himself to her; giving up his very soul to her tutelage, to become her pupil, her slave, her bondsman. She had rejected these advances; and the time for such exuberant submission, which must be founded on love and nourished by it, was now passed. Still all his wishes and endeavours were directed towards her peace, and his chief discomfort arose from the perception that he exerted himself in vain. If she were to continue inflexible in the line of conduct she now pursued, they must part. The combinations and occurrences of this senseless mode of intercourse were maddening to him. Yet he would not propose the separation. He was haunted by the fear of causing the death of one or other of the beings implicated in these events; and he could not persuade himself to undertake to direct the course of events, lest, ignorant of the land he traversed, he should lead those attached to the car into irremediable ruin.

After a discussion on this subject, which lasted for several hours, he took leave of his friends, and returned to town, unwilling to meet Perdita before us, conscious, as we all must be, of the thoughts uppermost in the minds of both. Perdita prepared to follow him with her child. Idris endeavoured to persuade her to remain. My poor sister looked at the counsellor with affright. She knew that Raymond had conversed with her; had he instigated this request?—was this to be the prelude to their eternal separation?—I have said, that the defects of her character awoke and acquired vigour from her unnatural position. She regarded with suspicion the invitation of Idris; she embraced me, as if she were about to be deprived of my affection also: calling me her more than brother, her only friend, her last hope, she pathetically conjured me not to cease to love her; and with encreased anxiety she departed for London, the scene and cause of all her misery.

The scenes that followed, convinced her that she had not yet fathomed the obscure gulph into which she had plunged. Her unhappiness assumed every day a new shape; every day some unexpected event seemed to close, while in fact it led onward, the train of calamities which now befell her.

The selected passion of the soul of Raymond was ambition. Readiness of talent, a capacity of entering into, and leading the dispositions of men; earnest desire of distinction were the awakeners and nurses of his ambition. But other ingredients mingled with these, and prevented him from becoming the calculating, determined character, which alone forms a successful hero. He was obstinate, but not firm; benevolent in his first movements; harsh and reckless when provoked. Above all, he was remorseless and unyielding in the pursuit of any object of desire, however lawless. Love of pleasure, and the softer sensibilities of our nature, made a prominent part of his character, conquering the conqueror; holding him in at the moment of acquisition; sweeping away ambition's web; making him forget the toil of weeks, for the sake of one moment's indulgence of the new and actual object of his wishes. Obeying these impulses, he had become the husband of Perdita: egged on by them, he found himself the lover of Evadne. He had now lost both. He had neither the ennobling self-gratulation, which constancy inspires, to console him, nor the voluptuous sense of abandonment to a forbidden, but intoxicating passion. His heart was exhausted by the recent events; his enjoyment of life was destroyed by the resentment of Perdita, and the flight of Evadne; and the inflexibility of the former, set the last seal upon the annihilation of his hopes. As long as their disunion remained a secret, he cherished an expectation of re-awakening past tenderness in her bosom; now that we were all made acquainted with these occurrences, and that Perdita, by declaring her resolves to others, in a manner pledged herself to their accomplishment, he gave up the idea of reunion as futile, and sought only, since he was unable to influence her to change, to reconcile himself to the present state of things. He made a vow against love and its train of struggles, disappointment and remorse, and sought in mere sensual enjoyment, a remedy for the injurious inroads of passion.

Debasement of character is the certain follower of such pursuits. Yet this consequence would not have been immediately remarkable, if Raymond had continued to apply himself to the execution of his plans for the public benefit, and the fulfilling his duties as Protector. But, extreme in all things, given up to immediate impressions, he entered with ardour into this new pursuit of pleasure, and followed up the incongruous intimacies occasioned by it without reflection or foresight. The council-chamber was deserted; the crowds which attended on him as agents to his various projects were neglected. Festivity, and even libertinism, became the order of the day.

Perdita beheld with affright the encreasing disorder. For a moment she thought that she could stem the torrent, and that Raymond could be induced to hear reason from her.—Vain hope! The moment of her influence was passed. He listened with haughtiness, replied disdainfully; and, if in truth, she succeeded in awakening his conscience, the sole effect was that he sought an opiate for the pang in oblivious riot. With the energy natural to her, Perdita then endeavoured to supply his place. Their still apparent union permitted her to do much; but no woman could, in the end, present a remedy to the encreasing negligence of the Protector; who, as if seized with a paroxysm of insanity, trampled on all ceremony, all order, all duty, and gave himself up to license.

Reports of these strange proceedings reached us, and we were undecided what method to adopt to restore our friend to himself and his country, when Perdita suddenly appeared among us. She detailed the progress of the mournful change, and entreated Adrian and myself to go up to London, and endeavour to remedy the encreasing evil:—"Tell him," she cried, "tell Lord Raymond, that my presence shall no longer annoy him. That he need not plunge into this destructive dissipation for the sake of disgusting me, and causing me to fly. This purpose is now accomplished; he will never see me more. But let me, it is my last entreaty, let me in the praises of his countrymen and the prosperity of England, find the choice of my youth justified."

During our ride up to town, Adrian and I discussed and argued upon Raymond's conduct, and his falling off from the hopes of permanent excellence on his part, which he had before given us cause to entertain. My friend and I had both been educated in one school, or rather I was his pupil in the opinion, that steady adherence to principle was the only road to honour; a ceaseless observance of the laws of general utility, the only conscientious aim of human ambition. But though we both entertained these ideas, we differed in their application. Resentment added also a sting to my censure; and I reprobated Raymond's conduct in severe terms. Adrian was more benign, more considerate. He admitted that the principles that I laid down were the best; but he denied that they were the only ones. Quoting the text, *there are many mansions in my father's house,* he insisted that the modes of becoming good or great, varied as much as the dispositions of men, of whom it might be said, as of the leaves of the forest, there were no two alike.

We arrived in London at about eleven at night. We conjectured, notwithstanding what we had heard, that we should find Raymond in St. Stephen's: thither we sped. The chamber was full—but there was no Protector; and there was an austere discontent manifest on the countenances of the leaders, and a whispering and busy tattle among the underlings, not less ominous. We hastened to the palace of the Protectorate. We found Raymond in his dining room with six others: the bottle was being pushed about merrily, and had made considerable inroads on the understanding of one or two. He who sat near Raymond was telling a story, which convulsed the rest with laughter.

Raymond sat among them, though while he entered into the spirit of the hour, his natural dignity never forsook him. He was gay, playful, fascinating—but never did he overstep the modesty of nature, or the respect due to himself, in his wildest sallies. Yet I own, that considering the task which Raymond had taken on himself as Protector of England, and the cares to which it became him to attend, I was exceedingly provoked to observe the worthless fellows on whom his time was wasted, and the jovial if not drunken spirit which seemed on the point of robbing him of his better self. I stood watching the scene, while Adrian flitted like a shadow in among them, and, by a word and look of sobriety, endeavoured to restore order in the assembly. Raymond expressed himself delighted to see him, declaring that he should make one in the festivity of the night.

This action of Adrian provoked me. I was indignant that he should sit at the same table with the companions of Raymond—men of abandoned characters, or rather without any, the refuse of high-bred luxury, the disgrace of their country. "Let me entreat Adrian," I cried, "not to comply: rather join with me in endeavouring to withdraw Lord Raymond from this scene, and restore him to other society."

"My good fellow," said Raymond, "this is neither the time nor place for the delivery of a moral lecture: take my word for it that my amusements and society are not so bad as you imagine. We are neither hypocrites or fools—for the rest, 'Dost thou think because thou art virtuous, there shall be no more cakes and ale?'"

I turned angrily away: "Verney," said Adrian, "you are very cynical: sit down; or if you will not, perhaps, as you are not a frequent visitor, Lord Raymond will humour you, and accompany us, as we had previously agreed upon, to parliament."

Raymond looked keenly at him; he could read benignity only in his gentle lineaments; he turned to me, observing with scorn my moody and stern demeanour. "Come," said Adrian, "I have promised for you, enable me to keep my engagement. Come with us." Raymond made an uneasy movement, and laconically replied—"I won't!"

The party in the mean time had broken up. They looked at the pictures, strolled into the other apartments, talked of billiards, and one by one vanished. Raymond strode angrily up and down the room. I stood ready to receive and reply to his reproaches. Adrian leaned against the wall. "This is infinitely ridiculous," he cried, "if you were school-boys, you could not conduct yourselves more unreasonably."

"You do not understand," said Raymond. "This is only part of a system:—a scheme of tyranny to which I will never submit. Because I am Protector of England, am I to be the only slave in its empire? My privacy invaded, my actions censured, my friends insulted? But I will get rid of the whole together.—Be you witnesses," and he took the star, insignia of office, from his breast, and threw it on the table. "I renounce my office, I abdicate my power—assume it who will!"

"Let him assume it," exclaimed Adrian, "who can pronounce himself, or whom the world will pronounce to be your superior. There does not exist the man in England with adequate presumption. Know yourself, Raymond, and your indignation will cease; your complacency return. A few months ago, whenever we prayed for the prosperity of our country, or our own, we at the same time prayed for the life and welfare of the Protector, as indissolubly linked to it. Your hours were devoted to our benefit, your ambition was to obtain our commendation. You decorated our towns with edifices, you bestowed on us useful establishments, you gifted the soil with abundant fertility. The powerful and unjust cowered at the steps of your judgment-seat, and the poor and oppressed arose like morn-awakened flowers under the sunshine of your protection.

"Can you wonder that we are all aghast and mourn, when this appears changed? But, come, this splenetic fit is already passed; resume your functions; your partizans will hail you; your enemies be silenced; our love, honour, and duty will again be manifested towards you. Master yourself, Raymond, and the world is subject to you."

"All this would be very good sense, if addressed to another," replied Raymond, moodily, "con the lesson yourself, and you, the first peer of the land, may become its sovereign. You the good, the wise, the just, may rule all hearts. But I perceive, too soon for my own happiness, too late for England's good, that I undertook a task to which I am unequal. I cannot rule myself. My passions are my masters; my smallest impulse my tyrant. Do you think that I renounced the Protectorate (and I have renounced it) in a fit of spleen? By the God that lives, I swear never to take up that bauble again; never again to burthen myself with the weight of care and misery, of which that is the visible sign.

"Once I desired to be a king. It was in the hey-day of youth, in the pride of boyish folly. I knew myself when I renounced it. I renounced it to gain—no matter what—for that also I have lost. For many months I have submitted to this mock majesty—this solemn jest. I am its dupe no longer. I will be free.

"I have lost that which adorned and dignified my life; that which linked me to other men. Again I am a solitary man; and I will become again, as in my early years, a wanderer, a soldier of fortune.

My friends, for Verney, I feel that you are my friend, do not endeavour to shake my resolve. Perdita, wedded to an imagination, careless of what is behind the veil, whose charactery is in truth faulty and vile, Perdita has renounced me. With her it was pretty enough to play a sovereign's part; and, as in the recesses of your beloved forest we acted masques, and imagined ourselves Arcadian shepherds, to please the fancy of the moment—so was I content, more for Perdita's sake than my own, to take on me the character of one of the great ones of the earth; to lead her behind the scenes of grandeur, to vary her life with a short act of magnificence and power. This was to be the colour; love and confidence the substance of our existence. But we must live, and not act our lives; pursuing the shadow, I lost the reality—now I renounce both.

"Adrian, I am about to return to Greece, to become again a soldier, perhaps a conqueror. Will you accompany me? You will behold new scenes; see a new people; witness the mighty struggle there going forward between civilization and barbarism; behold, and perhaps direct the efforts of a young and vigorous population, for liberty and order. Come with me. I have expected you. I waited for this moment; all is prepared;—will you accompany me?"

"I will," replied Adrian.

"Immediately?"

"To-morrow if you will."

"Reflect!" I cried.

"Wherefore?" asked Raymond—"My dear fellow, I have done nothing else than reflect on this step the live-long summer; and be assured that Adrian has condensed an age of reflection into this little moment. Do not talk of reflection; from this moment I abjure it; this is my only happy moment during a long interval of time. I must go, Lionel—the Gods will it; and I must. Do not endeavour to deprive me of my companion, the outcast's friend.

"One word more concerning unkind, unjust Perdita. For a time, I thought that, by watching a complying moment, fostering the still warm ashes, I might relume in her the flame of love. It is more cold within her, than a fire left by gypsies in winter-time, the spent embers crowned by a pyramid of snow. Then, in endeavouring to do violence to my own disposition, I made all worse than before. Still I think, that time, and even absence, may restore her to me. Remember, that I love her still, that my dearest hope is that she will again be mine. I know, though she does not, how false the veil is which she has spread over the reality—do not endeavour to rend this deceptive covering, but by degrees withdraw it. Present her with a mirror, in which she may know herself; and, when she is an adept in that necessary but difficult science, she will wonder at her present mistake, and hasten to restore to me, what is by right mine, her forgiveness, her kind thoughts, her love."

Chapter X

AFTER THESE EVENTS, it was long before we were able to attain any degree of composure. A moral tempest had wrecked our richly freighted vessel, and we, remnants of the diminished crew, were aghast at the losses and changes which we had undergone. Idris passionately loved her brother, and could ill brook an absence whose duration was uncertain; his society was dear and necessary to me—I had followed up my chosen literary occupations with delight under his tutorship and assistance; his mild philosophy, unerring reason, and enthusiastic friendship were the best ingredient, the exalted spirit of our circle; even the children bitterly regretted the loss of their kind playfellow. Deeper grief oppressed Perdita. In spite of resentment, by day and night she figured to herself the toils and dangers of the wanderers. Raymond absent, struggling with difficulties, lost to the power and rank of the Protectorate, exposed to the perils of war, became an object of anxious interest; not that she felt any inclination to recall him, if recall must imply a return to their former union. Such return she felt to be impossible; and while she believed it to be thus, and with anguish regretted that so it should be, she continued angry and impatient with him, who occasioned her misery. These perplexities and regrets caused her to bathe her pillow with nightly tears, and to reduce her in person and in mind to the shadow of what she had been. She sought solitude, and avoided us when in gaiety and unrestrained affection we met in a family circle. Lonely musings, interminable wanderings, and solemn music were her only pastimes. She neglected even her child; shutting her heart against all tenderness, she grew reserved towards me, her first and fast friend.

I could not see her thus lost, without exerting myself to remedy the evil—remediless I knew, if I could not in the end bring her to reconcile herself to Raymond. Before he went I used every argument, every persuasion to induce her to stop his journey. She answered the one with a gush of tears—telling me that to be persuaded—life and the goods of life were a cheap exchange. It was not will that she wanted, but the capacity; again and again she declared, it were as easy to enchain the sea, to put reins on the wind's viewless courses, as for her to take truth for falsehood, deceit for honesty, heartless communion for sincere, confiding love. She answered my reasonings more briefly, declaring with disdain, that the reason was hers; and, until I could persuade her that the past could be unacted, that maturity could go back to the cradle, and that all that was could become as though it had never been, it was useless to assure her that no real change had taken place in her fate. And thus with stern pride she suffered him to go, though her very heart-strings cracked at the fulfilling of the act, which rent from her all that made life valuable.

To change the scene for her, and even for ourselves, all unhinged by the cloud that had come over us, I persuaded my two remaining companions that it were better that we should absent ourselves for a time from Windsor. We visited the north of England, my native Ulswater, and lingered in scenes dear from a thousand associations. We lengthened our tour into Scotland, that we might see Loch Katrine and Loch Lomond; thence we crossed to Ireland, and passed several weeks in the neighbourhood of Killarney. The change of scene operated to a great degree as I expected; after a year's absence, Perdita returned in gentler and more docile mood to Windsor. The first sight of this place for a time unhinged her. Here every spot was distinct with associations now grown bitter. The forest glades, the ferny dells, and lawny uplands, the cultivated and cheerful country spread around the silver pathway of ancient Thames, all earth, air, and wave, took up one choral voice, inspired by memory, instinct with plaintive regret.

But my essay towards bringing her to a saner view of her own situation, did not end here. Perdita was still to a great degree uneducated. When first she left her peasant life, and resided with the elegant and cultivated Evadne, the only accomplishment she brought to any perfection was that of painting, for which she had a taste almost amounting to genius. This had occupied her in her lonely cottage, when she quitted her Greek friend's protection. Her pallet and easel were now thrown aside; did she try to paint, thronging recollections made her hand tremble, her eyes fill with tears. With this occupation she gave up almost every other; and her mind preyed upon itself almost to madness.

For my own part, since Adrian had first withdrawn me from my selvatic wilderness to his own paradise of order and beauty, I had been wedded to literature. I felt convinced that however it might have been in former times, in the present stage of the world, no man's faculties could be developed, no man's moral principle be enlarged and liberal, without an extensive acquaintance with books. To me they stood in the place of an active career, of ambition, and those palpable excitements necessary to the multitude. The collation of philosophical opinions, the study of historical facts, the acquirement of languages, were at once my recreation, and the serious aim of my life. I turned author myself. My productions however were sufficiently unpretending; they were confined to the biography of favourite historical characters, especially those whom I believed to have been traduced, or about whom clung obscurity and doubt.

As my authorship increased, I acquired new sympathies and pleasures. I found another and a valuable link to enchain me to my fellow-creatures; my point of sight was extended, and the inclinations and capacities of all human beings became deeply interesting to me. Kings have been called the fathers of their people. Suddenly I became as it were the father of all mankind. Posterity became my heirs. My thoughts were gems to enrich the treasure house of man's intellectual possessions; each sentiment was a precious gift I bestowed on them. Let not these aspirations be attributed to vanity. They were not expressed in words, nor even reduced to form in my own mind; but they filled my soul, exalting my thoughts, raising a glow of enthusiasm, and led me out of the obscure path in which I before walked, into the bright noon-enlightened highway of mankind, making me, citizen of the world, a candidate for immortal honors, an eager aspirant to the praise and sympathy of my fellow men.

No one certainly ever enjoyed the pleasures of composition more intensely than I. If I left the woods, the solemn music of the waving branches, and the majestic temple of nature, I sought the vast halls of the Castle, and looked over wide, fertile England, spread beneath our regal mount, and listened the while to inspiring strains of music. At such times solemn harmonies or spirit-stirring airs gave wings to my lagging thoughts, permitting them, methought, to penetrate the last veil of nature and her God, and to display the highest beauty in visible expression to the understandings of men. As the music went on, my ideas seemed to quit their mortal dwelling house; they shook their pinions and began a flight, sailing on the placid current of thought, filling the creation with new glory, and rousing sublime imagery that else had slept voiceless. Then I would hasten to my desk, weave the new-found web of mind in firm texture and brilliant colours, leaving the fashioning of the material to a calmer moment.

But this account, which might as properly belong to a former period of my life as to the present moment, leads me far afield. It was the pleasure I took in literature, the discipline of mind I found arise from it, that made me eager to lead Perdita to the same pursuits. I began with light hand and gentle allurement; first exciting her curiosity, and then satisfying it in such a way as might occasion her, at the same time that she half forgot her sorrows in occupation, to find in the hours that succeeded a reaction of benevolence and toleration.

Intellectual activity, though not directed towards books, had always been my sister's characteristic. It had been displayed early in life, leading her out to solitary musing among her native mountains, causing her to form innumerous combinations from common objects, giving strength to her perceptions, and swiftness to their arrangement. Love had come, as the rod of the master-prophet, to swallow up every minor propensity. Love had doubled all her excellencies, and placed a diadem on her genius. Was she to cease to love? Take the colours and odour from the rose, change the sweet nutriment of mother's milk to gall and poison; as easily might you wean Perdita from love. She grieved for the loss of Raymond with an anguish, that exiled all smile from her lips, and trenched sad lines on her brow of beauty. But each day seemed to change the nature of her suffering, and every succeeding hour forced her to alter (if so I may style it) the fashion of her soul's mourning garb. For a time music was able to satisfy the cravings of her mental hunger, and her melancholy thoughts renewed themselves in each change of key, and varied with every alteration in the strain. My schooling first impelled her towards books; and, if music had been the food of sorrow, the productions of the wise became its medicine.

The acquisition of unknown languages was too tedious an occupation, for one who referred every expression to the universe within, and read not, as many do, for the mere sake of filling up time; but who was still questioning herself and her author, moulding every idea in a thousand ways, ardently desirous for the discovery of truth in every sentence. She sought to improve her understanding; mechanically her heart and dispositions became soft and gentle under this benign discipline. After awhile she discovered, that amidst all her newly acquired knowledge, her own character, which formerly she fancied that she thoroughly understood, became the first in rank among the terræ incognitæ, the pathless wilds of a country that had no chart. Erringly and strangely she began the task of self-examination with self-condemnation. And then again she became aware of her own excellencies, and began to balance with juster scales the shades of good and evil. I, who longed beyond words, to restore her to the happiness it was still in her power to enjoy, watched with anxiety the result of these internal proceedings.

But man is a strange animal. We cannot calculate on his forces like that of an engine; and, though an impulse draw with a forty-horse power at what appears willing to yield to one, yet in contempt of calculation the movement is not effected. Neither grief, philosophy, nor love could make Perdita think with mildness of the dereliction of Raymond. She now took pleasure in my society; towards Idris she felt and displayed a full and affectionate sense of her worth—she restored to her child in abundant measure her tenderness and care. But I could discover, amidst all her repinings, deep resentment towards Raymond, and an unfading sense of injury, that plucked from me my hope, when I appeared nearest to its fulfilment. Among other painful restrictions, she has occasioned it to become a law among us, never to mention Raymond's name before her. She refused to read any communications from Greece, desiring me only to mention when any arrived, and whether the wanderers were well. It was curious that even little Clara observed this law towards her mother. This lovely child was nearly eight years of age. Formerly she had been a light-hearted infant, fanciful, but gay and childish. After the departure of her father, thought became impressed on her young brow. Children, unadepts in language, seldom find words to express their thoughts, nor could we tell in what manner the late events had impressed themselves on her mind. But certainly she had made deep observations while she noted in silence the changes that passed around her. She never mentioned her father to Perdita, she appeared half afraid when she spoke of him to me, and though I tried to draw her out on the subject, and to dispel the gloom that hung about her ideas concerning him, I could not succeed. Yet each foreign post-day she watched for the arrival of letters—knew the post mark, and watched me as I read. I found her often poring over the article of Greek intelligence in the newspaper.

There is no more painful sight than that of untimely care in children, and it was particularly observable in one whose disposition had heretofore been mirthful. Yet there was so much sweetness and docility about Clara, that your admiration was excited; and if the moods of mind are calculated to paint the cheek with beauty, and endow motions with grace, surely her contemplations must have been celestial; since every lineament was moulded into loveliness, and her motions were more harmonious than the elegant boundings of the fawns of her native forest. I sometimes expostulated with Perdita on the subject of her reserve; but she rejected my counsels, while her daughter's sensibility excited in her a tenderness still more passionate.

After the lapse of more than a year, Adrian returned from Greece.

When our exiles had first arrived, a truce was in existence between the Turks and Greeks; a truce that was as sleep to the mortal frame, signal of renewed activity on waking. With the numerous soldiers of Asia, with all of warlike stores, ships, and military engines, that wealth and power could command, the Turks at once resolved to crush an enemy, which creeping on by degrees, had from their stronghold in the Morea, acquired Thrace and Macedonia, and had led their armies even to the gates of Constantinople, while their extensive commercial relations gave every European nation an interest in their success. Greece prepared for a vigorous resistance; it rose to a man; and the women, sacrificing their costly ornaments, accoutred their sons for the war, and bade them conquer or die with the spirit of the Spartan mother. The talents and courage of Raymond were highly esteemed among the Greeks. Born at Athens, that city claimed him for her own, and by giving him the command of her peculiar division in the army, the commander-in-chief only possessed superior power. He was numbered among her citizens, his name was added to the list of Grecian heroes. His judgment, activity, and consummate bravery, justified their choice. The Earl of Windsor became a volunteer under his friend.

"It is well," said Adrian, "to prate of war in these pleasant shades, and with much ill-spent oil make a show of joy, because many thousand of our fellow-creatures leave with pain this sweet air and natal earth. I shall not be suspected of being averse to the Greek cause; I know and feel its necessity; it is beyond every other a good cause. I have defended it with my sword, and was willing that my spirit should be breathed out in its defence; freedom is of more worth than life, and the Greeks do well to defend their privilege unto death. But let us not deceive ourselves. The Turks are men; each fibre, each limb is as feeling as our own, and every spasm, be it mental or [bo] dily, is as truly felt in a Turk's heart or brain, as in a Greek's. The last action at which I was present was the taking of ———. The Turks resisted to the last, the garrison perished on the ramparts, and we entered by assault. Every breathing creature within the walls was massacred. Think you, amidst the shrieks of violated innocence and helpless infancy, I did not feel in every nerve the cry of a fellow being? They were men and women, the sufferers, before they were Mahometans, and when they rise turbanless from the grave, in what except their good or evil actions will they be the better or worse than we? Two soldiers contended for a girl, whose rich dress and extreme beauty excited the brutal appetites of these wretches, who, perhaps good men among their families, were changed by the fury of the moment into incarnated evils. An old man, with a silver beard, decrepid and bald, he might be her grandfather, interposed to save her; the battle axe of one of them clove his skull. I rushed to her defence, but rage made them blind and deaf; they did not distinguish my Christian garb or heed my words—words were blunt weapons then, for while war cried "havoc," and murder gave fit echo, how could I—

Turn back the tide of ills, relieving wrong
With mild accost of soothing eloquence?

One of the fellows, enraged at my interference, struck me with his bayonet in the side, and I fell senseless.

"This wound will probably shorten my life, having shattered a frame, weak of itself. But I am content to die. I have learnt in

Greece that one man, more or less, is of small import, while human bodies remain to fill up the thinned ranks of the soldiery; and that the identity of an individual may be overlooked, so that the muster roll contain its full numbers. All this has a different effect upon Raymond. He is able to contemplate the ideal of war, while I am sensible only to its realities. He is a soldier, a general. He can influence the blood-thirsty war-dogs, while I resist their propensities vainly. The cause is simple. Burke has said that, 'in all bodies those who would lead, must also, in a considerable degree, follow.'—I cannot follow; for I do not sympathize in their dreams of massacre and glory—to follow and to lead in such a career, is the natural bent of Raymond's mind. He is always successful, and bids fair, at the same time that he acquires high name and station for himself, to secure liberty, probably extended empire, to the Greeks."

Perdita's mind was not softened by this account. He, she thought, can be great and happy without me. Would that I also had a career! Would that I could freight some untried bark with all my hopes, energies, and desires, and launch it forth into the ocean of life—bound for some attainable point, with ambition or pleasure at the helm! But adverse winds detain me on shore; like Ulysses, I sit at the water's edge and weep. But my nerveless hands can neither fell the trees, nor smooth the planks. Under the influence of these melancholy thoughts, she became more than ever in love with sorrow. Yet Adrian's presence did some good; he at once broke through the law of silence observed concerning Raymond. At first she started from the unaccustomed sound; soon she got used to it and to love it, and she listened with avidity to the account of his achievements. Clara got rid also of her restraint; Adrian and she had been old playfellows; and now, as they walked or rode together, he yielded to her earnest entreaty, and repeated, for the hundredth time, some tale of her father's bravery, munificence, or justice.

Each vessel in the mean time brought exhilarating tidings from Greece. The presence of a friend in its armies and councils made us enter into the details with enthusiasm; and a short letter now and then from Raymond told us how he was engrossed by the interests of his adopted country. The Greeks were strongly attached to their commercial pursuits, and would have been satisfied with their present acquisitions, had not the Turks roused them by invasion. The patriots were victorious; a spirit of conquest was instilled; and already they looked on Constantinople as their own. Raymond rose perpetually in their estimation; but one man held a superior command to him in their armies. He was conspicuous for his conduct and choice of position in a battle fought in the plains of Thrace, on the banks of the Hebrus, which was to decide the fate of Islam. The Mahometans were defeated, and driven entirely from the country west of this river. The battle was sanguinary, the loss of the Turks apparently irreparable; the Greeks, in losing one man, forgot the nameless crowd strewed upon the bloody field, and they ceased to value themselves on a victory, which cost them—Raymond.

At the battle of Makri he had led the charge of cavalry, and pursued the fugitives even to the banks of the Hebrus. His favourite horse was found grazing by the margin of the tranquil river. It became a question whether he had fallen among the unrecognized; but no broken ornament or stained trapping betrayed his fate. It was suspected that the Turks, finding themselves possessed of so illustrious a captive, resolved to satisfy their cruelty rather than their avarice, and fearful of the interference of England, had come to the determination of concealing for ever the cold-blooded murder of the soldier they most hated and feared in the squadrons of their enemy.

Raymond was not forgotten in England. His abdication of the Protectorate had caused an unexampled sensation; and, when his magnificent and manly system was contrasted with the narrow views of succeeding politicians, the period of his elevation was referred to with sorrow. The perpetual recurrence of his name, joined to most honourable testimonials, in the Greek gazettes, kept up the interest he had excited. He seemed the favourite child of fortune, and his untimely loss eclipsed the world, and shewed forth the remnant of mankind with diminished lustre. They clung with eagerness to the hope held out that he might yet be alive. Their minister at Constantinople was urged to make the necessary perquisitions, and should his existence be ascertained, to demand his release. It was to be hoped that their efforts would succeed, and that though now a prisoner, the sport of cruelty and the mark of hate, he would be rescued from danger and restored to the happiness, power, and honour which he deserved.

The effect of this intelligence upon my sister was striking. She never for a moment credited the story of his death; she resolved instantly to go to Greece. Reasoning and persuasion were thrown away upon her; she would endure no hindrance, no delay. It may be advanced for a truth, that, if argument or entreaty can turn any one from a desperate purpose, whose motive and end depends on the strength of the affections only, then it is right so to turn them, since their docility shews, that neither the motive nor the end were of sufficient force to bear them through the obstacles attendant on their undertaking. If, on the contrary, they are proof against expostulation, this very steadiness is an omen of success; and it becomes the duty of those who love them, to assist in smoothing the obstructions in their path. Such sentiments actuated our little circle. Finding Perdita immoveable, we consulted as to the best means of furthering her purpose. She could not go alone to a country where she had no friends, where she might arrive only to hear the dreadful news, which must overwhelm her with grief and remorse. Adrian, whose health had always been weak, now suffered considerable aggravation of suffering from the effects of his wound. Idris could not endure to leave him in this state; nor was it right either to quit or take with us a young family for a journey of this description. I resolved at length to accompany Perdita. The separation from my Idris was painful—but necessity reconciled us to it in some degree: necessity and the hope of saving Raymond, and restoring him again to happiness and Perdita. No delay was to ensue. Two days after we came to our determination, we set out for Portsmouth, and embarked. The season was May, the weather stormless; we were promised a prosperous voyage. Cherishing the most fervent hopes, embarked on the waste ocean, we saw with delight the receding shore of Britain, and on the wings of desire outspeeded our well filled sails towards the South. The light curling waves bore us onward, and old ocean smiled at the freight of love and hope committed to his charge; it stroked gently its tempestuous plains, and the path was smoothed for us. Day and night the wind right aft, gave steady impulse to our keel—nor did rough gale, or treacherous sand, or destructive rock interpose an obstacle between my sister and the land which was to restore her to her first beloved,

Her dear heart's confessor—a heart within that heart.

Roger Dodsworth
The Reanimated Englishman

IT MAY BE remembered, that on the fourth of July last, a paragraph appeared in the papers importing that Dr. Hotham, of Northumberland, returning from Italy, over Mount St. Gothard, a score or two of years ago, had dug out from under an avalanche, in the neighbourhood of the mountain, a human being whose animation had been suspended by the action of the frost. Upon the application of the usual remedies, the patient was resuscitated, and discovered himself to be Mr. Dodsworth, the son of the antiquary Dodsworth, who perished in the reign of Charles I. He was thirty-seven years of age at the time of his inhumation, which had taken place as he was returning from Italy, in 1654. It was added that as soon as he was sufficiently recovered he would return to England, under the protection of his preserver. We have since heard no more of him, and various plans for public benefit, which have started in philanthropic minds on reading the statement, have already returned to their pristine nothingness. The antiquarian society had eaten their way to several votes for medals, and had already begun, in idea, to consider what prices it could afford to offer for Mr. Dodsworth's old clothes, and to conjecture what treasures in the way of pamphlet, old song, or autographic letter his pockets might contain. Poems from all quarters, of all kinds, elegiac, congratulatory, burlesque and allegoric, were half written. Mr. Godwin had suspended for the sake of such authentic information the history of the Commonwealth he had just begun. It is hard not only that the world should be baulked of these destined gifts from the talents of the country, but also that it should be promised and then deprived of a new subject of romantic wonder and scientific interest. A novel idea is worth much in the commonplace routine of life, but a new fact, an astonishment, a miracle, a palpable wandering from the course of things into apparent impossibilities, is a circumstance to which the imagination must cling with delight, and we say again that it is hard, very hard, that Mr. Dodsworth refuses to appear, and that the believers in his resuscitation are forced to undergo the sarcasms and triumphant arguments of those sceptics who always keep on the safe side of the hedge.

Now we do not believe that any contradiction or impossibility is attached to the adventures of this youthful antique. Animation (I believe physiologists agree) can as easily be suspended for an hundred or two years, as for as many seconds. A body hermetically sealed up by the frost, is of necessity preserved in its pristine entireness. That which is totally secluded from the action of external agency, can neither have any thing added to nor taken away from it: no decay can take place, for something can never become nothing; under the influence of that state of being which we call death, change but not annihilation removes from our sight the corporeal atoma; the earth receives sustenance from them, the air is fed by them, each element takes its own, thus seizing forcible repayment of what it had lent. But the elements that hovered round Mr. Dodsworth's icy shroud had no power to overcome the obstacle it presented. No zephyr could gather a hair from his head, nor could the influence of dewy night or genial morn penetrate his more than adamantine panoply. The story of the Seven Sleepers rests on a miraculous interposition—they slept. Mr. Dodsworth did not sleep; his breast never heaved, his pulses were stopped; death had his finger pressed on his lips which no breath might pass. He has removed it now, the grim shadow is vanquished, and stands wondering. His victim has cast from him the frosty spell, and arises as perfect a man as he had lain down an hundred and fifty years before. We have eagerly desired to be furnished with some particulars of his first conversations, and the mode in which he has learnt to adapt himself to his new scene of life. But since facts are denied to us, let us be permitted to indulge in conjecture. What his first words were may be guessed from the expressions used by people exposed to shorter accidents of the like nature. But as his powers return, the plot thickens. His dress had already excited Doctor Hotham's astonishment—the peaked beard—the love locks—the frill, which, until it was thawed, stood stiff under the mingled influence of starch and frost;

his dress fashioned like that of one of Vandyke's portraits, or (a more familiar similitude) Mr. Sapio's costume in Winter's Opera of the Oracle, his pointed shoes—all spoke of other times. The curiosity of his preserver was keenly awake, that of Mr. Dodsworth was about to be roused. But to be enabled to conjecture with any degree of likelihood the tenor of his first inquiries, we must endeavour to make out what part he played in his former life. He lived at the most interesting period of English History—he was lost to the world when Oliver Cromwell had arrived at the summit of his ambition, and in the eyes of all Europe the commonwealth of England appeared so established as to endure for ever. Charles I. was dead; Charles II. was an outcast, a beggar, bankrupt even in hope. Mr. Dodsworth's father, the antiquary, received a salary from the republican general, Lord Fairfax, who was himself a great lover of antiquities, and died the very year that his son went to his long, but not unending sleep, a curious coincidence this, for it would seem that our frost-preserved friend was returning to England on his father's death, to claim probably his inheritance—how short lived are human views! Where now is Mr. Dodsworth's patrimony? Where his co-heirs, executors, and fellow legatees? His protracted absence has, we should suppose, given the present possessors to his estate—the world's chronology is an hundred and seventy years older since he seceded from the busy scene, hands after hands have tilled his acres, and then become clods beneath them; we may be permitted to doubt whether one single particle of their surface is individually the same as those which were to have been his—the youthful soil would of itself reject the antique clay of its claimant.

Mr. Dodsworth, if we may judge from the circumstance of his being abroad, was no zealous commonwealth's man, yet his having chosen Italy as the country in which to make his tour and his projected return to England on his father's death, renders it probable that he was no violent loyalist. One of those men he seems to be (or to have been) who did not follow Cato's advice as recorded in the Pharsalia; a party, if to be of no party admits of such a term, which Dante recommends us utterly to despise, and which not unseldom falls between the two stools, a seat on either of which is so carefully avoided. Still Mr. Dodsworth could hardly fail to feel anxious for the latest news from his native country at so critical a period; his absence might have put his own property in jeopardy; we may imagine therefore that after his limbs had felt the cheerful return of circulation, and after he had refreshed himself with such of earth's products as from all analogy he never could have hoped to live to eat, after he had been told from what peril he had been rescued, and said a prayer thereon which even appeared enormously long to Dr. Hotham—we may imagine, we say, that his first question would be: "If any news had arrived lately from England?"

"I had letters yesterday," Dr. Hotham may well be supposed to reply.

"Indeed," cries Mr. Dodsworth, "and pray, sir, has any change for better or worse occurred in that poor distracted country?"

Dr. Hotham suspects a Radical, and coldly replies: "Why, sir, it would be difficult to say in what its distraction consists. People talk of starving manufacturers, bankruptcies, and the fall of the Joint Stock Companies—excrescences these, excrescences which will attach themselves to a state of full health. England, in fact, was never in a more prosperous condition."

Mr. Dodsworth now more than suspects the Republican, and, with what we have supposed to be his accustomed caution, sinks for awhile his loyalty, and in a moderate tone asks: "Do our governors look with careless eyes upon the symptoms of over-health?"

"Our governors," answers his preserver, "if you mean our ministry, are only too alive to temporary embarrassment." (We beg Doctor Hotham's pardon if we wrong him in making him a high Tory; such a quality appertains to our pure anticipated cognition of a Doctor, and such is the only cognizance that we have of this gentleman.) "It were to be wished that they showed themselves more firm—the king, God bless him!"

"Sir!" exclaims Mr. Dodsworth.

Doctor Hotham continues, not aware of the excessive astonishment exhibited by his patient: "The king, God bless him, spares immense sums from his privy purse for the relief of his subjects, and his example has been imitated by all the aristocracy and wealth of England."

"The King!" ejaculates Mr. Dodsworth.

"Yes, sir," emphatically rejoins his preserver; "the king, and I am happy to say that the prejudices that so unhappily and unwarrantably possessed the English people with regard to his Majesty are now, with a few" (with added severity) "and I may say contemptible exceptions, exchanged for dutiful love and such reverence as his talents, virtues, and paternal care deserve."

"Dear sir, you delight me," replies Mr. Dodsworth, while his loyalty late a tiny bud suddenly expands into full flower; "yet I hardly understand; the change is so sudden; and the man—Charles Stuart, King Charles, I may now call him, his murder is I trust execrated as it deserves?"

Dr. Hotham put his hand on the pulse of his patient—he feared an access of delirium from such a wandering from the subject. The pulse was calm, and Mr. Dodsworth continued: "That unfortunate martyr looking down from heaven is, I trust, appeased by the reverence paid to his name and the prayers dedicated to his memory. No sentiment, I think I may venture to assert, is so general in England as the compassion and love in which the memory of that hapless monarch is held?"

"And his son, who now reigns?—"

"Surely, sir, you forget; no son; that of course is impossible. No descendant of his fills the English throne, now worthily occupied by the house of Hanover. The despicable race of the Stuarts, long outcast and wandering, is now extinct, and the last days of the last Pretender to the crown of that family justified in the eyes of the world the sentence which ejected it from the kingdom for ever."

Such must have been Mr. Dodsworth's first lesson in politics. Soon, to the wonder of the preserver and preserved, the real state of the case must have been revealed; for a time, the strange and tremendous circumstance of his long trance may have threatened the wits of Mr. Dodsworth with a total overthrow. He had, as he crossed Mount Saint Gothard, mourned a father—now every human being he had ever seen is "lapped in lead," is dust, each voice he had ever heard is mute. The very sound of the English tongue is changed, as his experience in conversation with Dr. Hotham assures him. Empires, religions, races of men, have probably sprung up or faded; his own patrimony (the thought is idle, yet, without it, how can he live?) is sunk into the thirsty gulph that gapes ever greedy to swallow the past; his learning, his acquirements, are probably obsolete; with a bitter smile he thinks to himself, I must take to my father's profession, and turn antiquary. The familiar objects, thoughts, and habits of my boyhood, are now antiquities. He wonders where the hundred and sixty folio volumes of MS. that his father had compiled, and which, as a lad, he had regarded with religious reverence, now are—where—ah, where? His favourite play-mate, the friend of his later years, his destined and lovely bride; tears long frozen are uncongealed, and flow down his young old cheeks.

But we do not wish to be pathetic; surely since the days of the patriarchs, no fair lady had her death mourned by her lover so many years after it had taken place. Necessity, tyrant of the world, in some degree reconciles Mr. Dodsworth to his fate. At first he is persuaded that the later generation of man is much deteriorated from his contemporaries; they are neither so tall, so handsome, nor so intelligent. Then by degrees he begins to doubt his first impression. The ideas that had taken possession of his brain before his accident, and which had been frozen up for so many years, begin to thaw and dissolve away, making room for others. He dresses himself in the modern style, and does not object much to anything except the neck-cloth and hardboarded hat. He admires the texture of his shoes and stockings, and looks with admiration on a small Genevese watch, which he often consults, as if he were not yet assured that time had made progress in its accustomed manner, and as if he should find on its dial plate occular demonstration that he had exchanged his thirty-seventh year for his two hundredth and upwards, and had left A.D. 1654 far behind to find himself suddenly a beholder of the ways of men in this enlightened nineteenth century. His curiosity is insatiable; when he reads, his eyes cannot purvey fast enough to his mind, and every now and then he lights upon some inexplicable passage, some discovery and knowledge familiar to us, but undreamed of in his days, that throws him into wonder and interminable reverie. Indeed, he may be supposed to pass much of his time in that state, now and then interrupting himself with a royalist song against old Noll and the Roundheads, breaking off suddenly, and looking round fearfully to see who were his auditors, and on beholding the modern appearance of his friend the Doctor, sighing to think that it is no longer of import to any, whether he sing a cavalier catch or a puritanic psalm.

It were an endless task to develope all the philosophic ideas to which Mr. Dodsworth's resuscitation naturally gives birth. We should like much to converse with this gentleman, and still more to observe the progress of his mind, and the change of his ideas in his very novel situation. If he be a sprightly youth, fond of the shows of the world, careless of the higher human pursuits, he may proceed summarily to cast into the shade all trace of his former life, and endeavour to merge himself at once into the stream of humanity now flowing. It would be curious enough to observe the mistakes he would make, and the medley of manners which would thus be produced. He may think to enter into active life, become whig or tory as his inclinations lead, and get a seat in the, even to him, once called chapel of St. Stephens. He may content himself with turning contemplative philosopher, and find sufficient food for his mind in tracing the march of the human intellect, the changes which have been wrought in the dispositions, desires, and powers of mankind. Will he be an advocate for perfectibility or deterioration? He must admire our manufactures, the progress of science, the diffusion of knowledge, and the fresh spirit of enterprise characteristic of our countrymen. Will he find any individuals to be compared to the glorious spirits of his day? Moderate in his views as we have supposed him to be, he will probably fall at once into the temporising tone of mind now so much in vogue. He will be pleased to find a calm in politics; he will greatly admire the ministry who have succeeded in conciliating almost all parties—to find peace where he left feud. The same character which he bore a couple of hundred years ago, will influence him now; he will still be the moderate, peaceful, unenthusiastic Mr. Dodsworth that he was in 1647.

For notwithstanding education and circumstances may suffice to direct and form the rough material of the mind, it cannot create, nor give intellect, noble aspiration, and energetic constancy where dulness, wavering of purpose, and grovelling desires, are stamped by nature. Entertaining this belief we have (to forget Mr. Dodsworth for awhile) often made conjectures how such and such heroes of antiquity would act, if they were reborn in these times: and then awakened fancy has gone on to imagine that some of them are reborn; that according to the theory explained by Virgil in his sixth Æneid, every thousand years the dead return to life, and their souls endued with the same sensibilities and capacities as before, are turned naked of knowledge into this world, again to dress their skeleton powers in such habiliments as situation, education, and experience will furnish. Pythagoras, we are told, remembered many transmigrations of this sort, as having occurred to himself, though for a philosopher he made very little use of his anterior memories. It would prove an instructive school for kings and statesmen, and in fact for all human beings, called on as they are, to play their part on the stage of the world, could they remember what they had been. Thus we might obtain a glimpse of heaven and of hell, as, the secret of our former identity confined to our own bosoms, we winced or exulted in the blame or praise bestowed on our former selves. While the love of glory and posthumous reputation is as natural to man as his attachment to life itself, he must be, under such a state of things, tremblingly alive to the historic records of his honour or shame. The mild spirit of Fox would have been soothed by the recollection that he had played a worthy part as Marcus Antoninus—the former experiences of Alcibiades or even of the emasculated Steeny of James I. might have caused Sheridan to have refused to tread over again the same path of dazzling but fleeting brilliancy. The soul of our modern Corinna would have been purified and exalted by a consciousness that once it had given life to the form of Sappho. If at the present moment the witch, memory, were in a freak, to cause all the present generation to recollect that some ten centuries back they had been somebody else, would not several of our free thinking martyrs wonder to find that they had suffered as Christians under Domitian, while the judge as he passed sentence would suddenly become aware, that formerly he had condemned the saints of the early church to the torture, for not renouncing the religion he now upheld—nothing but benevolent actions and real goodness would come pure out of the ordeal. While it would be whimsical to perceive how some great men in parish affairs would strut under the consciousness that their hands had once held a sceptre, an honest artizan or pilfering domestic would find that he was little altered by being transformed into an idle noble or director of a joint stock company; in every way we may suppose that the humble would be exalted, and the noble and the proud would feel their stars and honours dwindle into baubles and child's play when they called to mind the lowly stations they had once occupied. If philosophical novels were in fashion, we conceive an excellent one might be written on the development of the same mind in various stations, in different periods of the world's history.

But to return to Mr. Dodsworth, and indeed with a few more words to bid him farewell. We entreat him no longer to bury himself in obscurity; or, if he modestly decline publicity, we beg him to make himself known personally to us. We have a thousand inquiries to make, doubts to clear up, facts to ascertain. If any fear that old habits and strangeness of appearance will make him ridiculous to those accustomed to associate with modern exquisites, we beg to assure him that we are not given to ridicule mere outward shows, and that worth and intrinsic excellence will always claim our respect.

This we say, if Mr. Dodsworth is alive. Perhaps he is again no more. Perhaps he opened his eyes only to shut them again more obstinately; perhaps his ancient clay could not thrive on the harvests of these latter days. After a little wonder; a little shuddering to find himself the dead alive—finding no affinity between himself and the present state of things—he has bidden once more an eternal farewell to the sun. Followed to his grave by his preserver and the wondering villagers, he may sleep the true death-sleep in the same valley where he so long reposed. Doctor Hotham may have erected a simple tablet over his twice-buried remains, inscribed—

To the Memory of R. Dodsworth,
An Englishman,
Born April 1, 1617; Died July 16, 1826; Aged 209.

An inscription which, if it were preserved during any terrible convulsion that caused the world to begin its life again, would occasion many learned disquisitions and ingenious theories concerning a race which authentic records showed to have secured the privilege of attaining so vast an age.

The False Rhyme

Come, tell me where the maid is found
Whose heart can love without deceit,
And I will range the world around
To sigh one moment at her feet.
Thomas Moore

On a fine July day, the fair Margaret, Queen of Navarre, then on a visit to her royal brother, had arranged a rural feast for the morning following, which Francis declined attending. He was melancholy; and the cause was said to be some lover's quarrel with a favourite dame. The morrow came, and dark rain and murky clouds destroyed at once the schemes of the courtly throng. Margaret was angry, and she grew weary: her only hope for amusement was in Francis, and he had shut himself up—an excellent reason why she should the more desire to see him. She entered his apartment: he was standing at the casement, against which the noisy shower beat, writing with a diamond on the glass. Two beautiful dogs were his sole companions. As Queen Margaret entered, he hastily let down the silken curtain before the window, and looked a little confused.

"What treason is this, my liege," said the queen, "which crimsons your cheek? I must see the same."

"It is treason," replied the king, "and therefore, sweet sister, thou mayest not see it."

This the more excited Margaret's curiosity, and a playful contest ensued: Francis at last yielded: he threw himself on a huge high-backed settee; and as the lady drew back the curtain with an arch smile, he grew grave and sentimental, as he reflected on the cause which had inspired his libel against all womankind.

"What have we here?" cried Margaret: "nay, this is lèse majesté—

'Souvent femme varie,
Bien fou qui s'y fie!'

Very little change would greatly amend your couplet:—would it not run better thus—

'Souvent homme varie,
Bien folle qui s'y fie'?

I could tell you twenty stories of man's inconstancy."

"I will be content with one true tale of woman's fidelity," said Francis, drily; "but do not provoke me. I would fain be at peace with the soft Mutabilities, for thy dear sake."

"I defy your grace," replied Margaret, rashly, "to instance the falsehood of one noble and well reputed dame."

"Not even Emilie de Lagny?" asked the king.

This was a sore subject for the queen. Emilie had been brought up in her own household, the most beautiful and the most virtuous of her maids of honour. She had long loved the Sire de Lagny, and their nuptials were celebrated with rejoicings but little ominous of the result. De Lagny was accused but a year after of traitorously yielding to the emperor a fortress under his command, and he was condemned to perpetual imprisonment. For some time Emilie seemed inconsolable, often visiting the miserable dungeon of her husband, and suffering on her return, from witnessing his wretchedness, such paroxysms of grief as threatened her life. Suddenly, in the midst of her sorrow, she disappeared; and inquiry only divulged the disgraceful fact, that she had escaped from France, bearing her jewels with her, and accompanied by her page, Robinet Leroux. It was whispered that, during their journey, the lady and the stripling often occupied one chamber; and Margaret, enraged at these discoveries, commanded that no further quest should be made for her lost favourite.

Taunted now by her brother, she defended Emilie, declaring that she believed her to be guiltless, even going so far as to boast that within a month she would bring proof of her innocence.

"Robinet was a pretty boy," said Francis, laughing.

"Let us make a bet," cried Margaret: "if I lose, I will bear this vile rhyme of thine as a motto to my shame to my grave; if I win—"

"I will break my window, and grant thee whatever boon thou askest."

The result of this bet was long sung by troubadour and minstrel. The queen employed a hundred emissaries—published rewards for any intelligence of Emilie—all in vain. The month was expiring, and Margaret would have given many bright jewels to redeem her word. On the eve of the fatal day, the jailor of the prison in which the Sire de Lagny was confined sought an audience of the queen; he brought her a message from the knight to say, that if the Lady Margaret would ask his pardon as her boon, and obtain from her royal brother that he might be brought before him, her bet was won. Fair Margaret was very joyful, and readily made the desired promise. Francis was unwilling to see his false servant, but he was in high good humour, for a cavalier had that morning brought intelligence of a victory over the Imperialists. The messenger himself was lauded in the despatches as the most fearless and bravest knight in France. The king loaded him with presents, only regretting that a vow prevented the soldier from raising his visor or declaring his name.

That same evening as the setting sun shone on the lattice on which the ungallant rhyme was traced, Francis reposed on the same settee, and the beautiful Queen of Navarre, with triumph in her bright eyes, sat beside him. Attended by guards, the prisoner was brought in: his frame was attenuated by privation, and he walked with tottering steps. He knelt at the feet of Francis, and uncovered his head; a quantity of rich golden hair then escaping, fell over the sunken cheeks and pallid brow of the suppliant. "We have treason here!" cried the king: "sir jailor, where is your prisoner?"

"Sire, blame him not," said the soft faltering voice of Emilie; "wiser men than he have been deceived by woman. My dear lord was guiltless of the crime for which he suffered. There was but one mode to save him:—I assumed his chains—he escaped with poor Robinet Leroux in my attire—he joined your army: the young and gallant cavalier who delivered the despatches to your grace, whom you overwhelmed with honours and reward, is my own Enguerrard de Lagny. I waited but for his arrival with testimonials of his innocence, to declare myself to my lady, the queen. Has she not won her bet? And the boon she asks——"

"Is de Lagny's pardon," said Margaret, as she also knelt to the king: "spare your faithful vassal, sire, and reward this lady's truth."

Francis first broke the false-speaking window, then he raised the ladies from their supplicatory posture.

In the tournament given to celebrate this "Triumph of Ladies," the Sire de Lagny bore off every prize; and surely there was more loveliness in Emilie's faded cheek—more grace in her emaciated form, type as they were of truest affection—than in the prouder bearing and fresher complexion of the most brilliant beauty in attendance on the courtly festival.

Transformation

Forthwith this frame of mine was wrench'd
With a woful agony,
Which forced me to begin my tale,
And then it set me free.
Since then, at an uncertain hour,
That agony returns;
And till my ghastly tale is told
This heart within me burns.
Coleridge's Ancient Mariner.

I HAVE HEARD it said, that, when any strange, supernatural, and necromantic adventure has occurred to a human being, that being, however desirous he may be to conceal the same, feels at certain periods torn up as it were by an intellectual earthquake, and is forced to bare the inner depths of his spirit to another. I am a witness of the truth of this. I have dearly sworn to myself never to reveal to human ears the horrors to which I once, in excess of fiendly pride, delivered myself over. The holy man who heard my confession, and reconciled me to the church, is dead. None knows that once——

Why should it not be thus? Why tell a tale of impious tempting of Providence, and soul-subduing humiliation? Why? answer me, ye who are wise in the secrets of human nature! I only know that so it is; and in spite of strong resolve—of a pride that too much masters me—of shame, and even of fear, so to render myself odious to my species—I must speak.

Genoa! my birth-place—proud city! looking upon the blue waves of the Mediterranean sea—dost thou remember me in my boyhood, when thy cliffs and promontories, thy bright sky and gay vineyards, were my world? Happy time! when to the young heart the narrow-bounded universe, which leaves, by its very limitation, free scope to the imagination, enchains our physical energies, and, sole period in our lives, innocence and enjoyment are united. Yet, who can look back to childhood, and not remember its sorrows and its harrowing fears? I was born with the most imperious, haughty, tameless spirit, with which ever mortal was gifted. I quailed before my father only; and he, generous and noble, but capricious and tyrannical, at once fostered and checked the wild impetuosity of my character, making obedience necessary, but inspiring no respect for the motives which guided his commands. To be a man, free, independent; or, in better words, insolent and domineering, was the hope and prayer of my rebel heart.

My father had one friend, a wealthy Genoese noble, who in a political tumult was suddenly sentenced to banishment, and his property confiscated. The Marchese Torella went into exile alone. Like my father, he was a widower: he had one child, the almost infant Juliet, who was left under my father's guardianship. I should certainly have been an unkind master to the lovely girl, but that I was forced by my position to become her protector. A variety of childish incidents all tended to one point,—to make Juliet see in me a rock of refuge; I in her, one, who must perish through the soft sensibility of her nature too rudely visited, but for my guardian care. We grew up together. The opening rose in May was not more sweet than this dear girl. An irradiation of beauty was spread over her face. Her form, her step, her voice—my heart weeps even now, to think of all of relying, gentle, loving, and pure, that was enshrined in that celestial tenement. When I was eleven and Juliet eight years of age, a cousin of mine, much older than either—he seemed to us a man—took great notice of my playmate; he called her his bride, and asked her to marry him. She refused, and he insisted, drawing her unwillingly towards him. With the countenance and emotions of a maniac I threw myself on him—I strove to draw his sword—I clung to his neck with the ferocious resolve to strangle him: he was obliged to call for assistance to disengage himself from me. On that night I led Juliet to the chapel of our house: I made her touch the sacred relics—I harrowed her child's heart, and profaned her child's lips with an oath, that she would be mine, and mine only.

Well, those days passed away. Torella returned in a few years, and became wealthier and more prosperous than ever. When I was seventeen, my father died; he had been magnificent to prodigality; Torella rejoiced that my minority would afford an opportunity for repairing my fortunes. Juliet and I had been affianced beside my father's deathbed—Torella was to be a second parent to me.

I desired to see the world, and I was indulged. I went to Florence, to Rome, to Naples; thence I passed to Toulon, and at length reached what had long been the bourne of my wishes, Paris. There was wild work in Paris then. The poor king, Charles the Sixth, now sane, now mad, now a monarch, now an abject slave, was the very mockery of humanity. The queen, the dauphin, the Duke of Burgundy, alternately friends and foes—now meeting in prodigal feasts, now shedding blood in rivalry—were blind to the miserable state of their country, and the dangers that impended over it, and gave themselves wholly up to dissolute enjoyment or savage strife. My character still followed me. I was arrogant and self-willed; I loved display, and above all, I threw all control far from me. Who could control me in Paris? My young friends were eager to foster passions which furnished them with pleasures. I was deemed handsome—I was master of every knightly accomplishment. I was disconnected with any political party. I grew a favourite with all: my presumption and arrogance were pardoned in one so young: I became a spoiled child. Who could control me? not the letters and advice of Torella—only strong necessity visiting me in the abhorred shape of an empty purse. But there were means to refill this void. Acre after acre, estate after estate, I sold. My dress, my jewels, my horses and their caparisons, were almost unrivalled in gorgeous Paris, while the lands of my inheritance passed into possession of others.

The Duke of Orleans was waylaid and murdered by the Duke of Burgundy. Fear and terror possessed all Paris. The dauphin and the queen shut themselves up; every pleasure was suspended. I grew weary of this state of things, and my heart yearned for my boyhood's haunts. I was nearly a beggar, yet still I would go there, claim my bride, and rebuild my fortunes. A few happy ventures as a merchant would make me rich again. Nevertheless, I would not return in humble guise. My last act was to dispose of my remaining estate near Albaro for half its worth, for ready money. Then I despatched all kinds of artificers, arras, furniture of regal splendour, to fit up the last relic of my inheritance, my palace in Genoa. I lingered a little longer yet, ashamed at the part of the prodigal returned, which I feared I should play. I sent my horses. One matchless Spanish jennet I despatched to my promised bride; its caparisons flamed with jewels and cloth of gold. In every part I caused to be entwined the initials of Juliet and her Guido. My present found favour in hers and in her father's eyes.

Still to return a proclaimed spendthrift, the mark of impertinent wonder, perhaps of scorn, and to encounter singly the reproaches or taunts of my fellow-citizens, was no alluring prospect. As a shield between me and censure, I invited some few of the most reckless of my comrades to accompany me: thus I went armed against the world, hiding a rankling feeling, half fear and half penitence, by bravado and an insolent display of satisfied vanity.

I arrived in Genoa. I trod the pavement of my ancestral palace. My proud step was no interpreter of my heart, for I deeply felt that, though surrounded by every luxury, I was a beggar. The first step I took in claiming Juliet must widely declare me such. I read contempt or pity in the looks of all. I fancied, so apt is conscience to imagine what it deserves, that rich and poor, young and old, all regarded me with derision. Torella came not near me. No wonder that my second father should expect a son's deference from me in waiting first on him. But, galled and stung by a sense of my follies and demerit, I strove to throw the blame on others. We kept nightly orgies in Palazzo Carega. To sleepless, riotous nights, followed listless, supine mornings. At the Ave Maria we showed our dainty persons in the streets, scoffing at the sober citizens, casting insolent glances on the shrinking women. Juliet was not among them—no, no; if she had been there, shame would have driven me away, if love had not brought me to her feet.

I grew tired of this. Suddenly I paid the Marchese a visit. He was at his villa, one among the many which deck the suburb of San Pietro d'Arena. It was the month of May—a month of May in that garden of the world—the blossoms of the fruit trees were fading among thick, green foliage; the vines were shooting forth; the ground strewed with the fallen olive blooms; the fire-fly was in the myrtle hedge; heaven and earth wore a mantle of surpassing beauty. Torella welcomed me kindly, though seriously; and even his shade of displeasure soon wore away. Some resemblance to my father—some look and tone of youthful ingenuousness, lurking still in spite of my misdeeds, softened the good old man's heart. He sent for his daughter—he presented me to her as her betrothed. The chamber became hallowed by a holy light as she entered. Hers was that cherub look, those large, soft eyes, full dimpled cheeks, and mouth of infantine sweetness, that expresses the rare union of happiness and love. Admiration first possessed me; she is mine! was the second proud emotion, and my lips curled with haughty triumph. I had not been the *enfant gâté*[1] of the beauties of France not to have learnt the art of pleasing the soft heart of woman. If towards men I was overbearing, the deference I paid to them was the more in contrast. I commenced my courtship by the display of a thousand gallantries to Juliet, who, vowed to me from infancy, had never admitted the devotion of others; and who, though accustomed to expressions of admiration, was uninitiated in the language of lovers.

For a few days all went well. Torella never alluded to my extravagance; he treated me as a favourite son. But the time came, as we discussed the preliminaries to my union with his daughter, when this fair face of things should be overcast. A contract had been drawn up in my father's lifetime. I had rendered this, in fact, void, by having squandered the whole of the wealth which was to have been shared by Juliet and myself. Torella, in consequence, chose to consider this bond as cancelled, and proposed another, in which, though the wealth he bestowed was immeasurably increased, there were so many restrictions as to the mode of spending it, that I, who saw independence only in free career being given to my own imperious will, taunted him as taking advantage of my situation, and refused utterly to subscribe to his conditions. The old man mildly strove to recall me to reason. Roused pride became the tyrant of my thought: I listened with indignaton—I repelled him with disdain.

"Juliet, thou art mine! Did we not interchange vows in our innocent childhood? are we not one in the sight of God? and shall thy cold-hearted, cold-blooded father divide us? Be generous, my love, be just; take not away a gift, last treasure of thy Guido—retract not thy vows—let us defy the world, and setting at nought the calculations of age, find in our mutual affection a refuge from every ill."

[1] Literally "spoiled child," but here "pampered darling."

Fiend I must have been, with such sophistry to endeavour to poison that sanctuary of holy thought and tender love. Juliet shrank from me affrighted. Her father was the best and kindest of men, and she strove to show me how, in obeying him, every good would follow. He would receive my tardy submission with warm affection; and generous pardon would follow my repentance. Profitless words for a young and gentle daughter to use to a man accustomed to make his will, law; and to feel in his own heart a despot so terrible and stern, that he could yield obedience to nought save his own imperious desires! My resentment grew with resistance; my wild companions were ready to add fuel to the flame. We laid a plan to carry off Juliet. At first it appeared to be crowned with success. Midway, on our return, we were overtaken by the agonized father and his attendants. A conflict ensued. Before the city guard came to decide the victory in favour of our antagonists, two of Torella's servitors were dangerously wounded.

This portion of my history weighs most heavily with me. Changed man as I am, I abhor myself in the recollection. May none who hear this tale ever have felt as I. A horse driven to fury by a rider armed with barbed spurs, was not more a slave than I, to the violent tyranny of my temper. A fiend possessed my soul, irritating it to madness. I felt the voice of conscience within me; but if I yielded to it for a brief interval, it was only to be a moment after torn, as by a whirlwind, away—borne along on the stream of desperate rage—the plaything of the storms engendered by pride. I was imprisoned, and, at the instance of Torella, set free. Again I returned to carry off both him and his child to France; which hapless country, then preyed on by freebooters and gangs of lawless soldiery, offered a grateful refuge to a criminal like me. Our plots were discovered. I was sentenced to banishment; and, as my debts were already enormous, my remaining property was put in the hands of commissioners for their payment. Torella again offered his mediation, requiring only my promise not to renew my abortive attempts on himself and his daughter. I spurned his offers, and fancied that I triumphed when I was thrust out from Genoa, a solitary and penniless exile. My companions were gone: they had been dismissed the city some weeks before, and were already in France. I was alone—friendless; with nor sword at my side, nor ducat in my purse.

I wandered along the sea-shore, a whirlwind of passion possessing and tearing my soul. It was as if a live coal had been set burning in my breast. At first I meditated on what *I should do*. I would join a band of freebooters. Revenge!—the word seemed balm to me:—I hugged it—caressed it—till, like a serpent, it stung me. Then again I would abjure and despise Genoa, that little corner of the world. I would return to Paris, where so many of my friends swarmed; where my services would be eagerly accepted; where I would carve out fortune with my sword, and might, through success, make my paltry birth-place, and the false Torella, rue the day when they drove me, a new Coriolanus, from her walls. I would return to Paris—thus, on foot—a beggar—and present myself in my poverty to those I had formerly entertained sumptuously? There was gall in the mere thought of it.

The reality of things began to dawn upon my mind, bringing despair in its train. For several months I had been a prisoner: the evils of my dungeon had whipped my soul to madness, but they had subdued my corporeal frame. I was weak and wan. Torella had used a thousand artifices to administer to my comfort; I had detected and scorned them all—and I reaped the harvest of my obduracy. What was to be done?—Should I crouch before my foe, and sue for forgiveness?—Die rather ten thousand deaths!—Never should they obtain that victory! Hate—I swore eternal hate! Hate from whom?—to whom?—From a wandering outcast—to a mighty noble. I and my feelings were nothing to them: already had they forgotten one so unworthy. And Juliet!—her angel-face and sylph-like form gleamed among the clouds of my despair with vain beauty; for I had lost her—the glory and flower of the world! Another will call her his!—that smile of paradise will bless another!

Even now my heart fails within me when I recur to this rout of grim-visaged ideas. Now subdued almost to tears, now raving in my agony, still I wandered along the rocky shore, which grew at each step wilder and more desolate. Hanging rocks and hoar precipices overlooked the tideless ocean; black caverns yawned; and for ever, among the seaworn recesses, murmured and dashed the unfruitful waters. Now my way was almost barred by an abrupt promontory, now rendered nearly impracticable by fragments fallen from the cliff. Evening was at hand, when, seaward, arose, as if on the waving of a wizard's wand, a murky web of clouds, blotting the late azure sky, and darkening and disturbing the till now placid deep. The clouds had strange fantastic shapes; and they changed, and mingled, and seemed to be driven about by a mighty spell. The waves raised their white crests; the thunder first muttered, then roared from across the waste of waters, which took a deep purple dye, flecked with foam. The spot where I stood, looked, on one side, to the wide-spread ocean; on the other, it was barred by a rugged promontory. Round this cape suddenly came, driven by the wind, a vessel. In vain the mariners tried to force a path for her to the open sea—the gale drove her on the rocks. It will perish!—all on board will perish!—Would I were among them! And to my young heart the idea of death came for the first time blended with that of joy. It was an awful sight to behold that vessel struggling with her fate. Hardly could I discern the sailors, but I heard them. It was soon all over!—A rock, just covered by the tossing waves, and so unperceived, lay in wait for its prey. A crash of thunder broke over my head at the moment that, with a frightful shock, the skiff dashed upon her unseen enemy. In a brief space of time she went to pieces. There I stood in safety; and there were my fellow-creatures, battling, how hopelessly, with annihilation. Methought I saw them struggling—too truly did I hear their shrieks, conquering the barking surges in their shrill agony. The dark breakers threw hither and thither the fragments of the wreck: soon it disappeared. I had been fascinated to gaze till the end: at last I sank on my knees—I covered my face with my hands: I again looked up; something was floating on the billows towards the shore. It neared and neared. Was that a human form?—It grew more distinct; and at last a mighty wave, lifting the whole freight, lodged it upon a rock. A human being bestriding a sea-chest!—A human being!—Yet was it one? Surely never such had existed before—a misshapen dwarf, with squinting eyes, distorted features, and body deformed, till it became a horror to behold. My blood, lately warming towards a fellow-being so snatched from a watery tomb, froze in my heart. The dwarf got off his chest; he tossed his straight, straggling hair from his odious visage:

"By St. Beelzebub!" he exclaimed, "I have been well bested." He looked round and saw me. "Oh, by the fiend! here is another ally of the mighty one. To what saint did you offer prayers, friend—if not to mine? Yet I remember you not on board."

I shrank from the monster and his blasphemy. Again he questioned me, and I muttered some inaudible reply. He continued:—

"Your voice is drowned by this dissonant roar. What a noise the big ocean makes! Schoolboys bursting from their prison are not louder than these waves set free to play. They disturb me. I will no more of their ill-timed brawling.—Silence, hoary One!—Winds, avaunt!—to your homes!—Clouds, fly to the antipodes, and leave our heaven clear!"

As he spoke, he stretched out his two long lank arms, that looked like spider's claws, and seemed to embrace with them the expanse before him. Was it a miracle? The clouds became broken, and fled; the azure sky first peeped out, and then was spread a calm field of blue above us; the stormy gale was exchanged to the softly breathing west; the sea grew calm; the waves dwindled to riplets.

"I like obedience even in these stupid elements," said the dwarf. "How much more in the tameless mind of man! It was a well got up storm, you must allow—and all of my own making."

It was tempting Providence to interchange talk with this magician. But *Power,* in all its shapes, is venerable to man. Awe, curiosity, a clinging fascination, drew me towards him.

"Come, don't be frightened, friend," said the wretch: "I am good-humoured when pleased; and something does please me in your well-proportioned body and handsome face, though you look a little woebegone. You have suffered a land—I, a sea wreck. Perhaps I can allay the tempest of your fortunes as I did my own. Shall we be friends?"—And he held out his hand; I could not touch it. "Well, then, companions—that will do as well. And now, while I rest after the buffeting I underwent just now, tell me why, young and gallant as you seem, you wander thus alone and downcast on this wild sea-shore."

The voice of the wretch was screeching and horrid, and his contortions as he spoke were frightful to behold. Yet he did gain a kind of influence over me, which I could not master, and I told him my tale. When it was ended, he laughed long and loud: the rocks echoed back the sound: hell seemed yelling around me.

"Oh, thou cousin of Lucifer!" said he; "so thou too hast fallen through thy pride; and, though bright as the son of Morning, thou art ready to give up thy good looks, thy bride, and thy well-being, rather than submit thee to the tyranny of good. I honour thy choice, by my soul!—So thou hast fled, and yield the day; and mean to starve on these rocks, and to let the birds peck out thy dead eyes, while thy enemy and thy betrothed rejoice in thy ruin. Thy pride is strangely akin to humility, methinks."

As he spoke, a thousand fanged thoughts stung me to the heart. "What would you that I should do?" I cried.

"I!—Oh, nothing, but lie down and say your prayers before you die. But, were I you, I know the deed that should be done."

I drew near him. His supernatural powers made him an oracle in my eyes; yet a strange unearthly thrill quivered through my frame as I said—"Speak!—teach me—what act do you advise?"

"Revenge thyself, man!—humble thy enemies!—set thy foot on the old man's neck, and possess thyself of his daughter!"

"To the east and west I turn," cried I, "and see no means! Had I gold, much could I achieve; but, poor and single, I am powerless."

The dwarf had been seated on his chest as he listened to my story. Now he got off; he touched a spring; it flew open!—What a mine of wealth—of blazing jewels, beaming gold, and pale silver—was displayed therein. A mad desire to possess this treasure was born within me.

"Doubtless," I said, "one so powerful as you could do all things."

"Nay," said the monster, humbly, "I am less omnipotent than I seem. Some things I possess which you may covet; but I would give them all for a small share, or even for a loan of what is yours."

"My possessions are at your service," I replied, bitterly—"my poverty, my exile, my disgrace—I make a free gift of them all."

"Good! I thank you. Add one other thing to your gift, and my treasure is yours."

"As nothing is my sole inheritance, what besides nothing would you have?"

"Your comely face and well-made limbs."

I shivered. Would this all-powerful monster murder me? I had no dagger. I forgot to pray—but I grew pale.

"I ask for a loan, not a gift," said the frightful thing: "lend me your body for three days—you shall have mine to cage your soul the while, and, in payment, my chest. What say you to the bargain?—Three short days."

We are told that it is dangerous to hold unlawful talk; and well do I prove the same. Tamely written down, it may seem incredible that I should lend any ear to this proposition; but, in spite of his unnatural ugliness, there was something fascinating in a being whose voice could govern earth, air, and sea. I felt a keen desire to comply; for with that chest I could command the world. My only hesitation resulted from a fear that he would not be true to his bargain. Then, I thought, I shall soon die here on these lonely sands, and the limbs he covets will be mine no more:—it is worth the chance. And, besides, I knew that, by all the rules of art-magic, there were formula and oaths which none of its practisers dared break. I hesitated to reply; and he went on, now displaying his wealth, now speaking of the petty price he demanded, till it seemed madness to refuse. Thus is it: place our bark in the current of the stream, and down, over fall and cataract it is hurried; give up our conduct to the wild torrent of passion, and we are away, we know not whither.

He swore many an oath, and I adjured him by many a sacred name; till I saw this wonder of power, this ruler of the elements, shiver like an autumn leaf before my words; and as if the spirit spake unwillingly and per force within him, at last, he, with broken voice, revealed the spell whereby he might be obliged, did he wish to play me false, to render up the unlawful spoil. Our warm life-blood must mingle to make and to mar the charm.

Enough of this unholy theme. I was persuaded—the thing was done. The morrow dawned upon me as I lay upon the shingles, and I knew not my own shadow as it fell from me. I felt myself changed to a shape of horror, and cursed my easy faith and blind credulity. The chest was there—there the gold and precious stones for which I had sold the frame of flesh which nature had given me. The sight a little stilled my emotions: three days would soon be gone.

They did pass. The dwarf had supplied me with a plenteous store of food. At first I could hardly walk, so strange and out of joint were all my limbs; and my voice—it was that of the fiend. But I kept silent, and turned my face to the sun, that I might not see my shadow, and counted the hours, and ruminated on my future conduct. To bring Torella to my feet—to possess my Juliet in spite of him—all this my wealth could easily achieve. During dark night I slept, and dreamt of the accomplishment of my desires. Two suns had set—the third dawned. I was agitated, fearful. Oh expectation, what a frightful thing art thou, when kindled more by fear than hope! How dost thou twist thyself round the heart, torturing its pulsations! How dost thou dart unknown pangs all through our feeble mechanism, now seeming to shiver us like broken glass, to nothingness—now giving us a fresh strength, which can *do* nothing, and so torments us by a sensation, such as the strong man must feel who cannot break his fetters, though they bend in his grasp. Slowly paced the bright, bright orb up the eastern sky; long it lingered in the zenith, and still more slowly wandered down the west: it touched the horizon's verge—it was lost! Its glories were on the summits of the cliff—they grew dun and gray. The evening star shone bright. He will soon be here.

He came not!—By the living heavens, he came not!—and night dragged out its weary length, and, in its decaying age, "day began to grizzle its dark hair;"[2] and the sun rose again on the most miserable wretch that ever upbraided its light. Three days thus I passed. The jewels and the gold—oh, how I abhorred them!

Well, well—I will not blacken these pages with demoniac ravings. All too terrible were the thoughts, the raging tumult of ideas that filled my soul. At the end of that time I slept; I had not before since the third sunset; and I dreamt that I was at Juliet's feet, and she smiled, and then she shrieked—for she saw my transformation—and again she smiled, for still her beautiful lover knelt before her. But it was not I—it was he, the fiend, arrayed in my limbs, speaking with my voice, winning her with my looks of love. I strove to warn her, but my tongue refused its office; I strove to tear him from her, but I was rooted to the ground—I awoke with the agony. There were the solitary hoar precipices—there the plashing sea, the quiet strand, and the blue sky over all. What did it mean? was my dream but a mirror of the truth? was he wooing and winning my betrothed? I would on the instant back to Genoa—but I was banished. I laughed—the dwarf's yell burst from my lips—*I* banished! O, no! they had not exiled the foul limbs I wore; I might with these enter, without fear of incurring the threatened penalty of death, my own, my native city.

I began to walk towards Genoa. I was somewhat accustomed to my distorted limbs; none were ever so ill adapted for a straightforward movement; it was with infinite difficulty that I proceeded. Then, too, I desired to avoid all the hamlets strewed here and there on the sea-beach, for I was unwilling to make a display of my hideousness. I was not quite sure that, if seen, the mere boys would not stone me to death as I passed, for a monster: some ungentle salutations I did receive from the few peasants or fishermen I chanced to meet. But it was dark night before I approached Genoa. The weather was so balmy and sweet that it struck me that the

[2] Lord Byron, *Werner* III.iv.152–53.

Marchese and his daughter would very probably have quitted the city for their country retreat. It was from Villa Torella that I had attempted to carry off Juliet; I had spent many an hour reconnoitring the spot, and knew each inch of ground in its vicinity. It was beautifully situated, embosomed in trees, on the margin of a stream. As I drew near, it became evident that my conjecture was right; nay, moreover, that the hours were being then devoted to feasting and merriment. For the house was lighted up; strains of soft and gay music were wafted towards me by the breeze. My heart sank within me. Such was the generous kindness of Torella's heart that I felt sure that he would not have indulged in public manifestations of rejoicing just after my unfortunate banishment, but for a cause I dared not dwell upon.

The country people were all alive and flocking about; it became necessary that I should study to conceal myself; and yet I longed to address some one, or to hear others discourse, or in any way to gain intelligence of what was really going on. At length, entering the walks that were in immediate vicinity to the mansion, I found one dark enough to veil my excessive frightfulness; and yet others as well as I were loitering in its shade. I soon gathered all I wanted to know—all that first made my very heart die with horror, and then boil with indignation. To-morrow Juliet was to be given to the penitent, reformed, beloved Guido—to-morrow my bride was to pledge her vows to a fiend from hell! And I did this!—my accursed pride—my demoniac violence and wicked self-idolatry had caused this act. For if I had acted as the wretch who had stolen my form had acted—if, with a mien at once yielding and dignified, I had presented myself to Torella, saying, I have done wrong, forgive me; I am unworthy of your angel-child, but permit me to claim her hereafter, when my altered conduct shall manifest that I abjure my vices, and endeavour to become in some sort worthy of her. I go to serve against the infidels; and when my zeal for religion and my true penitence for the past shall appear to you to cancel my crimes, permit me again to call myself your son. Thus had he spoken; and the penitent was welcomed even as the prodigal son of scripture: the fatted calf was killed for him; and he, still pursuing the same path, displayed such openhearted regret for his follies, so humble a concession of all his rights, and so ardent a resolve to reacquire them by a life of contrition and virtue, that he quickly conquered the kind, old man; and full pardon, and the gift of his lovely child, followed in swift succession.

O! had an angel from Paradise whispered to me to act thus! But now, what would be the innocent Juliet's fate? Would God permit the foul union—or, some prodigy destroying it, link the dishonoured name of Carega with the worst of crimes? To-morrow at dawn they were to be married: there was but one way to prevent this—to meet mine enemy, and to enforce the ratification of our agreement. I felt that this could only be done by a mortal struggle. I had no sword—if indeed my distorted arms could wield a soldier's weapon—but I had a dagger, and in that lay my every hope. There was no time for pondering or balancing nicely the question: I might die in the attempt; but besides the burning jealousy and despair of my own heart, honour, mere humanity, demanded that I should fall rather than not destroy the machinations of the fiend.

The guests departed—the lights began to disappear; it was evident that the inhabitants of the villa were seeking repose. I hid myself among the trees—the garden grew desert—the gates were closed—I wandered round and came under a window—ah! well did I know the same!—a soft twilight glimmered in the room—the curtains were half withdrawn. It was the temple of innocence and beauty. Its magnificence was tempered, as it were, by the slight disarrangements occasioned by its being dwelt in, and all the objects scattered around displayed the taste of her who hallowed it by her presence. I saw her enter with a quick light step—I saw her approach the window—she drew back the curtain yet further, and looked out into the night. Its breezy freshness played among her ringlets, and wafted them from the transparent marble of her brow. She clasped her hands, she raised her eyes to Heaven. I heard her voice. Guido! she softly murmured, Mine own Guido! and then, as if overcome by the fulness of her own heart, she sank on her knees:—her upraised eyes—her negligent but graceful attitude—the beaming thankfulness that lighted up her face—oh, these are tame words! Heart of mine, thou imagest ever, though thou canst not pourtray, the celestial beauty of that child of light and love.

I heard a step—a quick firm step along the shady avenue. Soon I saw a cavalier, richly dressed, young and, methought, graceful to look on, advance.—I hid myself yet closer.—The youth approached; he paused beneath the window. She arose, and again looking out she saw him, and said—I cannot, no, at this distant time I cannot record her terms of soft silver tenderness; to me they were spoken, but they were replied to by him.

"I will not go," he cried: "here where you have been, where your memory glides like some Heaven-visiting ghost, I will pass the long hours till we meet, never, my Juliet, again, day or night, to part. But do thou, my love, retire; the cold morn and fitful breeze will make thy cheek pale, and fill with languor thy love-lighted eyes. Ah, sweetest! could I press one kiss upon them, I could, methinks, repose."

And then he approached still nearer, and methought he was about to clamber into her chamber. I had hesitated, not to terrify her; now I was no longer master of myself. I rushed forward—I threw myself on him—I tore him away—I cried, "O loathsome and foul-shaped wretch!"

I need not repeat epithets, all tending, as it appeared, to rail at a person I at present feel some partiality for. A shriek rose from Juliet's lips. I neither heard nor saw—I *felt* only mine enemy, whose throat I grasped, and my dagger's hilt; he struggled, but could not escape: at length hoarsely he breathed these words: "Do!—strike home! destroy this body—you will still live: may your life be long and merry!"

The descending dagger was arrested at the word, and he, feeling my hold relax, extricated himself and drew his sword, while the uproar in the house, and flying of torches from one room to the other, showed that soon we should be separated—and I—oh! far better die: so that he did not survive, I cared not. In the midst of my frenzy there was much calculation:—fall I might, and so that he did not survive, I cared not for the death-blow I might deal against myself. While still, therefore, he thought I paused, and while I saw the villanous resolve to take advantage of my hesitation, in the sudden thrust he made at me, I threw myself on his sword, and at the same moment plunged my dagger, with a true desperate aim, in his side. We fell together, rolling over each other, and the tide of blood that flowed from the gaping wound of each mingled on the grass. More I know not—I fainted.

Again I returned to life: weak almost to death, I found myself stretched upon a bed—Juliet was kneeling beside it. Strange! my first broken request was for a mirror. I was so wan and ghastly, that my poor girl hesitated, as she told me afterwards; but, by the mass! I thought myself a right proper youth when I saw the dear reflection of my own well-known features. I confess it is a weakness, but I avow it, I do entertain a considerable affection for the countenance and limbs I behold, whenever I look at a glass; and have more mirrors in my house, and consult them oftener than any beauty in Venice. Before you too much condemn me, permit me to say that no one better knows than I the value of his own body; no one, probably, except myself, ever having had it stolen from him.

Incoherently I at first talked of the dwarf and his crimes, and reproached Juliet for her too easy admission of his love. She thought me raving, as well she might, and yet it was some time before I could prevail on myself to admit that the Guido whose penitence had won her back for me was myself; and while I cursed bitterly the monstrous dwarf, and blest the well-directed blow that had deprived him of life, I suddenly checked myself when I heard her say—Amen! knowing that him whom she reviled was my very self. A little reflection taught me silence—a little practice enabled me to speak of that frightful night without any very excessive blunder. The wound I had given myself was no mockery of one—it was long before I recovered—and as the benevolent and generous Torella sat beside me, talking such wisdom as might win friends to repentance, and mine own dear Juliet hovered near me, administering to my wants, and cheering me by her smiles, the work of my bodily cure and mental reform went on together. I have never, indeed, wholly recovered my strength—my cheek is paler since—my person a little bent. Juliet sometimes ventures to allude bitterly to the malice that caused this change, but I kiss her on the moment, and tell her all is for the best. I am a fonder and more faithful husband—and true is this—but for that wound, never had I called her mine.

I did not revisit the sea-shore, nor seek for the fiend's treasure; yet, while I ponder on the past, I often think, and my confessor was not backward in favouring the idea, that it might be a good rather than an evil spirit, sent by my guardian angel, to show me the folly and misery of pride. So well at least did I learn this lesson, roughly taught as I was, that I am known now by all my friends and fellow-citizens by the name of Guido il Cortese.

The Dream

Chi dice mal d'amore
Dice una falsità!
Italian Song[1]

THE TIME OF the occurrence of the little legend about to be narrated, was that of the commencement of the reign of Henry IV. of France, whose accession and conversion, while they brought peace to the kingdom whose throne he ascended, were inadequate to heal the deep wounds mutually inflicted by the inimical parties. Private feuds, and the memory of mortal injuries, existed between those now apparently united; and often did the hands that had clasped each other in seeming friendly greeting, involuntarily, as the grasp was released, clasp the dagger's hilt, as fitter spokesman to their passions than the words of courtesy that had just fallen from their lips. Many of the fiercer Catholics retreated to their distant provinces; and while they concealed in solitude their rankling discontent, not less keenly did they long for the day when they might show it openly. In a large and fortified chateau built on a rugged steep overlooking the Loire, not far from the town of Nantes, dwelt the last of her race and the heiress of their fortunes, the young and beautiful Countess de Villeneuve. She had spent the preceding year in complete solitude in her secluded abode; and the mourning she wore for a father and two brothers, the victims of the civil wars, was a graceful and good reason why she did not appear at court, and mingle with its festivities. But the orphan countess inherited a high name and broad lands; and it was soon signified to her that the

[1] "Whoever speaks badly about love / Utters a falsehood!"

king, her guardian, desired that she should bestow them, together with her hand, upon some noble whose birth and accomplishments should entitle him to the gift. Constance, in reply, expressed her intention of taking vows, and retiring to a convent. The king earnestly and resolutely forbade this act, believing such an idea to be the result of sensibility overwrought by sorrow, and relying on the hope that, after a time, the genial spirit of youth would break through this cloud.

A year passed, and still the countess persisted; and at last Henry, unwilling to exercise compulsion—desirous, too, of judging for himself of the motives that led one so beautiful, young, and gifted with fortune's favours, to desire to bury herself in a cloister—announced his intention, now that the period of her mourning was expired, of visiting her chateau; and if he brought not with him, the monarch said, inducement sufficient to change her design, he would yield his consent to its fulfillment.

Many a sad hour had Constance passed—many a day of tears, and many a night of restless misery. She had closed her gates against every visitant; and, like the Lady Olivia in "Twelfth Night," vowed herself to loneliness and weeping. Mistress of herself, she easily silenced the entreaties and remonstances of underlings, and nursed her grief as it had been the thing she loved. Yet it was too keen, too bitter, too burning, to be a favoured guest. In fact, Constance, young, ardent, and vivacious, battled with it, struggled, and longed to cast it off; but all that was joyful in itself, or fair in outward show, only served to renew it; and she could best support the burthen of her sorrow with patience, when, yielding to it, it oppressed but did not torture her.

Constance had left the castle to wander in the neighbouring grounds. Lofty and extensive as were the apartments of her abode, she felt pent up within their walls, beneath their fretted roofs. The clear sky, the spreading uplands, the antique wood, associated to her with every dear recollection of her past life, enticed her to spend hours and days beneath their leafy coverts. The motion and change eternally working, as the wind stirred among the boughs, or the journeying sun rained its beams through them, soothed and called her out of that dull sorrow which clutched her heart with so unrelenting a pang beneath her castle roof.

There was one spot on the verge of the well-wooded park, one nook of ground, whence she could discern the country extended beyond, yet which was in itself thick set with tall umbrageous trees—a spot which she had forsworn, yet whither unconsciously her steps for ever tended, and where now again, for the twentieth time that day, she had unaware found herself. She sat upon a grassy mound, and looked wistfully on the flowers she had herself planted to adorn the verdurous recess—to her the temple of memory and love. She held the letter from the king which was the parent to her of so much despair. Dejection sat upon her features, and her gentle heart asked fate why, so young, unprotected, and forsaken, she should have to struggle with this new form of wretchedness.

"I but ask," she thought, "to live in my father's halls—in the spot familiar to my infancy—to water with my frequent tears the graves of those I loved; and here in these woods, where such a mad dream of happiness was mine, to celebrate for ever the obsequies of Hope!"

A rustling among the boughs now met her ear—her heart beat quick—all again was still. "Foolish girl!" she half muttered: "dupe of thine own passionate fancy: because here we met; because seated here I have expected, and sounds like these have announced, his dear approach; so now every coney as it stirs, and every bird as it awakens silence, speaks of him. O Gaspar!—mine once—never again will this beloved spot be made glad by thee—never more!"

Again the bushes were stirred, and footsteps were heard in the brake. She rose; her heart beat high: it must be that silly Manon, with her impertinent entreaties for her to return. But the steps were firmer and slower than would be those of her waiting-woman; and now emerging from the shade, she too plainly discerned the intruder. Her first impulse was to fly:—but once again to see him—to hear his voice:—once again before she placed eternal vows between them, to stand together, and find the wide chasm filled which absence had made, could not injure the dead, and would soften the fatal sorrow that made her cheek so pale.

And now he was before her the same beloved one with whom she had exchanged vows of constancy. He, like her, seemed sad, nor could she resist the imploring glance that entreated her for one moment to remain.

"I come, lady," said the young knight, "without a hope to bend your inflexible will. I come but once again to see you, and to bid you farewell before I depart for the Holy Land. I come to beseech you not to immure yourself in the dark cloister to avoid one as hateful as myself:—one you will never see more. Whether I die or live in Palestine, France and I are parted for ever!"

"Palestine!" said Constance; "that were fearful, were it true; but King Henry will never so lose his favourite cavalier. The throne you helped to build, you still will guard. Nay, as I ever had power over thought of thine, go not to Palestine."

"One word of yours could detain me—one smile—Constance——" and the youthful lover knelt before her; but her harsher purpose was recalled by the image once so dear and familiar, now so strange and so forbidden.

"Linger no longer here!" she cried. "No smile, no word of mine will ever again be yours. Why are you here—here, where the spirits of the dead wander, and, claiming these shades as their own, curse the false girl who permits their murderer to disturb their sacred repose?"

"When love was young and you were kind," replied the knight, "you taught me to thread the intricacies of these woods—you welcomed me to this dear spot, where once you vowed to be my own—even beneath these ancient trees."

"A wicked sin it was," said Constance, "to unbar my father's doors to the son of his enemy, and dearly is it punished!"

The young knight gained courage as she spoke; yet he dared not move, lest she, who, every instant, appeared ready to take flight, should be startled from her momentary tranquillity; but he slowly replied:—"Those were happy days, Constance, full of terror and deep joy, when evening brought me to your feet; and while hate and vengeance were as its atmosphere to yonder frowning castle, this leafy, star-lit bower was the shrine of love."

"*Happy?*—miserable days!" echoed Constance; "when I imagined good could arise from failing in my duty, and that disobedience would be rewarded of God. Speak not of love, Gaspar!—a sea of blood divides us for ever! Approach me not! The dead and the beloved stand even now between us: their pale shadows warn me of my fault, and menace me for listening to their murderer."

"That am not I!" exclaimed the youth. "Behold, Constance, we are each the last of our race. Death has dealt cruelly with us, and we are alone. It was not so when first we loved—when parent, kinsman, brother, nay, my own mother breathed curses on the house of Villeneuve; and in spite of all I bless'd it. I saw thee, my lovely one, and bless'd it. The God of peace planted love in our hearts, and with mystery and secrecy we met during many a summer night in the moon-lit dells; and when daylight was abroad, in this sweet recess we fled to avoid its scrutiny, and here, even here, where now I kneel in supplication, we both knelt and made our vows.—Shall they be broken?"

Constance wept as her lover recalled the images of happy hours. "Never," she exclaimed, "O never! Thou knowest, or wilt soon know, Gaspar, the faith and resolves of one who dare not be yours. Was it for us to talk of love and happiness, when war, and hate, and blood were raging around? The fleeting flowers our young hands strewed were trampled by the deadly encounter of mortal foes. By your father's hand mine died; and little boots it to know whether, as my brother swore, and you deny, your hand did or did not deal the blow that destroyed him. You fought among those by whom he died. Say no more—no other word: it is impiety towards the unreposing dead to hear you. Go, Gaspar; forget me. Under the chivalrous and gallant Henry your career may be glorious; and many a fair girl will listen, as once I did, to your vows, and be made happy by them. Farewell! May the Virgin bless you! In my cell and cloister-home I will not forget the best Christian lesson—to pray for our enemies. Gaspar, farewell!"

She glided hastily from the bower: with swift steps she threaded the glade and sought the castle. Once within the seclusion of her own apartment she gave way to the burst of grief that tore her gentle bosom like a tempest; for hers was that worst sorrow which taints past joys, making remorse wait upon the memory of bliss, and linking love and fancied guilt in such fearful society as that of the tyrant when he bound a living body to a corpse. Suddenly a thought darted into her mind. At first she rejected it as puerile and superstitious; but it would not be driven away. She called hastily for her attendant. "Manon," she said, "didst thou ever sleep on St. Catherine's couch?"

Manon crossed herself. "Heaven forefend! None ever did, since I was born, but two: one fell into the Loire and was drowned; the other only looked upon the narrow bed, and returned to her own home without a word. It is an awful place; and if the votary have not led a pious and good life, woe betide the hour when she rests her head on the holy stone!"

Constance crossed herself also. "As for our lives, it is only through our Lord and the blessed saints that we can any of us hope for righteousness. I will sleep on that couch to-morrow night!"

"Dear, my lady! and the king arrives to-morrow."

"The more need that I resolve. It cannot be that misery so intense should dwell in any heart, and no cure be found. I had hoped to be the bringer of peace to our houses; and is the good work to be for me a crown of thorns? Heaven shall direct me. I will rest to-morrow night on St. Catherine's bed: and if, as I have heard, the saint deigns to direct her votaries in dreams, I will be guided by her; and believing that I act according to the dictates of Heaven, I shall feel resigned even to the worst."

The king was on his way to Nantes from Paris, and he slept on this night at a castle but a few miles distant. Before dawn a young cavalier was introduced into his chamber. The knight had a serious, nay, a sad aspect; and all beautiful as he was in feature and limb, looked way-worn and haggard. He stood silent in Henry's presence, who, alert and gay, turned his lively blue eyes upon his guest, saying gently, "So thou foundest her obdurate, Gaspar?"

"I found her resolved on our mutual misery. Alas! my liege, it is not, credit me, the least of my grief, that Constance sacrifices her own happiness when she destroys mine."

"And thou believest that she will say nay to the gaillard chevalier whom we ourselves present to her?"

"Oh! my liege, think not that thought! it cannot be. My heart deeply, most deeply, thanks you for your generous condescension. But she whom her lover's voice in solitude—whose entreaties, when memory and seclusion aided the spell—could not persuade, will resist even your majesty's commands. She is bent upon entering a cloister; and I, so please you, will now take my leave:—I am henceforth a soldier of the cross, and will die in Palestine."

"Gaspar," said the monarch, "I know woman better than thou. It is not by submission nor tearful plaints she is to be won. The death of her relatives naturally sits heavy at the young countess' heart; and nourishing in solitude her regret and her repentance, she fancies that Heaven itself forbids your union. Let the voice of the world reach her—the voice of earthly power and earthly kindness—the one commanding, the other pleading, and both finding response in her own heart—and by my fay and the Holy Cross, she will be yours. Let our plan still hold. And now to horse: the morning wears, and the sun is risen."

The king arrived at the bishop's palace, and proceeded forthwith to mass in the cathedral. A sumptuous dinner succeeded, and it was afternoon before the monarch proceeded through the town beside the Loire to where, a little above Nantes, the Chateau Villeneuve was situated. The young countess received him at the gate. Henry looked in vain for the cheek blanched by misery, the aspect of downcast despair which he had been taught to expect. Her cheek was flushed, her manner animated, her voice scarce tremulous. "She loves him not," thought Henry, "or already her heart has consented."

A collation was prepared for the monarch; and after some little hesitation, arising even from the cheerfulness of her mien, he mentioned the name of Gaspar. Constance blushed instead of turning pale, and replied very quickly, "To-morrow, good my liege; I ask for a respite but until tomorrow;—all will then be decided;—to-morrow I am vowed to God—or—"

She looked confused, and the king, at once surprised and pleased, said, "Then you hate not young De Vaudemont;—you forgive him for the inimical blood that warms his veins."

"We are taught that we should forgive, that we should love our enemies," the countess replied with some trepidation.

"Now by Saint Denis that is a right welcome answer for the nonce," said the king, laughing. "What ho! my faithful serving-man, Dan Apollo in disguise! come forward, and thank your lady for her love."

In such disguise as had concealed him from all, the cavalier had hung behind, and viewed with infinite surprise the demeanour and calm countenance of the lady. He could not hear her words: but was this even she whom he had seen trembling and weeping the evening before?—this she whose very heart was torn by conflicting passion?—who saw the pale ghosts of parent and kinsman stand between her and the lover whom more than her life she adored? It was a riddle hard to solve. The king's call was in unison with his impatience, and he sprang forward. He was at her feet; while she, still passion-driven, overwrought by the very calmness she had assumed, uttered one cry as she recognised him, and sank senseless on the floor.

All this was very unintelligible. Even when her attendants had brought her to life, another fit succeeded, and then passionate floods of tears; while the monarch, waiting in the hall, eyeing the half-eaten collation, and humming some romance in commemoration of woman's waywardness, knew not how to reply to Vaudemont's look of bitter disappointment and anxiety. At length the countess' chief attendant came with an apology: "her lady was ill, very ill. The next day she would throw herself at the king's feet, at once to solicit his excuse, and to disclose her purpose."

"To-morrow—again to-morrow!—Does to-morrow bear some charm, maiden?" said the king. "Can you read us the riddle, pretty one? What strange tale belongs to to-morrow, that all rests on its advent?"

Manon coloured, looked down, and hesitated. But Henry was no tyro in the art of enticing ladies' attendants to disclose their ladies' counsel. Manon was besides frightened by the countess' scheme, on which she was still obstinately bent, so she was the more readily induced to betray it. To sleep in St. Catherine's bed, to rest on a narrow ledge overhanging the deep rapid Loire, and if, as was most probable, the luckless dreamer escaped from falling into it, to take the disturbed visions that such uneasy slumber might produce for the dictate of Heaven, was a madness of which even Henry himself could scarcely deem any woman capable. But could Constance, her whose beauty was so highly intellectual, and whom he had heard perpetually praised for her strength of mind and talents, could she be so strangely infatuated! And can passion play such freaks with us?—like death, levelling even the aristocracy of the soul, and bringing noble and peasant, the wise and foolish, under one thraldom? It was strange—yet she must have her way. That she hesitated in her decision was much; and it was to be hoped that St. Catherine would play no ill-natured part. Should it be otherwise, a purpose to be swayed by a dream might be influenced by other waking thoughts. To the more material kind of danger some safeguard should be brought.

There is no feeling more awful than that which invades a weak human heart bent upon gratifying its ungovernable impulses in contradiction to the dictates of conscience. Forbidden pleasures are said to be the most agreeable:—it may be so to rude natures, to those who love to struggle, combat, and contend; who find happiness in a fray, and joy in the conflict of passion. But softer and sweeter was the gentle spirit of Constance; and love and duty contending crushed and tortured her poor heart. To commit her conduct to the inspirations of religion, or, if it was so to be named, of superstition, was a blessed relief. The very perils that threatened her undertaking gave a zest to it;—to dare for his sake was happiness;—the very difficulty of the way that led to the completion of her wishes, at once gratified her love and distracted her thoughts from her despair. Or if it was decreed that she must sacrifice all, the risk of danger and of death were of trifling import in comparison with the anguish which would then be her portion for ever.

The night threatened to be stormy—the raging wind shook the casements—and the trees waved their huge shadowy arms, as giants might in fantastic dance and mortal broil. Constance and Manon, unattended, quitted the chateau by a postern, and began to descend the hill side. The moon had not yet risen; and though the way was familiar to both, Manon tottered and trembled; while the countess, drawing her silken cloak round her, walked with a firm step down the steep. They came to the river's side, where a small boat was moored, and one man was in waiting. Constance stepped lightly in, and then aided her fearful companion. In a few moments they were in the middle of the stream. The warm, tempestuous, animating, equinoctial wind swept over them. For the first time since her mourning, a thrill of pleasure swelled the bosom of Constance. She hailed the emotion with double joy. It cannot be, she thought, that Heaven will forbid me to love one so brave, so generous, and so good as the noble Gaspar. Another I can never love; I shall die if divided from him: and this heart, these limbs, so alive with glowing sensation, are they already predestined to an early grave? Oh, no! life speaks aloud within them. I shall live to love. Do not all things love?—the winds as they whisper to the rushing waters? the waters as they kiss the flowery banks, and speed to mingle with the sea? Heaven and earth are sustained by, live through, love; and shall Constance alone, whose heart has ever been a deep, gushing, overflowing well of true affection, be compelled to set a stone upon the fount to lock it up for ever?

These thoughts bid fair for pleasant dreams; and perhaps the countess, an adept in the blind god's lore, therefore indulged them the more readily. But as thus she was engrossed by soft emotions, Manon caught her arm:—"Lady, look," she cried; "it comes—yet the oars have no sound. Now the Virgin shield us! Would we were at home!"

A dark boat glided by them. Four rowers, habited in black cloaks, pulled at oars which, as Manon said, gave no sound; another sat at the helm: like the rest, his person was veiled in a dark mantle, but he wore no cap; and though his face was turned from them, Constance recognized her lover. "Gaspar," she cried aloud, "dost thou live?"—but the figure in the boat neither turned its head nor replied, and quickly it was lost in the shadowy waters.

How changed now was the fair countess' reverie! Already Heaven had begun its spell, and unearthly forms were around, as she strained her eyes through the gloom. Now she saw and now she lost view of the bark that occasioned her terror; and now it seemed that another was there, which held the spirits of the dead; and her father waved to her from shore, and her brothers frowned on her.

Meanwhile they neared the landing. Her bark was moored in a little cove, and Constance stood upon the bank. Now she trembled, and half yielded to Manon's entreaty to return; till the unwise *suivante*[2] mentioned the king's and De Vaudemont's name, and spoke of the answer to be given to-morrow. What answer, if she turned back from her intent?

She now hurried forward up the broken ground of the bank, and then along its edge, till they came to a hill which abruptly hung over the tide. A small chapel stood near. With trembling fingers the countess drew forth the key and unlocked its door. They entered. It was dark—save that a little lamp, flickering in the wind, showed an uncertain light from before the figure of Saint Catherine. The two women knelt; they prayed; and then rising, with a cheerful accent the countess bade her attendant good night. She unlocked a little low iron door. It opened on a narrow cavern. The roar of waters was heard beyond. "Thou mayest not follow, my poor Manon," said Constance,—"nor dost thou much desire:—this adventure is for me alone."

It was hardly fair to leave the trembling servant in the chapel alone, who had neither hope nor fear, nor love nor grief, to beguile her; but, in those days, esquires and waiting-women often played the part of subalterns in the army, gaining knocks and no fame. Besides, Manon was safe in holy ground. The countess meanwhile

[2] "Waiting-maid."

pursued her way groping in the dark through the narrow tortuous passage. At length what seemed light to her long-darkened sense gleamed on her. She reached an open cavern in the overhanging hill's side, looking over the rushing tide beneath. She looked out upon the night. The waters of the Loire were speeding, as since that day have they ever sped—changeful, yet the same; the heavens were thickly veiled with clouds, and the wind in the trees was as mournful and ill-omened as if it rushed round a murderer's tomb. Constance shuddered a little, and looked upon her bed—a narrow ledge of earth and a moss-grown stone bordering on the very verge of the precipice. She doffed her mantle—such was one of the conditions of the spell;—she bowed her head, and loosened the tresses of her dark hair—she bared her feet—and thus, fully prepared for suffering to the utmost the chill influence of the cold night, she stretched herself on the narrow couch that scarce afforded room for her repose, and whence, if she moved in sleep, she must be precipitated into the cold waters below.

At first it seemed to her as if she never should sleep again. No great wonder that exposure to the blast and her perilous position should forbid her eyelids to close. At length she fell into a reverie so soft and soothing that she wished even to watch—and then by degrees her senses became confused—and now she was on St. Catherine's bed—the Loire rushing beneath, and the wild wind sweeping by—and now—O whither?—and what dreams did the saint send, to drive her to despair, or to bid her be blest for ever?

Beneath the rugged hill, upon the dark tide, another watched, who feared a thousand things, and scarce dared hope. He had meant to precede the lady on her way, but when he found that he had outstaid his time, with muffled oars and breathless haste he had shot by the bark that contained his Constance, nor even turned at her voice, fearful to incur her blame, and her commands to return. He had seen her emerge from the passage, and shuddered as she leant over the cliff. He saw her step forth, clad as she was in white, and could mark her as she lay on the ledge beetling above. What a vigil did the lovers keep!—she given up to visionary thoughts, he knowing—and the consciousness thrilled his bosom with strange emotion—that love, and love for him, had led her to that perilous couch; and that while dangers surrounded her in every shape, she was alive only to the small still voice that whispered to her heart the dream which was to decide their destinies. She slept perhaps—but he waked and watched; and night wore away, as, now praying, now entranced by alternating hope and fear, he sat in his boat, his eyes fixed on the white garb of the slumberer above.

Morning—was it morning that struggled in the clouds? Would morning ever come to waken her? And had she slept? and what dreams of weal or woe had peopled her sleep? Gaspar grew impatient. He commanded his boatmen still to wait, and he sprang forward, intent on clambering the precipice. In vain they urged the danger, nay, the impossibility of the attempt; he clung to the rugged face of the hill, and found footing where it would seem no footing was. The acclivity, indeed, was not high; the dangers of St. Catherine's bed arising from the likelihood that any one who slept on so narrow a couch would be precipitated into the waters beneath. Up the steep ascent Gaspar continued to toil, and at last reached the roots of a tree that grew near the summit. Aided by its branches, he made good his stand at the very extremity of the ledge, near the pillow on which lay the uncovered head of his beloved. Her hands were folded on her bosom; her dark hair fell round her throat and pillowed her cheek; her face was serene: sleep was there in all its innocence and in all its helplessness; every wilder emotion was hushed, and her bosom heaved in regular breathing. He could see her heart beat as it lifted her fair hands crossed above. No statue hewn of marble in monumental effigy was ever half so fair; and within that surpassing form dwelt a soul true, tender, self-devoted, and affectionate as ever warmed a human breast.

With what deep passion did Gaspar gaze, gathering hope from the placidity of her angel countenance! A smile wreathed her lips; and he too involuntarily smiled, as he hailed the happy omen; when suddenly her cheek was flushed, her bosom heaved, a tear stole from her dark lashes, and then a whole shower fell, as starting up she cried, "No!—he shall not die!—I will unloose his chains!—I will save him!" Gaspar's hand was there. He caught her light form ready to fall from the perilous couch. She opened her eyes and beheld her lover, who had watched over her dream of fate, and who had saved her.

Manon also had slept well, dreaming or not, and was startled in the morning to find that she waked surrounded by a crowd. The little desolate chapel was hung with tapestry—the altar adorned with golden chalices—the priest was chanting mass to a goodly array of kneeling knights. Manon saw that King Henry was there;

and she looked for another whom she found not, when the iron door of the cavern passage opened, and Gaspar de Vaudemont entered from it, leading the fair form of Constance; who, in her white robes and dark dishevelled hair, with a face in which smiles and blushes contended with deeper emotion, approached the altar, and kneeling with her lover, pronounced the vows that united them for ever.

It was long before the happy Gaspar could win from his lady the secret of her dream. In spite of the happiness she now enjoyed, she had suffered too much not to look back even with terror to those days when she thought love a crime, and every event connected with them wore an awful aspect. Many a vision, she said, she had that fearful night. She had seen the spirits of her father and brothers in Paradise; she had beheld Gaspar victoriously combating among the infidels; she had beheld him in King Henry's court, favoured and beloved, and she herself—now pining in a cloister, now a bride—now grateful to Heaven for the full measure of bliss presented to her, now weeping away her sad days—till suddenly she thought herself in Paynim land; and the saint herself, Saint Catherine, guiding her unseen through the city of the infidels. She entered a palace and beheld the miscreants rejoicing in victory; and then descending to the dungeons beneath, they groped their way through damp vaults, and low mildewed passages, to one cell, darker and more frightful than the rest. On the floor lay one with soiled and tattered garments, with unkempt locks and wild matted beard. His cheek was worn and thin; his eyes had lost their fire; his form was a mere skeleton; the chains hung loosely on the fleshless bones.

"And was it my appearance in that attractive state and winning costume that softened the hard heart of Constance?" asked Gaspar, smiling at this painting of what would never be.

"Even so," replied Constance; "for my heart whispered me that this was my doing: and who could recall the life that waned in your pulses—who restore, save the destroyer? My heart never warmed to my living happy knight as then it did to his wasted image, as it lay, in the visions of night, at my feet. A veil fell from my eyes; a darkness was dispelled from before me. Methought I then knew for the first time what life and what death was. I was bid believe that to make the living happy was not to injure the dead; and I felt how wicked and how vain was that false philosophy which placed virtue and good in hatred and unkindness. You should not die: I would loosen your chains and save you, and bid you live for love. I sprung forward, and the death I deprecated for you would, in my presumption, have been mine—then, when first I felt the real value of life—but that your arm was there to save me, your dear voice to bid me be blest for evermore."

The Mortal Immortal
A Tale

JULY 16, 1833.—This is a memorable anniversary for me; on it I complete my three hundred and twenty-third year!

The Wandering Jew?—certainly not. More than eighteen centuries have passed over his head. In comparison with him, I am a very young Immortal.

Am I, then, immortal? This is a question which I have asked myself, by day and night, for now three hundred and three years, and yet cannot answer it. I detected a gray hair amidst my brown locks this very day—that surely signifies decay. Yet it may have remained concealed there for three hundred years—for some persons have become entirely white-headed before twenty years of age.

I will tell my story, and my reader shall judge for me. I will tell my story, and so contrive to pass some few hours of a long eternity, become so wearisome to me. For ever! Can it be? to live for ever! I have heard of enchantments, in which the victims were plunged into a deep sleep, to wake, after a hundred years, as fresh as ever: I have heard of the Seven Sleepers—thus to be immortal would not be so burthensome: but, oh! the weight of never-ending time—the tedious passage of the still-succeeding hours! How happy was the fabled Nourjahad! But to my task.

All the world has heard of Cornelius Agrippa. His memory is as immortal as his arts have made me. All the world has also heard of his scholar, who, unawares, raised the foul fiend during his master's absence, and was destroyed by him. The report, true or false, of this accident, was attended with many inconveniences to the renowned philosopher. All his scholars at once deserted him—his servants disappeared. He had no one near him to put coals on his ever-burning fires while he slept, or to attend to the changeful colours of his medicines while he studied. Experiment after experiment failed, because one pair of hands was insufficient to complete them: the dark spirits laughed at him for not being able to retain a single mortal in his service.

I was then very young—very poor—and very much in love. I had been for about a year the pupil of Cornelius, though I was absent when this accident took place. On my return, my friends implored me not to return to the alchymist's abode. I trembled as I listened to the dire tale they told; I required no second warning; and when Cornelius came and offered me a purse of gold if I would remain under his roof, I felt as if Satan himself tempted me. My teeth chattered—my hair stood on end:—I ran off as fast as my trembling knees would permit.

My failing steps were directed whither for two years they had every evening been attracted,—a gently bubbling spring of pure living waters, beside which lingered a dark-haired girl, whose beaming eyes were fixed on the path I was accustomed each night to tread. I cannot remember the hour when I did not love Bertha; we had been neighbours and playmates from infancy—her parents, like mine, were of humble life, yet respectable—our attachment had been a source of pleasure to them. In an evil hour, a malignant fever carried off both her father and mother, and Bertha became an orphan. She would have found a home beneath my paternal roof, but, unfortunately, the old lady of the near castle, rich, childless, and solitary, declared her intention to adopt her. Henceforth Bertha was clad in silk—inhabited a marble palace—and was looked on as being highly favoured by fortune. But in her new situation among her new associates, Bertha remained true to the friend of her humbler days; she often visited the cottage of my father, and when forbidden to go thither, she would stray towards the neighbouring wood, and meet me beside its shady fountain.

She often declared that she owed no duty to her new protectress equal in sanctity to that which bound us. Yet still I was too poor to marry, and she grew weary of being tormented on my account. She had a haughty but an impatient spirit, and grew angry at the obstacles that prevented our union. We met now after an absence, and she had been sorely beset while I was away; she complained bitterly, and almost reproached me for being poor. I replied hastily,—

"I am honest, if I am poor!—were I not, I might soon become rich!"

This exclamation produced a thousand questions. I feared to shock her by owning the truth, but she drew it from me; and then, casting a look of disdain on me, she said—

"You pretend to love, and you fear to face the Devil for my sake!"

I protested that I had only dreaded to offend her;—while she dwelt on the magnitude of the reward that I should receive. Thus encouraged—shamed by her—led on by love and hope, laughing at my late fears, with quick steps and a light heart, I returned to accept the offers of the alchymist, and was instantly installed in my office.

A year passed away. I became possessed of no insignificant sum of money. Custom had banished my fears. In spite of the most painful vigilance, I had never detected the trace of a cloven foot; nor was the studious silence of our abode ever disturbed by demoniac howls. I still continued my stolen interviews with Bertha, and Hope dawned on me—Hope—but not perfect joy; for Bertha fancied that love and security were enemies, and her pleasure was to divide them in my bosom. Though true of heart, she was somewhat of a coquette in manner; and I was jealous as a Turk. She slighted me in a thousand ways, yet would never acknowledge herself to be in the wrong. She would drive me mad with anger, and then force me to beg her pardon. Sometimes she fancied that I was not sufficiently submissive, and then she had some story of a rival, favoured by her protectress. She was surrounded by silk-clad youths—the rich and gay——What chance had the sad-robed scholar of Cornelius compared with these?

On one occasion, the philosopher made such large demands upon my time, that I was unable to meet her as I was wont. He was engaged in some mighty work, and I was forced to remain, day and night, feeding his furnaces and watching his chemical preparations. Bertha waited for me in vain at the fountain. Her haughty spirit fired at this neglect; and when at last I stole out during the few short minutes allotted to me for slumber, and hoped to be consoled by her, she received me with disdain, dismissed me in scorn, and vowed that any man should possess her hand rather than he who could not be in two places at once for her sake. She would be revenged!—And truly she was. In my dingy retreat I heard that she had been hunting, attended by Albert Hoffer. Albert Hoffer was favoured by her protectress, and the three passed in cavalcade before my smoky window. Methought that they mentioned my name—it was followed by a laugh of derision, as her dark eyes glanced contemptuously towards my abode.

Jealousy, with all its venom, and all its misery, entered my breast. Now I shed a torrent of tears, to think that I should never call her mine; and, anon, I imprecated a thousand curses on her inconstancy. Yet, still I must stir the fires of the alchymist, still attend on the changes of his unintelligible medicines.

Cornelius had watched for three days and nights, nor closed his eyes. The progress of his alembics was slower than he expected: in spite of his anxiety, sleep weighed upon his eyelids. Again and again he threw off drowsiness with more than human energy; again and again it stole away his senses. He eyed his crucibles wistfully. "Not ready yet," he murmured; "will another night pass before the work is accomplished? Winzy, you are vigilant—you are faithful—you have slept, my boy—you slept last night. Look at that glass vessel. The liquid it contains is of a soft rose-colour: the moment it begins to change its hue, awaken me—till then I may close my eyes. First, it will turn white, and then emit golden flashes; but wait not till then; when the rose-colour fades, rouse me." I scarcely heard the last words, muttered, as they were, in sleep. Even then he did not quite yield to nature. "Winzy, my boy," he again said, "do not touch the vessel—do not put it to your lips; it is a philter—a philter to cure love; you would not cease to love your Bertha—beware to drink!"

And he slept. His venerable head sunk on his breast, and I scarce heard his regular breathing. For a few minutes I watched the vessel—the rosy hue of the liquid remained unchanged. Then my thoughts wandered—they visited the fountain, and dwelt on a thousand charming scenes never to be renewed—never! Serpents and adders were in my heart as the word "Never!" half formed itself on my lips. False girl!—false and cruel! Never more would she smile on me as that evening she smiled on Albert. Worthless, detested woman! I would not remain unrevenged—she should see Albert expire at her feet—she should die beneath my vengeance. She had smiled in disdain and triumph—she knew my wretchedness and her power. Yet what power had she?—the power of exciting my hate—my utter scorn—my—oh, all but indifference! Could

I attain that—could I regard her with careless eyes, transferring my rejected love to one fairer and more true, that were indeed a victory!

A bright flash darted before my eyes. I had forgotten the medicine of the adept; I gazed on it with wonder: flashes of admirable beauty, more bright than those which the diamond emits when the sun's rays are on it, glanced from the surface of the liquid; an odour the most fragrant and grateful stole over my sense; the vessel seemed one globe of living radiance, lovely to the eye, and most inviting to the taste. The first thought, instinctively inspired by the grosser sense, was, I will—I must drink. I raised the vessel to my lips. "It will cure me of love—of torture!" Already I had quaffed half of the most delicious liquor ever tasted by the palate of man, when the philosopher stirred. I started—I dropped the glass—the fluid flamed and glanced along the floor, while I felt Cornelius's gripe at my throat, as he shrieked aloud, "Wretch! you have destroyed the labour of my life!"

The philosopher was totally unaware that I had drunk any portion of his drug. His idea was, and I gave a tacit assent to it, that I had raised the vessel from curiosity, and that, frighted at its brightness, and the flashes of intense light it gave forth, I had let it fall. I never undeceived him. The fire of the medicine was quenched—the fragrance died away—he grew calm, as a philosopher should under the heaviest trials, and dismissed me to rest.

I will not attempt to describe the sleep of glory and bliss which bathed my soul in paradise during the remaining hours of that memorable night. Words would be faint and shallow types of my enjoyment, or of the gladness that possessed my bosom when I woke. I trod air—my thoughts were in heaven. Earth appeared heaven, and my inheritance upon it was to be one trance of delight. "This it is to be cured of love," I thought; "I will see Bertha this day, and she will find her lover cold and regardless; too happy to be disdainful, yet how utterly indifferent to her!"

The hours danced away. The philosopher, secure that he had once succeeded, and believing that he might again, began to concoct the same medicine once more. He was shut up with his books and drugs, and I had a holiday. I dressed myself with care; I looked in an old but polished shield, which served me for a mirror; methought my good looks had wonderfully improved. I hurried beyond the precincts of the town, joy in my soul, the beauty of heaven and earth around me. I turned my steps towards the castle—I could look on its lofty turrets with lightness of heart, for I was cured of love. My Bertha saw me afar off, as I came up the avenue. I know not what sudden impulse animated her bosom, but at the sight, she sprung with a light fawn-like bound down the marble steps, and was hastening towards me. But I had been perceived by another person. The old high-born hag, who called herself her protectress, and was her tyrant, had seen me, also; she hobbled, panting, up the terrace; a page, as ugly as herself, held up her train, and fanned her as she hurried along, and stopped my fair girl with a "How, now, my bold mistress? whither so fast? Back to your cage—hawks are abroad!"

Bertha clasped her hands—her eyes were still bent on my approaching figure. I saw the contest. How I abhorred the old crone who checked the kind impulses of my Bertha's softening heart. Hitherto, respect for her rank had caused me to avoid the lady of the castle; now I disdained such trivial considerations. I was cured of love, and lifted above all human fears; I hastened forwards, and soon reached the terrace. How lovely Bertha looked! her eyes flashing fire, her cheeks glowing with impatience and anger, she was a thousand times more graceful and charming than ever—I no longer loved—Oh! no, I adored—worshipped—idolized her!

She had that morning been persecuted, with more than usual vehemence, to consent to an immediate marriage with my rival. She was reproached with the encouragement that she had shown him—she was threatened with being turned out of doors with disgrace and shame. Her proud spirit rose in arms at the threat; but when she remembered the scorn that she had heaped upon me, and how, perhaps, she had thus lost one whom she now regarded as her only friend, she wept with remorse and rage. At that moment I appeared. "O, Winzy!" she exclaimed, "take me to your mother's cot; swiftly let me leave the detested luxuries and wretchedness of this noble dwelling—take me to poverty and happiness."

I clasped her in my arms with transport. The old lady was speechless with fury, and broke forth into invective only when we were far on our road to my natal cottage. My mother received the fair fugitive, escaped from a gilt cage to nature and liberty, with tenderness and joy; my father, who loved her, welcomed her heartily; it was a day of rejoicing, which did not need the addition of the celestial potion of the alchymist to steep me in delight.

Soon after this eventful day, I became the husband of Bertha. I ceased to be the scholar of Cornelius, but I continued his friend. I always felt grateful to him for having, unawares, procured me that delicious draught of a divine elixir, which, instead of curing me of love (sad cure! solitary and joyless remedy for evils which seem blessings to the memory), had inspired me with courage and resolution, thus winning for me an inestimable treasure in my Bertha.

I often called to mind that period of trance-like inebriation with wonder. The drink of Cornelius had not fulfilled the task for which he affirmed that it had been prepared, but its effects were more potent and blissful than words can express. They had faded by degrees, yet they lingered long—and painted life in hues of splendour. Bertha often wondered at my lightness of heart and unaccustomed gaiety; for, before, I had been rather serious, or even sad, in my disposition. She loved me the better for my cheerful temper, and our days were winged by joy.

Five years afterwards I was suddenly summoned to the bedside of the dying Cornelius. He had sent for me in haste, conjuring my instant presence. I found him stretched on his pallet, enfeebled even to death; all of life that yet remained animated his piercing eyes, and they were fixed on a glass vessel, full of a roseate liquid.

"Behold," he said, in a broken and inward voice, "the vanity of human wishes! a second time my hopes are about to be crowned, a second time they are destroyed. Look at that liquor—you remember five years ago I had prepared the same, with the same success;—then, as now, my thirsting lips expected to taste the immortal elixir—you dashed it from me! and at present it is too late."

He spoke with difficulty, and fell back on his pillow. I could not help saying,—

"How, revered master, can a cure for love restore you to life?"

A faint smile gleamed across his face as I listened earnestly to his scarcely intelligible answer.

"A cure for love and for all things—the Elixir of Immortality. Ah! if now I might drink, I should live for ever!"

As he spoke, a golden flash gleamed from the fluid; a well-remembered fragrance stole over the air; he raised himself, all weak as he was—strength seemed miraculously to re-enter his frame—he stretched forth his hand—a loud explosion startled me—a ray of fire shot up from the elixir, and the glass vessel which contained it was shivered to atoms! I turned my eyes towards the philosopher; he had fallen back—his eyes were glassy—his features rigid—he was dead!

But I lived, and was to live for ever! So said the unfortunate alchymist, and for a few days I believed his words. I remembered the glorious drunkenness that had followed my stolen draught. I reflected on the change I had felt in my frame—in my soul. The bounding elasticity of the one—the buoyant lightness of the other. I surveyed myself in a mirror, and could perceive no change in my features during the space of the five years which had elapsed. I remembered the radiant hues and grateful scent of that delicious beverage—worthy the gift it was capable of bestowing——I was, then, IMMORTAL!

A few days after I laughed at my credulity. The old proverb, that "a prophet is least regarded in his own country," was true with respect to me and my defunct master. I loved him as a man—I respected him as a sage—but I derided the notion that he could command the powers of darkness, and laughed at the superstitious fears with which he was regarded by the vulgar. He was a wise philosopher, but had no acquaintance with any spirits but those clad in flesh and blood. His science was simply human; and human science, I soon persuaded myself, could never conquer nature's laws so far as to imprison the soul for ever within its carnal habitation. Cornelius had brewed a soul-refreshing drink—more inebriating than wine—sweeter and more fragrant than any fruit: it possessed probably strong medicinal powers, imparting gladness to the heart and vigor to the limbs; but its effects would wear out; already were they diminished in my frame. I was a lucky fellow to have quaffed health and joyous spirits, and perhaps long life, at my master's hands; but my good fortune ended there: longevity was far different from immortality.

I continued to entertain this belief for many years. Sometimes a thought stole across me—Was the alchymist indeed deceived? But my habitual credence was, that I should meet the fate of all the children of Adam at my appointed time—a little late, but still at a natural age. Yet it was certain that I retained a wonderfully youthful look. I was laughed at for my vanity in consulting the mirror so often, but I consulted it in vain—my brow was untrenched—my cheeks—my eyes—my whole person continued as untarnished as in my twentieth year.

I was troubled. I looked at the faded beauty of Bertha—I seemed more like her son. By degrees our neighbours began to make similar observations, and I found at last that I went by the name of the Scholar bewitched. Bertha herself grew uneasy. She became jealous and peevish, and at length she began to question me. We had no children; we were all in all to each other; and though, as she grew older, her vivacious spirit became a little allied to ill-temper, and her beauty sadly diminished, I cherished her in my heart as the mistress I had idolized, the wife I had sought and won with such perfect love.

At last our situation became intolerable: Bertha was fifty—I twenty years of age. I had, in very shame, in some measure adopted the habits of a more advanced age; I no longer mingled in the dance among the young and gay, but my heart bounded along with them while I restrained my feet; and a sorry figure I cut among the Nestors of our village. But before the time I mention, things were altered—we were universally shunned; we were—at least, I was—reported to have kept up an iniquitous acquaintance with some of my former master's supposed friends. Poor Bertha was pitied, but deserted. I was regarded with horror and detestation.

What was to be done? we sat by our winter fire—poverty had made itself felt, for none would buy the produce of my farm; and often I had been forced to journey twenty miles, to some place where I was not known, to dispose of our property. It is true we had saved something for an evil day—that day was come.

We sat by our lone fireside—the old-hearted youth and his antiquated wife. Again Bertha insisted on knowing the truth; she recapitulated all she had ever heard said about me, and added her own observations. She conjured me to cast off the spell; she described how much more comely gray hairs were than my chestnut locks; she descanted on the reverence and respect due to age—how preferable to the slight regard paid to mere children: could I imagine that the despicable gifts of youth and good looks outweighed disgrace, hatred, and scorn? Nay, in the end I should be burnt as a dealer in the black art, while she, to whom I had not deigned to communicate any portion of my good fortune, might be stoned as my accomplice. At length she insinuated that I must share my secret with her, and bestow on her like benefits to those I myself enjoyed, or she would denounce me—and then she burst into tears.

Thus beset, methought it was the best way to tell the truth. I revealed it as tenderly as I could, and spoke only of a *very long life,* not of immortality—which representation, indeed, coincided best with my own ideas. When I ended, I rose and said,

"And now, my Bertha, will you denounce the lover of your youth?—You will not, I know. But it is too hard, my poor wife, that you should suffer from my ill-luck and the accursed arts of Cornelius. I will leave you—you have wealth enough, and friends will return in my absence. I will go; young as I seem, and strong as I am, I can work and gain my bread among strangers, unsuspected and unknown. I loved you in youth; God is my witness that I would not desert you in age, but that your safety and happiness require it."

I took my cap and moved towards the door; in a moment Bertha's arms were round my neck, and her lips were pressed to mine. "No, my husband, my Winzy," she said, "you shall not go alone—take me with you; we will remove from this place, and, as you say, among strangers we shall be unsuspected and safe. I am not so very old as quite to shame you, my Winzy; and I dare say the charm will soon wear off, and, with the blessing of God, you will become more elderly-looking, as is fitting; you shall not leave me."

I returned the good soul's embrace heartily. "I will not, my Bertha; but for your sake I had not thought of such a thing. I will be your true, faithful husband while you are spared to me, and do my duty by you to the last."

The next day we prepared secretly for our emigration. We were obliged to make great pecuniary sacrifices—it could not be helped. We realised a sum sufficient, at least, to maintain us while Bertha lived; and, without saying adieu to any one, quitted our native country to take refuge in a remote part of western France.

It was a cruel thing to transport poor Bertha from her native village, and the friends of her youth, to a new country, new language, new customs. The strange secret of my destiny rendered this removal immaterial to me; but I compassionated her deeply, and was glad to perceive that she found compensation for her misfortunes in a variety of little ridiculous circumstances. Away from all tell-tale chroniclers, she sought to decrease the apparent disparity of our ages by a thousand feminine arts—rouge, youthful dress, and assumed juvenility of manner. I could not be angry—Did not I myself wear a mask? Why quarrel with hers, because it was less successful? I grieved deeply when I remembered that this was my Bertha, whom I had loved so fondly, and won with such transport—the dark-eyed, dark-haired girl, with smiles of enchanting archness and a step like a fawn—this mincing, simpering, jealous old woman. I should have revered her gray locks and withered cheeks; but thus! It was my work, I knew; but I did not the less deplore this type of human weakness.

Her jealousy never slept. Her chief occupation was to discover that, in spite of outward appearances, I was myself growing old. I verily believe that the poor soul loved me truly in her heart, but never had woman so tormenting a mode of displaying fondness. She would discern wrinkles in my face and decrepitude in my walk, while I bounded along in youthful vigour, the youngest looking of twenty youths. I never dared address another woman: on one occasion, fancying that the belle of the village regarded me with favouring eyes, she bought me a gray wig. Her constant discourse among her acquaintances was, that though I looked so young, there was ruin at work within my frame; and she affirmed that the worst symptom about me was my apparent health. My youth was a disease, she said, and I ought at all times to prepare, if not for a sudden and awful death, at least to awake some morning white-headed, and bowed down with all the marks of advanced years. I let her talk—I often joined in her conjectures. Her warnings chimed in with my never-ceasing speculations concerning my state, and I took an earnest, though painful, interest in listening to all that her quick wit and excited imagination could say on the subject.

Why dwell on these minute circumstances? We lived on for many long years. Bertha became bed-rid and paralytic: I nursed her as a mother might a child. She grew peevish, and still harped upon one string—of how long I should survive her. It has ever been a source of consolation to me, that I performed my duty scrupulously towards her. She had been mine in youth, she was mine in age, and at last, when I heaped the sod over her corpse, I wept to feel that I had lost all that really bound me to humanity.

Since then how many have been my cares and woes, how few and empty my enjoyments! I pause here in my history—I will pursue it no further. A sailor without rudder or compass, tossed on a stormy sea—a traveller lost on a wide-spread heath, without landmark or star to guide him—such have I been: more lost, more hopeless than either. A nearing ship, a gleam from some far cot, may save them; but I have no beacon except the hope of death.

Death! mysterious, ill-visaged friend of weak humanity! Why alone of all mortals have you cast me from your sheltering fold? O, for the peace of the grave! the deep silence of the iron-bound tomb! that thought would cease to work in my brain, and my heart beat no more with emotions varied only by new forms of sadness!

Am I immortal? I return to my first question. In the first place, is it not more probable that the beverage of the alchymist was fraught rather with longevity than eternal life? Such is my hope. And then be it remembered, that I only drank *half* of the potion prepared by him. Was not the whole necessary to complete the charm? To have drained half the Elixir of Immortality is but to be half immortal—my For-ever is thus truncated and null.

But again, who shall number the years of the half of eternity? I often try to imagine by what rule the infinite may be divided. Sometimes I fancy age advancing upon me. One gray hair I have found. Fool! do I lament? Yes, the fear of age and death often creeps coldly into my heart; and the more I live, the more I dread death, even while I abhor life. Such an enigma is man—born to perish—when he wars, as I do, against the established laws of his nature.

But for this anomaly of feeling surely I might die: the medicine of the alchymist would not be proof against fire—sword—and the strangling waters. I have gazed upon the blue depths of many a placid lake, and the tumultuous rushing of many a mighty river, and have said, peace inhabits those waters; yet I have turned my steps away, to live yet another day. I have asked myself, whether suicide would be a crime in one to whom thus only the portals of the other world could be opened. I have done all, except presenting myself as a soldier or duellist, an object of destruction to my—no, *not* my fellow-mortals, and therefore I have shrunk away. They are not my fellows. The inextinguishable power of life in my frame, and their ephemeral existence, place us wide as the poles asunder. I could not raise a hand against the meanest or the most powerful among them.

Thus I have lived on for many a year—alone, and weary of myself—desirous of death, yet never dying—a mortal immortal. Neither ambition nor avarice can enter my mind, and the ardent love that gnaws at my heart, never to be returned—never to find an equal on which to expend itself—lives there only to torment me.

This very day I conceived a design by which I may end all—without self-slaughter, without making another man a Cain—an expedition, which mortal frame can never survive, even endued with the youth and strength that inhabits mine. Thus I shall put my immortality to the test, and rest for ever—or return, the wonder and benefactor of the human species.

Before I go, a miserable vanity has caused me to pen these pages. I would not die, and leave no name behind. Three centuries have passed since I quaffed the fatal beverage: another year shall not elapse before, encountering gigantic dangers—warring with the powers of frost in their home—beset by famine, toil, and tempest—I yield this body, too tenacious a cage for a soul which thirsts for freedom, to the destructive elements of air and water—or, if I survive, my name shall be recorded as one of the most famous among the sons of men; and, my task achieved, I shall adopt more resolute means, and, by scattering and annihilating the atoms that compose my frame, set at liberty the life imprisoned within, and so cruelly prevented from soaring from this dim earth to a sphere more congenial to its immortal essence.

On Ghosts

I look for ghosts—but none will force
Their way to me; 'tis falsely said
That there was ever intercourse
Between the living and the dead.
Wordsworth

WHAT A DIFFERENT earth do we inhabit from that on which our forefathers dwelt! The antediluvian world, strode over by mammoths, preyed upon by the megatherion, and peopled by the offspring of the Sons of God, is a better type of the earth of Homer, Herodotus, and Plato, than the hedged-in cornfields and measured hills of the present day. The globe was then encircled by a wall which paled in the bodies of men, whilst their feathered thoughts soared over the boundary; it had a brink, and in the deep profound which it overhung, men's imaginations, eagle-winged, dived and flew, and brought home strange tales to their believing auditors. Deep caverns harboured giants; cloudlike birds cast their shadows upon the plains; while far out at sea lay islands of bliss, the fair paradise of Atlantis or El Dorado sparkling with untold jewels. Where are they now? The Fortunate Isles have lost the glory that spread a halo round them; for who deems himself nearer to the golden age, because he touches at the Canaries on his voyage to India? Our only riddle is the rise of the Niger; the interior of New Holland, our only terra incognita; and our sole mare incognitum, the north-west passage. But these are tame wonders, lions in leash; we do not invest Mungo Park, or the Captain of the Hecla, with divine attributes; no one fancies that the waters of the unknown river bubble up from hell's fountains, no strange and weird power is supposed to guide the ice-berg, nor do we fable that a stray pick-pocket from Botany Bay has found the gardens of the Hesperides within the circuit of the Blue Mountains. What have we left to dream about? The clouds are no longer the charioted servants of the sun, nor does he any more bathe his glowing brow in the bath of Thetis; the rainbow has ceased to be the messenger of the Gods, and thunder is no longer their awful voice, warning man of that which is to come. We have the sun which has been weighed and measured, but not understood; we have the assemblage of the planets, the congregation of the stars, and the yet unshackled ministration of the winds:—such is the list of our ignorance.

Nor is the empire of the imagination less bounded in its own proper creations, than in those which were bestowed on it by the poor blind eyes of our ancestors. What has become of enchantresses with their palaces of crystal and dungeons of palpable darkness? What of fairies and their wands? What of witches and their familiars? and, last, what of ghosts, with beckoning hands and fleeting shapes, which quelled the soldier's brave heart, and made the murderer disclose to the astonished noon the veiled work of midnight? These which were realities to our forefathers, in our wiser age—

—— Characterless are grated
To dusty nothing.

Yet is it true that we do not believe in ghosts? There used to be several traditionary tales repeated, with their authorities, enough to stagger us when we consigned them to that place where that is which "is as though it had never been." But these are gone out of fashion. Brutus's dream has become a deception of his over-heated brain, Lord Lyttleton's vision is called a cheat; and one by one these inhabitants of deserted houses, moonlight glades, misty mountain tops, and midnight church-yards, have been ejected from their immemorial seats, and small thrill is felt when the dead majesty of Denmark blanches the cheek and unsettles the reason of his philosophic son.

But do none of us believe in ghosts? If this question be read at noonday, when—

Every little corner, nook, and hole,
Is penetrated with the insolent light—

at such a time derision is seated on the features of my reader. But let it be twelve at night in a lone house; take up, I beseech you, the story of the Bleeding Nun; or of the Statue, to which the bridegroom gave the wedding ring, and she came in the dead of night to claim him, tall, white, and cold; or of the Grandsire, who with shadowy form and breathless lips stood over the couch and kissed the foreheads of his sleeping grandchildren, and thus doomed them to their fated death; and let all these details be assisted by solitude, flapping curtains, rushing wind, a long and dusky passage, an half open door—O, then truly, another answer may be given, and many will request leave to sleep upon it, before they decide whether there be such a thing as a ghost in the world, or out of the world, if that phraseology be more spiritual. What is the meaning of this feeling?

For my own part, I never saw a ghost except once in a dream. I feared it in my sleep; I awoke trembling, and lights and the speech of others could hardly dissipate my fear. Some years ago I lost a friend, and a few months afterwards visited the house where I had last seen him. It was deserted, and though in the midst of a city, its vast halls and spacious apartments occasioned the same sense of loneliness as if it had been situated on an uninhabited heath. I walked through the vacant chambers by twilight, and none save I awakened the echoes of their pavement. The far mountains (visible from the upper windows) had lost their tinge of sunset; the tranquil atmosphere grew leaden coloured as the golden stars appeared in the firmament; no wind ruffled the shrunk-up river which crawled lazily through the deepest channel of its wide and empty bed; the chimes of the Ave Maria had ceased, and the bell hung moveless in the open belfry: beauty invested a reposing world, and awe was inspired by beauty only. I walked through the rooms filled with sensations of the most poignant grief. He had been there; his living frame had been caged by those walls, his breath had mingled with that atmosphere, his step had been on those stones, I thought:—the earth is a tomb, the gaudy sky a vault, we but walking corpses. The wind rising in the east rushed through the open casements, making them shake;—methought, I heard, I felt—I know not what—but I trembled. To have seen him but for a moment, I would have knelt until the stones had been worn by the impress, so I told myself, and so I knew a moment after, but then I trembled, awe-struck and fearful. Wherefore? There is something beyond us of which we are ignorant. The sun drawing up the vaporous air makes a void, and the wind rushes in to fill it,—thus beyond our soul's ken there is an empty space; and our hopes and fears, in gentle gales or terrific whirlwinds, occupy the vacuum; and if it does no more, it bestows on the feeling heart a belief that influences do exist to watch and guard us, though they be impalpable to the coarser faculties.

I have heard that when Coleridge was asked if he believed in ghosts,— he replied that he had seen too many to put any trust in their reality; and the person of the most lively imagination that I ever knew echoed this reply. But these were not real ghosts (pardon, unbelievers, my mode of speech) that they saw; they were shadows, phantoms unreal; that while they appalled the senses, yet carried no other feeling to the mind of others than delusion, and were viewed as we might view an optical deception which we see to be true with our eyes, and know to be false with our understandings. I speak of other shapes. The returning bride, who claims the fidelity of her betrothed; the murdered man who shakes to remorse the murderer's heart; ghosts that lift the curtains at the foot of your bed as the clock chimes one; who rise all pale and ghastly from the churchyard and haunt their ancient abodes; who, spoken to, reply; and whose cold unearthly touch makes the hair stand stark upon the head; the true old-fashioned, foretelling, flitting, gliding ghost,—who has seen such a one?

I have known two persons who at broad daylight have owned that they believed in ghosts, for that they had seen one. One of these was an Englishman, and the other an Italian. The former had lost a friend he dearly loved, who for awhile appeared to him nightly, gently stroking his cheek and spreading a serene calm over his mind. He did not fear the appearance, although he was somewhat awe-stricken as each night it glided into his chamber, and,

Ponsi del letto in su la sponda manca.

This visitation continued for several weeks, when by some accident he altered his residence, and then he saw it no more. Such a tale may easily be explained away;—but several years had passed, and he, a man of strong and virile intellect, said that "he had seen a ghost."

The Italian was a noble, a soldier, and by no means addicted to superstition: he had served in Napoleon's armies from early youth, and had been to Russia, had fought and bled, and been rewarded, and he unhesitatingly, and with deep relief, recounted his story.

This Chevalier, a young, and (somewhat a miraculous incident) a gallant Italian, was engaged in a duel with a brother officer, and wounded him in the arm. The subject of the duel was frivolous; and distressed therefore at its consequences he attended on his youthful adversary during his consequent illness, so that when the latter recovered they became firm and dear friends. They were quartered together at Milan, where the youth fell desperately in love with the wife of a musician, who disdained his passion, so that it preyed on his spirits and his health; he absented himself from all amusements, avoided all his brother officers, and his only consolation was to pour his love-sick plaints into the ear of the Chevalier, who strove in vain to inspire him either with indifference towards the fair disdainer, or to inculcate lessons of fortitude and heroism. As a last resource he urged him to ask leave of absence; and to seek, either in change of scene, or the amusement of hunting, some diversion to his passion. One evening the youth came to the Chevalier, and said, "Well, I have asked leave of absence, and am to have it early to-morrow morning, so lend me your fowling-piece and cartridges, for I shall go to hunt for a fortnight." The Chevalier gave him what he asked; among the shot there were a few bullets. "I will take these also," said the youth, "to secure myself against the attack of any wolf, for I mean to bury myself in the woods."

Although he had obtained that for which he came, the youth still lingered. He talked of the cruelty of his lady, lamented that she would not even permit him a hopeless attendance, but that she inexorably banished him from her sight, "so that," said he, "I have no hope but in oblivion." At length he rose to depart. He took the Chevalier's hand and said, "You will see her to-morrow, you will speak to her, and hear her speak; tell her, I entreat you, that our conversation to-night has been concerning her, and that her name was the last that I spoke." "Yes, yes," cried the Chevalier, "I will say any thing you please; but you must not talk of her any more, you must forget her." The youth embraced his friend with warmth, but the latter saw nothing more in it than the effects of his affection, combined with his melancholy at absenting himself from his mistress, whose name, joined to a tender farewell, was the last sound that he uttered.

When the Chevalier was on guard that night, he heard the report of a gun. He was at first troubled and agitated by it, but afterwards thought no more of it, and when relieved from guard went to bed, although he passed a restless, sleepless night. Early in the morning some one knocked at his door. It was a soldier, who said that he had got the young officer's leave of absence, and had taken it to his house; a servant had admitted him, and he had gone up stairs, but the room door of the officer was locked, and no one answered to his knocking, but something oozed through from under the door that looked like blood. The Chevalier, agitated and frightened at this account, hurried to his friend's house, burst open the door, and found him stretched on the ground—he had blown out his brains, and the body lay a headless trunk, cold, and stiff.

The shock and grief which the Chevalier experienced in consequence of this catastrophe produced a fever which lasted for some days. When he got well, he obtained leave of absence, and went into the country to try to divert his mind. One evening at moonlight, he was returning home from a walk, and passed through a lane with a hedge on both sides, so high that he could not see over them. The night was balmy; the bushes gleamed with fireflies, brighter than the stars which the moon had veiled with her silver light. Suddenly he heard a rustling near him, and the figure of his friend issued from the hedge and stood before him, mutilated as he had seen him after his death. This figure he saw several times, always in the same place. It was impalpable to the touch, motionless, except in its advance, and made no sign when it was addressed. Once the Chevalier took a friend with him to the spot. The same rustling was heard, the same shadow stept forth, his companion fled in horror, but the Chevalier staid, vainly endeavouring to discover what called his friend from his quiet tomb, and if any act of his might give repose to the restless shade.

Such are my two stories, and I record them the more willingly, since they occurred to men, and to individuals distinguished the one for courage and the other for sagacity. I will conclude my "modern instances," with a story told by M. G. Lewis, not probably so authentic as these, but perhaps more amusing. I relate it as nearly as possible in his own words.

"A gentleman journeying towards the house of a friend, who lived on the skirts of an extensive forest, in the east of Germany, lost his way. He wandered for some time among the trees, when he saw a light at a distance. On approaching it he was surprised to observe that it proceeded from the interior of a ruined monastery. Before he knocked at the gate he thought it proper to look through the window. He saw a number of cats assembled round a small grave, four of whom were at that moment letting down a coffin with a crown upon it. The gentleman startled at this unusual sight, and, imagining that he had arrived at the retreats of fiends or witches, mounted his horse and rode away with the utmost precipitation. He arrived at his friend's house at a late hour, who sate up waiting for him. On his arrival his friend questioned him as to the cause of the traces of agitation visible in his face. He began to recount his adventures after much hesitation, knowing that it was scarcely possible that his friend should give faith to his relation. No sooner had he mentioned the coffin with the crown upon it, than his friend's cat, who seemed to have been lying asleep before the fire, leaped up, crying out, 'Then I am king of the cats;' and then scrambled up the chimney, and was never seen more."

ΣΖ.

